CUVVIN BOOKS

Hook, Line & Sinker

HOOK, LINE & SINKER

Len Deighton

C

CENTURY

LONDON   SYDNEY   AUCKLAND   JOHANNESBURG

Copyright © Pluriform Publishing Company B.V. 1991

Spy Hook © B.V Holland Copyright Corporation 1988
Spy Line © B.V. Holland Copyright Corporation 1989
Spy Sinker © Pluriform Publishing Company B.V. 1990

All rights reserved

The right of Len Deighton to be identified as the author
of this work has been asserted by him in accordance with the
Copyright, Designs and Patents Act 1988.

First published in Great Britain in 1991 by
Random Century Group
20 Vauxhall Bridge Rd, London SW1V 2SA

Century Hutchinson South Africa (Pty) Ltd
PO Box 337, Bergvlei 2012, South Africa

Random Century Australia Pty Ltd
20 Alfred Street, Milsons Point, Sydney, NSW 2061
Australia

Random Century New Zealand Ltd
PO Box 40–086, Glenfield, Auckland 10
New Zealand

British Library Cataloguing in Publication Data

Deighton, Len
    Hook, line and sinker.
    I. Title
    823 [F]

ISBN 0–7126–4964–6

Photoset by Deltatype Ltd, Ellesmere Port
Printed and bound in Great Britain by
Mackays of Chatham PLC, Chatham, Kent

Berlin Game, *Mexico Set* and *London Match* together cover the period from spring 1983 until spring 1984.

Winter covers 1900 until 1945.

Spy Hook picks up the Bernard Samson story at the beginning of 1987 and *Spy Line* continues it into the summer of that same year.

Spy Sinker starts in September 1977 and ends in summer 1987. The stories can be read in any order and each one is complete in itself.

Len Deighton

SPY HOOK

1

When they ask me to become President of the United States I'm going to say, 'Except for Washington DC.' I'd finally decided while I was shaving in icy cold water without electric light, and signed all the necessary documentation as I plodded through the uncleared snow to wait for a taxi-cab that never came, and let the passing traffic spray Washington's special kind of sweet-smelling slush over me.

Now it was afternoon. I'd lunched and I was in a somewhat better mood. But this was turning out to be a long long day, and I'd left this little job for the last. I hadn't been looking forward to it. Now I kept glancing up at the clock, and through the window at the interminable snow falling steadily from a steely grey overcast, and wondering if I would be at the airport in time for the evening flight back to London, and whether it would be cancelled.

'If that's the good news,' said Jim Prettyman with an easy American grin, 'what's the bad news?' He was thirty-three years old, according to the briefing card, a slim, white-faced Londoner with sparse hair and rimless spectacles who had come from the London School of Economics with an awesome reputation as a mathematician and qualifications in accountancy, political studies and business management. I'd always got along very well with him – in fact we'd been friends – but he'd never made any secret of the extent of his ambitions, or of his impatience. The moment a faster bus came past, Jim leapt aboard, that was his way. I looked at him carefully. He could make a smile last a long time.

So he didn't want to go to London next month and give evidence. Well, that was what the Department in London had expected him to say. Jim Prettyman's reputation said he was not the sort of fellow who would go out of his way to do a favour for London Central: or anyone else.

I looked at the clock again and said nothing. I was sitting in a huge soft beige leather armchair. There was this wonderful smell of new leather that they spray inside cheap Japanese cars.

'More coffee, Bernie?' He scratched the side of his bony nose as if he was thinking of something else.

'Yes, please.' It was lousy coffee even by my low standards, but I suppose it was his way of showing that he wasn't trying to get rid of me, and my ineffectual way of disassociating myself from the men who'd sent the message I was about to give him. 'London might ask for you officially,' I said. I tried to make it sound friendly but it came out as a threat, which I suppose it was.

'Did London tell you to say that?' His secretary came and peered in through the half-open door – he must have pressed some hidden buzzer – and he said, 'Two more – regular.' She nodded and went out. It was all laconic and laid back and very American but then James Prettyman – or as it said on the oak and brass nameplate on his desk, Jay Prettyman – was very American. He was American in the way that English emigrants are in their first few years after applying for citizenship.

I'd been watching him carefully, trying to see into his mind, but his face gave no clue as to his real feelings. He was a tough customer, I'd always known that. My wife Fiona had said that, apart from me, Prettyman was the most ruthless man she'd ever met. But that didn't mean she didn't admire him for that and a lot of other things. He'd even got her interested in his time-wasting hobby of trying to decipher ancient Mesopotamian cuneiform scripts. But most of us had learned not to let him get started on the subject. Not surprising he'd ended his time running a desk in Codes and Ciphers.

'Yes,' I said, 'they told me to say it.' I looked at his office with its panelled walls that were made of some special kind of plastic on account of the fire department's regulations. And at the stern-faced President of Perimeter Security Guarantee Trust framed in gold, and the fancy reproduction antique bureau that might have concealed a drinks cupboard. I'd have given a lot for a stiff Scotch before facing that weather again.

'No chance! Look at this stuff.' He indicated the trays laden with paper-work, and the elaborate work station with the video screen that gave him access to one hundred and fifty major data bases. Alongside it, staring at us from a big solid silver frame, there was another reason: his brand-new American wife. She looked about eighteen but had a son at Harvard and two ex-husbands, to say nothing of a father who'd been a big-shot in the State Department. She was standing with him and a shiny Corvette in front of a big house with cherry trees in the garden. He grinned again. I could see why they didn't like him in London. He had no eyebrows and his eyes were narrow so that when he grinned those superwide mirthless grins with his white teeth just showing, he looked like the commander of a Japanese prison camp complaining that the POWs weren't bowing low enough.

'You could be in and out in one day,' I coaxed.

He was ready for that. 'A day to travel; a day to travel back. It would cost me three days' work and quite frankly, Bernie, those goddamned flights leave me bushed.'

'I thought you might like a chance to see the family,' I said. Then I waited while the secretary – a tall girl with amazingly long red tapering fingernails and a mane of silvery yellow wavy hair – brought in two paper cups of slot-machine coffee and put them down very delicately on his huge desk, together with two bright yellow paper napkins, two packets of artificial sweetener, two packets of 'non-dairy creamer' and two plastic stirrers. She smiled at me and then at Jim.

'Thank you, Charlene,' he said. He immediately reached for his coffee, looking at it as if he was going to enjoy it. After putting two sweetener pills and the white 'creamer' into it, and stirring energetic-ally, he sipped it and said, 'My mother died last August and Dad went to live in Geneva with my sister.'

Thank you London Research and Briefing, always there when you need them. I nodded. He'd made no mention of the English wife he'd divorced overnight in Mexico, the one who had refused to go and live in Washington despite the salary and the big house with the cherry trees in the garden: but it seemed better not to pursue that one. 'I'm sorry, Jim.' I was genuinely sorry about his mother. His parents had given me more than one sorely needed Sunday lunch and had looked after my two kids when the Greek au pair had a screaming row with my wife and left without notice. I drank some of the evil-tasting brew and started again. 'There's a lot of money – half a million perhaps – still unaccounted for. Someone must know about it: half a million. Pounds!'

'Well, I don't know about it.' His lips tightened.

'Come along, Jim. No one's shouting fire. The money is somewhere in Central Funding. Everyone knows that but there'll be no peace until the book-keepers find it and close the ledgers.'

'Why you?'

Good question. The true answer was that I'd become the dogsbody who got the jobs that no one else wanted. 'I was coming over anyway.'

'So they saved the price of an air ticket.' He drank more coffee and carefully wiped the extreme edge of his mouth with the bright yellow paper napkin. 'Thank God I'm through with all that penny-pinching crap in London. How the hell do you put up with it?' He drained the rest of his coffee. I suppose he'd developed a taste for it.

'Are you offering me a job?' I said, straight-faced and open-eyed. He frowned and for a moment looked flustered. The fact was that since my wife had defected to the Russians a few years before, my bona fides was dependent upon my contract with London Central. If they dispensed with my services, however elegantly it was done, I might suddenly start finding that my 'indefinite' US visa for 'unlimited' visits was not getting me through to where the baggage was waiting. Of course some really powerful independent corporation might be able to face down official disapproval, but powerful independent organisations, like these friendly folks Jim worked for, were usually hell-bent on keeping the government sweet.

'Another year like last year and we'll be laying off personnel,' he said awkwardly.

'How long will it take to get a cab?'

'It's not as if my drag-assing over to London would make a difference to you personally . . .'

'Someone told me that some cabs won't go to the airport in this kind of weather.' I wasn't going to crawl to him, no matter how urgent London was pretending it was.

'If it's for you, say the word. I owe you, Bernie. I owe you.' When I didn't react, he stood up. As if by magic the door opened and he told his secretary to phone the car pool and arrange a car for me. 'Do you have anything to pick up?'

'Straight to the airport,' I said. I had my shirts and underwear and shaving stuff in the leather bag that contained the faxed accounts and memos that the embassy had sent round to me in the middle of the night. I should have been showing them to Jim but showing him papers would make no difference. He was determined to tell London Central that he didn't give a damn about them or their problems. He knew he didn't have to worry. When he'd told them he was going to Washington to work, they'd taken his living accommodation to pieces and given him a vetting of the sort that you never get on joining: only on leaving. Especially if you work in Codes and Ciphers.

So Jim clean-as-a-whistle Prettyman had nothing to worry about. He'd always been a model employee: that was his modus operandi. Not even an office pencil or a packet of paper-clips. Rumours said the investigating team from K-7 were so frustrated that they'd taken away his wife's handwritten recipe book and looked at it under ultraviolet light. But Jim's ex-wife certainly wasn't the sort of woman who writes out recipes in longhand, so that might be a silly story: no one likes the people from K-7. There were lots of silly stories going round at the time; my wife had just defected, and everyone was nervous.

'You work with Bret Rensselaer. Talk to Bret: he knows where the bodies are buried.'

'Bret's not with us any more,' I reminded him. 'He was shot. In Berlin . . . a long time back.'

'Yeah; I forgot. Poor Bret, I heard about that. Bret sent me over here the first time I came. I have a lot to thank him for.'

'Why would Bret know?'

'About the slush fund Central Funding set up with the Germans? Are you kidding? Bret master-minded that whole business. He appointed the company directors – all front men of course – and squared it with the people who ran the bank.'

'Bret did?'

'The bank directors were in his pocket. They were all Bret's people and Bret briefed them.'

'It's news to me.'

'Sure. It's too bad. If half a million pounds took a walk, Bret was the man who might have pointed you in the right direction.' Jim Prettyman looked up to where his secretary stood at the door again. She must have nodded or something for Jim said, 'The car's there. No hurry but it's ready when you are.'

'Did you work with Bret?'

'On the German caper? I okayed the cash transfers when there was no one else around who was authorized to sign. But everything I did had already been okayed. I was never at the meetings. That was all kept behind closed doors. Shall I tell you something, I don't think there was ever one meeting held in the building. All I ever saw was cashier's chits with the authorized signatures: none of them I recognized.' He laughed reflectively. 'Any auditor worth a damn would immediately point out that every one of those damned signatures might have been written by Bret Rensselaer. For all the evidence I have, there never was a real committee. The whole thing could have been a complete fabrication dreamed up by Bret.'

I nodded soberly, but I must have looked puzzled as I picked up my bag and took my overcoat from his secretary.

Jim came with me over to the door, and through his secretary's office. With his hand on my shoulder he said, 'Sure, I know. Bret didn't dream it up. I'm just saying that's how secret it was. But when you talk to the others just remember that they were Bret Rensselaer's cronies. If one of them put his hand in the till, Bret will probably have covered it for him. Be your age, Bernie. These things happen: only rarely I know, but they happen. It's the way the world is.'

Jim walked with me to the elevator and pushed the buttons for me the way Americans do when they want to make sure you're leaving the building. He said we must get together again, have a meal and talk about the good times we had together in the old days. I said yes we must, and thanked him and said goodbye, but still the lift didn't come.

Jim pressed the button again and smiled a crooked little smile. He straightened up. 'Bernie,' he said suddenly and glanced around us and along the corridor to see that we were alone.

'Yes, Jim?'

He looked around again. Jim had always been a very careful fellow: it was why he'd got on so well. One of the reasons. 'This business in London . . .'

Again he paused. I thought for one terrible moment that he was going to admit to pocketing the missing money, and then implore me to help him cover it up, for old times' sake. Or something like that. It would have put me in a damned difficult position and my stomach turned at the thought of it. But I needn't have worried. Jim wasn't the sort who pleaded with anyone about anything.

'I won't come. You tell them that in London. They can try anything they like but I won't come.'

He seemed agitated. 'Okay, Jim,' I said. 'I'll tell them.'

'I'd love to see London again. I really miss the Smoke . . . We had some good times, didn't we, Bernie?'

'Yes, we did,' I said. Jim had always been a bit of a cold fish: I was surprised by this revelation.

'Remember when Fiona was frying the fish we caught and spilled the oil and set fire to the kitchen? You really flipped your lid.'

'She said you did it.'

He smiled. He seemed genuinely amused. This was the Jim I used to know. 'I never saw anyone move so fast. Fiona could handle just about anything that came along.' He paused. 'Until she met you. Yes, they were good times, Bernie.'

'Yes, they were.'

I thought he was softening and he must have seen that in my face for he said, 'But I'm not getting involved in any bloody inquiry. They are looking for someone to blame. You know that don't you?'

I said nothing. Jim said, 'Why choose you to come and ask me. . . ? Because if I don't go, you'll be the one they finger.'

I ignored that one. 'Wouldn't it be better to go over there and tell them what you know?' I suggested.

My reply did nothing to calm him. 'I don't know anything,' he said, raising his voice. 'Jesus Christ, Bernie, how can you be so blind? The Department is determined to get even with you.'

8

'Get even? For what?'

'For what your wife did.'

'That's not logical.'

'Revenge never is logical. Wise up. They'll get you; one way or the other. Even resigning from the Department – the way I did – makes them mad. They see it as a betrayal. They expect everyone to stay in harness for ever.'

'Like marriage,' I said.

'Till death do us part,' said Jim. 'Right. And they'll get you. Through your wife. Or maybe through your father. You see.'

The car of the lift arrived and I stepped into it. I thought he was coming with me. Had I known he wasn't I would never have let that reference to my father go unexplained. He put his foot inside and leaned round to press the button for the ground floor. By that time it was too late. 'Don't tip the driver,' said Jim, still smiling as the doors closed on me. 'It's against company policy.' The last I saw of him was that cold Cheshire Cat smile. It hung in my vision for a long time afterwards.

When I got outside in the street the snow was piling higher and higher, and the air was crammed full of huge snowflakes that came spinning down like sycamore seeds with engine failure.

'Where's your baggage?' said the driver. Getting out of the car he tossed the remainder of his coffee into the snow where it left a brown ridged crater that steamed like Vesuvius. He wasn't looking forward to a drive to the airport on a Friday afternoon, and you didn't have to be a psychologist to see that in his face.

'That's all,' I told him.

'You travel light, mister.' He opened the door for me and I settled down inside. The car was warm, I suppose he'd just come in from a job, expecting to be signed out and sent home. Now he was in a bad mood.

The traffic was slow even by Washington weekend standards. I thought about Jim while we crawled out to the airport. I suppose he wanted to get rid of me. There was no other reason why Jim would invent that ridiculous story about Bret Rensselaer. The idea of Bret being a party to any kind of financial swindle involving the government was so ludicrous that I didn't even give it careful thought. Perhaps I should have done.

The plane was half-empty. After a day like that, a lot of people had had enough, without enduring the tender loving care of any airline company plus the prospect of a diversion to Manchester. But at least the half-empty First Class cabin gave me enough leg-room. I accepted the offer of a glass of champagne with such enthusiasm that the stewardess finally left the bottle with me.

I read the dinner menu and tried not to think about Jim Prettyman. I hadn't pressed him hard enough. I'd resented the unexpected phone call from Morgan, the D-G's personal assistant. I'd planned to spend this afternoon shopping. Christmas was past and there were sale signs everywhere. I'd glimpsed a big model helicopter that my son Billy would have gone crazy about. London was always ready to provide me with yet another task that was nothing to do with me or my immediate work. I had the suspicion that this time I'd been chosen not because I happened to be in Washington but because London knew that Jim was an old friend who'd respond more readily to me than to anyone else in the Department. When this afternoon Jim had proved recalcitrant I had rather enjoyed the idea of passing his rude message back to that stupid man Morgan. Now it was too late I was beginning to have second thoughts. Perhaps I should have taken up his offer to do it as a personal favour to me.

I thought about Jim's warnings. He wasn't the only one who thought the Department might still be blaming me for my wife's defection. But the idea that they'd frame me for embezzlement was a new one. It would wipe me out, of course. No one would employ me if they made something like that stick. It was a nasty thought, and even worse was that throwaway line about getting to me through my father. How could they get to me through my father? My father didn't work for the Department any more. My father was dead.

I drank more champagne – fizzy wine is not worth drinking if you allow the chill to go off it – and finished the bottle before closing my eyes for a moment in an effort to remember exactly what Jim had said. I must have dozed off. I was tired: really tired.

The next thing I knew the stewardess was shaking me roughly and saying, 'Would you like breakfast, sir?'

'I haven't had dinner.'

'They tell us not to wake passengers who are asleep.'

'Breakfast?'

'We'll be landing at London Heathrow in about forty-five minutes.'

It was an airline breakfast: shrivelled bacon, a plastic egg with a small stale roll and UHT milk for the coffee. Even when starving hungry I found it very easy to resist. Oh well, the dinner I'd missed was probably no better, and at least the threatened diversion to sunny Manchester had been averted. I vividly remembered the last time I was forcibly flown to Manchester. The airline's senior staff all went and hid in the

10

toilets until the angry, unwashed, unfed passengers had been herded aboard the unheated train.

But soon I had my feet on the ground again in London. Waiting at the barrier there was my Gloria. She usually came to the airport to meet me, and there can be no greater love than that which brings someone on a voluntary visit to London Heathrow.

She looked radiant: tall, on tiptoe, waving madly. Her long naturally blonde hair and a tailored tan suede coat with its big fur collar made her shine like a beacon amongst the line of weary welcomers slumping – like drunks – across the rails in Terminal Three. And if she did flourish her Gucci handbag a bit too much and wear those big sun-glasses even at breakfast time in winter, well, one had to make allowances for the fact that she was only half my age.

'The car's outside,' she whispered as she released me from the tight embrace.

'It will be towed away by now.'

'Don't be a misery. It will be there.'

And it was of course. And the weathermen's threatened snow and ice had not materialized either. This part of England was bathed in bright early-morning sunshine and the sky was blue and almost completely clear. But it was damned cold. The weathermen said it was the coldest January since 1940, but who believes the weathermen?

'You won't know the house,' she boasted as she roared down the motorway in the yellow dented Mini, ignoring the speed limit, cutting in front of angry cabbies and hooting at sleepy bus drivers.

'You can't have done much in a week.'

'Ha, ha! Wait and see.'

'Better you tell me now,' I said with ill-concealed anxiety. 'You haven't knocked down the garden wall? Next door's rose beds . . .'

'Wait and see: wait and see!'

She let go of the wheel to pound a fist against my leg as if making sure I was really and truly flesh and blood. Did she realize what mixed feelings I had about moving out of the house in Marylebone? Not just because Marylebone was convenient and central but also because it was the first house I'd ever bought, albeit with the aid of a still outstanding mortgage that the bank only agreed to because of the intervention of my prosperous father-in-law. Well, Duke Street wasn't lost for ever. It was leased to four American bachelors with jobs in the City. Bankers. They were paying a handsome rent that not only covered the mortgage but gave me a house in the suburbs and some small change to face the expenses of looking after two motherless children.

11

Gloria was in her element since moving in to the new place. She didn't see it as a rather shabby semi-detached surburban house with its peeling stucco and truncated front garden and a side entrance that had been overlaid with concrete to make a place to park a car. For Gloria this was her chance to make me see how indispensable she was. It was her chance to get us away from the shadow of my wife Fiona. Number thirteen Balaklava Road was going to be our little nest, the place into which we settled down to live happily ever after, the way they do in the fairy stories that she was reading not so very long ago.

Don't get me wrong. I loved her. Desperately. When I was away I counted the days – even the hours sometimes – before we'd be together again. But that didn't mean that I couldn't see how ill-suited we were. She was just a child. Before me her boy-friends had been schoolkids: boys who helped with logarithms and irregular verbs. Sometime she was going to suddenly realize that there was a big wide world out there waiting for her. By that time perhaps I'd be depending on her. No perhaps about it. I was depending on her now.

'Did it all go all right?'

'All all right,' I said.

'Someone from Central Funding left a note on your desk . . . Half a dozen notes in fact. Something about Prettyman. It's a funny name, isn't it?'

'Nothing else?'

'No. It's all been very quiet in the office. Unusually quiet. Who is Prettyman?' she asked.

'A friend of mine. They want him to give evidence . . . some money they've lost.'

'And he stole it?' She was interested now.

'Jim? No. When Jim puts his hand in the till he'll come up with ten million or more.'

'I thought he was a friend of yours,' she said reproachfully.

'Only kidding.'

'So who did steal it?'

'No one stole anything. It's just the accountants getting their paper-work into the usual chaos.'

'Truly?'

'You know how long the cashier's office takes to clear expenses. Did you see all those queries they raised on last month's chit?'

'That's just your expenses, darling. Some people get them signed and paid within a week.' I smiled. I was glad to change the subject. Prettyman's warnings had left a dull feeling of fear in me. It was heavy in my guts, like indigestion.

12

We arrived at Balaklava Road in record time. It was a street of small Victorian houses with large bay windows. Here and there the fronts were picked out in tasteful pastel colours. It was Saturday: despite the early hour housewives were staggering home under the weight of frantic shopping, and husbands were cleaning their cars: everyone demonstrating that manic energy and determination that the British only devote to their hobbies.

The neighbour who shared our semi-detached house – an insurance salesman and passionate gardener – was planting his Christmas tree in the hard frozen soil of his front garden. He could have saved himself the trouble, they never grow: people say the dealers scald the roots. He waved with the garden trowel as we swept past him and into the narrow side entrance. It was a squeeze to get out.

Gloria opened the newly painted front door with a proud flourish. The hall had been repapered – large mustard-yellow flowers on curlicue stalks – and new hall carpet too. I admired the result. In the kitchen there were some primroses on the table which was set with our best chinaware. Cut-glass tumblers stood ready for orange juice, and rashers of smoked bacon were arranged by the stove alongside four brown eggs and a new Teflon frying pan.

I walked round the whole house with her and played my appointed role. The new curtains were wonderful; and if the brown leather three-piece was a bit low and so difficult to climb out of, with a remote control for the TV, what did it matter? But by the time we were back in the kitchen, a smell of good coffee in the air, and my breakfast spluttering in the pan, I knew she had something else to tell me. I decided it wasn't anything concerning the house. I decided it was probably nothing important. But I was wrong about that.

'I've given in my notice,' she said over her shoulder while standing at the stove. She'd threatened to leave the Department not once but several hundred times. Always until now she'd made me the sole focus of her anger and frustration. 'They promised to let me go to Cambridge. They promised!' She was getting angry at the thought of it. She looked up from the frying pan and waved the fork at me before again jabbing at the bacon.

'And now they won't? They said that?'

'I'll pay my own way. I have enough if I go carefully,' she said. 'I'll be twenty-three in June. Already I'll feel like an old lady, sitting with all those eighteen-year-old schoolkids.'

'What did they say?'

'Morgan stopped me in the corridor last week. Asked me how I was getting along. What about my place at Cambridge? I said. He didn't have the guts to tell me in the proper way. He said there was no money. Bastard! There's enough money for Morgan to go to conferences in Australia and that damned symposium in Toronto. Money enough for jaunts!'

I nodded. I can't say that Australia or Toronto were high on my list of places to jaunt in, but perhaps Morgan had his reasons. 'You didn't tell him that?'

'I damned well did. I let him have it. We were outside the Deputy's office. He must have heard every word. I hope he did.'

'You're a harridan,' I told her.

She slammed the plates on the table with a snarl and then, unable to keep up the display of fierce bad temper, she laughed. 'Yes, I am. You haven't seen that side of me yet.'

'What an extraordinary thing to say, my love.'

'You treat me like a backward child, Bernard. I'm not a fool.' I said nothing. The toast flung itself out of the machine with a loud clatter. She rescued both slices before they slid into the sink and put them on a plate alongside my eggs and bacon. Then, as I began to eat, she sat opposite me, her face cupped in her hands, elbows on the table, studying me as if I were an animal in the zoo. I was getting used to it now but it still made me uneasy. She watched me with a curiosity that was disconcerting. Sometimes I would look up from a book or finish talking on the phone to find her studying me with that same expression.

'When did you say the children would be home?' I asked.

'You didn't mind them going to the sale of work?'

'I don't know what a sale of work is,' I said, not without an element of truth.

'It's at the Church Hall in Sebastopol Road. People make cakes and pickles and knit tea cosies and donate unwanted Christmas presents. It's for Oxfam.'

'And why would Billy and Sally want to go?'

'I knew you'd be angry.'

'I'm not angry but why would they want to go?'

'There'll be toys and books and things too. It's a jumble sale really but the Women's Guild prefers to call it their New Year Sale of Work. It sounds better. I knew you wouldn't bring any presents back with you.'

'I tried. I wanted to, I really did.'

'I know, darling. That wasn't why the children wanted to be here when you arrived. I told them to go. It's good for them to be with other children. Changing schools isn't easy at that age. They left a lot of friends in London; they must make new ones round here. It's not easy, Bernie.' It was quite a speech; perhaps she'd had it all prepared.

'I know.' I was still examining the awful prospect of her taking a place at the university next October, or whenever it was the academic year started in such places. What was I going to do with this wretched house, far away from everyone I knew? And what about the children?

She must have seen my face. 'I'll be back every weekend,' she promised.

'You know that's impossible,' I told her. 'You'll be working damned hard. I know you; you'll want to do everything better than anyone's ever done it before.'

'It will be all right, darling,' she said. 'If we want it to be all right, it will be. You'll see.'

Muffin, our battered cat, came and tapped on the window. Muffin seemed to be the only member of the family who'd settled in to Balaklava Road without difficulties. And even Muffin stayed out all night sometimes.

2

There was another thing I didn't like about the suburbs: getting to work. I braved the morning traffic jams in my ageing Volvo but Gloria seldom came with me in the car. She enjoyed going on the train, at least she said she enjoyed it. She said it gave her time to think. But the 7.32 was always packed with people from even more outlying suburbs by the time it arrived. And I hated to stand all the way to Waterloo. Secondly there was the question of my assigned parking place. Already the hyenas were circling. The old man who ran Personnel Records had started hinting about a cash offer for it as soon as I registered my new address. You'll come in on the train now I suppose? No, I said sharply. No I won't. And apart from a couple of days when the old Volvo was having its transmission fixed, I hadn't. I calculated that five consecutive days in a row would be all I'd need to find my hard-won parking space reassigned to someone who'd make better use of it.

So on Monday I went by car and Gloria went by train. She arrived ahead of me, of course. The office is only two or three minutes' walk from Waterloo Station, while I had to drag through the traffic jams in Wimbledon.

I got into the office to find alarm and despondency spread right through the building. Dicky Cruyer was there already, a sure sign of a crisis. They must have phoned him at home and had him depart hurriedly from the leisurely breakfast he enjoys after jogging across Hampstead Heath. Even Sir Percy Babcock, the Deputy D-G, had dragged himself away from his law practice and found time to spare for an early morning session.

'Number Two Conference Room,' the girl waiting in the corridor said. She whispered in a way that revealed her pent-up excitement: as if this was the sort of day she'd been waiting for ever since beginning to type all those tedious reports for us. I suppose Dicky must have sent her to stand sentry outside my office. 'Sir Percy is chairing the meeting. They said you should join them as soon as you arrived.'

'Thanks, Mabel,' I said and gave her my coat and a leather case of very unimportant non-classified paper-work that I hoped she'd mislay. She smiled dutifully. Her name wasn't Mabel but I called them all Mabel and I suppose they'd got used to it.

Number Two was on the top floor, a narrow room that seated fourteen at a pinch and had a view right across to where the City's ugly tower blocks underpinned the low-grey cloud base.

'Samson! Good,' said the Deputy D-G when I went in. There was a notepad, a yellow pencil and a chair waiting for me and two more pristine pads and pencils that may or may not have been waiting for others who were arriving at work hoping their lateness would not be noticed. Bad luck.

'Have you heard?' Dicky asked.

I could see it was Dicky's baby. This was a German Desk crisis. It wasn't a routine briefing for the Deputy, or a conference to decide about annual leave rosters, or more questions about where Central Funding might have put the odd few hundred thousand pounds that Jim Prettyman authorized for Bret Rensselaer and Bret Rensselaer never got. This was serious. 'No,' I said. 'What's happened?'

'Bizet,' said Dicky, and went back to chewing his fingernail.

I knew the group; at least I knew them as well as a deskman sitting in London can know the people who do the real nasty dangerous work. Somewhere near Frankfurt an der Oder, right over there on East Germany's border with Poland. 'Poles,' I said, 'or that's how it started. Poles working in some sort of heavy industry.'

'That's right,' said Dicky judiciously. He had a folder and was looking at it to check how well my memory was working.

'What's happened?'

'It looks nasty,' said Dicky, unvanquished master of the nebulous answer on almost any subject except the gastronomic merits of expensive restaurants.

Billingsly, a bald-headed youngster from the Data Centre, tapped the palm of his hand with his heavy horn-rimmed spectacles and said, 'We seem to have lost more than one of them. That's always a bad sign.'

So even in the Data Centre they knew that. Things were looking up. 'Yes,' I said. 'That's always a bad sign.'

Billingsly looked at me as if I'd slapped his face. Uncordial now, he said, 'If you know anything else we can do . . .'

'Have you put out a contact string?' I asked.

Billingsly seemed to be unsure what a contact string – a roll-call for survivors – was. But eventually Harry Strang, an elderly gorilla from Operations, stopped scratching his cheek with the eraser end of his brand-new yellow pencil for enough time to answer me. 'Early yesterday morning.'

'It's too soon.'

'That's what I told the Deputy,' said Dicky Cruyer, nodding deferentially to Sir Percy. Dicky was looking more tired and ill every minute. He usually came down with something totally incapacitating in this sort of situation. It was the thought of making a decision, and signing it for all to see, that affected him.

'Mass,' said Harry Strang.

'They see each other at Sunday morning Mass,' explained Dicky Cruyer.

'No out-of-contact signals?' I asked.

'No,' said Strang. 'That's what makes it worrying.'

'Damn right,' I said. 'What else?'

There was a moment's silence. If I'd been paranoid I could easily have suspected that they wanted to keep me ignorant of the confirmation.

'Odds and ends,' said Billingsly.

Strang said, 'We have something from inside. Two men picked up for interrogation in the Frankfurt area.'

'Berlin.'

'Berlin? No Frankfurt,' said Billingsly.

I'd had enough of Billingsly by that time. They were all like him in the Data Centre: they thought we all needed a couple of megabytes of random access memory to get level with them.

'Don't act the bloody fool,' I told Strang. 'Is your information from Berlin or from Frankfurt?'

'Berlin,' said Strang. 'Normannenstrasse.' That was the big grey stone block in Berlin-Lichtenberg from which East Germany's Stasi – State Security Service – intimidated their world and poked their fingers into ours.

'Over a weekend,' I said. 'Doesn't sound good. If Frankfurt Stasi put that on the teleprinter they must think they have something worthwhile.'

'The question we're discussing,' said the Deputy with the gentle courtesy that barristers show when leading a nervous defendant into an irreversible admission of guilt, 'is whether to follow up.' He looked at me and tilted his head to one side as if seeing me better like that.

I stared back at him. He was a funny bright-eyed plump little man with a shiny pink face and hair brushed close against his skull. Black jacket, a waistcoat full of ancient pens and pencils, pinstripe trousers and the tie of some obscure public school held in place by a jewelled pin. A lawyer. If you saw him on the street you'd have thought him a down-at-heel solicitor or a barrister's clerk. In real life – which is to say outside this building – he ran one of the most successful law firms in London. Why he persevered with this unrewarding job I couldn't fathom, but he was only one step away from running the whole Department. The D-G was, after all, on his last legs. I said, 'You mean, should you put someone in to follow up?'

'Precisely,' said the Deputy. 'I think we'd all like to hear your views, Samson.'

I played for time. 'From Berlin Field Unit?' I said. 'Or from somewhere else?'

'I don't think BFU should come into this,' said Strang hastily. That was the voice of Operations.

He was right of course. Sending someone from West Berlin into such a situation would be madness. In a region like that any kind of stranger is immediately scrutinized by every damned secret policeman on duty and a few that aren't. 'You're probably right,' I said as if conceding something.

Strang said, 'They'd have him in the slammer before the ink was dry on the hotel register.'

'We have people nearer,' said the Deputy.

They were all looking at me now. This is why they'd waited for me to join them. They knew what the answer was going to be but they were going to make sure that it was me, an ex-Field Man, who would say it out loud. Then they could get on with their work, or their lunch, or doze off until the next crisis.

'We can't just leave them to it,' I said.

They all nodded. We had to agree the wrong answer first, that was the ethic of the Department.

'We've had good stuff from them,' Dicky said. 'Nothing big of course, they are only foundry workers, but they've never let us down.'

'I'd like to hear what Samson thinks,' said the Deputy. He had a slim gold pencil in his hand. He was leaning back in his chair, arm extended to his notepad. He looked up from whatever he was writing, stared at me and smiled encouragement.

'We'll have to let it go,' I said finally.

'Speak up,' said the Deputy in his housemaster voice.

I cleared my throat. 'There's nothing we can do,' I said rather louder. 'We'll just have to wait and see.'

They all turned to see the Deputy's reaction. 'I think that's sound,' he said at last. Dicky Cruyer smiled with relief at someone else making the decision. Especially a decision to do nothing. He wriggled about and ran his hand back through his curly hair, looking round the room and nodding. Then he looked over to where a clerk was keeping an account of what was said, to be sure he was writing it down.

Well I'd earned my wages for the day. I'd told them exactly what they wanted to hear. Now nothing would happen for a day or so, apart from a group of Polish workers having their fingernails torn out under hygienic conditions with a shorthand writer in attendance.

There was a knock at the door and a tray with tea and biscuits arrived. Billingsly, perhaps because he was the youngest and least arthritic of us, or because he wanted to impress the Deputy, distributed the cups and saucers and passed the milk and teapot along the polished table top.

'Chocolate oatmeal!' said Harry Strang. I looked up at him and he winked. Harry knew what it was all about. Harry had spent enough time at the sharp end to know what I was thinking.

Harry poured tea for me. I took it and drank some. It turned to acid in my stomach. The Deputy was leaning towards Billingsly to ask him something about the excessive 'down time' the computers in the Yellow Submarine were suffering lately. Billingsly said that you had to expect some trouble with these 'electronic toys'. The Deputy said not when you paid two million pounds for them you didn't.

'Biscuit?' said Harry Strang.

'No thanks.'

'You used to like chocolate oatmeal as I remember,' he said sardonically.

I leaned over to see what the Deputy had written on his notepad but it was just a pattern: a hundred wobbly concentric circles with a big dot in the middle. No escape; no solution; no nothing. It was the answer he wanted to his question, I suppose, and I had given it to him. Ten marks out of ten, Samson. Advance to Go and collect two hundred pounds.

It was only when the Deputy had finished his tea that protocol permitted even the busiest of us to take our leave. Just when the Deputy was moving towards the door, Morgan – the D-G's most obsequious acolyte – came in waxen-faced and complete with Melton overcoat carrying, like an altar candle, one of those short unfolding umbrellas. He said, in his singsong Welsh accent, 'Sorry I'm late, sir. I had the most awful and unexpected trouble with the motorcar.' He bit his lip. Exertion and anxiety had made his face even paler than usual.

The Deputy was annoyed but allowed no more than a trace of it to show. 'We managed without you, Morgan,' he said.

As the Deputy marched out Morgan looked at me with a deep hatred that he made no attempt to hide. Perhaps he thought his humiliation was all my fault or perhaps he blamed me for being there when it happened. Either way, if the Department ever needed someone to bury me Morgan would be an enthusiastic volunteer. Perhaps he was already working on it.

I went downstairs, relieved to get out of that meeting even if it meant sitting in my cramped little office and trying to see over the top of the uncompleted paper-work. I stared at the cluttered table near the window, and more specifically at two boxes in beautiful Christmas wrappings, one marked 'Billy' and the other 'Sally'. They'd been delivered by the Harrods van together with the cards that said 'With dearest love from Mummy' but not in Fiona's handwriting. I should have given them to the children before Christmas but I'd left them there and tried not to look at them. She'd sent presents on previous Christmases and I'd put them under the tree. The children had read the cards without comment. But this year we'd spent Christmas in our new little home and somehow I didn't want Fiona to intrude into it. The move had given me a chance to get rid of Fiona's clothes and personal things. I wanted to start again, but that didn't make it any easier to confront those two bright boxes waiting for me every time I went into my office.

My desk was a mess. My secretary, Brenda, had been covering for two filing clerks who were sick or pregnant or some damned thing, so I tried to sort out a week of muddle that had accumulated on my desk in my absence.

The first things I came across were the red-labelled 'urgent' messages about Prettyman. My God, last Thursday there must have been new messages, requests, assignments and words of advice landing on my desk every half hour. Thank heavens Brenda had enough sense not to forward it all to Washington. Well, now I was back in London, and they could get someone else to go and bully Jim Prettyman into coming back here to be roasted by a committee of time-serving old flower-pots from Central Funding who were desperately looking for some unfortunate upon whom to dump the blame for their own inadequacies.

I was putting it all into the classified waste when I noticed the signature. Billingsly. Billingsly! It was damned odd that Billingsly hadn't mentioned it to me this morning in Number Two Conference Room. He hadn't even asked me what happened. His passion, if not to say obsession, for getting Prettyman here had undergone some abrupt traumatic change. That was the way it went with people like Billingsly –and many others in the Department – who alternated displays of panic and amnesia with disconcerting suddenness.

21

I threw the notes into the basket and forgot about it. There was no point in stirring trouble for Jim Prettyman. In my opinion he was a fool to suddenly get on his high horse about something so mundane. He could have testified and been the golden boy: he could have declined without upsetting them. But I think he liked confrontation. I decided to smooth things over as much as I could. When it came to writing the report I wouldn't say he'd refused point-blank: I'd say he was thinking about it. Until they asked for the report, I'd say nothing at all.

I didn't see Gloria until we had lunch together in the restaurant. Her fluent Hungarian had recently brought her a job downstairs: promotion, more pay and much more responsibility. I suppose they thought that it would be enough to make her forget the promises they'd made about paying her wages while she was at Cambridge. Her new job meant that I saw much less of her and so lunch had become the time when our domestic questions were settled: would it look too pushy to invite the Cruyers for dinner? Who had the receipt for the dry-cleaning? Why had I opened a new tin of cat-food for Muffin when the last one was still half-full?

I asked her if anything more had been said about her resignation, secretly hoping, I suppose, that she might have changed her mind. She hadn't. When I broached the subject over the 'mushroom quiche with winter salad' she told me that she'd had an answer from a friend of hers about some comfortable rooms in Cambridge that she could probably rent.

'What am I going to do with the house?'

'Not so loud, darling,' she said. We kept up this absurd pretence that our co-workers – or such of them as might be interested – didn't know we were living together. 'I'll keep paying half the rent. I told you that.'

'It's nothing to do with the rent,' I said. 'It's simply that I wouldn't have taken on a place out in the sticks so I could sit there every night on my own, watching TV and saving up my laundry until I've got enough to make a full load for the washing machine.'

That produced the flicker of a grin. She leaned closer to me and said, 'After you find out how much dirty laundry the children have every day, you won't be worrying about filling up the machine: you'll be looking for a place where you can get washing powder wholesale.' She sipped some apple juice with added vitamin C. 'You've got a nanny for the children. You'll have that nice Mrs Palmer coming in every day to tidy round. I'll be back every weekend: I don't know what you are worrying about.'

'I wish you'd be a little more realistic. Cambridge is a damned long

22

way away from Balaklava Road. The weekend traffic will be horrendous, the railway service is even worse and in any case you'll have your studying to do.'

'I wish I could make you stop worrying,' she said. 'Are you ill? You haven't been yourself since coming back from Washington. Did something go wrong there?'

'If I'd known what you were going to do I would have made different plans.'

'I told you. I told you over and over.' She looked down and continued to eat her winter salad as if there was no more to be said. In a way she was right. She had told me time and time again. She'd been telling me for years that she was going to go to Cambridge and get this honours degree in PPE that she'd set her heart on. She'd told me so many times that I'd long since ceased to give it any credence. When she told me that she'd actually resigned I was astounded.

'I thought it would be next year,' I said lamely.

'You thought it would be never,' she said curtly. Then she looked up and gave me a wonderful smile. One thing about this damned business of going to Cambridge. It had put her into an incomparably sunny mood. Or was that simply the result of seeing me discomfited?

3

It was Gloria's evening for visiting parents. Tuesday she had an evening class in mathematics, Wednesday economics and Thursday evening she visited her parents. She apportioned time for such things, so that I sometimes wondered if I was one of her duties, or time off.

I stayed working for an extra hour or so until there was a phone call from Mr Gaskell, a recently retired artillery sergeant-major who'd taken over security duties at reception. 'There is a lady here. Asking for you by name. Mr Samson.' The security man's hoarse whisper was confidential to the point of being conspiratorial. I wondered if this was in deference to my professional or social obligations.

'Does she have a name, Mr Gaskell?'

'Lucinda Matthews.' I had the feeling that he was reading from the slip that visitors have to fill out.

The name meant nothing to me but I thought it better not to say so. 'I'll be down,' I said.

'That would be best,' said the security man. 'I can't let her upstairs into the building. You understand, Mr Samson?'

'I understand.' I looked out of the window. The low grey cloud that had darkened the sky all day seemed to have come even lower, and in the air there were tiny flickers of light; harbingers of the snow that had been forecast. Just the sight of it was enough to make me shiver.

By the time I'd locked away my work, checked the filing cabinets and got down to the lobby the mysterious Lucinda had gone.

'A nice little person, sir,' Gaskell confided when I asked what the woman was like. He was standing by the reception desk in his dark blue commissionaire's uniform, tapping his fingers nervously upon the pile of dog-eared magazines that were loaned to visitors who spent a long time waiting here in the draughty lobby. 'Well turned-out; a lady, if you know my meaning.'

I had no notion of his meaning. Gaskell spoke a language that seemed to be entirely his own. He was especially cryptic about dress, rank and class, perhaps because of the social no-man's-land that all senior NCOs inhabit. I'd had these elliptical utterances from Gaskell before, about all kinds of things. I never knew what he was talking about. 'Where did she say she'd meet me?'

'She'd put the car on the pavement, sir. I had to ask her to move it. You know the regulations.'

'Yes, I know.'

'Car bombs and that sort of thing.' No matter how much he rambled, his voice always had the confident tone of an orderly room: an orderly room under his command.

'Where did she say she'd meet me?' I asked yet again. I looked out through the glass doors. The snow had started and was falling fast and in big flakes. The ground was cold, so that it was not melting: it was going to lie. It didn't need more than a couple of cupfuls of that sprinkled over the Metropolis before the public transportation systems all came to a complete halt. Gloria would be at her parents' house by now. She'd gone by train. I wondered if she'd now decide to stay overnight at her parents', or if she'd expect me to go and collect her in the car. Her parents lived at Epsom; too damned near our little nest at Raynes Park for my liking. Gloria said I was frightened of her father. I wasn't frightened of him, but I didn't relish facing intensive questioning from a Hungarian dentist about my relationship with his young daughter.

Gaskell was talking again. 'Lovely vehicle. A dark green Mercedes. Gleaming! Waxed! Someone is looking after it, you could see that. You'd never get a lady polishing a car. It's not in their nature.'

'Where did she go, Mr Gaskell?'

'I told her the best car park for her would be Elephant and Castle.' He went to the map on the wall to show me where the Elephant and Castle was. Gaskell was a big man and he'd retired at fifty. I wondered why he hadn't found a pub to manage. He would have been wonderful behind a bar counter. The previous week, when I'd been asking him about the train service to Portsmouth, he'd confided to me – amid a barrage of other information – that that's what he would have liked to be doing.

'Never mind the car park, Mr Gaskell. I need to know where she's meeting me.'

'Sandy's,' he said at last. 'You knew it well, she said.' He watched me carefully. Ever since our office address had been so widely published, thanks to the public-spirited endeavours of 'investigative journalists', there had been strict instructions that staff must not frequent any local bars, pubs or clubs because of the regular presence of eavesdroppers of various kinds, amateur and professional.

'I wish you'd write these things down,' I said. 'I've never heard of it. Do you know where she means? Is it a café, or what?'

'Not a café I've heard of,' said Gaskell, frowning and sucking his teeth. 'Nowhere near here with a name like that.' And then, as he remembered, his face lit up. 'Big Henry's! That's what she said: Big Henry's.'

'Big Henty's,' I said, correcting him. 'Tower Bridge Road. Yes, I know it.'

Yes, I knew it and my heart sank. I knew exactly the kind of 'informant' who was likely to be waiting for me in Big Henty's: an ear-bender with open palm outstretched. And I had planned an evening at home alone with a coal fire, the carcass of Sunday's duck, a bottle of wine and a book. I looked at the door and I looked at Gaskell. And I wondered if the sensible thing wouldn't be to forget about Lucinda, and whoever she was fronting for, and drive straight home and ignore the whole thing. The chances were that I'd never hear from the mysterious Lucinda again. This town was filled with people who knew me a long time ago and suddenly remembered me when they needed a few pounds from the public purse in exchange for some ancient and unreliable intelligence material.

'If you'd like me to come along, Mr Samson . . .' said Gaskell suddenly, and allowed his offer to hang in the air.

So Gaskell thought there was some strong-arm business in the offing. Well he was a game fellow. Surely he was too old for that sort of thing: and certainly I was.

'That's very kind of you, Mr Gaskell,' I said, 'but the prospect is boredom rather than any rough stuff.'

'Whatever you say,' said Gaskell, unable to keep the disappointment from his voice.

It was the margin of disbelief that made me feel I had to follow it up. I didn't want it to look as if I was nervous. Dammit! why wasn't I brave enough not to care what the Gaskells of this world thought about me?

Tower Bridge Road is a major south London thoroughfare that leads to the river, or rather to the curious neo-Gothic bridge which, for many foreigners, symbolizes the capital. This is Southwark. From here Chaucer's pilgrims set out for Canterbury; and a couple of centuries later Shakespeare's Globe theatre was built upon the marshes. For Victorian London this shopping street, with a dozen brightly lit pubs, barrel organs and late-night street markets, was the centre of one of the capital's most vigorous neighbourhoods. Here filthy slums, smoke-darkened factories and crowded sweat-shops stood side by side with neat leafy squares where scrawny clerks and pot-bellied shopkeepers asserted their social superiority.

26

Now it is dark and squalid and silent. Well-intentioned bureaucrats nowadays sent shop assistants home early, street traders were banished, almost empty pubs sold highly taxed watery lager and the factories were derelict: a textbook example of urban blight, with yuppies nibbling the leafy bits.

Back in the days before women's lib, designer jeans and deep-dish pizza, Big Henty's snooker hall with its 'ten full-size tables, fully licensed bar and hot food' was the Athenaeum of Southwark. The narrow doorway and its dimly lit staircase gave entry to a cavernous hall conveniently sited over a particularly good eel and pie shop.

Now, alas, the eel and pie shop was a video rental 'club' where posters in primary colours depicted half-naked film stars firing heavy machine guns from the hip. But in its essentials Big Henty's was largely unchanged. The lighting was exactly the same as I remembered it, and any snooker hall is judged on its lighting. Although it was very quiet every table was in use. The green baize table tops glowed like ten large aquariums, their water still, until suddenly across them brightly coloured fish darted, snapped and disappeared.

Big Henty wasn't there of course. Big Henty died in 1905. Now the hall was run by a thin white-faced fellow of about forty. He supervised the bar. There was not a wide choice: these snooker-playing men didn't appreciate the curious fizzy mixtures that keep barmen busy in cocktail bars. At Big Henty's you drank whisky or vodka; strong ale or Guinness with tonic and soda water for the abstemious. For the hungry there were 'toasted' sandwiches that came soft, warm and plastic-wrapped from the microwave oven.

'Evening, Bernard. Started to snow, has it?' What a memory the man had. It was years since I'd been here. He picked up his lighted cigarette from the Johnny Walker ashtray, and inhaled on it briefly before putting it back into position. I remembered his chain-smoking, the way he lit one cigarette from another but put them in his mouth only rarely. I'd brought Dicky Cruyer here one evening long ago to make contact with a loud-mouthed fellow who worked in the East German embassy. It had come to nothing, but I remember Dicky describing the barman as the keeper of the sacred flame.

I responded, 'Half of Guinness . . . Sydney.' His name came to me in that moment of desperation. 'Yes, the snow is starting to pile up.'

It was bottled Guinness of course. This was not the place that a connoisseur of stout and porter would come to savour beverages tapped from the wood. But he poured it down the side of the glass holding his thumb under the point of impact to show he knew the folklore, and he put exactly the right size head of light brown foam upon the black beer. 'In the back room.' Delicately he shook the last drops from the bottle and tossed it away without a glance. 'Your friend. In the back room. Behind Table Four.'

I picked up my glass of beer and sipped. Then I turned slowly to survey the room. Big Henty's back room had proved its worth to numerous fugitives over the years. It had always been tolerated by authority. The CID officers from Borough High Street police station found it a convenient place to meet their informants. I walked across the hall. Beyond the tasselled and fringed lights that hung over the snooker tables, the room was dark. The spectators – not many this evening – sat on wooden benches along the walls, their grey faces no more than smudges, their dark clothes invisible.

Walking unhurriedly, and pausing to watch a tricky shot, I took my beer across to table number four. One of the players, a man in the favoured costume of dark trousers, loose-collared white shirt and unbuttoned waistcoat, moved the scoreboard pointer and watched me with expression-less eyes as I opened the door marked 'Staff' and went inside.

There was a smell of soap and disinfectant. It was a small storeroom with a window through which the snooker hall could be seen if you pulled aside the dirty net curtain. On the other side of the room there was another window, a larger one that looked down upon Tower Bridge Road. From the street below there came the sound of cars slurping through the slush.

'Bernard.' It was a woman's voice. 'I thought you weren't going to come.'

I sat down on the bench before I recognized her in the dim light. 'Cindy!' I said. 'Good God, Cindy!'

'You'd forgotten I existed.'

'Of course I hadn't.' I'd only forgotten that Cindy Prettyman's full name was Lucinda, and that she might have reverted to her maiden name. 'Can I get you a drink?'

She held up her glass. 'It's tonic water. I'm not drinking these days.'

'I just didn't expect you here,' I said. I looked through the net curtain at the tables.

'Why not?'

'Yes, why not?' I said and laughed briefly. 'When I think how many times Jim made me swear I was giving up the game for ever.' In the old days, when Jim Prettyman was working alongside me, he taught me to play snooker. He played an exhibition class game, and his wife Cindy was something of an expert too.

Cindy was older than Jim by a year or two. Her father was a steel worker in Scunthorpe: a socialist of the old school. She'd got a scholarship to Reading University. She said she'd never had any ambition but for a career in the Civil Service since her schooldays. I don't know if it was true but it went down well at the Selection Board. She wanted Treasury but got Foreign Office, and eventually got Jim Prettyman who went there too. Then Jim came over to work in the Department and I saw a lot of him. We used to come here, me, Fiona, Jim and Cindy, after work on Fridays. We'd play snooker to decide who would buy dinner at Enzo's, a little Italian restaurant in Old Kent Road. Invariably it was me. It was a joke really; my way of repaying him for the lesson. And I was the eldest and making more money. Then the Prettymans moved out of town to Edgware. Jim got a rise and bought a full-size table of his own, and then we stopped coming to Big Henty's. And Jim invited us over to his place for Sunday lunch, and a game, sometimes. But it was never the same after that.

'Do you still play?' she asked.

'It's been years. And you?'

'Not since Jim went.'

'I'm sorry about what happened, Cindy.'

'Jim and me. Yes, I wanted to talk to you about that. You saw him on Friday.'

'Yes, how do you know?'

'Charlene. I've been talking to her a lot lately.'

'Charlene?'

'Charlene Birkett. The tall girl we used to let our upstairs flat to . . . in Edgware. Now she's Jim's secretary.'

'I saw her. I didn't recognize her. I thought she was American.' So that's why she'd smiled at me: I thought it was my animal magnetism.

'Yes,' said Cindy, 'she went to New York and couldn't get a job until Jim fixed up for her to work for him. There was never anything between them,' she added hurriedly. 'Charlene's a sweet girl. They say she's really blossomed since living there and wearing contact lenses.'

'I remember her,' I said. I did remember her; a stooped, mousy girl with glasses and frizzy hair, quite unlike the shapely Amazon I'd seen in Jim's office. 'Yes, she's changed a lot.'

'People do change when they live in America.'

'But you didn't want to go?'

'America? My dad would have died.' You could hear the northern accent now. 'I didn't want to change.' Then she said, solemnly, 'Oh, doesn't that sound awful? I didn't mean that exactly.'

'People go there and they get richer,' I said. 'That's what the real change is.'

'Jim got the divorce in Mexico,' she said. 'Someone told me that it's not really legal. A friend of mine: she works in the American embassy. She said Mexican marriages and divorces aren't legal here. Is that true, Bernard?'

'I don't imagine that the Mexican ambassador is living in sin, if that's what you mean.'

'But how do I stand, Bernard? He married this other woman. I mean, how do I stand now?'

'Didn't you talk to him about it?' My eyes had become accustomed to the darkness now and I could see her better. She hadn't changed much, she was the same tiny bundle of brains and nervous energy. She was short with a full figure but had never been plump. She was attractive in an austere way with dark hair that she kept short so it would be no trouble to her. But her nose was reddened as if she had a cold and her eyes were watery.

'He asked me to go with him.' She was proud of that and she wanted me to know.

'I know he did. He told everyone that you would change your mind.'

'No. I had my job!' she said, her voice rising as if to repeat the arguments they'd had about it.

'It's a difficult decision,' I said to calm her. In the silence there was a sudden loud throbbing noise close by. She jumped almost out of her skin. Then she realized that it was the freezer cabinet in the corner and she smiled.

'Perhaps I should have done. It would have been better I suppose.'

'It's too late now, Cindy,' I said hurriedly before she started to go weepy on me.

'I know; I know; I know.' She got a handkerchief from her pocket but rolled it up and gripped it tight in her red-knuckled hand as if resolving not to sob.

'Perhaps you should see a lawyer,' I said.

'What do they know?' she said contemptuously. 'I've seen three lawyers. They pass you on one from the other like a parcel, and by the time I was finished paying out all the fees I knew that some law books say one thing and other law books say different.'

'The lawyers can quote from the law books until they are blue in the face,' I said. 'But eventually people have to sort out the solutions with each other. Going to lawyers is just an expensive way of putting off what you're going to have to do anyway.'

30

'Is that what you really think, Bernard?'

'More or less,' I said. 'Buying a house, making a will, getting divorced. Providing you know what you want, you don't need a lawyer for any of that.'

'Yes,' she said. 'What's more important than getting married, and you don't go to a lawyer to do that.'

'In foreign countries you do,' I told her. 'Couples don't get married without signing a marriage contract. They never have this sort of problem that you have. They decide it all beforehand.'

'It sounds a bit cold-blooded.'

'Maybe it is, but marriage can be a bit too hot-blooded too.'

'Was yours?' She released her grip on the tiny handkerchief and spread it out on her lap to see the coloured border and the embroidered initials LP.

'My marriage?' I said. 'Too hot-blooded?'

'Yes.'

'Perhaps.' I sipped my drink. It was a long time since I'd had one of these heavy bitter-tasting brews. I wiped the froth from my lips; it was good. 'I thought I knew Fiona, but I suppose I didn't know her well enough.'

'She was so lovely. I know she loved you, Bernard.'

'I think she did.'

'She showed me that fantastic engagement ring and said, Bernie sold his Ferrari to buy that for me.'

'It sounds like a line from afternoon television,' I said, 'but it was a very old battered Ferrari.'

'She loved you, Bernard.'

'People change, Cindy. You said that yourself.'

'Did it affect the children much?'

'Billy seemed to take it in his stride but Sally . . . She was all right until I took a girl-friend home. Lots of crying at night. But I think she's adjusted now.' I said it more because I wanted it to be true than because I believed it. I worried about the children, worried a lot, but that was none of Cindy's business.

'Gloria Kent, the one you work with?'

This Cindy knew everything. Well, the FO had always been Whitehall's gossip exchange. 'That's right,' I said.

'It's difficult for children,' said Cindy. 'I suppose I should be thankful that we didn't have any.'

'You're right,' I said. I drank some Guinness and sneaked a look at the time.

'But on the other hand, if we'd had kids perhaps Jim wouldn't have wanted to go so much. He wanted to prove himself, you see. Lately I've wondered if he blamed himself that we never were able to have children.'

'Jim was talking about that time when the kitchen caught fire,' I said.

'Jim spilled the oil. He's always been clumsy.'

'Fiona didn't do it?'

'She took the blame,' said Cindy with a sigh. 'Jim could never admit to making a mistake. That was his nature.'

'Yes, Fiona took the blame,' I said. 'She told me Jim did it but she really took the blame . . . the insurance . . . everything.'

'Fiona was a remarkable woman, Bernard, you know that. Fiona had such self-confidence that blame never touched her. I admired her. I would have given almost anything to have been like Fiona, she was always so calm and poised.'

I didn't respond. Cindy drank some of her tonic water and smoothed her dress and cleared her throat and then said, 'The reason I wanted to talk to you, Bernard, is to see what the Department will do.'

'What the Department will do?' I said. I was puzzled.

'Do about Jim,' said Cindy. I could see her squeezing the handkerchief in repeated movements, like someone exercising their hands.

'About Jim.' I blew dust from my spectacle lenses and began to polish them. They'd picked up grease from the air and polishing just made them more smeary. The only way to get them clean was to wash them with kitchen detergent under the warm tap. The optician advised against this method but I went on doing it anyway. 'I'm not sure what you mean, Cindy.'

'Will they pay me or this American woman, this so-called "wife",' she said angrily.

'Pay you?' I put my glasses on and looked at her.

'Don't be so difficult, Bernard. I must know. I must. Surely you can see that.'

'Pay you what?'

Her face changed. 'Holy Mary!' she said in that way that only church-going Catholics say such things. 'You don't know!' It was a lament. 'Jim is dead. They killed him Friday night when he left the office after seeing you. They shot him. Six bullets.'

'Last Friday.'

'In the car park. It was dark. He didn't stand a chance. There were two of them; waiting for him. No one told you?'

'No.'

32

'Don't think me callous, Bernard. But I want to put in a claim for his pension before this other woman. What should I do?'

'Is there a pension, Cindy? I would have thought all that would have been wound up when he left.'

'Left? He's never stopped working for the Department.'

'You're wrong about that, Cindy,' I said.

She became excited. 'Do you think I don't know! By God, I saw . . .' she stopped suddenly, as if she might be saying something I wasn't entitled to know.

'I was there in Washington asking him to come to London to give evidence. He wouldn't come,' I explained quietly.

'That was the cover-up, Bernard,' she said. She had her temper under control now but she was still angry. 'They wanted him in London but it was going to be done as if he came under protest.'

'It fooled me,' I said.

'Jim got into very deep water,' she said. 'Was it the money you had to talk to him about?'

I nodded.

'Jim arranged all that,' she said sadly. 'Millions and millions of pounds in some secret foreign bank account. A lot of people were empowered to sign: Jim was one of them.'

'You're not saying that Jim was killed because of this, are you Cindy?'

'What was it then: robbery?' she said scornfully.

'Washington is a rough place,' I told her.

'Two men; six bullets?' she said. 'Damned funny thieves.'

'Let me get you a proper drink, Cindy. I need time to think about all this.'

4

I was in Dicky Cruyer's very comfortable office, sitting in his Eames chair and waiting for him to return from his meeting with the Deputy. He'd promised to be no more than ten minutes, but what the Deputy had to say to him took longer than that.

When Dicky arrived he made every effort to look his youthful carefree self, but I guessed that the Deputy had given him a severe wigging about the Bizet crisis. 'All okay?' I said.

For a moment he looked at me as if trying to remember who I was, and what I was doing here. He ran his fingers back through his curly hair. He was slim; and handsome in a little-boy way which he cultivated assiduously.

'The Deputy has to be kept up to date,' said Dicky, indicating a measured amount of condescension about the Deputy's inexperience. As long as Sir Henry, the Director-General, had been coming in regularly, the Deputy, Sir Percy Babcock, had scarcely shown his face in the building. But since the old man's attendance had become intermittent, the Deputy had taken command with all the zeal of the newly converted. The first major change he wrought was to tell Dicky to wear clothes more in keeping with his responsibilities. Dicky's extensive wardrobe of faded designer jeans, trainers and tartan shirts, and the gold medallion that he wore at his neck, had not been seen recently. Now, in line with the rest of the male staff, he was wearing a suit every day. I found it difficult to adjust to this new sober Dicky.

'You weren't at Charles Billingsly's farewell gathering last night,' said Dicky. 'Champagne . . . very stylish.'

'I didn't hear about it,' I said. Billingsly – German Desk's more or less useless Data Centre liaison man – wasn't a close friend of mine. I suppose he thought I might drink too much of his expensive fizz. 'Are we getting rid of him?'

'A super hush-hush assignment to Honkers. Forty-eight hours' notice is all they gave him. So he didn't let you know about the party? Well, it was all a rush for him.'

'What would Hong Kong need him for?'

'No one knows, not even Charles. Hurry and wait. That's how it goes isn't it?'

'Maybe the Deputy just wanted to get rid of him,' I suggested.

Dicky's eyes glittered. After his little session on the carpet it probably made him wonder if he might not one day find himself on a fast plane to distant places. 'Get rid of Charles, why?'

'I've no idea,' I said.

'No. Charles is a good sort.'

Unbid, Dicky's secretary arrived with a large silver-plated tray bearing the Spode chinaware and a large pot of freshly ground coffee made just the way Dicky liked it. I suppose she hoped it would put Dicky into a better frame of mind as sometimes a heavy shot of caffeine did. He bent over it and gave low murmurs of approval before pouring some coffee for himself. Then he went and sat down behind the big rosewood table that he used as his desk before he tasted the coffee appreciatively. 'Damn good!' he pronounced and drank some more. 'Pour yourself a cup,' he said when he was quite sure it was okay.

I took one of the warmed cups, poured some for myself and added cream. It always came with cream, even though Dicky drank his coffee black. I often wondered why. For a moment we drank our coffee in silence. I had the feeling that Dicky needed five minutes to recover from his meeting.

'He's become an absolute despot lately,' said Dicky at last. Having devoured a large cup of coffee he took a small cigar from his pocket, lit it and blew smoke. 'I wish I could make him understand that it's not like running his law firm. I can't get a book down from the shelf and read the answers to him.'

'He'll get the hang of it,' I said.

'In time, he will,' agreed Dicky. 'But by then I'll be old and grey.' That might be quite a long time, for Dicky was young and fit and two years my junior. He flicked ash into the big cut-glass ashtray on his desk and kept looking at the carpet as if lost in thought.

I pulled my paper-work from its cardboard folder and said, 'Do you want to run through this stuff?' I brandished it at him but he continued to stare at the carpet.

'He's talking about vertical reorganization.'

I said, 'What's that?'

Dicky, short-listed for the Stalin Prize in office politics, said, 'Jesus Christ, Bernard. Vertical planning! Dividing the German Desk up into groups region by region. He told me that I'd have Berlin, as if that would make me overjoyed. Berlin! With other desks for Bonn and Hamburg and so on. A separate unit would liaise with the Americans in Munich. Can you imagine it!'

'That idea has been kicking around for ages,' I said. I began to sort out the work I'd brought for him. I knew that getting him to look at it would be difficult in his present agitated mood, so I put the papers that required a signature on top. There were five of them.

'It's ridiculous!' said Dicky so loudly that his secretary looked in through the door to see if everything was all right. She was a new secretary or she would have made herself scarce when there was a chance of encountering Dicky's little tantrums.

'It will happen sooner or later I suppose,' I said. I got my pen out so that Dicky could sign while he talked about something else. Sometimes it was easier like that.

'You'd heard about it before?' said Dicky incredulously, suddenly realizing what I'd said.

'Oh, yes. A year or more ago but it had some other name then.'

'Ye gods, Bernard! I wish you'd told me.'

I put the papers on his desk and gave him the ballpoint pen and watched him sign his name. I hadn't heard of the vertical planning scheme before, of course, but guessed that the Deputy had simply invented something that would goad Dicky into more energetic action, and I thought it better not to let the old boy down. 'And these you should look at,' I said, indicating the most important ones.

'You'll have to go and see Frank,' he said as he signed the final one and plucked at the corners of the rest of the stuff to see if anything looked interesting enough to read.

'Okay,' I said. He looked up at me. He'd expected me to object to a trip to Berlin but he'd caught me at a good time. It was a month or more since I'd been to Berlin and there were reasons both official and social for a trip there. 'And what do I tell Frank?' I wanted to get it clear because we had this absurd system in which Dicky and Frank Harrington – the Berlin 'resident' and as old as Methuselah – had equal authority.

He looked up from the carpet and said, 'I don't want to rub Frank up the wrong way. It's not up to me to tell him how to run his Berlin Field Unit. Frank knows more about the operations side of his bailiwick than all the rest of us put together.' That was all true, of course, but it wasn't often the line Dicky took.

'We're talking about Bizet, I take it?'

'Right. Frank may want to put someone in. After all, Frankfurt an der Oder is only a stone's throw from where he is.'

'It's not the distance, Dicky. It's . . .'

He immediately held up his hand in defence. 'Sure. I know I know I know.'

'Are you hoping he'll have done something already?'

'I just want his advice,' said Dicky.

'Well, we both know what Frank's advice will be,' I said. 'Do nothing. Just the same advice that he gives us about everything.'

'Frank's been there a long time,' said Dicky, who had survived many a crisis and reshuffle on 'do nothing' policies.

I made sure Dicky had signed everything in the right place. Then I drank the coffee and left it at that for a bit. But this seemed a good opportunity to quiz him about the Prettyman business. 'Remember Prettyman?' I said as casually as I could manage.

'Should I?'

'Jim Prettyman: ended up in "black boxes". Left and went to America.'

'Codes and Ciphers, downstairs?' It was a not a region into which Dicky ever ventured.

'He was on the Special Operations committee with Bret. He was always trying to organize holidays where you could look at tombs and no one ever put their name down. Wonderful snooker player. Don't you remember how we went to Big Henty's one night and he made some fantastic break?'

'I've never been to Big Henty's in my life.'

'Of course you have, Dicky. Lots of times. Jim Prettyman. A young fellow who got that job in Washington.'

'Sometimes I think you must know everyone in this building,' said Dicky.

'I thought you knew him,' I said lamely.

'A word to the wise, Bernard.' Dicky was holding a finger aloft as if testing for the direction of the wind. 'If I was in this room talking to you about this Prettyman fellow you'd change the subject to talk about Frank Harrington and the Bizet business. No offence intended, old chum, but it's true. Think about it.'

'I'm sure you're right, Dicky.'

'You must try and concentrate upon the subject in hand. Have you ever done any yoga?' He pushed aside the papers that I'd suggested he should read.

'No, Dicky,' I said.

'I did a lot of yoga at one time.' He ran a finger across the papers as if reading the contents list. 'It trains the mind: helps the power of concentration.'

'I'll look into that,' I promised, taking from him the signed papers

37

that Dicky had decided not to read, and stuffing them into the cardboard folder.

When I stood up, Dicky, still looking at the carpet, said, 'My mother's cousin died and left me a big lion skin. I was wondering whether to have it in here.'

'It would look just right,' I said, indicating the antique furniture and the framed photos that covered the wall behind him.

'I had it in the drawing room at home but some of our friends made a bit of fuss about shooting rare animals and that sort of thing.'

'Don't worry about that, Dicky,' I said. 'That's just because they're jealous.'

'That's just what I told Daphne,' he said. 'After all, the damned thing's dead. I can't bring a lion back to life can I?'

5

Many civilians have a lifelong obsession about what it would be like to be in the army. Some like the idea of uniforms, horses, trumpets and flags; others just want clearly expressed orders, and a chance to carry them out in exchange for hot meals on the table every day. For some men the army represents a challenge they never faced; for others a cloistered cosy masculine retreat from reality.

Which of these aspects of the soldier's life Frank Harrington found attractive – or whether it was something entirely different – I never knew. But whenever Frank was not in his office, nor in the splendid Grunewald mansion that he'd arranged should be one of the 'perks' of being the Berlin Resident, I knew I'd find him in some squalid dug-out, sitting in the middle of a bunch of begrimed infantry officers, looking thoroughly happy as he told them how to fight their war.

This day, dressed in borrowed army togs with mud on his knees and elbows, he was delivered to the Grunewald house in a big army staff car.

'I'm awfully sorry, Frank,' I said.

'I was only playing soldiers,' he said in that disarming way he had. 'And Dicky said it was urgent.'

He looked as if he was going to conduct me straight into his study. 'It's not so urgent that you can't change and take a shower,' I said. I gave him the report from London.

He took it and shook it at his ear to listen for its rattle. He grinned. We both knew Dicky. 'Go into the drawing room and get yourself a drink, Bernard,' he said. 'Ring for Tarrant if you can't find what you want. You're going to eat with me I hope?'

'Yes. I'd like that, Frank.'

He was a wellspring of cheer after his day with the soldiers. Halfway up the stairs he turned to say, 'Welcome home, Bernard,' knowing how delighted I would be at such a greeting. For no matter where I went or what I did, Berlin would always be home for me. My father had been Resident long ago – before they were provided with a grand mansion in which to live and an entertainment allowance – and Berlin held all my happy childhood recollections.

When after thirty minutes or more Frank returned he was dressed in what for him were informal clothes: an old grey herringbone tweed jacket and flannels, but the starched shirt and striped tie wouldn't have disgraced any Mess. Just as I was able to make new clothes look shabby, so Frank was able to invest even his oldest garments with a spruce look. His cuffs emerged just the right amount and there was a moiré kerchief in his top pocket and hand-sewn Oxfords that were polished to perfection. He went across to the drinks trolley and poured himself a large Plymouth gin with a dash of bitters. 'What have you got there?' he asked.

'I'm all right, Frank,' I said.

'Wouldn't you rather have a real drink?'

'I'm trying to cut back on the hard stuff, Frank.'

'That bottle must have been on that trolley for years. Is it still all right?' He picked up the bottle I'd poured my drink from, and studied the label with interest, and then he looked at me. 'Vermouth? That's not like you, Bernard.'

'Delicious,' I said.

He came and sat opposite me. His face had the war-painted look that dedicated skiers wore at this time of the year. His skin was dark, with pale surrounds where his goggles had been. Frank knew a thing or two about the good life. I didn't ask after his wife. She spent most of the time at their house in England nowadays. She had never liked Berlin, and rumours said there had been a row when Frank accepted the invitation to stay on past his official retirement date.

He'd read the interim report in his bath, he told me. We knew that it had been roughly cobbled together in London and we both knew it was just a lengthy way of saying nothing at all. He flicked through it very quickly again and said, 'Does Dicky want me to deposit someone in there?'

'He's going to great pains not to say so,' I said.

'I'll do anything for the poor bastards who are in trouble,' he said. 'But this is Berlin. I can't think of anyone here who could go to Frankfurt an der bloody Oder and do anything to help them.' He touched his blunt military moustache. It was going very grey.

'They don't like to sit in London doing nothing,' I said.

'How do they think I like it?' said Frank. Just for a moment his face and his voice revealed the strain of the job. I suppose there were plenty of agents being picked up all the time but it was only when there was monitored Soviet radio traffic about them that London got interested and concerned. 'The army got wind of it,' said Frank. 'They're keen to try their hand.'

He must have seen my face go white, and my teeth clench, or

40

whatever happened when I became so terrified that I wanted to scream. 'The army?' I said, holding tight to my drink and keeping my voice under control.

'The Brigadier was reminding me about the Military Mission staff we have with the Russian army headquarters. They are able to move about a little more freely nowadays.'

'What else did your Brigadier say?'

'He was quoting the behaviour of these GRU bastards our chaps have to put up with at Bunde. Counting those with the French army at Baden-Baden, and those with the Yanks, there are about fifty Soviet Military Mission staffers. GRU agents every one, and many of them with scientific training. They wear leather jackets over their uniforms and deliberately muddy their car registration plates so they're not recognized while they go pushing their way into, and photographing, everything that interests them.' He grinned. ' "What about tit for tat?" that's what the Brigadier says.'

'You didn't tell your army pal about Bizet?'

'I'm not senile, Bernard.'

'The idea of some keen young subaltern sniffing around in Frankfurt an der Oder is enough to give me a nightmare.'

'I shouldn't have mentioned it.'

'You said the army had wind of it,' I reminded him.

'Did I? I should have said that the army know we have a crisis of some sort.' He looked at me and added, 'They have a good radio monitoring service, Bernard.'

'For listening to Russian army signals.'

'Along the border, that is true. But here in Berlin – right in the middle of the DDR – they hear all the domestic stuff. They monitor GRU and KGB traffic; they like to know what's going on. I would never object to that, Bernard. In an outpost like this, the army need to keep a finger on the pulse.'

'Maybe I will have something stronger,' I said. But at that moment Frank's German maid came in to say dinner was served.

I pushed all my worries, about what Frank might have said to his army cronies, to the back of my mind. We sat in the grand dining room, just me and Frank at one end of the long polished table. He'd had someone decant a bottle of really good claret: the empty bottle was on the sideboard. It was something of an honour. Frank kept his best wines for people either important enough to merit them, or choosy enough to notice. He poured some for me to taste when the egg and bacon tart arrived. The portions were very small. I suspected that the

41

cook was trying to eke out Frank's meal and make enough for me. Frank seemed not to notice. He wanted to hear all the latest gossip from the Department, and I told him how the Deputy was slowly but surely changing the Department to his own wishes.

From my own point of view I rather welcomed the new ideas. It was time the old gang were shaken up a bit. Frank agreed, but with less enthusiasm.

'I'm too old to welcome changes just for the sake of change, Bernard. I was in the Department with your father back in 1943. I did a training course with Sir Henry Clevemore – "Pimples" we called him – a damned great hulking kid. He fell into a drainage ditch on one of the assault courses. It needed four of us to haul him out.' He drank some more wine, and after a reflective pause added, 'My wife says I've given my life to the Department, and a large chunk of her life too!' It was a heartfelt declaration of pride, resentment and regret.

He went on talking about the Department through the cottage pie, the bread and butter pudding and the Cheddar cheese. No matter how long he lived here, and how assimilated he became, the output from Frank's kitchen remained defiantly British public school. I was happy to listen to him, especially when he mentioned my father. He knew that of course, and all the stories he told showed my father in such a glorious light that I knew he was just putting it on for me. 'Your dad sat for days and days in some filthy apartment with only this German fellow for company: arguing and swearing most of the time according to your dad's account. They were waiting for news of Hitler's assassination. When the news that the assassination attempt had failed, in came this Gestapo agent. Your dad was ready to jump out of the window but it turned out that it was the other chap's brother . . . I'm probably getting it all muddled,' said Frank with a smile. 'And I'm sure it was all just one of your father's yarns. But whenever your dad could be persuaded to tell that story he'd have me, and everyone else, in fits of laughter.' Frank had some more wine and ate some cheese. 'None of the rest of us had ever been in Nazi Germany of course. We hung on your dad's every word. Sometimes he'd be pulling our leg mercilessly.'

'The other day someone hinted that the Department might get to me through my father,' I said as casually as I could.

'Pressure you?'

'That was the implication. How could they do that, Frank? Did Dad do anything . . .'

'Are you serious, Bernard?'

'I want to know, Frank.'

'Then may I suggest you seek clarification from whoever gave you this bizarre idea.'

I changed the subject. 'And Fiona?' I asked as casually as I was able.

He looked up sharply. I suppose he knew how much I still missed her. 'She keeps a very low profile.'

'But she's still in East Berlin?'

'Very much so. Flourishing, or so I hear. Why?'

'I was just curious.'

'Put her out of your mind, Bernard. It's all over now. I suffered for you but now it's time to forget the past. Tell me about the new house. Do the children like having a garden?'

Our conversation was devoted to domestic small-talk. By the time we went back to the drawing room to drink coffee, Frank was in a mellow mood. I said, 'Remember the last time we were together in this room, Frank?'

He looked at me and after a moment's thought said, 'The night you came over asking me to get Bret Rensselaer off the hook. It is really that long ago? Three years?'

'You were packing your Duke Ellington records,' I said. 'They were all across the floor here.'

'I thought I was retiring and going back to England.' He looked round remembering it all and said, 'It changed my life, I suppose. By now I would have been pensioned off and growing roses.'

'And been Sir Frank Harrington,' I said. 'I'm sorry about the way it all worked out, Frank.' It was generally agreed that the débâcle resulting from my intervention had deprived Frank of the knighthood he'd set his heart on. London Central had been saved from humiliation, by my warning and Frank's unilateral action, but they'd still not forgiven either of us. We'd been proved right, and for the mandarins of the Foreign Office that was a rare and unpardonable sin.

'It must be nearly three years,' he said, unrolling his tobacco pouch and stuffing his Balkan Sobranie tobacco into the bowl of a curly pipe. Oh God, was Frank going to smoke that pipe of his? 'I was disappointed at the time but I've got over it now.'

'I suppose Bret got the worst of it.'

'I suppose so,' said Frank, lighting his pipe.

'Last I heard he was having night and day nursing care and sinking fast,' I said. 'He's not still alive?'

Frank took his time getting his pipe going before he replied. Then he said, 'Bret hung on for a long time but now he's gone.' He smiled in that distant way of his and started puffing contentedly. I moved back from

43

him. I could never get used to Frank's pipe. He said, 'That's not to be repeated. Perhaps I shouldn't have told you. I was told in confidence; the Department have said nothing yet.'

'Poor Bret. That night I flew out of Berlin there was a roomful of men in white coats swearing he couldn't live beyond the weekend.'

'His brother arrived with some damned American general in tow. Bret was hauled aboard a US Air Force plane and flown out. I heard they'd put him into that hospital in Washington, where they treat the US Presidents. He was in all kinds of hospitals for a long time: you know what the Americans are like. And then he went to convalesce in a house he owns in the Virgin Islands. He sent me a postcard from there; "Wish you were here", palm trees and a beach. Berlin was deep under snow and the central heating was giving trouble. I didn't think it was so funny at the time. I wondered if he meant that he wished I'd stopped the bullet that he'd taken. I don't know. I never will know, I suppose.'

I said nothing.

There was a lot of prodding at the tobacco. Frank had a special little steel device for pushing it around. He tended that pipe like some Scots engineer at the boiler of an ancient and well beloved tramp steamer. And it gave him time to think about what he was going to say. 'I've never been told officially, of course. I thought it was funny, the way that Bret always made such a big performance of being English. And then he's injured and he's off to America.' Another pause. 'As I say, Bret never died officially; he just faded away.'

'Like old soldiers,' I said.

'What? Oh, yes, I see what you mean.'

Then the conversation moved to other matters. I asked about Frank's son, an airline pilot who'd recently gone from British Airways to one of the domestic airlines. He was flying smaller planes on shorter routes but he was at home with his wife almost every night and making more money too. In the old days Frank's son had often got to Berlin, but nowadays it was not on any of his routes and Frank admitted that sometimes he felt lonely.

I looked around. The house was all beautifully kept up but it was a dark echoing place for one man on his own. I remembered how, many years ago, Frank told me that marriage didn't fit very well with men 'in our line of business – women don't like secrets to which they are not a party'. I'd thought about it ever since.

Frank asked about mutual friends in Washington DC and after talking about some of them I said, 'Do you remember Jim Prettyman?'

'Prettyman? No,' said Frank with conviction. Then Frank asked if everything was all right between me and Gloria. I said it was, because the ever-growing fear that I had, about becoming too dependent upon her, seemed too trivial and childish to discuss.

'Not thinking of marrying again?' Frank asked.

'I'm not free to marry,' I reminded him. 'I'm still legally married to Fiona, aren't I?'

'Of course.'

'I have a nasty feeling she'll try for custody of the children again,' I said. I hadn't intended to tell him but I'd got to the point where I had to tell someone.

'I hope not, Bernard.'

'I had a formal letter from my father-in-law. He wants regular access to the children.'

He took his pipe from his mouth. 'And you think he's in touch with Fiona?'

'I'm not going to rule it out; he's a two-faced old bastard.'

'Don't meet trouble halfway, Bernard. What does Gloria think?'

'I haven't told her yet.'

'Bernard you are an ass. You must stop treating her as if she's half-witted. A woman's point of view, Bernard.'

'You're right,' I said.

'Yes, I am. Stop brooding. Talk to her. She must know the children by now.'

'I'd better get going, Frank,' I said. 'It's been like old times.'

'I'm glad you stayed to dinner. I wish I'd known you were coming, I could have laid on some decent grub for you.'

'It was just like home,' I said.

'Have you got a car?' he asked.

'Yes, thanks.'

'I wish you wouldn't rent cars at the airport. It's not good security.'

'I suppose you're right,' I admitted.

His pipe was burning fiercely now, its smoke so dense that Frank's eyes were half-closed against it. 'Staying with Frau Hennig?' He always called her Frau Hennig. I don't think he liked her very much but he hid his emotions about her as he did about a lot of other things.

'Yes,' I said. Out of the corner of my eye I saw Tarrant glide in, scowling. Frank's longtime valet always materialized like the ghost of Hamlet's father. I swear he listened at the door. How else could he appear at the exact right – or sometimes no less exact wrong – moment?

When Frank turned to him, Tarrant said, 'Colonel Hampshire phoned to say Headquarters won the tournament.'

45

I looked at Frank, who took the pipe from his mouth, smiled at me and said, 'Bridge.'

So I'd dragged Frank from some damned Officers' Mess bridge final. No doubt the meal we'd eaten was Tarrant's supper. But appearances could be deceptive; Tarrant's big eyebrows were always lowered menacingly, like a bull about to charge. Perhaps he wasn't hungry and resentful: maybe he was drunk.

'Thank you, Tarrant. You can go to bed. I'll see Mr Samson out.'

'Very good, sir.'

'Don't go,' said Frank to me. 'Let's open a bottle of tawny and make a night of it.'

Frank's choice in vintage port was always a temptation but I declined. 'I must put my head round the door before Lisl goes to sleep,' I said, looking at my watch.

'And what time is that?'

'Pretty damned late,' I admitted.

'You heard she's closing down?'

'The hotel? No more than that. Werner wrote me one of his cryptic notes but that's all he said.'

'It's too much for her,' said Frank, 'and those bloody people who work for her turn up only when they feel like it.'

'You don't mean Klara?' Klara was Lisl Hennig's maid and had been for countless ages.

'No, not Klara, of course not. But Klara is very old now. They're a couple of very old ladies. They should both be in a nursing home, not trying to cope with all the problems of a broken-down hotel.'

'What will Lisl do?'

'If she takes the advice everyone is giving her, she'll sell the place.'

'She's borrowed on it,' I said.

He prodded the pipe. 'If I know anything about the mentality of bank managers, the bank won't have loaned her more than half of what it will fetch on the market.'

'I suppose you're right.'

'She'd have enough cash to live her last few years in comfort.'

'But the house means such a lot to her.'

'She can't have it both ways,' said Frank.

'I can't imagine coming to Berlin and not being able to go to Lisl's,' I said selfishly. My father had been billeted in that house, and eventually my mother took me there to join him. We lived there all through my schooldays and my youth. Every room, every stick of furniture, every bit of frayed carpet held memories for me. I suppose that was why I was pleased that so little was done to bring it up to date. It was my private museum of nostalgia, and the thought of being deprived of it filled me with dread. It was tantamount to someone wrenching from me memories of my father.

'Just one?' said Frank. He laid his pipe on the ashtray with reverential care, and went to the drinks trolley. 'I'm opening the bottle anyway.'

'Yes, thanks,' I said changing my mind and sitting down again while Frank poured a glass of his tawny port for me. I said, 'The last time I was at Lisl's, only three rooms were occupied.'

'That's only half of the trouble,' said Frank. 'The doctor said running that place is too much for her. He told Werner that he wouldn't give her more than six months if she doesn't rest completely.'

'Poor Lisl.'

'Yes, poor Lisl,' said Frank handing me a brimming glass of port wine. There was a sardonic note in his voice: he usually called her Frau Hennig.

'I know you never liked her,' I said.

'Come, Bernard. That's not true.' He picked up his pipe and got it going again.

'Isn't it?'

'I said she was a Nazi,' he said in a measured way and smiled to acknowledge his dissembling.

'That's nonsense.' She was like a second mother to me. Even if Frank was like a second father I wasn't going to let him get away with such damaging generalizations about her.

'The Hennigs were social climbers in Hitler's time,' said Frank. 'Her husband was a member of the Party, and a lot of the people she mixed with were damned shady.'

'For instance?'

'Don't get so defensive, Bernard. Lisl and her friends were enthusiastic Hitler supporters right up to the time when the Red Army started waving a flag from the Brandenburger Tor.' He sipped. 'And even after that she only learned to keep her political opinions to herself.'

'Maybe,' I said grudgingly. It was true that Lisl had always had a quick eye for any failings of socialism.

'And that Lothar Koch . . . Well, we've been through all that before.'

Frank was convinced that Lothar Koch, an old friend of Lisl's, had some sort of Nazi past. One of Frank's German pals said Koch was a Gestapo man but there were always stories about people being Gestapo men, and Frank had said the same thing about many other people. Sometimes I thought Frank spent more time worrying about the Nazis than he did about the Russians. But that was something common to a lot of the old-timers.

'Lothar Koch was just a clerk,' I said. I emptied my glass and got to my feet. 'And you're just a romantic, Frank, that's your problem. You're still hoping that Martin Bormann will be discovered helping Hitler to type his memoirs in a tin hut in the rain forest.'

Still puffing his pipe Frank got to his feet and gave me one of his 'we'll-see-one-day' smiles. When we got to the door he said, 'I'll acknowledge Dicky's memo on the teleprinter, and we'll get together late tomorrow so you can take a verbal back to him. Will that suit you?'

'Just right! I wanted to have a day sightseeing,' I said.

He nodded knowingly and without enthusiasm. Frank didn't approve of some of my Berlin acquaintances. 'I thought you might,' he said.

It was about one-thirty when I got back to Lisl Hennig's little hotel. I'd arranged that Klara should leave the door unlatched for me. I crept up the grand front staircase under crippled cherubs that were yellowing and cobwebbed. A tiny shaded table lamp in the bar spilled its meagre light across the parquet floor of the salon, where the enormous baroque mirrors – stained and speckled – dimly reflected the tables set ready for breakfast.

The pantry near the back stairs had been converted to a bedroom for Lisl Hennig when her arthritis made the stairs a torment to her. There was a wedge of yellow light under her door and a curious intermittent buzzing noise. I tapped lightly.

'Come in, Bernd,' she called, with no hint in her voice of the frailty I'd been led to expect. She was sitting up in bed, looking as perky as ever: cushions and pillows behind her and newspapers all over the red and green quilt. Reading newspapers was Lisl's obsession.

Parchment lampshades made the light rich and golden and made a halo of her disarranged hair. She had a small plastic box in her hands and she was pushing and pulling at it. 'Look at this, Bernd! Just look at it!'

She fiddled with the little box again. A loud buzz with a metallic rattle came from behind me. I was visibly startled and Lisl laughed.

'Look at it, Bernd. Careful now! Isn't that wonderful!' She chuckled with delight. I jumped aside as a small olive-coloured jeep came rattling across the carpet, but it swerved aside and rushed headlong at the fireplace, hitting the brass fender with a loud clang before reversing and swinging round – antenna wobbling – to race across the room again.

Lisl, who was wrestling with the controls of this little radio-controlled toy, was almost hysterical with joy. 'Have you ever seen anything like it, Bernd?'

'No,' I said. Not wanting to tell her that every toy shop in the Western world was awash with such amusements.

'It's for Klara's nephew's son,' she said, although why Lisl should be playing with it in the small hours was left unexplained. She put the control box alongside a glass of wine on the bedside table where the wind-up gramophone, and a pile of old 78 records, were at her elbow. 'Give me a kiss, Bernd!' she ordered.

I rescued the little toy jeep from where it had come to a halt on the rumpled carpet and gave her an affectionate hug and kiss. She smelled of snuff, a heavy spicy mixture that she'd spilled down the front of her bed jacket. The idea of losing this crazy old woman was a terrible prospect. She was no less dear to me than my mother.

'How did you get in?' she said and glared at me. I moved back from her, trying to think of a suitable answer. She put on her glasses so that she could see better. 'How did you get in?'

'I . . .'

'Did that wretched girl leave the door on the latch?' she said angrily. 'The times I've told her. We could all be murdered in our beds.' She hit the newspaper with her loose fingers so that it made a loud smack. 'Doesn't she read the papers? People are murdered for ten marks in this town nowadays . . . muggers! heroin addicts! perverts! violent criminals of all kinds. You only have to go a hundred metres to the Ku-Damm to see them parading up and down! How can she leave the door wide open? I told her to wait up until you arrived. Stupid girl!'

The 'stupid girl' was almost Lisl's age and would be up at the crack of dawn collecting the breakfast rolls, making coffee, slicing the sausage and the cheese, and boiling the eggs that are the essential constituents of a German breakfast. Klara deserved her sleep but I didn't point this out to Lisl. It was better to let her simmer down.

'Where have you been?'

'I had dinner with Frank.'

'Frank Harrington: that snake in the grass!'

'What has Frank done?'

'Oh, yes, he's an Englishman. You'd have to defend him.'

'I'm not defending him. I don't know what he's done to upset you,' I said.

'He's all schmaltz when he wants something but he thinks only of himself. He's a pig.'

'What did Frank do?' I asked.

'Do you want a drink?'

'No thanks, Lisl.'

Thus reassured she drank some of her sherry, or whatever it was, and said, 'My double suite on the first floor had a new bathroom only a year or two ago. It's beautiful. It's as good as anywhere in any hotel in Berlin.'

'But Frank's got this big house, Lisl.'

She waved her hand to tell me I'd got it wrong. 'For Sir Clevemore. He stayed here long ago when your father was here. That's before he became a "sir" and he'd be happy to stay here now. I know he would.'

'Sir Henry?'

'Clevemore.'

'Yes, I know.'

'Frank got him a suite at the Kempi. Think of the expense. He would have been happier here. I know he would.'

'When are we talking about?'

'A month . . . two months ago. Not more.'

'You must have made a mistake. Sir Henry has been sick for nearly six months. And he hasn't been in Berlin for about five years.'

'Klara saw him in the lobby of the Kempi. She has a friend who works there.'

'It wasn't Sir Henry. I told you: he's sick.'

'Don't be so obstinate, Bernd. Klara spoke with him. He recognized her. I was so angry. I was going to ring Frank Harrington but Klara persuaded me not to.'

'Klara got it wrong,' I said. I didn't like to say that it was the sort of story that Klara had been known to invent just to needle her autocratic and exasperating employer.

'It's a beautiful suite,' said Lisl. 'You haven't seen that bathroom since it was done. Bidet, thermostatic control for the taps, mirrored walls. Beautiful!'

'Well, it wasn't Sir Henry,' I said. 'So you can sleep easy on that one. I would know if Sir Henry came to Berlin.'

'Why would you know?' she said. She grinned from ear to ear, delighted to catch me out in a self-contradiction, for I'd always kept up the pretence that I worked for a pharmaceutical company.

'I get to hear these things,' I said unconvincingly.

'Good night, Bernd,' she said still smiling. I kissed her again and went upstairs to bed.

As my foot touched the first stair there came a sudden blast of sound. A Dixieland band, with too much brass, giving 'I'm for ever blowing bubbles' a cruel battering. The volume was ear-splitting. No wonder Lisl's hotel wasn't overcrowded.

I had my usual garret room at the top of the house. It was a room I'd had as a child, a cramped room, overlooking the back of the house and the courtyard. It was chilly at this time of year. The effects of the hot-water pump didn't seem to reach up to the top of the house nowadays, so the massive radiator was no more than tepid. But the indomitable Klara had put a hot-water bottle between the crisp linen of my bed and I climbed into it content.

Perhaps I should have been more restrained when drinking my way through Frank's big pot of strong coffee, for I remained awake for hours thinking about Fiona who would by now be tucked up in bed somewhere just a few blocks away. In my mind's eye I saw her so clearly. Would she be alone or were there two people in that bed? A deluge of memories came flooding into my mind. But I forced myself to think of other matters. Lisl and what would become of the old house after she sold it. It was a valuable site: so near the Ku-Damm. Any speculator would do what all speculators do everywhere: chase out the residents and the family-owned shops and old-fashioned eating places, bulldoze everything in sight to build ugly concrete and glass offices that yielded high rent for landlords and high taxes for the government. It was a depressing thought.

And I thought about Klara's provocative little story about spotting the Director-General in the Hotel Kempinski. It didn't make sense for a number of reasons. First the D-G was sick and had been for months. Secondly he hated to travel anywhere outside England. The only official trip he'd done, apart from the odd conference in Washington DC, was to the Far East. As far as I could remember the D-G hadn't visited Berlin for at least five years. And, thirdly, had he come he wouldn't have taken a room in a big Berlin hotel: he'd have been Frank's house-guest, or if it was official, been a guest of the general commanding the British forces. But where Klara's story really rang false was saying that the D-G recognized her. The D-G couldn't remember the name of his own Labrador dog without having Morgan – his faithful attendant –prompt him.

I tried to sleep but sleep didn't come. There was so much to think about. And I couldn't help noticing the promptness with which Frank had denied knowing Jim Prettyman. He hadn't hemmed and hawed or asked why I'd mentioned his name. It was a flat no and a change of subject. It wasn't like Frank's normal behaviour to be so lacking in curiosity: in fact it wasn't like anyone's normal behaviour.

6

'I told Willi not to put that damned machine in here,' Werner said, looking up from his big plate of beef to where two white-coated surgeons were poking screwdrivers deep into the entrails of an old jukebox that had clearly been kicked into silence. Willi Leuschner, the proprietor, watched as grim-faced as any grieving relative. Apparently certain pop-music aficionados of the late evening hours voted with their feet.

We were sitting in one of the booths near the window. When we were kids we had all firmly believed that the people in the window seats got bigger portions to attract passers-by. I still don't know whether it's true or not but it wasn't something that either of us wanted to take a chance on.

'You can't trust music critics,' I said. 'Toscanini could have told him that.'

'I'll bet that his jukebox is not insured,' said Werner. He had the sort of mind that thought in terms of expenditure, percentages, interest rates, risk and insurance.

'It was offered cheap,' I explained. 'Willi thought it would bring more teenagers.'

'He'd make a lot of money from penniless teenagers, wouldn't he?' said Werner with heavy irony. 'He should be glad they keep away, not trying to find a way of attracting them.'

Even after a lifetime's friendship, Werner could still surprise me. It was his often expressed view that juvenile delinquency was to be blamed on TV, single-parent families, unemployment or too much sugar in the diet. Was this new reactionary stand against teenagers a sign that Werner was growing old, the way I'd been all my life?

Werner made his money by avalizing: which means he financed East European exports to the West with hard currency borrowed from anywhere he could get it. He paid high interest and he lived on narrow margins. It was a tough way to make a living but Werner seemed to flourish on the hazards and difficulties of this curious bywater of the financial world. Like many of his rivals he had no banking experience, and his formal education went no further than the legerdemain that comes from prodding a Japanese calculator.

'I thought you liked young people, Werner,' I said.

He looked at me and scowled. He was always accusing me of being intolerant and narrow-minded, but on the issue of keeping my haunts Jungend-frei I was with him, and so were a lot of Berliners. You don't have to walk far down Potsdamer Strasse before starting to believe that universal military conscription for teenagers might be a good idea.

There was something different about Werner today. It wasn't his new beard – a fine full-set with moustache – when it was fully grown he'd look like a prosperous Edwardian beer baron or some business associate of Sir Basil Zaharoff. It wasn't just that he was noticeably overweight, he was always overweight between his dedicated slimming regimes; nor the fact that he'd arrived absurdly early for our appointment. But he was unusually restless. While waiting for the meal to arrive he'd fidgeted with the salt and pepper as well as tugging at his earlobes and pinching his nose and staring out of the window as if his mind was somewhere else. I wondered if he was thinking of some other appointment he had, for Werner, in his tailormade suit and silk shirt, was not dressed for this sort of eating-place.

We were in Leuschner's, a once famous and fashionable café near Potsdamerplatz. It was shabby now and almost empty. It had been like this for many years, for the great expanse of Potsdamerplatz – once the busiest traffic intersection in all Europe – was now a still and silent place where armed sentries patrol constantly between the massed barbed wire and, with a compassion not extended to their fellow-countrymen, carefully restrain their attack-trained dogs from running into the minefields. And as the district became a backwater, Café Leuschner became the sort of place where men were cautious what they said to strangers, and policemen came regularly to inspect everyone's identity papers.

Once great luxury hotels stood here, adjacent to the mighty Anhalter railway terminal, that was the biggest in the world. The posters in the museum listed one hundred and forty-five trains arriving each day, eighty-two of them long-distance luxury expresses that came complete with cocktail bars, sleeping compartments and diners. Beneath the road, by means of a specially constructed tunnel, baggage porters, labouring under steamer trunks and cases made of the hides of crocodile and pig, and smartly dressed pages conducted the arriving passengers under the swirling traffic, directly into the plush foyer of the famous Excelsior Hotel next door. Here they would be conveniently close to the fine shops of Leipziger Strasse, the embassies, palaces and grand houses that adjoined the Tiergarten, and the government offices of the newly created German Reich and the Palace of its Emperor. By day the traffic seemed never-ending; and the night-life continued until breakfast was served free to any reveller who was still awake.

Now the Anhalter Bahnhof is gone, except for a large section of old yellow brickwork that used to be the ticket hall. In summer it is lost amid a tangle of weeds. Behind it, as Werner and I had discovered in our schooldays, there is a vast no-man's-land of rusting rails, collapsed roundhouses, skeletons of old sleeping cars and signal boxes complete with handles that could be pulled. No one has passed this way since the last train left for Magdeburg in April 1945. It remains empty except for a few tramps and fugitives who spend a night sheltering in the wrecked buildings but find them too inhospitable even for their stark needs.

Grimy and neglected, this is a neighbourhood of derelict bombed buildings, roofless façades that might look like some phony cityscape built for a film, except that they are so filthy. Now this place, which once seemed like the centre of all Europe, is nothing. It is just a place past which traffic hurries to get to the newspaper offices of Kochstrasse, or to Checkpoint Charlie, which is only a short distance along this garbage-littered thoroughfare that skirts the Wall.

But Café Leuschner remains. Willi Leuschner, despite such lapses as installing a jukebox, knows how to tap a glass of strong Berlin Beer, and his Austrian wife still produces once a week the best Tafelspitz in town. And the tender boiled beef comes with little potato dumplings and the cabbage is cooked in dripping and has carraway seeds to flavour it.

As Werner came to the end of his huge portion of beef, dipping the final forkful into rather too much horseradish, it was time to tackle again the subject I'd come here to talk to him about. I said, 'Well, I thought Lisl looked awfully well.'

'You only saw her for five minutes,' said Werner, wiping the final smear of horseradish from his plate with a crust of bread roll. Frau Leuschner's powerful horseradish did not affect Werner as it did me.

'She was sleeping this morning so I didn't want to disturb her.' I put the prongs of my fork into the horseradish I'd abandoned, and tasted it again. It was very very hot.

'She's a stupid old woman,' said Werner, with a sudden paroxysm of uncharacteristic bitterness. It was a measure of his frustration. 'The doctor told her again and again to lose weight and take things easy. She drinks, she smokes, she gets excited, she argues and loses her temper. It's absurd.' Perhaps it wasn't bitterness so much as grief that I heard in his voice.

'You say she had a stroke?'

'The hospital gave her tests and said they couldn't be sure.' He put the last piece of bread in his mouth and chewed it. 'But either way she'll have to have a complete rest.'

'Who will arrange about selling the house?' Even as I said it I realized what a big task was involved. There would be meetings with the property agents and with the bank, a lawyer and a tax accountant too, plus all the form-filling and petty bureaucratic rigmarole that makes such simple transactions into a nightmare. 'It would be better if we could persuade Lisl to go away until it's all done. Perhaps we could find a place in Baden-Baden. She's always talked about taking a holiday in Baden one day.'

He looked at me and gave a twisted little smile. 'And which of us is going to explain all this to Lisl?' he asked.

Willi Leuschner came over to the table to clear the plates. 'What are you two having now?' said Willi. 'Bread pudding?' Willi was my age but his head was bald, and the big curly moustache that he'd grown as a joke was grey with age and yellow with nicotine.

He always used the familiar 'du', for all three of us had been to school together, and we understood each other better than we understood our wives. In my case much better than I understood my wife. Certainly Willi knew that Werner and I could eat unlimited amounts of the old wartime recipe that Frau Leuschner had elevated to haute cuisine by the addition of eggs and cream. He didn't wait for an affirmative. He wiped the plastic table with a cloth and balanced the mustard pot and beer glasses on top of the plates and cutlery with a skill of long practice. Willi's father had commanded a forbidding maître d', a dozen waiters in tail coats and bow ties, with white-jacketed youngsters to assist them. Now Willi and his brother had only a couple of young draft-dodgers to help, and both those helpers were apt to arrive in the morning glassy-eyed and trembling.

'I know what you're thinking, Werner,' I said, once Willi had gone.

'What am I thinking?' He was looking through the big plate glass windows at the almost deserted street. Yesterday's snow had gone but the temperature had dropped, and every Berliner could recognize that low grey sky from which much more snow would come.

'You think it's easy for me to come breezing into town and talk about Lisl, and then I go home leaving you to do the things that have to be done.'

'It's not the same for you, Bernie,' he said. 'Lisl is my problem, not yours.'

'She's only got us,' I said. 'Whatever has to be done, we'll do it

55

together. I'll get leave.' Werner nodded mournfully so I tried to be brisk. 'Selling the house shouldn't be too difficult. But we'll have to arrange somewhere for Lisl to go. Somewhere she'll like,' I added vaguely.

'I'm a Jew,' said Werner suddenly. 'I was born in the war. My name is Jacob like my grandfather but they called me Werner because it was more Aryan. Lisl hid my parents. She made no money out of it, my parents had no money. She risked her life. The Nazis put people into camps for much less. I don't know why she took such a risk. Sometimes I ask myself if I'd do the things she did to help comparative strangers. And to tell you the truth I'm not sure. But Lisl hid them and when I was born she hid me. And when my parents died Lisl brought me up as if I was her own child. Now do you understand?'

'We do it together,' I said.

'Do what?'

'Sell the house. Get Lisl into some nice residential home. Klara too.'

'Are you crazy?' said Werner. 'You'd never get her out of that house in a million years.'

I looked at him. He had that inscrutable expression he'd developed as a schoolboy. 'So what are you saying? Are they going to pull the house down around her?'

'I'm going to run the hotel,' said Werner. He stared at me defensively as if expecting strenuous opposition or a burst of laughter.

'Run the hotel?'

He became defensive in the face of my amazement. 'I grew up with her, didn't I? I used to do the accounts. I know enough.'

'She'll not let you change anything,' I warned him.

'I'll run it my way,' he said quietly. It was so easy to forget the hard centre inside that sugar coating. But Werner could be tough too.

'And make it pay?'

'It only has to tick over.'

'And what about the avalizing? What about your own work?'

'I'm winding it up.'

'You'd better think it over, Werner,' I said in alarm as the implications struck me.

'I've made my decision.'

'Where will you live?'

He smiled at my consternation; perhaps that was the only compensation for him, maybe he'd been looking forward to it. 'One of those upstairs rooms, I'm moving out of my apartment.'

'What about Zena?' I asked. I couldn't imagine his young, tough, snobbish wife adapting to one of Lisl's upstairs rooms or even to the suite with the refurbished bathroom of which Lisl was so proud.

'It's difficult for Zena to understand,' said Werner.

'I imagine it is.'

'Zena says she has no debt to Lisl, and in a way she's right,' he said sadly.

'For richer for poorer . . . with all my worldly debts . . . Or is it different now there's women's lib?'

'I wish you'd got to know Zena better. She's not selfish. Not as selfish as you think,' he amended, as he realized just what he was claiming.

'So what's Zena going to do?'

'She'll stay in the apartment in Dahlem. It's just as well really when you think of all that furniture we have there. We couldn't move it to Lisl's, could we?'

'It's a big step, Werner.' He was giving up his work, his luxury apartment and, by the sound of it, losing his wife too. He'd lost her before; Zena's constancy to Werner wasn't something the poets wrote sonnets about. Limericks, maybe. I suppose that's why I detested her so much.

'There's no alternative, Bernie. If I did anything less for Lisl I'd never be able to face myself again, would I?'

I looked at him. Werner was a good man. Perhaps he was the only truly good person I'd ever met. What could I say except, 'You're right, Werner. It's the only thing to do.'

'Maybe it will work out very well,' said Werner, trying desperately to see the best side of it. 'If the hotel could get some more holiday bookings, I could pay off the bank loan. I'm going to talk to some of the travel companies.'

He seemed serious about it. Didn't he know that travel companies wanted only cheap bleak 200-room shoe boxes, run by sixteen year-old high school dropouts who don't speak any known language? What would a travel company do with a small comfortable hotel run by humans? 'Good idea, Werner,' I said.

'Of course, I can't wind up my business overnight,' he said. 'I have a few deals outstanding.'

'How often do you go over there nowadays?' I asked. Werner's business required regular visits to DDR government officials in East Berlin. I didn't ask him whether he was still reporting back to our people in Frank's office. It was better that I didn't know.

'Not so often. Nowadays I can sometimes arrange a few of the preliminaries on the phone.'

'Is it getting better?'

'Not better; different. They are better at covering up than they used to be; better too at understanding what upsets the Western press.' It was a harsh verdict coming from Werner, who tried always to be objective in such off-the-cuff remarks about the East.

'How is Normannenstrasse these days?'

'Very happy,' said Werner.

'Tell me more.'

'The East Germans are number one on Moscow's hit parade. Prague is no longer the centre of Russian penetration of the West and our friends in Normannenstrasse are rubbing their hands in glee.'

'I heard the Stasi was getting a big shake-up over there.'

'One by one the old gang are being got rid of. The same with the administration. It's a smaller and better organization these days.'

'Okay.'

'Of course the KGB monitors it from day to day. If things are not going well, Moscow makes its displeasure known.'

'Ever hear anything about that fellow Erich Stinnes?'

'He's the Moscow liaison. He got a big promotion.'

'Stinnes?'

'The KGB is riding high: no financial cutbacks for them. And the Americans are still running their networks from their embassies, and all US embassies are bugged from roof to cellar. They never learn.'

'Is my wife involved in this reorganization?' I asked.

'Isn't that who we're talking about?' said Werner. 'She helped you with that "Structure Report" didn't she?'

I didn't reply. For ages now many had been saying that our networks should be organized quite separately from the embassies and other diplomatic establishments. I'd spent a long time on a report about it, on the bottom of which Dicky Cruyer gladly signed his name. A lot of people, me included, thought that it would mean another big promotion for Dicky. It was the best work of that kind I've ever done and I was proud of it. Some said that it must inevitably lead to a reorganization. But we reckoned without the Foreign Office. Even getting the D-G to submit the report was difficult. When the mandarins at the Foreign Office read it they stamped on it with such force that the whole building trembled. The Secret Intelligence Service was going to remain a part of the Foreign Office, its submissions rated no more important than those from a medium-sized embassy in Africa. Our offices would remain inside embassies, and if that meant that everyone knew where to find us, too bad chaps! It was a depressing thought. And Fiona knew the whole story.

We sat in silence, watching the street where traffic raced past and some people waiting to cross the road were hunched against the bitter-cold wind. 'There is the matter of inheritance,' I said finally. I suppose we'd both been thinking of Lisl all the time.

'The hotel?' said Werner.

'You might work yourself to death and then find she's left the place to a dog's home.'

'Dog's home?' said Werner puzzled. It was of course an entirely English concept: old German ladies were unlikely to bequeath their entire estates for the welfare of unwanted canines.

'To some charity,' I explained.

'I'm not doing it to get the house,' said Werner.

'No need to get irritable,' I said. 'But it's something you should settle before you start.'

'Don't be stupid, Bernie. How can I sit down with Lisl and tell her to write her Will in my favour?' I didn't try to answer through the sudden bellow of discordant sound that came from the jukebox. But after a few bars to test it the mechanic switched it off and started to replace the coloured panels.

'She has no other relatives, does she?'

'Yes she has,' said Werner. 'There was a sister who died in the war and another – Inge Winter – even older than Lisl. She used to live in France. Childless and probably dead by now. Lisl said I met her once when she came to Berlin but I don't remember it. She has some sort of claim to the house. Lisl once told me that her father left it to both daughters but only Lisl wanted to live in it. But it was half Inge Winter's. And apart from the sister, there could be relatives of Lisl's late husband Erich. I must talk to her again.'

'If Lisl said half the house belonged to her sister, the sister might be a signatory for the bank loan.'

'I know,' said Werner rubbing his moustache. 'I was wondering if that's why the sister came to Berlin.'

'You'd better ask the bank,' I said.

'The bank won't reveal anything to me without Lisl's permission.' He rubbed his moustache again. 'It itches,' he explained.

'It will have to be sorted out,' I said. 'I'll talk to her.'

'No you won't,' said Werner immediately. 'It would spoil everything. It's got to look as though I *want* to go and run the place. It's got to seem as though she's doing *me* the favour. Surely you see that?'

It was a long time before I nodded. But Werner was right. He must have spent a lot of sleepless nights working it all out. 'Shall I find out if the sister is still alive?' I offered to do it more because I wanted to appease my conscience than because I thought it would lead anywhere, or be of any practical use.

Perhaps Werner understood what my motives were. He said, 'That would be really useful, Bernie. If you could find out about the sister that would be the most important problem solved. I've got the last address she used in France. I got it out of that big green address book Lisl keeps in the office. I don't know when it dates back to.' He looked across to the bar counter where Willi Leuschner had been operating the chrome espresso machine, and said, 'Willi's coming with the bread pudding.'

'And about time.'

'He'll want to sit down and chat,' Werner warned. 'Don't mention anything about the hotel for the time being. I'll phone and give you the sister's address.'

'Take a day or so to think it all over,' I suggested. Willi was coming this way now, carrying the desserts and the coffees and some Kipferl – sweet crescent-shaped biscuits – that always marked the end of any of Werner's diets. 'It's a big step.'

'I've thought it over,' said Werner firmly and with just a trace of sadness. 'It's what I've got to do.'

France, I thought. Why do I have to say such silly things? How the hell am I going to get time off and go to France to trace a sister who is undoubtedly long since dead and gone? And anyway wasn't one Lisl in my life enough?

7

'We could have bought a microwave oven,' said Gloria suddenly and spontaneously.

'Is that what you want? A microwave oven?'

'With the money this damned flight is costing us,' she explained bitterly.

'Oh,' I said. 'Yes.' She was making a list in her head. She did this sometimes. And the longer the list got the more bitter hatred she had for the air line and its management. Fortunately for the air line's management none of them were sitting in the seat next to Gloria on the flight to Nice. I was sitting there. 'It's a rip-off,' she said.

'Everyone knows it's a rip-off,' I said. 'So drink the nice warm *café*, unwrap your processed *fromage* and enjoy the *ambiance*.'

The Plexiglass windows were scratched so that even the dense grey cloud looked cross-hatched. Gloria did not respond, nor eat the items set before her on the tiny plastic tray. She got nail varnish from the big handbag she always carried, and began doing something with her fingernails. This was always a dire portent.

I suppose I should have told her, right from the beginning, that our journey was made to fulfil a promise I'd made about finding Lisl Hennig's sister. I should have realized that Gloria would be angry when the truth was revealed, and that I'd have to tell her sooner rather than later.

Looking back on it, I don't know why I chose the airport departure lounge to tell Gloria the real reason for the trip. She was unhappy to hear that this was not actually the 'mad lovers' weekend' that I'd let her think of it as. She called me names, and did it so loudly that some people on the next seat took their children out of earshot.

It was at times like that I tried to analyse the essence of my relationship with Gloria. My contemporaries – married men in their forties – were not reluctant to give me their own interpretations of my romance with this beautiful twenty-two-year-old. Sometimes these took the form of serious 'talks', sometimes anecdotes about mythical friends, and sometimes they were just lewd jokes. Oddly enough it was the envious comments that offended me. I wished they would try to understand that such relationships are complex and this love affair was more complex than most.

Sitting on the plane, with no work to do and nothing to read except the 'flight magazine', I thought about it. I tried to compare this relationship with Gloria to the one I'd had with Fiona, my wife whose fortieth birthday would be coming up soon. She'd always said she dreaded her fortieth birthday. This 'dread' had begun as a sort of joke, and my response was to promise that we'd celebrate it in style. But now she'd be celebrating it in East Berlin with Russian champagne no doubt, and perhaps some caviar too. Fiona loved caviar.

Would I have got as far as London Heathrow with Fiona and still been trying to pretend that we were embarking on some madcap romantic escapade? No. But the fact of the matter was that such a romantic escapade would have had a very, very limited appeal to my wife Fiona. Wait a moment! Was that true? Surely the real reason I wouldn't have told her that this was a 'surprise getaway' was that my wife would not have believed for one instant that a sudden invitation to fly to Nice would be a romantic escapade. My wife Fiona knew me too well; that was the truth of it.

But at Nice the sun was shining, and it did not take very much to restore Gloria to her usual light-hearted self. In fact, it took no more than renting a car for our trip to the last known address of Inge Winter. At work Gloria had seen me dictating and conversing in German, and sometimes my imperfect Russian was used too. So she was ill-prepared for my halting French.

It went wrong right from the start. The beautifully coiffured young French woman at the car rental desk was understandably irritated when I tried to interpose news about my need for a car into a private conversation she was having with her female colleague. She didn't hide her irritation. She spoke rapidly and with a strong Provençal accent that I couldn't follow.

When finally I appealed to Gloria for help in translating this girl's rapid instructions about finding the vehicle, Gloria's jubilation knew no bounds. 'No compree!' she said and laughed and clapped her hands with joy.

Despite Gloria's uncooperative attitude we found the car, a small white Renault hatchback that must have been sitting in the rental car pound for many winter days, for it did not start easily.

But once away, and on to the Autoroute heading west, all was well. Gloria was laughing and I was finally persuaded that it had all been very amusing.

It was only a few minutes along the Autoroute before the Antibes exit. On this occasion, determined not to provide more laughs for

Gloria I had a handful of small change ready to pay the Autoroute charge. Now, with Gloria bent low over a map, we began to thread our way through the back roads towards Grasse.

Once off the Autoroute you find another France. Here in this hilly backwater there is little sign of the ostentatious wealth that marks the coastline of the Riviera. Rolls-Royces, Cadillacs and Ferraris are here replaced by brightly painted little vans and antique Ladas that bump over the large pot-holes and splash through the ochre-coloured pools that are the legacy of steady winter rain. Here is a landscape where nothing is ever completed. Partially built houses – their innards skeletal grey blocks, fresh cement and ganglia of wiring – stand alongside half-demolished old farm buildings. Ladders, broken bidets and abandoned bath tubs mark the terraces of olive trees. Heaps of sand – eroded by the rain storms – are piled alongside bricks, sheets of galvanized metal and half-completed scaffolding. The fruit of urban squalor litters the fields where the most profitable cash crop is the maison secondaire.

But 'Le Mas des Vignes Blanches' was not such a place. Here, on the south-facing brow of a hill, there was a Prussian interlude in the Gallic landscape. The house had once been a place from which some lucky landowner surveyed his vineyards. Now the hillsides were disfigured with a pox of development, an infection inevitably rendered more virulent by the thin crescent of Mediterranean which shone pale blue beyond the next hill.

The house was surrounded with a box hedge but the white wooden gates were open, and I drove up the well-kept gravel path. The main building must have been well over a hundred years old. It wasn't the grim rectangular shape that northern landowners favoured. This was a house built for the Provençal climate, two stories with shuttered windows, vines climbing across the façade, some mature palm trees – fronds thrashing in the wind – and a gigantic cactus, pale green and still, like a huge prehensile sea creature waiting to attack.

At the back of the house I could see a cobbled courtyard, swept and scrubbed to a cleanliness that is unusual hereabouts. From the coachhouse jutted the rear ends of a big Mercedes and a pale blue BMW. Behind that there was a large garden with neatly pruned fruit trees espaliered on the walls. I noticed the lawns in particular. In this part of the world – where fierce sunshine parches the land – a well-tended lawn is the sign of eccentric foreign tastes, of a passionate concern for gardens, or wealth.

On the small secluded front terrace there was a selection of garden furniture: some fancy metal chairs arranged around a large glass-topped table and a couple of recliners. But despite the sunshine, it was not really a day for sitting outside. The wind was unrelenting, and here on the hill even the tall conifers whipped with each gust of it. Gloria turned up her collar as we stood waiting for someone to respond to the jangling bell.

The woman who answered the door was about forty years old. She was attractive looking in that honest way that country people sometimes are, a strong big-boned woman with quick intelligent eyes and greying hair that she'd done nothing to darken. 'Frau Winter?' I said.

'My name is Winter,' she said. 'But I am Ingrid.' She opened the door to us and, as if needing something to say, added, 'It is confusing that I have the same initial as my mother.' Having noted our cheap rented car, she gave all her attention to Gloria and was no doubt trying to guess our relationship. 'You want Mama. Are you Mr Samson?' Her English was excellent, with an edge of accent that was more German than French. Her dress was a green, floral-patterned Liberty fabric cut to an old-fashioned design with lacy white high collar and cuffs. It was hard to know whether she was poor and out of style, or whether she was following the trendy ideas that are de rigueur at smart dinner parties in big towns.

'That's right,' I said. I'd written to say that I was an old friend of Lisl, a writer, researching for a book that was to be set in Berlin before the war. Since I would be in the neighbourhood, I wondered if she would allow me to visit her and perhaps share some of her memories. There had been no reply to the letter. Perhaps they were hoping that I wouldn't show up.

'Let me take your coats. It's so cold today. Usually at this time of year we are lunching outside.' Her nails were short and cared for but her hands were reddened as if with housework. There was an expensive-looking wristwatch and some gold rings and a bracelet but no wedding ring.

I murmured some banalities about the winters getting colder each year, while she got a better look at us. So there was a daughter. She didn't look anything like Lisl, but I remembered seeing an old photo of Lisl's mother in a large hat and a long dress with leg-of-mutton sleeves: she was a big woman too. 'How is your mother?' I asked while Gloria took the opportunity to look at herself in the hall mirror and tease her hair out with her fingertips.

'She goes up and down, Mr Samson. Today is one of her better days. But I must ask you not to stay too long. She gets tired.'

'Of course.'

We went into the large drawing room. Several big radiators kept the room warm despite large windows that provided a view of the front lawn. The floor was of the red tile that is common in this region; here and there some patterned carpets were arranged. On the wall there was one big painting that dominated the room. It was a typical eighteenth-century battle scene; handsome officers in bright uniforms sat on prancing chargers and waved swords, while far away serried ranks of stunted anonymous figures were killing each other in the smoke. Two white sofas and a couple of matching armchairs were arranged at one end of the room and an old woman in a plain black dress sat in the ugly sort of high chair from which people with stiff joints find it possible to get up.

'How do you do, Mr Samson?' she said as her daughter went through the formalities with us, and studied Gloria carefully before nodding to her. Lisl's sister was not at all like Lisl. She was a slight, shrivelled figure, with skin like speckled yellow parchment and thinning white hair that looked as if it might have been specially washed and set for this visit. I looked at her with interest: she was even older than Lisl, goodness knows how old that would make her. But this was a woman who had come to terms with ageing. She hadn't dyed her hair or painted her face or stuck on to her eyelids the false lashes that Lisl liked to wear if visitors came. But despite all the differences, there was no mistaking the facial resemblance to her sister. She had the same determined jaw and the large eyes and the mouth that could go so easily from smile to snarl.

'So you are a friend of my sister?' Her words were English, her pronunciation stridently American, but her sentences were formed in a mind that thought in German. I moved a little closer to her so she did not have to raise her voice.

'I've known her a long time,' I said. 'I saw her only a couple of weeks ago.'

'She is well?' She looked up at the daughter and said, 'Are you bringing tea?' The younger woman gave a filial smile and went out of the room.

I hesitated about the right way to describe Lisl's health. I didn't want to frighten her. 'She might have had a slight stroke,' I said tentatively. 'Very slight. Even the hospital doctors are not sure.'

'And this is why you have come?' I noticed her eyes now. They were like the eyes of a cat; green and deep and luminous. Eyes of a sort I'd never seen before.

This old woman certainly didn't beat about the bush. 'No,' I said.

'But it means she'll have to give up the hotel. Her doctor insists it's too much for her.'

'Of course it is. Everyone is telling her that at some time or other.'

'It was your father's house?' I said.

'Sure. It has many wonderful memories for me.'

'It's a magnificent old place,' I said. 'I wish I could have seen it in your father's time. But the entrance steps make it difficult for Lisl. She needs to live somewhere where everything is on the ground floor.'

'So. And who is caring for her?'

'Have you heard of Werner Volkmann?'

'The Jew?'

'The boy she brought up.'

'That Jew family she hid away on the top floor. Yes, my sister was completely crazy. I was living in Berlin until 1945. Even me she never told! Can you believe that from her own sister she'd keep such a thing secret? I visited her there, it was partly my house.'

'It's astonishing,' I said dutifully.

'So the Jewish kid she raised is looking after her.' She nodded.

'He's not a kid any more,' I said.

'I guess not. So what's he getting out of it?'

'Nothing,' I said. 'He feels he owes it to Lisl.'

'He figures he's going to inherit the house. Is that it?' She gave a malicious little chuckle and looked at Gloria. Gloria was sitting on a carved wooden chair: she shifted uncomfortably.

'Not as far as I know,' I said defensively. So bang goes the whole purpose of coming all the way here. Did this vituperative old woman deliberately manoeuvre me into that denial? I couldn't decide. I was still thinking about it when the daughter arrived with tea and that sort of open apple tart in which the thin slices of fruit are carefully arranged in fanlike patterns.

'Ingrid made that,' said the old woman when she saw the way I was looking at it.

'It looks wonderful,' I said, without adding that after the 'light meal' on the plane almost anything would look wonderful. Gloria made appreciative noises too and the daughter cut us big slices.

During tea I asked the old woman about life in Berlin before the war. She had a good memory and answered clearly and fully but the answers she gave were the standard answers that people who lived under the Third Reich give to foreigners and strangers of any kind.

After forty-five minutes or so I could see she was tiring. I suggested that we should leave. The old woman said she wanted to go on longer but the daughter gave me an almost imperceptible movement of the head and said, 'They have to go, Mama. They have things to do.' The daughter could also show a hard edge.

'Are you just passing through?' Ingrid asked politely while she was handing our coats.

'We are booked in to the big hotel on the road this side of Valbonne,' I said.

'They say it's very comfortable,' she said.

'I'll write up my notes tonight,' I said. 'Perhaps if I have any supplementary questions, I could phone you?'

'Mama doesn't have many visitors,' she said. It was not meant to sound like an encouragement.

When we reached the hotel it was not the 'honeymoon hotel' that I'd described to Gloria. It was at the end of a long winding road – broken surfaced and pot-holed as are all local roads in this region – and behind it there was an abandoned quarry. In a bold spirit of enterprise someone seemed to have fashioned a car park gate from two cartwheels, but on closer inspection it was a prefabricated plastic contraption. A few genuine old wine barrels were arranged across the patio, and in them some rhododendrons and camellias were struggling to stay alive. The hotel was a pink stucco building with shiny plastic tiles.

At the far end of the car park there was an out-building in which some derelict motor vehicles of indeterminate shape and marque were rusting away undisturbed by human hand. We parked beside a new Peugeot station wagon and a van that carried advertisements for a butcher's shop in Valbonne. A large sign said that all cars were parked at owner's risk and another pointed the way to an empty swimming pool which was partially repainted in a vivid shade of cerulean blue.

But once inside everything looked up. The dining room was clean and rather elegant, set with starched cloths and shining glass and cutlery. And there was a big log fire in the bar.

Gloria went straight upstairs to bathe and change but I went into the bar and warmed my hands at the fire and tried the Armagnac that the barman said was especially good. Gloria didn't enjoy alcohol: she preferred orange juice or yogurt or even Seven-Up. It was another manifestation of the generation gap I suppose. Concurring with the barman's verdict I took a second Armagnac up to our room, where Gloria had just finished taking her bath. 'The water is hot,' she called happily. She walked across the room stark naked and said, 'Have a shower, darling. It will cheer you up.'

'I'm cheered up already,' I said, watching her.

All the way from Le Mas des Vignes Blanches to the hotel, she'd kept quiet, giving me time to think about the Winter woman. But when I said, 'So what did you think of her?' Gloria was ready to explode with indignation.

'What a cow!' said Gloria, dabbing herself with a towel.

'If I have to be knocked out in the first round it's a consolation to know it's done by a world champion,' I said.

'She trapped you.'

'And you have to admire the skill of it,' I said. 'She sensed what we'd come for even before we started talking. It was quick and clever. You have to admit that.'

'What a vicious old moo,' said Gloria.

'Are you going to put some clothes on?'

'Why?'

'It's distracting.'

She came and kissed me. 'You smell of booze,' she said and I stretched out my arms to embrace her. 'Well, that's very reassuring, darling. Sometimes I think I've lost the art of being distracting.'

I reached for her.

'No no no! What time's dinner? Stop it! There's no time. I said what time's dinner.'

'It's too late to think of that now,' I said. And it was.

Afterwards, when we were sitting quietly together, she said, 'What are you, Bernard?'

'What do you mean?'

'Are you English, or German, or nothing? I'm a nothing. I used to think I was English but I'm a nothing.'

'I used to think that I was German,' I said. 'At least I used to think that my German friends thought I was a Berliner, which is even better. Then one day I was playing cards with Lisl and an old man named Koch, and they just took it for granted that I was an Englishman and had never been anything else. I was hurt.'

'But you wanted it both ways, darling. You wanted your English friends to treat you like an Englishman, while your German friends thought of you as one of them.'

'I suppose I did.'

'My parents are Hungarian but I've never been to Hungary. I grew up in England and always thought of myself as one hundred per cent English. I was a super-patriot. Being English was all I had to hang on to. I learned all those wonderful Shakespeare speeches about England and chided anyone who said a word against the Queen or wouldn't stand up for the National Anthem. Then one day one of the girls at school told me the truth about myself.'

'Truth?'

'You Hungarians, she said. All the other girls were there watching us, I wasn't going to let it go. She knew that. I told her I was born in England. She said, if you were born in an orange box, would that make you an orange? The other girls laughed. I cried all night.'

'My poor love.'

'I'm a nothing. It doesn't matter. I'm used to the idea now.'

'Here's to us nothings,' I said holding the last of my Armagnac aloft before drinking it.

'We'll miss dinner unless you hurry,' she said. 'Go and have a shower.'

8

There was no breakfast room of course. In this sort of French hotel there never is. And unlike Gloria I don't like eating food in bed. Thus she was propped up in bed, the tray balanced on her thighs, and I was halfway through my second cup of coffee, and eating Gloria's second brioche – 'You are a fool, darling. You've had two already' – when the phone rang.

I knew it would be the Winter woman. No one else knew where I was. Contrary to regulations I'd not left a contact number at the office. People who left overseas contact numbers were likely to find themselves answering questions about where they'd been and why.

'This is Ingrid Winter. Mama is feeling rather fit today. She wonders if you'd like to join us for lunch.'

'Thank you: I would.' Gloria had used the extra earpiece that all French phones have, and was waving a hand, in case her violently shaking head escaped my attention. 'But Miss Kent has an appointment in Cannes. She could drop me and pick me up, if you'd suggest convenient times.'

'Eleven and three,' said the daughter without hesitation. The Winter family seemed to have answers ready for everything.

Gloria dropped me at the gate a few minutes early. It was better that way when dealing with Germans. 'So! Exactly on time,' said Ingrid Winter as she opened the door to me. It was a statement of warm approval. We went through the same formalities as before, talking about the weather as I gave her my coat, but today she proved far more affable. 'Let me close the door quickly: that yellow dust gets everywhere when the wind is from the south. The Sirocco. It's hard to believe that the sand could be blown all the way from the Sahara isn't it?'

'Yes,' I said.

She locked my raincoat away in a closet painted with big orange flowers. 'My mother is a very old lady, Mr Samson.' I said yes, of course she was, and then Ingrid Winter looked at me as if to convey some special meaning, apprehension almost. Then she said, 'A very old lady.' She paused. 'Komm!'

With that she turned and walked not into the drawing room we'd used the previous afternoon but along a tiled corridor, hung with old engravings of ancient German cities, to a room at the back.

It had not always been a bedroom of course. Like Lisl she'd had a downstairs room converted to her use. Few people of Inge Winter's age wanted to go upstairs to bed.

She was not in bed. She was wearing the sort of grey woollen dress provided to poor patients in State hospitals, and sitting in a large angular armchair with a heavy cashmere shawl draped round her thin shoulders. 'Sit down,' she told me. 'Do you want a drink of any sort?'

'No thank you,' I said. Well, now I understood Ingrid's fears. This wasn't a bedroom it was a shrine. It wasn't simply that Inge Winter had surrounded herself with pictures and mementoes of times past – many old people do that – it was the ones she'd chosen that provided the surprise. The top of a large side-table was crowded with framed photos; the sort of collection that actors and actresses seem to need to reassure themselves of the undying affection that their colleagues have promised them. But these were not film stars.

The large silver-framed photo of Adolf Hitler had been carefully placed in a commanding position. I'd seen such photos before: it was one of the sepia-toned official portraits by Hoffmann that Hitler had given to visiting dignitaries or old comrades. But this one was not just perfunctorily signed with the scratchy little abbreviated signature normally seen on such likenesses. This was carefully autographed with greetings to Herr and Frau Winter. It was not the only picture of Hitler. There was a shiny press photo of a handsome middle-aged couple standing with Hitler and a big dog on a terrace, with high snow-capped mountains in the background. Berchtesgaden probably, the Berghof. Prewar because Hitler was not in uniform. He was wearing a light-coloured suit, one hand stretched towards the dog as if about to stroke it. The woman was a rather beautiful Inge Winter, with long shiny hair and wearing the angular padded fashions of the nineteen thirties. The man – presumably Herr Winter – slightly too plump for his dark pinstripe suit, had been caught with his mouth half-open so that he looked surprised and slightly ridiculous. But perhaps that was a small price to pay for being thus recorded consorting with the Führer. I couldn't bring my eyes away from the collection of pictures. Here were signed photos of Josef Goebbels with his wife and all the children; greetings from a black uniformed blank-faced Himmler; a broadly smiling, soft focused and carefully retouched Herman Göring; and a flamboyantly inscribed picture of Fritz Esser, with whom Göring faced

71

the judges at Nuremberg. The Winters had found welcome in the very top echelons of Nazi society. So where did that put her sister Lisl?

'People usually do nowadays,' said the old woman. 'There's far too much drinking.' Without giving me much of a chance to answer she reached over for one of the pictures. Holding it in her hand, she looked at her daughter and said in rapid German. 'Leave us alone, Ingrid. You can call us when lunch is ready.'

'Yes, Mama.'

When I said how pleased I was that she'd spared time to see me again, I automatically continued in German.

The old woman's face lit up in a way that I wouldn't have thought possible. 'Such beautiful German . . . You are German?'

'I think I am,' I said. 'But my German friends seem doubtful.'

'You are a Berliner?' She was still holding the photo but seemed to have forgotten about it.

'I grew up there.'

'I hear you speak and I am drinking a glass of champagne. If only my daughter didn't have that dreadful Bavarian growl. Why didn't you tell me yesterday? Oh, how splendid that my daughter made me ask you back today.'

'Your daughter made you ask me?'

'She thinks I am being too Prussian about the house,' she smiled grimly, as one Prussian to another. 'She thinks I should let Lisl give it to the wretched Jew, if that's what she wants to do. Poor Lisl was always the simpleton of the family. That's why she married that piano player.' It was a relief to hear her speaking German instead of her uncertain English with its terrible accent, the sort of accent people only acquire when they come to a language late in life. I suppose that's how I spoke French. But Inge Winter's German was – apart from a few dated words and expressions – as clear and as fresh as if she'd come from Berlin yesterday.

She looked at me. I was expected to respond to her daughter's offer of the house. 'That's very generous, Frau Winter.'

'It makes no difference to me. Everything will be Ingrid's when I die. She might as well decide now.'

'Lisl has borrowed money on the house I believe.'

She ignored that. 'Ingrid says it's too much trouble for nothing. Perhaps she's right. She knows more than I do about these things.'

'There will be taxes and so on . . .'

'And Ingrid says it's better that we don't have to go to all the trouble of filing accounts and submitting tax forms. Who would I find here who knew about German tax?'

I didn't answer. Considering how many rich Germans had big houses on the Riviera – and the fleets of huge German-registered yachts that crowded local ports and marinas – I would have thought it a not insurmountable problem.

'But I have things there in the house,' she said. 'Personal things.'

'I can't think there would be any difficulty about that,' I said.

'The ormolu clock. My mother was so insistent that I should have it. Do you remember seeing it?'

'Yes,' I said. Who could forget it: a huge horrid thing with angels and drgons and horses and goodness knows what else jumping about all over the mantelshelf. And if you missed seeing it, there was every chance that its resonant chimes would keep you awake all night. But I could see a complication just the same; Lisl had often expressed her fondness for that dreadful object.

'And some other oddments. Photos of my parents, a tiny embroidered cushion I had when I was a little girl. Some papers, keepsakes, diaries, letters and things that belonged to my husband. I'll send Ingrid to Berlin to get them. It would be tragic if they were thrown away.'

'Nothing will happen as quickly as that,' I said. I was fearful that she'd phone Lisl before Werner had spoken to her. Then there would be a fearful rumpus.

'Just private papers,' she said. 'Things that are of no concern to anyone but me.' She nodded. 'Ingrid will find them for me. Then Lisl can have the house.' She looked down at her hands and became aware of the photo she was holding. She passed it to me. 'My wedding,' she announced.

I looked at it. It had been an elaborate ceremony. She was standing on the steps of some grand building in a magnificent wedding gown – there were pages behind her to hold the train of it – and her husband was in the dress uniform of some smart Prussian regiment. Deployed on the higher steps there was a sword-brandishing honour guard of army officers, each one accompanied by a bridesmaid in the old German style. On each side the guests were arrayed: a handsome naval officer, high-ranking Brownshirts and SS officers, richly caparisoned Nazi party officials and other elaborate uniforms of obscure Nazi organizations.

'Do you see Lisl there?' she said with an arch smile.

'No.'

'She's with the civilian.' It was easy to spot them now; he was virtually the only man there without uniform. 'Poor Erich,' she said and

73

gave a snigger of laughter. Once no doubt this cruel joke against Lisl's piano player husband had been a telling blow. But this old woman didn't seem to realize that history had decided in Erich Hennig's favour.

I slid the photo back into its narrow allotment of space on the table.

'Just private papers,' she said again. 'Things that are of no concern to anyone but me.'

Promptly at one o'clock her daughter called us for lunch in the small dining room which looked on to the courtyard. The old woman walked there, slowly but without assistance, and continued to talk all through the meal. It was always about Berlin.

'I know Berlin not at all,' said Ingrid, 'but for my mother there is no other town like it.'

It was enough to start another story about her happy prewar days in the capital. Sometimes the old woman's stories were told with such gusto that she seemed to forget that I was there with her daughter. She seemed to be speaking to other people and she larded her stories with '. . . and you remember that stuff that Fritz liked to drink . . .' or '. . . that table that Pauli and I always reserved at the Königin on Ku-Damm . . .' Once in the middle of a story about the gala ball she'd attended in 1938, she said to Ingrid, 'What was the name of that place where Göring had that wonderful ball?'

'Haus der Flieger,' said Ingrid. I must have looked puzzled for she added, 'I know all Mama's stories very well by now, Herr Samson.'

After lunch her mother quietened. Ingrid said, 'My mother gets tired. I think she should have a little sleep now.'

'Of course. Can I help?'

'She likes to walk on her own. I think she's all right.' I waited while Ingrid took her mother to her room again. There was still another quarter of an hour before Gloria was due to collect me so Ingrid invited me to sit in the kitchen and share a second pot of coffee she was just about to make for herself. I accepted.

Ingrid Winter seemed a pleasant woman, who waved away my suggestions that forgoing a share in the house was a generous thing to do. 'When Mama dies, and Tante Lisl dies,' she said, not using any of the common euphemisms for death, 'I will have no use for a house in Berlin.'

'You prefer France?' I asked.

She looked at me for a moment before answering. 'Mama likes the climate.' There was no indication about her own likes and dislikes.

'Most people do,' I said.

She didn't respond. She poured more coffee for me and said, 'You mustn't take any notice of what Mama says.'

'She's a wonderful old woman considering her age.'

'That may be true but she is mischievous: old people often like to make trouble. They are like children in that respect.'

'I see,' I said and hoped she would explain.

'She tells lies.' Perhaps seeing that these allegations had little effect upon me she became more specific. 'She pretends to believe everything but her brain works like lightning. She pretends to believe that you're a writer but she knows who you are.' She waited.

'Does she?' I said in a bored voice and sipped some coffee.

'She knew before you arrived. She knew your father a long time ago: before the war she said it was. She told me your father was an English spy. She says you're probably a spy too.'

'She is a very old woman.'

'Mama said your father killed her husband.'

'She said that?'

'In those very words. She said, "This man's father killed my darling husband" and said I must be on my guard against you.'

'You've been very frank, Fräulein Winter, and I appreciate it, but I truly can't fathom what your mother was referring to. My father was a British army officer but he was not a fighting soldier. He was stationed in Berlin after the war, she might have met him then. Before the war he was a travelling salesman. It seems very unlikely that she could have met him before the war.'

Ingrid Winter shrugged. She was not going to vouch for the accuracy of anything her mother said.

There was a peremptory toot on a car horn and I got up to go. When Ingrid Winter handed me my coat we were back to discussing the vagaries of the weather again. As I said goodbye to her I found myself wondering why her mother might have said 'killed my darling husband' rather than 'killed your father'. I didn't know much about Inge Winter's husband except what I'd heard from Lisl; that Paul Winter had been some kind of civil servant working in one of the Berlin ministries, and that he'd died somewhere in southern Germany in the aftermath of the war. Now that I'd met Ingrid – this woman of whom her aunt Lisl knew nothing – I could only say that there were a lot of things about the Winter family that I didn't understand, including what my father might have had to do with them.

9

We spent the last evening of that hectic weekend in Provence at the nearby home of Gloria's 'uncle'. Gloria's parents were Hungarian; and this old friend wasn't actually a kinsman, except in the way that all Hungarian exiles are a family of crazy, congenial, exasperating individuals who, no matter how reclusive their mode of living, keep amazingly well informed about the activities of their 'relatives'.

Zu he called her. All her Hungarian friends called her Zu. It was short for Zsuzsa, the name she'd been given by her parents. This 'Dodo' lived in an isolated tumbledown cottage. It was on a hillside, sandwiched between a minuscule vineyard and the weed-infested ground of an abandoned olive oil mill. One small section of earth had been partitioned off to be Dodo's garden, where the remaining leaves of last year's winter vegetables were being devoured by slugs. Perched precariously over a drainage ditch at the front there was a battered Deux Chevaux with one headlight missing.

He was introduced to me as 'Dodo', and judging by the vigorous way he shook my hand was happy enough to be called that. My first impression was of a man in his middle sixties, a short fat noisy fellow who any casting director would engage to play the role of a lovable Hungarian refugee. He had a lot of pure white hair that was brushed straight back, and a large unruly moustache that was somewhat greyer. His face was ruddy, the result perhaps of his drinking, for the whole house was littered with bottles, both full and empty, and he seemed quite merry by the time we arrived. To what extent his imbibing advanced his linguistic ability I'm not sure but his English was almost accentless and fluent, and – apart from a tendency to call everyone 'darling' – his syntax had only the imperfections of the natives.

He wore old brown corduroy trousers that had, in places, whitened and worn to the under-fabric. His shaggy crimson roll-neck sweater came almost to his knees and his scuffed leather boots had zipper sides and two-inch heels. He gave us wine and sat us down on the long lumpy chintz-covered sofa, in front of the blazing fire, and talked without taking breath.

His house was about thirty kilometres from Le Mas des Vignes Blanches, where the Winters lived, but he seemed to know all about

76

them. 'The Hitler woman' the locals called Inge Winter, for some talkative plumber had been there to fix a pipe and broadcast news of the old woman's photo of Hitler all round the neighbourhood.

When he heard that we'd visited his mysterious neighbours he added to my knowledge, telling amusing stories about Inge's father-in-law – old Harald Winter – who'd been a rich businessman. Vienna abounded with all sorts of tales about him; his motorcars, his violent temper, his unrelenting vengeance, the titled ladies seen with him in his box at the opera, huge sums of money spent on amazing jewellery for women he was pursuing, his ridiculous duel with old Professor Doktor Schneider, the gynaecologist who delivered his second son.

'In my father's time, Harry Winter was the talk of Vienna; even now the older people still tell stories about him. Most of the yarns are nonsense I suspect. But he did keep a very beautiful mistress in Vienna. This I know is true because I saw her many times. I was studying chemistry in Vienna in 1942 and living with my aunt, who was her dressmaker for many years. The mistress was a bit down on her luck by that time: the war was on, the Nazis were running Austria and she was a Jew. She was Hungarian and she liked to gossip in her native language. Then one day she didn't turn up for a fitting; we heard later that she'd been taken off to a camp. Not all the money in the world could save you from the Gestapo.' Having said this he sniffed, and went to stir something in the kitchen. When he returned he heaved a big log on to the fire. It was wet and it sizzled in the red-hot embers.

Dodo's little home was as different as could be from the well ordered good taste of the Winters' house. The Winter mansion had a Spartan luxury but Dodo's 'glory hole' was a wonderful squalor. Half the south-facing wall had been replaced by sliding glass doors and through them – just visible in the twilight – there was a ramshackle terrace. In retirement he'd become a painter. The only other sizeable room in the house faced north and he'd put a skylight into it and used it as a studio. He showed us around it. There were some half-finished canvases: landscapes, bold, careless, competent pastiches of Van Gogh's Provençal work. Most of them were variations of the same view: his valley at dawn, at dusk and at many of the stages between. He claimed to have a gallery in Cannes where his works were sold. Perhaps it wouldn't be too difficult to sell such colourful pictures to the rich tourists who came here in the holidays.

When we returned from our tour of the premises the damp log in the living room fireplace oozed blue smoke that billowed into the room, blackening still more the painted walls and irritating the eyes. Gloria set

77

the table that was conveniently near the door of the kitchen. Behind it stood a massive carved wardrobe that almost touched the ceiling. Its doors missing, it had been provided with unpainted shelves for hundreds of books. Philosophy, history, chemistry, art, dictionaries, detective stories, biographies, they were crammed together in anarchic disorder. Everything was worn, stained, bent or slightly broken.

When we sat down at the big table, he pulled a wheelback chair into position for me and the arm of it came away in his hand. He roared with laughter and thumped it back into position with a deftness that had obviously come from practice. He laughed often, and when he did his open mouth revealed gold molars only slightly more yellow than the rest of his teeth.

I knew of course that we'd come here because Gloria wanted to show me to 'Dodo' and that his approval would be important to her. And in turn, important to me. In loco parentis, he eyed me warily and asked me the casual sort of questions that parents ask their beloved daughter's suitors. But his heart wasn't in it. That role was soon forgotten and he was laying down the law about art:

'Titian loved reds and blues. Look at any of his paintings and you'll see that. That's why he was always painting auburn-haired models. Wonderful women: he knew a thing or two about women, eh?' A roar of laughter and a quick drink. 'And look at his later work . . . never mind *The Assumption of the Virgin*, or any of that . . . Look at the real Titians: he was putting the paint on with his fingertips. He was the first Impressionist: that's the only word you can use. I'll tell you, darling, Titian was a giant.'

Or on Gloria's interest in British higher education:

'You won't learn anything worth knowing at Oxford or Cambridge. But I'm glad to hear you're not going to study Modern Languages. I had a graduate here last year: he couldn't even read a menu, darling! What are quenelles, he asked me. Ignorant beyond belief! And his accent was unimaginable. The only people who can understand an Englishman speaking French are people who have been taught French in England.'

Or about gambling:

'Use two dice and you change the odds of course. Why, I've seen men backing the same odds on two as on six.'

Gloria provided the cue. 'Shouldn't they have?' she asked.

He swung round to the fire and, supporting himself with a hand on each armrest of his dining chair, he aimed a kick at the log so that it exploded in sparks. 'Naw! With two dice? No! You can throw six so many different ways. You can get it with two threes; with a four and a two; four and a two the other way; a five and a one; five and a one the other way. That makes five different ways. But you have only one chance to get two; both dice have to come up right for you. Same with getting twelve.'

He swung back to face us and reverted to being Gloria's guardian. He looked at Gloria and then examined me as if trying to decide if my motives were honourable. What he decided did not show on his face. He was remarkably good at concealing his feelings when he was so inclined.

Art and science and cookery and politics and weather forecasting and ancient Greek architecture, and every so often there came that penetrating stare. And so for the whole evening he was roaring down the motorways of conversation and then slamming on the brakes as he remembered I was the man who was taking his old friend's little girl to bed every night.

It was during one of these abrupt pauses in the conversation that he suddenly extended his fist so it was only a few inches from my nose. I stared at him and made no move. Click! There was the handle of a flick-knife concealed in his hand and now its blade snapped forward so that its shiny point was almost touching my eye.

'Dodo!' Gloria yelled in alarm.

Slowly he drew his knife back and folded the blade back into the handle. 'Ha ha. I wanted to see what this fellow had in him,' he said and sounded disappointed that I'd been able to conceal my alarm.

'I don't like that sort of joke,' she said.

Gloria had bought two bottles of Hine brandy in the duty-free shop, and Dodo had got the cork out of the first one before we were far through his front door. I stuck to the local rosé wine, a light and refreshing drink, but Dodo favoured the Hine through the black olives, the chicken and vegetable stew, the goat cheese and the bowl of apples and oranges that followed. By the end of the meal, he was uncorking the second bottle and when we went out on his patio to see the view, he was talking loud enough to be heard in Nice. The sky was clear and every star in the sky was gathering over his house but it was damned cold and the chilly air had no discernible effect upon his ebullience. 'It's cold,' I said. 'Damned cold.'

'One hundred and fifty years,' he answered and wiped drink from his chin. 'And the walls are a metre thick, darling.'

Gloria laughed. 'Shall we go back inside?' she said. I suppose she was used to him.

He held tight to the balcony to get back in through the sliding door.

Even so, he collided with the fly screen and banged his head on the door's edge.

Despite all his shouting about it not being necessary, Gloria went in to the kitchen to wash the dishes. In an attempt to show him what a good-hearted and inoffensive fellow I was, I tried to follow her but he pulled me aside with a rough tug at my sleeve.

'Leave her alone, darling,' he said gruffly. 'She'll do what she wants to do. Zu has always been like that.' He poured more wine for me and topped up his tumbler of brandy. 'She's a wonderful girl.'

'Yes, she is,' I said.

'You're a lucky man: do you know that?' His voice was soft but his eyes were hard. I was on my guard all the time and he knew that, and seemed to enjoy it.

'Yes, I do.'

He went suddenly quiet. He was staring out through the glass door at the lights that wound up into the hills: orange lights and blue lights and sometimes the headlights of cars that shone suddenly and then disappeared like fireflies on a summer's evening. The wonderful view seemed to wreak some profound change upon him. Perhaps it has that effect upon people who spend most of their working days studying the same landscape, its colours, patterns and contradictions. When he spoke again his voice was soft and sober. 'Make the most of every minute,' he said. 'You'll lose her, you know.'

'Will I?' I kept my voice level.

He sipped his brandy and smiled sadly. 'She adores you of course. Any fool could see that. I could see it in her eyes as soon as you walked into the house. Never takes her eyes off you. But she's just a child. She has a life ahead of her. How old are you . . . over forty. Right?'

'Yes,' I said.

'She's determined on this university business. You'll not persuade her otherwise. She'll go to college. And there she'll meet brilliant people of her own age, and because they are at college they'll all end up sharing the same appalling tastes and the same half-baked opinions. We're old fossils. We're part of another world. A world of dinosaurs.' He swigged his brandy and poured more. There was a lot of spite in him. His friendly advice was really a way of hurting me. And it was a method difficult to counter.

I said, 'Yes, thanks a lot Dodo. But the way I see it, you are indisputably an old tyrannosaurus but I'm a young dynamic brilliant individual in the prime of life, and Gloria is an immature youngster.'

He laughed loudly enough to rupture my eardrums and he grabbed my shoulder to save himself from falling over.

'Zu, darling!' he shouted gleefully and loud enough for her to hear him from the kitchen. 'Where did you find this lunatic?'

She came from the kitchen wiping her hands on a tea-towel decorated with a picture of the Mona Lisa smoking a big cigar. 'Are you on some sort of diet, Dodo?' she asked. 'How can you eat three dozen eggs?'

For a moment words did not come but then he stammered and said that they were the finest eggs he'd ever eaten and a nearby farmer supplied him but he had to take a lot at a time. 'Have some,' he offered.

'I'm not that fond of eggs,' said Gloria. 'They are bad for you.'

'Rubbish, darling. Arrant rubbish. A newly laid soft-boiled egg is the most easily digested protein food I know. I love eggs. And there are so many delicious ways of cooking them.'

'They won't be so newly laid by the time you get through three dozen of them,' said Gloria with devastating feminine logic. She smiled. 'We must be leaving you, Dodo.'

'Sit down for a moment longer, darling,' he pleaded. 'I have so few visitors nowadays and you haven't told me the latest news of your parents and all our friends in London.'

For the next ten minutes or so they talked of the family. Small-talk of Gloria's father's dental practice and her mother's charity committees. Dodo listened politely and with ever more glazed eyes.

At 10.25 exactly – I looked at my watch to see the time – Dodo threw himself up to his full height, drank to the health of 'Zu and her lunatic' and having upended his glass, bent and fell full-length on to the floor with a horrifying crash. The tumbler broke, and there was a flare from the log fire as brandy splashed on the embers.

Gloria looked at me, expecting me to revive him, but I just shrugged at her. He groaned and moved enough to reassure her that he wasn't dead. Having stretched himself across the carpet before the fire, he began to snore heavily. Gloria's attempts to wake him failed.

'I shouldn't have brought the brandy for him,' Gloria said. 'He has liver trouble.'

'And I can understand why,' I said.

'We must try and get him on to his bed,' she said. 'We can lift him between us.'

'He looks comfortable enough,' I said.

'You're a callous swine,' said Gloria. So I got his boots off and carried him into his bedroom and dumped him on to his bed.

In his tiny bedroom one more surprise awaited us. A table had been hidden in here. It was laden with pots of colour, a kitchen measuring spoon, a bottle of vinegar and a bottle of linseed oil. Balanced on a jug there was a muslin strainer through which raw beaten egg had been poured, and in the rubbish bin under the table there were half a dozen broken egg shells. Propped against the wall there was another panel, unpainted but smooth and shiny with its beautifully prepared chalk gesso ground.

'What the hell is this?' I said, looking at the half-finished painting leaning against the table. It was quite different to anything we'd seen in the living room or the studio: a Renaissance street scene – a procession – painted on a large wooden panel about five feet long. The colours were weird but the drawings were exact. 'What strange colouring,' I said.

'It's just the underpainting,' explained Gloria. 'He'll put coloured glazes over that to create deep luminous colours.'

'You seem to know all about it.'

'I was an au pair girl in Nice. I used to come up here on my afternoons off. Sometimes I helped him. He's a sweet man. Do you know what it is?' Gloria asked.

'Egg tempera painting, I suppose. But why on long panels?'

'Renaissance marriage chests.'

'I don't get it.'

'He paints forgeries. He sells them through a dealer in Munich.'

'And buyers are fooled?'

'They are authenticated by international art experts. Often famous museums buy them.'

'And he gets away with that?'

'Now it's new . . . unfinished. It will be stained and varnished and damaged so that it looks very old.'

'And fool museums?' I persisted.

'Museum directors are not saints, Bernard.'

'And there goes another illusion! So Dodo's rich?'

'No, they take him a long time to do, and the dealers won't pay much: there are other forgers ready and willing to supply them.'

'So why. . . ?'

'Does he do it?' she finished the question for me. 'The deception . . . the fraud, the deceit is what amuses him. He can be cruel. When you get to know him better, perhaps you'll see what makes him do it.'

The old man groaned and seemed about to wake up but he turned over and went back to sleep breathing heavily. Gloria bent over and stroked his head affectionately. 'The dealers make the big profits. Poor Dodo.'

'You knew all along? You were teasing him about the eggs in his refrigerator?'

82

She nodded. 'Dodo is notorious. He claims to have painted a wonderful "School of Uccello" marriage chest that ended up in the Louvre. Dodo bought dozens of coloured postcards of it, and used them as Christmas cards last year. I thought he'd end up in prison, but no one knows whether that was just Dodo's idea of a joke. Hungarians have all got a strange sense of humour.'

'I wondered about that,' I said.

'He knows about chemistry. It amuses him to reproduce the pigments, and age the wood and the other materials. He's awfully clever.'

The old man stirred again and put a hand to his head where he'd banged it in falling. 'Oh my God!' he groaned.

'You're all right,' I told him.

'He can't hear you; he's talking in his sleep,' said Gloria. 'You do that sometimes.'

'Oh yes,' I scoffed at the suggestion.

'Last week you woke up. You were calling out crazy things.' She put an arm round me in a protective gesture.

'What things?'

'They're killing him; they're killing him.'

'I never talk in my sleep,' I said.

'Have it your own way,' said Gloria. But she was right. Three nights in a row I'd woken up after a nightmare about Jim Prettyman. 'They're killing Jim!' is what I'd shouted. I remember it only too well. In the dream, no matter how urgently I shouted at the passers-by, none of them would take any notice of me.

'Look at these photos,' said Gloria, unrolling some old prints that had been curled up on a cluttered side-table. 'Wasn't he a handsome young brute?'

A slim youthful athletic Dodo was in a group with half a dozen such youngsters and an older man whose face I knew well. Three of them were seated on wicker chairs in front of a garden hut. A man in the front row had a foot upon a board that said 'The Prussians'.

'Probably a tennis tournament,' explained Gloria. 'He was a wonderful tennis player.'

'Something like that,' I said, although I knew in fact that it was nothing of the kind. The older man was an old Berlin hand named John 'Lange' Koby – a contemporary of my father – and his 'Prussians' were the intelligence teams that he ran into the Russian zone of Germany. So Dodo had been an agent.

'Did Dodo ever work with your father?' I asked her.

'In Hungary?' I nodded. 'Intelligence gathering?' She had such a delicate way of putting things. 'Not as far as I know.' She took the photo from me. 'Is that a team?'

'That's the American: Lange Koby,' I said.

She looked at the photo with renewed interest now that she knew that they were field agents. 'Yes, he's much older than the others. He's still alive isn't he?'

'Lives in Berlin. Sometimes I run into him. My father detested Lange. But Lange was all right.'

'Why?'

'He detested all those Americans who Lange ran. He used to say, "German Americans are American Germans." He had an obsession about them.'

'I've never heard you criticize your father before,' said Gloria.

'Maybe he had his reasons,' I said defensively. 'Let's go.'

'Are you sure Dodo will be all right?'

'He'll be all right,' I said.

'You do like him, don't you?'

'Yes,' I said.

At that first meeting I did like him: I must have been raving mad.

10

'It went well, I thought,' Dicky Cruyer said with a hint of modest pride. He was carrying illustration boards and now he put them on the floor and leaned them against the leg of his fine rosewood table.

I came into the room still trying to read the notes I'd scribbled during the babble, indignation and dismay that were always the hallmark of Tuesday mornings. I wasn't giving my whole attention to Dicky and that was the sort of thing he noticed. I looked up and grunted.

'I said,' Dicky repeated slowly, having given me a good-natured smile, 'that I thought it all went very well.' I must have looked puzzled. 'In the departmental get-together.' He tapped the brass barometer that he'd lately added to the furnishings of his working space. Or maybe he was tapping the temperature, or the time in New York City.

'Oh yes,' I said. 'Very well indeed.'

Well, why wouldn't it go to his satisfaction? What Dicky Cruyer, my immediate boss, called a 'departmental get-together' took place in one of the conference rooms every Tuesday morning. At one time it took place in Dicky's office, but the German Station Controller's empire had grown since then: we needed a larger room nowadays because Tuesday morning had become a chance for Dicky to rehearse the lectures he gave to the indefatigable mandarins of the Foreign Office. It was usually a mad scramble of last-minute paper-work but today he'd used satellite photos and had pretty coloured diagrams – pie-charts, stacked bars and line-graphs – prepared in the new 'art department' and an 'operator' came and put them on the projector. Dicky prodded the screen with a telescopic rod and looked round the darkened room in case anyone had lit a cigarette.

The get-together was also the opportunity for Dicky to allocate work to his subordinates, arbitrate between them and start thinking about the monthly report that would have to be on the Director-General's desk first thing on Friday morning. That is to say he got me to start thinking about it because I always had to write it.

'It's simply a matter of motivating them all,' said Dicky, sitting at his rosewood table and straightening out a wire paper-clip. 'I want them to feel . . .'

'Part of a team,' I supplied.

'That's right,' he said. Then, detecting what he thought might be a note of sarcasm in my voice, he frowned. 'You have a lot to learn about being part of a team, Bernard,' he said.

'I know,' I said. 'I think the school I went to didn't emphasize the team spirit nearly enough.'

'That lousy school in Berlin,' he said. 'I never understood why your father let you go to a little local school like that. There were schools for the sons of British officers weren't there?'

'He said it would be good for my German.'

'And it was,' conceded Dicky. 'But you must have been the only English child there. It made you into a loner, Bernard.'

'I suppose it did.'

'And you're proud of that, I know. But a loner is a misfit, Bernard. I wish I could make you see that.'

'I'll need your notes, Dicky.'

'Notes?'

'To do the D-G's report.'

'Not much in the way of notes today, Bernard,' he said proudly. 'I'm getting the hang of these Tuesday morning talks nowadays. I improvise as I go along.'

Oh my God! I should have listened to what he was saying. 'Any rough notes will do.'

'Just write it the way I delivered it.'

'It's a matter of emphasis, Dicky.'

He threw the straightened wire clip into his large glass ashtray and looked at me sharply. 'A matter of emphasis' was Dicky's roundabout way of admitting total ignorance. Hurriedly I added, 'It's so technical.'

Dicky softened somewhat. He liked being 'technical'. Until recently Dicky's lectures had been a simple résumé of the everyday work of the office. But now he'd decided that the way ahead was the path of hi-tech. So he'd become a minor expert – and a major bore – on such subjects as 'photo-interpretation of intelligence obtained by unmanned vehicles' and 'optical cameras, line-scan and radar sensors that provide mono-chrome, colour, false-colour and infra-red imagery'.

'I think I explained it all carefully,' Dicky said.

'Yes, you did,' I said and bent over far enough to flip through the cardboard-mounted pictures he'd used, in the hope that they would all be suitably captioned. To some extent they were: 'SLRR sideways-looking reconnaissance radar' the first one said, and there was a neat red arrow to show which way was up. And 'IRLS infra-red line scan photo showing various radiometric temperatures of target area at noon.

Notice buildings occupied by personnel, and the transport vehicles at bottom right of photo. Compare with photo of same area at midnight.'

'Don't take that material away with you,' Dicky warned. 'I'll need those pictures tomorrow, and I promised the people at Joint Air Reconnaissance that they'd have them back in perfect condition: no fingerprints or bent corners.'

'No, I won't take them,' I promised and slid the illustrations back in place. I was hopeless at understanding such things. I began to wonder which one of Dicky's staff, present at this morning's meeting, might have remembered his discourse well enough to recapitulate and explain it to me. But I couldn't think of anyone who gave Dicky their undivided attention during the Tuesday morning meetings. Our most assiduous note-taker, Charlie Billingsly, was now in Hong Kong and Harry Strang, with his prodigious memory, had artfully contrived an urgent phone call that granted him escape just five minutes into Dicky's dissertation. I said, 'But you used to be strongly opposed to all this stuff from JARIC, and the satellite material too.'

'We have to move with the times, Bernard.' Dicky looked down at the appointments book that his secretary had left open for him. 'Oh, by the bye,' he said casually. Too casually. 'You keep mentioning that fellow Prettyman . . .'

'I don't keep mentioning him,' I said. 'I mentioned him once. You said you didn't remember him.'

'I don't want to quibble,' said Dicky. 'The point is that his wife has been making a nuisance of herself lately. She cornered Morgan when he was in the FO the other day. Started on about a pension and all that kind of stuff.'

'His widow,' I said.

'Verily! Widow. I said widow.'

'You said wife.'

'Wife. Widow. What damned difference does it make.'

'It makes a difference to Jim Prettyman,' I said. 'It makes him dead.'

'Whatever she is, I don't want anyone encouraging her.'

'Encouraging her to do what?'

'I wish you wouldn't be so otiose,' said Dicky. He'd been reading *Vocabulary Means Power* again, I noticed that it was missing from the shelf behind his desk. 'She shouldn't be button-holing senior staff. It would serve her right if Morgan made an official complaint about her.'

'She wields a lot of clout over there,' I reminded him. 'I wouldn't advise Morgan to make an enemy of her. He might end up on his arse.'

Dicky wet his thin lips and nodded. 'Yes. Well. You're right. Morgan knows that. Far better that we all close ranks and ignore her.'

'Jim Prettyman was one of us,' I said. 'He worked downstairs.'

'That was a long time ago. No one told him to go and work in Washington DC. What a place that is! My God, that town has some of the worst crime figures in the whole of North America.' So Dicky had been doing his homework.

I said, 'This is not official then? This . . . this not encouraging Prettyman's widow?'

He looked at me and then looked out of the window. 'It's not official,' he said with measured care. 'It's good advice. It's advice that might save someone a lot of trouble and grief.'

'That's what I wanted to know,' I said. 'Shall we get the heading for the D-G's report?'

'Very well,' said Dicky. He looked at me and nodded again. I wondered if he knew that Cindy Matthews – one-time Mrs Prettyman –had invited me to a dinner party that evening.

'And by the way, Dicky,' I said. 'That lion looks very good on the floor in here.'

Mrs Cindy Matthews, as she styled herself, lived in considerable comfort. There was new Italian furniture, old French wine, a Swiss dishwasher and the sort of Japanese hi-fi that comes with a thick instruction manual. They'd never faced the expense that children bring of course, and I suppose the rise in London house prices had provided them with a fat profit on the big house they'd been buying in Edgware. Now she lived in a tiny house off the King's Road, a thoroughfare noted for its punks, pubs and exotic boutiques. It was no more than four small rooms placed one upon the other, with the lowest one – a kitchen and dining room – below street level. But it was a fashionable choice: the sort of house that estate agents called 'bijou' and newly divorced advertising men hankered after.

There were candles and pink roses on the dining table, and solid silver cutlery, and more drinking glasses than I could count. Through the front window we could see the ankles of people walking past the house, and they could see what we were eating. Which is perhaps why we had the sort of meal that women's magazines photograph from above. Three paper-thin slices of avocado arranged alongside a tiny puddle of tomato sauce and a slice of kiwi fruit. The second course was three thin slices of duck breast with a segment of mango and a lettuce leaf. We ended with a thin slice of Cindy's delicious home-made chocolate roulade. I ate a lot of bread and cheese.

Cindy was a small pale-faced young woman with pointed nose and little cupid's bow mouth. She had her wavy brunette hair cut short. I suppose it was easier to arrange and more suited to her senior position. Her dress was equally severe: plain brown wool and simply cut. She'd always been brimful of nervous energy, and arranging this dinner party had not lessened her restless anxiety. Now she fussed about the table, asking everyone whether they wanted more champagne, Perrier or Chablis, wholemeal or white rolls, and making sure that everyone had a table napkin. There was a tacit sigh of relief when she finally sat down.

It was a planned evening. Cindy always planned everything in advance. The food was measured, the cooking times synchronized, the white wines were chilled and reds at the right temperature. The rolls were warmed, the butter soft, the guests carefully prompted and the conversation predictable. It wasn't one of those evenings when you can hardly squeeze a word into the gabble, the guests stay too late, drink too much and lurch out of the house excitedly scribbling each other's phone numbers into their Filofax notebooks. It was dull.

Perhaps it was a tribute to Cindy's planning that she'd invited me on an evening when Gloria did a class in mathematics, part of her determination to do well at university, and so I went along to dinner on my own.

The evening started off very sedately, as evenings were likely to do when Sir Giles Streeply-Cox was the guest of honour. A muscular old man with bushy white Pickwickian sideburns and a florid complexion, 'Creepy-Pox', had been the scourge of the Foreign Office in his day. Ministers and Ambassadors went in terror of him. Since retirement he lived in Suffolk and grew roses while his wife made picture frames for all the local watercolour artists. But the old man was still attending enough committees to get his fares and expenses paid when he came to London.

It was the first time I'd ever seen the fearful Creepy close-to, but this evening he was on his best behaviour. Cindy knew exactly how to handle him. She let him play the part of the charming old great man of Whitehall. He slipped into this role effortlessly but there was no mistaking the ogre that lurked behind the smiles and self-deprecating asides. Lady Streeply-Cox said little. She was of a generation that was taught not to mention the food or the table arrangements, and talking about her husband's work was as bad as talking about TV. So she sat and smiled at her husband's jokes, which meant she didn't have much to do all evening.

There were two Diplomatic Corps people. Harry Baxter, a middle-aged second secretary from our embassy in Berne, and his wife Pat. She had a heavy gold necklace, pink-tinted hair and told old jokes – with punch-lines in schweizer-deutsch – about bankers with unpronounceable names.

When Cindy asked Baxter what exciting things had been happening in Berne lately, old Streeply-Cox answered for him by saying the only exciting thing that happened to the diplomatic staff in Berne was losing their bread crusts in the fondue. At which both Streeply-Coxes laughed shrilly.

There was a young couple too. Simon was a shy young chap in his early twenties who'd been teaching English in a private school in Bavaria. It was not an experience he'd enjoyed. 'You see these mean little German kids and you understand why the Germans have started so many wars,' he said. 'And you see those teachers and you know why the Germans lost them.' Now Simon had become a theatre critic on a giveaway magazine and achieved a reputation as a perfectionist and connoisseur by condemning everything he wrote about. With him there was a quiet girl with smudged lipstick. She was wearing a man's tweed jacket many sizes too big for her. They smiled at each other all through dinner and left early.

After dinner we all went upstairs and had coffee and drinks in a room with an elaborate gas fire that hissed loudly. Creepy had one demi-tasse of decaffeinated coffee and a chocolate mint, then his wife swigged down two large brandies and drove him home.

The couple from Berne stayed on for another half-hour or so. Cindy having indicated that she wanted a word with me, I remained behind. 'What do you think of him?' she said after all the other guests had left.

'Old Creepy? He's a barrel of fun,' I said.

'Don't take him for a fool,' Cindy warned. 'He knows his way around.'

I had a feeling that Creepy was there to impress me with the sort of contacts she had, the sort of influence she could wield behind the scenes in the Foreign Office corridors if she needed a show of strength. 'Did you want to talk to me?'

'Yes, Bernard, I did.'

'Give me another drink,' I said.

She got the bottle of Scotch from the side-table and put it in front of me, on a copy of *Nouvelle Cuisine* magazine. On the cover it said, 'Ten easy steps to a sure-fire chocolate roulade'. She didn't pour it, she walked across to the fireplace and fiddled with something on the mantelpiece. 'Ever since poor Jim was murdered . . .' she began without turning round.

I suppose I guessed – in fact dreaded – what was coming because I immediately tried to head it off. 'Is murdered the right word?' I said.

She rounded on me. 'Two men wait for him and shoot him dead? Six bullets? What do you call it Bernard? It's a damned bizarre way to commit suicide, isn't it?'

'Yes, go on.' I dropped some ice into my glass and poured myself a generous drink.

'I asked about the funeral. I told them I wanted to go and asked them for the fare.'

'And?'

'It's all over and done with. Cremated!' She used the word as if it was an obscenity, as perhaps for her it was. 'Cremated! Not a word to me about what I'd like done for my husband.' Her voice was bitter. As a Catholic she felt herself doubly wronged. 'Oh, and there's something for you.'

She gave me a cardboard box. I opened it and found a pile of papers about ancient Mesopotamian tomb inscriptions. It was all neatly arranged and included ones that Fiona had worked on. I recognized her handwriting. 'For me?' I said. 'In Jim's Will?'

'There was no Will; just a letter Jim had left with his lawyer. Things to be done after he died. It's witnessed. It's legal they say.'

'Are you sure he wanted me to have it? I was never interested.'

'Perhaps he wanted you to send it to Fiona,' she said. 'But don't give it back to me. I've got enough on my mind without all the tricks and puzzles of the Ancient World.'

I nodded. She'd always been sarcastic about Jim's hobby and I suppose I had too.

'I've been trying to find out more exactly what Jim was doing when he died,' she said and there was a significant pause.

'Tell me.' I knew she was going to tell me anyway.

'I started with the money,' she said. I nodded. The Foreign Office handled our budget. It was one aspect of our work that she might have been able to pry into.

'Money?' I said.

'The money that's supposed to be missing. The money you went to Washington to ask Jim about.'

'Just for the record, Cindy, I didn't go to Washington to ask Jim anything. That extra little job was dumped upon me after I got there.'

She was unconvinced. 'Maybe. Maybe not,' she said. 'When we've got to the bottom of it you might find that it was all arranged right from the start.'

'That what was arranged?'

'Having you in Washington at the right time to do that "little extra job".'

'No. Cindy . . .'

'Mother of God! Will you listen to me, Bernard, and stop interrupting. The fund that Jim arranged. There was a lot of money laundered through a couple of banks in Gibraltar and Austria. Backwards and forwards it went so it's damned difficult to trace it. It seems to have ended up in an account in Germany. All that money was moved and invested six months before your wife defected.'

'So what?'

'Before!'

'I heard you.'

'Don't you see?'

'See what?'

'Suppose I told you that this fund was set up by your wife Fiona? Suppose I said that this was a KGB slush fund?'

'A KGB what?' I said rather more loudly than I intended. 'And Jim could sign? You told me Jim could sign.'

She smiled knowingly. 'Exactly. That was the cunning of it. Suppose Fiona set up the funding of a KGB network and used SIS money and people to operate it? Do you see the elegance of it?'

'Frankly, no,' I said. I wasn't going to make it easy for her. If she wanted to sell me her crackpot hypothesis she'd have to take me through it theorem by theorem.

'Financing a secret network is the most difficult and dangerous part of any secret operation. You don't have to be working on your side of the river to know that, Bernard.'

'Yes, I think I read that somewhere,' I said. But sarcasm wasn't going to stop her.

'Don't be stupid, Bernard. I know how it all works.'

I drank her whisky and didn't answer.

'I must have a cigarette,' she said. 'I'm trying to give up but I must have one now.' She got an unopened pack from a brass bowl on the bookshelf and took her time lighting up. Her hands were shaking, and the flaming match emphasized the movement, but that might have been because she craved the cigarette. I watched her with interest. The people in the Foreign Office knew things that we never found out about until it was too late. She said, 'If Fiona set up a clandestine bank account and had our own people run it under strict secrecy, it would be the best and most secret way to supply funds to enemy agents wouldn't it?' She was calmer now that she was smoking the cigarette.

'But if you have found out about it, how secret is that?'

She had an answer. 'Because Fiona defected. That upset everything.'

'And you are saying that Jim went to Washington because Fiona defected? That Jim was a KGB agent?'

'Maybe.' That was the weakest link: I could see that in her face. 'I keep thinking about it. I really don't know.'

'Not Jim. Of all people, not Jim. And even if you were right, why the hell would he run to America, the heartland of capitalism?'

'I only said maybe. More probably Fiona fooled everyone into thinking it was official. How could they guess it was money for the KGB?'

'But the money is missing,' I pointed out.

'They can't find the account,' she said. 'The whole damned account. And they are only guessing at how much might be in it: one estimate said four million pounds. No one in the FO or the Department will admit to knowing anything about it. The cashier knows the money is missing but that's all.'

'That only means that he doesn't have the right piece of paper with an appropriate signature on it. That's what the cashier means by money missing.'

'This was real money, Bernard, and someone got their hands on it.'

I shook my head. It was beyond me. 'Did you get all this from "our man in Berne"?' I said, referring to the Baxters.

'They're old friends. He knows his way around but he hasn't got anywhere so far.'

'But there must be a departmental record of who was named as the account holder.'

'Yes, Jim.'

'And who else?'

She shrugged. 'We don't even know where the account is,' she said and blew smoke hard through pursed lips. 'I'm not going to let it go, Bernard.'

'What will you do?'

'What do you suggest?'

'The Deputy D-G is very energetic these days,' I offered. 'You might find some way of talking to him.'

'How can we be sure it doesn't go up that far?'

For a moment I didn't follow her. Then I did. 'Working for the KGB? The Deputy? Sir Percy Babcock?'

'No need to shout, Bernard. Yes, the Deputy. You read the newspapers. You know the score.'

'If I know the score it's not because I read the newspapers,' I said. 'No one is above suspicion these days.'

'You're going to talk to Five?' And already I was wondering whether it was better to jump out of the window or ring for an ambulance.

She was horrified at the idea. 'MI5? The Home Office? No, no, no. They'd know nothing about our Central Funding. And I work for the Foreign Office. That would be more than my job's worth, Bernard.'

'So what else can you do? You're not thinking of trying to lobby the Cabinet Office are you?'

'Are you saying that you won't help?'

So that was it. I drank some of my whisky, took a deep breath and said, 'What do you want me to do, Cindy?'

'We've got to go through the files and find the orders that created the account.'

'You said you've tried that already,' I pointed out.

'But not in the Data Centre,' she said.

'The Yellow Submarine? Jesus Christ, Cindy! You're not serious. And anyway you're not allowed there.' I could have bitten my tongue off.

'No,' she said. 'But you are, Bernard. You're always in and out of there.' I'd walked right into it. I took a good mouthful of booze and swallowed it quickly.

'Cindy . . .'

Hurriedly she explained her theory. 'The computer will have it in cross-reference. That's how computers work, isn't it? Instead of me rummaging through hundreds of files, we'd only have to give the computer one hard fact to access everything.'

'And what hard fact could we give it?'

'Jim. Jim was a trustee or a signatory or something. Key him into the computer and we'll get everything we need.'

So this was why I'd been invited along. And Creepy was there to reassure me that Cindy had friends at court, just in case. 'Well, wait a minute, Cindy,' I said as the full awful implications of it hit me.

She said, 'We must see who else had access to it before they are murdered too.'

It was then that I began to think Jim's death had deranged her. 'You think Jim was murdered because he was a signatory to the bank account?'

'Yes. That's exactly what I think, Bernard,' she said.

I watched her as she lit a cigarette. 'I'll see what I can find out,' I promised. 'Maybe there's another way.'

'The Data Centre is our only chance,' said Cindy.

'We could both be fired, Cindy. Are you sure it's worth it?' I asked. Having been warned off by Dicky I wanted to see if she had an explanation.

But she was like a woman possessed. 'There's something damned odd going on,' she said. 'Everything to do with this bloody bank account is so damned well covered. I've handled some sensitive material Bernard but I've never heard of anything buried as deep as this one. There is no paper: no files on it, no memos, no records. No one knows anything.'

'Don't know or won't tell? It might just have a very high clearance.'

'Someone is damned scared. Someone in the Department, I mean. Someone is so damned scared that they had Jim murdered.'

'We're not sure of that.'

'I'm sure,' she said. 'And no one is going to shut me up.'

'Cindy,' I said, and paused wondering how to put it to her. 'Don't be offended. But there's something you must tell me. Truly.'

'Spit it out, Bernard.'

'You're not just putting this pressure on to the Department as a way to get Jim's pension, are you?'

She smiled one of her special Mona Lisa smiles. 'They've agreed that already,' she said.

'They have?'

'They're paying a full pension to me and a full pension to this American woman who says she married Jim in Mexico.'

'They admitted Jim was still working for the Department?' Now I was surprised.

'They admit nothing. It's one of those "in full and final settlement" contracts. Sign here and shut up.'

'That's unusual,' I allowed.

'Unusual?' she chortled. 'Jesus! It's bloody unprecedented. It's not the way the Department works, is it? They didn't hesitate, didn't confirm with anyone or check anything I said. Okay, they said. Just like that.'

'Who authorized it?'

A scornful little laugh. 'No one knows. They said it was in the file.'

'How could it be in the file?' I said. There couldn't be anything in the file about paying out two pensions to two wives of someone who'd stopped working for the Department years before.

'Exactly,' she said. 'Someone is damned scared.'

'Scared,' I said, 'yes.' She was right: it was me.

95

11

Thursday was not a good day. I had to go down into the 'Yellow Submarine'. The Data Centre was just about the only part of the Foreign Office where Cindy Matthews would not be able to stroll past the security guard with some casual chat about getting the tin of biscuits for the Minister's afternoon tea. They were fussy here: uniformed guards with hats on. A photo identity check at the ground floor entrance and more checks at the software library level and video at the third and deepest level where the secrets were really kept under lock and key.

After my wife defected it was several weeks, nearly three months in fact, before I was required to go down into the Submarine again. I had begun to believe that my security clearance had been downgraded and that I'd never see the inside of the place again, but then one day Dicky stayed at home with a head-cold and something was wanted urgently and I was the only one in the office who knew how to work the consoles down there and they sent me. From that time onwards everything was back to normal again as far as I could tell. But with the Department you can never be sure. It's not like a Michelin guide: they don't publish a book each spring so you can find out how the inspectors feel about you.

So I was happy enough to sit at the keyboard and tell the machine my name, grade and department and wait for it to come up with the request for my secret access number. It meant that I was still one of the nation's trusted. Once the machine had okayed my number I spent a couple of hours sitting there, rolling around on one of those uncomfortable little typist chairs, calling up answers on the display screen and printing out yards of pale-green security bumf for Dicky. When I had finished everything he wanted I sat there for a moment. I knew I should get up and go straight back to the office. But I couldn't resist probing into the machinery just once. Just so I could go back to Cindy and tell her that I'd tried. And also to satisfy my own curiosity.

I keyed it in: 'PRETTYMAN, JAMES.'

The machine gurgled before providing a 'Menu' from which I selected BIOG. More soft clattering came from deep inside the machine before Prettyman's twenty-two-page-long service biography came up on the screen. I pushed the control arrow buttons to get to the end of it and found it ended with a summary of Prettyman's last report. This was the standard Civil Service file in which one's immediate superior comments on 'judgement, political sense, power of analysis and foresight' but it didn't say whether Prettyman had retired from the Department or continued to work for it. When I pressed the machine for supplementary material I got the word REVISE.

So I pursued PRETTYMAN J BIOG REVISE and got REFER FILE FO FX MI 123/456, which seemed an unlikely number for a file. I tried to access that file and found ACCESS DENIED ENTER ARCTIC NUMBER.

I couldn't tell the machine the 'Arctic' number it wanted because I didn't even know what an Arctic number was. I looked at my watch. I still had plenty of time to spare before my appointment with Dicky. Dicky had been in a very good mood for the last few days. The Bizet crisis seemed to have faded. There had been no hard news but he told the Department that the Stasi prosecution office were about to release our men because of insufficient evidence and managed to imply that it was all his doing. It was a total fabrication, but when Dicky needed good news he never hesitated to invent some. Once, when I'd tackled him about it, he said it was the only way of getting the old man off his back.

Today Dicky had gone to lunch with his old friend and one-time colleague Henry Tiptree, who'd left his cosy Foreign Office desk for a job with a small merchant bank in the newly deregulated City. Morgan had gone to lunch with them too. Morgan used to be a hatchet man and general factotum for the Director-General but since the D-G's appearances had become fewer and further between, Morgan had nothing to do but pass queries to the Deputy D-G's office and blow smoke at the ceilings of the City's private dining rooms. I suspected that Morgan and Dicky were cautiously investigating their chances of getting one of the six-figure City salaries that I kept reading about in *The Economist*. In any case, Tiptree, Morgan and Dicky were not likely to finish judging the Havanas and old tawny port until three at the earliest, which is why I'd brought my packet of sandwiches to the Submarine.

So I tried again. I entered the company for which Prettyman worked in Washington. TRANSFER LOAD then PERIMETER SECURITY GUARANTEE TRUST.

The machine purred contentedly and then the screen filled. Here it all was: the address of the headquarters, computed world assets, stock market price and names of president and vice presidents of the PSGT. This wasn't what I wanted so I entered PRETTYMAN into the PSGT queries space. Hiccups. Then I got REFER FILE FO FX MI 123/456.

I went back to REGISTRY ONE and entered that file number. On the screen came the same message as before: ACCESS DENIED ENTER ARCTIC NUMBER. It was a merry-go-round. Had I not been seeking specific information it would not have seemed sinister. Had I not chosen those particular subjects it would not have produced the coincidence.

Now I tried another angle. The data bank held details of departmental employees past and present. I entered the name of my wife SAMSON, FIONA and entered the UPDATE command for the final part of her file.

No surprise now. Up came that damned bogus number that couldn't possibly have come from the normal filing system; REFER FILE FO FX MI 123/456. And of course the subsequent keying was answered by the inevitable request for the ARCTIC NUMBER. So whatever the Arctic number was, it would give an enquirer answers about Jim Prettyman, his US employers – almost certainly a front for some sort of illicit business – and whatever my wife Fiona was doing during those final weeks before her defection.

I went and walked around for a few minutes. Level Three was especially depressing. On one wall the long open room had dark metal shelving packed with spools and huge 12-platter disk packs, and other examples of sophisticated computer software. Another long wall was occupied with the work stations and on the third wall there was a series of desks and soft chairs that were allocated to senior staff. The last wall was of glass, and behind it the toilers came hauling trolleys piled with paper which the machines consumed with terrible appetites.

I stretched my legs and racked my brains. I even drank some of the concoction that the 'beverage dispenser' classified as coffee. I went to the toilet. For many months the question 'Is there intelligent life in the Data Centre?' had been posed in neat handwriting on the wall there. Now someone had scrawled 'Yes but I'm only visiting' below it. The graffito was the only sign of real human life displayed anywhere, for the staff assigned here soon became as robotic as the machines they operated and serviced. I went back to my work station.

I continued for another hour but it was no use. The damned machine always defeated me. In the old days everything was in Registry, and no matter that the flies were grimy, and you had to take your own soap and towel down there, at least if you couldn't find what you wanted there was always someone to show you the bottom shelf where the missing file was put because it was too heavy, or the top shelf where it was put because it was never asked for, or the door it was put against because someone had stolen the wedge that kept the door open. I preferred Registry.

'Where did you have lunch today?' Gloria asked me in that cheerful casual voice that she assumes when suspicion warps her soul. She wasn't visiting her parents this evening: they were at a dentist's convention in Madrid.

'The Submarine,' I said. We were at home and about to have dinner. I was sitting watching the seven o'clock Channel Four news. Gale-force winds were 'lashing the coastline' and bringing 'chaos' and 'havoc' in the way that the weather is apt to do when camera crews have no real news to record. As if to bring the news home to me the window panes rattled and the wind howled loudly through the little trees in the garden. Gloria on her way to the dining room put two glasses of chilled white wine on to the side-table. She was trying to wean me off the hard liquor.

'In the Submarine?' she said with a slight smile and a voice brimming with that malicious one-sided delight for which the Germans coined the word Schadenfreude. 'How perfectly awful!' She laughed.

'Rubber sandwiches from the Dinky Deli,' I added just to complete her pleasure.

'But you weren't back until nearly four,' she called. I could see her in the dining room. She was setting the table for dinner. She did it with the same careful attention she gave to everything. Knives, forks and spoons were aligned with the plastic place-mats; serving spoons guarded the mustard, salt and pepper-mill. The napkins were folded and put into position with mathematical accuracy. Satisfied with the table she came back to where I was sitting, perched herself on the arm of the sofa and took a small sip of her wine.

'I had a meeting at four . . . with Dicky.' I switched off the TV. It was just a regurgitation of ancient happenings. I suppose the news has to be expanded to fit into its allotted time slot.

'The whole afternoon down there? Whatever were you doing?'

'I stayed on tinkering with the files. I do sometimes.'

'Jim Prettyman?'

She knew me too well. 'That sort of thing,' I admitted.

'Any luck?'

'The same all the time. Have you ever heard of an Arctic coding?'

'No, but there have been a dozen new coding levels in the past year. And there are new top-level data-bank names coming in every month these days.'

'I kept getting the same Access Denied signal from everything I tried.'

'You were trying different ways to get the same data?'

'I spent well over an hour at it.'

'I wish you'd told me, darling,' she said, her voice changing to one of concern.

'Why?'

'I know those machines. I spent a month down there until you rescued me. Remember?'

'I was working those machines . . .' I almost said before she was born, but the difference in our ages was not something I wanted to keep reminding myself about. '. . . years ago,' I finished lamely.

'Then you should know about "sneaky-peak",' she said.

'Who, or what in hell is sneaky-peak?'

'If you'd taken proper training, instead of just tapping away and hoping for the best, you'd not do silly things.'

'What are you talking about?' I said.

'When you get any sort of Access Denied signal the machine flags it and records your name and number.'

'Does it?' I asked as she went into the hall and called upstairs to where Billy and Sally were supposed to be doing their homework under the supervision of Doris.

'Dinner, children! Are you ready, Doris?'

She came back into the room and added, 'And that's not all. It lists every file you fail to access. When the Data Security Clerks run their analysis program they can see exactly what it is you were trying to get that is beyond your security clearance.'

'I didn't know that.'

'Obviously, darling.' A kitchen timer sounded and she uttered a muffled Hungarian curse that I'd learned to recognize, and went to the kitchen to get our dinner.

I got up and followed her and watched her getting bright new pots from the oven and loading them on to the trolley. 'You don't know how often they run their security program, do you?'

'Make yourself useful,' she said, and left me with the trolley. I pushed it into the dining room. 'You can't erase it, darling. If that's what you're hoping for, forget it.'

Sally and Billy came in carrying their school books. Billy was fourteen and had suddenly grown tall. He had wire bracing on his teeth. It must have been uncomfortable but he never complained. He was a stoic. Sally was a couple of years younger, still very much a child, and still suffering from the loss of her mother. The truth was that both children missed their mother. They never said so, they kept their grief hidden deep inside and I could find no way of even beginning to console them.

Gloria had made it a routine to check their homework after dinner each evening. She was wonderful to them. Sometimes they seemed to learn more from her in their half an hour of cheerful instruction than they learned all day at school. And Gloria had gained the children's confidence by means of these lessons and that was no less important to all of us. And yet I sometimes wondered if the children didn't resent the happiness I'd found with Gloria. I suspected that they wanted me to bear my rightful share of their sorrow.

'Hands washed?'

'Yes, Auntie Gloria,' they both choroused with their palms held high. Doris held her hands up too and smiled shyly. Newly slimmed, this quiet – and hitherto overweight – girl from a little village in Devon had been with the children a long time now. Having started as a nanny she now shuttled them back and forth to their respective schools, gave Sally some lunch at home, did some shopping and scorched my shirts. She was of about Gloria's age and sometimes I wondered what she really thought about Gloria setting up home with me. But there would be little chance of her confiding any such thoughts to me. In my presence Doris was inscrutable, but with the children I could often hear her yelling and joining in their noisy games.

'Billy can plug the trolley into the electricity socket for me,' said Gloria. I sat down. Doris was fidgeting with the cutlery. Abstaining from eating chocolate seemed to have given her chronic withdrawal symptoms.

The trolley with the built-in warmer – to say nothing of the brightly coloured casseroles, and striped pot-holders – was Gloria's idea. It was going to revolutionize our lives, as well as being wonderful when we gave dinner parties.

'Chipolata sausages!' I said. 'And Uncle Ben rice! My favourites.'

Gloria didn't respond. It was the third time in a week we'd had those damned pork sausages. Perhaps if I'd had a proper lunch I would have had sense enough to keep a civil tongue in my head.

Gloria didn't look at me, she was serving the children. 'The rice is a bit burned,' she told them. 'But if you don't take it from the bottom it will be all right.'

She served two sausages to each of us. She'd had the heat too high and they were black and shrunken. She put the rest of them back on the warmer. Then she gave us all some spinach. It was watery.

101

Having served the meal she sat down and took an unusually large swig of her wine before starting to eat.

'I'm sorry,' I said in the hope of breaking her tight-lipped silence.

In a voice unnaturally high she said, 'I'm no good at cooking, Bernard. You knew that. I never pretended otherwise.' The children looked at Doris, and Doris looked down at her plate.

'It's delicious,' I said.

'Don't bloody well patronize me!' she said loudly and angrily. 'It's absolutely awful. Do you think I don't know it's all spoiled?'

The children looked at her with that dispassionate interest that children show for events outside their experience. 'Don't cry, Auntie Gloria,' said Sally. 'You can have my sausage: it's almost not burned at all.'

Gloria got to her feet and rushed from the room. The children looked at me to see what I would do.

'Carry on eating your supper, children,' I said. 'I must go and see Auntie Gloria.'

'Give her a big kiss, Daddy,' advised Sally. 'That's sure to make everything all right.'

Doris took the mustard away from Billy and said, 'Mustard is not good for children.'

Some days with Gloria were idyllic. And not just days. For week after week we lived in such harmony and happiness that I could hardly believe my good fortune. But at other times we clashed. And when one thing went wrong, other discords followed like hammer blows. Lately there had been more and more of these disagreements and I knew that the fault was usually mine.

'Don't switch on the light,' she said quietly. I went into the bedroom expecting to face a tirade. Instead I found Gloria inappropriately apologetic. The only light came from the bedside clock-radio but it was enough to see that she was crying. 'It's no good, Bernard,' she said. She was sprawled across the bed, the corner of an embroidered handkerchief held tightly in her teeth as if she was trying to summon up enough courage to eat it. 'I try and try but it's no use.'

'It's my fault,' I said and bent over and kissed her.

She lifted her face to me but her expression was unchanging. 'It's no one's fault,' she said sadly. 'You try. I know you do.'

I sat on the bed and touched her bare arm. 'Living together is not easy,' I said. 'It takes time to adjust.'

For a few moments neither of us spoke. I was tempted to suggest that we sent Doris off to cooking classes. But a man who lives in a house with two women knows better than to sprinkle even a mote of dust upon the delicate balance of power.

'It's your wife,' said Gloria suddenly.

'Fiona? What do you mean?'

'She was the right one for you.'

'Don't talk nonsense.'

'She was beautiful and clever.' Gloria wiped her nose. 'When you were with Fiona everything was always perfect. I know it was.'

For a moment I said nothing. I could take all this admiration of Fiona from everyone except Gloria. I didn't want Gloria implying that I'd been a lucky fellow; I wanted her to say how fortunate Fiona had been to capture me. 'We had more help,' I said.

'She was rich,' said Gloria and the tears came to her eyes again.

'It's better the way we are.'

She seemed not to hear me. When she spoke her voice came from very far away. 'When I first saw you I wanted you so much, Bernard.' She sniffed. 'I thought I'd be able to make you so happy. I so envied your wife.'

'I didn't know you ever met my wife.'

'Of course I saw her about. Everyone admired her. They said she was one of the cleverest women to ever come and work in the Department. People said she would be the first woman Director General.'

'Well, people were wrong.'

'Yes, I was wrong too,' said Gloria. 'Wrong about everything. You'll never be happy with me, Bernard. You're too demanding.'

'Demanding? What are you talking about?' Too late I recognized that it had been my cue to say how happy I was with her.

'That's right; get angry.'

'I'm not getting angry,' I said very quietly.

'It's just as well that I'm going to Cambridge.'

She was determined to feel sorry for herself. There was nothing I could say. I gave her a kiss but she didn't respond. Her grief was not to be assuaged.

'Perhaps Doris could help more,' I said very tentatively.

Gloria looked at me and gave a bitter smile. 'Doris has given notice,' she said.

'Doris? Not Doris.'

'She says it's boring here in the suburbs.'

'Jesus Christ!' I said. 'Of course it is. Why else does she think we came here?'

'She had her friends in central London. She went to discos there.'

'Doris had friends?'

'Don't be a pig.'

'She can go up on the train.'

'Once a week. It's not much fun for her. She's still young.'

'We're all still young!' I said. 'Do you think I don't want to go with Doris's friends to discos?'

'Making jokes won't help you,' said Gloria doggedly. 'We'll be in a terrible mess when she goes. It won't be easy to get someone who will get on well with the children.' Outside the rain kept coming down, thrashing through the apple tree and banging on the windows, while the wind buffeted against the chimney stack and screamed through the TV antenna. 'I'm going to see what the agency can offer, but we might have to pay more around here. The woman in the agency says this is a particularly high-wages area.'

'I bet she did,' I said.

Then the telephone rang on my side of the bed. I went to get it. It was Werner. 'I've got to see you,' he said. He sounded excited, or as near excited as the phlegmatic Werner ever got.

'Where are you?' I asked.

'I'm in London. I'm in a little apartment in Ebury Street, near Victoria Station.'

'I don't understand.'

'I flew to Gatwick.'

'What's happened?'

'We must talk.'

'We've got a spare room. Have you got wheels?'

'Better you come here, Bernard.'

'To Victoria? It will take half an hour. More perhaps.' The idea of dragging up to central London again appalled me.

'It's serious,' said Werner.

I capped the phone. 'It's Werner,' I explained. 'He says he's got to see me. He wouldn't say that unless it was really urgent.'

Gloria gave a little shrug and closed her eyes.

12

I didn't realize what had happened to some of those little hotels in Ebury Street. It used to be a no-man's-land, where the rucksack-laden hordes from the bus terminal met the smart set of Belgravia. In a curious juxtapositioning that is peculiarly English, Ebury Street provided Belgravia with its expensive little boutiques and chic restaurants and offered budget-conscious travellers cheap overnight lodging. But change was inevitable and Werner had found a small but luxuriously appointed suite 'all major credit cards accepted' with twenty-four-hour service and security, rubber plants in the lobby and Dom Pérignon in the refrigerator.

'Have you eaten?' said Werner as soon as he opened the door to me.
'Not really.'
'Good. I've booked a table for us. It's just round the corner. I read a rave review of it in a flight magazine coming over.' He said it in a distracted way, as if his mind was really on something entirely different.
'Wonderful,' I said.
'No,' said Werner. 'I think it might really be good.' He looked at his watch. He was agitated: I knew the signs. 'The magazine said the fresh salmon mousse is very good,' he said as if not totally convinced.
'How did you find this hotel, Werner?' He was my best friend, but I never really understood Werner in the way I understood other people I'd known for a long time. He was not just secretive; he masked his real feelings by assuming others. When he was happy, he looked sad. When he made a rib-tickling joke, he scowled as if resenting laughter. Winning, he looked like a loser. Was that because he was a Jew? Did he feel he had to conceal his true feelings from a hostile world?
'It's an apartment, a service apartment, not a hotel,' he corrected me. The rich of course have more words than the rest of us, for they have more goods and services at their disposal. 'A fellow I do business with at Kleinwort Benson keeps it as his London base. He said I could use it. Champagne? Whisky or anything?'
'A glass of wine,' I said.
He stepped into the tiny kitchen. It was just a fluorescent-lit box, designed to encourage the use of the 'service' rather than a place to do any proper cooking. He took a bottle of wine from the refrigerator, a

Meursault; the bottle was full but uncorked as if he'd guessed what I would like to drink, and prepared for my arrival. He poured a good measure into a Waterford wineglass and put the bottle back again. The refrigerator's machinery began to purr, setting off a soft rattle of vibrating bottles.

'Happy days, Werner,' I said before I drank.

He smiled soberly and picked up his wallet from a side-table and made sure his credit cards were all there before putting it in his pocket. Meursault: it was a luxury I particularly enjoyed. I suppose Werner could have guzzled it all day long if he'd had a mind to.

Most people were hurtled through life on a financial switchback, a roller-coaster that decided for them whether they must economize or splurge. Not Werner; Werner always had enough. He decided what he wanted – anything: whether it was a little place round the corner that did a good salmon mousse, or a splendid new car – and put his hand in his pocket and bought it. Mind you, Werner's needs were modest: he didn't hanker for yachts or private planes, keep mistresses, gamble or throw lots of extravagant parties. Werner simply had money more than sufficient for his needs. I envied his unbudgeted easygoing lifestyle; he made me feel like a money-grubbing wage-slave because, I suppose, that's exactly what I am.

I took my wine and sat down in one of the soft leather armchairs and waited for him to tell me what was distressing him so much that he would fly to London and drag me up here to talk with him. I looked around. So it was an apartment. Yes, I could see that now. It was not quite like a hotel suite; it looked lived in. Glenn Gould was playing Bach uncharacteristically softly on the CD player, and there were two big hideous modern paintings on the walls, instead of the tasteful lithographs that architects and interior designers bought wholesale.

It was a place used by men who were away from home. You could tell that from the books. As well as year after year of outdated restaurant guides, street maps and museum catalogues, there were the sort of books that help pass the time when all the work is done. Dog-eared detective stories of the sort that can be read over and over again without any feeling of repetition, very thin books by thin lady novelists who win prizes, and very thick ones by thick lady novelists who don't. And a whole shelf full of biographies from Mother Teresa to Lord Olivier via 'Streisand the Woman and the Legend'. Long long hours away from home.

Werner had responded to my toast by drinking some mineral water from a cut-glass tumbler. It had a lemon slice in it and ice too. It was as if he wanted to pretend it was a real drink. He sank down into an armchair and sighed. The black beard – now closely trimmed – suited him. He didn't look like a hippie or an art teacher, it was more formal than that. But formality ended at the neck. His clothes were casual, a black long-sleeve woollen pullover, matching trousers, rainbow-striped silk shirt and shiny patent shoes. His hair was thick and dark, his pose relaxed: only his eyes were worried. 'It's Zena.' He reached across to get a coaster from the shelf and moved my wineglass on to it so it would not mark the polished side-table. Werner was house-trained.

Oh, no, I thought. Not an evening of talking about that wife of his, it was more than even a best friend should be expected to endure. 'What about Zena?' I said, trying to make my voice warm and concerned.

'More precisely, that damned Frank Harrington,' said Werner bitterly. 'I know what Frank means to you, Bernie, but he's a bastard. He really is.' He watched me to see if I would take offence on Frank's behalf, and he pinched his nose as he often did when distressed.

'Frank?' Frank Harrington was an amazingly successful womanizer. Linking Frank and Zena's names meant only one thing to me. Some years back, Frank and Zena had had a tempestuous affair. Like some nineteenth-century rake, he'd even set her up in a little house to await his visits. Then – the way I heard it – Zena got fed up with sitting waiting for Frank to find time for her. There was nothing of the nineteenth-century mistress about Zena. Since then I suspected that Zena had found other men, but always she returned to poor old Werner. In the long term he was the only one who would put up with her. 'Frank and Zena?'

'Not like that,' said Werner hurriedly. 'He's using her for departmental work. It's dangerous, Bernie. Bloody dangerous. She's never done anything like that before.'

'You'd better start at the beginning,' I said.

'Zena has relatives in the East. She takes them food and presents. You know . . .'

'Yes, you told me.' I reached for the little bowl of salted almonds but there were only a couple of broken pieces left buried under salt and bits of skin. I suppose Werner had eaten them while sitting here waiting for me and worrying.

'She went over there last week.' In German over there – 'druben' – meant only one thing, it meant the other side of the Wall. 'Now I've discovered that that bloody Frank asked her to look up someone for him.'

'One of our people?' I said guardedly.

'Of course. Who else would they be if Frank wants her to look them up for him?'

'I suppose so,' I conceded.

'Frankfurt an der Oder,' said Werner. 'You know what we're talking about don't you?' Despite the level voice he was angry now: damned angry, and somewhere in the back of his mind he was implicating me in this development of which I knew nothing, and preferred to know nothing.

'That's just speculation,' I said and waited to see if he'd say it wasn't.

'Why ask Zena?' His face was distorted as he bit his lip with rage and anxiety. 'He has his own people to do that kind of work.'

'Yes,' I admitted.

'It's Bizet. He's trying to reopen a contact string.'

'She'll be all right, Werner,' I said. I sympathized with Werner's anger but I'd been at the sharp end of operations. From the field agent's point of view it sometimes looked like good sense to send legitimate travellers such as Zena into these touchy situations. They are told nothing, so they know nothing. Usually they get away scot-free.

My apparent indifference to Zena's plight made him angrier than ever but as usual he smiled. He leaned back on the sofa and stroked the house-phone as if it was a pet cat. From the street outside there was the growling sound of the long-distance buses that had to turn into a narrow sidestreet to get to the bus terminal. 'I want you to do something,' he said.

'What do you want me to do?'

'Get her out,' he said. His fingers were twitching on the phone. He reached for the handpiece, called reception and, without asking me what I wanted to eat, told them he wanted the restaurant dinner sent round for us. He spoke rapidly into the phone ordering two portions of the very good salmon mousse and a couple of fillet steaks – one rare and one well done – and whatever went with it. Then he put the phone down, turned and looked at me. 'It's getting late,' he explained, 'the kitchen will close soon.'

I said, 'You don't really want the Department to bring her out, do you? From what you've told me, there's nothing to suggest she's in any kind of danger. I imagine Frank just asked her to make a couple of phone calls, or knock at a door. If I go rushing in to the office demanding a full-scale rescue attempt, everyone will think I've taken leave of my senses. And, quite honestly Werner, it might be putting Zena into a worse position than she is.' What I didn't add was that there was no chance at all that Dicky, or anyone in authority at the office,

108

would countermand Frank's actions on my say-so. It sounded as if Frank had been made 'file officer' and his word would be law.

'How dare Frank ask Zena to help him?' Was that the real focus of Werner's rage: Frank Harrington? They'd never seen eye to eye. Even before Frank stole Werner's wife, he'd eased Werner out of the Berlin Field Unit. Now there was no way to convince Werner that Frank was what he was: a very experienced departmental administrator, and an archetypal 'English gentleman' who not only knew how to attract adventuresome young women but often fell prey to them.

And I could hardly tell Werner that his wife should have learned to stay away from Frank by now. So I said, 'When is she due back?'

'Monday.' He touched his beard. Glenn Gould finished playing but after a couple of clicks Art Tatum started. Werner liked the piano. In the old days he used to play at all the most rowdy Berlin parties. Seeing him now it was difficult to believe the things we had done in Berlin back in those days when we were young.

'She'll be all right,' I said.

Unconvinced by my reassurances he nodded without replying, and studied his glass of mineral water suspiciously before taking a sip of it. We sat for a moment in silence. Then he looked at me, gave me a little shrug and a smile and, noticing that my glass was empty, he got up and went to the refrigerator and brought more wine for me.

I watched him carefully. There was more to it – some other aspect to the story – but I didn't press him for more details. His anger had peaked. It was better for him to simmer down.

There was a tap at the door and – like some sort of well rehearsed cabaret act – a uniformed man from the reception desk helped a restaurant waiter to set up two folding chairs, a folding table, and an array of tableware. There were steaks and some spinach keeping warm on a chafing dish. The portions of fish mousse, which the waiter insisted upon showing us, were under the heavy dome-shaped silver covers that are always needed to keep microscopic portions of food from escaping.

It wasn't until they'd gone and we were seated at the table eating the mousse that Werner mentioned Zena again. 'I love her. I can't help that, Bernie.'

'I know, Werner.' The salmon mousse was sinking into a puddle of bright green sauce; a pink, tilted slab with fragments of vegetable looking out of it, like passengers waiting for a rescue boat. I ate it quickly.

'So I worry,' said Werner, and he shrugged in a gesture of resignation. I felt sorry for him. It wasn't easy to imagine being in love with Zena. That some man might murder her, or join the Foreign Legion to escape her, was simple to envisage. But love her: no. 'She's the only woman for me.' He said it defensively, almost apologetically.

Sometimes I think he loved her because she was incapable of loving anyone. A friend of mine once explained the lifetime he'd given to the study of reptiles by saying that he was fascinated by their complete lack of any response to affection. And I think Werner's relationship with Zena was like that. She seemed to have no real feelings about anyone alive or dead. People were all the same for her, and she dealt with them by means of a curious highly developed sense of self-imposed and carefully apportioned 'justice' that some of her critics had called 'fascistic'.

But it was no use talking to Werner about Zena. For him she could do no wrong. I remember him falling in love with girls at school. His love was boundless; the respect he showed for them usually earned only their withering contempt, so that eventually Werner's ardour faded and died. So I thought it would be when Zena came along. But Zena wasn't so profligate with Werner's love. She welcomed his affection, she encouraged him and knew how to handle Werner so that she could do almost anything with him.

Werner picked at the fish mousse. It was dry and completely tasteless, only the creamy watercress sauce had any flavour. It was salty. 'Refrigerated and then warmed in a micro-wave,' said Werner knowledgeably. He pushed the mousse aside and started on the steak as I'd already done. 'It looks as if you liked the mousse,' he said accusingly.

'It was delicious,' I said. 'But I'm beginning to think that this is your well-done fillet.' By that time I'd already eaten some of his steak. Silently he passed the untouched underdone one to me and took what was left of the steak I'd half-eaten. 'Sorry, Werner,' I said.

'You eat everything,' he said. 'Even at school you ate everything.'

'You won't like the underdone one,' I told him, and offered it back to him.

He declined. 'I know,' he said.

To change the subject I said, 'How is the hotel?'

'It's going all right,' he said sharply. Then he added, 'Did I tell you that that damned woman Ingrid Winter insists on coming to Berlin?'

'She wants some things,' I said, keeping it vague.

'She wants to help,' said Werner as if it was the direst threat in his vocabulary.

'Tell her you don't need help.' It seemed simple enough.

'I can't stop her coming. She's Lisl's niece . . .'

'. . . and she has a claim on the house. Yes, you'd better be nice to her, Werner, or she could upset the whole apple-cart.'

'Just as long as she doesn't get in the way,' he said ominously. Werner was in a bad mood.

I decided I might as well face it. He wasn't going to simmer down. 'Are you going to tell me about Zena?' I said as casually as I could.

'Tell you what?'

'You're not worried about what could happen to her for knocking on the wrong door in Frankfurt an der Oder, Werner. Not Zena, she'd talk her way out of that one with a paper bag over her head.'

He looked at me with that impassive look I knew so well and then chewed a piece of steak before replying. 'I should have given you some red wine,' he said. 'I've got some for you.'

'Never mind the wine. What's the real story?'

He dabbed his lips with a dinner napkin and said, 'Zena's uncle has a wonderful collection of very old books and crucifixes, icons and things . . .' He looked at me. I stared back at him and said nothing. Werner amended it to, 'Maybe he buys them . . . I'm not sure.'

'And maybe he's not her uncle,' I suggested.

'Oh, I think he's her . . . Well, yes maybe an old friend. Yes, sometimes he buys these things from Poles who come into East Germany looking for work. Bibles mostly: seventeenth-century. He's an expert on early Christian art.'

'And Zena smuggles them back to the West, and they are sold in those elegant shops in Munich where orthodontists go to furnish their Schlösser.'

Werner wasn't listening. 'Zena doesn't understand how they work,' he said lugubriously.

'How who work?'

'The Stasi. If she goes calling, the way Frank has told her to, they'll just follow her day after day to see where she goes. But Zena won't realize that. The whole lot of them will go into the bag. They'll accuse her of stealing State art treasures or something.'

'The People's art treasures,' I corrected him. 'Yes, well they won't like the idea of her exporting antiques without a licence.' I tried to make it sound like a minor misdeed, a technical infraction of a customs regulation. 'But Frank wouldn't know anything about that, of course.'

Without answering Werner got up and went to the tiny kitchen. He came back with the half-empty bottle of Meursault and a wineglass for himself. He poured more wine for me and some for himself too and put the bottle on the table, having put a coaster into position for it. I

111

watched him drink. He pulled a face like a small child asked to swallow some nasty medicine. Werner knew a lot about wine but he always treated it like sour grape juice. 'Suppose Frank knew all about Zena and the antique books?' Werner said slowly and carefully. 'After all, Frank is supposed to be running an intelligence service, isn't he?'

'Yes,' I said, ignoring the sarcasm.

'And suppose Frank had reason to believe that by delivering poor Zena to the Stasi he'd get them to lay off his Bizet people. Maybe let them get away?'

I said nothing. I sipped my wine and tried to conceal my thoughts. Then bloody good for Frank, I thought. But it all sounded highly unlikely. I suspected that Frank was still too fond of Zena to throw her to the wolves. But if he'd worked out some bizarre deal that got two or three of our people off the hook, in exchange for a ring of cheap crooks who were running a racket involving religious antiques, books, and God knows what else, stuff that might well have been stolen in the first place, then good for Frank. I would be all in favour of a deal like that. So I said nothing.

'Don't forget it's Zena,' said Werner.

No, don't forget it's Zena. That would make a swop like that a real public benefit. 'No,' I said. 'It's her I'm thinking about.'

'He's a bloody Judas,' said Werner. He drank some more wine but seemed no more happy with the taste of it than he was the first time.

'Have you got any reason to think so?' I asked.

'I feel it in my guts,' said Werner in a voice I didn't recognize.

'Frank wouldn't do a thing like that,' I said, more to calm Werner than because I completely believed it. Frank liked Zena but Frank could be ruthless: I knew it and so did Werner. And so, if she had any brains, did the wretched Zena.

'Yes, Frank would!' snapped Werner. 'It's just the sort of thing he would do. It's the sort of thing the English are notorious for. You know that.'

'Perfidious Albion?' I said.

He didn't think that was funny. He didn't answer or even look at me. He just sat there with his face tight, his eyes watery and his big hands clenched together so tightly that the knuckles whitened.

I'd never seen him in such a state before. Whether it was concern for Zena or a burning hatred for Frank, it was eating him up. I watched him biting his lip with rage and I worried about him. I'd seen men wound up this tight before; and I'd seen them snap. 'I'll see what I can do,' I said, but it was too late for such offers.

Through gritted teeth Werner said, 'First thing tomorrow morning I'm going to the office. I'll find the D-G and make him do something. Make him!'

'I wouldn't advise that, Werner,' I said anxiously. 'No, Werner, I really wouldn't.' The idea of this black-bearded Werner shouting and struggling in the lobby of London Central with the redoubtable Sergeant-Major Gaskell trying to subdue him, and the questions that would inevitably be directed at me in consequence, was something I didn't care to contemplate. I tipped the rest of the Meursault into my glass. It was warm; I suppose he'd not put the bottle back into the refrigerator. All in all, Thursday was not a good day.

13

I have always been a light sleeper: it's a part of the job. But it wasn't the low rumble of the motorcycle that awakened me – they come roaring past at all hours of the night – it was the silence that followed its engine being switched off. By the time the garden gate clicked I was fully awake. I heard the footsteps – high heel boots on the stone paving – and I rolled out of bed before the brief ring of the doorbell awakened Gloria.

'Three thirty!' I heard Gloria say sleepily as I went out of the bedroom. She sounded surprised; she had a lot to learn about the demands the Department made on its middle management. I went downstairs two steps at a time, to answer it before Doris and the children were disturbed. But before I got to the bottom of the stairs the caller tried again: more insistent this time, two long rings.

'Okay okay okay,' I said irritably.

'Sorry governor, I thought you hadn't heard.' The caller was a tall thin young man dressed entirely in shiny black leather like some apparition from a bad dream. 'Mr Samson?' Over his arm he had a black shiny helmet, and there was a battered leather pouch slung from his neck.

'Yes?'

'Have you got something to identify yourself, sir?' he said, without saying what I was supposed to produce. That was the way regulations said it should be done, but I'd got used to a more vernacular style from the messengers I knew.

So it was a new man. 'What about this?' I said and, from behind the half-open door, I brought the Mauser 9-mm into view.

He grinned, 'Yeah, I reckon that'll do,' he said. He opened the pouch and from it took one of the large buff envelopes that the Department uses to circulate its bad news.

'Samson, B,' I said just to get him off the hook. 'Any verbal?'

'You're to open it right away. That's all.'

'Why not,' I said. 'I'll need something to help me back to sleep.'

'Goodnight, governor. Sorry to disturb you.'

'Next time,' I said, 'don't ring the bell. Just breathe heavily through the letter-box.'

'What is it, darling?' asked Gloria, coming downstairs slowly like a chorus girl in a Busby Berkeley musical. She was not fully awake. Blonde hair disarranged, she was dressed in the big fluffy white Descamps bathrobe that I'd bought her for Christmas. She looked wonderful.

'A messenger.' I tore open the big brown envelope. Inside there was an airline ticket from London Heathrow to Los Angeles International by the flight that left at nine am – that is to say in less than six hours time – and a note, curt and typed on office paper bearing the usual rubber stamps:

Dear Bernard,
    You'll be met on arrival. Sorry about the short notice but the Washington office works five hours later than we do, and someone there arranged with the Deputy that this one should be down to you, and only you,
        Yours apologetically,
        Harry (N.D.O. Ops.)

I recognized the sprawling handwriting. So poor old Harry Strang was still on the roster for night duty in Operations. I suppose he must have felt sorry for himself too for he'd scribbled on the bottom of the note 'Some people have all the luck!' I suppose for someone sitting up all night in Operations and listening to the rain, the prospect of immediate transportation to sunny California must have seemed attractive.

To me it didn't. At least it didn't until I recalled Werner's threat to go into the office this morning, and tackle the D-G head-on.

'They can't make you go,' said Gloria, who had leaned over my shoulder to read the note.

'No,' I agreed. 'I can always start drawing unemployment benefit.'

'It doesn't even say how long you'll be away,' she said, in such a way as to leave me in doubt about how she would respond to such a peremptory command.

'I'm sorry,' I said.

'You promised to look at the garage door.'

'It just needs a new hinge,' I told her. 'There's a place near Waterloo Station. I'll get it next week.'

'I'll pack your bag.' She looked at the clock on the mantelpiece. 'It's not worth going back to bed.'

'I said I'm sorry,' I reminded her.

'The weekends are the only time we have together,' she said. 'Why couldn't it wait till Monday?'

115

'I'll try and find something exciting for Billy's birthday.'

'Bring yourself back,' said Gloria and kissed me tenderly. 'I worry about you . . . when they send you off on these urgent jobs with that damned "Briefing on Arrival" rubber stamp, I worry about you.'

'It won't be anything dangerous,' I said. 'I'll be sitting beside a pool all weekend.'

'They've specifically asked for you, Bernard,' she said.

I nodded. It was not a flattering assumption but she was right. They hadn't asked for me on account of my social contacts or my scholarship. 'I'll wear the water-wings and stay away from the deep end,' I promised.

'What will you do when you get there?'

'It's "Briefing on Arrival", sweetheart. That means they haven't yet decided.'

'Seriously. How will you recognize them?'

'It doesn't work like that, darling. They'll have a photo of me. I won't know them until they come up to me and introduce themselves.'

'And how will you know that person is the genuine contact?'

'He'll show me my photo.'

'It's all carefully arranged,' she said with a note of approval in her voice. She liked everything to be well arranged.

'It's all in the Notes and Amendments,' I said.

'But always the same airline, Bernard? That seems bad security.'

'There must be a reason,' I said. 'How about making me a cup of coffee while I pack my bag?'

'Everything's clean. Your shirts are on hangers in the wardrobe, so don't start shouting when you find the chest of drawers empty.'

'I won't shout about shirts,' I promised, and kissed her. 'And if I do, rip more buttons off.'

'I do love you, Bernard.' She put both arms round me and hugged me tight. 'I want to have you for ever and ever.'

'Then that's the way it will be,' I promised with the sort of unthinking impetuosity that I am prey to when rudely awakened in such early hours of the morning.

For a moment she just held me, crushing me so that I could hardly breathe, then into my ear she said, 'And I love the children, Bernard. Don't worry about them.'

The children missed their real mother, of course, and I knew how hard Gloria worked to replace her. It wasn't easy for her. Cambridge, just unremitting hard work, must have been an attractive prospect at times.

116

Almost every seat was taken in First Class. Wide-awake young men, with well cut suits and large gold wristwatches, were shuffling papers that came from pigskin document cases, or tapping at tiny portable computers with hinged screens. Many of them declined the champagne and worked right through the meal service: reading reports, ticking at accounts and underlining bits of 'projections' with coloured markers.

The man in the next seat to mine was from the same mould but considerably less dedicated. Edwin Woosnam – 'a Welsh name although I've never been there: can you believe it?' – an overweight fellow with thick eyebrows, thin lips and the sort of nose they create from putty for amateur productions of *Julius Caesar*. My desire to catch up on lost sleep was frustrated by his friendliness.

He was, he told me, the senior partner of a 'development company' in Glasgow. His firm was building eight 600-room hotels in towns around the world and he told me all about it. 'Outdoor pool, that's important. The hotel owners need a picture on the brochure that makes it look like the weather is good enough for swimming all year round.' Throaty chuckle and a quick sip of champagne. 'Penthouses at the top, leisure centres in the basement and en-suite bathrooms throughout. Find a big cheap site – I mean really big – and after the hotel is up, shops and apartment blocks will follow. The neighbourhood is upgraded. You can't go wrong on an investment like that. It's like money in the bank. As long as the local labour is cheap, it doesn't matter where you site the hotel, half these idiot tourists don't even know which country they're in.'

But otherwise Mr Woosnam proved a congenial companion, with an endless supply of stories. '. . .You can't tell the Greeks anything. I showed this foreman – Popopopolis, or something, you know what those names are like – I showed him the schedule, and told him the eighth floor should be all complete by now. And he got angry. It was complete, he shouted. He shook his fist and waved his arms and went rushing along the girders, jumped through a doorway and fell all the way into the basement. Eight storeys! Killed of course. We had terrible trouble getting a new foreman at that time of year. Another month and it wouldn't have mattered so much.' He took a drink.

'Ha ha ha. Some people just won't listen. Perhaps you find that in your business too,' said Woosnam, but before I could agree he was off again. 'I was with one of our site surveyors in Bombay and he was laughing and making jokes about the way the Indians build their lashed-up wooden scaffolding. I told him that he'd be laughing on the other side of his face when he put up steel scaffolding and the heat of the sun twisted it into a corkscrew and his project collapsed. Bloody architects! They come straight from college, and they know it all. That's the trouble nowadays. I'll give you another example . . .' And so it went on. He was good entertainment but his affability precluded all chance of slumber.

'Travel much?' he said as I began to doze.

'No,' I said.

'I travel all the time. Flying across the Atlantic is exciting for you of course, but it's just a bore for me.' He looked at me to see my reaction.

'Yes,' I said and tried to look excited.

'And what line are you in? No, don't tell me. I'm good at guessing what people do for a living. Insurance?'

'Chemicals.' I usually say that because it's so vague and also because I have a prepared line of chat about pharmaceuticals should my bluff be called.

'All right,' he said, reluctant to admit to error. 'Not a salesman though. You haven't got the pushy temperament you need for the Sales side.'

'No, not Sales,' I agreed.

'Keep an eye on my briefcase while I go to the toilet will you? Once they start the meal service everyone will jump up and want to go. It's always like that.'

The toy meal came and went. The captain's carefully modulated voice recited the names of places that were hidden far beneath the clouds. The great aluminium tube droned on, its weary cargo of unwashed, red-eyed travellers numbed with alcohol and crippled with indigestion. Duty-free baubles were interminably hustled by stewardesses who went, eyes averted, past bawling babies and harassed mothers. Over the public-address system came more names of equally invisible towns. The shutters were closed against the daylight and the cabin darkened. Blurred ghosts of tiny unrecognizable actors postured on the pale screens while their strident voices assaulted the inner ear from plastic tubes. We raced after the sun and chased a never-ending day. Tortured by the poker-red glare of the sun, dazzled by the white clouds, one by one the heads of the passengers lolled and bent as they succumbed to their misery, and sought escape in fitful sleep.

'This is your captain speaking . . .'

We'd arrived in Los Angeles: now came the worst part, the line-up at US Customs and Immigration. It took well over an hour standing in line, disconsolately kicking my baggage forward a few inches at a time. But finally I was grudgingly admitted to America.

'Hi there! Mr Samson? Did you have a nice flight?' He was chewing gum, a suntanned man about thirty years old with patient eyes, stretch pants, a half-eaten hamburger and a half-read paperback edition of *War and Peace*: everything necessary for meeting someone at LAX. We walked through the crowded concourse and into the mêlée of cabs and cars and buses that served this vast and trainless town.

'Buddy Breukink,' the man introduced himself. He flicked a finger at the dented, unpainted metal case that I'd wrenched from the carousel. 'Is this all your baggage?' If everyone kept saying that to me I was going to start feeling socially disadvantaged.

'That's right,' I said. He took my bag and the corrugated case. I didn't know whether I should politely wrest it from him. There was no way to discover if he was just a driver, sent to collect me, or a senior executive who was going to pick up the bills and give me my orders. The US of A is like that. He marched off and I followed him. He hadn't been through the formalities but I didn't press it. He didn't look the type who would regularly read and update the Notes and Amendments.

'Hungry? We have more than a hour's ride.' He had a sly gap-toothed smile, as if he knew something that the rest of the world didn't know. It wasn't something to be taken personally.

'I'll survive,' I promised. My blood-sugar wasn't so low that I wanted an airport hamburger.

'The buggy's across the street.' He was a coffee-shop cowboy: a tall, slim fellow with a superfluity of good large teeth, tan-coloured tight-fitting trousers, short-sleeve white shirt and a big brown stetson with a bright band of feathers round it. In keeping with the outfit, Buddy Breukink climbed into a jeep, a brand-new Wrangler soft-top complete with phone, personalized plates – BB GUN – and roll bar.

He threw my baggage and Tolstoy into the back before carefully placing his beautiful stetson in a box there. He got in and pushed a lot of buttons, a coded signal to activate his car phone. 'Have to make sure none of these parking-lot jockeys make a long long call to their folks in Bogota,' he said, as if a short freebie hello to Mexico City might be okay with him. He smiled to himself and cleared half a dozen audio cassettes from the passenger seat and dumped them into a box. When he turned the ignition key the tape recorder started playing 'Pavarotti's Greatest Hits' or more specifically 'Funiculi, funicula' delivered in ear-splitting fortissimos. 'It's kind of classical,' he explained with a hint of apology.

He gunned the engine impatiently. 'Let's go!' he yelled even louder

119

than Pavarotti; and even before I was strapped in, the wheels were burning rubber and we were out of the car park and off down the highway.

I had arrived in the New World and was as bemused as Columbus. In this part of the world it was already spring, the air was warm and the sky was that pale shade of blue that portends a steep rise in temperature. The noisy downtown streets were crowded with black roaring Porsches and white Rolls-Royce convertibles, shouting kids rattled round on roller skates and pretty girls preened in sun-tops and shorts.

Up the ramp. On the Freeway that stretches across the city, the anarchy of the busy streets ended. Apart from some kids racing past in a dented pickup, restrained drivers observed lane discipline and moved at a steady pace. The wind roared through the jeep's open sides and threatened to blow me from my seat. I huddled down to shelter behind the windscreen. Buddy turned the music louder and looked at me and grinned.

'Funiculi,' sung Buddy between chewing. 'Funicula.'

Once clear of the 'international airport', its mañana-minded airline staff and its hard-eyed bureaucrats, Southern California reaches out to its visitors. The warmth of the sun, the sight of the San Gabriel mountains, dry winds from the desert, the bitter herbal smells of the brushwood flowers, the orange poppies in the bright green landscape that has not yet suffered the cruel heat of summer; at this time of year all these things urge me to stay for ever.

Racing along the road that is slung roof-high above the city, there was a view of the whole of Los Angeles from the ocean to the mountains. Clusters of tall buildings at Century City, and more at Broadway, dominated a town of modest little suburban houses squeezed between pools and palms. Soon Buddy took an off-ramp and cut across town to pick up the Pacific Coast Highway and go north following the signs that point the way to Santa Barbara and eventually San Francisco. At Malibu the traffic thinned, and we sped past an ever more varied selection of elaborate and eccentric beach houses: until houses, and even seafood restaurants, ended and the road followed the very edge of the continent. Here the Pacific Ocean relentlessly assaulted the seashore. Huge green breakers exploded into lacy foam and a mist of water vapour, and roared so loudly that the noise of them could be heard above the sound of the jeep's engine, and that of the music.

Buddy took the gum from his mouth and pitched it out on to the road. 'They told me you'd ask questions,' he confided.

'No,' I said.

'And they said I shouldn't tell you anything.'

'It's working out just fine,' I said.

He nodded, and dodged round a big articulated truck marked Budweiser, before flattening the gas pedal against the floor and showing me what speed his jeep would do.

We passed the place where agile figures dangling from hang-gliders threw themselves off the high cliffs and did figure of eights above the highway and the Pacific Ocean before landing on the narrow strip of beach that provided their only chance of survival. We passed the offshore oil-rigs, standing like anchored aircraft carriers in the mist. By the time we turned off the Pacific Coast Highway into a narrow 'Seven mile canyon' we were well past the county line and into Ventura. And I was getting hungry.

It was a private road, narrow and pot-holed. On the corner a tall wooden post was nailed with half a dozen signs in varying degrees of deterioration: 'Schuster Ranch', 'Greentops quarter-horse Stud – no visits', 'Ogarkov', 'D and M Bishop', 'Rattlesnake Computer Labs' and 'Highacres'. As the jeep climbed up the dirt road into the canyon I wondered which of those establishments we were going to. But as we passed all the mailboxes on the roadside it became clear that we were heading up to some unmarked property nearer the summit.

We were about three miles up the canyon, and high enough to get glimpses of the ocean far below us, when we came to gates in a high chain-link fence that stretched on either side as far as I could see. Alongside the gate a sign said, 'La Buona Nova. Private Property. Beware guard dogs.' Buddy steered the jeep to within reaching distance of a small box on a metal post. He pressed a red button and spoke into the box. 'Hi there! It's Buddy with the visitor. Open up will yuh?'

With a hesitant, jerky motion, and a loud grinding of hidden mechanical devices, the gates slowly opened. From the box a tinny voice said, 'Hang in to see the gates click shut, Buddy. Last week's rain seems to have gotten to them.'

We drove inside and Buddy did as he'd been told. I could see no buildings anywhere but I had the feeling that we were being kept under observation by whoever the tinny voice belonged to. 'Keep your hands inside the car,' Buddy advised. 'Those darn dogs run free in this outer compound.'

We continued up the dirt road, always climbing and leaving hairpins of dust on the trail behind us. Then suddenly, around a spur, another chain fence came into view. There was another gate and a small hut.

121

Inside this second perimeter fence there were three figures. At first they looked like a man with his two children, but when I got closer I could see it was a huge man with two Mexicans. They were guards. The white man had his belt slung under a big gut. He wore a stetson, starched khakis, high boots and had a shield-shaped gold badge on his shirt. In his hand he held a small transceiver. The Mexicans wore dark brown shirts and one of them had a shotgun. Like the chainlink fence, the men looked fresh and well cared for. One of the Mexicans opened the gate and the big man waved us through.

It was still another mile or more to where a cluster of low pink stucco buildings with red-tiled roofs sat tight just below the summit of the hill. The buildings were of indeterminate age, and designed in the style that Californians call Spanish. Passing a couple of mud-spattered Japanese pickups, Buddy parked the jeep in a cool barnlike building which already held an old Cadillac Seville and a Lamborghini. Buddy put on his stetson, looked at himself in the wing mirror to adjust the brim, and then took my bags. With my jacket over my arm, and sweating in the afternoon heat, I followed him. The main buildings were two storeys high and provided views westwards to the ocean. On the east side they sheltered a wide patio of patterned tiles and a pool about twenty-five yards along. The pool was blue and limpid, with just enough breeze from the ocean to dimple the surface of the water. There was no one to be seen except in the pool, where a slim middle-aged woman was swimming in the gentle dog-paddle style that ensures that your eye make-up doesn't get splashed. At the side of the pool where she'd been sitting there was a big pink towel, bottles of sun-oil and other cosmetics, a brush and comb and a hand-mirror. Leaning against the chair there was a half-completed watercolour painting of bougainvillaea flowers. Beside it there was a large paint box and a jar of brushes.

'Hello, Buddy,' called the lady in the pool without interrupting her swim. 'What's the traffic like? Hi there, Mr Samson. Welcome to La Buona Nova.'

Without slowing his pace Buddy called, 'We came up the PCH, Mrs O'Raffety, but if you're going to town, go through the canyon.' He swivelled his head for long enough to give her one of his sly, gap-toothed smiles. I waved to her and said thanks but had to hurry to follow him.

He went up two steps to an arcaded passageway which provided shady access to, and held chairs and tables for, three guest suites that occupied one side of the building. One of the outdoor tables still had the remains of breakfast: a vacuum coffee pot, a glass jug of juice and expensive-looking tableware of a sort that Gloria would have liked. Buddy opened the door and led the way into the last suite. It was decorated in a theme of pink and white. On the walls there were three framed landscape paintings, amateurish watercolours of local scenes that I was inclined to authenticate as O'Raffety originals.

'Mrs O'Raffety is my mother-in-law,' Buddy explained without being asked. 'She's sixty years old. She owns this whole setup.' He put the bags down and opening the door of the huge green and white tiled bathroom said, 'This is your suite. Switch the air to the way you want it.' He indicated a control panel on the wall. 'You've got time for a swim before lunch. Swim suits in the closet and a slew of towels in the other room.'

'Lunch? Isn't it a bit late for lunch?' The afternoon had almost gone.

'I guess, but Mrs O' Raffety eats any time. She said she'd wait for you.'

'That's very nice of her,' I said.

The large brown-tinted windows gave a view of the patio area. Mrs O'Raffety was still swimming slowly down the pool. There was a look of stern determination on her face. I watched her as she reached the deep end and steered round majestically, like the Queen Elizabeth coming in to Southampton. I could see her more clearly from here. The swimming produced a look of concentration on her face so that, despite the trim figure, and the Beverly Hills beauty treatments, she looked every bit of her sixty years. 'It's quite a place,' I said, realizing that some such response was expected from me.

'She'd get three million dollars – maybe more – if she wanted to sell. There's all that land.'

'And is she going to sell?' I said, hoping to find out more about my mysterious hostess, and why I had been brought here.

'Mrs O'Raffety? She'll never sell. She's got all the money she needs.'

'Do you live here too?' I asked. I was trying to guess at his position in the household.

'I have a beautiful home: three bedrooms, pool, jacuzzi, everything. We passed it on the way up here: the place with the big palm trees.'

'Oh, yes,' I said, although I hadn't noticed such a place.

'My marriage went wrong,' he said. 'Charly – that's Mrs O'Raffety's daughter – left me. She married a movie actor we met at a benefit dinner. He never seemed to get the right kind of parts, so they went to live in Florida. They have a lovely home just outside Palm Beach.' He said it without rancour – or any emotion – as a man might talk of people he'd only read about in the gossip columns.

'But you stayed with Mrs O'Raffety?'

'Well, I had to stay,' said Buddy. 'I'm Mrs O'Raffety's attorney. I handle things for her.'

'Oh, yes, of course.'

'You have your swim, Mr Samson. The water's kept at eighty degrees. Mrs O'Raffety has to swim on account of her bad back, but she can't abide cold water.' He stared through the window to watch her swimming. There was a fixed expression on his face that could have been concern for her.

'And who is Mr O'Raffety?' I said.

'Who is Mr O'Raffety?' Buddy was puzzled by my question.

'Yes. Who is Mr O'Raffety? What does he do for a living?'

Buddy's face relaxed. 'Oh, I get you,' he said. 'What does he do for a living. Well, Shaun O'Raffety was Mrs O'Raffety's hairdresser: L.A. . . . a fancy place on Rodeo Drive.' Buddy rubbed his face. 'Way back before my time, of course. It didn't last long. She gave him the money to buy a bar in Boston. She hasn't seen him in ten years but sometimes I have to go and get him out of trouble.'

'Trouble?'

'Money trouble. Women trouble. Tax return trouble. Bookies or fist-fights in the bar so that the cops get mad. Never anything bad. Old Shaun is an Irishman. No real harm in him. He just can't choose carefully enough: not his clients, his friends or his women.'

'Except in the case of Mrs O'Raffety,' I said.

For a moment I thought Buddy was going to take offence, but he contained himself and said, 'Yeah. Except in the case of Mrs O'Raffety.' The smile was noticeably absent.

'Since you're Mrs O'Raffety's attorney, Buddy, perhaps you could explain why I've been brought here.'

He looked at me as if trying to help, trying to guess the answer. 'Socializing isn't my bag,' said Buddy. He was silent for a few moments, as if regretting telling me about his employer and mother-in-law. Then he said, 'Mrs O'Raffety has a social secretary to handle the invites: weekend guests and cocktails and dinner parties and suchlike.'

'But just between the two of us, Buddy, I've never even heard of Mrs O'Raffety.'

'Then maybe you are here to visit one of Mrs O'Raffety's permanent guests. Do you know Mr Rensselaer? He lives in the house with the big bougainvillaea.'

'Bret Rensselaer?'

'That's correct.'

124

'He's dead.'

'No sir.'

Everyone knew Bret was dead. If Frank Harrington said he was dead; he was dead. Frank was always right about things like that. Bret died of gunshot wounds resulting from a gun-battle in Berlin nearly three years ago. I was only a couple of yards away. I saw him fall; I heard him scream. 'Bret Rensselaer,' I said carefully. 'About sixty years old. Blond hair. Tall. Thin.'

'You've got him. White hair now but that's him all right. He's been sick. Real bad. An auto accident somewhere in Europe. Mrs O'Raffety brought him here. She had that guest house remodelled and fixed up a beautiful room with equipment where he could do his special exercises and stuff. He could hardly walk when he first arrived. One or other of the therapy nurses comes up here every day, even Sunday.' He looked at the expression on my face. 'You knew him in Europe, maybe?'

'I knew him very well,' I said.

'Isn't that something.' Buddy Breukink nodded. 'Yeah, he's some kind of distant relation to Mrs O'Raffety. Old Cy Rensselaer – the famous one they named the automobile for – was Mrs O'Rafferty's grandfather.'

'I see.' So Bret Rensselaer really was still alive and they'd brought me all this way to see him. Why?

125

14

We ate lunch very late. Mrs Helena O'Raffety didn't eat much. Perhaps she'd had lots of other lunches earlier in the day. But she kept her salad scared, moving it around the huge pink plate like a cop harassing a drunk.

'I'm a European,' she said. She'd been explaining that she was, at heart, quite unlike her native Californian friends and acquaintances. 'When I was very young I always said that one day I'd buy a little apartment in Berlin, but when I got there, it seemed such a sad place. And so dirty. Everything I wore got sooty. So I never got around to it.' She sighed and this time speared a segment of peeled tomato and ate it.

'It gets cold in Berlin,' I told her. I looked at the sun glittering on the blue water of the pool beside us and the brightly coloured tropical flowers. I smelled the wild sage, breathed the clean air off the ocean and watched the hawks slowly circling high above us. We were a long way from Berlin.

'Is that right?' she said exhibiting only mild interest. 'I've only been twice; both times in the fall. I always take vacations in the fall. It stays warm and the resorts are not so crowded.' As if to offset the simplicity of her blue cotton beach dress she wore lots of jewellery: a gold chain necklace, half a dozen rings and a gold watch with diamonds around the face. Now she touched the rings on her fingers, twisting them as if they were uncomfortable, or perhaps to make sure they were all still there.

From the garage at the back there was the sudden sound of the Wrangler being started and gunned impatiently. I'd got used to Buddy Breukink's manner by now and I recognized his touch. Varoom, varoom, varoom, went the engine. Mrs O'Raffety looked up to the sky with a pained expression. It wouldn't require an overdeveloped imagination to see suppressed rage in just about everything that Buddy did.

'They quarrelled about the education of my little grandson Peter.' No need for her to say who she was talking about. 'Buddy has his own ideas but my daughter wants him brought up in the Jewish faith.' She drank some iced tea.

I was fully occupied with the elaborate 'lobster salad' that had been put before me. Every salad vegetable I'd ever heard of – from Shiitaki mushrooms to lotus root – made a decorative jardinière for half a dozen baby lobster tails in rich mayonnaise. On a separate pink plate there was a hot baked potato heaped with sour cream and garnished with small pieces of crispy bacon. Salads in California are not designed for weight-loss. I looked up from my plate. Mrs O'Raffety was looking at me quizzically. She waited until I nodded.

'It's solely a question of the female line,' she explained, prodding at a radish that rolled over and escaped. 'My mother was a Jew, so I am a Jew. Therefore my daughter is a Jew and so her son is a Jew. Buddy just can't seem to understand that.'

'Perhaps,' I ventured, 'it's difficult to reconcile with a mother-in-law named O'Raffety.'

She looked at me with a stern expression I'd noticed when she was swimming. Her eyes were glacial blue. 'Maybe it is,' she conceded. 'Maybe it is. Mind you, I'm not strict. We don't eat kosher. You can't with Mexican kitchen staff.'

'And where is your little grandson now?'

'In Florida. Last week Buddy was taking lunch with a private detective. I'm frightened he's got some plan to take the child away somewhere.'

'Kidnap him?'

'Buddy gets emotional.'

'But he's a lawyer.'

'Even lawyers get emotional,' she said, dismissing the subject without entirely condemning such emotion. As the sound of Buddy's jeep receded she went back to the subject of being European. 'I was born in Berlin,' she told me. 'I have relatives in Berlin. Maybe one day I'll seek them out. But then I ask myself: who needs more relatives.' She toyed with a pack of Marlboro cigarettes, and a gold lighter, as if trying to resist temptation.

'You came to America as a child?'

She nodded. 'But lost the language. A few years back I started taking German lessons, but I just couldn't seem to get the hang of it. All those bothersome verbs . . .' She laughed. 'More wine?'

'Thank you.'

She plucked the bottle from the bucket. 'A friend of mine – not far from here – makes it. His Chablis is excellent, the rosé is good – wonderful colour – but the red doesn't quite come off so I keep to the French reds.' She poured the remainder of the wine into my glass. She called all white wines Chablis; everyone in California seemed to do that.

'What about you, Mrs O'Raffety?' I said. She never invited me to call her by her first name and I noticed that even her son-in-law addressed her in that same formal way, so she must have liked being Mrs O'Raffety. She had, I suppose, paid enough for the privilege.

'I take only half a glass. Chablis affects the joints you know, it's the uric acid.'

'I didn't know that.'

The bottle dripping from the ice water, had made her fingers wet. Fastidiously she dried her hands on a pink towel before touching the cigarettes again. 'You're easy to talk to,' she said, looking at me through narrowed eyes as if my appearance might explain it. 'Did anyone ever tell you that? It's a gift being a good listener. You listen but show no curiosity; I suppose that's the secret.'

'Perhaps it is,' I said.

'You can't imagine how excited Bret was to hear you were actually coming.'

'I'm looking forward to seeing him again.'

'He's with the physiotherapist right now. Miss a session and he's set back a week: that's what the doctor says, and he's right. I know. All my life I've suffered with this darn disc of mine.' She touched her back as if remembering the pain.

When I finished the lobster salad a servant magically appeared to remove the plates to a side-table: mine totally cleaned and Mrs O'Raffety's still laden with food.

'Do you mind if I smoke, Mr Samson?'

The Mexican servant – a muscular middle-aged man with the tight skin and passive face of the Indian – waited for her orders. There was not only a dignity about him, there was an element of repressed strength, like a fierce dog that was awaiting the order to spring.

I felt like inviting Mrs O'Raffety to call me Bernard, but she was the sort of woman who might decline such an invitation. 'It's your home,' I told her.

'And my lungs. Yes, that's what Buddy tells me.' She gave a throaty little laugh and tugged a cigarette from the pack on the table. The servant bent over and lit it for her. 'Now Mr Samson: fresh strawberries? Raspberries? Cook's home-made blueberry pie? What else is there, Luis?' There was something disconcerting about the way that California's menus defied the strictures of the seasons. 'The pies are just gorgeous,' she added but didn't ask for any.

When I'd decided upon blueberry pie and icecream, and the silent Luis had departed to get it, Mrs O'Raffety said, 'You'll notice the change in him. Bret, I mean, he's not the man he used to be.' She looked at the burning tip of her cigarette. 'He'll want to tell you how tough he is, of course. Men are like that, I know. But don't encourage him to do anything stupid, will you?'

'What sort of stupid thing is he likely to do?'

'The physician has him on drugs up here.' She held her hand up to her head. 'And he has to rest in the afternoon too. He's sick.'

'The surgeons in Berlin didn't expect him to survive,' I said. 'He's lucky to have you to look after him, Mrs O'Raffety.'

'What else could I do? The hospital bills were piling up, and Bret had some lousy British insurance scheme that didn't even cover the cost of his room.' She smoked her cigarette. 'I got Buddy to try getting more money from them but you know what insurance companies are like.'

'You were the good Samaritan,' I said.

'Who else did he have who would take him? And I was related to him in a crazy roundabout way. Not kin. My grandfather married Bret's widowed mother. She changed the children's names to Rensselaer. Bret's real name was Turner.'

'He was married,' I said.

'Do you know his wife?' She flicked ash into the ashtray.

'No.'

'I contacted her. I wrote and told her Bret was on the point of death. No reply. She never even sent a get-well card.' Mrs O'Raffety inhaled deeply and blew smoke in a manner that displayed her contempt. She reminded me of Cindy Matthews just for a moment. They were both women who knew what they wanted.

'Perhaps she'd moved house,' I suggested.

'Buddy got someone on to that. She cashes her alimony check every month without fail. She got my letter all right. She's taken all the money from him and doesn't give a damn. How can a woman behave that way?' She drank iced tea and waited while a huge portion of blueberry pie with icecream and whipped cream was put on the table for me. Then she said, 'Bret and I were kids together. I was crazy about him. I guess I always figured we'd be married. Then one day he went downtown and joined the Navy. I waited for him. Waited and waited and waited. The war ended but he never came back.'

'Never came back?'

'Never came back to live hereabouts. London, Berlin. I got letters and cards from him. Long letters sometimes but the letters never said the one thing I wanted to hear.'

I started eating my pie.

'You didn't think you were going to hear the confessions of a lonely old lady. Well, I don't know what got me started. You knowing Bret, I suppose. The only other acquaintance Bret and I have in common is that bitch of a wife of his.'

'So you know her?' She had spoken of her distantly, as if she existed only as a spender of Bret's money.

'Nikki? Sure I know her. I knew what would happen to that marriage right from the start. Right from the moment she told me she was going to marry him. Sometimes I think she only went for him because she knew how much I would suffer.'

'Is she from around here?'

'Nikki Foster? Her folks had a shoe store in Santa Barbara. She was at school with me. She always was a little bitch.'

'How long did it last?'

'Eight long miserable years they lived together, or so I understand. I've never spoken to Bret about her and he never mentions her name.'

'And he had a brother.'

'Sheldon.' She gave an enigmatic little chuckle. 'Ever met him?'

'No,' I said.

'Big man in Washington DC. Big, big man. A nice enough guy but always on his way to somewhere better: know what I mean?'

'I know what you mean.'

She lowered her voice. 'And none of them seem to have any money. What did they do with all that Rensselaer money? That's what I'd like to know. Old Cy Rensselaer must have been sitting on a fortune when he died. Surely Bret couldn't have given so much of it to that awful woman. But if not, where did it go?'

I don't know what I was expecting but Bret Rensselaer, when I finally got to see him, looked far from fit and well. He was somewhere about sixty, a slim, tailored figure in white cotton slacks, white tee shirt and white gym shoes. It could have been the height of fashion but on his frail figure the outfit looked institutional. He smiled. He'd kept that tight-jawed smile and he'd kept his hair.

But now he'd aged. His cheeks were drawn and his face wrinkled. And yet something of that former youth had been replaced with distinction, as a film star might age and become a president. He was doing some gentle arm exercises when I entered the room. 'Bernard,' he called amiably. His exertions had made him a little out of breath. 'Sorry to be so elusive, Bernard, but there's no way they'll let me break this routine.' He always put the accent on the second half of my name, and hearing him say it in that low burring accent brought back memories. I looked around at this private gym. Someone had spent a lot of money on it: the upstairs had been ripped out to make a 'cathedral' ceiling, there were polished wood bars right across one wall, and a picture window in the other. The floor was wood blocks and the room was equipped with an exercise bicycle, a rowing machine and a big steel frame with a seat inside, and weights and pulleys, like some instrument of torture. Bret was inside it pulling and pushing levers. 'It's time I finished,' he said.

It was that moment of the late afternoon when nature comes to a complete standstill. Even up here on the hillside, there was no wind, not a leaf moved and no birds flew. The afternoon sun – now low and far away over the Pacific Ocean – gilded everything, and the air was heavy and suffocating. It was at this moment that sunlight coming through the big window painted Bret – and the machine that encaged him – gold, so that he looked like the statue of a remote, wrinkled and pagan god.

'I hear they're getting you ready for the Decathlon.'

Bret looked gratified by this silly compliment. He smiled the shy fleeting smile that he'd used on the best-shaped girls from the typing pool and rubbed his face. 'Three hours a day but it pays off. In just the last two months I'm really getting back into shape,' he said. He climbed out of his machine and wiped his forehead with a towel.

'Sounds grim.'

'And with an ex-Marine Corps medic to put you through it, it is grim,' said Bret with that proud masochistic relish that all men are prone to at times. 'I even went skiing.'

'Not bad!'

'Sun Valley. Just a weekend. Easy slopes: no black runs or double diamonds.' He shook my hand and gripped it tight. For a moment we stood looking at each other. Despite all our ups and downs I liked him and I suppose he knew that. Three years ago when he'd really been in trouble it was me he came to and for some stupid reason that I could not fathom I was proud of that. But Bret had spent too much of his life with the rich and powerful, and he'd developed the hard carapace that all such people use to hide their innermost feelings. He smiled as he let go of my hand and punched my arm gently. 'Jesus Christ! It's good to see you, Bernard. How is everything in the Department?'

'We're managing, but only just.'

'But Dicky never got Europe?'

'No.'

'Well, that's just as well. He's not ready for that one yet. How are you getting along with the Deputy? I hear he's kicking ass.' He indicated that I should sit down on the bench and I did so.

'We see a lot more of him,' I admitted.

'That's good. A Deputy with a knighthood hasn't got so much to work for,' said Bret. 'I suppose he wants to show he's keen.'

'He didn't get the K for working in the Department,' I pointed out.

'Is that a cry from the heart?' said Bret, and laughed a sober little laugh that didn't strain his muscles.

I hadn't meant to criticize the Deputy's lack of experience but it reminded me that a chat with Bret was like a session on a polygraph. And as soon as the subject of honours and titles came up Bret's face took on a predatory look. It always amazed me that educated and sophisticated people such as Bret, Dicky and Frank were so besotted by these incongruous and inconvenient devices. But that's how the system worked: and at least it cost the taxpayer nothing. 'The Deputy will be all right,' I said. 'But a lot of people don't like new ideas, no matter who's selling them.'

'Frank Harrington for instance,' said Bret.

He'd hit it right on the nose, of course. Frank – so near to retirement – would oppose change of any sort. 'I get to hear things, Bernard. Even over here I get to know what's going on. The D-G tells me what's what.'

'The D-G does?'

'Not personally,' said Bret.

'We hardly ever see him nowadays,' I said. 'Everyone says he's sick and going to retire early.'

'And let the Deputy take over . . . Yes, I hear the same stories, but I wouldn't write the D-G out of the script too early. The old devil likes to be a back-seat driver.'

'I should come out here and talk to you more often, Bret,' I said admiringly.

'Maybe you should, Bernard,' he said. 'Sometimes an onlooker sees the game more clearly than the players.'

'But do any of the team take advice from the stands?'

'That's the same old Bernard I used to know,' he said in a manner which might, or might not, have been sarcastic. 'And your lovely Gloria? Is that still going strong?'

'She's a good kid,' I said vaguely enough for him to see that I didn't want to talk about it.

'I heard you'd set up house with her.'

Damn him, I thought, but I kept my composure. 'I rented the town house and got a mortgage on a place in the suburbs.'

132

'You can never go wrong with real estate,' he said.

'I'll go wrong with it if my father-in-law turns nasty,' I said. 'He guaranteed the mortgage. Even the bank doesn't know I'm renting it yet.'

'That will be all right, Bernard. Maybe they'll inch your payments up but they won't give you a bad time.'

'Half the house belongs to Fiona. If her father claimed it on her behalf I'd be into a legal wrangle.'

'You did get legal advice?' he asked.

'No, I'm trying not to think about it.'

Bret pulled a face of disapproval. People like Bret got legal advice before taking a second helping of carbohydrates. 'The Department would help,' said Bret in that authoritative way he was inclined to voice his speculations.

'We'll see,' I said. I was in fact somewhat fortified by his encouragement, no matter how flimsy it was.

'You don't think Fiona might come back?' he said. He put on a cardigan. The sun had gone now and there was a drop in the temperature.

'Come back!' I said. 'How could she? She'd find herself in the Old Bailey.'

'Stranger things have happened,' said Bret. 'How long has she been away?'

'A long while.'

'Bide your time,' said Bret. 'You're not thinking of getting married again are you?'

'Not yet,' I said.

He nodded. 'Come back to me,' said Bret. 'Any problem about the house or your father-in-law, or anything like that, you come back to me. Phone here; leave a number where I can reach you. Understand?'

'Why you, Bret? I mean thanks. But why you?'

'Ever hear of the Benevolent Fund?' said Bret, and without waiting for me to say no I hadn't, he added, 'They recently made me the President of the Fund. It's an honorary title but it gives me a chance to keep in touch. And the Fund is for this kind of problem.'

'Benevolent Fund?'

'These problems are not of your making, Bernard. Sure your wife defected but there's no way that can be laid at your door. It's the Department's problem and they'll do what they can.' He stopped studying his fingernails for long enough to give me a sincere look straight in the eyes.

133

I said, 'I envy you your faith in the Department's charity and understanding, Bret. Maybe that's what keeps you going.'

'It comes with being an Anglophile, Bernard.' He put both hands in his pockets and grinned. 'And talking about your marriage, what do you hear about Fiona?'

'She's working for the other side,' I said stolidly. He knew I didn't want to discuss any of this but it didn't deter him. I'd been hoping to hear why he'd been playing possum all this time, but he was obviously unwilling to confide in me.

'No messages? Nothing? She must miss the children.'

I said, 'She'd be crazy to have the children there with her. It wouldn't be good for them, and her new bosses would hold the children ransom if she ever strayed out of line.'

'Fiona is probably trusted, Bernard. She gave up a lot: children, husband, family, home, career. She gave up everything. It's my guess they trust her over there.' He fiddled with the controls of the exercise bicycle. It was like Bret; he always had to fidget with something. Always had to interfere, his critics said. He pushed the pedal down so that the mechanism made a noise. 'But a lot of people find it impossible to live over there. Don't give up hope yet.'

'Well, I guess you didn't have me come all the way to California to talk about Fiona,' I said.

He looked up sharply. Years back I'd suspected him of having an affair with Fiona. They seemed to enjoy each other's company in a way that I envied. I was no longer jealous – we'd both lost her – but my suspicion, and his awareness of it, cast a shadow upon our relationship. 'Well in a way, yes I did.' Big smile. 'I had some papers for London. Someone had to come, and they sent you, which makes me very happy.'

'Don't give me all that shit,' I said. 'I'm grown up now. If there's something to say, say it and get it over with.'

'What do you mean?'

'What do I mean? I'll tell you what I mean. First, Harry Strang, not being in on the joke, whatever the joke is, told me that I was assigned at the particular request of the Washington Field Unit. Secondly, when I get here and open my suitcase, I find that it's all been searched very carefully. Not hurriedly ransacked and turned over the way a thief does it, or the orderly and systematic "authorized" way customs do it. But turned right over just the same.'

'Airport security,' said Bret sharply. 'Don't be so paranoid, Bernard.'

'I thought you'd say that, Bret. So what about my hand baggage?

What about the chatty Mr Woosnam or whatever his real name was, who just happens to get the seat next to mine and goes through my bag while I'm in the toilet?'

'You can't be sure,' said Bret.

'Sure it happened? Or sure it was the Department?'

Bret smiled. 'Bernard, Bernard, Bernard,' he said, shaking his head in disbelief. I was paranoid: the matter of my baggage was another example of my foolishness. There was nothing to be gained from trying to pursue the subject. 'Sit back, and let's talk.'

I sat back.

'Years ago – before Fiona took a walk – I was given a job to do. Operation Hook it was called. It was designed to move some money around the globe. In those days I was always liable to get saddled with those finance jobs. There was no one else upstairs who knew anything about nuts-and-bolts finance.'

'With Prettyman?'

'Right. Prettyman was assigned to me to oversee the facts and figures.'

'Prettyman was on the Special Operations Committee with you.'

'I wouldn't make too much of that,' said Bret. 'It might have looked good on his CV but as far as that Committee was concerned he was just a glorified book-keeper.'

'But he reported back to Central Funding,' I said. 'Reported directly back to them. In effect Prettyman was their man on the Committee.'

'You have been doing your homework,' said Bret, piqued that I should have known anything about it. 'Yes, Prettyman reported back directly to Funding, because I suggested that we did it that way. It saved me having to sign everything, and answer questions, at a time when I was out of London a lot.'

'Operation Hook? I've never heard of it.'

'And why should you? Almost no one heard of it. It was very "need to know" . . . the D-G, me . . . even Prettyman didn't know all the details.'

I looked at him waving his hands about.

'Prettyman signed the cheques,' I said.

'I don't know who told you that. It's true he counter-signed the cheques. But that was just a belt-and-braces device the D-G added, to monitor spending. The cheques had the amount and the date filled in – so that Prettyman could watch the cash-flow – but he wasn't a party to the rest of it, payees and so on.'

'And suddenly Prettyman goes to Codes and Ciphers. Fiona defects.

135

Prettyman goes to Washington. Is it all connected in some way I don't see? What was it all for?'

'It's still going,' said Bret. 'It's still damned hot.'

'Going where?' I said.

He hesitated and wet his lips. 'This is still very touchy stuff, Bernard.'

'Okay.'

Another hesitation and more chewing of the lip. 'Embassy penetration.'

'I thought Ravenscroft had taken all that embassy stuff across the river. He's got a dozen people over there. What do they do all day?'

'Hook is quite different. Ravenscroft knows nothing about it.'

'So Ravenscroft and his people were moved because they were compromised?'

He shrugged. 'I couldn't say. Embassy penetration work is constantly compromised. You know that. A defector goes, and they tighten up, and Ravenscroft's life becomes more tricky for a while.' He looked at me. 'But Hook is not in Ravenscroft's class. A lot of money is involved. Hook is for really big fish.'

'I learn more from you in five minutes than I find out in the office after a year of asking questions.'

'Because I want you to stop asking questions,' said Bret. A new firmer voice now, and not so friendly. 'You're poking into things that don't concern you, Bernard. You could blow the whole show for us.' He was angry, and his angry words turned into a cough so that he had to pat his chest to recover his breath.

'Is that why I was sent here?'

'In a way,' said Bret. He cleared his throat.

'Just let me get this straight,' I said. 'You set up a lot of companies and bank accounts for this "Hook" business so you could move cash without Central Funding having any record?'

'Embassies,' said Bret. 'East European embassies. Not many people. Even I don't have the details. That's how it's run. And it makes sense that way. Because if someone in Funding had the ledgers every one of our sources could be endangered.' I looked at him. 'Big fish, Bernard . . .'

'And Prettyman knew about all this?'

'Prettyman knew only what he had to be told, plus whatever he could guess.'

'And how much was that?'

'Only Prettyman can answer that one.'

'And Prettyman is dead.'

'That's right,' said Bret. 'He's dead.'

'And you want me to forget the whole thing?'

'Some bloody fool of a book-keeper got his figures wrong. Panic. And suddenly it seemed like getting Prettyman back to London was the best way to sort out the muddle.'

'But now it's sorted out?'

'It was an accountant's mistake. A glitch like that happens now and again.'

'Okay, Bret. Can I go now?'

'It's no use getting tough,' warned Bret. 'This business is nothing to do with you. I don't want you prying into it. I'm asking you to back off because lives are at stake. If you're too dumb to see there's no other way . . .'

'Then what?'

'This is official,' he said. 'It's not just me asking you on a personal basis, it's an official order.'

'Oh, I've got that one written down and learned by heart,' I said. 'My baggage wasn't turned over because there was any chance of finding something I was hiding. I'm too long in the tooth for that one. My checked baggage was searched to show me that you were on the side of the angels. Right, Bret? Was that your idea, Bret? Did you ask London Central Operations to turn me over? Harry Strang was it? Harry's a good enough fellow. Tough, efficient and experienced enough to arrange a small detail like that. And near enough to his pension not to be tempted to confide in me that it was going to happen. Right, Bret?'

'You're your own worst enemy, Bernard.'

'Not while you're around, Bret.'

'Think it over, Bernard. Sleep on it. But make quite sure you know what's at stake.' He turned his eyes away from me and found an excuse to fiddle with the bicycle.

'Innocent lives, you mean?' I asked sarcastically. 'Or my job?'

'Both, Bernard.' He was being tough now: all that Benevolent Fund script was shredded. This was the real Bret: steely-eyed and contemptuous.

'Is this the sort of ultimatum you put to Jim Prettyman?' I asked. 'Was he his own worst enemy, until you came along? Did he give your "official order" a thumbs down so you had to have some boys from out of town blow him away in the car park?'

The shake of his head was almost imperceptible. Bret's expression had locked up tight. The gold had gone from the sunlight; he looked old and tired and wrinkled. He'd never come back and work in the

137

Department again, I was certain of that. Bret's time had come and gone. His voice was little more than a whisper as he said, 'I think you've said enough, Bernard. More than enough, in fact. We'll talk again in the morning. You're booked on the London flight tomorrow.'

I didn't answer. In a way I felt sorry for him, doing his exercises every day, and trying to keep in touch with the Department, and even interfere in what went on there. Telling himself that one day it would all be like it was before, and hoping that his chance of a knighthood wasn't irretrievably lost.

I stood up. So it was the stick and carrot. Play ball with Bret and I even get help with the mortgage: but keep looking into things that don't concern me and I'll lose my job, and maybe lose it the way Jim Prettyman lost his job. Feet first.

Or had I misunderstood him?

15

Disorientated and jet-lagged, my mind reeling with memories, I slept badly that night. That damned house was never quiet, not even in the small hours. Not only was there the relentless whine and hum of machinery close by but I heard footsteps outside my open window and muttered words in that thick accented Spanish that Mexican expatriates acquire in Southern California. I closed the window, but from behind the house there came the sounds of guard dogs crashing through the undergrowth and throwing their weight against the tall chainlink fence that surrounded the house and kept the animals in the outer perimeter. Perhaps the animals sensed the coming storm, for soon after that came the crash of thunder, gusting winds and rain beating on the window and drumming against the metal pool furniture on the patio.

The storm passed over rapidly, as storms out of the Pacific so often do, and about four o'clock in the morning a new series of loud buzzes and resonant droning of some nearby machines began. It was no good, I couldn't sleep. I got up to search for the source of the noise. Dressed in one of the smart towelling robes that Mrs O'Raffety thoughtfully provided for her guests, I explored the whitewashed corridor. Here were doors to the pantry, the larder, the kitchen and various store rooms. The main lighting was not working – perhaps the storm had caused a failure – but low-wattage emergency lights were bright enough for me to see the way.

I passed the boiler room and the fuse boxes and the piled cartons of bottled water that Mrs O'Raffety believed was so good for the digestion. The mechanical sounds grew louder as I got to the low wooden door next to the kitchen servery. The key was left in a big brass-bound lock. By now I'd come far enough around the house to be behind the guest rooms.

I opened the door and stepped cautiously inside. The hum of machinery was louder now and I could see a short flight of worn steps leading down into a low-ceilinged cellar. Along one wall there were four control panels lit with flickering numbers and programs. The glimmer of orange light from them was enough to reflect the large puddle that had formed on the uneven flagstones of the floor. It was the laundry room, with a battery of washing and drying machines. On the top of one of the dryers there was an empty beer can and some cigarette butts. The machines were aligned along the wall that I guessed must back on to mine. From somewhere close by I heard a cough and an exclamation of anger. It was one of the Mexicans.

I went past the machines to find another room: the door was ajar and there was bright light inside. I opened the door. Four men were seated round a table playing cards: three Mexicans and Buddy. He was wearing his stetson. It was tilted well forward over his brow. There was money on the table, some cans of beer and a bottle of whisky. Propped against the wall there was a pump-handle shotgun. The machinery sounded loud in here but the men seemed to be inured to it.

'Hi there, Bernard. I knew it was you,' murmured Buddy. He hadn't looked up from his cards. The three Mexicans had turned their heads and were studying me with a passive but unwelcoming curiosity. All three of them were men in their mid-thirties; tough-looking men with close-cropped hair and weather-beaten faces. 'Want to sit in?'

'No,' I said. 'I couldn't sleep.'

'I wouldn't go strolling around at this time of night,' said Buddy, rearranging the cards he was holding. 'The night-shift guards are too damned trigger-happy.'

'Is that so?' I said.

Now, for the first time, he looked up and studied me with the same discontent that he'd given to his hand of cards. 'Yes, Bernard. It is so.' He wet his lips. 'We had a break-in last month. Some young punk got past our little soldiers, over the outer fence, past the dogs, cut his way through the inner fence using bolt-cutters, opened the security bolt on Mr Rensselaer's office, and tried to lever open the goddamned desk. How do you like that! Mrs O'Raffety fired the whole army. She said they were asleep or drunk or spaced-out or something. She's wrong about that, but new brooms sweep clean. These new recruits are hungry, and raring to do things right. Know what I mean?'

'I didn't know Mr Rensselaer had an office,' I said.

'A kind of sitting room,' amended Buddy and shrugged. 'If you want to see my cards . . .'

'No,' I said. 'No, I don't.'

'These guys are taking me to the cleaners,' complained Buddy light-heartedly. He poured himself a drink and swallowed it quickly.

'What happened to the kid?' I said.

'The kid? Oh, the punk who got in. I'm not sure, but he won't be operating bolt-cutters in the foreseeable future. An excited *soldado* with a shotgun was a bit too close. Both barrels. He'd lost a lot of blood by the

140

time we got him to the hospital. And then of course there was hassle about whether he had Blue Cross insurance before they'd take a look at him.'

'That was a tough decision for you,' I said.

'Nothing tough about it,' said Buddy. 'I'll make damn sure Mrs O'Raffety doesn't find herself paying the medical bills for any stiff who comes up here to rob her. It was bad enough clearing up the blood, and repairing the damage he did. So I told the night nurse I found him bleeding on the highway, and I had these guys with me to say the same.' He nodded at the three Mexicans.

'You think of everything, Buddy.'

He looked up and smiled. 'You know something, Bernard. That joker wasn't carrying a weapon, and that's darned unusual in these parts. He had a camera in his pocket. Olympus: a darn good camera too, I've still got it somewhere. A macro lens and loaded with slow black and white film. That's the kind of outfit you'd need to photograph a document. I said that to Mr Rensselaer at the time but he just smiled and said maybe.'

'I'll try sleeping again.'

'What about a shot of Scotch?'

'No thanks,' I said. 'I'm trying to give it up.'

I went back to bed and put a pillow over my head to keep the sound of the machines from my ears. It was getting light when eventually I went to sleep. A deep sleep from which I was roused by the buzzing of my little alarm clock.

The next morning brought a sudden taste of winter. The temperature had dropped, so that I went digging into my bag for a sweater. The Pacific Ocean was greenish-grey with dirty white crests that broke off the waves to make a trail of spray. Overhead the dark clouds were low enough to skim the tops of the hills, and even the water in the pool had lost its clarity and colour.

Time passed slowly. The London plane was not due to depart until the early evening. It was too cold to sit outside, and there was nowhere to go walking, for beyond the wire the dogs ran free. I swam in the heated pool which steamed like soup in the cold air. By ten o'clock the rain had started again. I drank lots of coffee and read old issues of *National Geographic Magazine*. The 'family room' was big, with dark oak beams in the ceiling and a life-size painting, in Modigliani style, of Mrs O'Raffety in a flouncy pink dress. Mrs O'Raffety was there in person, and so were Bret and Buddy. There was not much talking. A

141

jumbo-sized TV, tuned to a football game, had been wheeled into position before us. No one watched it but it provided an excuse for not speaking.

We sat sprawling on long chintz-covered sofas, arranged around a low oak table. On it there stood a gigantic array of flowers in an ornamental bowl that bore the gold sticker of a Los Angeles florist. In a huge stone fireplace some large logs burned brightly, their flames fanned by the wind that howled in the chimney and was still fierce enough to whip the palm fronds.

Both Mrs O'Raffety and Bret missed lunch. Buddy and I ate hamburgers and Caesar salad from trays that we balanced on our knees as we all sat round the fire. They were huge burgers, as good as I've ever tasted, with about half a pound of beef in each one. But Buddy only picked at his meal. He said he'd slept badly. He said he was sick but he managed to eat all his French fries.

Outside the weather got worse and worse all morning until the grey cloud reached down and enveloped us, cutting visibility to almost nothing, and Mrs O'Raffety made Buddy phone the airport to be sure the planes were still flying.

For the rest of the afternoon Mrs O'Raffety – in red trousers and long pink crocheted top – exchanged small talk with her son-in-law, politely including me in the exchanges whenever a chance came along. Bret turned his head as if to show interest in what was said but contributed very little. He looked older and more frail. Buddy had confided that Bret had bad days and this was obviously one of them. His face was lined and haggard. His clothes – dark blue open-neck linen shirt, dark trousers and polished shoes – worn in response to the colder weather emphasized his age.

Mrs O'Raffety said, 'Are you sure you can't stay another day, Mr Samson? It's such a pity to come to Southern California and just stay overnight.'

'Maybe Mr Samson has a family,' said Buddy.

'Yes,' I said. 'Two children, a boy and a girl.'

'Do they swim?' said Mrs O'Raffety.

'More or less,' I said.

'You should have brought them,' she said in that artless way that rich people have of overlooking financial obstacles. 'Wouldn't they just love that pool.'

'It's a wonderful place you have here,' I said.

She smiled and pushed back the sleeves of her open-work jumper in a nervous mannerism that was typical of her. 'Bret used to call it

142

"paradise off the bone",' she said sadly. It was impossible to miss the implication that Bret was not calling it that these days.

Bret made a real attempt to smile but got stuck about halfway through trying. 'Why "off the bone"?' I asked.

'Like fish in a restaurant,' she explained. 'Every little thing done for you. Enjoy. Enjoy.'

Bret looked at me: I smiled. Bret scowled. Bret said, 'For God's sake, Bernard, come to your senses.' His voice was quiet but the bitterness of his tone was enough to make Mrs O'Raffety stare at him in surprise.

'Whatever are you talking about, Bret?' she said.

But he gave no sign of having heard her. His eyes fixed on me and the expression on his face was fiercer than I'd ever seen before. His voice was a growl. 'You goddamn pinbrain! Search your mind! Search your mind!' He got up from his low seat and then walked from the room.

No one said anything. Bret's outburst had embarrassed Mrs O'Raffety, and Buddy took his cues from her. They sat there looking at the flower arrangement as if they'd not heard Bret and not noticed him get up and leave.

It was a long time before she spoke. Then she said, 'Bret resents his infirmity. I remember him at high school: a lion! Such an active man all his life . . . it's so difficult for him to adjust to being sick.'

'Is he often angry like this?' I asked.

'No,' said Buddy. 'Your visit seems to have upset him.'

'Of course it hasn't,' said Mrs O'Raffety, who knew how to be the perfect hostess. 'It's just that meeting Mr Samson makes Bret remember the times when he was fit and well.'

'Some days he's just fine,' said Buddy. He reached for the coffee pot that was keeping hot on the serving trolley. 'More?'

'Thanks,' I said.

'Sure,' said Buddy. 'And some days I see him standing by the pool with an expression on his face so that I think he's going to throw himself in and stay under.'

'Buddy! How can you say such a thing?'

'I'm sorry Mrs O'Raffety but it's true.'

'He has to find himself,' said Mrs O'Raffety.

'Sure,' said Buddy, hastily trying to assuage his employer's alarm. 'He has to find himself. That's what I mean.'

We took the coast road back. Buddy wasn't feeling so good and so one of the servants – Joey, a small belligerent little Mexican who'd been playing cards the previous night – was driving Buddy's jeep and leaning forward staring into the white mist and muttering that we should have taken the canyon road and gone inland to the Freeway instead.

'Buddy should be doing this himself,' complained the driver for the hundredth time. 'I don't like this kind of weather.' The fog rolled in from the Ocean and swirled around us so that sudden glimpses of the highway opened up and were as quickly gone.

'Buddy felt ill,' I said. Car headlights flashed past. A dozen black leather motorcyclists went with suicidal disregard into the white wall of fog, and were swallowed up with such suddenness that even the sound of the bikes was gone.

'Ill!' said Joey. 'Drunk, you mean.' The rain was suddenly fiercer. The grey shapes of enormous trucks came looming from the white gloom, adorned with a multitude of little orange lights, like ships lit up for a regatta.

When I didn't respond Joey said, 'Mrs O'Raffety doesn't know but she'll find out.'

'Doesn't know what?'

'That he's a lush. That guy puts down a fifth of bourbon like it's Coca Cola. He's been doing that ever since his wife dumped him.'

'Poor Buddy,' I said.

'The sonuvabitch deserves all he gets.'

'Is that so?' I said.

In response to my unasked question Joey looked at me and grinned. 'I'm leaving next week. I'm going to work for my brother-in-law in San Diego. Buddy can shove his job.'

A few miles short of Malibu we were stopped by a line of flares burning bright in the roadway. Half a dozen big trucks were parked at the roadside. A man in a tan-coloured shirt emerged from the mist. Los Angeles County Sheriff said the badge on his arm. With him there were two Highway Patrol cops in yellow oilskins; a big fellow and a girl. They were all very wet.

'Pull over,' the cop told Joey, pointing to the roadside.

'What's wrong?' The slap and buzz of the wipers seemed unnaturally loud. 'A slide?'

'Behind the white Caddie.' The man from the Sheriff's Office indicated an open patch of ground where several patient drivers were parked and waiting for the road to be cleared. The cop's face was running with rainwater that dropped from the peak of his cap, his shirt was black with rain. He wasn't in the mood for a long discussion.

'We've got a plane to catch: international,' said Joey.

The cop looked at him with a blank expression. 'Just let the ambulance through.' The cop squeegeed the water from his face, using the edge of his hand.

'What happened?'

The ambulance moved slowly past. The cop spoke like a swimmer too, in brief breathless sentences. 'A big truck – artic – jack-knifed. No way you'll get past.'

'Any other route we can take?' Joey asked.

'Sure but you'd add an hour to your trip.' The cop squinted into the rain. 'LAX, you say? There are a couple of guys in a big old Lincoln limo. They said they were going to turn around and head back downtown. They'd maybe take your passenger.'

'Where are they?'

'Other side of the wreck. Maybe they left already but I could try.' He switched on his transceiver. There was a burst of static and the cop said, 'That big dark blue limo still there, Pete?'

There was a scarcely intelligible affirmative from the radio. The cop said, 'Ask them if they'd take someone in a hurry to get to LAX.'

With bag in hand I picked my way past a line of cars and the monster-sized truck that was askew across the highway and completely blocked the road both ways. I found the limousine waiting for me and by that time – despite my plastic raincoat – I was very wet too.

The man beside the driver got out into the heavy rain and opened the rear door for me, and that's the kind of thing you do only if you've got a job you are determined to keep. Now I could see the man in the back: a short thickset man with a rotund belly. He wore an expensive three-piece dark blue suit – gold pocket watch chain well evidenced – and a shirt with a gold collar pin below the tight knot of a very conservative striped tie. It was too Wall Street for the Pacific Coast Highway, where pants and matching jackets went out of fashion with laced corsets and high hats.

'Bernie. Jump in,' said the well dressed man in the back. His voice was low, soft and attractive; like his car.

I hesitated no more than a moment. Wet, stranded and without transport I was in no position to decline and Posh Harry knew that. He smiled a welcome that had an element of smug satisfaction in it, and revealed a lot of teeth and some expensive dentistry. I climbed in beside him. Or as beside him as I had to be on a soft leather seat wide enough for four.

'What's the game?' I said. I was angry at the simple trick.

'Take Mr Samson's bag,' Posh Harry told the man in the front seat.

145

'It's valuable,' I protested.

'Valuable,' scoffed Harry. 'What do you think is going to happen to it? You think I've got some dwarf hidden in the trunk to ransack your baggage on the way to the airport?'

'Maybe,' I said.

'Maybe!' He laughed. 'Did you hear that?' he asked the men in the front. 'This guy is a real pro. From this one you could learn a thing or two.' And then, in case they were taking him seriously, he laughed. 'So nurse the bag, Bernie, if that's the way you prefer it. Let's go, driver! This man has a plane to catch.'

'You didn't do all this just for me?' I asked cautiously. But how could they have collared me so neatly without positioning the truck as well?

'Not my style, baby,' said Posh Harry. He paused before adding, 'But my boss: it sure is her style!'

One of the men in the front laughed softly enough not to interrupt but loud enough to be heard.

'Her?' I said.

'We got a female Station Chief here. You mean you hadn't heard? Yup. We've got a "Chieftess" running things.' He laughed.

'A woman!'

He waved a manicured hand in a dismissive gesture of impatience. 'You guys in London know all that stuff. It was in the monthly briefing last September.'

'In London there were bets on which one of your LA men was calling himself Brigette,' I said.

'You bastard!' said Harry. He sniggered.

The driver said, 'Right on! Half those young guys in the office have got earrings and permanent waves. Faggots!'

'It was Brigette's idea,' insisted Harry. 'I told her I knew you. I wanted to phone Bret and keep it all cool but she had her mind all made up. She said we'd have to pay for the truck rental anyway. The ambulance was her idea: a nice touch huh? It was all fixed up by then so she insisted we go ahead. Not like the old days, eh Bernie?'

'Is that her real name: Brigette?'

'She's a hard-nosed little lady,' said Harry with respect. 'She runs that office . . . I mean those guys jump. Not like the old days, Bernie. I mean it.'

'So what's this really about then?' I said, now that the mandatory exchange about the CIA's first female Station Chief was over and done with.

'It's about Bret,' said Posh Harry. 'It's about Bret Rensselaer.'

146

Delicately he scratched his cheek with the nail of his little finger so that I saw his starched linen cuffs and the gold cuff-links. His complexion was yellow enough to suggest Japanese blood but his hands were paler. And his nails were carefully manicured. It was in line with his natty appearance. I'd never seen him anything but perfectly haircut and shaved with talc on his chin and a discreet smell of aftershave in the air. His clothes were always new looking and a perfect fit, so that he was like a carefully assembled plastic toy. Perhaps it says more about me —or about the gangster films of my childhood – that I always saw in his polished appearance a certain hint of menace.

'Yeah?' I said.

'The word is, that you have some kind of feud – some kind of private vendetta – with Bret.' Very serious now: with the smile gone, hands loosely clasped across his belly like a temple Buddha taking a day off.

'And?'

'Private vendettas don't get the rent paid. Vendettas are turn-offs, Bernie. Bad news for Bret: bad news for you: bad news for London and bad news for us.'

'Who's "us"?'

'Don't put me through the mangle, baby; the laundry's dried and aired. You know who us is. Us is the Company.'

'And what in hell has it got to do with you?'

Hand raised in a gesture of pacification. 'Did I handle this all wrong? Maybe we could start over? Right?'

'I'm not likely to get out and walk,' I said.

'No. Sure.' He sat well back in his seat and watched me from under lowered eyelids as he picked up the pieces of good will and figured how to glue it all back together again. Posh Harry was pretty good at that kind of thing. For years he'd been a Mr Fixit, working both sides of the street, and he only got paid when everyone was happy.

We drove on in silence. I put my bag between my feet and turned away to watch the rain falling on the millionaires' shacks that line this part of the beach. Here and there I saw groups of surfers in shiny black rubber wet-suits. Anyone crazy enough to go looking for big waves in the Pacific Ocean was not deterred by bad weather.

I sat back in my seat and stole a glance at Posh Harry. I'd heard that he'd taken a permanent job with the CIA. Some said he'd never been anything but their paid mouthpiece, but I doubted that. I'd known him a long time. I'd watched him scratching a living in that shady world where secret information is bought and sold like gilts and pork bellies. He'd always been something of an enigma, an Hawaiian who'd taken to

Europe in a way that few strangers ever do. Posh Harry's mastery of the German language – grammar, pronunciation and idiom – belied the rather casual, relaxed demeanour he liked to display. Adult foreigners who will devote enough time and energy to acquire German like this have to be dedicated, demented or Dutch.

'Why would you care?' I asked him. 'What's Bret to you?'

'They like him,' said Harry.

'Brigette you mean?'

'I mean Washington,' he said.

'Is Bret so important to the boys in Langley?' I asked very casually.

Like a scalded cat he jumped aside from the implication of that one. 'Don't get me wrong,' said Harry. 'Bret is not a CIA employee and he never has been.' There was an old-fashioned formality about that statement and about the way he said it.

'Everyone keeps telling me that,' I said. By 'everyone' I meant Posh Harry. We'd been all through this years ago.

With ostentatious patience he said, 'Everyone keeps telling you that because it's true.'

'Washington?'

'Will you listen, Bernard. Bret is not – repeat not – an Agency employee. We know nothing about what Bret does for you. I wish the hell we did.'

'Did you put someone over the fence there last month, Harry? Was that one of your people trying to get a line on Bret?'

Harry looked at me for a moment and then said, 'Someone got shot up there. An intruder was hurt bad. Yes, I heard about that.'

'A friendly Agency gumshoe dropping in to pass the time of day? Off the record,' I coaxed. 'Was that one of yours?'

But Harry would not be coaxed into an admission like that. 'I'm not talking about the Agency; I'm talking about Capitol Hill, Bret's got some good friends there. His family deploy a lot of muscle in that town. They won't stand by while Bret is smeared.'

'While Bret is smeared? Harry, I wish I knew what you're talking about,' I said. 'I didn't know Bret was still alive until I got here.'

'Don't snow me, Bernie. Dead or alive, you've been bad-mouthing Bret Rensselaer. Don't deny it.'

I felt a sudden pang of fear. There were three of them. There were plenty of lonely stretches of coastline nearby and the desert. With more boldness than I felt I said, 'Put away the brass knuckles Harry. That's not your style.' But rumours from long ago said it was exactly his style.

He smiled. 'They said you were becoming paranoid.'

'You get that way when jerks shanghai you on the highway and bury you under horse-manure.'

He ignored that and said, 'This guy Woosnam for instance. This guy is a kosher businessman.'

'What?'

'Bret came through to the office last night and asked for an urgent check-up on the passenger you sat next to on the plane. He's a nothing, Bernard. A two-bit building contractor who made it big in real estate. That's what I mean about you being paranoid.'

'Bret asked? About Woosnam?' I said.

'Sure. Bret came on the phone. The way I heard it, Bret was mad. He wanted to know if we'd put someone on the plane with you but I knew we hadn't. We didn't even know you were coming until you'd arrived. Bret persuaded someone to make it a number one priority. Dig out this Woosnam baby, and dig him out fast. So they made the airline go through the manifests. They dug people out of their beds and had them working all night. They weren't pleased, I can tell you. It being a weekend too.'

'And Woosnam wasn't working for London Central?'

'Jesus Christ. Even now you don't believe me. I can see it in your face.'

'Who cares,' I said.

'I care. Bret cares. Everyone who likes you cares. We wonder what's happening to you, Bernard baby.'

I made a noise to indicate that I didn't want to talk about the wretched Mr Woosnam. Posh Harry nodded sagely and leaned forward to push a button that made the glass partition slide into position, so the men in front couldn't hear us. Although if this was the kind of CIA limo I think it was, there would be a hidden tape recorder button built into the upholstery so that Brigette, and God knows who else, would be able to refer to a transcript of what I said. Or was I becoming paranoid?

'Let's talk turkey, Bernie. Let's cut out all the crap, eh?'

'Which crap was that, Harry?'

He ignored my question. He looked out of the car to see how near LA International we were and decided to get to the point. 'Listen,' he said. 'Big men in Washington hear you are running around trying to pin some old London screw-up on to Bret . . . Well, Washington gets touchy. They talk to your people in London Central. They say, shit or get off the pot. What charges? they ask. Where's the evidence? They want to know, Bernard. Because they don't like the way Bret is expected to take all your lousy flak without getting a proper chance to

149

answer.' Just for a moment there had been a glimpse of the real Posh Harry: the savage little guy inside this soft smiling cerebral Charlie Chan.

'If Bret thinks that . . .' I started to say.

'Hold the phone, Bernie.' The amiable smile was back in place. 'I'm saying that this is the way Washington sees it. Maybe they got it wrong, but that's the way it was looking to them, by the time they got on to London Central and started asking questions.'

'And what did London say?' I said with genuine interest.

'London said just what Washington expected them to say. They said this was just Bernie Samson, on a one-man crusade that had no official authorization. London said they'd talk to Bernard Samson and cool him off a little.'

'And how did Washington feel about that?'

'Washington said that was good. These big men in Washington said that if a little help was needed in cooling this maverick Brit off, they'd be happy to arrange for someone to break his arms in several places just to show him that his extra-curricular energies would be better employed with wine, women and song.'

'In a manner of speaking,' I said.

'Sure, in a manner of speaking, Bernie.' No smiles now, just blank face and cold stare before Posh Harry turned away to look out at the neon signs and the restaurant forecourts that were packed with the cars of people who liked their lunch to go on till sundown. He touched the condensation that had formed on the windows and seemed surprised when a dribble of water ran down the glass. 'Because these big men in Washington don't believe what your people tell them,' said Harry, talking to the window. 'They don't think London really have got some wild man who likes to go off to stir the dirt on his own time.'

'No?'

'No. Washington think he's on assignment. They wonder if maybe those bastards in London Central are getting ready for the big reshuffle that their deck of marked cards has needed so long.'

'Tell me more about that,' I said. 'I'd like to know.'

He turned his head and gave me a slow toothy smile. 'They think your top guys are very clever at burying the bodies in a neighbour's yard.'

Now I was beginning to see it. 'London Central are going to blame some of their disasters on Bret?'

'It would be a way of handling it,' said Harry.

'A bit far-fetched, isn't it?'

Harry gave a tight-lipped smile and didn't answer. We both knew it wasn't far-fetched. We knew it was exactly the way that our masters handled their difficulties. And anyway I didn't feel like working hard to convince him that London Central wouldn't do anything like that. The alternative would focus the wrath of Bret's Washington fan club upon me. And I have always been opposed to violence, even when it's in a manner of speaking.

16

Sunday lunchtime; London Heathrow; no Gloria to meet me. It was not a warm homecoming. An overtired customs man demanded that the box of official papers that Bret had dumped on me should be opened for his inspection. My inclination was to hand it over, but I waited until the duty Special Branch officer finished his late breakfast of fried egg and sausages so that he could come down – egg on his tie – and explain to all concerned that I was permitted to enter the United Kingdom with the box closed and locked and its contents not scrutinized by Her Majesty's Customs.

The unnecessary delay was especially galling because I was certain that the paper-work in the box was of no great importance or secrecy: my errand was the Department's excuse to have me cross the water and be rattled, wrung and reassured by lovable Bret Rensselaer. Whether my encounter with Posh Harry was also part of my Department's plan was something I hadn't yet decided, but probably not. They would not relish the message that Posh Harry conveyed to me.

And when I got to number thirteen Balaklava Road the house was dark and empty. A hastily scribbled message stuck on the oven door said that Gloria's mother was sick and she'd had to go to see her. The word 'had' underlined three times. The children were on a trip to the Zoo with some 'very nice' schoolfriends.

It was difficult for Gloria. She knew that I was likely to be examining her priorities in anything to do with my children. Her parents were not enthusiastic about our domestic arrangements. And I was very much aware of the fact that her mother was only three years older than I was. So were they!

Sunday lunch is a sacred ritual for Englishmen of my generation. You eat at home. With luck it's raining so you can't work in the garden. You monitor the open fire diligently, while sipping an aperitif of your choice. Should a mood of desperate intellectuality overcome you, you might peruse the Sunday papers, reassured by the certainty that there will be no news in them. At the appointed time, with an appreciative family audience, you carve thin slices from a large piece of roasted meat and, if possible, serve cabbage, roasted potatoes and Yorkshire pudding. You divide it unevenly amongst the family according to

152

whim. You eventually do the same with a sweet, stodgy, cooked dessert that is accompanied by both custard and cream. You doze.

No matter how German some others said I was, no matter what my tastes were for foreign food, foreign heating systems, foreign cars and foreign bodies, in the matter of Sunday lunch I was resolutely English.

That was why I was so unhappy at the idea of eating the cold ham and salad that Gloria had left for me. So I took the car and went to Alfonso's – a small Italian restaurant in Wimbledon. An establishment which, after taking the children to see *Così fan tutte*, our family called Don Alfonso's. Alfonso himself was, of course, Spanish, and although willing to tackle an Italian menu in Wimbledon he was not so foolish as to offer British cooking of any sort. Certainly not Sunday lunch.

That Sunday, Alfonso's was crowded with noisy people who didn't know that a home-cooked lunch is an established English tradition. There were lots of children in evidence and two loaded dessert trolleys awaited the onslaught. From the amplifier there came a scratchy rendition of 'Volare' sung in an Italian falsetto with massed guitar accompaniment. It came around about every thirty minutes.

'Have the *aragosta fra Diavolo*,' Alfonso advised, having poured me a glass of white wine and twisted the bottle to reveal an impressive Soave label. 'Drink! Drink! It's on the house, Mr Samson.' Only the most unperceptive of customers could have mistaken Alfonso for an Italian, despite his having lived in Rome for eight years. He had the lively and unscrupulous salesmanship of the Roman, incongruously coupled with the relentless melancholy of Iberia. I sipped the wine and kept my eyes down on the menu. 'Lobster cooked in wine with tomato. Really delicious,' he added persuasively.

'Frozen lobster?' I enquired. He watched one of his newest young waiters trying to prise baked lasagne from the metal dish to which it had stuck. It almost fell from his hands. Only with commendable self-control did Alfonso restrain himself from rushing across the room to do it himself.

He turned back again and his anxiety was manifested in his reply. 'You think I wade through the paddling pool on Wimbledon Common to trap them? Frozen? Sure. Frozen.'

'I don't like frozen lobster,' I said. 'And I don't like anything that's going to be "Diavolo".'

Zzzwhoof. Sharp intake of breath. 'So what happened to you this morning? Get out of bed on the wrong side?'

'I didn't get out of bed: I haven't been to bed. I've been on a bloody aeroplane all night.' Now we both watched the mad waiter as a gigantic serving spoon, heavily laden with pasta and sauce, made a perilous journey across the table to the plate. By a miracle it got there: no one got splattered. Alfonso breathed out and said, 'Okay okay okay. Sorry I asked. Have a little more Soave. Shall I ask the chef to cook you a lovely half lobster without the chilli? Just a little melted butter?'

'What will frozen lobster taste of without the chilli?' I asked.

'Oh dear! Oh dear! No lovely lady. That's the trouble. Is this what you're like when you're on your own?'

'I'm not on my own: I've got you here selling me a lunch.'

'Something very light,' he said. He always said 'something very light' even if he was going to suggest pork and dumplings. I know because he often suggested pork and dumplings and I often ate it. 'Fish. A beautiful unfrozen red mullet baked with olives. Green salad. Start with a half portion of risotto.'

'Okay.'

'And a carafe of this Soave?'

'Are you crazy, Al? Everyone knows Italian restaurants manufacture their booze in a garden shed. Soave maybe, but I'll have a bottle with a cork in it.'

'You're a cynic, Mr Samson,' he said.

'And I'm paranoid with it,' I said. 'Everyone says so.'

I ate my meal in solitude, watching my fellow-customers getting drunk and noisy. The yellow dented Mini arrived when I was having coffee. She found a place to park immediately outside. She did it with style and economy of effort, even if one wheel did end up on the pavement.

Gloria entered the dining room with all the joyful energy of show-biz: without arm-waving or shouting she was able to ensure that no one failed to look up. Even drunk I could not have done it like her; perhaps that's what I found so attractive about her. She was everything I could not be. A big kiss and a hug. 'I'm bloody starved, darling,' she said. 'How did it go in California?' Another kiss. 'Did you swim?' Alfonso took her coat and pulled out a chair for her. She said, 'Am I too late to eat, Alfonso darling?'

'How could I send you away hungry, beautiful lady?' He gave her coat to a waiter and reached for the cutlery from another table and arranged a setting before her with surprising speed.

After no more than a glance at the menu, Gloria said, 'Could I have that delicious calves liver dish you do with onions and sage? And start with the marinaded mushrooms?' She was like that: she could make up her mind very quickly about almost everything. I often wondered whether she had her answers prepared in advance. Or was it that she simply didn't care very much about the consequences of these things she was so quick to decide upon?

'Perfect,' said Al, as if no one had ever thought of such a meal before. And then, as he thought about it again, 'Absolutely perfect!' He poured her some wine and held the bottle up to the light, as if worried that the wine left would be insufficient for us.

'How's your mother?' I said in an attempt to lower the temperature.

'She'll live.'

'What was it?' I said.

'Poor Mummy is doing her dramatic Hungarian number. She thinks Daddy is getting tired of her.'

'And is he?'

'I suppose so. Good God! I don't know. They've been married for twenty-five years. It wouldn't be amazing if he was starting to feel a bit imprisoned. I've seen some gorgeous patients at his surgery. And they all adore him.'

'Imprisoned by marriage?'

'It happens. They haven't got much in common.'

I was surprised to find her so resigned. 'But they are both expatriate Hungarians. They came here together and set up a new life.'

'Now they both speak excellent English and my sisters are away at school and I have left home. There is not so much binding them together.'

'And people say *I'm* a cynic.'

'I'm not being cynical. I'm stating facts.'

'Did you tell your mother this?'

'I wrapped it up a bit.'

'I hope you wrapped it up a lot. She must be depressed beyond measure. And maybe your father is not chasing other women. Or even feeling imprisoned.'

She sipped some wine, looked me in the eyes and then gave me a slow smile. 'You're a romantic really, Bernard. An old-fashioned romantic. Perhaps that's why I fell for you so badly.'

She smiled again. Her blonde hair had been rearranged so that she had a fringe to just above her eyebrows. She was so beautiful. 'Your new hair-do looks good,' I said.

She touched her hair. 'Do you really like it?'

'Yes.' I couldn't bear being separated from her, not even for a day or two. The prospect of her going to Cambridge was unendurable. She pursed her lips to offer a kiss.

'I love you, Gloria,' I said without meaning to.

She smiled and fidgeted with the cutlery. She seemed slightly agitated and I wondered if perhaps she was more worried about her mother than she was prepared to admit.

'I saw Bret Rensselaer,' I said. 'Everyone thought he was dead but he's convalescing.'

'You saw Bret Rensselaer?' She wasn't as surprised by the news as I'd been, but then Bret Rensselaer had been gone for years.

'He was in a filthy temper. I suppose being chronically sick makes you moody.'

'But he's recuperating?'

'He seems to have found a rich old lady. She said they were childhood sweethearts.'

'How sweet,' said Gloria.

'With a very nice little spread in Ventura County. I can't think why he'd want to get well.'

'What a rotten thing to say, darling,' she said. 'That spoils everything; that's not romantic at all.' Her marinaded mushrooms arrived and as she started eating she said, 'Well, you chose exactly the right day to disappear as usual.'

'I did?'

'Friday morning. First your old friend Werner Volkmann arrived, tight-lipped and glaring. From what I understand he's accusing Frank Harrington of sending his wife off on a suicide mission to Frankfurt an der Oder. He was furious! I stayed out of sight.'

'What happened?'

She continued eating and then said, 'After a lot of toing and froing, and Dicky complaining of a headache and saying he would have to go to the doctor, it was decided that the Deputy would talk to Werner.'

'The Deputy?'

'Well, he was demanding to see the bloody D-G, no less. Dicky told him the D-G was away sick but Mr Volkmann wasn't buying that one. It was obvious that seeing Dicky would only put his back up worse, so the Deputy offered to handle it.'

'Good on the Deputy,' I said.

'Sir Percy is all right. He's got guts and he's willing to make decisions.'

'And there are not many people in London Central who answer to that description.'

'And meeting the Deputy calmed Werner down. It was when he thought they were trying to get rid of him that he got really angry.'

'And an angry Werner is not a pretty sight.'

'I was surprised. Dicky was too. I think it's that damned beard. Dicky was frightened of him. Dicky took refuge in Morgan's room and closed the door, not noticing that I was standing there. He said to Morgan that all these field agents are yobs. When he realized that I'd overheard him, he smiled as if to make it into a joke.'

'What did the Deputy say to Werner?'

'No one knows. There was just the two of them. They were together for nearly an hour; I don't know whether that means they got along just fine, or that they were at each other's throats, but Volkmann came out all smiles so I suppose the Deputy did a good job.'

'I'm damned glad I missed it,' I said.

'Did you know he was going along to raise hell?'

'He may have mentioned it.'

'You bastard.'

'What did I do?'

'You could have talked him round the other night. You let him come into the office and raise hell. That amused you I suppose?' She said it without bitterness. In some ways I suspected that the notion of me as a trouble-maker was not unattractive to her.

'Maybe I could have done: maybe not. But it's not as simple as it looks. This is part of Werner's on-going feud with Frank Harrington. Werner has always hated Frank and I'm determined not to be in the middle of any dispute between those two. I'd end up losing two good friends and I haven't got enough friends to risk losing two of the best ones, in order to smooth things along for Dicky and Morgan and the rest of them in the office.'

'You were lucky to avoid it all. Then yesterday your friend Lucinda came to call.'

'Cindy Prettyman?'

'Lucinda Matthews she calls herself nowadays. She was most particular about that.'

'She came to the office?'

'No, this was Saturday, she came to Balaklava Road. I was in and out with the car. I'd left the garage door open on account of that broken hinge, so she walked right in on me. I cursed. I was trying to get the children's laundry done so that Mrs Palmer could help with the ironing.'

'What did she want?'

'The usual. Her husband's "murder" and the KGB slush fund and the conspiracy behind it. You know.'

'Did she tell you all that?'

'I thought she'd never stop. Finally I said you'd get together with her one day next week. Not at the office, she says, because someone might see you together. If you ask me, darling, she's off her head.'

'Has something new happened?'

'She said I was to tell you that she has a new line on the money. And she wants a box of papers she gave you. She thinks they might contain a clue.'

'She won't get much joy from that stuff,' I said. 'Unless she's suddenly taken up archaeology.' Without intending to, I sighed deeply. I was not ready to face Cindy again.

'She said you'd want to know. She's heard of some money being moved. They are running scared, she says. They must realize that someone is on to them. All that sort of thing. She's bonkers.'

'Cindy has been working hard.'

Gloria wasn't too keen to endorse this praise for Cindy. 'She doesn't know what she's talking about,' said Gloria. 'A lot of hot money is being pulled out of German banks and companies right now. It's because the Bonn government is bringing in new laws. The EEC have instructed them to bring German corporate balance sheets into line with those of other countries. Until now German private banks and private corporations haven't had to reveal their profits. By next year it won't be so easy to bury money in a bank or corporation. Central Funding is sure to be preparing for that change.'

'I thought the German banks reported everything to the German tax authorities. I thought Germany didn't have hot money.'

Gloria shook her head. 'They only have to report their customers' money darling. Their own money, and all the rich pickings they make, are kept secret. You know what all those bloody High Street banks are like: well, German banks are ten times worse.'

'How do you know all this?'

'My economics classes. The West German financial markets is my special subject.'

'Did you tell Cindy this?'

'She thinks I'm your dumb blonde. She didn't come round to talk to me.' Gloria's grilled liver arrived. It looked good: I stole a piece of sauté potato and let her eat her lunch in peace.

'I suppose eventually I'll have to talk to Cindy. I owe it to Jim.'

'She says phone her at home and she'll meet you at the weekend.' Gloria abandoned her liver and put her knife and fork down. It was a different tone of voice now: serious and concerned. 'I really do think she's unbalanced, Bernard. She parked her car miles away, in front of Inkerman Villas. I told her it was private parking there, and she might get towed away, but she wouldn't listen. She kept looking out of the window as though someone might have followed her. When I asked her what was the matter, she said she was just admiring the view. She has a mad sort of look in her eyes. She's scary.'

'I'll have to phone her,' I said while searching my mind for excuses not to. 'But I wish she'd leave me out of it. I've already ruffled Bret's feathers, and I ask myself what for? I've got enough work, and enough enemies, without looking for more.'

'You said you wanted to get to the bottom of it,' said Gloria.

'But I just can't spare any more time. It's just another one of the Department's little secrets, and if they are so determined that it remains a mystery; then let it stay a mystery. Everything I encounter mystifies me, I don't need any more.'

'Do I mystify you, my poor darling?' She reached out and stroked my hand.

'You especially,' I said.

'Do you think Alfonso would give me a bag so I can take the rest of my liver home for Muffin?' she said without expecting a reply, and added, 'Your friend Cindy won't let it go so easily.'

'She has more spare time than I do, and she likes these "causes". Cindy's always been a bit like that: animal welfare, women priests, diesel emission is killing the trees. She has to have a cause.'

'I think she's abnormal,' said Gloria in that flat casual voice that suggested that she didn't care one way or the other. She had switched off now. Gloria could do that. It was a knack I would dearly like to acquire. Suddenly she raised an arm and shouted, 'Can I have some coffee, Alfonso?'

'Make that two,' I called to him but he gave no sign of having heard me.

'I'm sorry,' she said, 'I forgot that you don't like me to order things when I'm with you.'

'Are you wrapping that liver up in your handkerchief. Ugh!'

'Muffin loves liver.' She put the little parcel in her handbag as the coffee arrived.

'I shouldn't be drinking coffee,' I said. 'I need to go to bed.'

'The children won't be home until supper. Maybe I will go to bed too,' she said artlessly.

'Race you home!'

17

There was plenty of work waiting for me in the office. At the top of the pile, flagged and beribboned, was a Ministry of Defence request for details of Semtex, a Czechoslovak explosive exported through the DDR and now being used in home made 'bean can grenades' and causing casualties in Northern Ireland. Under it there were some confidential questions about the Leipzig Trade Fair and – with only a number one priority – some supplements from the Minister that must be ready for parliamentary question time.

It was one of the natural laws of departmental life that the sort of files that Dicky chose to keep on his desk, while he worried about his career and vacillated about expedient courses of action, were always the ones that ultimately required the most urgent response from me when he finally dumped them on my desk. My work was not made easier by the cryptic thoughts and instructions that Dicky shared with me as each flat file was dropped into my tray.

'Just keep it warm until we hear who's going to be on the committee,' Dicky would say. Or, 'Tell the old bastard to get stuffed but keep him sweet'; 'This might work out if they find the right people but make sure it doesn't bounce back our way'; and his standard reaction: 'Find out what they really expect and maybe we'll be able to meet them halfway'. These were the sort of arcane instructions I was trying to implement on Tuesday while Dicky was gone to wherever he went when there was work in the offing. And Dicky wanted everything done by the end of the day.

By the time a debonair Frank Harrington looked into my little office and invited me to go for a quick lunch, I was glassy-eyed. 'You'll do yourself an injury if you try and work your way through this lot before going home,' said Frank, running the tip of an index finger across the cover of a fat file for which some unfortunate had analysed, in considerable detail, the various types of East European shops where only Western currency was accepted. Here were tables and estimates, comments and balance sheets, from Pewex in Poland, Tuwex in Czechoslovakia, Korekom in Bulgaria, compared point by point with Intershops in East Germany.

Without picking it up, Frank flicked open the file carefully so as not

160

to get his hands dirty. 'Would you believe I saw this in the tray on the old man's desk on the day I got the Berlin job?'

'Of course I would,' I said.

'It's got fatter over the years, of course,' said Frank, who probably wanted to be congratulated on his phenomenal memory. He hooked his tightly rolled umbrella on the desk edge and then consulted his gold pocket watch as if to confirm that it was lunchtime. 'Heave all this aside, Bernard. Let me buy you a pint of Guinness and a pork pie.' The illusion that Englishmen wanted a pub lunch every day was something that many expatriates cherished, so I smiled. Frank was looking very trim. He had been upstairs talking to the Deputy and was dressed in a three-piece grey worsted with gold watch-chain, wide-striped Jermyn Street shirt and a new Eton tie, of which Frank seemed to have an inexhaustible supply.

My tie was plain and polyester, and my watch Japanese and plastic. I was weary and my ears were ringing with the sound of Dicky's voice. I'd been listening to the dictating machine, taking notes from a long rambling disquisition that Dicky had passed to me to 'get into shape'. It was going to be a long job. Dicky was not good at getting his arguments into proper order, and those passages where he was consistent and logical were riddled with inaccurate 'facts'. I pushed the work aside and said, 'What about next week, Frank? I'm in Berlin on Wednesday.'

Frank didn't leave. 'A very quick lunch, Bernard.'

I looked up to see him standing in the doorway with a forced smile on his face. It wasn't until then I realized how much such little things meant to him.

I knew of course that Frank had always looked upon me as a surrogate son. Several people had remarked on it, usually at times when I was being especially rude or making Frank's life difficult. Even Frank himself had more than once referred to some undefined responsibility he'd owed to my father. But Frank took it too seriously. More than once he'd risked his career to help me, and to tell the truth that made me uncomfortably indebted to him. Father–son relationships seldom run smoothly, and true to my role I'd taken considerably more from him than I ever gave, and I confess I resented being obliged to anyone, even Frank.

'You're right, Frank. To hell with it!' I took the tape cassette from the machine and locked it in my desk drawer. Maybe I should have sent it to the KGB to promote more confusion amongst the opposition. Frank reached for my coat.

Frank always had a car and driver during his visits to London. It was one of the desirable perks of his job in Berlin. We went off to a 'small City wine bar'; but because this was Frank Harrington's idea, the bar was not in the City. It was south of the Thames in that borough of London which is enigmatically called the 'the Borough'. In a street of rundown Victorian houses off the Old Kent Road its entrance was a doorway marked only by a small polished brass plate of the sort that marks the offices of lawyers and dentists. A long underground corridor eventually opened upon a gloomy cellar with heavy pillars and low vaulting. The brickwork was painted a shiny bottle-green. Small blackboards were chalked with tempting vintage wines that were today available by the glass. A bar counter occupied most of one wall of the largest 'room' and in the adjoining areas spotlights picked out small tables where shrill businessmen drank their vintage clarets and ports, nibbled at their expensive cold snacks and tried to look like tycoons avoiding the TV crews while concluding multi-million dollar City deals.

'Like it?' said Frank proudly.

'Wonderful, Frank.'

'Charming little place, eh? And no chance of meeting any of our people here, that's what I like about it.' By 'our' people he meant important Whitehall bureaucrats. He was right.

An old man dressed in appropriate wine cellar style – white shirt, bow tie and long apron – showed us to places set ready at the counter. Frank was obviously known and welcomed there, and when I saw how much he spent on a bottle of Château Palmer 1966 I could understand why. But Frank's discursive survey of the wine list, and its extravagant outcome, was part of the paternal role he had to demonstrate.

With due ceremony the bottle was opened, the cork sniffed. Poured, swirled and tasted. Frank puckered his lips, bared his teeth and pronounced it 'drinkable'. We laughed.

It was another immutable aspect of Frank's character that, along with his superlative wine, he ate, without adverse comment, yellowing Stilton, a desiccated hunk of pork pie and squashy white bread.

I could see he had something to tell me, but I contributed my share of office small-talk and let him take his time. When he'd eaten his segment of pork pie – each mouthful spread with a large dollop of fierce English mustard – he poured a second glass of claret for both of us and said, 'That bloody Zena.' He said it quietly but with feeling. 'I could kill her.'

I looked at him with interest. In the past Frank had always indulged Zena. Infatuated was the only word for it. 'Is she all right?' I asked

162

casually between pieces of pork pie. 'She was off to Frankfurt an der Oder, the last I heard of her. Werner was worried.'

He looked at me as if trying to decide how much I knew, and then said, 'She was running up and down on the Berlin–Warsaw express.'

'The "paradise train"? What for?' I asked but I'd already guessed the answer.

'Black market. You've been on that train: you know.'

Yes, I'd been on that train and I knew. Once over the Polish border it became an oriental bazaar. Black-market traders – and in the subtle nuances of East Bloc social life, brown- and grey-market traders too – moved from compartment to compartment buying and selling everything from Scotch whisky to Black & Decker power tools. I remember loud Polish voices and hands waving bundles of dollar bills and suitcases almost bursting with pop music records and cartons of Marlboro cigarettes. The 'paradise train' would provide plenty of opportunities to buy rare artefacts and manuscripts. 'What was Zena doing on the train?' I asked.

'They picked her up coming back . . . on the platform at Friedrichstrasse. It sounds as if they were tipped off.'

'Where is she now?'

'They let her go.'

'What did she have?'

'Old engravings. And an icon and a Bible. They confiscated everything and let her go.'

'She was lucky,' I said.

'She told them she'd happily take a receipt for only one item and they could divide the rest of it up between them.'

'I still say she was lucky. An offer like that to the wrong man and she'd end up with ten years for attempted bribery.'

Frank looked at me and said, 'She's a good judge of men, Bernard.'

There was no answer to that. I sipped the lovely Château Palmer and nodded. The wine was coming to life now, a wonderful combination of half-forgotten fragrances.

The anger that the memory of Zena had regenerated now subsided again. 'Silly little cow,' he said, with a measure of affection in his voice. He smiled. 'What about a pudding, Bernard? I believe they do a splendid apple crumble here.'

'No thanks, Frank. Just coffee.'

'Werner came to London. He went into the office on Friday and kicked up no end of fuss,' said Frank. 'I was in Berlin, of course. By the time the Deputy came through to me, I'd heard that Zena was safe at home. I was able to tell him that all was well. I came out of it smelling of roses.'

'I wasn't in London,' I said. 'I was in California.'

'I'll have a savoury: Angels on Horseback, they do it rather well here. Sure you won't have something?' When I shook my head he called to the waiter and ordered it. 'I must say, Sir Percy is doing a damned good job,' said Frank.

But I wasn't going to let him steer the conversation round to the Deputy's abilities or lack of them. 'Did you know that Bret is alive? I saw him in California.'

'Bret?' He looked at me full in the eye. 'Yes, the old man told me . . . a couple of days ago.'

'Were you surprised?'

'I was damned annoyed,' said Frank. 'The old man had actually heard me say that Bret was dead and had never contradicted me or confided the truth of the matter.'

'Why?'

'God knows. The old man can be a bit childish at times. He just laughed and said Bret deserved a bit of peace. And yet it was the old man who told me Bret was dead. It was a little supper party at the Kempi; there were other people present: outsiders. I couldn't pursue it. Perhaps I should have done.'

'But why say he was dead? What was it all about?'

'You saw him: I didn't. What did Bret tell you?'

'I didn't ask him why he wasn't dead,' I replied woodenly.

Frank preferred to see it as a harmless subterfuge. 'Bret was at death's door. What difference did it make? Perhaps it was better security to say he was dead.'

'But you don't know of any special reason?'

'No, I don't Bernard.' He drank some more wine, studied its colour and gave it great attention.

I said, 'Posh Harry button-holed me over there.' Frank raised an eyebrow. 'He wanted to tell me that, whatever Bret was doing, Washington like it.'

'Well, Posh Harry would know. He's landed a cushy job,' said Frank. 'They use him like an errand boy but his starting salary is more like a king's ransom.'

'Sounds just like my job,' I said, 'apart from the salary.'

'Why did Posh Harry button-hole you?'

'He said I was asking too many questions.'

'Mistaken identity. That doesn't sound at all like you,' said Frank with his laborious sense of humour. 'Questions about Bret?'

'Fiona was involved. Some kind of financial bore-hole. A lot of money. Prettyman was a signatory . . . probably a go-between for Central Funding.'

'You're not still going around saying Prettyman was murdered, are you? I looked at the homicide figures for Washington – it's horrific – and I know the Deputy arranged for the FBI to take a special look at the Prettyman killing. There's nothing to support the idea of it being anything but the casual sort of murder that muggers commit over there. A miserable business, but nothing there to justify any further investigation.'

'It seemed like a chance to find out more about Fiona.'

'I thought we'd found out all there was to find out about Fiona.'

'Her motives. Her accomplices and so on.'

'I'd imagine the Department followed up every lead, Bernard. For months afterwards they were sniffing around everyone who'd even heard of Fiona.'

'Even you?'

'No one is above suspicion in that sort of inquiry, Bernard. I would have thought you'd know that better than anyone. The D-G had the Minister breathing down his neck for week after week. I think that was what made the old man ill.'

'Is the D-G really ill?' I said. 'Or is it just a stunt so he can retire early or do something else?' Frank and the old man had been together during the war, they were close friends.

'Sir Henry's not around very much is he? They're probably letting him work out the contract for the sake of his pension. But I can't see him taking up the reins again.'

'Will Sir Percy take over?'

'No one knows at present. They say the PM is very keen to have someone from outside . . . putting one of the younger Law Lords into the driver's seat might ease the pressure on her to have a Parliamentary Committee sitting in judgment on everything we do.'

Frank's 'Angels on Horseback' arrived; a couple of cooked oysters wrapped in fried bacon and balanced on a triangle of warm toast. Frank liked savouries. At his dinner parties he stubbornly kept to the Victorian tradition of serving such salty, fiery tidbits after the dessert. 'Clears a chap's palate for the port,' he'd explained to me more than once. Now he ate it with a relish that he'd not shown for anything else except the claret, and said nothing until it was finished and the plate removed.

Then he wiped his lips with one of the huge linen napkins and said, 'You're miffed aren't you, Bernard?'

'Miffed?'

Frank grinned. 'You're put out. Don't pretend you're not.'

'Why would I be?' I insisted.

'I'm not such an old fool,' said Frank. 'You're remembering that recently I said Sir Henry hadn't been to Berlin for many years. Now I've told you that he was at the Kempi hosting a supper party and your ears are flapping. Right, Bernard?'

'It's not important,' I said.

'Exactly. The "need to know" principle: the only people told the secrets are those who need to know. Not those who simply want to find out.' He lifted the wine bottle to pour more but the waiter had done it already. The bottle was empty. 'A dead soldier!' said Frank holding the bottle aloft. 'And dead men tell no tales, eh? So what about a glass of Madeira?'

'No more for me, Frank,' I said, 'or 'I'll fall asleep over my desk.'

'Quite right. What was I saying? Yes, need to know.'

'You were telling me not to put my nose into matters not my concern.'

'Not at all. I was simply explaining to you the policy of the Department. I heard that you were on another of your crusades. I'm just trying to convince you that there's nothing personal about it. Any extra-curricular activities of that sort, by any employee, worries Internal Security.'

'Thanks.'

'You're not still trying to find a mole?' He smiled again. Frank had a resolute faith in his superiors, providing they had attended the right schools, or done well in the army. For him any such suspicions were genuinely comical.

'No, Frank. No, I'm not.'

'I'm on your side, Bernard.'

'I know you are, Frank.'

'But you do have enemies – or perhaps more accurately rivals – and I don't want them to be given an excuse to clobber you.'

'Yes.'

'You're what . . .' he paused no more than a moment, 'forty-four last birthday.' So Frank even had my birthdays registered in his memory.

I grunted an affirmative.

'With those two lovely kids you should be thinking more about your career, not seeing how many different ways you can upset the chaps on the top floor.' Another pause while that sank in. 'That's just a word to the wise, Bernard.' He dropped his napkin on the table and got to his feet to show me that his little lecture was at an end.

'Okay, Frank,' I said. 'Strictly need to know, from now onwards and for ever more.'

'That's a sensible fellow,' said Frank. 'Think of the children, Bernard. They rely on you now that Fiona's gone.'

'I know they do, Frank.'

I hadn't promised Frank Harrington anything I hadn't already promised myself. It seemed as if everyone in the Western world was keen to tell me that Bret Rensselaer was clean-cut, upright and true. It would have been stupid in the light of so many reassurances to continue poking and probing into the work he was doing before my wife Fiona defected.

That afternoon I went back to work with renewed vigour. By Thursday my desk – despite a second onslaught from Dicky's out-tray – was virtually clear. To celebrate my new freedom from extra-curricular detective work I took Gloria and the children for a weekend in the country. It was the new girl's first weekend off, having worked for us for no less than six days. We started early Saturday morning. In a ten-acre field near Bath we visited a 'Steam Engine Rally', a collection of ancient steam-powered machines: harvesters, roundabouts, tractors and rollers. All working. The children adored every moment of it. Gloria seemed to become even younger and more beautiful. Despite the constant presence of the children she kept saying how wonderful it was to have me to herself. I think it was the first time that all four of us discovered that we were a family, a happy family. Even twelve-year-old Sally, who'd hitherto shown a certain reserve about Gloria, now embraced her in a way I'd almost stopped hoping for. Billy – usually so prosaic and self-contained – took Gloria for a walk and told her the story of his life, and gave her a few hints and tips on handling the new girl's 'ratty' moods, which seemed to be frequent and varied. I was not optimistic about the girl. Doris, I now realized, wasn't so bad after all.

On Saturday evening we found Everton, a pretty little village. We had dinner in the hotel. It was a long drive back to London, so on impulse we stayed there overnight. Gloria with feminine foresight had put some overnight things, including the children's toothbrushes and pyjamas – and even the spare elastic bands Billy had to put on his wired teeth – into a bag in the back of the car. I remembered that weekend for ever afterwards. Gloria's future education was not discussed. On Sunday morning we all went for a walk across the fields without seeing another soul. We followed a stream that was filled with fish and ended up in a tiny riverside pub decorated with photos, theatre programmes, playbills and other mementoes of Maria Callas. We drank a bottle of Pol Roger. Billy got very muddy and Sally picked flowers. Gloria told me that it could be like this for ever and ever, and I allowed myself to believe her.

The children were growing up so fast that I could hardly reconcile this tall young fellow walking alongside me with the child that Billy had been only a few months ago. 'Girls don't understand about moving,' he said, as if continuing a conversation we'd already started, although in fact we'd been giving all our attention to the prospect of scrambling across a stream.

'Sally you mean?'

'Yes, she had these special friends at her school in Marylebone.'

'More special than your friends?' I said.

'It's all right now. She likes it at the new place. Girls only want to talk about clothes,' said Billy, 'so it hardly matters where she is.'

'And what about you?'

'I'm going to join the Vintage Car Club.'

I concealed my surprise. 'Are you old enough? Don't you have to have a car?'

'They will probably let me help . . . fixing the engines and pumping up the tyres.' He looked at me. 'I like our new house, Dad. So does Sally. So don't worry about us.'

'I'll go first,' I said and I took his arm and swung him across the water. He was heavy, damned heavy. I would never carry him on my shoulder again.

Now it was Billy's turn to extend a hand to me. And when I'd negotiated the steep muddy bank he said, 'I saw Grandpa the other day.'

'Grandpa?'

'He's got a new car, a Bentley turbo, dark blue. He came to the school.'

'You spoke to him?'

'He drove us home.'

'I thought nanny met you.'

'She came too.'

'I should have taken you to see him,' I said.

'He said we could have a holiday with him. He's going to Turkey. He might drive there: drive all the way.'

'Grandpa? You're not making this up, Billy?'

'Could we go, Daddy? Perhaps in the Bentley.'

'Did you tell Auntie Gloria about this?'

Billy looked contrite. He stared down at his muddy shoes and spoke quietly. 'She said I wasn't to tell you. She said you'd worry.'

'No, it's all right, Billy. I'll have to see about it. Maybe I'll talk to Grandpa.'

'Thank you, Daddy. Thank you, thank you!' Billy hugged me and said, 'Do you think Grandpa would let me sit up front?'

'Turkey is a long way away,' I said.

'There's Sally and Auntie Gloria,' he shouted. 'They must have found a way across the stream.'

So it had started. If it was simply a matter of going on holiday, why hadn't Fiona's father come to me and asked? Turkey: the USSR just a stone's throw away. The idea of my children being there with my meddlesome father-in-law filled me with dread.

Billy's little story cast a grey shadow across our idyll, but it was that bloody old fool Dodo who caused all the trouble to start again for me. At our first meeting in France I'd seen him as an amiable eccentric, a cultured old man who occasionally took too much to drink. Now I was to encounter the malicious, self-aggrandizing belligerent old drunk that was really him.

Although it was never confirmed, I have no doubt that Gloria's mother had spoken on the phone with him and poured her heart out about being neglected and lonely. Gloria said that in some unspecified time in the distant past the old man had always been fond of her mother. Dodo however told everyone he met in London that he was 'on business'. Whatever the reason, Dodo suddenly appeared in London, dressed up in an old but beautifully cut Glen Urquhart suit, and for the first week he was staying in the Ritz; a room with a view across the park.

He had contacts of course. Not only expatriate Hungarians and the people he'd known during his time in Vienna, but 'departmental' people too. For Dodo had been one of Lange's 'Prussians' and for some people that was commendation beyond compare. He'd also played some unrevealed part in the Budapest network of which Gloria's father had been a member before escaping across the border. And Dodo was a man who could be relied upon to keep in touch, so 'old pals' from the Treasury and the Foreign Office took Dodo to lunch at the Reform and the Travellers.

He liked to go to parties. He went to embassy parties, show-biz parties, 'society' parties and literary parties. How much time he spent with Gloria's parents, and whether they talked about me, and speculated upon the work I did, was never established. But by the time I encountered him again, Dodo was disturbingly well informed about me.

Dodo's invitation to have drinks with 'friends of mine – Thursday 6–8pm or as long as people stay . . .' at a smart address in Chapel Street near Eaton Square was scribbled on Ritz notepaper and arrived in the post on Wednesday morning. It was not adequate preparation for what we met there. We arrived at a small town house typical of London South West One. Outside in the street there were expensive motorcars, and a formally dressed butler opened the door. Many of the guests were in evening clothes and the women in long dresses. There was the sound of live music and loud laughter. Gloria cursed under her breath, for she was wearing a tweed suit that had been relegated to her working day, and she'd not had time to fix her hair.

The whole house was given over to the party and there were guests in every room. In the first room we entered there was a young man in evening clothes and two girls in party dresses seemingly engrossed in a large illustrated book. We left them to their reading and went to the next room, where two men were dispensing drinks from behind a trestle table. 'Hungarian wines,' said the barman when I asked what they were. 'Only Hungarian wines.' I took the biggest measure and, with drinks in hand, we went upstairs in search of the gypsy band. 'It's a zimbalon,' said Gloria when she heard the strings. 'Hungarian music. Wherever would Dodo find someone to play a zimbalon?'

'Now's your chance to ask him,' I said.

Dodo was coming down the upper stairs with a drink in his hand and a happy smile on his face. His hair had been neatly trimmed but the dinner suit he wore had seen better days and with it he was wearing blue suede shoes with odd laces and red socks. He grinned even more as he caught sight of us. He was not the sort of man who felt disadvantaged by old clothes. On the contrary, he seemed to like old garments as he liked old books and old wines, and he paid no regard to Gloria's distress at feeling so inappropriately dressed.

He'd already had a few drinks, and wasted little time on greetings before telling us about some of the distinguished guests. 'The chap you saw me with on the stairs is the power behind the scenes with Lufthansa. He used to have a room across the hall from me when I lived in that dreadful flea-pit in Kohlmarkt. Now of course it's one of the most fashionable streets in Vienna.' Dodo led us into the room where the gypsy band was playing. It was dark, with only candle-light flickering on the faces of the musicians and revealing the rapt expressions on the shadowed faces of the audience.

'Were they playing czardas?' Gloria said with such urgency that I suddenly saw a new aspect of her revealed.

170

'Of course, darling Zu,' said Uncle Dodo.

'How clever you are,' she told him, all worries about her clothes and hair forgotten. She gave him a sudden kiss and said something in Hungarian. He laughed. I felt excluded.

'Are you from Budapest?' I asked him, more to make conversation than because I truly wanted to know.

'All Hungarians are from Budapest,' he said.

Gloria said, 'Yes, we all love Budapest.' She looked at Dodo and reflectively said, 'You're right: all Hungarians feel at home in Budapest.'

'Even you gypsies,' said Uncle Dodo as the slow gypsy music started again, and Gloria began to sway with its rhythm.

'Did Zu ever tell you your fortune?' he asked me.

'No,' I said.

'With the tarot cards?'

'No, Dodo,' said Gloria. 'Sometimes it's better not to know what the cards say.' The subject was closed.

'Have you eaten?' he asked.

When told we hadn't he took us down to the kitchen, where two frantic cooks were slaving to produce a tableful of exotic dishes. Gloria and Dodo vied to name for me the different dishes, and disputed the authentic recipes for them. I tried everything. Veal strips in sour cream, garlicky stewed beef cubes with rich red paprika. There were breadcrumbed fried chicken pieces, boiled pork with horseradish and river fish flavoured with garlic and ginger. It was not the food I'd ever encountered in modern Hungary, a country where cooks render meat stew completely tasteless and measure each portion with government-issued 100-gram ladles.

'So you like Hungarian food, eh?' said Dodo. The only really good meal I'd eaten there was at a big country house near Lake Balaton. The food from Käfer in Munich, smuggled over the border. My host was a black-market dealer who had a security colonel as the guest of honour. But when Dodo said, as everyone has to say, that the Hungarians eat damned well nowadays and that Budapest is fast becoming a place for gourmets to journey to, I nodded and smiled and gobbled my food and said yes it was.

After eating we wandered off to find a place where we could sit down in comfort. The rooms had emptied as the gypsy band drew many of the guests upstairs. In the corner of this room there was a large table with posters and brochures advertising a new book called *The Wonderful World of Hungarian Cooking*. I realized that the egregious Dodo had

171

simply helped us to gatecrash a particularly lavish publication party. He saw me looking at the display and he smiled without offering any explanation. He was like that.

A waiter, in a smart white jacket and gold shoulder loops, came over to us and offered coffee and small jam-filled pancakes. Dodo declined the food so that he could go on with his stories about his youth in Vienna. 'The landlady – as mean and venal as only Viennese landladies can be – had a Schiele charcoal portrait hanging in her kitchen. Her kitchen! She'd wrung it from the poor devil for some insignificantly small debt. She didn't even appreciate her good fortune. The old cow! She'd rather have a coloured one, she kept saying. Well, all those coloured Schiele pictures had the coloured wash applied long after the drawing was complete. Anyone with any taste at all would have preferred this delicate charcoal portrait . . . a young woman. It might have been Schiele's wife Edith. That would have made it more valuable of course.' I tried not to listen to him. Another waiter looked into the room. Dodo hurriedly downed the rest of his whisky and waved an arm for more without even looking to see if the waiter had noticed. 'Those were the days!' said Dodo and sat back red-faced and breathing heavily. It wasn't clear whether he was referring to Schiele's times in Vienna, or his own. I didn't ask. There were not many respites from Dodo's remorseless chatter and I was beginning to get a headache.

But there was little chance of him remaining quiet for more than a moment or two. In record time a double Scotch arrived and Dodo was off on another story.

He was well oiled by the time the coffee waiter returned with offers of second helpings, and Dodo's cheerfulness had turned to his own jocular sort of sarcasm that was edged with hostility. He put a heavy hand on my shoulder. 'We know – those of us who have had the honour to work for Her Majesty's Government in positions of trust and danger – that fortune favours the brave. Right, Bernard right?'

He'd made similar remarks earlier in the evening and now I decided not to let it go. 'I'm not sure I know what you mean,' I said. Gloria glanced at him and at me, having heard the irritation in my voice.

'A field agent who is smart doesn't get paid off with an MBE and a big thank you. A clever field agent knows he can get a sackful of gold sovereigns and knows there are more where they came from. See what I mean?'

'No,' I said.

He hit my shoulder again in a gesture that he probably thought

172

fraternal. 'And so he should be. I'm not against that. Let the people at the sharp end make a bit of money. It's only right and fair.'

'Do you mean Daddy?' Gloria asked. Her voice too had a note of warning, had he been sober enough to heed it.

He made a hissing sound and said, 'Darling, what your dear father was paid – and what I got – was chicken feed compared with what those in the know can tuck away. If you haven't discovered that by now, Bernard will fill in the details.'

'I never met any rich field agents,' I said.

'Really, darling, no?' A slowly expanding artful grin illuminated his whole face.

'What do you mean?' I asked him.

'If you want to pretend you don't know what I'm talking about then so be it.' He drank his whisky, spilling some down his chin, and turned his head away.

'You'd better tell me,' I said.

'Damn it!' Big smile. 'You and that wife of yours.'

'Me and that wife of mine . . . what?'

'Come along, darling.' A knowing grin. 'Your wife was in Operations, right? She was a trustee for some kind of "sinking fund". She disappeared and so did all the money. Don't tell me that you didn't get your hands on a few pounds, or that some of it wasn't put away in the children's names somewhere.'

'Uncle Dodo, that's enough,' said Gloria sharply.

'Let him go on,' I said. 'I want to hear more.'

Like a cunning little animal his eyes went from one to the other of us. 'Berlin, the Ku-Damm,' he said meaningfully.

'What about it?'

'Schneider, von Schild und Weber.'

'It sounds like a bank,' I said.

'It is a bank,' said Dodo with great satisfaction, as if his argument was already won. 'It is a bank.'

'So what?'

'You want me to go on, darling?'

'Yes, I do.'

'Weber – grandson of the original partner – handles special financial matters for the British government. That's where your money came from.' He recited it as if I was trying to make a fool of him.

'Money? What money? And how did I get it?' I asked, convinced now that he was crazy, as well as drunk.

'You're a signatory to the account.'

173

'Rubbish.'

'It's a fact, and easily proved or disproved.' The waiter came and put a small plate of chocolate mints on the table. Dodo didn't offer them round, he peeled the wrapping from one, inspected it and popped it into his mouth.

'Who told you all this?' I said.

Still chewing the mint, Dodo said, 'I've known young Weber for years. When I was pensioned off from the Department, it was Weber's father who arranged everything for me.'

I looked at him, trying to see into his mind. He chewed at the mint and stared at me with unseeing eyes.

'You're always in Berlin, darling. Go to the Ku-Damm and have a word with Weber.'

'Maybe I shall.'

'The money is sure to be held in short-term bonds. It's the way they do it. A dozen or more signatories to the account – no less! – but there have to be two different signatures. You and your wife, for instance.'

'A dozen signatories?'

'Don't pretend to be so naïve, darling. That's a common device, we all know that.' The malevolence was unbridled now.

'Bogus names?' said Gloria.

'No need to use bogus names. Use real names. It disguises the purpose of the fund, and can give an account a bit of class if someone came snooping around. Providing the signatories don't find out about it.'

'Perhaps that's how Bernard's name got there,' said Gloria softly. She obviously believed Dodo's story.

Dodo's beady eyes were almost hypnotic. There was something frightening about him: a whiff of evil. 'If you never got your hands on any of that loot, you've really been swindled darling.' He laughed softly enough to show that it wasn't a possibility he would spare much time pondering. Then he looked at Gloria, inviting her to join in the fun. When she looked away he picked up his drink and swilled down a good mouthful of it. 'Must go,' he said. 'Must go.'

I didn't get up. I let the old fool heave himself to his feet and stagger off in the direction of the door. Gloria and I sat together in silence for a few minutes. Finally, in what was doubtless an attempt to pacify me about Dodo's offensiveness, she said, 'He was in a funny mood tonight.'

'And I needed a good laugh,' I said.

18

It was the day before I was due to pay my regular visit to Berlin that Werner phoned and asked me if I was coming with only hand baggage. I was. Such visits required only a document case big enough to hold pyjamas and shaving gear.

'Could you bring a parcel for me? I wouldn't ask you but Ingrid needs it urgently.'

'Ingrid?' I said. 'Who's Ingrid?'

'Ingrid Winter. Lisl's niece. She's helping me in the hotel.'

'Oh, is she?'

'It will be heavy,' he said apologetically. 'It's curtain material from Peter Jones, the department store in Sloane Square. Ingrid says she can't get the patterns she wants anywhere in Berlin.'

'Okay, Werner. I said okay.'

'Wait till you see the hotel. Almost everything is changed, Bernie. You'll never recognize the place.'

Oh, my God! I thought. 'And how is Lisl taking to all the changes?'

'Lisl?' said Werner as if having difficulty in remembering who Lisl was. 'Lisl loves the changes. Lisl says it's wonderful.'

'She does?'

'We wouldn't do anything Lisl didn't like, Bernie. You know that. It's Lisl we're doing it for isn't it?'

'And Lisl likes it?'

'Of course she does. I've just told you she does.'

'See you tomorrow, Werner.'

'And it's bulky too.'

'Stop worrying, Werner. I said I'll bring it.'

'If the customs want to charge: pay. Ingrid wants to get the curtain people started on the work.'

'Okay.'

'You'll stay the night? Here? We have room.'

'Thanks Werner. Yes, I'd like that.'

'Ingrid cooks a great Hoppel-Poppel.'

'I haven't eaten Hoppel-Poppel in twenty years,' I said. 'Not a real one.'

'With fresh herbs,' said Werner, 'that's the secret. Fresh eggs and fresh herbs.'

'Sounds like Ingrid is not getting in the way,' I said.

'Oh, no,' said Werner. 'She's not getting in the way at all.'

I cursed Werner, Ingrid and the roll of curtain material before I got to Berlin-Tegel. The customs man watched me struggling with it and just grinned. In Berlin even the customs men are human.

Werner struggled to get it into the back seat of his brand-new silver 7 series BMW, and even then the end of the roll of cloth protruded through the open window. 'This isn't you, Werner,' I said as he roared off into the traffic with an insolent skill that I never knew he had. 'This flashy new fashionable car with the big engine. It's not you, Werner.'

'I've changed, Bernie,' he said.

'Because of running the hotel?'

'That's right. Because I'm running the hotel,' and he smiled at some secret joke as he went weaving through the fast-moving traffic that fills West Berlin at this time of the morning. The heater was on, there were grey clouds overhead and it was beginning to rain. Berliners were still wrapped up in their heavy clothes. Spring doesn't hurry on its way to Berlin.

He dropped me at Frank Harrington's office. Once there I started to earn my pay. Frank, and a couple of his senior people, plodded with me through the latest London directives. Every few minutes there would be some expletive or a sharp intake of breath as I revealed a particularly impractical or ill-advised notion that had sprung from London Central's committees. I was only there to take the brunt of the Field Office objections, and everyone present recognized that as my role. So I smiled and shrugged and wriggled and prevaricated as they hit me over the head with their reasoned objections. And eventually the game ended and, our role-playing abandoned, I was allowed to resume the more comfortable persona of Bernard Samson, former Berlin Field Unit agent.

It was six-thirty by the time I finished work. The rain had come and gone but there was still a drizzle. The offices had emptied and the streets were crowded. Like rivers of flame the flashing signs made brightly coloured reflections in the wet streets. The car took me to Lisl Hennig's hotel. As I got out of it I stood in the rain and examined the façade apprehensively, but whatever changes Werner had wrought they were not to be seen from the street. This was the same old house that I'd known all my life. They were all the same, these Ku-Damm houses near the Zoo. They were built at the turn of the century by speculative builders for nouveau riche businessmen, and the adornments of bearded gods and buxom nymphs were chosen from catalogues by those who wanted to customize their homes. Some of them were grotesquely overdone.

Since then the Red Army's artillery, and the Anglo-American bombing fleets, had added further distinguishing features to all the buildings of Berlin, so that Lisl's house was scarred and chipped with a pox of splinter damage. The fighting done, the roof had been renewed and the decorated window surrounds of the upper storey had been shoddily and hastily patched up. Real repairs were forty years overdue.

I pushed through the heavy doors and went up the front stairs. The carpet was new, a rich ruby red, and the brass handrail was polished so it shone like gold. There was a sparkling chandelier over the stairs, and the elaborate mirrors on the walls had been cleaned so that they repeated my reflections a thousand times. No sooner had I started up the stairs than I heard the piano. 'Embrace me, my sweet embraceable you . . .' And then a sudden cascade of improvised harmonies. It was Werner at the keys. I would recognize his silky ebullient style anywhere. Something almost spiritual happened to Werner when he sat at the piano.

'. . . my irreplaceable you.' Someone had moved the grand piano so that it was in the centre of the 'salon'. And either it had been painted white or it was a new piano. There were comfortable soft brown leather armchairs too. And all Lisl's signed souvenir photos of Berlin personalities of long ago had been cleaned and newly arranged, one close upon the other, to cover the whole wall. Who wasn't represented there? Here were Einstein, Furtwängler, Strauss, Goebbels, Dietrich, Piscator, Brecht, Weil, and the photos were signed with extravagant declarations of affection for Lisl or for her mother – Frau Wisliceny – who'd once played hostess to all Berlin.

There were not many hotel guests to be seen. Just a party of four Danes who were chatting animatedly as if unaware of the music, and a desiccated couple sitting at the bar, drinking colourful cocktails and glaring at each other. I caught a brief glimpse of Ingrid Winter as she came down the stairs with a tray. She was wearing another of her stylish 'farmer's wife goes to church' dresses. This one had a high lacy neckline and long ankle-length skirt. She smiled at me.

Werner looked up from the keyboard. He saw me and stopped playing. 'Bernie! I told you to phone. I was going to come and fetch you. The rain is terrible . . .' He looked at my wet coat.

'Frank arranged a car.'

From her chair in the corner Lisl called imperiously, 'What are you doing, Bernd? Come and give your Lisl a kiss!' She was in good voice whatever her infirmities. She was dressed in a flowing red robe. Her face was carefully painted and she had false eyelashes which she fluttered like a schoolgirl. As I leaned over her, the smell of perfume was almost overwhelming. 'Your coat is wet, Bernd,' she said. 'Take it off. Tell Klara to dry it in the kitchen.'

'It's all right, Lisl,' I said.

'Do as I say, Bernd. Don't be so stubborn.' I took the coat off and gave it to the aged Klara who appeared from nowhere. 'And then go down to the boiler room. The pump is giving trouble again. I told them you were always able to mend it.'

'I'll try,' I promised without conviction. Lisl was determined to believe that I had spent my childhood performing all kind of mechanical miracles with the antiquated electricity system and the heating. It wasn't true of course. The idea that Bernd would fix it had been Tante Lisl's way of deferring as long as possible the inevitable replacement of aged and broken machinery.

'The hotel is looking wonderful, Lisl.'

She grunted as if she hadn't properly heard me, but the one-sided little smile she gave was enough to tell me how pleased she was with Werner's refurbishment.

I could not really be expected to cure the pump of its chronic arrhythmias: it was too far gone. Werner came with me to the subterranean boiler room and we examined the incontinent old brute with its dribbled rust and flaking insulation. In an attempt to justify Lisl's confidence in me I gave the meter a tap, rapped upon the pump casing and repeatedly touched warm pipes that should have been hot enough to scorch the flesh. 'It's not just the boiler. The whole system will have to be renewed,' said Werner. 'But I'm praying that it will last out till next year.'

'Yes,' I said. We continued to look at it in the hope that it would suddenly come to life. Then Ingrid Winter joined us. She said nothing. She just stood with us staring at the boiler. I stole a look at her. She was a handsome woman with a lovely complexion and clear eyes that shone when she looked at you. She glowed with the quiet vocational self-assurance that you hope to see in a nurse.

'It's not only the money,' explained Werner to no one in particular. 'We'll have to change all the pipes and radiators. There will be dust and noise in every room. If we had to do that in the winter it would mean closing the hotel completely . . .'

'Couldn't you change the boiler first?' I suggested. 'Then do the plumbing and piping piece by piece?'

'The plumber says we can't,' said Werner. He knew my ignorance about such matters was profound, and the look he gave me let me know that he knew. 'The sort of boiler we'll need for all the new bathrooms just wouldn't operate with the old plumbing. It's very old.'

Ingrid Winter said, 'Perhaps we should talk to some other heating engineer, Werner.'

Her accent was the rounded one of southern Bavaria: not one of those raw back-country accents, just a slight burr. But there was some inflection of Ingrid Winter's voice, some tiny change of pitch or of tone, that made me look at Werner. He stared back at me and gave the same mirthless smile that I remembered from our schooldays together. Werner once confided that it was his 'inscrutable' expression but 'guilty' would have been a better description.

Werner said, 'Old Heinmuller knows the system very well, Ingrid. It was him and his father who got it going again after the bombing in the war.'

'We'll have to do something, Werner dear,' she said, and this time was unable to conceal the intimacy in her voice. There existed between them that intuitive sympathy and unspoken understanding for which Goethe coined the word *Wahlverwandtschaft*.

'While we're here alone, Ingrid, tell Bernie about the Hungarian.' He touched her arm. 'Tell him what you told me, Ingrid.'

She hesitated and then said, 'Perhaps I shouldn't have said anything . . . But the other evening I was telling Werner about my mother and about that awful Hungarian man who lives nearby.'

'Dodo?' I said.

'Yes. He calls himself Dodo.'

'What about him?'

'He's a pathetic little man,' said Ingrid. 'I've never liked him. I wish Mother wouldn't invite him to the house. He's always leering at me.' She paused and looked closely at the lagging on the boiler pipes. 'It should be cleaned away,' she said. 'I hate dirt.'

'When was it last cleaned and serviced?' I said. She seemed ill at ease. I wanted to give her a chance to compose herself. 'I remember once a fellow came and replaced a nozzle or something, and it started working perfectly again.'

'We've tried nozzles,' said Werner impatiently. To Ingrid he said, 'Tell Bernie what they said about his father. And your father. It's better that he knows.'

Ingrid looked at me, obviously not wanting to tell me anything at all.

'I'd like to hear, Ingrid,' I said, trying to make it easier for her.

'You remember what I told you when you visited my mother?'

'Yes,' I said.

'I upset you. I know I did. I'm sorry.'

'No matter.'

'Most of what I know comes from Dodo: he's not a reliable source.'

'But tell me anyway.'

'All we've ever been told officially is that Paul Winter was killed after the war ended. An accidental shooting.'

'By the Americans,' said Werner.

'Let me tell it, Werner.'

'I'm sorry, Ingrid.'

'They said he was escaping,' she said. 'But they always say that, don't they?'

'Yes,' I said. 'They always say that.'

'It was Dodo who brought it all up again. He kept on at my mother about it. You probably know how he goes on. She listens to him. He was a Nazi; that's why he gets on so well with Mother.'

'A Nazi?' I said.

Werner said, 'He worked for Gehlen. The Abwehr recruited him at Vienna University. When the war ended, and Gehlen started working for the Americans, Dodo worked for Lange.'

I looked at Werner and tried to guess where my father fitted into all this. Werner smiled nervously, wondering perhaps if he should have brought up the subject of my father. Ingrid said, 'Dodo is a trouble-maker. Some people are like that, aren't they?' She looked at me expecting a response, so I nodded.

She said, 'He is a troubled, morbid creature. And he drinks too much and becomes maudlin. Full of self-pity. Hungarians have the highest suicide rate in the world: four times as many as Americans, and still climbing.' Ingrid broke off, doubtless remembering that Gloria was Hungarian too. Flushed with embarrassment she turned back to the boiler and said, 'We could get it cleaned and serviced and see what happens. Even when the pump keeps working, the water doesn't get really hot.'

'Lisl should have fitted a bigger one when she had it renewed,' I said. I reached out with both hands and slapped the boiler twice, encouragingly, as a Neapolitan platoon commander might slap the shoulders of a man ordered out on a dangerous mission. It made no difference.

For a moment I thought she'd decided to say no more, then she said, 'Dodo urged my mother to sue the American army.'

'That sounds like Dodo,' I said.

'Get compensation for Paul Winter's death. It was a shooting accident.'

'It's a bit late now, isn't it? And I thought you said he was shot while trying to escape,' I said.

'Ingrid said that the Americans gave that as their excuse.'

'Dodo told my mother the Americans would pay a lot of money. He said they wouldn't want it all dragged up.'

I grunted to express my doubts about Dodo's theory.

'My Uncle Peter was a colonel in the American army. He was shot in the same incident. Dodo says they were on a secret mission.'

I said. 'What's all this got to do with my father?'

'He was there,' said Ingrid.

'Where?' I said.

'Berchtesgaden,' said Ingrid. 'The inquiry said that he was the one who shot Paul Winter.'

'I think you must have made a mistake,' I said. 'Werner knew my father. He will tell you . . . anyone will tell you . . .' I shrugged. 'My father wasn't a shooting soldier. He worked in intelligence.'

'He shot Paul Winter,' said Ingrid coldly and calmly. 'Paul Winter was a war criminal . . . or so it was alleged. Your father was an officer on duty with the army that had conquered us. There probably was a cover-up. Such things happen when there are wars.'

I said nothing. There was nothing to say. She obviously believed what she said, but she wasn't getting angry. She was more embarrassed than angry. I suppose she had no recollection of her father. He was no more than a name to her, and that's how she spoke of him.

When it seemed that Ingrid didn't want to tell me more, Werner said, 'Dodo used the American Freedom of Information Act and had someone go through the US army archives. He didn't find much except that an American colonel and a German civilian – both named Winter – died of gunshot wounds. It was night and snowing. The court of inquiry recorded it as an accident. No one was punished.'

'Are you sure my father was there? Berchtesgaden was in the American Zone. Why would my father be with the Americans?'

'Captain Brian Samson,' said Ingrid. 'He gave evidence to the inquiry. A sworn statement from him – and many other documents were listed – but Dodo couldn't get transcripts.'

Werner said, 'That damned Dodo is a dangerous little swine. If he's determined to make trouble . . .'

He didn't finish. He didn't have to. Werner knew me well enough to appreciate how much any kind of blemish on my father's career would hurt me. 'I have no quarrel with Dodo,' I said.

'He resents you,' said Ingrid. 'After your visit to him he came to see Mama. Dodo really hates you.'

'Why should he hate me?'

'She's Hungarian, isn't she?'

'Yes, she's Hungarian,' I said.

'And Dodo's a close friend of her family,' said Ingrid with that decisive finality with which women pronounce upon such relationships. 'To him you are a meddlesome foreign intruder . . .' She didn't finish. There was no need to. I nodded. Ingrid was right and I knew the rest of it. It was easy to see myself as a middle-aged lecher taking advantage of this innocent young girl. It would be more than enough to trigger an unstable personality like Dodo. If it was the other way round, if that dreadful Dodo was living with the young daughter of one of my old friends I would be angry too. Angry beyond measure.

'Yes,' I said.

'There is always electricity,' said Ingrid.

'Is there?' I said.

'To heat the water,' said Ingrid. 'We could even have small electric heaters in each bathroom. Then water from the boiler would just be used by the kitchen.'

I was angry at the injustice of it. I looked at the boiler and kicked it at the place where the water went into the pump. Nothing happened so I kicked it again, harder. It gave a whirring sound. Ingrid and Werner looked at me with new respect. For a moment or two we watched to see if it would keep going, and Werner touched it to be sure it was getting hot again. It got hotter. 'What about a drink?' said Werner.

'I thought you'd never ask,' I said.

'And then Ingrid will cook the Hoppel-Poppel. She has everything ready. She cooks it in goose dripping.'

'If you want to wash or anything, your top-floor bathroom will have plenty of hot water. It gets it straight from the tank.'

'Thanks Ingrid.'

'Your room is just the same as it was. Werner wanted to have it repapered and refurbished as a surprise for you but I said it would be better to ask you first. I said you might like it just the way it is.' She looked at me and her face said how sorry she was to have been a conveyor of unpleasant news to Werner's friend.

'I like it the way it is,' I admitted.

'It was nice of you to bring the curtain material. Werner said you wouldn't mind.'

'In goose dripping, eh?' I said. 'Ingrid, you're some woman!'

Werner smiled. He was smiling a lot lately.

19

Having returned to London with the malicious drunken defamations of Dodo still ringing in my mind, I left a message for Cindy Prettyman or Matthews as, despite the Prettyman pension, she was determined to be known. She called back almost immediately. I expected her to be annoyed that I'd not contacted her earlier, but she had no recriminations. She was sweet and elated. Friday evening would be just fine for her. A hotel in Bayswater? Any way you want to play it, Cindy. Before I rang off, I heard the pips going. So she'd gone out of the office and called from a pay phone. Pay phone? And a hotel in Bayswater? Oh well, Cindy had always been a bit weird.

I had to talk to her. Dodo's various bombshells, whether true or entirely nonsense, made it all the more urgent. And delicate little assignments like nosing into the tight little empire of Schneider, von Schild and Weber was best done via the big anonymous facilities of the Foreign Office, rather than the parochial ones of my Department, where all concerned would know, or guess, that the request had come from me. I'd come out of it with a lot of explaining to do if any of Dodo's exotic allegations proved true.

'I hate the idea of you confiding in that woman,' said Gloria when I got home that night. 'She's so . . .' Gloria paused to think of the word, '. . . cold-blooded.'

'Is she?'

'When are you seeing her?'

'Friday evening, from the office.'

'Can I come?' said Gloria.

'Of course.'

'I'd be intruding.'

'No, do come along. She won't be expecting dinner. A drink, she said.' I watched Gloria carefully. In all our years together, my wife – Fiona – had never revealed a trace of jealousy or suspicion, but Gloria scrutinized every female acquaintance as a possible paramour. She especially examined the motives of unattached females, and those from my past. In all these respects Cindy loomed large.

'If you're sure,' said Gloria.

'You might have to close your ears,' I warned. I meant of course that there would be things said that I might later officially deny, that Cindy might later deny and that, if Gloria was going to be there, she'd have to be prepared to deny too. Deny on oath.

I think Gloria understood. 'I'll make a trip to the Ladies, that will give her a chance to say anything confidential.'

In the event Gloria decided not to come after all. I suppose she just wanted to see whether I'd say no, and how I would do it. I knew these little 'tests' she gave me were all part of her insecurity. Sometimes I wondered whether her plan to go to university was a test, designed to push me into a proposal of marriage.

Meanwhile, that Friday evening, I went to meet Cindy alone. It was just as well. Cindy was not in the best of moods. She was rather distracted, and it would not have improved her humour to see Gloria tagging along behind me. Cindy regarded her as a very junior civil servant who had come trespassing on the old friendship we'd once had.

'Your blonde interlude' is how Cindy referred to Gloria. It summed up what she thought of the relationship: its participants, its incongruity, its frivolity and its impermanence.

I let it go. She smiled in a fashion that both gave emphasis to what she'd said, and noted my passive acceptance of the judgment she'd passed. Cindy was an attractive woman, sexy in the way that health and energy so often are. But I'd never envied Jim. Cindy was too devious and manipulative and I was not good at handling her.

She was in a room on the second floor, sitting on the bed smoking a cigarette. Beside her there was a tray with a teapot and milk and cup – just one cup – and a big Martini ashtray with lots of lipstick-marked cigarette butts. Cindy's attempt to give up smoking seemed to have been abandoned. She asked me if I wanted a drink. I should have said no but I said I'd have a Scotch and I gave her the box with the photos of the tomb inscriptions and the deciphering attempts, or rather I tried to give it to her. She waved it away with a world-weary flick of splayed fingers. 'I don't want it.'

'Gloria said . . .'

'I've changed my mind. Keep it.'

'There's nothing there that will shed any light on Jim or his work,' I told her. 'I'll stake my life on that.'

She shrugged and touched her hair.

We wasted a lot of time getting the hotel staff to supply drinks, and while we waited we passed the time talking about nothing in particular. It was not my idea of an enjoyable evening out. Cindy had chosen the venue; The Grand & International, a seedy old hotel standing on the northern edge of Kensington Gardens, and hiding behind the Chinese restaurants of Queensway.

She'd coped with getting the room, paying in advance and arranging to occupy it without luggage and entertain a male visitor for an hour or so. I looked at her in her smart green and black plaid jacket and matching skirt. A boxy imitation fur coat was thrown across the bed. She wasn't tall and graceful in the way that Gloria was but she had a shapely figure and the way she was lounging across the pillows did everything to emphasize it. I wondered what they made of her downstairs at the desk. Or had reception clerks in this part of the town stopped wondering about their clients?

It was probably one of their best rooms, but it was a squalid place by any standards. A flyblown mirror surmounted a cracked blue china sink. The bed was big with a quilted headboard and grey sheets. Cindy said it was suitably anonymous but I think she was confusing anonymity with discomfort – many people did. But if 'The G and I', an amalgamation of two Victorian monoliths, was somewhere that Cindy was in no danger of seeing anyone she knew, the same could not be said for me.

I'd been in this place many times. I'd brought a lovely old Sauer automatic pistol to the bar there back in 1974. I'd sold it to a man named Max, who died saving my life during the last 'illegal' border crossing I ever made. It was a good little gun: its blueing had worn but it had been little used. At the time its double action was better than anything else manufactured, but I suspect that Max selected it because during the war it had been the favoured side-arm of high-ranking German officers. Max was as anti-Nazi as anyone I knew, but he had a healthy respect for their choice of weapons.

There was hardly a day went by when I didn't think of Max. Like Dodo, he had been one of 'Koby's Prussians', an American Prussian in this case, for Max was one of those curious men who drift from place to place and from job to job. And somehow the towns they go to are all troublespots, and the jobs they find are always violent and dangerous jobs, and usually illegal too. But Max was different to all the others, an ex New York police detective who fretted and worried and looked after everyone he worked with, especially me, the youngest member of his team.

Max had the most amazing memory for poetry, and his quotes ranged from Goethe to Gilbert & Sullivan librettos. I could usually keep up with his Goethe: 'Kennst du das Land, wo die Zitronen blühn?' but his Gilbert was what I always remembered him for:

'When you're lying awake with a dismal headache,
    and repose is taboo'd by anxiety,
I conceive you may use any language you choose
    to indulge in, without impropriety.'

and of course, sung with verve and derision, for Max was not an
uncritical admirer of his British allies:

'For he might have been a Roosian,
A French, or Turk, or Proosian,
    Or perhaps Ital-ian!
But in spite of all temptations
To belong to other nations,
    He remains an Englishman!'

Some of Gilbert's phrases were too cryptic for Max. As the only
Englishman with whom Max was regularly in contact, I was expected to
decipher all the 'Britishisms' and explain such Gilbertian inexplicables
as 'A Sewell & Cross young man, A Howell & James young man'. Poor
Max, I never did find out for him.

And yet there was nothing so inexplicable as Max himself. He was his
own worst enemy, if my father was to be believed, but my father
detested Max. In fact he detested 'Lange' Koby and all of what he called
'the American freebooters' in Berlin. That's why my father stayed clear
of them.

'Are you listening, Bernard?' I was jolted from my memories by
Cindy.

'Yes, Cindy, of course I am.' I suppose I hadn't nodded and smiled
frequently enough while listening to her small-talk.

'I'm going to Strasbourg,' she said suddenly, and she had all my
attention. With the cigarette still in her hand, she made a movement
that left a thin trail of smoke. Then she touched her hair; it was shiny
and curly and looked as if she'd been to the hairdresser. Her hair always
looked like that.

'On holiday?'

'God-a-mercy! Don't be stupid, Bernard. Who would go to
Strasbourg on holiday?' She waved the cigarette in the air, and a long
section of ash fell on the bedcover.

'A job?'

'Don't be so dense, Bernie. The bloody European Parliament is
there, isn't it?' As if angry about the marked bedcover, she stubbed her

cigarette into the ashtray, pushing it down in a punitive action that deformed its shape and left it bent and broken.

'And that's who you'll be working for?' I wondered why the hell she hadn't mentioned it earlier, when we'd been talking about the weather and how difficult it was to get seats for the Royal Opera House unless you knew someone. But then I realized that she didn't want to tell me until I'd had a drink.

'The pay is terrific and I'll have no trouble selling my place in London. The estate agent is putting an ad. in next Sunday's papers. He says I'll have hordes of people after it. He said that if I spent a bit of money on the kitchen and bathroom he could get another fifteen grand but I just don't have the time.'

'I see.'

'You're not interested, I suppose?'

'Interested in what?'

'What's wrong with you tonight, Bernie? Are you interested in buying my house? I'd sooner it went to a friend.'

'I've just moved,' I said. 'I couldn't go through packing and unpacking again.'

'Yes. I forgot. You're in the sticks. I couldn't live in the suburbs again. It's a slow death.'

'Yes, well, I'm not in a hurry,' I said. I felt as if I'd just been given a swift kick in the guts. I'd come here believing that Cindy was even more determined than I was to get to the bottom of the mystery, and now I found she wasn't interested in anything but selling her bloody house. Tentatively, and keeping Dodo out of it, I said, 'I think I might have had a breakthrough on the matter of the German bank account.'

She had started rummaging through the expensive crocodile handbag that never left her side. 'Good,' she said looking down into the handbag and showing little or no interest in anything I might have discovered.

I persisted. 'I hear it's a bank called Schneider, von Schild and Weber. I found it in the Berlin phone book. We'll need more details.'

'I'll be in Strasbourg as from the end of next week.' From the handbag she brought her pack of cigarettes and a gold lighter.

'That's damned sudden.'

Without hurrying she lit her cigarette, blew a lot of smoke high into the air and said, 'Sir Giles put my name in.'

'Creepy-Pox strikes again.'

She gave a fixed smile to show that she didn't think it was amusing but wasn't going to make an issue of it.

'It's a plum job. The vacancy came up out of the blue. That's why I got it. The fellow there now has AIDS. Two others shortlisted for the job are both family men with children at school. They wouldn't move at such short notice. No, I have to be there next week.'

I swallowed the angry words that first came to mind and said, 'But the last time we talked, you said that no one was going to shut you up. You said you weren't going to let it go.'

'I've got my life to lead, Bernard.'

'So now you want me to forget it?'

'Don't shout, Bernie. I thought you'd be pleased and wish me good luck. I'm not telling you what to do, Bernie. If you want to continue and solve your whodunnit I'm not going to stop you.'

Patiently and quietly I said, 'Cindy, this isn't a whodunnit. If it's what I think it is – what we both think it is – it's the biggest KGB penetration of our department ever.'

'Is it?' She didn't give a damn. It was as if I was talking to a stranger. This wasn't the woman who'd vowed to uncover the truth about the murder of her ex-husband.

'Even if I'm wrong,' I said, 'we're still talking about embezzlement on a mammoth scale: millions!'

'I thought the same at first,' she said very calmly and very condescendingly. 'But when you consider it more carefully, it's difficult to sustain the notion that there's some gigantic financial swindle, and that the D-G is in on it.' She smiled one of her saccharine smiles to emphasize the absurdity of that suggestion.

'The D-G has virtually disappeared.' I was exaggerating only slightly; he was very seldom in the office these days.

'Is the disappearance of the D-G all part of this plot?' she said with that same stupid smile on her face.

'I'm not joking, Cindy,' I said. Only with considerable difficulty did I resist telling the stupid bitch that she was the one who'd started all this. And she was the one who set up this discreet meeting and used a pay phone to do so.

'I'm not joking either, Bernie. So just answer my question: are you saying there is a conspiracy in which Bret Rensselaer, Frank Harrington, the Deputy and maybe Dicky Cruyer are all implicated?'

It was such an absurd misrepresentation of anything I'd ever thought that I didn't know where to start refuting it. I said, 'Let us suppose that just one really irreproachable individual . . .'

'The D-G,' she said, like a particularly haughty member of the audience choosing a card for an amateur conjuror.

189

'Okay. For the sake of argument, let's say the D-G is a party to some big swindle. Surely you see that the structure of the Department is such that no one would believe it. Frank, Dicky, Bret and all the others would simply stand firm and say everything's fine.'

'And you're the little boy telling the Emperor he has no clothes?'

'Just because everyone says there is nothing wrong, we shouldn't refuse to examine it more closely. Strange things happen in the place where I go to work. I'm not talking about the Ministry of Education or the Department of Health and Social Services, Cindy. I'm talking about the place the rough stuff is arranged.'

'If you want my advice . . .' She slid off the bed and stood up. Having eased her shoes half off her feet she squeezed back into them, putting all her weight on first one foot then the other. 'You should stop beating your head against a brick wall.'

'You make it sound like I enjoy beating my head against a brick wall.'

She smoothed her lapels and reached for her coat. 'I think you want to destroy yourself. It's something to do with Fiona leaving you. Perhaps you feel guilty in some way. But all those theories you dream up . . . I mean, they never come to anything do they? Don't you see that inside you there is some kind of worm that is eating you up? I suppose you desperately want to believe that all the world is wrong, and only Bernard Samson is right.' She snapped her handbag lock closed. 'Forget all this crap, Bernard. Life is too short to rectify all the world's wrongs. It took me a long time to see that, but from now on I live my life. I'm not going to change the world.'

'There's one small thing you could do before you go to Strasbourg.'

'Not before I go, and not after I get there either. I don't want to know, Bernie. Do I have to draw a diagram for you?'

I looked at her and she stared back. She was not in any way hostile, not even tough. She was just a woman who'd made up her mind. There was no way to change it. 'Okay, Cindy. Have a good time in Strasbourg.'

She smiled, visibly relieved by my friendly tone of voice. 'God willing, I'll find some nice young sexy Frenchman and get married.' She drew the window curtain aside to see if it was raining. It was. She buttoned up her coat. 'Do you want to buy the Mercedes, Bernard? Dark green 380 SE. It's only two years old; it does twenty-five to a gallon.'

'I can't afford it, Cindy.'

'That's on the motorway, of course. In town, more like twenty.' When she got to the doorway she stopped. Just for a moment I thought she was going to say she'd help after all but she said, 'The steering is on

190

the wrong side for the Continent, and I can buy a tax-free car when I'm there, so I'll have to sell it.'

We walked down the stairs in silence. When we got to the brightly lit foyer she stopped and delved into her handbag until she found a white plastic rain hat. There was no one there, even the reception desk was unmanned. Cindy walked over to look in the mirror and be sure her hair was tucked away. 'Everything else I'm taking with me,' she said while looking at herself in the mirror. 'Furniture and TV and video and hi-fi. That sort of thing is very expensive in France.'

'Your TV won't work in France,' I said. 'They have a different system.'

She didn't look at me. She turned and pushed the main door open and went out into the night without saying goodbye. The heavy doors slammed behind her with a soft thud. She thought I was trying to annoy her.

It was a long walk to where I'd left the car. The street was noisy and crowded with people and cruising traffic of all kinds. Young couples, skinheads, punks, freaks, whores of all sexes, cops and robbers too. Painted faces whitened under the bright neon. I found my car still in one piece. No sooner had I pulled away from the kerb than another car was taking my place in the narrow parking slot.

The rain got heavier. My old Volvo stuttered and choked in the heavy downpour. Maybe they didn't have rain in Sweden. So I thought about Cindy's Mercedes all the way home: British racing green; paintwork waxed so that even Mr Gaskell approved, and a Vee-eight engine. I wondered what she was asking for it.

When I got to Balaklava Road the downstairs lights were out. The children were in bed and nanny was watching a TV play in her room. Gloria wasn't there. I'd forgotten that she'd changed the night for visiting her parents to Friday. She probably never had the slightest intention of joining me and Cindy for our little drink and discussion in town. Gloria knew she could depend upon me to forget which evenings she went out.

I opened a tin of sardines and a bottle of white burgundy. I put a tape of *Citizen Kane* in the video and ate my supper from a tray on my knees. But I spent all the time thinking about Bret Rensselaer's anger, Jim Prettyman's murder, Dodo's diatribe and Cindy Matthews' sudden change of mind.

By the time Gloria got home I was in bed. I wasn't surprised that she was late. I guessed that it was something to do with this 'crisis' that her mother said threatened their marriage.

191

Whatever domestic crisis she'd attended, Gloria didn't arrive back low-spirited. In fact she was bubbling with excitement. I knew what she'd be like even before she came into the house. Her old yellow Mini could only just be fitted into the space between the kitchen and the fence to which our neighbour's cosseted wistaria clung. Even then it meant squeezing out on the passenger side. This tricky feat was not something that Gloria always felt willing to attempt, but on this night I heard her bump over the kerb and, with no slackening of speed, on to the garden path and stop with a squeal of brakes. She gave the accelerator a little jab of satisfaction before switching off the ignition. I could visualize the smile on her face.

'Hello, darling,' she said as she tiptoed into the bedroom still carrying the plastic bag that I knew contained one of her mother's Hungarian walnut cakes and a tub of home-made liptoi cheese, pickles and all sorts of other things that her family felt she needed regular supplies of when not living at home. 'How was Mrs Prettyman?'

'Suddenly silent.'

Gloria looked at me, trying to read the expression on my face. 'Has someone put a gun at her head?'

I laughed. 'Right,' I said. 'A golden gun. Suddenly she's been offered a plum job with the Strasbourg bureaucrats, lots of money, little or no tax. God knows what else.'

'You don't think . . .'

'I don't know.'

'I wouldn't like to be trying to bribe her,' said Gloria.

'Because she'd ask for more than you had to offer?'

'No, I don't mean that. I just think she'd be touchy. I'd worry that she might write it all down and take it to the newspapers.'

'It's just a soft job in Strasbourg,' I said. 'Not even the reporters from the tabloids could make that into a bribe, unless Cindy declared herself so incompetent that the offer was ridiculously inappropriate.'

'I suppose so.' She put the bag of Hungarian delicacies on the dressing table and began to undress.

'What is it?' I asked, for she had the sort of self-satisfied grin on her face that usually meant I'd done something careless, like locking the cat in the broom closet or absent-mindedly picking up the milkman's money and putting it in my pocket.

'Nothing,' she said, though I could tell by the wanton abandon with which she disrobed and threw aside her clothes that there was some kind of joke to share. But I thought it would be something about her parents or

192

the latest about the egregious Dodo, who'd now been given temporary rent-free use of a comfortable little house near Kingston on Thames.

'That bank,' she said as she got between the sheets and huddled against me. 'Guess who owns that bank?'

'Bank? Schneider, von Schild . . .'

'And Weber,' she supplied still grinning at her cleverness and at the joke that was to come. 'Yes, that's the bank, my darling. Guess who owns it.'

'Not Mr Schneider, Mr von Schild and Mr Weber?'

'Your precious Bret Rensselaer, that's who.'

'What?'

'I knew that would bring you fully awake.'

'I was already fully awake.'

'At least, it belongs to the Rensselaer family.'

'How did you find out?'

'I didn't have to raid the Yellow Submarine darling. It's public knowledge. Even German banks have to make ownership declarations. My teacher at the Economics class got it from an ordinary data-bank listing. He phoned me back in half an hour and had its history.'

'I should have checked that out.'

'Well, you didn't; I did,' she chuckled like a baby.

'You're such a clever girl,' I said.

'So you've noticed?'

'That you're a clever girl? Yes, I've noticed.'

'Don't do that . . . at least, don't do it yet.'

'The Rensselaer family?'

'Are you ready for the details? Hold on to your hat, lover, here goes. Back in 1925 a man named Cyrus Rensselaer bought shares in a California bank group. Bret and his brothers worked for them, I guess they had directorships or something. I can get more details . . . Then, sometime in the Second World War, the old man died. Under the terms of his Will the shares went into a trust, of which Bret's mother was the beneficiary. In a complicated share issue and merger in 1953 the Californian bank became a part of Calibank (International) Serco which began large-scale buying of other banks. One shareholding they acquired gave them a majority holding in Schneider, von Schild and Weber.'

'Anything else?'

'Anything else, he says! My darling, you're insatiable. Has anyone ever told you that?'

'I plead the Fifth Amendment,' I said.

193

20

Only desperation would have provoked me to set out on a journey to see Silas Gaunt that Saturday. He'd retired from the Department many years before but he remained one of the most influential individuals in what Dicky Cruyer delicately called 'the intelligence community'. Uncle Silas knew everything and knew everyone. He had been close to my father over many years; was distantly related to my mother-in-law, and was Billy's godfather.

Perhaps I should have visited him more regularly, but he was devoted to my wife Fiona, and her departure had distanced Silas from me. He wasn't likely to appreciate my arriving arm in arm with Gloria, and yet it was a damned long journey to do alone. Now I was doing it alone, and as I drove through a pale prostrate landscape that had still not loosened the shackles of winter, I had a chance to think about what I might say to him. How did I start? Jim Prettyman was dead and Bret Rensselaer was suddenly alive, but neither metamorphosis was going to help me. Dodo was telling anyone who'd listen that I'd been conspiring with Fiona to swindle the Department; while my prime helper, Cindy Prettyman, was suffering the selective amnesia that valued promotion sometimes brings.

'Uncle' Silas lived at 'Whitelands' a middle-sized farm in the Cotswolds, a picturesque place of tan-coloured stone with ill-fitting doors, creaking floorboards and low beams that split the skulls of the tall and unwary. Silas must have been exceptionally wary, for he was a giant of a man and so fat that he was scarcely able to squeeze through some of the narrower doors. Some nineteenth-century tycoon had redone the interior to his own taste, so that there was a surfeit of mahogany and ornamental tiles, and a scarcity of bathrooms. But it suited Silas, and somehow it was difficult to imagine him in any other environment.

In the day time he kept busy. There were discussions with his farm manager, and his house-keeper Mrs Porter, and with the lady from the village who came to deal with his mail but who seemed unable to deal with any telephone caller without coming downstairs and dragging Silas upstairs to the one and only phone.

I was sitting waiting for Silas to return from upstairs. The narrow stone-framed windows let in only a thin slice of grey afternoon light. The log fire burning brightly in the big stone hearth filled the air with a smoky perfume and provided the light by which to see the drawing room with its battered old sofa and uncomfortable chairs, their shapes only vaguely apparent under the baggy chintz covers. In front of the fire there was a tray with the remains of our tea: silver teapot, the last couple of Mrs Porter's freshly made scones and a pot of jam with a handwritten label saying 'Whitelands – strawberry'. It might have been a hundred years ago but for the big hi-fi speakers that stood in the far corners of the room. This was where Silas spent his evenings listening to his opera records and drinking his way through his remarkable cellar.

'Sorry about these interruptions,' he said as he fiddled to close the ancient brass door latch. He clapped his hands and then went to warm them at the fire. 'Fresh tea?'

'I've had enough tea,' I said.

'And it's too early for a drink,' said Silas.

I didn't reply.

'You tell me a lot of things,' he said, pouring the last tepid remains of the tea into his cup. 'And you want me to make them fit together nicely, like pieces of a jigsaw.' He sipped the cold tea but pulled a face and abandoned it. 'But I don't see any causal connection.' Sniff. 'Either it's much colder today or I'm getting flu . . . or maybe both. So this accountant fellow, Prettyman, was killed in Washington by some hooligan, and now his wife has been promoted? Well, jolly good, I say. Why shouldn't the poor woman be promoted? I've always thought we should look after our own people to the best of our ability.'

There was a long silent rumination until I helped him remember the rest of it. 'And then there was Bret Rensselaer,' I said.

'Yes, poor Bret. An awfully good chap, Bret; injured on duty. An episode in the very best traditions of the service, if I may say so. Yet, you seem indignant that he survived.'

'I was surprised to see him arise from the dead.'

'I can't see what you're getting at,' said Uncle Silas. 'Aren't you pleased by that either?' he scratched his crotch unselfconsciously. He was a strange old devil; fat and dishevelled, with a coarse humour and biting wit that was not funny to those who found it directed at them.

'There are too many things happening . . . funny things.'

'I really don't follow your reasoning Bernard.' He shook his head. 'I really don't.' Uncle Silas had always been able to twist the facts to suit his hypothesis. 'It's not a bit of good, you sitting there glaring at me, dear boy.' He paused to take out a big red cotton handkerchief and blow his nose violently. 'I'm trying to prevent you making a bloody fool of yourself.'

'By doing what?'

'By bursting in on poor old Dodo and giving him the third degree.' Old Silas must have been the last living person still using expressions like third degree.

'Did you know him well?'

'Yes, I remember him well,' said Silas, sitting back in his armchair and staring into the fire. 'His real name was Theodor – Theodor Kiss – so he preferred to be Dodo. A keen worker: bright as a button. A good science degree at Vienna University and a good administrative knack. Lots of languages and dialects too. Dodo could effortlessly pass himself off as a German. Or as an Austrian. Effortlessly!'

'Amazing,' I said.

'Oh, I know you can do the same thing, Bernard. But it's quite an unusual feat. Not many Germans can do it, as I know to my cost. Yes, Dodo was a remarkable linguist.'

'He worked for Gehlen,' I said, to remind Silas that this paragon was an ex-Nazi.

'Most of the best ones had worked for him. They were the only experienced people available for hire. Of course, I never used any of them,' said Silas, perhaps wanting to deflect my wrath. 'Not directly. I stayed clear of Gehlen's ex-employees. Lange Koby took him away with the rest of his gang . . . What did he call them. . . ?'

'Prussians,' I supplied.

'Yes, "Koby's Prussians", that's right. How could I forget that? My memory is going wonky these days.'

I said nothing.

'Your father too. He wouldn't go near any of them. He was upset when you worked for Lange Koby.'

'I teamed up with Max,' I said. 'Koby came as part of the deal.'

Silas sniffed. 'You should have stayed with your father, Bernard.'

'I know,' I said. He'd touched a nerve.

We sat silent for a few minutes. 'Your Dodo is all right,' said Silas, as if he'd been thinking deeply about it. 'Perhaps a bit too keen to demonstrate his valour, but so were all the ones who'd changed sides. But Dodo, when he settled down he became a loyal, sensible agent; the sort of fellow I would have expected you to be specially sympathetic towards. A man like that must be excused an indiscretion now and again. What?' He got out his handkerchief and wiped his nose.

'Indiscretion?'

196

'I'd say the same for you, Bernard,' he added before my indignation boiled over. 'Have said it, in fact,' he persisted, to make sure I knew I was indebted to him.

He stopped, perhaps waiting for some gesture of appreciation or agreement. I nodded without putting too much into it. Ever since arriving here I had been considering ways to ask him about the mad allegations about my father. Silas had known my father as well as anyone still alive. They'd served together in Berlin, and in London too. Silas Gaunt could solve just about any mystery that arose out of my father's service if he wanted to. If he wanted to; there's the rub. Silas Gaunt was not a man much given to revealing secrets, even to those entitled to know. And this wasn't the time to ask. That much was clear just from looking at the old man's face. He was not enjoying my visit, despite all the smiles and nods and pleasantries. Perhaps he was just worried about me. Or about Fiona or about my children. Or about Dodo. 'I know you have, Silas,' I said. 'I appreciate it.'

'I want you to promise not to go in there ranting and raving,' said Silas. 'I want you to promise to go along there and talk to him in a conciliatory manner that will make him see your point of view.'

'I'll try,' I said.

'We all have a lot of old comrades in common: the Gebhart twins, "Baron" Busch who took you to Leipzig, Oscar Rhine who said he could swim across Lübeck Bay but couldn't . . . ' Silas had tried to make light of his list of departed colleagues but couldn't maintain the levity. He wiped his nose and tried again. 'We all grieve for the same old friends, Bernard: you, me, Dodo . . . No sense in quarrelling amongst ourselves.'

'No,' I said.

'He's been in the business even longer than you have,' said Silas, 'so don't start talking down to him.' This was Silas at his avuncular worst. Sometimes I wondered if he ever spoke to the D-G like this, for I knew that Silas regarded all of us as children attempting a man's job at which he'd excelled.

'No, Silas,' I said, and I must have allowed some trace of my scepticism to show, for there was a twitch of the face that I'd learned to recognize as a sign of anger to come.

But the anger didn't come, or at least it didn't show. 'Tell me again about Bret Rensselaer; is he coming back to work?'

'No chance,' I said. 'He's too sick and too old.'

'They say he wanted Berlin,' said Silas.

'Yes,' I said. 'At the time the rumours said Frank would get his K and retire, and Bret would get Berlin.'

197

'And then Bret would get his K and retire,' said Silas, completing the scenario that everyone had said was inevitable up to the time that things went wrong and Bret got shot. 'So what was the long-term plan for Berlin?'

I looked at him and wondered what everyone in the Department must have wondered at some time or other: why Silas Gaunt had never got the knighthood that usually came with such retirements. 'Come along, Silas,' I said. 'You know more about what goes on in the minds of the men on the top floor than I will ever find out. You tell me.'

'Seriously, Bernard. What do you think was the plan? If Frank had been bowler-hatted and replaced by Bret, Bret could only have had that job until his retirement came up. And they could hardly have asked for a special dispensation to keep Bret there.'

'I suppose you are right,' I said. 'I never get to thinking about such long-term possibilities.'

'Then that's a pity,' said Silas, lowering his voice as if saying something confidential and important, a trick he'd developed from his briefing days. 'Perhaps if you gave your mind to such things you wouldn't be getting yourself into such deep water as you are now in.'

'Wouldn't I?'

'Could Dicky Cruyer hold down the Berlin job?' His voice was still soft.

'He wants it,' I said.

'Dicky has no German contacts does he? None that are worth a damn anyway. The Berlin job must have someone with flair, someone with a feeling for the streets, someone who can smell what's going on, quite apart from the departmental input.'

'Someone like Frank?'

'Frank, like your father, was a protégé of mine. Yes. Frank has done well there. But age slows a man down. Berlin is a job for someone more resilient, someone much younger who gets out and about. Frank spends too much time at home playing his damned gramophone records.'

'Yes,' I said, and nodded seriously. Gramophone records? Silas knew about Frank's extra-marital amours as well as I did but he preferred to tell the story his way. He was always like that.

'I get the idea, Silas,' I said. The idea was that if I was a good little chap, and didn't keep spreading alarm and despondency with my extra-curricular questions, I might get Berlin. I didn't believe it.

'Do you? I'm so glad,' he said. I got to my feet. 'As a favour to me, Bernard, could you hold off for a couple of days or so. . . ? On the Dodo fellow.'

'I was going over there tonight. He's always home on a Saturday evening,' I said. 'There's some programme he watches on TV.'

'Just until next week. A cooling off period, eh? Better for all concerned, dear boy.'

I looked up at Silas. He was giving me good advice but I was wound up tight and ready to confront the little swine. He stared at me, not giving an inch. 'If you insist,' I said reluctantly.

'You won't regret your decision,' said Silas. 'I'll talk to the old man about it. And about you.'

'Thanks for giving me your time, Silas.'

'Why don't you hang on for supper? We'll have a game of billiards.' He held his handkerchief in front of him as if transfixed. For one awful moment I thought he was having a heart attack or some other serious affliction, but then his nose twitched and he sneezed.

'You should be in bed, Silas,' I said. 'You've got flu.'

He didn't persist. Silas was old and set in his ways. He didn't like visits at short notice and he didn't want unscheduled dinner guests. He wiped his nose and said, 'No news from your wife?'

'Nothing.'

'It must be difficult for you but don't give up,' said Silas. 'When are you going to bring the children to see me?'

I looked up in surprise. It had never occurred to me that Silas would welcome such an intrusion into his jealously guarded little world. 'Any time,' I said awkwardly. 'Today week? Lunch?'

'Splendid!' He looked out of the window and said, 'I'll tell Mrs Porter to be sure the sirloin is underdone. And a Charlotte Russe to follow? Billy likes that doesn't he?'

The old man's eye for detail could still astound me; so he'd noticed Billy's appetite for Mrs Porter's rare roast beef and the Charlotte Russe. 'Yes, we all do,' I said.

'We don't have to tempt you; you like everything,' said Silas dismissively. 'Sometimes I wish you were more selective.'

I took it as a comment upon aspects of my life other than my appetite for Charlotte Russe, but I didn't pursue it.

At the time I undertook not to see Dodo I meant it. But it was a resolve hard to stick to as I drove back to London, turning over in my mind everything that had happened.

By the time I got to the outer suburbs I had decided to disregard Silas' request to lay off Dodo. All my instincts told me to go for him and go now.

Dodo had emerged as a truly remarkable freeloader, so I was not surprised that he'd obtained the rent-free use of a house. It belonged to a Hungarian couple he'd met through Gloria's parents. The owners were having a winter holiday in Madeira. It was an elegant old house in Hampton Wick. Positioned between the river and the grounds of Hampton Court Palace, it stood in a quiet back street of early Victorian houses of varying shapes and sizes.

It was growing dark by the time I arrived, the sky purple with that hazy moon that is said to portend rain. The street lamps showed that number eighteen stood alone and back from the road. Rising over its eight-foot-tall garden wall I could see its intricate ironwork balcony, complete with curving pagoda-style top. The contrived seclusion, and the delicacy of the design, immediately suggested it as the sort of villa in which some alluring concubine might have passed her long lonely days.

The wrought-iron gate gave on to a small front garden. I stood there a moment and looked again at the house. The curtains were carelessly closed so that chinks of light were to be seen in almost every window. It was a bitterly cold night and the only sounds to be heard came from cars going along the main road towards Kingston Bridge.

I went up the steps to the bright green front door. There was no doorbell so I hammered loudly, using a brass lion's-head knocker. There was a long time before I heard movement inside. I had the feeling that someone might have gone to one of the upstairs windows to see who it was. Eventually the door opened to reveal Dodo. He was dressed in a white roll-neck sweater, grey cotton jacket, grey cord slacks and loafers with leather tassels. 'Ahhh! Good evening!' he said. 'So you tracked me down.'

'Can I come in?'

He didn't answer immediately. He clung to the door edge and looked me up and down. 'Very well,' he said without much enthusiasm. 'Come in and have a drink.'

He led the way through the hall, past the bentwood coatstand and the big mirror. He didn't suggest that I should take off my overcoat. He ushered me into a room at the back. It was a large room with a grand piano, a couple of easy chairs and some small antique tables cluttered with an array of snuff boxes and chinaware. The Victorian wallpaper provided a jungle of printed vegetation and the only light came from a brass fixture that directed all its rays upon the sheet music displayed on the piano.

The room smelled musty and unused, the window was shuttered and the piano wore a grey sheen of dust. Dodo turned to face me. 'Now what is it?' he said. His voice was hard and belligerent and his eyes glittered fiercely. I guessed he'd been on the booze but you could never be sure of anything with Dodo.

'Listen, Dodo,' I said. 'We'd better get one thing straight . . .'

He had moved as if reaching past me, but smoothly and without warning he straightened, and bringing his fist forward slammed me in the guts with enough force to wind me. As I bent forward, choking for air, the edge of his hand came down upon the side of my neck. It was a very well-placed karate chop and the pain of it set fire to every nerve in my body.

As I was doubled over and coughing my dinner up he lashed out with a vicious kick. But with my head down I saw his foot coming and lurched aside so that his shoe did no more than graze my arm.

My overcoat had protected me against the full effect of his blows. Had Dodo got me to take off my overcoat in the hall I would by then have been laid out. Another kick but wide of the mark this time. I reached out in the hope of grabbing his foot but he was too fast for me. Too fast and too experienced. I had underestimated Dodo all along the line: underestimated his brains, his influence, his malevolence and his physical strength.

Still in pain I straightened up. I backed away from him and felt the piano behind me. I welcomed the support it provided and for a moment rested against it and waited for Dodo's next move. The light from the piano was fully in his eyes. His kicks and punches had caused him some exertion but he was reluctant to give me any chance to recover. He came at me again, slower this time, his hands high and his feet well apart. I took a deep breath; I knew if he placed them right, a couple of those chops would put my lights out.

'Gaah!' He gave a sudden cry and lunged at me. Or was it just a feint to see how I'd react? I sank down a little and kicked out at his guts but didn't connect. My foot made an arc in empty air but the threat of it made him hesitate. Then he ducked his head and reached out with a jab that hit my arm and sent a pain down to my hand. But I went for him then. I went in close swinging my fist, embracing him with a punch that landed in his kidney and produced an angry little grunt of pain. For a moment we stood grappling like partners on the dance floor, then he pushed away, hammering a couple of blows at my chest as we broke.

He stepped back and was almost lost in the shadows of the dark room. We stood apart panting heavily and staring at each other. The element of surprise was gone and I was getting his measure. Dodo was no boxer. If I could get him toe to toe, trading blows, I could knock him unconscious. But that was a big if. From the street there came the sound of a car moving slowly. Dodo cocked his head to listen but after a moment or two the car revved up and moved on.

Click! The flick-knife was in his hand, and as he inched forward the light shone on the blade. He was holding it low and pointed upwards, the way a man holds a knife when he means business. 'I'll teach you a lesson, Samson,' he promised in that low growl he produced when being especially venomous. 'Slice you up!' His face was flushed and he was over-salivating.

I moved sideways. Now the support that the piano had provided became a trap. I didn't want to be impaled. I dragged my scarf from my neck and flipped it around my hand to provide a flimsy glove. I edged sideways more. From the corner of my eye I chose the largest glass ornament within reach, a big cut-glass pineapple with silver leaves. I grabbed it and threw it with all my force. It hit him in the chest and he grunted and reeled back, banging against a table so that a dozen pieces of chinaware went crashing to the floor. But it didn't provide me with the chance I was hoping for. Dodo swore softly, some Hungarian curse, and kept his balance without looking round to see what he'd done.

When he came at me again I was trying to unlock the old-fashioned shutters and get to the french windows that opened on to the garden. I turned back to face him and kicked high trying to knock the knife from his hand but he was ready for that. He avoided the blow and smiled with satisfaction.

He closed again. My back crashed against the shutter and behind it a pane of glass cracked like a pistol shot. Dodo's knife came at me, ripping through my coat. I grabbed at his wrist and for a moment held it. We were close: he stank of whisky. He wrenched hard to get free and desperately I butted him in the face. 'Bastard!' he called as he escaped my grip and backed off. A tiny red worm crawled from his nostril, slid over his mouth and dripped from his chin. 'Bastard!' he said again. He moved the flick-knife to his left hand and reached under his jacket. Now there was a gun in his hand, a silly little toy designed for a lady's handbag but it would be enough to settle things.

And that was also the moment when I realized I couldn't beat him. Dodo had the staying power, the confidence, the ruthless determination to win at any cost that makes an Olympic champion.

And it was at that moment that I had the feeling that Dodo had known I was coming. He was prepared for me. He hadn't wanted to talk with me, he didn't ask me what I was there for. He put a gun and a knife in his belt and waited for me to arrive. How could he have guessed that I was on my way?

'Say your prayers, Samson.' With studied glee he took the gun into his left hand. He wanted me to understand what he meant by it. The gun was to be his insurance policy: Dodo was going to use the knife on me. He moved closer but he was wary now. He wouldn't be caught again by my kicks, butts or jabs. I tried to guess his intentions. He would have to cripple me with the knife lest I wrench the gun from him. 'Say your prayers,' he whispered softly.

I was frightened and he could see it. I had no plan to tackle him: he'd chosen his position well. There were no more objects handy for me to throw at him, no rugs under him, no doors or windows for me to escape through. And the sole light was no longer in his eyes; it was in mine. That was why I didn't see clearly what happened next.

Over Dodo's shoulder I saw a figure coming silently through the door behind him. The intruder moved quietly and with the grace of a dancer. A slim man, wearing a short black car coat and a close-fitting cap. In a balletic movement he raised his hand high in the air, as if trying to touch the ceiling. And he brought it down in a vertical movement that ended with the thud of something hard hitting Dodo's skull.

Dodo gave a gasp like the air escaping from a balloon and collapsed to sprawl senseless upon the carpet. Then suddenly the dark room seemed to be full of men. Someone pushed me flat against a wall and frisked me while others were searching the house and searching Dodo's body too.

'Sit down, Bernie. Sit down and catch your breath.' Someone handed me a glass of whisky and I drank gratefully.

'That was a close one, eh?'

I knew the voice. Prettyman. 'Jim!' I said. 'Jesus! Is it really you, Jim. What. . . ? Why. . . ?'

I looked at him but he gave no sign of friendliness. 'Deep cover, Bernie.'

'Cindy thinks you're dead. What's all this about?' Outside in the hall I could hear the squawks and hisses of a two-way radio. Drawers were being pulled open and doors closed. 'What in hell is it all about?'

'You know better than to ask me that, Bernie.'

'For the Department?' He didn't answer.

He stared at me. His skin was white and his face hard like a waxwork figure. He said, 'I've got to get you out of here. Can you drive yourself home?'

I couldn't resist leaning forward and touching his arm. 'Is this why you sent me that box of ancient scripts and stuff? To keep for you? Was I supposed to guess that you weren't really dead?'

He flinched away from my touch. He got up and looked round the shadowy room. 'Maybe,' he said. He was near the piano. Reflectively he reached down and picked out a few bass notes. The room was dark, so that the lamp on the piano made a hard light upon the keyboard and his seemingly disembodied fingers.

'Jim,' I said. 'Who ordered you to disappear? Is it something to do with Fiona?'

Unhurriedly he hit a few more notes to complete a doleful little melody. Then he looked up and said, 'Bernie, it's time you realized that the Department isn't run for your benefit. There's nothing in Command Rules that says we have to clear everything with Bernard Samson before an Operation is okayed.'

'I'm talking about my wife, Jim,' I said angrily.

'Well, I'm not talking about her: not to you, not to anyone. Now shut up and get out of here. Go home and forget everything, and leave me to sort out this bloody mess you've created.'

'Or else?'

There was a pause. I met his gaze. 'Or else I include you in the report. You were told not to contact Dodo but you can't leave anything alone, can you, Bernie? You've just got to keep poking that nose of yours into everything.'

'So Silas Gaunt sent you here?'

He played a minor chord and held it. 'I told you to get going, so get going.' He closed the piano. 'Think you can drive?'

I gulped the rest of the whisky and got to my feet. I was still shaky. 'Okay, Jim,' I said.

'Just for old times' sake, I'll keep you out of it. Don't forget now. If anyone wants to know – and I do mean anyone – you went straight home.' He was watching me and now, for the first time, he smiled, but he didn't put a lot of energy into it. 'Don't drop me into it.' I thought he would offer his hand but he turned away and prodded Dodo's inert shape with the toe of his shoe. 'Come on, Dodo,' he said. 'The fight is over.'

21

'Go to jail!' It was not unexpected. There was a measure of inevitability to every game of chance.

I sometimes wonder if the reservations and doubts that my generation showed for capitalism were the legacy of being bankrupted and humiliated by our parents in those Sunday afternoon Monopoly games. Billy and Sally will not be similarly assailed; for them Monopoly games are simply a time when family discussions, reminiscences, stories and jokes (Waiter, waiter, this Pekin Duck is rubbery. Chinese waiter: thank you sir) are punctuated by desultory throws of the dice.

'Go to jail, go directly to jail. Do not pass Go. Do not collect two hundred pounds.' Oh, well.

This was my family now: three children in effect, for seeing Gloria with my children was to recognize the way that she was just a grown-up child with all the sudden changes of mood that children believe normal. I looked at her that Sunday afternoon. It was a promise of spring to come, the sun shone from a blue sky, and we sat in the dilapidated conservatory that, more than any other thing, had made Gloria want to live in Balaklava Road. The potted plants and flowers that filled every shelf had been bought at the local garden centre but the effect was green and luxuriant, and for Gloria effect was everything.

The sun gave new life to Gloria, as it does to so many women, and I had never seen her looking so beautiful as she did that day. The sunshine had turned her blonde hair to the colour of pale butter. Her high cheekbones and wonderful teeth made her broad smile infectious and despite my misery – or perhaps because of it – I fell in love with her all over again.

Not once but often I had wondered how I would have survived that terrible time after Fiona's defection without Gloria there at my side. Apart from working all week, studying for university and attending to the household chores she cared for my children and worried about me. Most of all she renewed my self-respect at a time when my male ego was badly bruised by Fiona's departure.

I guess I should have told her all this but I never did. At the bad times when I needed her most I had no stamina for such tributes, and when things were going well between us there seemed to be no need of them.

'You can't move, you're in jail,' said Sally. 'You'll have to throw a double six.'

'Yes, I'm in jail.' I said. 'I forgot.'

Sally laughed.

I wondered if the children were aware of the difficulties that their mother's defection had brought. They were always polite to Gloria and occasionally affectionate but there was no way that she could replace their mother. At best they treated her as an elder sister, and the authority they granted her was on that basis. I worried about them, and work was not going well. Dicky Cruyer complained that I was not working hard enough to clear my desk. I countered that I was getting too many messenger-boy trips to Berlin but Dicky laughed and said that the Berlin jaunts were one of the best perks of the job. And Dicky was right. I liked the trips to Berlin. I'd be desolated to be deprived of the chance to see my friends there.

Were all the people I'd always trusted and depended on working against me? Perhaps I was beginning to go mad: or maybe I was far gone! At nights I stayed awake, trying to figure out what might be going on. I went to a pharmacy and bought sleeping tablets that had no discernible effect. Something more powerful would have required a prescription from the doctor, and regulations for senior staff said that any medical consultations of any sort have to be reported. Better to stay awake. But I felt more and more exhausted. By Wednesday I had decided that the only possible way of escaping from this nightmare was to talk to someone at the very top. Since the Deputy was a new boy and something of an unknown quantity this meant the Director-General, Sir Henry Clevemore. The only remaining task was to locate him; I was determined to do this before my next Berlin trip.

Apart from some spells in a nursing home, Sir Henry lived in a big stockbroker-Tudor mansion near Cambridge. In the distant past I had taken urgent papers there. Once I'd even been given lunch by the old man; a privilege so rarely granted to anyone but his immediate associates that Dicky interrogated me afterwards and wanted to know every word uttered.

How often Sir Henry came to London nowadays no one on my floor seemed to know. As far as the staff were concerned he was only to be glimpsed now and again emerging from – or disappearing into – the car of the express lift that took him to his top floor office, his face gloomy and his back hunched.

Sir Henry's office was still there and still unchanged; a desperate muddle of books, files, ornaments, mementoes and souvenirs too cheap and ugly to be enshrined in his richly furnished home but too imbued with memories to be thrown away.

The irrepressible and ever enchanting Gloria provided an answer to my problem when she invited a friend of hers to sit down with us in the canteen for lunch. Peggy Collier, a prematurely grey-haired lady who'd befriended Gloria right from the first day she'd come to work here, said something that indicated that Sir Henry must be in London every Friday. Peggy said that every Friday at noon she had a box of 'current and vital' papers ready and waiting for the D-G. It was delivered to the Cavalry Club in Piccadilly. Also I remembered that the Operations log-book showed the Cavalry Club as the contact number for the Deputy D-G every Friday afternoon.

Peggy said a special messenger brought the document box back to the office at varying times between five and seven pm. It was poor old Peggy who had to wait for the box to arrive, and then refile all the documents the D-G had been looking through. Sometimes – in fact quite frequently – this meant that Peg did not get home in time to prepare a proper meal for her husband, Jerry – spelled with a J because it was short for Jerome not Gerald – who worked as a fully qualified accountant for the local office of the Inspector of Inland Revenue and so was always home early, not having the train journey which Peggy had to endure from the office on account of the absurd rents they charge anywhere near the centre of town, and anyway wasn't the rent they paid out in the suburbs where they lived next door to Jerry's mother enough? And who wants a cold meal at night after a long day's work, although by the time you've dished up a cold meal it has taken almost as long as cooking? And who can afford the price you have to pay in the little shop just along the road from the bus stop that stays open to midnight – it's run by foreigners but no matter what you say those people don't mind hard work and that's something you can't say about some of the English people Peg knows – but really the prices they charge for ready-prepared food. They have pork pies, cooked chicken or those foreign sausages that are all meat and Jerry likes but which Peg finds funny tasting on account of the way they are full of chemicals or anyway that's what the papers say, still you can't believe everything you read in the papers can you?

'Who takes the box?' I asked.

'Anyone cleared to carry "Top Secret",' said Peg.

'I see,' I said.

'And his dog,' said Peggy. 'The driver takes the box and the dog. The dog walks in Green Park.'

The Cavalry Club is not one of those 'gentleman's Clubs' which have been infiltrated by advertising men and actors. The only time outsiders gained access to these sacred portals was in January 1976 when members of the newly closed Guards' Club were allowed in. The quiet dignity of this old house at the Hyde Park Corner end of Piccadilly fits well with its elite and clannish membership. Reminded of their reputation for consuming more French champagne than any comparable establishment, these clubbable cavalrymen are likely to account for it by the popularity their premises enjoy as a venue for regimental events and the private cocktail parties that are so often to be heard even in the quiet of the library.

Sir Henry Clevemore was in the otherwise unoccupied writing room when I took his document box to him. He always chose this room, which was on the ground floor. It is different to all the other rooms in the Club, for it can be entered from the street without passing through the main entrance and answering questions from the men behind the desk. Here were stored cocktail party chairs and a billiard table that the committee didn't want to throw away. The room smelled of ancient leather and scented polish and Sir Henry was alone there. There were no cocktail parties to be heard, only the sound of buses crawling along the rainswept street outside. Sir Henry was sitting before a writing desk at the window, with a frantic wide-nostrilled charger of the Light Brigade thundering through the oilpaint above him. Beneath the vivid painting – framed and reverently positioned – there were pressed flowers collected from the 'Valley of Death' and a lock of hair from Wellington's favourite charger.

'Oh, it's you,' said Sir Henry vaguely, his arms extended to take the document box.

'Yes, Sir Henry,' I said as I handed it to him. 'I was hoping that you'd grant me a few minutes of your time.'

He frowned as I put the box on the table in front of him. It was not done of course. Decent chaps didn't bamboozle their way into a fellow's club and then corner them for a chat. But he managed a brief and mandatory smile before reaching into his pocket and bringing out a key on a long silver chain.

'Of course, of course. Splendid! My pleasure entirely.' He was still hoping that he'd misheard, that I would say goodbye, and go away and leave him to his paper-work.

'Samson, sir. German Desk.'

He raised his eyes to me and rubbed his face like a man coming out of a deep sleep. Eventually he said, 'Ummmm. Brian Samson. Of course.'

208

He was a strange old fellow, a gangling, uncoordinated emaciated teddy bear, the bruin-like effect heightened by the ginger-coloured rough tweed jacket he was wearing, and his long hair. His face was more wrinkled than I remembered and his complexion had darkened with that mauvish colour that sickness sometimes brings.

'Brian Samson was my father, sir. My name is Bernard Samson.' The D-G put on his spectacles and for a moment he stared at me quizzically. This action disarranged his hair so that demoniacal tufts appeared above each ear. The lenses glinted in the light from the window. The frames were incongruously small for his long droopy face and did not fit properly upon his nose.

'Bernard Samson. Yes, yes. Of course it is.' He unlocked the box and opened it to get a glimpse of the papers. He was excited now, like a child with a box of new toys. Without looking up – and without much conviction – he said, 'If we can find that waiter we'll get you a cup of coffee . . . or a drink.'

'Nothing for me, thank you, Sir Henry. I must get back to the office. I'm going to Berlin this afternoon.' I reached out for the lid of the box and firmly and gently closed it.

He looked up at me in amazement. Such insubordination was like a physical assault, but I enjoyed the shining armour of the self-righteous innocent. He did not voice his anger. He was a luminary of the expensive end of the British education system which specializes in genial, courteous philistines. So, concealing his impatience, he invited me to sit down and take as long as I wished to tell him whatever I had to say.

There were plenty of stories that said the old man was non compos mentis, but any concern I had about explaining my worries to a potty boss were soon gone. I decided to leave out my visit to Dodo in Hampton Wick and my strange encounter with Jim Prettyman. If the Department said Jim was dead, then dead he would remain. As soon as I began Sir Henry was bright-eyed and alert. As I told him what I had discovered about the funds passed over to Bret Rensselaer's company, and what I could guess about the way in which the money had been moved from place to place before going to the Berlin bank, he interrupted me with pertinent comments.

At times he was well ahead of me, and more than once I was unable to understand fully the import of his questions. But he was an old-timer and too much of a pro to reveal the extent of his knowledge or the degree of his fears. This didn't surprise me. On the contrary I fully expected any Director-General stolidly to deny suggestions of treason or malfeasance, or even a possibility that any member of staff might be getting a second biscuit with their afternoon tea.

'Do you garden?' he said, suddenly changing the subject.

'Garden, sir?'

'Dammit man, garden.' He gave a genial smile. 'Dig the soil, grow flowers and shrubs and vegetables and fruit?'

I remembered Sir Henry's twenty-acre garden and the men I'd seen labouring in it. In his lapel he wore a small white rose, a mark of the rural Yorkshire upbringing of which he was so proud. 'No, sir. I don't garden. Not really.'

'A man needs a garden, I've always said so.' He looked at me over his spectacles. 'Not even a little patch?'

'I have a little patch,' I admitted, remembering the wilderness of weeds and nettles at the rear of Balaklava Road.

'July is my favourite month in the garden, Simpson. Can you guess why?' He raised a finger.

'I don't think I can, sir.'

'By July everything that's coming up is up. Some lovely things are ready for cropping: raspberries, red currants and cherries, as well as your beans and potatoes . . .' He paused and fixed me with his eyes. 'But if any of them haven't appeared above ground, Simpson. If your seeds failed to germinate or got washed out in the rains or frozen by late frosts . . .' His finger pointed. 'There's still time to plant. Right? July. Nothing you can't plant in July, Simpson. It's not too late to start again. Now do you follow me?'

'I see what you mean, sir,' I said.

'I love my vegetable garden, Simpson. There's nothing finer than to eat the crop you've planted with your own hands. I'm sure you know that.'

'Yes, I do, sir.'

'*Our* world is like an onion, Simpson,' he said with heavy significance, his voice growing hoarser by the minute. 'The Department I mean, of course. I told the PM that once, when she was complaining about our unorthodox methods. Each layer of the onion fits closely upon its neighbour but each layer is separate and independent: terra incognita. Follow me, Simpson?'

'Yes, Sir Henry.'

Thus reassured he said, '*Omne ignotum pro magnifico:* are you familiar with that splendid notion, Simpson?' Characteristically unwilling to take a chance, he explained it in a soft aside. 'Anything little known is assumed to be wonderful. The watchword of the service, Simpson . . . at least the watchword of the appropriations wallahs, eh?' He laughed.

'Yes, sir,' I said, 'Tacitus, wasn't it?'

His eyes flickered behind the spectacle lenses; a glass-eyed old teddy suddenly come to life. He cleared his throat. 'Awww! Yes. Read Tacitus have you? Remember any more of it, Simpson?'

'*Omnium consensu capax imperii nisi imperasset,*' I quoted and, after giving him a moment to digest it, I took a leaf out of his book and told him what it meant. 'Everyone thought him capable of exercising authority until he tried it.'

The watery eyes gave me a steady stare. 'Haw! A palpable hit! I take your point, young man. You're wondering if I am capable of exercising my authority. Is that it?'

'No, Sir Henry, of course I'm not.'

He scratched his nose. 'Exercising it forcefully enough to explore the substance of your fears and concerns.' He turned his head and coughed in a quiet gentlemanly way.

'No, sir.' I got to my feet to take leave of him.

He looked up at me. 'Have no fear, my boy. I'll act on your information. I'll root through every aspect of this matter until no shadow of a doubt remains.'

'Thank you, sir.' He heaved himself up to offer his hand in farewell and his spectacles fell off. He caught them in mid-fall. I suppose it happened to him a lot.

Once outside in Piccadilly I looked at my watch. I had more than enough time to pick up my case from the office, take the car to Ebury Street and pick up Werner, who'd been in London shopping and was booked on the same plane back to Berlin-Tegel. So I walked towards Fortnum's and the prospect of a cup of coffee. I wanted just a moment to myself. I needed time to think.

There were dark clouds racing over the tree tops of Green Park and the drizzle of rain had now become spasmodic heavy showers and gusting winds. Tourists trudged through the downpour with grim determination. On the park side of the street the artists who displayed their paintings there had covered them with sheets of plastic and gone to find shelter behind the colonnade of the Ritz Hotel. As I passed Green Park tube station a woman's umbrella was blown inside out, and a man's wide-brimmed felt hat went flying away into the traffic. The hat bounced, a car swerved to avoid it but a bus rolled over it and a man selling newspapers laughed grimly. There was a rumble of thunder. It was cold and wet; it was a thoroughly miserable day; it was London in winter.

For some there is a perverse satisfaction to walking in the rain: it provides a privacy that a stroll in good weather does not. Passers-by bowed their heads, and butted into the downpour oblivious of anything but their own discomfort. I recalled my conversation with the Director-General and wondered if I had handled it right. There was something curious about the old man's demeanour. Not that he wasn't concerned: I'd never seen him more disturbed. Not that he wasn't prepared to listen: he weighed my every word. But something . . .

I turned into Fortnum's entrance and went through the food store to the tea shop at the back. It was crowded with ladies with blue hair and crocodile handbags, the sort of ladies who have little white dogs waiting for them at home. Perhaps I'd chosen a bad time. I sat at the counter and had a cup of coffee and a Danish pastry. It was delicious. I sat there thinking for some time. When I finished that coffee I ordered another. It was then that I realized what I'd found odd about my conversation with the Director-General. No matter how outrageous my story and my theories might have sounded to him, he had shown no indignation, no anger; not even surprise.

I must have lost track of time, for I suddenly looked at my watch and realized that my schedule was tight. But I hurried and by the time I got to Ebury Street I was only a few minutes late. Werner – with that dedicated punctuality that is inherently German – was waiting for me on the pavement, briefcase packed, bills paid, black Burberry raincoat buttoned and umbrella up. At his feet there was a large carton marked 'chinaware very fragile'. 'Sorry, Werner,' I said in apology for my late arrival. 'Everything took a bit longer than expected.'

'Plenty of time,' said Werner. The driver opened the door for him and then heaved the carton of chinaware into the boot. It looked damned heavy. Werner made no comment about this huge and cumbersome item of baggage. He reached over to put his umbrella in the front seat alongside the driver and then took off his trilby hat to make sure his ticket was inside it. Werner kept tickets and things in his hatband. He was the only person I know who did that.

The car dropped us at Victoria Station so that we could catch one of the direct trains for Gatwick Airport. A porter took the carton of chinaware on a barrow, with Werner fussing around to make sure it didn't get knocked. The train was almost empty. We had no difficulty finding a place to ourselves. Werner was wearing a new suit – a lightweight grey mohair – and looking rather more rakish than the sober fellow I'd known so well. But he hung his umbrella so it would drain on to the floor, carefully folded his raincoat and placed his hat and his briefcase on the rack. No matter how rakish he looked Werner had

212

been house-trained by the indomitable Zena. 'Plates and cups and so on,' said Werner, touching the carton delicately with the toe of his polished shoe.

'Yes,' I said. I could think of nothing to add.

Once the train started its journey he said, 'In Berlin I suppose you'll be going to see Koby?'

'Lange Koby? Maybe.' Koby lived in a squalid apartment near Potsdamer Platz and held court for foreign journalists and writers who were writing about 'the real Berlin'. I didn't enjoy my visits there.

'If this Dodo worked for him, Lange might be able to tell you something.'

I didn't tell Werner that I'd seen Prettyman or grappled with Dodo; I hadn't told anyone. 'Perhaps. But that was all a long time ago, Werner. Dodo was just a nasty little spear-carrier. I don't see how Lange can know anything about Bret and the money and all the things that really matter.'

'Lange usually knows all the scandal,' said Werner without admiration.

I leaned forward to him and said, 'I told the old man everything I know . . . damn nearly everything,' I amended it. 'From now onwards it's the D-G's problem, Werner. His problem, not my problem.'

Werner looked at me and nodded as if thinking about it. 'Does that mean you're going to drop the Bret business?'

'I might,' I admitted.

'Let it go, Bernard. It's eating you up.'

'If only I knew what part Fiona played in that fiddle.'

'Fiona?'

'She had her hands on that money, Werner. I remember seeing the bank papers – statements – in the drawer where she kept her household accounts and money for Mrs Dias our cleaning woman.'

'Before Fiona defected, you mean?'

'Yes, years ago. I was looking for the car keys . . . Schneider, von Schild und Weber . . . I knew that damned name was familiar, and last night I remembered why.'

'Why would Fiona have the Berlin Bank accounts?'

'At the time I thought it was some stuff from the office . . . forgeries even. There were a lot of zeros on those sheets, Werner. Millions and millions of Deutsche Marks. Now I realize it was real and the money was hers. Or at least, in her keeping.'

'Fiona's money? A secret account?'

'Banks send the statements to the account holder, Werner. There is no getting away from that.'

'It's too late now,' said Werner. 'She's gone.'

'I told the old man everything I know,' I said again as if to remind myself of what I'd done. 'From now onwards it's his problem, Werner. His problem, not my problem.'

'You said that already,' said Werner.

'I left Ingrid out of it. There was no point in telling him all that rigmarole about her mother and Dodo.'

'Nor the stuff about your father,' said Werner.

'That's right,' I said. 'Do you think I should have told him that?'

'Either the Department authorized what Bret has been doing with the money, or Bret and Fiona have been stealing it,' said Werner with his usual devastating simplicity. 'Didn't the old man give any indication of knowing?'

'Perhaps he's the greatest actor in the world, but it seemed like he was hearing it all for the first time.'

'They say he's meshugga.'

'No sign of that today.'

'You did the right thing, Bernie. I'm sure of it. Now forget it and stop brooding.'

I looked at his big package. 'So what did you buy in London that I couldn't be trusted with?'

He smiled. 'We felt we couldn't use you like a courier service.'

'I'm in Berlin every week the way things are now. I'll bring whatever you need.'

'Ingrid wants the hotel to look more homely. She likes all these English fabrics and English china; little floral patterns. She says the hotel is too inhospitable-looking, too institutional.'

'It's a Berlin hotel; it looks German.'

'Times change, Bernie.'

'I thought Lisl told you her sister was childless,' I said. 'What did she say when Ingrid arrived?'

He nodded, and then said, 'Lisl knew about Ingrid but Ingrid is illegitimate. She has no legal claim on the hotel.'

'Are you in love with Ingrid?'

'Me? In love with Ingrid?'

'Don't stall, Werner. We know each other too well.'

'Yes, I'm in love with Ingrid,' said Werner somewhat apprehensively.

'Does Zena know?' I asked.

'Zena will be all right,' said Werner confidentially. 'I'll give her a lot of money and she'll be satisfied.'

I said nothing. It was true, of course. It was a bleak comment on Zena and her marriage but there was no arguing with it.

'Zena's in Munich. I keep hoping she'll meet someone . . .' Werner looked at me and smiled. 'Yes, me and Ingrid . . . We're happy together. Of course it will all take time . . .'

'That's wonderful, Werner.'

'You never liked Zena, I know.'

'Ingrid is a very attractive woman, Werner.'

'You do like her?'

'Yes, I do.'

'She's never been married. She might find it difficult to adjust to married life at her age.'

'You're both young, Werner. What the hell . . .'

'That's what Ingrid says,' said Werner.

'Gatwick Airport' said the voice of the train conductor over the speakers; the train was slowing.

'Thanks Bernie,' he said. 'You've helped me.'

'Any time, Werner.'

The plane took off on time. It was a small private company, Dan-Air, and the stewardesses smile and they give you real coffee. Once above the clouds the sun shone brightly. Despite the emptiness of the train the plane was filled. I asked Werner about his progress with Lisl's hotel and I unleashed a long and enthusiastic account of his hopes and hard work. And Werner wasn't too selfish to include Ingrid Winter's contribution. On the contrary, his praise and admiration for her were very apparent. At times he seemed to be giving her too much credit but I listened patiently and made the right noises at appropriate times. Werner was in love and people who are in love are good company only for their beloved.

I looked at the landscape passing below. Germany: there was no mistaking it. The people of Europe may grow more and more alike in their choice of cars, their clothes, their TV programmes and their junk food, but our landscapes reveal our true nature. There is no rural West Germany. The German landscape is ordered, angular and built-upon, so that cows must share their Lebensraum with apartment blocks, and forest trees measure the factory chimneys. Towns are allotted foliage under which to hide their ugly shopping plazas but huntsmen must stalk their prey between the parked cars and swimming pools of an unending suburbia.

But once across the East-West frontier the landscape is lonely and

215

tranquil. The Democratic Republic enjoys an agricultural landscape not yet sullied by shiny cars and new houses. Here the farms are old and picturesque. Big breeds of horses have stubbornly resisted the tractors and men and women still do the hard work.

It was a lovely evening when we landed in Berlin, this glittering little capitalist island, with its tall concrete office blocks and sparkling streets, set in a vast green ocean of grassy communism. The sun was low and orange-coloured. Tall cumulus dominated the eastern skies, while to the west the grey storm clouds were smudged and streaked across the sky as if some angry god had been trying to erase them.

I came down the steps from the plane carrying Werner's briefcase while he staggered under the weight of the chinaware. Ahead of us the other passengers straggled on their way to customs and immigration.

Berlin-Tegel is in the French Sector of occupied Berlin. This small airport is technically under the control of the French air force. So the incongruous presence of four British military policemen was especially noticeable, if not to say disturbing. They were dressed in that unnaturally perfect way that only military policemen can manage. Their shoes were gleaming, their buttons bright and their khaki had knife-edge creases in all the places where creases were supposed to be.

And if the incongruous presence of British 'redcaps' was not enough, I now noticed that one of them was a captain. Such men are not commonly seen standing and staring in public places, for MP captains do not patrol airports to make sure there are no squaddies going around improperly dressed. A quick glance round revealed two British army vehicles – a khaki car and a van – drawn up on the apron. Behind them there was a blue van bearing the winged badges of l'armée de l'air. A few yards behind that there was a civilian police car too. Inside it there were a couple of cops in summer uniforms. Quite a police presence for a virtually empty airport.

As we walked across the apron the four British MPs straightened up and stared at us. Then the captain strode forward on a path that intercepted us.

'Excuse me, gentlemen,' said the British captain. He was a diffident young man with a large moustache that was less than bushy. 'Which of you is Mr Samson?'

Always afterwards I wondered exactly what made Werner unhesitatingly say, 'I'm Bernard Samson. What is it, Captain?'

Werner could smell trouble, that's why he said it. He could smell trouble even before I got a whiff of it, and that was very quick indeed.

'I'll have to ask you to come with me,' said the Captain. He glanced at

216

the sergeant – a burly forty-year-old with a pistol on his belt – and the looks they exchanged told me everything I needed to know.

'Come with you?' said Werner. 'Why?'

'It's better if we sort it out in the office,' said the captain, with a hint of nervousness in his voice.

'I'd better go with him, Werner,' said Werner, continuing the act.

I nodded. Surely the soldiers could hear Werner's German accent. But perhaps they hadn't been told that Bernard Samson was English.

As if demonstrating something to me, Werner turned to the captain and said, 'Am I under arrest?'

'Well . . .' said the captain. He'd obviously been told that arresting a man in public was something of a last resort, something you only did when sweet talk failed. 'No. That is . . . Only if you refuse to come.'

'We'll sort it out at your office,' said Werner. 'It's a stupid mistake.'

'I'm sure it is,' said the captain with marked relief. 'Perhaps your friend will take the package.'

'I'll take it,' I said.

The captain turned to one of the corporals and said, 'Help the gentleman, Corporal. Take the parcel for him.'

I had Werner's briefcase in my hand. It contained his passport and all sorts of other personal papers. If they took Werner to their police office, it might take an hour or two before they discovered that he was the wrong man. So I followed the corporal and Werner's parcel of chinaware and left Werner to his fate.

With the military policeman acting as my escort my passage through customs and immigration got no more than a nod. In the forecourt there were lines of taxi cabs. My cab driver was an unshaven youngster in a dirty red tee shirt with the heraldic device of Harvard University crudely printed on the front. 'I want an address in Oranienburger Strasse. I know it by sight . . . go to the Wittenau S-Bahn station.' I said it in slow German, in earshot of the soldier. It would give them a confusing start, for Oranienburger Strasse stretches across town from the airport to Hermsdorf. Not the sort of street in which you'd want to start a door-to-door inquiry.

Once the taxi was clear of the airport I told the driver that I'd changed my mind. I wanted to go to Zoo Station. He looked at me and gave a knowing smile that was inimitably *berlinerisch*.

'Zoo Station,' he said. It was a squalid place, the Times Square of West Berlin. '*Alles klar.*' In that district there was no shortage of people who would help a fugitive to hide from authority of any kind. The cab driver probably thought I was outsmarting the army cops, and he approved.

217

Yes, I thought, everything is clear. No sooner had I finished talking to him than the bloody D-G signalled to Berlin to have me arrested. It was artful to do it in Berlin. Here the army was king. Here I had no civil liberties that couldn't be overruled by regulations that dated from wartime. Here I could be locked away and forgotten. Yes, alles klar, Sir Henry. I am hooked.

22

Don't ask me what I hoped to achieve. I don't know what I was trying to do beyond gain time enough to collect my thoughts and see some way of extricating myself from this mess.

My mind worked frantically. I dismissed the idea of picking up the Smith & Wesson snub-nosed .38 and five hundred pounds' worth of mixed currency small denomination paper money that I used to keep in Lisl's safe but now kept in a twenty-four-hour safe-deposit box in the Ku-Damm. Neither ready cash nor flying lead would help me if the Department was after my blood. I dismissed too the Austrian passport that was sewn into the lining of a suitcase in a room in Marienfelde. I could become Austrian, if I raised my voice an octave and kept a tight grip on my nose. But what for; by Monday they would have good recent photos of me circulated, and being a phoney Austrian wouldn't help.

A taxi took Werner's box of china round to the hotel with a note for Ingrid Winter that I'd gone with Werner to the cinema. For anyone who knew us well, the idea of such an excursion was absurd. But Ingrid didn't know us very well, and it was the only excuse I could think of that would prevent her making inquiries about us for two or three hours.

Some of my actions were less well reasoned. As if driven by some demon from my over-active past, I took a second cab and asked for Checkpoint Charlie. It was almost night by now but my world was tilting towards the sun and it was not dark. My cab edged through the traffic as battalions of weary tourists wandered aimlessly around the neon and concrete charms of the Europa Centre and chewed popcorn and 'curry-wurst'.

'Checkpoint Charlie?' said the driver again just to be sure.

'Yes,' I said.

Once clear of the crowds we headed for the Canal. This quiet section of the city provides the shortest route to Checkpoint Charlie. No tourists walked the gently curving banks of the Landwehr Canal and yet there was more history in this short stretch than in the entire length of the Kurfursten Damm.

It was not always such a neglected backwater. The street names of yesterday tell their own story. Bendlerstrasse, from which the Wehrmacht marched to conquer Europe, is now named after

219

Stauffenberg, architect of the failed anti-Nazi putsch. But is there some militaristic ambition burning deep inside the town planners who keep Bendler Bridge still Bendler Bridge?

Here on the canal bank is the building where Admiral Canaris, Hitler's chief of military intelligence, sat in his office plotting against his master. And into these murky waters the battered body of Rosa Luxemburg was thrown by the army's assassins.

Soon the dark tree-lined canal was left behind and the taxi was in Kreuzberg, speeding past Leuschner's Café and along Koch Strasse – Berlin's Fleet Street – and to the Friedrichstrasse intersection that provides a view into the heart of East Berlin.

I paid off the cab and made a point of asking the American soldier on duty in the temporary hut, which has been positioned there for forty years, what time the checkpoint closed. It never closed, he told me; never! It was enough to make sure he remembered me passing through. If I was going to leave a trail that the MPs would follow, it would be better to make it wide and deep. The Department would not be fooled, but on past performance it would take a little time to get them into action. A Friday evening: Dicky Cruyer would have to be got back to his office from somewhere where the fishing and shooting was good and the telephoning demonstrably bad.

On the Western side of Checkpoint Charlie you'll find only a couple of well laid-back GIs lounging in a hut, but the Eastern side is crowded with gun-toting men in uniforms deliberately designed in the pattern of the old Prussian armies. I gave my passport to the surly DDR frontier guard who showed it to his senior officer who pushed it through the slot under the glass window. There it was photographed and put under the lights to find any secret marks that previous DDR frontier police might have put there. They gripped my passport with that proprietorial manner that all bureaucrats adopt towards identity papers. For men who man frontiers regard passports and manifests as communications to them from other bureaucrats in other lands. The bearers of such paper are no more than lowly messengers.

As a thinly disguised tax, all visitors are made to exchange Western money for DDR currency at an exorbitant rate. I paid. Guards came and went. Tourists formed a line. Buses and private cars crawled through and were examined underneath with the aid of large wheeled mirrors. A shiny new black Mercedes, flying the flag of some remote and impoverished African nation, was halted at the barrier behind a US army jeep that was demonstrating the victorious armies' right to patrol both sides of the city. The DDR guards did everything with a studied slowness. It all takes time: here everything takes time. And some of the victors have to be kept in their place.

East Berlin is virtually the only place to find a regime staunch and wholehearted in its application of the teachings of Karl Marx. Why not? Who could have doubted that the Germans, who had given such unquestioning faith and loyalty – not to mention countless million lives – to Kaiser Wilhelm and Adolf Hitler, would soldier on, long after Marxism had perished at its own hand and been relegated to the levelled Führerbunker of history.

The taller buildings around the shanty-town of huts that is Checkpoint Charlie give the feeling of being in an arena. So do the banners and the slogans. But the bellicose themes have gone. It is a time of retrenchment. The communist propaganda has abandoned the promises of outstripping the West in prosperity or converting it politically. Now the messages stress continuity and security and tell the proletariat to be grateful.

Emerging from Checkpoint Charlie you can see all the way to Friedrichstrasse station. There, a steel bridge crossing the street cuts a pattern in the indigo sky. Across the bridge go the trains that connect Paris with Warsaw and eventually Moscow, but the bridge itself is also the Friedrichstrasse station platform of the elevated S-Bahn, the commuter line that runs through both East and West Berlin.

The sight of the bridge gives the impression that the station is only a short walk, but the distance is deceptive and as I walked up Friedrichstrasse – past the blackened and pockmarked shells of bombed buildings that people said were owned by mysterious Swiss companies that even the DDR did not wish to offend – I remembered too late that it's worth getting a cab that short distance when one is in a hurry.

The S-Bahn station Friedrichstrasse provides another demonstration of the enormous workforce that the DDR devotes to manning the Wall. I went through its agonizingly slow passport control – there are even more checks on people leaving than on those entering – and eventually went through the tunnel and up to the platform.

The station is a huge open-ended hangar-like building with overhead gantries patrolled by guards brandishing machine guns. The S-Bahn's rolling stock, like the stations and the track, are ancient and dilapidated. The train came rattling in, its windows dirty and the lights dim. I got in. It was almost empty: those privileged few permitted to cross the border are not to be found travelling westwards at this time of evening. It took only a few minutes to clatter over the Wall. The 'anti-fascist

221

protection barrier' is particularly deep and formidable here where the railway crosses the Alexander Ufer: perhaps the sight of it is intended to be a deterrent.

There is an almost audible sigh of relief from the passengers who alight at Zoo Station. I had to change trains for Grunewald, but there was only a minute or two to wait and it was quicker than taking a cab and getting tangled up in the Ku-Damm traffic which would be thick at this time.

From the station I walked to Frank Harrington's home. I approached it carefully in case there was anyone waiting for me. It seemed unlikely. The standard procedure was to cover the frontier crossing points – those for German nationals as well as the ones for foreigners – and the airport. On a Friday night at short notice that would provide more than enough problems. Frank as the Berlin chief was already given special protection by the civil police. My guess was that whoever was allotting the personnel would decide that Frank couldn't be afforded a car and a three-shift watch. They would describe me as a fugitive special category three: 'possibly armed but not dangerous'.

It was Axel Mauser – one of the kids at school here – who first showed me the proper way to climb drainpipes. Until then I'd been using my hands and getting my clothes into a terrible state. It was Axel who said, 'Climb ropes with your hands; drainpipes with your feet' and showed me how the burglars did it without getting their hands dirty. I don't know who showed Axel how to do it: his father probably. His father, Rolf Mauser, used to work in the hotel for Lisl. Rolf Mauser was an unscrupulous old crook. I'd believe almost anything of Rolf.

I was remembering all that as I climbed into the upstairs master bedroom of Frank's big house in Grunewald. There were no burglar alarms at the back. I knew where all the burglar alarms were. I'd helped Frank decide where to put them. And Frank always kept the bathroom window ajar. Frank was a fresh-air fiend. He'd often told me it was unhealthy to close the bedroom windows no matter how cold it was. Sometimes I think that's why his wife doesn't like living with him; she can't stand those freezing cold bedrooms. I told Fiona that once: she said don't be ridiculous but it didn't seem ridiculous to me. I can't stand cold bedrooms: I prefer unhealthy warmth.

Frank wasn't in bed of course, I knew he wouldn't be. That's why I got in upstairs. I got through the window and then had to stand there, carefully removing from the sill about three hundred bottles, tubes and sprays of bath oil, shaving soap, hair shampoo, toothpaste and God knows what. What could Frank ever want with all that stuff? Or was it the unredeemed property of Frank's girl-friends?

Finally I made a foot space on the window sill and from there I could step down into the bath and . . . Jesus, there was water in the bath. Lots of water! What did that bloody Tarrant do if he couldn't even make sure the bath was drained properly? My shoe was full of soapy water. How disgusting! I didn't like Frank's valet and the feeling was mutual. I suppose, if I was to examine my feelings closely, the principal reason I didn't just knock on Frank's front door was because I wouldn't trust that bloody man Tarrant as far as I could throw him. In a jam like the one I was now in, I would give Tarrant just three minutes before catching sight of me and getting on the blower and reporting me. Less than three minutes: thirty seconds.

Frank was downstairs. I knew where he was. I'd known it even when I was on the back lawn looking up at the drainpipes. He was sitting in the drawing room playing his Duke Ellington records. That's what Frank usually did when he was alone in the house. Volume up really loud, so that you could hear the drums and brass section halfway along the street. Frank said the only way you could really appreciate these old records was to have them as loud as the original band had been when making them, but I think Frank was going deaf.

It was the 1940 band – the best Ellington band ever in my opinion, although Frank didn't agree – playing 'Cotton Tail'. No wonder Frank didn't hear me come into the room. I could have been driving a combine harvester and still he wouldn't have heard me above the surging beat of the Ellington band.

Frank was sitting in a chair positioned exactly in line with his two giant speakers. He was dressed in a yellow sweater with a Paisley-patterned silk scarf tucked into his open-neck shirt. It was all very Noel Coward except for the big curly pipe in his fist and the clouds of fierce-smelling tobacco smoke that made me want to cough. He was bent low reading the small print on a record label. I waited for him to look up. I said, 'Hello, Frank,' as casually as I could say it.

'Hello, Bernard,' said Frank and held his pipe aloft to caution me. 'Listen to Ben Webster.'

Listen to him. How could I do anything else, the tenor sax solo went through my head like a power drill. But when the immortal Webster had finished, Frank turned the volume down so it was merely very loud.

'Whisky, Bernard?' said Frank. He was already pouring it.

'Thanks,' I said gratefully.

'I enjoy seeing you any time, Bernard. But I wish you'd just knock on the front door, the way other visitors do.'

If Frank knew there was a warrant out for me, he was staying very cool. 'Why?' I said and drank some whisky. Laphroaig: he knew I liked it.

'So you don't make such a mess on the carpet,' said Frank with a fleeting grin to offset his complaint.

I looked at the carpet. My wet shoe had left marks all the way to the door, and right through the house probably. 'I'm sorry, Frank.'

'Why do you have to do everything arse upwards Bernard? It makes life so difficult for your friends.' Frank had always taken his paternal role seriously, and his way of demonstrating it was to be there when I needed him. Sometimes I wondered what kind of man my father must have been to have made a friendship so deep and binding that I was still drawing upon its capital. 'You're too old now for tricks like climbing up to that damned bathroom. You used to do that when you were very young. Remember?'

'Did I?'

'I left the light on in the bathroom so you wouldn't fall off the ledge and break your neck.'

'You heard what happened?' I said, not being able to endure another moment of Frank's small-talk.

'I knew you'd come to me,' Frank said, walking towards me with a whisky bottle. He couldn't resist it. It was the sort of complacent statement my mother made. Why did he have to be such an old woman? Couldn't he see how it spoiled everything? I let him pour me another drink. It was a wonder he was able to resist telling me I drank too much, but he'd probably find some way to work it into the conversation before long.

'When did you hear?' I asked.

'That the old man wanted you collared? I got a "confidential" on the printer about four o'clock. But then a cancellation came through.' He smiled. 'Reading between the lines, someone in London must have decided that the old man had gone completely batty. Then, after an hour or more, the same message was repeated. This time with the names of both the D-G and the Deputy on it.' He looked at the carpet. 'It's not grease is it?'

'It's water,' I said.

'If it's grease or oil, tell me now so I can leave a note for Tarrant to do something about it before it soaks in.'

'I told you, Frank. It's water.'

'Keep your hair on, Bernard.'

'So I'm still on the arrest list?'

224

'I'm afraid you are. Your ruse with your friend Werner Volkmann didn't fool the army very long.'

'Long enough.'

'For you to do a bunk, yes. But Captain Berry got the devil of a rocket.'

'Captain Berry?'

'The provost captain. I hear the commanding general wants him to face a court. Poor little bugger.'

'Screw Captain Berry,' I said. 'I have no tears to shed for MP captains who want to throw me into the slammer.' I looked at the clock on the mantelpiece.

Frank saw me looking at it and said, 'They won't come here searching for you.'

'What's it all about, Frank?'

'I was hoping you'd tell me, Bernard.'

'I went to see the old man and reported all that stuff about Bret Rensselaer and the bank funds.'

'I thought you were going to abandon all that nonsense,' said Frank wearily.

'Did they tell you what the charges against me might be?'

'No.'

'Were they planning to hold me here, or ship me back to the UK?'

'I don't know, Bernard. I really don't know.'

'You're the Head of Berlin Station, Frank.'

'I'm telling the truth, Bernard. I don't bloody well know.'

'It's about Fiona, isn't it?'

'Fiona?' said Frank, and seemed genuinely puzzled.

'Is Fiona still working for the Department?'

It took the wind out of his sails. He drank some of whatever he was drinking and looked at me for what seemed a long time. 'I wish I could say yes, Bernard. I really do.'

'Because that's the only conclusion that makes sense.'

'Makes sense how?'

'What would Bret Rensselaer be doing with umpteen million dollars?'

'I can think of a lot of things,' said Frank, who was not very fond of Bret Rensselaer.

'Money. You know what a tight rein the Department keep on their cash. You can't really believe Central Funding let millions out of their sight and forget who they'd given it to.'

'Umm.' He smoked his pipe and thought about it.

225

I said, 'That sort of money is stashed away in secret accounts for pay-outs. For pay-outs, Frank.'

'In California?'

'No. Not California. When I talked to Bret in California, no one, except the Americans, was getting agitated. It was when I traced the money to Berlin that the excitement began.'

'Berlin?'

'So they didn't tell you that? Schneider, von Schild and Weber, right here on the Ku-Damm.'

He touched his moustache with the mouthpiece of his pipe. 'Even so, I'm still not sure . . .'

'Suppose Fiona's defection was the end of a very long-term plan. Suppose she is doing her own thing over there in East Berlin. She'd need lots of money, and she'd need it right here in Berlin where it's easy to get to.'

'To pay her own agents?'

'Good grief, Frank, I don't have to tell you what she'd need money for. Sure. For all kinds of things: agents, bribes, expenses. You know how it adds up.'

Frank touched my shoulder. 'I wish I could believe it. But I'm Head of Station here, as you just reminded me. No one would be planted there without my say-so. You know that, Bernard. Stop fooling yourself, it's not your style.'

'Suppose it was kept very tight; Bret Rensselaer as the case officer . . .'

'And the D-G getting direct authorization from the Cabinet Office? It's an ingenious explanation but I fear the true explanation is simpler and less palatable.' A puff at his pipe. 'The Berlin Head of Station is always informed. Even the D-G wouldn't defy that operational rule. It's been like that ever since your father's time. It would be unprecedented.'

'So is having a senior employee arrested at the airport,' I said.

'The D-G is a stick-in-the-mud. I know him, Bernard. We trained together in the war. He's careful to a fault. He just wouldn't go along with such a hazardous scheme.'

'To get an agent into the Stasi at the very top? A trusted agent at committee level? That's what Fiona is now. You told me that yourself.'

'Now calm down, Bernard. I can see why this scenario appeals to you. Fiona is rehabilitated and you have taken on the Department and penetrated their most jealously guarded secret.'

And, he might have added, made Bret into Fiona's colleague instead of her paramour. 'So what is your explanation?'

'A deadly dull one, I'm afraid. But after a lifetime in the service, you look back and see how much time you've wasted chasing bizarre solutions while the true answer was banal, obvious and under your nose the whole while.'

'Fiona leaving her home and children and going to work for the Stasi? Bret embezzling millions of departmental funds and sitting in California pretending to be penniless? Prettyman reassigned from Washington and his wife told he was dead? Uncle Silas telling me what a wonderful fellow Dodo is, while getting on the phone to have him roughed up and silenced? Except I got there first. A warrant issued for my arrest because I tell the D-G about it? Is this the deadly dull explanation that has the ring of truth?'

Frank looked at me. This was the first mention I'd made of Silas Gaunt's duplicity – I'd not even told Werner – and I watched Frank carefully. He nodded as if considering everything I'd said but showed no surprise. 'The last one certainly does,' he said grimly. 'I tore it off the printer myself this evening. Do you want to see it?'

'The old man wants me held because he's frightened that my inquiries are going to blow Fiona's cover. They got me to California just so that Bret could persuade me to forget the whole thing. They sent Charlie Billingsly to Hong Kong because of what he might have seen on the computer about Bret's bogus companies. They gave Cindy Prettyman a nice job in Strasbourg to keep her quiet. They panicked at the idea of Dodo loud-mouthing their secrets, and chose Prettyman to lean on him.'

'It's all very circumstantial,' said Frank. But I had his attention now.

'I suppose they are desperate, but I didn't realize how desperate until I landed here. When I took my questions to the D-G they couldn't think of anything to do with me except to put me in the cooler while they worked out how to shut me up.'

Frank looked at me pitifully and said, 'You'd better sit down, Bernard. There's something else you should know.'

I sat down. 'What?' I said.

'It's not like that. When the second teleprinter message came through I phoned London for clarification. I thought . . . under the circumstances . . .'

'You spoke to the D-G? This afternoon?'

'No but I had a word with the Deputy.'

'And?'

'Sir Percy told me in confidence.'

'Told you what?'

'They've opened an Orange File, Bernard.'

'On me?'

There was still a chance for him to say no but he didn't say no. He said, 'Ladbrook is coming on the plane tomorrow.'

'Jesus Christ!' I said. An Orange File is only started when someone in the Department is accused of treachery, and prima facie evidence has already been collected against them. Ladbrook is the senior interrogator. Ladbrook prepares the prosecution.

'Now do you see?' Frank asked.

'You still don't believe me do you, Frank?'

'I don't dare believe you,' he said.

'What?'

'I'd rather believe that you were guilty than believe that Fiona was over there playing a double game. Especially if you have started tongues waggling. Have you thought about what you are saying? Have you thought what it would mean for her if they tumbled to her? You'd face prison, but if she got to committee level and betrayed them they'd . . .'
He stopped. We were both thinking of Melnikoff, who'd reported back to one of Silas' networks. Over a dozen eye-witnesses had watched Melnikoff being pushed alive into a factory furnace. The KGB had wanted it talked about. 'Be careful how you declare your innocence,' said Frank. 'You could be signing your wife's death warrant; whether what you say is true, or not true.'

I sat down. It was all happening too quickly. I felt like vomiting but I got myself under control and looked at my watch. 'I'd better get out of here.' I hated this room. All the worst things that ever happened to me seemed to happen in this room, but I suppose that was because when something bad happened to me I came running along to Frank. I said, 'Don't you think Tarrant . . .'

'I gave Tarrant the evening off. Is there anything . . . ?'

'You've done your bit already, Frank.'

'I'm sorry, Bernard.'

'What's wrong with them all, Frank? Why can't they just call the dogs off?'

'Whatever the real truth may be, you'll never get a completely clean bill of health. Not after your wife defected. Surely you can see that.'

'No, I can't.'

'Whether your alarming theory is right or whether it is wrong, the Department still can't risk it, Bernard. There were voices who wanted you sacked within hours of her going. They get the wind up when you start nosing around. It scares them. You must see how difficult it is for them.'

228

I got to my feet. 'Have you got any money, Frank?'

'A thousand sterling. Will that be enough?'

'I didn't reckon on being an Orange File. I thought it really was some sort of mistake. Some over-zealous interpretation of the old man's suggestion . . .'

'It's here in the desk.' He found the money quickly, as he'd found the tumbler and the ice and the bottle of Laphroaig. I suppose he'd had everything ready. He walked with me to the front door and looked out into the Berlin night. Perhaps he was making sure there were no men on watch. 'Take this scarf, Bernard. It's bloody cold tonight.' When I shook hands with him he said, 'Good luck, Bernard,' and was reluctant to release my hand. 'What will you do now?' he asked.

I looked at the skyline. Even from here I could see the glow from the floodlights that the DDR used to illuminate their Wall. I shrugged. I didn't know. 'I . . . I'm sorry . . . about the marks on the carpet.' I nodded my thanks and turned away.

'It doesn't matter,' said Frank. 'As long as it's not grease.'

SPY LINE

1

'Glasnost is trying to escape over the Wall, and getting shot with a *silenced* machine gun!' said Kleindorf. 'That's the latest joke from over there.' He spoke just loudly enough to make himself heard above the strident sound of the piano. His English had an American accent that he sometimes sharpened.

I laughed as much as I could now that he'd told me it was a joke. I'd heard it before and anyway Kleindorf was hopeless at telling jokes: even good jokes.

Kleindorf took the cigar from his mouth, blew smoke at the ceiling and tapped ash into an ashtray. Why he was so finicky I don't know; the whole damned room was like a used ashtray. Magically the smoke appeared above his head, writhing and coiling, like angry grey serpents trapped inside the spotlight's beam.

I laughed too much, it encouraged him to try another one. 'Pretty faces look alike but an ugly face is ugly in its own way,' said Kleindorf.

'Tolstoy never said that,' I told him. I'd willingly play the straight man for anyone who might tell me things I wanted to know.

'Sure he did; he was sitting at the bar over there when he said it.'

Apart from regular glances to see how I was taking his jokes, he never took his eyes off his dancers. The five tall toothy girls just found room on the cramped little stage, and even then the one on the end had to watch where she was kicking. But Rudolf Kleindorf – 'Der grosse Kleiner' as he was more usually known – evidenced the truth of his little joke. The dancers – smiles fixed and eyes wide – were distinguished only by varying cellulite and different choices in hair dye, while Rudi's large lop-sided nose was surmounted by amazingly wild and bushy eyebrows. The permanent scowl and his dark-ringed eyes made unique a face that had worn out many bodies, not a few of them his own.

I looked at my watch. It was nearly four in the morning. I was dirty, smelly and unshaven. I needed a hot bath and a change of clothes. 'I'm tired,' I said. 'I must get some sleep.'

Kleindorf took the large cigar from his mouth, blew smoke, and shouted, 'We'll go on to Singing in the Rain, get the umbrellas!' The piano stopped abruptly and the dancers collapsed with loud groans, bending, stretching and slumping against the scenery like a lot of rag dolls tipped from a toybox. Their bodies were shiny with sweat. 'What kind of business am I in where I am working at three o'clock in the morning?' he complained as he flashed the gold Rolex from under his starched linen cuffs. He was a moody, mysterious man and there were all manner of stories about him, many of them depicting him as bad-tempered and inclined to violent rages.

I looked round 'Babylon'. It was gloomy. The fans were off and the place smelled of sweat, cheap cosmetics, ash and spilled drinks, as all such places do when the customers have departed. The long chromium and mirror bar, glittering with every kind of booze you could name, was shuttered and padlocked. His clients had gone to other drinking places, for there are many in Berlin which don't get going until three in the morning. Now Babylon grew cold. During the war this cellar had been reinforced with steel girders to provide a shelter from the bombing but the wartime concrete seemed to exude chilly damp. Two blocks away down Potsdamerstrasse one of these shelters had for years provided Berlin with cultivated mushrooms until the health authorities con-demned it.

It was the 'carnival finale' that had made the mess. Paper streamers webbed tables still cluttered with wine bottles and glasses. There were balloons everywhere – some of them already wrinkled and shrinking – cardboard beer mats, torn receipts, drinks lists and litter of all descriptions. No one was doing anything to clear it all up. There would be plenty of time in the morning to do that. The gates of Babylon didn't open until after dark.

'Why don't you rehearse the new show in the daytime, Rudi?' I asked. No one called him Der Grosse to his face, not even me and I'd known him almost all my life.

His big nose twitched. 'These bimbos work all day; that's why we go through the routines so long after my bedtime.' It was a stern German voice no matter how colloquial his English. His voice was low and hoarse, the result no doubt of his devotion to the maduro leaf Havanas that were aged for at least six years before he'd put one to his lips.

'Work at what?' He dismissed this question with a wave of his cigar. 'They're all moonlighting for me. Why do you think they want to be paid in cash?'

'They will be tired tomorrow.'

'Yah. You buy an icebox and the door falls off, you'll know why. One of these dolls went to sleep on the line. Right?'

'Right.' I looked at the women with new interest. They were pretty

234

but none of them were really young. How could they work all day and half the night too?

The pianist shuffled quickly through his music and found the sheets required. His fingers found the melody. The dancers put on their smiles and went into the routine. Kleindorf blew smoke. No one knew his age. He must have been on the wrong side of sixty, but that was about all he was on the wrong side of, for he always had a huge bundle of high-denomination paper money in his pocket and a beautiful woman at his beck and call. His suits, shirts and shoes were the finest that Berlin outfitters could provide, and outside on the kerb there was a magnificent old Maserati Ghibli with the 4.9 litre engine option. It was a connoisseur's car that he'd had completely rebuilt and kept in tune so that it could take him down the Autobahn to West Germany at 170 mph. For years I'd been hinting that I would enjoy a chance to drive it but the cunning old devil pretended not to understand.

One persistent rumour said the Kleindorfs were Prussian aristocracy, that his grandfather General Freiherr Rudolf von Kleindorf had commanded one of the Kaiser's best divisions in the 1918 offensives, but I never heard Rudi make such claims. 'Der Grosse' said his money came from 'car-wash parlours' in Encino, Southern California. Certainly not much of it could have come from this shabby Berlin dive. Only the most intrepid tourist ventured into a place of this kind, and unless they had money to burn they were soon made to feel unwelcome. Some said Rudi kept the club going for his own amusement but others guessed that he needed this place, not just to chat with his cronies but because Rudi's back bar was one of the best listening points in the whole of this gossip-ridden city. Such men gravitated to Rudi and he encouraged them, for his reputation as a man who knew what was going on gave him an importance that he seemed to need. Rudi's barman knew that he must provide free drinks for certain men and women: hotel doormen, private secretaries, telephone workers, detectives, military government officials and sharp-eared waiters who worked in the city's private dining rooms. Even Berlin's police officials – notoriously reluctant to use paid informants – came to Rudi's bar when all else failed.

How Babylon kept going was one of Berlin's many unsolved mysteries. Even on a gala night alcohol sales didn't pay the rent. The sort of people who sat out front and watched the show were not big spenders: their livers were not up to it. They were the geriatrics of Berlin's underworld; arthritic ex-burglars, incoherent con-men and palsied forgers; men whose time had long since passed. They arrived

235

too early, nursed their drinks, leered at the girls, took their pills with a glass of water and told each other their stories of long ago. There were others of course: sometimes some of the smart set – Berlin's *Hautevolee* in fur coats and evening dress – popped in to see how the other half lived. But they were always on their way to somewhere else. And Babylon had never been a fashionable place for 'the young': this wasn't a place to buy smack, crack, angel-dust, solvents or any of the other powdered luxuries that the Mohican haircut crowd bartered upstairs on the street. Rudi was fanatically strict about that.

'For God's sake stop rattling that ice around. If you want another drink, say so.'

'No thanks, Rudi. I'm dead tired, I've got to get some sleep.'

'Can't you sit still? What's wrong with you?'

'I was a hyper-active child.'

'Could be you have this new virus that's going around. It's nasty. My manager is in the clinic. He's been away two weeks. That's why I'm here.'

'Yes, you told me.'

'You're so pale. Are you eating?'

'You sound like my mother,' I said.

'Are you sleeping well, Bernd? I think you should see a doctor. My fellow in Wannsee has done wonders for me. He gave me a series of injections – some new hormone stuff from Switzerland – and put me on a strict diet.' He touched the lemon slice floating in the glass of water in front of him. 'And I feel wonderful!'

I drank the final dregs of my scotch but there was no more than a drip or two left. 'I don't need any doctors. I'm all right.'

'You don't look all right. You look bloody ill. I've never seen you so pale and tired-looking.'

'It's late.'

'I'm twice your age, Bernd,' he said in a voice that mixed self-satisfaction and reproof. It wasn't true: he couldn't have been more than fifteen years older than me but I could see he was irritable and I didn't argue about it. Sometimes I felt sorry for him. Years back Rudi had bullied his only son into taking a regular commission in the Bundeswehr. The kid had done well enough but he was too soft for even the modern army. He'd taken an overdose and been found dead in the barrack room in Hamburg. The inquest said it was an accident. Rudi never mentioned it but everyone knew that he'd blamed himself. His wife left him and he'd never been the same again after losing the boy: his eyes had lost their sheen, they'd become hard and glittering. 'And I thought you'd cut out the smoking,' he said.

'I do it all the time.'

'Cigars are not so dangerous,' he said and puffed contentedly.

'Nothing else then?' I persisted. 'No other news?'

'Deputy Führer Hess died . . .' he said sarcastically. 'He used to live in Wilhelmstrasse – number forty-six – after he moved to Spandau we saw very little of him.'

'I'm serious,' I persisted.

'Then I must tell you the real hot news, Bernd: you! People are saying that some maniac drove a truck at you when you were crossing Waltersdorfer Chaussee. At speed! Nearly killed you, they say.'

I stared at him. I said nothing.

He sniffed and said, 'People asked what was a nice boy like Bernd Samson doing down there where the world ends. Nothing there but that ancient checkpoint. You can't get anywhere down there: you can't even get to Waltersdorfer, there's a Wall in the way.'

'What did you say?' I asked.

'I'll tell you what's there, I told them. Memories.' He smoked his cigar and scrutinized the burning end of it as a philatelist might study a rare stamp. 'Memories,' he said again. 'Was I right, Bernd?'

'Where's Waltersdorfer Chaussee?' I said. 'Is that one of those fancy streets in Nikolassee?'

'Rudow. They buried that fellow Max Busby in the graveyard down there, if I remember rightly. It took a lot of wheeling and dealing to get the body back. When they shoot someone on their side of the Wall they don't usually prove very cooperative about the remains.'

'Is that so?' I said. I kept hoping he'd insist upon me having another shot of his whisky but he didn't.

'Ever get scared, Bernd? Ever wake up at night and fancy you hear the footsteps in the hall?'

'Scared of what?'

'I heard your own people have a warrant out for you.'

'Did you?'

'Berlin is not a good town for a man on the run,' he said reflectively, almost as if I wasn't there. 'Your people and the Americans still have military powers. They can censor mail, tap phones and jail anyone they want out of the way. They even have the death penalty at their disposal.' He looked at me as if a thought had suddenly come into his mind. 'Did you see that item in the newspaper about the residents of Gatow taking their complaints about the British army to the High Court in London? Apparently the British army commander in Berlin told the court that since he was the legitimate successor to Hitler he could do anything he wished.' A tiny smile as if it caused him pain. 'Berlin is not a good place for a man on the run, Bernd.'

'Who says I'm on the run?'

'You're the only man I know who both sides would be pleased to be rid of,' said Rudi. Perhaps he'd had a specially bad day. There was a streak of cruelty in him and it was never far from the surface. 'If you were found dead tonight there'd be ten thousand suspects: KGB, CIA, even your own people.' A chuckle. 'How did you make so many enemies, Bernd?'

'I don't have any enemies, Rudi,' I said. 'Not that kind of enemies.'

'Then why do you come here dressed in those old clothes and with a gun in your pocket?' I said nothing, I didn't even move. So he'd noticed the pistol, that was damned careless of me. I was losing my touch. 'Frightened of being robbed, Bernd? I can understand it; seeing how prosperous you are looking these days.'

'You've had your fun, Rudi,' I said. 'Now tell me what I want to know, so I can go home and get some sleep.'

'And what do you want to know?'

'Where the hell has Lange Koby gone?'

'I told you, I don't know. Why should I know anything about that schmuck?' It is not a word a German uses lightly: I guessed they'd had a row, perhaps a serious quarrel.

'Because Lange was always in here and now he's missing. His phone doesn't answer and no one comes to the door.'

'How should I know anything about Lange?'

'Because you were his very close pal.'

'Of Lange?' The sour little grin he gave me made me angry.

'Yes, of Lange, you bastard. You two were as thick . . .'

'As thick as thieves. Is that what you were going to say, Bernd?' Despite the darkness, the sound of the piano and the way in which we were both speaking softly, the dancers seemed to guess that we were quarrelling. In some strange way there was an anxiety communicated to them. The smiles were slipping and their voices became more shrill.

'That's right. That's what I was going to say.'

'Knock louder,' said Rudi dismissively. 'Maybe his bell push is out of order.' From upstairs I heard the loud slam of the front door. Werner Volkmann came down the beautiful chrome spiral staircase and slid into the room in that demonstratively apologetic way that he always assumed when I was keeping him up too late. 'All okay?' I asked him. Werner nodded. Kleindorf looked round to see who it was and then turned back to watch the weary dancers entangle umbrellas as they danced into the non-existent wings and cannoned against the wall.

238

Werner didn't sit down. He gripped a chairback with both hands and stood there waiting for me to get up and go. I'd been at school, not far from here, with Werner Jacob Volkmann. He remained my closest friend. He was a big fellow and his overcoat, with its large curly astrakhan collar, made him even bigger. The ferocious beard had gone – eliminated by a chance remark from Ingrid, the lady in his life – and it was my guess that soon the moustache would go too.

'A drink, Werner?' said Rudi.

'No thanks.' Although Werner's tone showed no sign of impatience I felt bound to leave.

Werner was another one who wanted to believe I was in danger. For weeks now he'd insisted upon checking the street before letting me take my chances coming out of doorways. It was carrying caution a bit too far but Werner Volkmann was a prudent man; and he worried about me.

'Well, goodnight, Rudi,' I said.

'Goodnight, Bernd,' he said, still looking at the stage. 'If I get a postcard from Lange I'll let you put the postmark under your microscope.'

'Thanks for the drink, Rudi.'

'Any time, Bernd.' He gestured with the cigar. 'Knock louder. Maybe Lange is getting a little deaf.'

Outside, the garbage-littered Potsdamerstrasse was cold and snow was falling. This lovely boulevard now led to nowhere but the Wall and had become the focus of a sleazy district where sex, souvenirs, junk food and denim were on sale. Beside the Babylon's inconspicuous doorway, harsh blue fluorescent lights showed a curtained shop window and customers in the Lebanese café. Men with knitted hats and curly moustaches bent low over their plates eating shreds of roasted soybean cut from the imitation shawarma that revolved on a spit in the window. Across the road a drunk was crouching unsteadily at the door of a massage parlour, rapping upon it while shouting angrily through the letter-box.

Werner's limp was always worse in the cold weather. His leg had been broken in three places when he surprised three DDR agents rifling his apartment. They threw him out of the window. That was a long time ago but the limp was still there.

It was while we were walking carefully upon the icy pavement that three youths came running from a nearby shop. Turks: thin wiry youngsters in jeans and tee shirts, seemingly impervious to the stark cold. They ran straight at us, their feet pounding and faces contorted into the ugly expressions that come with such exertions. They were all brandishing sticks. Breathlessly the leader screamed something in Turkish that I couldn't understand and the other two swerved out into the road as if to get behind us.

My gun was in my hand without my making any conscious decision about needing it. I reached out and steadied myself against the cold stone wall as I took aim.

'Bernie! Bernie! Bernie!' I heard Werner shout with a note of horrified alarm that was so unfamiliar that I froze.

It was at that moment that I felt the sharp blow as Werner's arm knocked my gun up.

'They're just kids, Bernie. Just kids!'

The boys ran on past us shouting and shoving and jostling as they played some ritual of which we were not a part. I put away my gun and said, 'I'm getting jumpy.'

'You over-reacted,' said Werner. 'I do it all the time.' But he looked at me in a way that belied his words. The car was at the kerbside. I climbed in beside him. Werner said, 'Why not put the gun into the glove compartment?'

'Because I might want to shoot somebody,' I said, irritable at being treated like a child, although by then I should have become used to Werner's nannying. He shrugged and switched the heater on so that a blast of hot air hit me. We sat there in silence for a moment. I was trembling, the warmth comforted me. Huge silver coins smacked against the windscreen glass, turned to icy slush and then dribbled away. It was a red VW Golf that the dealer had lent him while his new BMW was being repaired. He still didn't drive away: we sat there with the engine running. Werner was watching his mirror and waiting until all other traffic was clear. Then he let in the clutch and, with a squeal of injured rubber, he did a U-turn and sped away, cutting through the backstreets, past the derelict railway yards to Yorckstrasse and then to my squat in Kreuzberg.

Beyond the snow clouds the first light of day was peering through the narrow lattice of morning. There was no room in the sky for pink or red. Berlin's dawn can be bleak and colourless, like the grey stone city which reflects its light.

My pad was not in that part of Kreuzberg that is slowly being yuppified with smart little eating places, and apartment blocks with newly painted front doors that ask you who you are when you press the bell push. Kreuzberg 36 was up against the Wall: a place where the cops walked in pairs and stepped carefully over the winos and the excrement.

We passed a derelict apartment block that had been patched up to

240

house 'alternative' ventures: shops for bean sprouts and broken bicycles, a cooperative kindergarten, a feminist art gallery and a workshop that printed Marxist books, pamphlets and leaflets; mostly leaflets. In the street outside this block – dressed in traditional Turkish clothes, face obscured by a scarf – there was a young woman diligently spraying a slogan on the wall.

The block in which I was living had on its façade two enormous angels wielding machine guns and surrounded by men in top hats standing under huge irregular patches of colour that was the under-painting for clouds. It was to have been a gigantic political mural called 'the massacre of the innocents' but the artist died of a drug overdose soon after getting the money for the paint.

Werner insisted upon coming inside with me. He wanted to make sure that no unfriendly visitor was waiting to surprise me in my little apartment which opened off the rear courtyard. 'You needn't worry about that, Werner,' I told him. 'I don't think the Department will locate me here, and even if they did, would Frank find anyone stouthearted enough to venture into this part of town?'

'Better safe than sorry,' said Werner. From the other end of the hallway there came the sound of Indian music. Werner opened the door cautiously and switched on the light. It was a bare low-wattage bulb suspended from the ceiling. He looked round the squalid room; the paper was hanging off the damp plaster and my bed was a dirty mattress and a couple of blankets. On the wall there was a tattered poster: a pig wearing a policeman's uniform. I'd done very little to change anything since moving in; I didn't want to attract attention. So I endured life in this dark hovel: sharing – with everyone living in the rooms around this Hinterhof – one bathroom and two primitive toilets the pungent smell of which pervaded the whole place. 'We'll have to find you somewhere better than this, Bernie.' The Indian music stopped. 'Somewhere the Department can't get you.'

'I don't think they care any more, Werner.' I looked round the room trying to see it with his eyes, but I'd grown used to the squalor.

'The Department? Then why try to arrest you?' He looked at me. I tried to see what was going on in his mind but with Werner I could never be quite sure.

'That was weeks ago. Maybe I've played into their hands. I've put myself into prison, haven't I? And they don't even have the bother or the expense of it. They are ignoring me like a parent might deliberately ignore some child who misbehaves. Did I tell you that they are still paying my salary into the bank?'

'Yes, you told me.' Werner sounded disappointed. Perhaps he enjoyed the vicarious excitement of my being on the run and didn't want to be deprived of it. 'They want to keep their options open.'

'They wanted me silenced and out of circulation. And that's what I am.'

'Don't count on anything, Bernie. They might just be waiting for you to make a move. You said they are vindictive.'

'Maybe I did but I'm tired now, Werner. I must get some sleep.' Before I could even take my coat off a very slim young man came into the room. He was dark-skinned, with large brown eyes, pockmarked face and close-cropped hair, a Tamil. Sri Lanka had provided Berlin's most recent influx of immigrants. He slept all day and stayed awake all night playing ragas on a cassette player. 'Hello, Johnny,' said Werner coldly. They had taken an instant dislike to each other at the first meeting. Werner disapproved of Johnny's indolence: Johnny disapproved of Werner's affluence.

'All right?' Johnny asked. He'd appointed himself to the role of my guardian in exchange for the German lessons I gave him. I don't know which of us had the best out of that deal: I suspect that neither of us gained anything. He'd arrived in East Berlin a zealous Marxist but his faith had not endured the rigours of life in the German Democratic Republic. Now, like so many others, he had moved to the West and was reconstructing a philosophy from ecology, pop music, mysticism, anti-Americanism and dope.

'Yes, thanks, Johnny,' I said. 'I'm just going to bed.'

'There is someone to see you,' said Johnny.

'At four in the morning?' said Werner and glanced at me.

'Name?' I said.

Suddenly there was a screech from across the courtyard. A door banged open and a man staggered out backwards and fell down with a sickening thud of a head hitting the cobbles. Through the dirty window I could see by the yellow light from an open door. A middle-aged woman – dressed in a short skirt and bra – and a long-haired young man carrying a bottle came out and looked down at the still figure. The woman, her feet bare, kicked the recumbent man without putting much effort into it. Then she went inside and returned with a man's hat and coat and a canvas bag and threw them down alongside him. The young man came out with a jug of water and poured it over the man on the ground. The door slammed loudly as they both went back inside.

'He'll freeze to death,' said the always concerned Werner. But even as he said it the figure moved and dragged itself away.

'He said he was a business acquaintance,' continued Johnny, who remained entirely indifferent to the arguments of the Silesian family on the other side of the yard. I nodded and thought about it. People announcing themselves as business acquaintances put me in mind of cheap brown envelopes marked confidential, and are as welcome. 'I told him to wait upstairs with Spengler.'

'I'd better see who it is,' I said.

I plodded upstairs. This sort of old Berlin block had no numbers on the doors but I knew the little musty room where Spengler lived. The lock was long since broken. I went in. Spengler – a young chess-playing alcoholic who Johnny met after being arrested at a political demonstration – was sitting on the floor drinking from a bottle of apple schnapps. The room smelled noticeably more foul than the rest of the building. Sitting on the only chair in the room there was a man trying not to inhale. He was wearing a Melton overcoat, and new string-backed gloves. On his head he had a brown felt hat.

'Hello, Bernd,' said Spengler. He wore an earring and steel-rimmed glasses. His hair was long and very dirty. His name wasn't really Spengler. No one knew his real name. Rumours said he was a Swede who exchanged his passport for the identity papers of a man named Spengler so that he could collect welfare money, while the real Spengler went to the USA. He was growing a straggling beard to assist the deception.

'You looking for me?' I asked the man in the hat.

'Samson?' He got to his feet and looked me up and down. He kept it formal. 'How do you do. My name is Teacher. I have a message for you.' His precise English public school accent, his pursed lips and hunched shoulders displayed his distaste for this seedy dwelling, and perhaps for me too. God knows how long he'd been waiting for me; top marks for tenacity.

'What is it?'

'I . . .'

'It's all right,' I told him. 'Spengler's brain was softened by alcohol years ago.' A dazed smile crossed Spengler's white face as he heard and understood my words.

The visitor, still doubtful, looked round again before picking his words carefully. 'Someone is coming over tomorrow morning. Frank Harrington is inviting you to sit in. He guarantees your personal freedom.'

'Tomorrow is Sunday,' I reminded him.

'That's right, Sunday.'

'Thanks very much,' I said. 'Where?'

'I'll collect you,' said the man. 'Nine o'clock?'

'Fine,' I told him.

He nodded goodbye without smiling and eased his way past me, keeping the skirt of his overcoat from touching anything that might carry infection. It was not easy. I suppose he'd been expecting me to shout with joy. Anyone from the Field Unit – even a messenger – must have sniffed out something of my present predicament: disgraced ex-field agent with a warrant extant. Being invited to the official interrogation of a newly arrived defector from the East brought an amazing change of status.

'You're going?' Werner asked after the front door banged. He was watching over the balcony to be sure the visitor actually departed.

'Yes, I'm going.'

'It might be a trap,' he warned.

'They know where to find me, Werner,' I said, making him the butt of my anger. I knew that Frank had sent his stooge along as a way of demonstrating how easy it was to pick me up if he felt inclined.

'Have a drink,' said Spengler, from where he was still sprawled on the floor. He pushed his bent glasses up on his nose and prodded the buttons on the machine he was holding so that the little lights flashed. He'd finally found new batteries for his pocket chess computer and despite his alcoholic daze he was engaging it in combat. Sometimes I wondered what sort of genius he would be if he ever sobered up.

'No thanks,' I said. 'I've got to get some sleep.'

2

Take me to a safe house blindfolded and I'd know it for what it was. Werner once said they smelled of electricity, by which he meant that smell of ancient dust that the static electricity holds captive in the shutters, curtains and carpets of such dreary unlived-in places.

My father said it was not a smell but rather the absence of smells that distinguishes them. They don't smell of cooking or of children, fresh flowers or love. Safe houses, said my father, smelled of nothing. But reflexes conditioned to such environmental stimuli found hanging in the air the subtle perfume of fear, a fragrance instantly recognized by those prone to visceral terror. Somewhere beyond the faint and fleeting bouquet of stale urine, sweat, vomit and faeces there is an astringent and deceptive musky sweetness. I smelled fear now in this lovely old house in Charlottenburg.

Perhaps this young fellow Teacher smelled something of it too, for his chatter dried up after we entered the elegant mirrored lobby and walked past the silent concierge who'd come out of the wooden cubicle from where every visitor was inspected. The concierge was plump, an elderly man with grey hair, a big moustache and heavy features. He wore a Sunday church-going black three-piece suit of heavy serge that had gone shiny on the sleeves. There was something anachronistic about his appearance; he was the sort of Berliner better suited to cheering Kaiser Wilhelm in faded sepia photos. A fully grown German shepherd dog came out of the door too. It growled at us. Teacher ignored dog and master and started up the carpeted staircase. His footfalls were silent. He spoke over his shoulder. 'Are you married?' he said suddenly as if he'd been thinking of it all along.

'Separated,' I said.

'I'm married,' he said in that definitive way that suggested fatalism. He gripped the keys so tight that his knuckles whitened.

The wrought-iron baluster was a delicate tracery of leaves and flowers that spiralled up to a great glass skylight at the top of the building. Through its glass came the colourless glare of a snow-laden sky, filling the oval-shaped stairwell all the way down to the patterns of the marble hall but leaving the staircase in shadow.

I had never been here before or even learned of its existence. As I

245

followed Teacher into an apartment on the second floor I heard the steady tapping of a manual typewriter. Not the heavy thud of a big office machine, this was the lighter patter of a small portable, the sort of machine that interrogators carry with them.

At first I thought the interrogation – or debriefing as they were delicately termed – had ended, that our visitor was waiting to initial his statement. But I was wrong. Teacher took me along the corridor to a sitting room with long windows one of which gave on to a small cast-iron balcony. There was a view of the bare-limbed trees in the park and, over the rooftops, a glimpse of the figure surmounting the dome of the eighteenth-century palace from which the district gets its name.

Most safe houses were shabby, their tidiness arising out of neglect and austerity, but this ante-room was in superb condition, the wall-coverings, carpets and paintwork cared for with a pride and devotion that only Germans gave to their houses.

A slim horsy woman, about thirty-five years old, came into the room from another door. She gave Teacher a somewhat lacklustre greeting and, head held high, she peered myopically at me and sniffed loudly. 'Hello, Pinky,' I said. Her name was Penelope but everyone had always called her Pinky. At one time in London she'd worked as an assistant to my wife but my wife had got rid of her. Fiona said Pinky couldn't spell.

Pinky gave a sudden smile of recognition and a loud 'Hello, Bernard. Long time no see.' She was wearing a cocktail dress and pearls. It would have been easy to think she was one of the German staff, all of whom always looked as if they were dressed for a smart Berlin-style cocktail party. At this time of the year most of the British female staff wore frayed cardigans and baggy tweed jackets. Perhaps it was her Sunday outfit. Pinky swung her electric smile to beam upon Teacher and in her clipped accent said, 'Oh well, chaps. Must get on. Must get on.' She rubbed her hands together briskly, getting the circulation going, as she went through the other door and out into the corridor. That was something else about safe houses: they were always freezing cold.

'He's inside now,' said Teacher, his head inclining to indicate the room from which Pinky had emerged. 'The shorthand clerk is still there. They'll tell us when.' So far he'd confided nothing, except that the debriefing was of a man called Valeri – obviously a cover name – and that permission for me to sit in on the debriefing was conditional upon my not speaking to Valeri directly, nor joining in any general discussion.

I sank down on to the couch and closed my eyes for a moment. These things could take a long time. Teacher seemed to have survived his sleepless night unscathed but I was weary. I was reluctant to admit it but I was too old to enjoy life in a slum. I needed regular hot baths with expensive soap and thick towels and a bed with clean sheets and a room with a lock on the door. To some extent I was perhaps identifying with the mysterious escaper next door, who was no doubt desirous of all those same luxuries.

I sat there for nearly half an hour, dozing off to sleep once or twice. I was woken by the sound of an argument coming, not from the room in which the debriefing was taking place but from the room with the typewriter. The typewriting had stopped. The arguing voices were women's, the argument was quiet and restrained in the way that the English voice their most bitter resentments. I couldn't hear the actual words but there was a resignation to the exchange that suggested a familiar routine. When the door opened again an elderly secretary they called the Duchess came into the room. She saw me and smiled, then she put two dinner plates, some cutlery and a brown paper bag, inside which some bread rolls could be glimpsed, on to a small table.

The Duchess was a thin and frail Welsh woman but her appearance was deceptive, for she had the daring, stamina and tenacity of a prize-fighter. God knows how old she was: she had worked for the Berlin office for countless years. Her memory was prodigious and she also claimed to be able to foretell the future by reading palms and working out horoscopes and so on. She was unmarried and lived in an apartment in Dahlem with a hundred cats, and moon charts and books on the occult, or so it was said. Some people were afraid of her. Frank Harrington made jokes about her being a witch but I noticed that even Frank would think twice before confronting her.

The arrival of the dinner plates was a bad sign: someone was preparing for the debriefing to continue until nightfall. 'You're looking well, Mr Samson,' she said. 'Very fit.' She looked at my scuffed leather jacket and rumpled trousers and seemed to decide that they were occasioned by my official duties.

'Thank you,' I said. I suppose she was referring to my hungry body, drawn face and the anxiety I felt, and no doubt displayed. Usually I was plump, unfit and happy. An angry cat came into the room, its fur rumpled, eyes wide and manner agitated. It glared around as if it was some unfortunate visitor suddenly transformed into this feline form.

But I recognized this elderly creature as 'Jackdaw'. The Duchess took it everywhere and it slumbered on her lap while she worked at her desk. Now, dumped to the floor, it was outraged. It went and sank its claws into the sofa. 'Jackdaw! Stop it!' said the Duchess and the cat stopped.

'Would you like a cup of tea, Mr Samson?' she asked, her Welsh accent as strong as ever.

'Yes. Thank you,' I said gratified that she'd recognized me after a long time away.

'Sugar? Milk?'

'Both please.'

'And you, Mr Teacher?' she asked my companion. She didn't ask him how he drank it. I suppose she knew already.

Drinking tea with the Duchess gave me an opportunity to study this fellow Teacher in a way that I hadn't been able to the night before. He was about thirty years old, a slight, unsmiling man with dark hair, cut short and carefully parted. The waistcoat of his dark blue suit was a curious design, double-breasted with ivory buttons and wide lapels. Was it a relic of a cherished bachelorhood, or the *cri de coeur* of a man consigned to a career of interminable anonymity? His face was deeply lined, with thin lips and eyes that stared revealing no feelings except perhaps unrelieved sadness.

While we were drinking our cups of tea the Duchess spoke of former times in the Berlin office and she mentioned the way that Werner Volkmann had made an hotel off Ku-Damm into a 'cosy haven for some of the old crowd'. She knew Werner was my close friend and that's probably why she told me. Although she intended nothing but praise, I was not sure that her description augured well for its commercial success, for most of the 'old crowd' were noisy and demanding. They were not the sort of customers who would do much for the profit and loss account. We chatted on until, providing an example of the sort of considered guess that had helped her reputation for sorcery, she said that I'd be invited to go inside in ten minutes' time. She was almost exactly right.

I went in quietly. Two men sat facing each other at either side of the superb mahogany dining table. Its surface was protected by a sheet of glass. Around it there were eight reproduction Hepplewhite dining chairs, six of them empty, except that one was draped with a shapeless blue jacket. A cheap cut-glass chandelier was suspended over one end of the table, revealing that the table had been moved away from the window, for even here in Charlottenburg windows could prove dangerous. One of the men was smoking. He was in shirt-sleeves and loosened tie. The window was open a couple of inches so that a draught made the curtain sway gently but didn't disperse the blue haze of cigarette smoke. The distinctive pungent reek of coarse East German tobacco took me by the throat. Smoking was one of the few pleasures

248

still freely available in the East and there was neither official disapproval nor social hostility towards it over there.

The man called Valeri was quite elderly for an active agent. His high cheekbones and narrow eyes gave him that almost oriental appearance that is not unusual in Eastern Europe. His complexion was like polished red jasper, flecked with darker marks and shiny like a wet pebble found on a beach. His thick brown hair – darkened and glossy with dressing – was long. He'd combed it straight back, so it covered the tops of his ears to make a shiny helmet. His eyes flickered to see me as I came through the door but his head didn't move, and his high-pitched voice continued without faltering.

Sitting across the table from him, legs crossed in a languid posture, there was a fresh-faced young man named Larry Bower, a Cambridge graduate. His hair was fair and wavy, and he wore it long in a style that I'd heard described as Byronic, although the only picture of Byron that I could call to mind showed him with short back and sides. In contrast to the coarse ill-fitting clothes of Valeri, Bower was wearing a well-tailored fawn Saxony check suit, soft yellow cotton shirt, Wykehamist tie and yellow pullover. They were speaking German, in which Larry was fluent, as might be expected of a man with a German wife and a Rhineland beer baron grandfather named Bauer. In an armchair in the corner a grey-haired clerk bent over her notebook.

Bower raised his eyes to me as I came in. His face hardly changed but I knew him well enough to recognize a fleeting look that expressed his weariness and exasperation. I sat down in one of the soft armchairs from which I could see both men. 'Now once again,' said Bower, 'this new Moscow liaison man.' As if reflecting on their conversation he swung round in his chair to look out of the window.

'Not new,' said Valeri. 'He's been there years.'

'Oh, how many years?' said Bower in a bored voice, still looking out of the window.

'I told you,' said Valeri. 'Four years.'

Bower leaned forward to touch the radiator as if checking to see if it was warm. 'Four years.'

'*About* four years,' he replied defensively.

It was all part of the game: Bower's studied apathy and his getting facts wrong to see if the interviewee changed or misremembered his story. Valeri knew that, and he did not enjoy the mistrust that such routines implied. None of us did. 'Would you show me again?' Bower asked, pushing a battered cardboard box across the table.

Valeri opened the box and searched through a lot of dog-eared

249

postcard-sized photographs. He took his time in doing it and I knew he was relaxing for a moment. Even for a man like this – one of our own people as far as we knew – the prolonged ordeal of questioning could tighten the strings of the mind until they snapped.

He got to the end of the first batch of photos and started on the second pile. 'Take your time,' said Bower as if he didn't know what a welcome respite it was.

Until four years before, such identity photos had been pasted into large leather-bound ledgers. But then the KGB spread alarm and confusion in our ranks by instructing three of their doubles to select the same picture, in the same position on the same page, to identify a man named Peter Underlet as a spy, a KGB colonel. In fact Underlet's photo was one of a number that had been included only as a control. Poor Underlet. His photo should never have been used for such purposes. He was a CIA case officer, and since case officers have always been the most desirable targets for both sides, Underlet was turned inside out. Even after the KGB's trick was confirmed, Underlet never got his senior position back: he was posted to some lousy job in Jakarta. That had all happened at the time my wife Fiona went to work for the other side. If it was a way of deflecting the CIA's fury and contempt, it worked. I suppose that diversion suited us as much as it did the KGB. At the time I'd wondered if it was Fiona's idea: we both knew Peter Underlet and his wife. Fiona seemed to like them.

'This one,' said Valeri, selecting a photo and placing it carefully on the table apart from the others. I stood up so that I could see it better.

'So that's him,' said Bower, feigning interest, as if they'd not been through it all before. He picked up the photo and studied it. Then he passed it to me. 'Handsome brute, eh? Know him by any chance?'

I looked at it. I knew the man well. He called himself Erich Stinnes. He was a senior KGB man in East Berlin. It was said that he was the liaison man between the Moscow and the East German security service. It must have been a recent photo, for he'd grown fatter since the last time I'd seen him. But he still hadn't lost the last of his thinning hair and the hard eyes behind the small lenses of his glasses were just as fierce as ever. 'It's no one I've seen before,' I said, handing the picture back to Bower. 'Is he someone we've had contact with?'

'Not as far as I know,' said Bower. To Valeri he said, 'Describe the deliveries again.'

'The second Thursday of every month . . . The KGB courier.'

'And you saw him open it?' persisted Bower.

'Only the once but everyone knows . . .'

'Everyone?'

'In his office. In fact, it's the talk of Karlshorst.'

Bower gave a sardonic smile. 'That the KGB liaison is sniffing his way to dreamland on the second Thursday of every month? And Moscow does nothing?'

'Things are different now,' said Valeri adamantly, his face unchanging.

'Sounds like it,' said Bower, not concealing his disbelief.

'Take it or leave it,' said Valeri. 'But I saw him shake the white powder into his hand.'

'And sniff it?'

'I was going out of the room. I told you. I shut the door quickly, I wasn't looking for trouble.'

'And yet you could see it was white powder?'

'I wish I'd never mentioned the damned stuff.' I had him sized up now. He was a typical old-time Communist, one of the exiles who'd spent the war years in Moscow. Many such men had been trained for high posts in the Germany that Stalin conquered. What was the story behind this one? Why had he come to work for us? Blackmail? Had he committed some crime – political or secular – or was he not of the hard stuff of which leaders are made? Or was he simply one of those awkward individuals who thought for themselves?

'No comment,' said Bower in a tired voice and looked at his watch.

Valeri said, 'Next week I'll watch more carefully.'

I noticed Bower stiffen. It was a damned careless remark for an active agent to make. I was not supposed to discover that this Valeri was a double; going in and out regularly. It was the sort of slip of the tongue that kills men. Valeri was tired. I pretended not to have noticed the lapse.

Bower did the same. He should have noted it and cautioned the man but he gave an almost indiscernible shake of the head to the shorthand clerk before turning his eyes to me. Levelly he asked, 'Is that any use?' It was my signal to depart.

'Not as far as I can see.'

'Frank wanted you to know,' he added just in case I missed the message to get out of there and let him continue his difficult job.

'Where is he?'

'He had to leave.' Bower picked up the phone and said they'd break for lunch in thirty minutes. I wondered if it was a ploy. Interrogators did such things sometimes, letting the time stretch on and on to increase the tension.

251

I got to my feet. 'Tell him thanks,' I said. He nodded.

I went out to where Teacher was waiting in the ante-room. He didn't say 'All right?' or make any of the usual polite inquiries. Interrogations are like sacramental confessions: they take place and are seen to take place but no reference to them is ever made. 'Are you returning me to Kreuzberg?' I asked him.

'If that's where you want to be,' said Teacher.

We said our goodbyes to the Duchess and went downstairs to be let out of the double-locked front door by the guardian.

The streets were empty. There is something soul-destroying about the German *Ladenschlussgesetz* – a trade-union-inspired law that closes all the shops most of the time – and right across the land, weekends in Germany are a mind-numbing experience. Tourists roam aimlessly. Residents desperate for food and drink scour the streets hoping to find a *Tante Emma Laden* where a shopkeeper willing to break the law will sell a loaf, a chocolate bar or a litre of milk from the back door.

As we drove through the desolate streets, I said to Teacher, 'Are you my keeper?'

Teacher looked at me blankly.

I asked him again. 'Are you assigned to be my keeper?'

'I don't know what a keeper is.'

'They have them in zoos. They look after the animals.'

'Is that what you need, a keeper?'

'Is this Frank's idea?'

'Frank?'

'Don't bullshit me, Teacher. I was taking this town to pieces when you were in knee pants.'

'Frank knows nothing about you coming here,' he said mechanically. It contradicted everything he'd previously said but he wanted to end the conversation by making me realize that he was just obeying instructions: Frank's instructions.

'And Frank keeps out of the way so that he can truthfully tell London that he's not seen me.'

Teacher peered about him and seemed unsure of which way to go. He slowed to read the street signs. I left him to figure it out. Eventually he said, 'And that annoys you?'

'Why shouldn't it?'

'Because if Frank had any sense he'd toss you on to the London plane, and let you and London work it all out together,' said Teacher.

'That's what you'd do?'

'Damned right I would,' said Teacher.

We drove along Heer Strasse, which on a weekday would have been filled with traffic. Every now and again there had been a dusty glint in the air as a flurry offered a sample of the promised snow. Now it began in earnest. Large spiky flakes came spinning down. Time and time again the last snow had come, and still the cold persisted, reminding those from other climates that Berlin was on the edge of Asia.

In what was either carelessness or an attempt to impress me with his knowledge of Berlin, Teacher turned off and tried to find a shortcut round the Exhibition Grounds. Twice he came to a dead end. Finally I took pity on him and directed him to Halensee. Then, as we got to Kurfürstendamm, he sat back in his seat, sighed and said, 'I suppose I am your keeper.'

'And?'

'Frank might like to hear your reactions.'

'Berlin is the heroin capital of the world,' I said.

'I read that in *Die Welt*,' said Teacher.

I ignored the sarcasm. 'It all comes through Schönefeld airport. Those bastards make sure it keeps moving to this side of the Wall.'

'If it *all* comes here, then it makes sense that someone might try sending a little of it back,' said Teacher.

'Stinnes is top brass nowadays. He'd have a lot to lose. I can't swallow the idea that he's having an army courier pick up consignments of heroin – or whatever it is – in the West.'

'But?'

'Yes, there is a but. Stinnes knows the score. He's spent a lot of time in the West. He's an active womanizer and some types of hard drugs connect with sexual activity.'

'Connect? Connect how?'

'A lot of people use drugs only when they jump into bed. I could perhaps see Stinnes in that category.'

'So I tell Frank you think it's possible.'

'Only possible; not likely.'

'A nuance,' said Teacher.

'Once upon a time this fellow Stinnes was stringing me along . . . He told me he wanted to come across to us.'

'KGB? Enrolled?'

'That's what he said.'

'And you swallowed it?'

'I urged caution.'

'That's the best way: cover all the exits,' said Teacher. He was not

253

one of my most fervent admirers. I suspected that Frank had painted me too golden.

'Anyway: once bitten twice shy.'

'I'll tell Frank exactly what you said,' he promised.

'This is not the way to Kreuzberg.'

'Don't get alarmed. I thought I'd give you lunch before you go back to that slum.' I wondered if that too was Frank's idea. Mr Teacher didn't look like a man much given to impulsive gestures.

'Thanks.'

'I live in Wilmersdorf. My wife always has too much food in the house. Will that be okay?'

'Thanks,' I said.

'I've given my expenses a beating this month. I had a wedding anniversary.'

By the time we arrived in Wilmersdorf the streets were wrapped in a fragile tissue of snow. Teacher lived in a smart new apartment block. He parked in the underground car park that served the building. It was well lit and heated: luxury compared with Kreuzberg. We took the elevator to his apartment on the fourth floor.

He rang the bell while opening the door with his key. Once inside he called to his wife. 'Clemmie? Clem, are you there?'

Her voice replied from somewhere upstairs, 'Where the hell have you been? Do you know what time it is?'

'Clemmie—'

She still didn't appear. 'I've eaten my lunch. You'll have to make do with an egg or something.'

Standing awkwardly in the hall he looked at the empty landing and then at me and smiled ruefully. 'Egg okay? Clemmie will make omelettes.'

'Wonderful.'

'I've brought a colleague home,' he called loudly.

His wife came down the stairs, skittish and smiling. She was worth waiting for; young, long-legged and shapely. She touched her carefully arranged hair and flashed her eyes at me. She looked as if her make-up was newly applied. Her smile froze as she noticed some flecks of snow on his coat. 'My God! When does summer come to this damned town?' she said, holding him personally responsible.

'Clemmie,' said Teacher after she'd offered her cheek to be kissed, 'this is Bernard Samson, from the office.'

'The famous Bernard Samson?' she asked with a throaty chuckle. Her voice was lower now and her genial mockery was not unattractive.

254

'I suppose so,' I said. So much for Teacher's ingenuous inquiry about whether I was married. Even his wife knew all about me.

'Take off your coat, Bernard,' she said in a jokey flirtatious way that seemed to come naturally to her. Perhaps the dour Teacher was attracted to her on that account. She took my old coat, draped it on a wooden hanger marked Disneyland Hotel Anaheim, California and hung it in an antique walnut closet.

She was wearing a lot of perfume and a button-through dress of light green wool, large earrings and a gold necklace. It was not the sort of outfit you'd put on to go to church. She must have been six or eight years younger than her husband and I wondered if she was trying to acquire the pushy determination that young wives need to survive the social demands of a Berlin posting.

'Bernard Samson: secret agent! I've never met a real secret agent before.'

'That was long ago,' said Teacher in an attempt to warn her off.

'Not so long ago,' she said archly. 'He's so young. What is it like to be a secret agent, Bernard? You don't mind if I call you Bernard, do you?'

'Of course not,' I said awkwardly.

'And you call me Clemmie.' She took my arm in a gesture of mock confidentiality. 'Tell me what it's like. Please.'

'It's like being a down-at-heel Private Eye,' I said. 'In a land where being a Private Eye will get you thirty years in the slammer. Or worse.'

'Find something for us to eat, Clemmie,' said Teacher in a way that suggested that his acute embarrassment was turning to anger. 'We're starved.'

'Darling, it's Sunday. Let's celebrate. Let's open that lovely tin of sevruga that you got from someone I'm not allowed to inquire about,' she said.

'Wonderful idea,' said Teacher and sounded relieved at this suggestion. But he still did not look happy. I suppose he never did.

Clemmie went into the kitchen to find the caviar while Teacher took me into the sitting room and asked me what I wanted to drink.

'Do you have vodka?' I asked.

'Stolichnaya, or Zubrovka or a German one?' He set up some glasses.

'Zubrovka.'

'I'll get it from the fridge. Make yourself at home.'

Left alone I looked around. It is not what guests are expected to do but I can never resist. It was a small but comfortable apartment with a huge sofa, a big hi-fi and a long shelf of compact discs – mostly outmoded pop groups – that I guessed were Clemmie's. On the coffee table there was a photo album, the sort of leather-bound tasselled one in which people record an elaborate wedding. It bulged with extra pictures and programmes. I opened it. Every page contained photos of Clemmie: on the athletic field, running the 1,000 metres, hurdling, getting medals, waving silver cups. The pages were lovingly captioned in copperplate writing. Tucked into the back she was to be seen in already yellowing sports pages torn from the sort of local newspaper that carries large adverts for beauty salons and nursing homes. In all the pictures she looked so young: so very very young. She must have been here looking through it when she heard us at the door, and then rushed upstairs to put on fresh make-up. Poor Clemmie.

The apartment block was new and the walls were thin. As Teacher went into the kitchen I heard his wife speak loudly, 'Jesus Christ, Jeremy! Why did you bring him here?'

'I didn't have cash or I would have taken us all to a restaurant.'

'Restaurant. . . ? If the office hear all this, you'll be in a row.'

'Frank said give him lunch. Frank likes him.'

'Frank likes everyone until the crunch comes.'

'I'm assigned to him.'

'You should never have agreed to do it.'

'There was no one else.'

'You told me he was a pariah, and that's what you'll end up as if you don't keep the swine at arm's length.'

'I wish you'd let me do things my way.'

'It was letting you do things your way that brought us to this bloody town.'

'We'll have a nice long leave in six months.'

'Another six months here with these bloody krauts and I'll go round the bend,' she said.

There was the sound of a refrigerator door closing loudly, and of ice-cubes going into a jug.

'You don't have to put up with them,' she said. Her voice was shrill now. 'Pushing and elbowing their way in front of you at the check-outs. I hate the bloody Germans. And I hate this terrible winter weather that goes on and on and on. I can't stand it here!'

'I know, darling.' His voice remained soft and affectionate. 'But please try.'

When he returned he poured two large measures of vodka and we drank them in silence. I suppose he knew how thin the walls were.

It was not an easy lunch. We consumed 250 grams of Russian sevruga virtually in silence. With it we had rye bread and vodka. 'The spring catch,' said Teacher knowledgeably as he tasted the caviar. 'That's always the best.'

Unsure of an appropriate response to that sort of remark I just said it was delicious.

Clemmie's mascara was smudged. She responded minimally to her husband's small-talk. She wouldn't have a drink: she kept to water. I felt sorry for both of them. I wanted to tell them it didn't matter. I wanted to tell her it was just the Berlin Blues, the claustrophobic time that all the wives suffered when they were first posted to 'the island'. But I was too cowardly. I just contributed to the small-talk and pretended not to notice that they were having a private and personal row in silence.

'Keep going!' I told Teacher as he began to slow down to let me out of the car.

'What?'

'Keep-going keep-going keep-going!'

'What's the matter with you?' he said, but he kept going and passed the car that had attracted my notice. It was parked right outside my front door.

'Turn right and go right round the block.'

'What did you see? A car you recognize?'

I made a prevaricating noise.

'What then?' he persisted.

'A car I didn't recognize.'

'Which one?'

'The black Audi . . . Too smart for this street.'

'You're getting jumpy, Samson. There's nothing wrong, I'll bet you . . .'

As he was speaking a police car cruised slowly past us, but Teacher gave no sign of noticing it. I suppose he had other things on his mind. 'Perhaps you're right,' I said. 'I am a bit jumpy. I remember now it belongs to my landlady's brother.'

'There you are,' said Teacher. 'I told you there was nothing wrong.'

'I need a good night's sleep. Let me off on the corner. I must buy some cigarettes.'

He stopped the car outside the shop. 'Closed,' he said.

'They have a machine in the hallway.'

'Righto.'

I opened the car door. 'Thanks for sharing your caviar. And tell Clemmie thanks too. Sorry if I outstayed my welcome.' He'd let me have a hot shower. I felt better but couldn't help wondering if the grime was going to block the drain. I was grateful. 'And best wishes to Frank,' I added as an afterthought.

He nodded. 'I was on the phone to him. Frank says you're to keep away from Rudi Kleindorf.'

'Forget about the good wishes.'

He gave a grim little smile and revved the motor and pulled away as soon as I closed the door. He was worried about his wife. I took a deep breath. The air was thick with the stink from the lignite-burning power stations that the DDR have on all sides of the city. It killed the trees, burned the back of the throat and filled the nostrils with soot. It was the Berlinerluft.

I let Teacher's car go out of sight before cautiously returning down the street to rap on the window of the red VW Golf. Werner reached over to unlock the door and I got into the back seat.

'Thank God. You're all right, Bernie?'

'Why wouldn't I be?'

'Where have you been?' Werner was good at hiding his feelings but there was no doubt about his agitated state.

'What does it matter?' I said. 'What's going on?'

'Spengler is dead. Someone murdered him.'

Bile rose in my throat. I was too old for rough stuff: too old, too involved, too married, too soft. 'Murdered him? When?'

'I was going to ask you,' said Werner.

'What's that mean, Werner? Do you think I'd murder the poor little sod?' Werner's manner annoyed me. I'd liked Spengler.

'I saw Johnny. He was looking for you, to warn you that the cops were here.'

'Is Johnny all right?'

'Johnny is at the Polizeipräsidium answering questions. They're holding him.'

'He has no papers,' I said.

'Right. So they'll put him through the wringer.'

'Don't worry. Johnny's a good kid,' I said.

'If he has to choose between deportation to Sri Lanka or spilling his guts, he'll tell them anything he knows,' said Werner with stolid logic.

'He knows nothing,' I said.

'He might make some damaging guesses, Bernie.'

'Shit!' I rubbed my face and tried to remember anything compromising Johnny might have seen or overheard.

'Get down, the cops are coming out,' said Werner. I crouched down on the floor out of sight. There was a strong smell of rubber floor mats. Werner had moved the front seats well forward to give me plenty of room. Werner thought of everything. Under his calm, logical and conventional exterior there lurked an all-consuming passion, if not to say obsession, with espionage. Werner followed the published, and unpublished, sagas of the cold war with the same sort of dedication that other men gave to the fluctuating fortunes of football teams. Werner

259

would have been the perfect spy: except that perfect spies, like perfect husbands, are too predictable to survive in a world where fortune favours the impulsive.

Two uniformed cops walked past going to their car. I heard one of them say, '*Mit der Dummheit kämpfen Götter selbst vergebens*' – With stupidity the gods themselves struggle in vain.

'Schiller,' said Werner, equally dividing pride with admiration.

'Maybe he's studying to be a sergeant,' I said.

'Someone put a plastic bag over Spengler's head and suffocated him,' said Werner after the policemen had got into their car and departed. 'I suppose he was drunk and didn't make much resistance.'

'The police are unlikely to give it too much attention,' I said. A dead junkie in this section of Kreuzberg was not the sort of newsbreak for which press photographers jostle. It was unlikely to make even a filler on an inside page.

'Spengler was sleeping on your bed,' said Werner. 'Someone was trying to kill *you*.'

'Who wants to kill me?' I said.

Werner wiped his nose very carefully with a big white handkerchief. 'You've had a lot of strain lately, Bernie. I'm not sure that I could have handled it. You need a rest, a real rest.'

'Don't baby me along,' I said. 'What are you trying to tell me?'

He frowned, trying to decide how to say what he wanted to say. 'You're going through a funny time; you're not thinking straight any more.'

'Just tell me who would want to kill me.'

'I knew I'd upset you.'

'You're not upsetting me but tell me.'

Werner shrugged.

'That's right,' I said. 'Everybody says my life is in danger but no one knows from who.'

'You've stirred up a hornet's nest, Bernie. Your own people wanted to arrest you, the Americans thought you were trying to make trouble for them and God knows what Moscow makes of it all . . .'

He was beginning to sound like Rudi Kleindorf; in fact, he was beginning to sound like a whole lot of people who couldn't resist giving me good advice. I said, 'Will you drive me over to Lange's place?'

For a moment he thought about it. 'There's no one there.'

'How do you know?' I said.

'I've phoned him every day, just the way you asked. I've sent letters too.'

260

'I'm going to beat on his door. Perhaps Der Grosse wasn't kidding. Maybe Lange is playing deaf: maybe he's in there.'

'Not answering the phone and not opening his mail? That's not like Lange.' Lange was an American who'd lived in Berlin since it was first built. Werner disliked him. In fact it was hard to think of anyone who was fond of Lange except his long-suffering wife: and she visited relatives several times a year.

'Maybe he's going through a funny time too,' I said.

'I'll come with you.'

'Just drop me outside.'

'You'll need a ride back,' said Werner in that plaintive, martyred tone he used when indulging me in my most excruciating foolishness.

When we reached the street where John 'Lange' Koby lived I thought Werner was going to drive away and leave me to it, but the hesitation he showed was fleeting and he waved away my suggestions that I go up there alone.

Dating from the last century it was a great grey apartment block typical of the whole city. Since my previous visit the front door had been painted and so had the lobby, and one side of the entrance hall had two lines of new tin post-boxes, each one bearing a tenant's name. But once up the first staircase all attempts at improvement ceased. On each landing a press-button timer switch provided a dim light and a brief view of walls upon which sprayed graffiti proclaimed the superiority of football teams and pop groups, or simply made the whorls and zigzag patterns that proclaim that graffiti need not be a monopoly of the literate.

Lange's apartment was on the top floor. The door was old and scuffed, the bell push had had its label torn off as if someone had wanted the name removed. Several times I pressed the bell but heard no sound from within. I knocked, first with my knuckles and then with a coin I found in my pocket.

The coin gave me an idea. 'Give me some money,' I told Werner.

Obliging as ever he opened his wallet and offered it. I took a hundred-mark note and tore it gently in half. Using Werner's slim silver pencil, I wrote 'Lange – open up you bastard' on one half of the note and pushed it under the door.

'He's not there,' said Werner, understandably disconcerted by my capricious disposal of his money. 'There's no light.'

Werner meant there was no light escaping round the door or from the transom. I didn't remind him that John Lange Koby had been in the espionage game a very long time indeed. Whatever one thought of him –

and my own feelings were mixed – he knew a thing or two about fieldcraft. He wasn't the sort of man who would pretend he was out of town while letting light escape from cracks around his front door.

I put a finger to my lips and no sooner had I done so than the timer switch made a loud plop and we were in darkness. We stood there a long time. It seemed like hours although it was probably no more than three minutes.

Suddenly the door bolts were snapped back with a sound like gunshots. Werner gasped: he was startled and so was I. Lange recognized that and laughed at us. 'Step inside folks,' he said. He held out his hand and I gave it the slap that he expected as a greeting. Only a glimmer of light escaped from his front door. 'Bernard! You four-eyed son of a bitch!' Looking over my shoulder he said, 'And who's this well-dressed gent with false moustache and big red plastic nose? Can it be Werner Volkmann?' I felt Werner stiffen with anger. Lange continued, not expecting a reply, 'I thought you guys were Jehovah's Witnesses! The hallelujah peddlers have been round just about every night this week. Then I thought to myself, "It's Sunday, it's got to be their day off!" ' He laughed.

Lange read my written message again and tucked the half banknote into the pocket of his shirt as we went inside. In the entrance there was an inlaid walnut hallstand with a mirror and hooks for coats, a shelf for hats and a rack for sticks and umbrellas. He took Werner's hat and overcoat and showed us how it worked. It took up almost all the width of the corridor and we had to squeeze past it. I noticed that Lange didn't switch on the light until the front door was closed again. He didn't want to be silhouetted in the doorway. Was he afraid of something, or someone? No, not Lange: that belligerent old bastard was fearless. He pushed aside a heavy curtain. The curtain was in fact an old grey *Wehrmacht* blanket, complete with the stripe that tells you which end is for your feet. It hung from a rail on big wooden rings. It kept the cold draught out and also prevented any light escaping from the sitting room.

They only had one big comfortable room in which to sit and watch television, so Lange used it as his study too. There were bookshelves filling one wall from floor to ceiling, and even then books were double-banked and stuffed horizontally into every available space. An old school-desk near the window held more books and papers and a big old-fashioned office typewriter upon which German newspapers and a cup and saucer were precariously balanced.

'Look who finally found out where we live,' Lange said to his wife in the throaty Bogart voice that suited his American drawl. He was a gaunt figure, pens and pencils in the pocket of his faded plaid shirt, and baggy flannel trousers held up by an ancient US army canvas belt.

His wife came to greet us. Face carefully made-up, hair short and neatly combed, Gerda was still pretty in a severe spinsterish style. 'Bernard dear! And Werner too. How nice to see you.' She was a diminutive figure, especially when standing next to her tall husband. Gerda was German; very German. They met here in the ruins in 1945. At that time she was an opera singer and I can remember how, years later, she was still being stopped on the street by people who remembered her and wanted her autograph. That was a long time ago, and now her career was relegated to the history books, but even in her cheap little black dress she had some arcane magic that I could not define, and sometimes I could imagine her singing Sophie in *Der Rosenkavalier* the way she had that evening in 1943 when she brought the *Staatsoper* audience to its feet and became a star overnight.

'We tried to phone,' explained Werner apologetically.

'You are looking well,' said Gerda, studying Werner with great interest. 'You look most distinguished.' She looked at me. 'You too, Bernard,' she added politely, although I think my long hair and dirty clothes disturbed her. 'Would you prefer tea or coffee?' Gerda asked.

'Or wine?' said Lange.

'Tea or coffee,' I said hurriedly. Each harvest Gerda made enough plum wine to keep Lange going all year. I dread to think how much that must have been, for Lange drank it by the pint. It tasted like paint remover.

'Plum wine,' said Lange. 'Gerda makes it.'

'Do you really, Gerda?' I said. 'What a shame. Plum wine brings me out in spots.'

Lange scowled. Gerda said, 'Lange drinks too much of it. It's not good for him.'

'He looks fit on it,' I pointed out, and considering that this huge aggressive fellow was in his middle seventies, or beyond, was almost enough to convert me to Gerda's jungle juice.

We sat down on the lumpy sofa while Mrs Koby went off to the kitchen to make some tea for us. Lange hovered over us. He'd not changed much since the last time I'd seen him. In fact he'd changed very little from the ferocious tyrant I'd worked for long long ago. He was a craggy man. I remember someone in the office saying that they'd rather tackle the north face of the Eiger than Lange in a bad mood, and Frank Harrington had replied that there was not much in it. Ever since then I'd thought of Lange as some dangerous piece of granite: sharp and unyielding, his topsoil long since eroded so that his rugged countenance was bare and pitiless.

'What can I do for you boys?' he said with the urgent politeness with which a shopkeeper might greet a customer arriving a moment or two before closing time.

'I need advice, Lange.'

'Ah, advice. Everybody wants it: nobody takes it. What can I tell you?'

'Tell me about the Wall.'

'What do you want to know?'

'Escaping. I'm out of touch these days. Bring me up to date.'

He stared at me for a moment as if thinking about my request. 'Forget glasnost,' said Lange. 'If that's what you've come here to ask me. No one's told those frontier guards about glasnost. They are still spending money improving the minefields and barbed wire. Things are still the same over there: they still shoot any poor bastard who looks like he might want to leave their part of town.'

'So I hear,' I said.

'Then where do I start?'

'At the beginning.'

'Berlin Wall. About 100 miles of it surrounds West Berlin. Built Sunday morning August 1961 . . . Hell, Bernard, you were here!'

'That's okay. Just tell me the way you tell the foreign journalists. I need to go through it all again.'

A flicker of a smile acknowledged my gibe. 'Okay. At first the hastily built Wall was a bit ramshackle and it was comparatively easy for someone young, fit and determined to get through.'

'How?'

'I remember the sewers being used. The sewers couldn't be bricked off without a monumental engineering job. One of my boys came through a sewer in Klein-Machnow. A week after the Wall went up. The gooks had used metal fencing so as not to impede the sewage flow. My guys from this side waded through the sewage to cut the grilles with bolt-cutters and got him out. But after that things gradually got tougher. They got sneaky: welded steel grids into position and put alarms and booby-traps down there – put them under the level of the sewage so we couldn't see them. The only escape using the sewers that I heard of in the last few years were both East German sewage workers who had the opportunity to loosen the grid well in advance.'

'So then came the tunnels,' I said.

'No, at first came all the scramble escapes. People using ladders and mattresses to get across places where barbed wire was the main obstacle. And there were desperate people in those buildings right on the border: leaping from upstairs windows and being caught in a *Sprungtuch* by obliging firemen. It all made great pictures and sold newspapers but it didn't last long.'

'And cars,' said Werner.

'Sure cars: lots of cars – remember that little bubble car . . . some poor guy squeezed into the gas tank space? But they wised up real fast. And they got rid of any Berlin kids serving as *Grenztruppen* – too soft they said – and brought some real hard-nosed bastards from the provinces, trigger-happy country boys who didn't like Berliners anyway. They soon made that sort of gimmick impossible.'

'False papers?'

'You must know more about that than I do,' said Lange. 'I remember a few individuals getting through on all kinds of Rube Goldberg devices. You British have double passports for married couples and that provided some opportunities for amateur label fakers, until the gooks over there started stamping "travelling alone" on the papers and keeping a photo of people who went through the control to prevent the wrong one from using the papers to come back.'

'People escaped in gliders, hang-gliders, microlites and even hot-air balloons,' said Werner helpfully. He was looking at me with some curiosity, trying to guess why I'd got Lange started on one of his favourite topics.

'Oh, sure,' said Lange. 'No end of lunatic contraptions and some of them worked. But only the really cheap ideas were safe and reliable.'

'Cheap?' I said. I hadn't heard this theory before.

'The more money that went into an escape the greater the number of people involved in it, and so the greater the risk. One way to defray the cost was to sell it to newspapers, magazines or TV stations. You could sometimes raise the money that way but it always meant having cameramen hanging around on street corners or leaning out of upstairs windows. Some of those young reporters didn't know their ass from their elbow. The pros would steer clear of any escapes the media were involved with.'

'The tunnels were the best,' pronounced Werner, who'd become interested in Lange's lecture despite himself.

'Until the DDR made the 100-metre restricted area, all along their side of the Wall, tunnels were okay. But after that it was a long way to go, and you needed ventilation and engineers who knew what they were doing. And they had to dig out a lot of earth. They couldn't take too long completing the job or the word would get out. So tunnels needed two, sometimes three, dozen diggers and earth-movers. A lot of bags to fill; a lot of fetching and carrying. So you're asking too many people to keep their mouths shut. You trust a secret to that many people and, on the law of averages, at least one of them is going to gossip about it. And Berliners like to gossip.'

I said nothing. Mrs Koby came in with the tea. Upon the tray there was a silver teapot and four blue cups and saucers with gilt rims. They might have been heirlooms or a job lot from the flea-market at the old Tauentzienstrasse S-Bahn station. Gerda poured out the tea and passed round the sugar and the little blue plate with four chocolate 'cigarettes'. Lange got a refill of his plum wine: he preferred that. He took a swig of it and wiped his mouth with a big wine-stained handkerchief.

Lange hadn't stopped: he was just getting going. 'Over there, the Wall had become big business. There was a department of highly paid bureaucrats just to administer it. You know how it is: give a bureaucrat a clapboard doghouse to look after and you end up with a luxury zoo complete with an administration office block. So the Wall kept getting bigger and better and more and more men were assigned to it. Men to guard it, men to survey it and repair it, men to write reports about it, reports that came complete with cost-estimates, photos, plans and diagrams. And not just guards: architects, draftsmen, surveyors and all the infra-structure of offices, with clerks who have to have pension schemes and all the rest of it.'

'You make your point, Lange,' I said.

He gave no sign of having heard. He poured more wine and drank it. It smelled syrupy, like some fancy sort of cough medicine. I was glad to be allergic to it. He said, 'Wasteful, yes, but the Wall got to be more and more formidable every week.'

'More tea, Bernard,' said Gerda Koby. 'It's such a long time since we last saw you.'

If Gerda thought that might be enough to change the subject she was very much mistaken. Lange said, 'Frank Harrington sent agents in, and brought them out, by the U-Bahn system. I'm not sure how he worked it: they say he dug some kind of little connecting tunnel from one track to the next so he could get out in Stadtmitte where the West trains pass under the East Sector. That was very clever of Frank,' said Lange, who was not renowned for his praise of anything the Department did.

'Yes, Frank is clever,' I said. He looked at me and nodded. He seemed to know that Frank had deposited me into the East by means of that very tunnel.

'Trouble came when the gooks got wind of it. They staked it out and dumped a pineapple down the manhole just as two of Frank's people were getting ready to climb out of it. The dispatching officer was blown off his feet . . . and he was two hundred yards along the tunnel! Frank wasn't around: he was apple-polishing in London at the time, telling everyone about the coming knighthood that he never got.'

I wasn't going to talk about Frank Harrington; not to Lange I wasn't. 'So the diplomatic cars are the only way,' I said.

'For a time that was true,' said Lange with a wintry smile. 'I could tell you of African diplomats who put a lot of money into their pockets at ten thousand dollars a trip with an escapee in the trunk. But a couple of years ago they stopped a big black Mercedes with diplomatic plates at Checkpoint Charlie and fumigated it on account of what was described as "an outbreak of cattle disease". Whatever they used to fumigate that car put paid to a 32-year-old crane operator from Rostock who was locked in the trunk. They say his relatives in Toronto, Canada, had paid for the escape.'

'The guards opened the trunk of a diplomatic car?' asked Werner.

'No. They didn't have to,' said Lange grimly. 'Maybe that poison gas was only intended to give some young escaper a bad headache but when the trunk was opened on this side, the fellow inside was dead. Hear about that, Bernard?' he asked me.

'Not the way you tell it,' I admitted.

'Well that's what happened. I saw the car. There were ventilation holes drilled into the trunk from underneath to save an escaper from suffocating. The guards must have known that, and known where the vents were.'

'What happened?' asked Werner.

'The quick-thinking African diplomat turned around and took the corpse back to East Berlin and into his embassy. The corpse became an African national by means of pre-dated papers. Death in an embassy: death certificate signed by an African medico so no inquiries by the East German police. Quiet funeral. Buried in a cemetery in Marzahn. But here's the big boffola: not knowing the full story, some jerk working for the Foreign Affairs Committee of the Volkskammer thinks a gesture of sympathy is required. So – on behalf of the government and people of the DDR – they send an enormous wreath in which the words "peace, trust and friendship" are made from miniature roses. It was only on the grave for a day or two then it was discreetly removed by someone from

267

the Stasi.' Lange laughed loudly. 'Cheer up, Bernie,' he said and laughed some more.

'I thought you'd have good news for me, Lange. I thought things had eased up.'

'And don't imagine going through Hungary or Czechoslovakia is any easier. It's tight everywhere. When you read how many people have been killed crossing the Wall you should add on the hundreds that have quietly bled to death somewhere out of sight on the other side.'

'That's good tea, Gerda,' I said. I never knew whether to call her Mrs Lange or Gerda. She was one of those old-fashioned Germans who prefer all the formalities: on the other hand she was married to Lange.

'Bringing someone out, Bernie?' said Lange. 'Someone rich, I hope. Someone who can pay.'

'Werner's brother-in-law in Cottbus,' I said. 'No money, no nothing.'

Werner, who knew nothing of any brother-in-law in Cottbus, looked rattled but he recovered immediately and backed me up gamely. 'I've promised,' said Werner and sat back and smiled unconvincingly.

Lange looked from one of us to the other. 'Can he get to East Berlin?'

'He'll be here with his son,' Werner improvised. 'For the Free German Youth festival in summer.'

Lange nodded. Werner was a far better liar than I ever imagined. I wondered if it was a skill that he'd developed while married to the shrewish Zena. 'You haven't got a lot of time then,' said Lange.

'There must be a way,' said Werner. He looked at his watch and got to his feet. He wanted to leave before I got him more deeply involved in this fairy tale.

'Let me think about it,' said Lange as he got Werner's coat and hat. 'You didn't have an overcoat, Bernie?'

'No,' I said.

'Aren't you cold, Bernard?' said Gerda.

'No, never,' I said.

'Leave him alone,' said Lange. He opened the door for us but before it was open wide enough for us to leave he said, 'Where's the other half of that banknote, Bernard?'

I gave it to him.

Lange put it in his pocket and said, 'Half a banknote is no good to anybody. Right, Bernie?'

'That's right, Lange,' I said. 'I knew you'd quickly tumble to that.'

'There's a lot of things I quickly tumble to,' he said ominously.

'Oh, what else?' I said as we went out.

'Like there not being a *Freie Deutsche Jugend* festival in Berlin this summer.'

'Maybe Werner got it wrong,' I said. 'Maybe it was the *Gesellschaft für Sport und Technik* that have their Festival in East Berlin this summer.'

'Yeah,' said Lange, calling after us in that hoarse voice of his, 'and maybe it's the CIA having a gumshoe festival in West Berlin this summer.'

'Berlin is wonderful in the summer,' I said. 'Just about everyone comes here.'

I heard Lange close the door with a loud bang and slam the bolts back into place with a display of surplus energy that is often the sign of bad temper.

As we were going downstairs Werner said, 'Is it your wife Fiona? Are you going to try to get her out?'

I didn't answer. The timeswitch plopped and we continued downstairs in darkness.

Vexed at my failure to answer him, Werner said somewhat petulantly, 'That was my hundred marks you gave Lange.'

'Well,' I explained, 'it's your brother-in-law isn't it?'

4

Some men are born hoteliers, others strive to acquire hotels, but Werner Volkmann was one of those rare birds who have a hotel thrust upon them. It would be difficult to imagine any man in the whole world less ready to become a hotel manager than my good friend Werner Volkmann. His dedication to Tante Lisl, the old woman who had brought him up when he was orphaned, compelled him to take over from her when she became too old and sick to continue her despotic reign.

It was not a sumptuous establishment but the neighbourhood could hardly be more central. Before the war it had been Lisl's family home, set in the fashionable New West End. In 1945 the division of the city between the Russians and the Western Allies had made Der Neuer Westen the centre of 'capitalist Berlin'.

Werner was making changes, but sensitive to Lisl's feelings, for she was still in residence and monitored every new curtain and every drip of paint, the modifications did little to change the character of this appealing old place where so much of the interior was the same as it had been for fifty or more years.

After we left Lange Koby's apartment that evening I let Werner persuade me to move in to his hotel. There was little reason to suffer the dirt and discomfort of my Kreuzberg slum now that Frank Harrington had demonstrated his office's ability to put a finger out and reach me any time they chose.

Before going to bed Werner offered me a drink. We walked through the newly refurbished bar – there was no one else there – to the small office at the back. He poured me a big measure of scotch whisky with not much soda. Werner drank soda water with just a splash of Underberg in it. I looked around. An amazing transformation had taken place, especially pleasing for anyone who'd known Werner back in the old days. It had become a den and Werner's treasures had miraculously resurfaced. There was a lion's head: a moth-eaten old fellow upon whose wooden mounting some drunken wag had neatly inscribed *felis leo venerabilis*. Next to it on the wall hung an antique clock. It had a chipped wooden case upon the front panel of which a bucolic scene was unconvincingly depicted. It ticked loudly and was

270

eight minutes slow but it was virtually the only thing he possessed which had belonged to his parents. Hanging from the ceiling there was the model Dornier flying boat that Werner had toiled so long to construct: twelve engines, and if you lifted up each and every cowling the engine detail could be seen inside. I remember Werner working on those tiny engines: he was in a vile temper for over a week.

We'd done no more than say how well Lange looked and what a fierce old devil he was when Ingrid Winter came into the room.

'Bernie is staying here with us,' Werner said rather more sadly than I would have hoped, but then Werner was like that.

Ingrid had come into the room without my noticing. 'Oh, that's good,' she said. It would be easy to see Ingrid as a timid, self-effacing spinster, for she was always willing to appear in this guise. Her greying hair, which she did nothing to tint, her quiet voice and her style of floral-patterned woollen dresses all contributed to this picture. But even on our short acquaintance I'd discovered that Ingrid was a creature of fortitude and strength. Werner had discovered the same thing, and more, for the relationship between them was close. 'That woman was here again,' she told Werner in a voice tinged with disapproval.

'The Duchess?'

'The Englishwoman. The woman you said was a busybody.'

Werner looked at me and grinned selfconsciously. 'What did she want?'

'The Duchess likes it here,' I interjected. 'She hopes it's becoming a sort of club for the people she knows.'

Werner's face tightened. Ingrid was watching him as I spoke but her face showed no emotion, not even reflecting that of Werner. Werner looked at me and said, 'Ingrid thinks there is more to it than that.'

'What sort of more?'

'I told her about Frank,' said Werner as if that would explain everything. When I didn't react he added, 'Frank wants to use this place. It's obvious.'

'It's not obvious to me, Werner,' I said. 'Use it how?'

Werner poured himself more soda water and added no more than a drop of Underberg which only just coloured it. He took a sip of it and said, 'I think Frank has ordered his people to come here. They'll return to the office and report to him every word they hear and everything they see. It will all go on file.' This mild paranoia – complete with his rather endearing picture of Frank's rigorous and capable administration – provided a perfect example of Werner's ingrained Germanic thinking. In fact, Frank was typically English. Idle and congenial, Frank was an easygoing time-server who'd muster neither the energy nor the inclination to organize such a venture.

Werner on the other hand was provincial and narrow-minded in the way that Germans are prey to being. These differing attitudes were fundamental to their enmity, but I would never tell either of them what I thought. Werner would have been horrified: he always thought of himself as a cosmopolitan liberal. But of course all wealthy well-travelled bigots make that claim.

'As long as they pay cash for their drinks,' I said.

This flippancy did not please Werner. 'I don't mind Frank's people coming here but I don't want them to monopolize the place and try to turn it into some awful sort of English pub. And anyway, Bernie,' he added in a very quiet measured voice, as if talking to a small child, 'if you're here, they'll spy on you.'

Any difficulty I might have had in answering Werner was removed by Ingrid. I had a feeling she was not listening to us very carefully. Perhaps she was already familiar with Werner's suspicions about the Departmental personnel transmogrifying his bar. During a lapse in the conversation she said, 'There is something else. I heard them talking about Bernard. And about his wife.'

My wife! My wife! Now she had all my attention, and I wanted to hear all about it. She said that the Duchess had come into the bar in the early evening. She'd ordered a gin and tonic and read the *Daily Express*. Werner had recently started to provide the hotel with French and English, as well as German, daily papers, impaling them upon wooden *Zeitunghälter* and hanging them alongside the coat rack. Two other Department people – a man and a woman – came in soon afterwards and invited the Duchess to join them.

I recognized Ingrid's description of the second woman of this trio. The voice, the Burberry scarf, the horseshoe-shaped diamond brooch. It was Pinky: there was only one Pinky, and thank God for that. Her daddy owned race horses, mumsie hunted foxes, and her brother's nightclub adventures were regularly chronicled in the gossip columns. I remembered her when she'd come to work in the Department. She was newly divorced from 'Bang-bang' Canon, a captain in the Horse Guards who went into insurance. She said she couldn't stand the sight of him in mufti but that might have been her sense of humour. Pinky started using her maiden name again when Bang-bang went to prison for fraud.

From across the other side of the bar Ingrid had heard Pinky say in her shrill Home-Counties voice, 'When a man loses his wife it looks like carelessness, darling.' And laughing loudly and calling for another drink.

'What about the telephone?' the man asked. Long fair wavy hair parted high, almost centre. Check-patterned suit and mustard-coloured shirt. Larry Bower, taking Pinky in for a drink on their way back from a hard day's work at the safe house in Charlottenburg.

Pinky said, 'His phones were tapped from the first moment she walked out. That's the drill. The transcripts go to Frank.'

'Eventually they'll fire him,' said Bower.

Pinky said, 'You know how the Department works, darling: they have to make sure about him. It will take time. They'll get rid of him when it suits them.'

'I never met her,' said Bower. 'What sort of woman was she?'

The Duchess answered the question, 'Very beautiful. But I could never understand why she married him. Every man who clapped eyes on her wanted her, she has a sort of magic I suppose. Some women are lucky like that.'

'I never got to know her,' said Pinky. 'No one did. She wasn't a woman's woman, if you know what I mean.'

'I think she spent a lot of money on clothes,' said the Duchess. 'But in all fairness I have to say that she could wear an old sweater and jeans and make herself look like . . .'

'A film star?' supplied Bower.

'No,' said Pinky. 'Never like a film star. She wasn't brainless, darling! Men can't abide the notion that beautiful women can be brainy. But they can.'

'Yes, but what sort of woman was she really?' said Bower. 'Everyone's talking about her but no one seems to really know her.'

'An absolute cow!' answered Pinky.

'Sometimes an absolute cow can be a good wife,' said the Duchess.

'Oh no!' said Pinky. 'She made his life a misery. Everyone knew that.'

'He seems to be managing without her,' said Bower.

'He's something of a play-actor,' said the Duchess sadly. 'He always has been.'

'He can put down a few,' said Bower.

'I've never seen him drunk,' said the Duchess.

'Have you not, darling? My goodness yes but he can hold it. Let's face it, he was never really one of us, was he?' said Pinky.

'He hasn't got a bean, you know,' said the Duchess.

'But there were no papers missing?' said Bower.

Pinky said, 'Not as far as anyone can see . . . But who knows what was copied?'

'She phoned Frank, you say?' the Duchess asked.

'Early this morning, at his home,' said Pinky, who seemed to know everything. 'I don't know how she had that number. It's changed regularly.'

'You don't think that she . . . and Frank . . .' said Bower.

'Having it off with Frank?' Pinky's laugh ended in a giggle. 'Good old Frank! Not my type, darling, but it's astounding how the ladies zero in on the poor old thing.' Then in a more serious voice, 'No, I don't think there could be anything like that.'

'Not in the dim and distant past?' said Bower.

'No, not even in the dim and distant past.' This time the Duchess answered, firmly closing that door.

'So did Frank tell him?' said Bower.

'Tell hubbie?' Pinky said. 'About the phone call . . . No. And no one knows what she said. We just know that Frank cancelled all his appointments and ordered his car brought round the front . . . driving himself. No one knows where he went. Of course Frank's sudden departure may have nothing to do with it. You know what Frank is like. He might have just decided to spend the day with his army cronies or play golf or something.'

'I just hope,' said the Duchess, 'that it's not all going to start all over again.'

'Drinky for Pinky, darling,' said Pinky to Bower.

Bower said, 'All what start all over again?'

'You'll soon know,' said the Duchess. 'Life becomes hell for everyone once one of these security purges begin. Internal Security arrive and it's questions, questions, questions.'

'Drinky for Pinky, darling. Drinky for Pinky.'

'The same again three times,' Bower called across the bar to Ingrid. Then five cheerful Australians came in. They were on some government-financed jaunt; buying ten thousand hospital beds or something of that sort. They'd spent all day at a huge residential complex where internationally renowned architects had competed to produce the world's ugliest apartment blocks. The Aussies needed a drink and, pleased to hear English spoken after a long day, joined the Duchess and her friends for a boozy evening. The conversation turned to lighter matters, such as why the Germans invaded Poland.

I thanked Ingrid for passing on to me the gist of this conversation she'd overheard. Then I quickly downed another stiff drink and went up to bed.

I had my usual room. It was a tiny garret at the top of the house, the sort of place which inspired Puccini to orchestrate Mimi's demise. It was a long walk to the bathroom. The floral wallpaper's big flowers and whirling acanthus leaves had gone dark brown with age, so that the pattern was almost invisible, and there in the corner was a little chest of drawers that had once held my stamp collection, my home-made lock picks and the secret hoard of Nazi badges which my father had forbidden me to collect.

The bed was made up ready for me. There was a pair of pyjamas wrapped round a hot water bottle. It was all as if Werner had guessed that it was just a matter of time before I saw sense.

I undressed and got into bed, put my pistol in my shoe so I could reach it easily and went straight off to sleep. I must have been very tired, for I had plenty to stay awake and worry about.

5

Lisl's hotel – or perhaps what I should more appropriately call Werner and Ingrid's hotel – did not run to phones in every room. The next morning at eight o'clock there was a tap at the door. It was Richard, one of Lisl's employees whom Werner had kept on. 'Herr Bernd,' he said. 'A gentleman phoned, Herr Bernd. Herr Teacher. He comes here. Twelve hours sharply.' He was a nervous young man who had come to Berlin, as many such German youngsters came, to avoid being drafted into the Bundeswehr. He got a job at Lisl's and met a girl and now he had no plans to return to his parents in Bremen. Every now and again his father phoned to ask if Richard was 'keeping out of trouble'. Usually the phone calls came late at night and usually his father sounded drunk.

Sometimes I wished Richard would not persist in using English when speaking to me but he was determined to improve his languages. His ambition was to work on the reception desk of some very big luxury hotel, but he'd asked me not to reveal this to Lisl. So I kept his secret and I answered him in English telling him that I would be having lunch downstairs and that if my visitor Herr Teacher was early he should put him in the bar and invite him to join me for lunch.

Richard said, 'It is exactly as you say, Herr Bernd.' He blinked nervously. He had a comprehensive store of phrases that he could deliver in reasonable English. His problem lay in putting these fragments together so that the joins didn't show.

'Thank you, Richard.'

'You are hotly welcome, Herr Bernd. Have a nice day.'

'You too, Richard,' I said.

Once awake I was overcome with a desperate need for a cup of hot strong coffee. So at nine fifteen I was sitting in the dining room – the breakfast room was being completely re-done – with Lisl, who was waving her hand to obtain a pot of coffee from Klara. The faithful Klara wore an old-fashioned starched white apron with lacy edges on the bib. Lisl invariably referred to her as *das Dienstmädchen*, as if she was some newly employed teenage serving-girl, but Klara was amazingly old. She was thin and wiry, a birdlike creature with bright little eyes and grey hair drawn back into a tight bun at the nape of her neck, a style in vogue

276

when she was young. She was bent from a lifetime of hard work, having toiled for Lisl since long before the house became a hotel.

'And this time,' Lisl told Klara emphatically, 'put less coffee in the pot.'

'Some people like strong coffee,' I told Lisl but Lisl waved a hand to tell Klara to pay no heed to me.

When Klara was out of earshot, Lisl explained in a loud and earnest voice, 'She wastes coffee. It's so expensive. Do you know how much I pay for that coffee?'

From the corner of my eye I saw Klara turn her head to hear better what Lisl was saying. I was about to reply that it was time that Lisl stopped thinking about such things, and left the account books to Werner and Ingrid. But the last time I'd said something like that it unleashed upon me an indignant tirade forcefully assuring me that she was not too old to know how the hotel should be run. I suppose Werner and Ingrid had found some way of handling Lisl, for she gave no sign of resenting any of the changes they'd made.

This dining room for instance had been totally refurbished. All the panelling had been stripped back to the natural wood and the nondescript prints had been junked in favour of some contemporary water-colours: Berlin street scenes by a local artist. They went well with a cruel George Grosz drawing which was the only item retained from the former decoration. The picture had always hung beside this table – which was near a window that gave on to the courtyard – and this was where Lisl liked to sit for lunch. One of Lisl's more spiteful critics once said she was like a George Grosz drawing: black and white, a person of extremes, a jagged caricature of Berlin in the Thirties. And today this obese woman, with her long-sleeved black dress and darkly mascaraed penetrating eyes, did look the part.

The coffee came and Klara poured some into my cup. It was a thin brew with neither aroma nor colour. I didn't remark on it and Lisl pretended not to notice that it had come at all. Lisl sipped some milk – she wasn't drinking coffee these days. She was very slowly working her way through a red apple with a piece of Swiss Emmenthal and a slice of black rye bread. Her arthritic old hand – pale and spotted and heavy with diamond rings – held a sharp kitchen knife and cut from the apple a very small piece. She took it between finger and thumb and ate carefully, making sure that she didn't smudge her bright red lipstick.

'Werner has his own ideas,' said Lisl suddenly. She said it as if we'd both been talking about him, as if she was replying to a question. 'Werner has his own ideas and he is determined.'

'What ideas?'

'He has been back through the records, and is using that word process machine to write letters to all the people who have stayed here over the last five years or more. Also he keeps a record of all the guests, their names, their wives' names and what they liked to eat and any problems we have had with them.'

'Excellent,' I said. She pulled a face, so I said, 'You don't think that's the way to do it?'

'For years I have run the hotel without such things,' said Lisl. She didn't say it *wasn't* the way to do it. Lisl would sit on the fence until Werner's new ideas were tested. That was Lisl's way. She didn't like to be proved wrong.

'Werner is very clever at business affairs,' I said.

'And the bridge evenings,' said Lisl. 'Frank Harrington's people come for the bridge evenings. The British like bridge, don't they?'

'Some of them,' I said.

Lisl laughed grimly. She could usually thrash me at bridge. When she laughed her huge frame wobbled and the glossy satin dress rippled. She reached up and touched the corner of her eye with her little finger. It was a delicate gesture with which she tested the adhesion of her large false eyelashes. 'Werner is like a son to me.'

'He's very fond of you, Lisl,' I said. I suppose I should have told her that Werner loved her, for the sort of sacrifices Werner was making to run this place left no doubt of that.

'And loves the house,' said Lisl. She picked up another little piece of apple and crunched it noisily, looking down at her plate again as if not interested in my response.

'Yes,' I said. I'd never thought of that before but Werner had been born here during the war. It was the home in which he grew up as a tiny child. The house must have even more sentimental associations for him than it did for me, and yet in all our conversations he'd never expressed any feelings about the place. But how selfish of me not to see what was now so obvious. 'And you have your niece here too,' I said.

'Ingrid.' Lisl cleared her throat and nodded. 'She is my niece.'

'Yes,' I said. Since Lisl had repeatedly told anyone who would listen that Ingrid was her sister's illegitimate daughter, and therefore was *not* her niece, I interpreted this admission as substantial progress for Ingrid.

'Are you going somewhere?' she asked truculently. 'You keep looking at your watch.'

'I'm going to the bank. There should be money waiting for me and I owe money to Frank.'

278

'Frank has plenty of money,' said Lisl. She shifted about in her chair. It was her way of dismissing both Frank's generosity as a lender and my integrity in reimbursing him. As I got up to go she said, 'And I must get you to sort out all that stuff of your father's some time.'

'What stuff?'

'There's a gun and a uniform full of moth holes – he never wore it except when they ordered him to wear it – and there's the cot your mother lent to Frau Grieben across the street, and books in English – Dickens, I think – the footstool and a mattress. Then there's a big bundle of papers: bills and that sort of thing. I would have thrown it all away but I thought you might want to sort through it.'

'What sort of papers?'

'They were in that old desk your father used. He forgot to empty it. He left in a hurry. He said he'd be back and collect it but he forgot. You know how absent-minded he could be sometimes. Then I started using that room as storage space and I forgot too.'

'Where is it all now?'

'And account books and bundles of correspondence. Nothing important or he would have written and asked me for it. If you don't want it I'll just throw it all out, but Werner wants me to clear everything out of the storeroom. It's going to be made into a bathroom.'

'I'd like to sort through it.'

'That's all he thinks about; bathrooms. You can't rent a bathroom.'

'Yes, I'd like to sort through it, Lisl.'

'He'll end up with *fewer* bedrooms. So how will that earn more money?'

'When can I look at it?'

'Now don't be a nuisance, Bernd. It's locked up and quite safe. That room is crammed full of all sorts of junk and there's nowhere else to put it. Next week . . . the week after. I don't know. I just wanted to know if you wanted it all.'

'Yes, Lisl,' I said. 'Thank you.'

'And buy me the *Guide Michelin* for France. The new one! It's just come out. I don't want the old one mind.'

'The Michelin hotel guide to France!' For years now Lisl had rarely emerged from the hotel except to go to the bank. Since the heart attack she hadn't even done that. 'Are you going to France?' I asked. I wondered if she had some crazy plan to visit her sister Inge who lived there.

'Why shouldn't I go to France? Werner's running things, isn't he? They keep telling me to go away for a rest.'

Werner was thinking of putting Lisl into a nursing home but I could see no way of explaining that to her. 'The new Michelin France,' I said. 'I'll get one.'

'I want to see which are the best restaurants,' said Lisl blithely. I wondered if she was joking but you couldn't always be sure.

I spent the rest of the morning strolling along Ku-Damm. The snow had gone and the sunlight was diamond hard. The clouds were torn to shreds to reveal jagged shapes of blue, but under such skies the temperature always remains bitterly cold. Soviet jet fighters were making ear-splitting sonic bangs, part of the systematic harassment that capitalism's easternmost outpost was subjected to. After a visit to the bank I browsed in the bookshops and looked round Wertheim's department store. The food counters in the basement sold all sorts of magnificent snacks. I drank a glass of strong German beer and ate a couple of Bismarck herrings. For an hour the prospect of a lunch meeting that would be discordant, if not to say an outright conflict, was forgotten. My problems vanished. Around me there were the ever cheerful voices of Berliners. To my ears their quips and curses were unlike any others, for Berlin was home to me. I was again a child, ready to race back along the Ku-Damm to find my mother at the stove and father at the lunch table waiting for me at the top of that funny old house that we called home.

Time passes quickly when such a mood of content settles the mind. I had to hurry to get back to Lisl's for noon. When I went into the bar there was no sign of Teacher. I sat down and read the paper. At half past twelve a man came in and looked round to find me, but it was not Teacher: it was the Berlin resident, Frank Harrington. He took off his hat. 'Bernard! How good to see you.' His manner and his warm greeting gave no clue to the reason for this change of plan and I immediately decided that his presence was in some way connected with the enigmatic exchange that Ingrid had overheard.

Perhaps it was Frank's paternal attitude to me that made his behaviour so unvarying. I do believe that if I surprised Frank by landing on his side of the moon unexpectedly he would not be startled. Nonchalantly he'd say, 'Bernard! How good to see you,' and offer me a drink or tell me I was not getting enough exercise.

'I heard you were out of town, Frank.'

'London overnight. Just one of the chores of the job.'

'Of course.' I tried to see in his face what might be in store but Frank's wrinkled face was as genial as ever. 'I went to the bank this morning,' I said. 'I have a draft to repay the thousand pounds you let me have.' I gave it to him. He folded it and put it in his wallet without reading it.

He wet his lips and said, 'Do you think your friend Werner could conjure up a drink?' His feeling that this might be beyond Werner's abilities, or that Werner might be disposed to prevent him having a drink, was evident in his voice. Coat still on, hat in hand, he looked round the room in a way that was almost furtive. Frank had never been fond of Lisl or Werner or the hotel. It seemed his unease at being here was increased now that Werner had taken charge.

'Klara!' I said. I did not have to speak loudly, for the old woman had positioned herself ready to take Frank's hat and coat. 'A double gin and tonic for my guest.'

'Plymouth gin with Schweppes?' said Klara, who apparently knew better than I did what Frank drank. She took Frank's trenchcoat, felt hat and rolled umbrella.

'Yes, Plymouth with tonic,' said Frank. 'No ice.' He didn't immediately sit down in the chair I had pulled out for him but stood there, preoccupied, as if unable to remember what he'd come to tell me. He sighed before sinking down on to the newly chintz-covered banquette. 'Yes, just one of the chores of the job,' he said. 'And it's the sort of task I could be very happy without at this time.' He looked tired. Frank was somewhere in his middle sixties. Not so old perhaps, but they'd asked him to stay on at a time when he'd got all ready to retire. From that time onwards some of the zeal had gone out of him.

Or perhaps that was just my fancy, for today Frank had the sort of appearance that almost restored my faith in the British public school system. He radiated fidelity, trustworthiness and good breeding. His hair was wavy and greying, but not so wavy that he looked like a ladies' man and not so grey that he looked like he couldn't be. Even the wrinkles in his face were the sort of wrinkles that make him look like a good-natured outdoors man. And of course Frank had a valet to press his Savile Row suits and polish his hand-sewn shoes and make sure his Jermyn Street shirts had exactly the right amount of starch in the collars.

'You heard about my son?' He was rummaging through his pockets. The question was put in that casual manner and tone of voice that, with a certain sort of Englishman, indicates a matter of vital importance.

'No,' I said. 'What about him?' Frank had never made any secret of his hope that his son would find a place in the Diplomatic Service. He'd prepared the ground well in advance. So when the boy came down from

Cambridge with the declared intention of getting a commercial pilot's licence, Frank still didn't take it too seriously. It was only after he'd seen him flying the routes for a few years that Frank reluctantly faced the fact that his son was going to live a life of his own.

'Failed his medical.'

'Frank, I'm so sorry.'

'Yes, for an airline pilot that's a sentence of death. He said that to me on the phone. "It's a sentence of death, Dad." Until that very moment I don't think I understood what that damned flying job meant to him.' Frank wet his lips nervously; I knew that I was the first person to whom he'd confided his true feelings. 'Flying. It must be so boring. So repetitious.' This was of course exactly the superior attitude that his son had so resented, and which had created the unsurmountable barrier between them. 'Not much of a job for a fellow with a good degree, I would have thought.' He looked at me quizzically and then realized that I didn't have a college degree of any kind.

'What will he do?' I asked hurriedly to cover his discomfort.

'He's still in a state of shock,' said Frank and gave a little laugh, trying to hide the distress he felt at the abrupt ending of his son's career.

'It will be all right,' I said, improvising as I went. 'They'll find him a ground job. He'll end up with a seat on the board.' I knew that such a tedious administrative job would be something that Frank would really approve.

'There are too many of them,' said Frank. 'Too many unemployed aviators who don't know anything except how to drive an airbus. He'd be no damned use behind a desk, Bernard, you know that.' Frank had been going through his pocket in a distracted way; finally he brought out a yellow oilskin tobacco pouch. From his top pocket he got out his cherry-wood pipe and blew through it experimentally before he snapped open the pouch.

'I'm not sure they permit smoking in here any more, Frank,' I said.

'Nonsense,' said Frank. He sat down and began pushing tobacco into the bowl of his pipe and pressing it down with his thumb.

Klara brought Frank's gin and tonic. As she set it down before him she saw his pipe and said, '*Hier darf nicht geraucht werden, Herr Harrington.*'

'Fiddlesticks!' said Frank.

Despite Frank's devastating smile, Klara waggled a finger at him and said, '*Die Pfeife! Die Pfeife ist strenglich verboten!*'

Frank kept smiling and said nothing. Klara looked at me and pulled a fierce face that asked me how Lisl would deal with such a dilemma.

Then she shrugged her shoulders and marched off. I don't think Klara cared very much whether guests smoked in the dining room: she'd done her duty as laid down by Lisl. That was enough.

Perhaps Klara's warning took effect, for Frank continued to toy with his smoking equipment but did not light up. At first I thought his mind was still wholly occupied with the consequences of his son's failure to pass his pilot's medical, but there was something else. 'But I bring good news for you, Bernard,' he said.

'What's that, Frank?' I said.

'You're free.' Perhaps my face didn't show the joy that he'd anticipated for he added, 'Free to go to England. All charges dropped. No board to face, not even a tribunal.'

'I see,' I said.

'I don't think you understand what I'm telling you. All charges against you are to be dropped.'

'I thought you said they *had been* dropped.'

'You're in a captious mood today, Bernard.'

'Perhaps. But which is it?'

He coughed. Was it a sign of nervousness, the way the interrogation teams said, or was it something that came with that damned pipe tobacco? 'A couple of formalities still remain. Nothing more, I assure you.'

'Either or,' I said. 'Did London send you to hold a pistol to my head?' I looked out of the window. The blue sky had only been a brief interlude, a deception. Now it had clouded over and it looked like more snow, or with the thermometer going up, rain.

'Come along, Bernard. It's nothing like that.'

'What formalities?'

He tapped the table with his pipe. 'Well, we wouldn't want you selling your memoirs to one of the Sunday papers.' He smiled as if the restriction was upon something outrageous like leaping from the topmost pinnacle of Big Ben holding an umbrella. 'We don't want you starting an action in the High Court.' Another big smile.

'Wait a minute, Frank. Action in the High Court? I couldn't do that if I was still working for the Department.' I looked at him: his expression was unchanging. I said, 'Was that order for my arrest just some bizarre way of getting rid of me? Did they want me to run? Was someone half hoping that I might go East?'

'God forbid!' A gust of air rattled the windows like some demon trying to break in. Despite the double windows, the noise of the wind continued low and undulating, crooning a lament.

'From the Department's point of view that would make things easier, wouldn't it? If I ran East I'd be labelled a defector . . . For their reputation that would be marginally better than having me in an English courtroom, or even facing a military court in Berlin.'

'Bernard, please. They are simply asking for a signed supplementary agreement, covering the matters of confidence, contract and official secrets and so on. Formalities; just as I said.'

'Are you telling me I'm fired? Is that the "final solution" to the Samson problem? I'm to be tightly gagged and put out to grass?'

'Hold your horses, Bernard.'

'Then tell me, Frank. But tell me straight.'

'They want you to resign . . . They suggest you give a year's notice. You'll work the year normally.'

'Severance pay? Pension rights?'

'To be agreed.'

'Oh, I see the hand of Morgan in this one. I work a year relegated to some remote job where nothing classified will pass across my desk. If I behave myself and keep my mouth shut, and sign a hundred forms to make sure I can't say a word to anyone without dire consequences, then I will tiptoe off stage and get my pension. But if I shake rattle and roll during that twelve months, I'm cut off without the proverbial penny.'

'These matters always have two sides, Bernard.'

'But am I right?'

'That would be one way of looking at it. But I hope you'll see that it's good for you too. It's a chance to cut loose from an impossible situation.'

'The answer is no,' I said.

'Wait a minute, Bernard.'

'I've done nothing dishonest. They know that. Jesus! When Fiona took off I faced positive vetting teams from the Ministry of Defence and the Cabinet Office. They pronounced me clean and I am still. That's why they've dropped this lunatic plan of arresting me. The lawyers have told them that there is no case for me to answer. Not even here in occupied Berlin, where they can virtually invent their own laws. If they'd arrested me in England I would have been headline news, and by now the Department would be looking damned stupid.'

'Well, yes,' said Frank with what might have been a sigh. 'In fact I understand the Deputy discussed you, and the order to arrest you, with someone from the Attorney-General's office.'

'And came out with his arse in a sling.'

'I don't know what was said.' He was looking down and giving all his attention to his tobacco pouch. Frank's position as Berlin Head of Station had brought him into many head-on collisions with London Central. He couldn't entirely conceal his pleasure at the hash London had made of this whole business. That he was being asked to pull their coals from the fire must have made it even more piquant.

'I'm not resigning,' I told him. 'I'll work the year as they suggest but only if I continue in the same job. If in twelve months' time the Department still wants my head we'll talk about compensation then.'

'I don't see the difference, Bernard.'

'Don't you, Frank? The difference is that if I resign now it's like admitting that I've done something wrong: that I've sold secrets to a foreign power or taken the office pencils home. If they employ me normally for another year it will be a tacit admission that I was wrongly accused.'

'They won't like that answer,' said Frank. 'They are very keen to get it settled very quickly.' The wind came again, fiercer now. When the wind abated it would rain.

'I'll bet they are. Well, we can get it settled very quickly, if that's what they want. I'll fax my story to the *New York Times*.'

For a moment Frank didn't react. Then he rubbed his face and said, 'Don't make jokes like that, Bernard. I shudder to think of the damage that would be inflicted upon all of us if you did something silly.'

'Okay, Frank. I'll stop making jokes like that but you tell London that it's my deal or nothing.'

He kept his voice low and measured. 'I don't know anyone who has your knowledge – and your instinct – for what's happening here, Bernard. Your time in the field added to time on the German Desk in London makes you a key person, and so a prime target. You've seen the Department at work since you were on your father's knee. Surely you can see why they worry so much.'

'Yes, Frank. So you tell London that it's my deal or nothing.'

'They'll not be threatened, Bernard.'

'That has a sinister ring to it, Frank.'

'Did it? I'm truly sorry, that's not at all what I intended to convey. I was trying to point out that your approach is ill-considered. Their offer is made in good faith. Must you throw it back into their face?'

'I'm not resigning.'

'Go back to London. I'll arrange everything. Go to the office and work normally. Let the resignation issue stand for the time being while I talk to the old man.'

'There remains the question of Fiona,' I said.

Frank flinched as if I'd struck him. 'We can't discuss your wife.'

'I've got to know whether Fiona defected or went over there continuing to work for the Department.'

Frank stared at me. His face was like stone without even a flicker of sentience.

I said, 'Very well: you can't tell me officially, and I understand that, Frank. But it's my wife. I've got to know.'

I waited for him to frame an answer that would comply with his sense of propriety but he still didn't speak.

'Fiona was sent, right? She's working for us still?' Frank's face was the same Frank I'd known since childhood, but those pitiless eyes revealed a Frank that I'd always said did not exist. This tough unbending reaction to my question did not cause me to hate him: on the contrary it made me want his help and assistance even more. That of course was the secret of Frank's success over these many years; I'd taken a long time to discover it. 'Right?' I seemed to see in his eyes an affirmative. I felt sure that Frank wouldn't allow me to harbour the dangerous belief that Fiona was innocent if she was really a dedicated opponent.

After what seemed an age Frank said, 'I forbid you to discuss Fiona with me or with anyone else. I told you I would do my best to find out what you want to know. Meanwhile you must keep completely silent. Put her out of your mind.'

'Okay.'

'And I mean it.'

'I said okay.'

Frank relaxed a little. He said, 'I take it you'll want to go to London as soon as possible?' I nodded. 'You must have a lot of things to attend to.'

He looked at me for a moment before putting his hand in his pocket and putting a foolscap-sized white envelope on the table in front of me.

I looked at him and smiled. He'd outmanoeuvred me, and been so confident about being able to do so that he'd brought the airline ticket with him. 'Checkmate in three moves, eh Frank?' I smiled and tried not to sound too bitter.

'I thought you would want to see Gloria and the children as soon as possible.' He touched the ticket and moved it a fraction of an inch closer to me. 'You'll be with them tonight. Go in to the office tomorrow and work as usual. I'll phone you at home to tell you what's happening.' He was careful to keep any note of triumph out of his voice. From his tone and demeanour you'd have thought we were fellow sufferers with the same misfortune.

'Thanks, Frank,' I said, picking up the ticket. 'What happened to our colleague Teacher today?'

'You won't regret it, Bernard. I'm giving you good advice, the sort your dad would have given you.' A pause as he breathed deeply and no doubt congratulated himself upon getting a chance to change the subject. 'Teacher. Yes. A spot of bother,' said Frank, picking up his pipe and touching it to his lips. 'His wife skedaddled. An awfully nice girl. Extremely intelligent. Clementine: gorgeous looking creature: wonderful figure. Ever meet her?'

I nodded. Frank had a sharp eye for desirable young females with wonderful figures. His eyes stared into the distance as he remembered her.

'She went off with some flashy Yankee film producer. Met him for the first time ten days ago. Women are so impulsive aren't they? What provokes a young wife to such a headstrong act?' The wind had dropped now. The sky had darkened. At any moment it would rain.

'Poor old Teacher,' I said. 'He seemed to be very fond of her.' Now I realized why the beautiful Clemmie had become so agitated when I had lunch there on Sunday. Never mind her shouting about me being a pariah, my guess is that she thought the Department had got wind of her plans and sent me to spy on her.

'This wretched American has taken her to a film festival in Warsaw. Warsaw! Alarm bells started ringing I can tell you. London over-reacted: the telex got red-hot! "Do this; don't do that; disregard previous message; provide present whereabouts." You know. Luckily Mrs Teacher must have realized what trouble she was causing us. She phoned me from her hotel in Warsaw and explained, in guarded terms, that it was just a domestic rift. She had, she said, fallen in love for the very first time. Deep sighs and all. Says she'll never go back to her husband. They plan to fly on to a film festival in Japan and then to America. She wants to live in Beverly Hills. She said that I was not to worry.' Frank blew through his pipe and gave me a worried smile. 'So I'm not worrying.'

So that was what the Duchess and co. had been so excited about. They'd been talking about the Teachers: not about me and Fiona. 'And London?'

'London Central have professional worriers on the staff. But there's no way we can have our chaps lock their wives in the broom cupboard while they're out at work, eh?' He began to push tobacco into the bowl of his pipe. 'It's a pity in some ways we can't.'

There was the gentle noise of rain dabbing the windows. At first there were huge raindrops that came at measured intervals but soon the drops dribbled and joined and made rivulets and bent the trees and distorted the outside world beyond recognition.

6

I am not paranoid. That is to say I am not paranoid to the extent of distrusting everyone around me. Only some of them. When I went into the office next morning all seemed normal: too normal. When I'd finished looking at my own desk, I was summoned upstairs. Dicky Cruyer, German Desk supremo and my immediate superior, was in a singular mood that I could almost describe as jovial.

'Good morning, Bernard!' he said and smiled. He was a slim bony man with pale complexion and a golliwog-style head of curly hair that I suspected he regularly had permed.

During my few weeks of living rough in Berlin I'd reconciled myself to the idea that I would never again see this office. Never again see England, in fact. So now I looked round Dicky's office and marvelled at it as if seeing it all for the first time. I examined anew the magnificent rosewood table that Dicky used instead of a desk, and behind it the wall filled with photos, mostly of Dicky. I inspected the soft black leather Eames chair and matching footstool and the slightly mangy lion skin on the floor which I noticed he'd positioned less obtrusively. I looked at it all with a feeling of wonder.

'I hope you're in a mood for hard work,' said Dicky. 'There is plenty to do now your holiday is over.' He leaned forward, elbows on table with fingertips touching. He was in shirt-sleeves with bright red braces and a floral patterned bow tie. The Deputy had objected to Dicky's denim and leather and now he wore suits in the office, but the newly acquired loud ties and bright braces were a subtle erosion of these dress restrictions.

I looked at him. 'Yes, I am.' He smiled. Did he really think I'd been on holiday? There was no way I could tell from his warm relaxed friendly smile. But the way he touched his fingertips together in a rapid succession of staccato taps betrayed what I judged to be an underlying nervousness.

'The Deputy Controller Europe wants a pow-wow at ten-thirty. You'd better come along too. Take notes.'

'What about?' The Deputy Controller Europe was an Australian named Augustus Stowe. Dicky imperfectly concealed his envy of Stowe and usually referred to him by his title, with sarcastic emphasis as if the position Stowe occupied was self-evidently unsuited to the man's abilities. This attitude to Stowe, complete with whispered doubts about his competence, was shared by some of Dicky's immediate circle. Stowe, a formidable childhood prodigy, had stayed on to teach Logic at Perth University, and some now slightingly referred to him as 'Doctor Stowe' as if a man with a doctorate was too unworldly for the Department.

'There are a number of things,' said Dicky vaguely. It was Dicky's way of admitting that he hadn't the slightest idea. I suspected that Dicky was intimidated by Stowe, who had a savage temper when any shortcomings were uncovered and so Dicky's meetings with him were sometimes less than convivial. 'Coffee?'

'Yes, please.' Whatever shortcomings Dicky had they did not extend to his talent for self-preservation or to his coffee. Chagga, from Mr Higgins' new shop in Duke Street. Dicky sent motorcycle messengers to collect it. One day someone would ask what urgent secret dispatches were coming in aromatic brown packets from Mr Higgins two or three times a week.

'Capital!' said Dicky as his secretary brought in a polished wooden tray with steaming glass jug, the Spode chinaware and creamer. The cups contained hot water: Dicky said warmed cups were a vital contribution to the flavour. He tipped the hot water into a bowl and poured out his own coffee first. When tasting it he frowned with eyes half-closed and jug held poised. 'Even better than the last lot,' he pronounced.

'Is Stowe gunning for me?'

'He's gunning for someone,' said Dicky.

Dicky looked out of his window while he drank. The weather system that had Berlin still gripped in winter temperatures had loosened its hold on England, where a succession of highs had provided enough warmth to coax the trees into bud and bathe the streets in a deceptively golden morning sunlight. It was a false summer, the sort of day when a man leaves home without an overcoat and comes back with pneumonia.

At ten-thirty I made my way to the room of the Deputy Europe. I remembered this room when it was decorated to the expensive and somewhat avant-garde taste of Bret Rensselaer – chrome, glass, black leather and deep carpet – but now all that was gone. To say it was bare would be a gross understatement. It was even without floor covering. The walls still had the coat of grey-green underpaint that marked Bret's departure. Where once there had been an exquisite Dürer, now hung the standard portrait of the Queen. Stowe's desk was a metal one of the

290

sort used in the typing pool, and his chair was of the back-breaking design that the Ministry of Works used to discourage visitors from sitting too long in the reception area downstairs.

Dicky Cruyer was already there. He'd put his jacket on over his bright red braces, which I interpreted as a gesture of deference. Possibly their meeting had started earlier. Dicky liked to arrange an opportunity for a confidential chat before the real business started. He was perched on a metal chair with uneven feet so that it moved a fraction of an inch when he shifted his weight. All three of the visitors' chairs in this room had the same defect. I'd heard someone say the Deputy Controller had arranged for the chairs to be bent but I thought it unlikely that Stowe required any such psychological devices for discomforting his visitors.

Augustus Stowe had jet-black hair. As well as supplying an abundant moustache, this same black hair grew from inside his ears and straggled from his nostrils; it appeared in tufts on his cheeks and great tangles of it covered the backs of his hands. Strange then that he was so bald. The carefully combed hair, and the sideburns, only emphasized the perfect shiny pink dome of his head.

'No good sitting there scratching your arse, Dicky. Some bugger will have to go,' said Stowe with the antipodean directness of manner that had earned him few friends in the Department. 'You could go yourself,' he suggested in a way that implied that this would be a last and desperate resort.

'Leave it with me, Gus,' said Dicky.

Although it wouldn't be his style to comment on such a thing, I had the feeling that Stowe didn't like being called Gus. I wondered if Dicky failed to realize this, or whether it was deliberate provocation. 'No, Dicky,' said Stowe. 'When I leave things with you, they end up back in my tray six weeks later – flagged urgent.'

Dicky pressed his fingers against his thin bloodless lips, as if suppressing a temptation to smile at such a good joke. 'Bernard could go,' Dicky offered. 'He could manage it.'

'Manage it!' scoffed Stowe in his flat Australian growl. 'Of course. That's just what I've been saying. Any bloody fool could manage it.'

'Bernard knows Vienna,' said Dicky.

It wasn't true by any means but I didn't contradict Dicky, and he knew I wouldn't. It simply wasn't done to contradict your boss in front of a superior. 'Do you, Bernard?' said Stowe. There was a fat old fly buzzing round his head. He waved it away with a rather regal gesture.

'I was there with Harry Lime,' I said.

Stowe gave me a brief disparaging smile. 'Vienna is only part of it,' he said. He was not an easy man to fool, although perhaps that wouldn't have been so evident to anyone meeting him for the first time. Stowe was wearing a grey three-piece suit of curious weave, a lumpy knitted tie and zip-sided high boots. All of his clothes looked like theatrical costume rummaged from the hamper of some long-defunct repertory company. Even his wristwatch was an unusual trapezoid shape, its crystal discoloured brown, so that to see the time he had to bring his wrist close up to his face.

To peer at his watch he'd taken off his heavy tortoiseshell glasses. The stylish spectacles were an incongruous aspect of Stowe. One would have expected him to wear small circular gold-rimmed glasses, bent and perhaps secured with a piece of flesh-coloured sticking plaster. These spectacles were expensive and modern, and after looking at his wristwatch he brandished them as if wanting to make the most of them.

'And Bernard has good Russian,' said Dicky.

'They will all speak English,' Stowe said, looking again at his watch.

'Not amongst themselves,' said Dicky. 'Bernard will be able to understand what they say to each other.'

'Ummm,' said Stowe. 'What's the time?' He was twisting the crown of the watch to adjust the hands.

'Ten fifty-two,' said Dicky.

'You're not empowered to make any concessions,' Stowe told me solemnly. 'Listen to what these hoodlums have to say. If you think it's all baloney, come back and say so. But no deals. And come straight back. No sightseeing tours on the blue Danube, or tasting the May wine at the *heuriger* houses in Grinzing. Right?' Even Stowe could not resist telling us he'd been there.

'Of course,' said Dicky. The fly buzzed round Dicky now. Dicky gave no sign of noticing it and it flew away.

'And lastly, I don't want any of our bloody Yankee friends mixed up in it,' said Stowe as he opened a folder and turned its pages. Dicky looked at me and gave me a fleeting smile. I saw then that Dicky was not intimidated as much as discomposed by Stowe. He didn't know whether to respond with Stowe's same bar-room vernacular or keep him at his distance with deference and good manners.

'How would they get mixed up in it?' asked Dicky.

Stowe referred to his notes. The fly alighted on a page and walked insolently across the heading. 'They'll be on to any of our people arriving in Vienna. They'll be on to them right away.' With a surprising speed his hand shot forward. His fingers flicked and closed tightly upon the fly, but when he opened his fingers there was no fly.

'Do you think so, Gus?' said Dicky.

He gave a crafty smile. 'I'm bloody sure so. I worked with the Yanks in Korea. Corps headquarters: I know what they're like.' He wiped his hand on his trouser leg just as if the remains of the fly had been upon it. Perhaps it itched.

'What *are* they like?' said Dicky, dutifully providing the cue for which Stowe waited.

Stowe looked at Dicky, and sniffed in the contemptuous manner of a practised lecturer. 'It is in the character of your average American, an aspect of his history, that he is curious by nature, resourceful by upbringing and empirical by training,' said Stowe. 'In other words: Yanks are nosy interfering bastards. Stay clear of them.' He made an unsuccessful grab at the fly, and then waved at it angrily as it flew away. 'And I don't want one of you big spenders checking into the Vienna Hilton with your dark glasses on, and asking the desk clerk if they have a night-safe and telex facilities. Got it?'

Dicky, whose tastes for expense-account high living were directed more to the grandeur of the Imperial, nodded agreement.

Stowe must have guessed from the look on my face that Dicky hadn't told me much about the subject under discussion. In fact Dicky had told me nothing. Stowe said, 'You're having one of those off-the-record meetings with people from the other side.' Facing my blank look he added, 'Russkies, I mean. Don't ask me who or how or where, because I'm not allowed to tell you.'

'Yes, sir,' I said.

'Top priority, so we can assume they have some bloody complaint to whine about. There will be threats too if I know anything about the way these bastards operate. Stonewall all the time, and don't get ruffled.'

'Is it something Vienna Field Unit could do?' I asked as diffidently as I was able. 'I've never known any of them to become even slightly ruffled.'

Stowe touched his bald head very delicately almost as if he was smoothing his hair. He must have thought the fly had settled upon his head but in fact it was tramping across his desk. For a moment he seemed to forget the conversation we were having, then he looked at me. 'I told you: we've got to avoid the Yanks.' His eyes fixed on me, he added, 'Vienna is packed with Yanks . . . CIA I mean.'

So it wasn't tourists or encyclopaedia salesmen he was worried about.

'Why would the CIA be interested?' I asked. 'Or do you mean we are going to send someone to Vienna for every off-the-record contact?'

Slowly a smile came to Stowe's face. It was not much of a smile but what it lacked in joy it made up for in guile. 'Very good, Bernard!' he said, and there was in his voice a note of approval that I had not heard before. 'Very good!' He turned his head to share the fun with Dicky. Dicky gave a dutiful smirk that revealed that he didn't know what the hell was going on. I recognized it easily: it was one of Dicky's standard expressions.

But soon I saw that Stowe's pleasure was feigned; the way he reacted to what he judged to be insubordinate questioning. Speaking slowly Stowe said, 'I know the CIA are interested, Bernard, because a little bird told me. And if I'm told to make sure such events go smoothly in the future, maybe I *will* send someone to Vienna every time. And it might bloody well be you. Would you like that, Bernard?'

I didn't answer. Dicky smiled to show that now he knew what Stowe was talking about. Helpfully he said, 'So you think the Vienna CIA will try to interfere, Gus?'

'I *know* they bloody will,' he said. 'Brody, the Vienna Station Chief, is an old sparring partner of mine. He'll screw this one up for us if he gets half a chance.'

'And he knows it's on?' I asked.

'Joe Brody is a tough old bastard,' said Stowe. 'And he's very good at guessing.'

Stowe stared at me and nodded his head. I wondered if that was intended to be some special warning for me.

'What do you make the time now?' Stowe asked while he was tapping his watch. Dicky told him having consulted an elaborate wristwatch that had a tachometer, a perpetual calendar programmed to allow for leap years until the year 2100 and a little moon that waxed and waned. Stowe growled and hit his old timepiece with the flat of his hand, as if punishing it for failing to meet requirements.

Dicky got to his feet. 'Okay, Gus. I'll come back to you with some ideas tomorrow.' As Stowe opened his mouth to object Dicky said, 'Or perhaps this afternoon.'

'Jesus Christ, Dicky,' Stowe said. 'I know how jealously you guard your little realm, and about this overdeveloped *amour propre* that is a byword of all dealings with German Desk. But if you think I don't know you went to the Deputy D-G last week demanding Bernard's return because he was the only man for this job, you'd better think again.'

Dicky's face went bright red with anger, or with embarrassment, or perhaps a combination of those emotions over which English gentlemen have been supposed to exercise complete control. No doubt my presence added to his discomfort. 'Did Sir Percy tell you that?' Dicky stammered.

'A little spy told me,' said Stowe abrasively. Then: 'Yes, what do you think Sir Percy and I talk about at the briefing, except what all you bloody Controllers go snivelling to him about?'

Dicky was standing now, and he gripped the back of the chair he'd been occupying, like a prisoner in the dock. Flustered he said, 'I merely said, confirmed that is . . . I told Sir Percy no more than I told you . . . that . . .'

'That Bernard could manage it? Yes, right. Well, why come in here pretending you hadn't already gone above my head?' The fly appeared, did a circuit and went into a holding pattern around Stowe's cranium.

'I assure you that using Bernard was not my idea,' said Dicky indignantly. Stowe smiled grimly.

So that was it. This meeting had been called specifically to stage a Departmental brawl, and it was now evident that the clash was not really about who should attend an off-the-record meeting with a KGB delegation. This bare-knuckle contest was calculated to rebuff some rash attempt by Dicky to assail Stowe's territory. It was my bad luck to be the blunt instrument that Stowe had chosen to beat upon Dicky's head.

In the manner of the English, Dicky's voice had grown quieter as he became angry. Now he weighed his words carefully as he went into an involved explanation. Dicky was so offended that it made me wonder if he was telling the truth. In that case it would mean that the Deputy had arranged my recall, and pretended that it was at Dicky's request to conceal the fact from Stowe.

I was determined to get out of this quarrel. 'May I get back to my desk?' I asked. 'I'm expecting an important phone call.' Stowe waved a hand in the air in a gesture that might have signalled agreement to my leaving the room but which might have been rejecting something Dicky was saying. Or might have been a bid for the fly.

As I was leaving the room, Stowe's words overlaid Dicky's and Dicky said, 'Look here, Gus, I give you my solemn word that Bernard wasn't mentioned . . .' and then sat down again as if he was going to be there a long time.

With a sigh of relief I stepped out into the corridor. The fly came with me.

★

That evening I was very happy to get back to my little house in Balaklava Road. Until now I had not felt much affection for this cramped and inconvenient suburban house, but after my cold and lonely bed in Berlin it had become a paradise. My unexpected arrival the previous evening had been discounted. Tonight was to be my welcome home.

The children had painted a bright banner – Welcome Home Daddy – and draped it across the fireplace where a real fire was flickering. Even though half of me was a Berliner, the sight of a coal fire always made me appreciate the many subtle joys of coming home. My wonderful Gloria had prepared a truly miraculous meal, as good as anything any local restaurant could have provided. She'd chilled a bottle of Bollinger and I sat in our neat little front room with the children squatting on the carpet and demanding to hear about my adventures in Berlin. Gloria had told them only that I was away on duty. After a couple of glasses of champagne on an empty stomach, I invented an involved story about tracking down a gang of thieves, keeping the narrative sufficiently improbable to get a few laughs.

I was more and more surprised at the manner in which the children were maturing. Amongst their ideas and jokes – comparatively adult and sophisticated for the most part – the evidence of some childish pleasure would break in. Requests for a silly game or a treasure hunt or infantile song. How lucky I was to be with them while they grew up. What misplaced sense of patriotic duty persuaded Fiona to be elsewhere? And was her choice of priorities some bounden commitment that enslaved only the middle classes? I'd grown up amongst working-class boys from communities where nothing preceded family loyalty. Fiona had inflicted her moral obligations upon me and the children. She had forced us to contribute to her sacrifice. Why should I not feel grievously wronged?

A timer pinged. Effortlessly Gloria led the way into the dining room where the table was set with our best china and glass. When the dinner came it was delicious. 'Would champagne be all right with the whole meal?' 'Can a fish swim?' Another bottle of Bollinger and a risotto made with porcini. After that there was baked lobster. Then a soft Brie with French bread. And, to finish, huge apples baked with honey and raisins. A big jug of rich egg custard came with it. It was a perfect end to a wonderful meal. Sally sorted out each and every raisin and arranged them around the edge of her plate but Sally always did that. Billy counted them, 'Rich man, poor man, beggarman, thief . . .' to foretell that Sally would marry a beggarman. Sally said she'd always hated that

296

rhyme and Gloria – optimist, feminist and mathematician – rejected it as inaccurate on the grounds that it gave a girl only one chance in four of a desirable partner.

The children were both in that no-man's-land between childhood and adult life. Billy was dedicated to motorcars and beautiful handwriting. Sally was chosen to play Portia in *Julius Caesar* and gave us her rendition of her favourite scene. Her Teddy Bear played Brutus.

> 'Within the bond of marriage, tell me, Brutus,
> Is it excepted I should know no secrets
> That appertain to you?'

Dismissing the marital prophecy we all declared it to be a memorable family occasion.

'The children are old enough now to enjoy celebrating together as a family,' said Gloria after they had been put to bed. She was standing looking into the dying embers of the open fire.

'I'll never forget this evening,' I said. 'Never.'

She turned. 'I love you, Bernard,' said Gloria as if she'd never said it before. 'Now before I sit down, do you want a drink or anything?'

'And I love you, Gloria,' I said. I'd resisted voicing my feelings for too long because I still felt a tinge of guilt about the difference in our ages but my time away from her had changed things. Now I was happy to tell her how I felt. 'You are wonderful,' I said, taking her hand and pulling her down to sit with me on the sofa. 'You work miracles for all of us. I should be asking you what I can do for you.'

Her face was very close. She looked sad as she put a hand on my cheek as if touching a statue, a precious statue but a statue nevertheless. She looked into my eyes as if seeing me for the very first time and said, 'Sometimes, Bernard, I wish you would say you loved me without my saying it to you first.'

'I'm sorry, darling. Did the children thank you for that delicious meal?'

'Yes. They are lovely children, Bernard.'

'You are good for all of us,' I said.

'I got all the food from Alfonso's,' she confessed in the little-girl voice she affected sometimes. 'Except the baked apples. I did the baked apples myself. And the egg custard.'

'The baked apples were the best part of the welcome home.'

'I hope the best part of the welcome home is yet to come,' she said archly.

'Let's see,' I said. She switched out the light. It was a full moon and the back garden was swamped with that horrid blue sheen that made it look like a picture on television. I hate moonlight.

'What is it?'

'It's good to be home,' I said, staring at the ugly little garden. She came up behind me and put her arm round me.

'Don't go away again,' she said. 'Not ever. Promise?'

'I promise.' This was no time to reveal that Dicky and Stowe had got a little jaunt to Vienna lined up for me. She might have thought that I welcomed the prospect and the truth was that I had some irrational dread of it. Vienna was not a big city and never has been: it is a little provincial town where narrow-minded peasants go to the opera, instead of the pig market, to exchange spiteful gossip. At least that's the way I saw it: in the past Vienna had not been a lucky town for me.

7

I remember telling a young probationer named MacKenzie that the more casual the briefing was, the more hazardous the operation you were heading into. It was the glib sort of remark that one was inclined to provide to youngsters like MacKenzie who hung upon every word and wanted to do everything the way it was done in the training school. But I was to be given plenty of time to think about the truth of it. When, afterwards, I considered the way in which I'd been brought into the Vienna operation, I inclined to the view that Stowe had been given no alternative: that he was instructed to choose me to go.

The operation was called Fledermaus, not 'Operation Fledermaus' since it had been decided that the frequency rate of the word 'operation', and the way in which it was always followed by a code name, made it too vulnerable to the opposition's computerized code breaking.

Certainly Fledermaus was cloaked in Departmental secrecy. These BOA – Briefing On Arrival – jobs always made me a little nervous, there being no way of preparing myself for whatever was to be done. It seemed as if the determination to keep this task secret from the Americans had resulted in a strictness of documentation, a signals discipline and a delicacy of application that were seldom achieved when the aim was no greater than keeping things secret from the KGB.

I flew to Salzburg, a glittering toytown dominated by an eleventh-century fortress with a widely advertised torture chamber. The narrow streets of the town are crammed with backpack tourists for twelve months of every year, and postcards, icecreams and souvenirs are readily available. My hotel – like almost everywhere else in Austria – was not far from a house in which the seemingly restless Wolfgang Amadeus Mozart once resided.

My arrival had been timed to coincide with an important philatelic auction and I checked into the hotel together with a dozen or more stamp dealers who'd come in on the same flight. Their entries in the book showed a selection of home addresses including Chicago, Hamburg and Zurich. On the reception desk a cardboard sign depicted a youthful Julie Andrews, arms outstretched, singing 'The Sound of Music tour – visit the places where the film was shot.' Behind the desk sat a fragile-looking old man in a black suit and stiff collar. He used a pen that had to be dipped in an inkwell and rocked a blotter upon each entry.

The hotel was gloomy, spacious and comfortable. It was the old-fashioned sort of grand hotel still to be widely found in Austria, and the sweet synthetic scent of polish hung in the air: an indication of manual work. An ancient lift, crafted of brass and mahogany, lurched upwards inside a wire box with a wheezing sound, and sudden rattles, that persuaded me to use the stairs for the duration of my visit. There was even a man in black waistcoat and green baize apron to carry my bag.

An Austrian named Otto Hoffmann had met me at the airport and made sure I got a comfortable room in the hotel. 'At the back overlooking the river,' he said in his powerful Austrian accent, and a chilly draught hit me as he opened the window and peered out to be sure the water was still there. 'No traffic noise, no smells of cooking, no noise from the terrace café. Tip the porter ten schillings.' I did so.

Hoffmann was about forty years old, a short, hyperactive man with merry little eyes, a turned up nose and smiling mouth. His manner plus his large forehead, his pale unwrinkled skin, the way his small features were set in his globular head, and his sparse hair, all gave him the appearance of an inebriated baby. I don't know how much Hoffmann had been told about 'Fledermaus' but he never mentioned that name. He knew that my cover story of being a stamp dealer was completely untrue and he'd obviously been chosen for his knowledge of philately.

'And now I shall buy you a drink,' he said as he closed the inner window and put his hand on the radiator to be sure the furnace was working. He meant a cup of weak tea. Because he kept his money in his back pocket, in a large roll secured with a rubber band, he had a disconcerting habit of tapping his behind to make sure his money was still there. He did this now.

He briefed me while we were sitting in the hotel lounge. It was a cavernous place with a celestial dome where angels cavorted and from which hung an impressive cut-glass chandelier. Around the walls there were potted plants set between other small tables and soft chairs where fellow guests, unable or unwilling to face the crowded streets, sat drinking lemon tea in tall glasses together with the rich pastries, or gargantuan fruit and icecream concoctions, that punctuate the long Austrian days.

He ordered two teas and a rum baba. He told me they were delicious here but I was trying to give up rum babas.

'The auction sale consists almost entirely of Austrian and German material,' he told me. 'Of course the biggest market for that is Austria and Germany, but there will be American dealers, bidding as high as the present exchange rate of the dollar permits. Also there will be compatriots of yours from London. London is an important trading centre for philatelic material, and there are still many important German and Austrian collectors there. Mostly they are refugees who fled the Nazis and stayed in England afterwards.'

The waitress brought our order promptly. The tea came in a glass, its elaborate silver-plated holder fitted with a clip from which a spoon was suspended. She put two large chunks of lemon on the table and splashed a generous amount of an alcoholic liquid upon a shiny sponge cake which bore a crown of whipped cream. 'Are you sure. . . ?' Hoffmann asked again. I shook my head. The waitress scribbled a bill, put it on the table and sped away.

'And what am I doing here?' I asked, keeping my voice low.

He frowned. Then, as he understood me, he twitched his nose. On the table he had two beautiful catalogues. He passed one to me. It was an inch thick, its coloured cover, magnificent art paper and superbly printed illustrations, making it look more like an expensive book of art reproductions than a commercial catalogue. They must have cost a fortune to produce. He opened it to show me the pictures of stamps and old envelopes, tapping the pages as some picture caught his attention. 'Most of the really good items are from the old German states. Württemberg and Braunschweig, with a few rarities from Oldenburg, Hannover and so on. Here too are some choice things from old German colonies: mail from China, Morocco, New Guinea, Togo, Samoa.'

As he leafed through the catalogue Herr Hoffmann lost the thread of his conversation. His eyes settled upon one page of the catalogue. 'Some of these Togo covers sound wonderful,' he said in an awed voice, and read the descriptions with such concentration that his lips quivered. But he tore himself away from the wonderful offerings to show me the auction schedule printed on the inside cover. The hours – eight o'clock in the morning until approximately three o'clock in the afternoon, with an hour off for lunch – were listed to show the numbered Lots that would be offered in each session. There were several thousand Lots for the sale, which would last five days. 'Some rich collectors employ agents to come to the auction and buy selected items on their behalf. The agent gets a nice fee. You will be such a person.'

'Why don't they bid by post?'

He gave a slight grin. 'Some collectors are suspicious of these auctions. When you bid by post the amount you authorize the auctioneer to spend is supposed to be your tip-top offer. The auction

301

house undertakes to charge you no more than one step above the next best bid.' He squeezed lemon into his tea and chased a pip around with his spoon but, after testing the side of his glass with his fingertips, decided it was too hot to drink.

'And?'

He gave another sly grin; his face slipped naturally into this expression, so that it was hard to know whether he was amused or not. 'Whenever I bid by post it always seems that someone has mysteriously kept bidding right up to one step below my maximum offer. I find I always pay the whole of whatever I bid.' He picked up his fork and looked at his cake with the concentration a demolition expert gives to placing dynamite.

'So collectors have agents who make sure the bids and the bidders are real?' I said.

'Exactly. Even then it is difficult to know if there is a swindle. Sometimes there will be an auction official on the phone taking phone bids and the auctioneer will have in front of him the postal bids. It is difficult to be sure exactly what is happening.' His conversation had been marked by the little smiles but now he became serious as he took his fork and ate a section of his rum baba. 'The pastry chef is Viennese,' he confided as he savoured it.

'And what else will the agent have to do?'

'He should have examined the Lots for which he is going to bid, to make sure they are not damaged, or repaired or forgeries.'

'Are there many forgeries about?'

'There are some Lots in this auction with estimated prices of about one hundred thousand U.S. dollars. That is a great deal of money by any standards. Many people pay less than that for the lease of a house to live in.'

'You make your point, Mr Hoffmann,' I said. 'But don't the auction houses have experts? Don't they know enough about stamps to recognize a forgery?'

'Of course they do. But auction houses get their percentage of the sale price. What inducement do they have for detecting a forgery? And what do they do then – accuse their customer of dishonesty? If the forgery is sold they get a nice share of the money. If they send it back they lose a customer and make an enemy and lose their percentage too.' He stopped abruptly and ate some cake. Two men who'd been sitting at a nearby table had got up and were walking out. They were Americans to judge by their clothes and their voices, neatly dressed with fresh faces and polished shoes.

'You make them all sound like a lot of crooks,' I said.

'I hope I don't. I know dealers I would trust my life to. But it is a precarious trade,' said Hoffmann and smiled as if that was what he liked about it. I had the feeling that the idea of selling forgeries did not offend him in the way that it should have done. I wondered if he was in some way connected with the forgeries that the Department commissioned from time to time. Reading my mind perhaps, he gave me a sly grin.

'Are the people here all dealers?'

He looked round the sepulchral lounge. Waitresses in formal black dresses and white starched aprons padded silently to and fro across the white marble floor with trays of teas and cakes. The men, a mixed collection but for the most part middle-aged or elderly, were bent low, scribbling annotations in their catalogues and whispering conspiratorially to each other, rather as we were. 'I know most of them,' he said.

'And all men?'

'Yes, I don't know of one important female stamp dealer. There are virtually no female collectors even. Should a woman inherit a collection she sells almost immediately: you can depend upon it.' He decided his tea was cool enough to drink and tasted it.

I was flipping through the catalogue. 'How do they decide the estimated price?' I asked.

'Don't take much notice of that,' he said. 'That's just to whet your appetite. The estimated prices are far below what the auctioneer expects to get.'

'How much below?'

'There is no way to answer such a question. Auction houses vary. Crazy things happen. Sometimes two agents arrive, both instructed with buy bids.'

'What is a buy bid?'

'It means buy at any price.'

'At any price?'

'The craving – the reckless lust – that some collectors show for an item they particularly want is difficult to describe. Some collectors become unbalanced, there is no other word to describe it.' He fastidiously wiped his fingers on the napkin and then brought from his pocket a small folder of tough clear plastic. Inside it there was a used envelope (or what I'd learned to call a cover) with a stamp (or what I'd learned to call an adhesive) on it. 'Look at that.'

He handed me a white envelope adorned with quite an assortment of stamps and postmarks. Smudged and discoloured, it had been readdressed twice and was such a mess that I would probably have thrown it straight into the waste bin had I found it on my desk. It meant nothing to me but I looked at it with the kind of reverence he obviously expected of me. 'Most attractive,' I said.

'A man went to prison for that,' said Hoffmann. 'A respected man, chief clerk in an insurance office. He was a customer of mine: nearly fifty years old, with three children and a pensionable job. He had a decent little collection. I'd provided quite a lot of the things myself. He was knowledgeable about his own speciality. He regularly gave talks, and displayed his stamps to philatelic societies. Then he heard that a well-known collector had died and he knew that this cover was amongst the collection. It would be the gem that completed his collection. He asked me if I could find out when it was coming on the market. He was determined. By a lucky chance I knew about it. I guessed the widow would dispose of everything: they always do. You don't like to go sniffing round too soon. It upsets the family. On the other hand if you wait too long some other dealer will go in there and pick up the whole collection . . . buy it up for nothing sometimes, when the relatives don't know what they have inherited. There are some unscrupulous people in this business, I can tell you.'

'I'm beginning to believe it,' I said.

'Is there something wrong with your tea?'

'No. It's delicious.'

'You're not drinking it.'

'I'll get around to it.'

'The widow was a rich woman. The collection was unimportant to her. When I went there and asked her about the collection she decided to make me her agent, to value and then sell the whole lot of it. It put me in a difficult position in respect of the other collector but I never really considered that he was seriously in the market for it anyway. There are only thought to be four or five covers like that one. The last time one of them was auctioned it fetched fifty thousand dollars and that was almost ten years ago. Even if this one fetched no more than that one did, my insurance company friend just didn't have access to that sort of money.'

I looked at the cover. 'Fifty thousand dollars?' Could it be true?

Hoffmann nodded. No smile this time. They were serious people, these philatelists. 'In this year's catalogue the adhesives alone are listed at nearly that – of course catalogue values don't mean a lot – but I have a prospect in Munich . . . He's phoned me three times about it. He is becoming demented with the thought of owning it and insists that I let him see it . . . I am interested in hearing his assessment of its value. He spends a lot on his collection.'

'And your insurance friend?'

'The fool! He stole the money from his company. Filed a false claim, forged a cheque and made it payable to himself. Can you believe it? He was detected immediately. Pleaded guilty. His company said they had to prosecute him. There were too many other employees who might try the same trick. They were right of course, and he knows that. I went to see him yesterday.'

'In prison?' I handed the cover back to Hoffmann.

'Yes, in Graz. I gave evidence for him at the trial. I said he was honest and of good character but of course the evidence said he was a thief.'

'He must have been pleased to see you,' I said.

'I'm selling his collection too. He's flat broke now; the lawyers took his last penny. He's selling everything.' Hoffmann put the cover back into his pocket.

'Aren't you nervous about carrying a valuable thing like that?'

'Nervous? No.'

'What was the sentence?'

'My client?' He spoke through a mouthful of baba.

'The insurance man.'

He took his time in swallowing cake and then took some tea. 'Five years. I took him a colour photo of that cover.' He tapped his pocket. 'And the prison governor gave him special permission to have the picture in his cell.' Hoffmann sipped tea. 'The joke is that I'm beginning to think it's a forgery. In which case it's worthless.' He laughed down at his plate as if trying to resist it but finally ate the last of the cake.

'Did you know that right from the start?'

'Not for sure.' He wiped his lips.

'You suspected it?'

'I put it under the ultraviolet light. You can't be too careful. Then I took it to someone who knows. I'm still not certain one way or the other.' He drank more tea. 'Are you sure you wouldn't like a cream cake? They are delectable here, as light as a feather.'

'No thanks.'

'It's a weakness of mine,' he confessed. He'd finished the baba but left a huge blob of thick cream on the side of his plate. 'Not even apple strudel?'

'No.'

'You go into the auction and bid for Lot Number 584. It will come up in the morning at about ten o'clock but it would be safer if you were there a little early.' I looked at him. I recognized that this was my

305

briefing: London Central had sent me here to buy. 'Pay cash for it. It is estimated at one thousand schillings. I will leave you three thousand Austrian schillings; that should be enough. Take it to Vienna and phone von Staiger. You've heard of the Baron, I suppose?'

'No,' I said.

He looked surprised. 'You won't actually meet him but there will be instructions for you.' He passed me a visiting card. Its printed content consisted only of Staiger's name and title and the description 'Investment Consultant'. In minuscule handwriting a Vienna address had been added in pencil. The use of aristocratic titles was illegal in Austria but Staiger, like many others, seemed not to care about that.

From his back pocket Hoffmann took his roll of money and counted out the Austrian notes. With it there was a small printed receipt form, of the sort sold in stationery shops. 'Sign there please,' he said.

I signed for the money. 'You won't be at the auction tomorrow?'

'Alas, no. I go to Munich tonight.' He smiled as he made sure my signature was legible and put the receipt away in his wallet. 'Hold up one of the number cards to bid. Sit at the front where the auctioneer can see you and then no one else in the room knows you are bidding. Your Lot will be ready for collection about five minutes after you've bought it. By paying cash you won't have to establish your credit or say who you are.'

'Will I be seeing you again?'

'I don't think so,' he said. He waved a spoon at me.

'Is there anything else you are going to tell me?'

'No,' he said. 'From this point onwards Baron Staiger runs the show.' He used his fork to scoop up the huge dollop of cream and put it in his mouth. There was a look of pure bliss on his face as he held it on his tongue and then swallowed it. 'You haven't drunk your tea,' he said.

'No,' I said.

He got up and clicked his heels as he said goodbye. I sat there for a few minutes more sipping my tea and looking round the room. I noticed he'd left me with the bill.

I took the catalogue Hoffmann had left for me and strolled out on to the terrace that overlooked the River Salzach. It was too chilly for anyone else to be seated there but I relished the idea of being alone.

I looked up Lot Number 584. It came in the section of the auction designated 'Deutsches Reich Flugpost – Zeppelinbelege' and was written in that unrestrained prose style used by men selling time-share apartments on the Costa Brava.

Lot 584. Sieger Katalog 62B. Brief. Bunttafel IV. ÖS 1,000, – 1930 Südamerikafahrt, Paraguaypost. Schmuckbrief mit Flugpost-marken, entwertet mit violettem Paraguay-Zeppelin-Sonderstempel 'Por Zeppelin' dazu violetter Paraguay-Flugpoststempel 16. 5. Brief nach Deutschland, in dieser Erh. ungewöhnl. schöner und *extrem seltener Beleg, Spitzenbeleg für den grossen Sammler.*

From which I gathered that in 1930 the cover illustrated in colour on Plate 4 was expected to fetch one thousand Austrian schillings. It had been sent from Paraguay on the *Graf Zeppelin* airship with all the necessary postal formalities, and having become a great philatelic rarity it was available as centrepiece for some 'big collector'.

The colour photo showed a well preserved light blue envelope with several different rubber stamps and adhesives, addressed to a Herr Davis in Bremen. It didn't look like anything worth a thousand schillings.

As I was sitting there by the river and staring up at the Hohensalzburg fortress that blocked off half the skyline, the glass doors swung open and a man joined me on the terrace. At first he seemed unaware of my presence. He walked across to the metal balcony and checked how far there was to fall, the way most people do.

As the man turned to obtain a better view of the castle across the river I had a chance to study him. It was one of the Americans I'd seen earlier. He was dressed in a short forest-green hunter's coat, fashionably equipped with big pockets, straps and loops. His hair was streaked with grey and neatly trimmed and on his head he wore a smart loden cap. He spoke without preamble. 'When I visited Mozart's birthplace yesterday it was one of the greatest experiences of my life.' He had a rich cowboy voice that belied his declared emotion. 'Number nine Getreidegasse: ever been there?'

'Once . . . a long time back,' I said.

'You need to go real early,' he went on. 'It soon gets to be full of these pimple-faced backpackers drinking Coke out of cans.'

'I'll watch out for that,' I said and opened my catalogue hoping he'd go away.

'Mozart gets himself born on the third floor, and that's inconvenient, so they only let you look at the museum downstairs. It's kind of dumb, isn't it?'

'I suppose so.'

'I really go for Mozart,' he said. '*Così fan tutte* has got to be the ultimate musical experience. Sure, critics go for *Don Giovanni*, and

Mozart's wife Constanze said the maestro rated *Idomeneo* number one, but *Idomeneo* was his first smash hit. The sort of box office receipts *Idomeneo* rang up in Munich made young Wolfgang a star. But *Così* has real class. Consider the psychological insight, the dramatic integrity and the musical elegance. Yes, sir, and it is sweet, sweet all the way through. I play *Così* in the car: I know every note, every word. My theory is that those two girls weren't fooled by the disguises: they wanted to have fun swapping partners. That's what it's really about: swapping. Mozart couldn't make that clear because it would have been too shocking. But think about it.'

'I will,' I promised.

'And shall I tell you something about that great little guy? He could compose in his head: reams of music. Then he'd sit down and write it all out. And do you know, he'd let his wife prattle on about her tea parties and be saying "So what did you say?" and "What did she tell you?" And all the time he'd be writing out the score of a Requiem or an opera or a string quartet, keeping up a conversation at the same time. How do you like that?'

'It's not easy to do,' I said feelingly.

'I can see you want to get back to your catalogue. I know there's some kind of big-deal stamp collectors' shindig in the hotel. But I never reckoned you as a stamp collector, Bernie.'

I tried not to react suddenly. I slowly raised my eyes to his and said, 'I collect airmail covers.'

He smiled. 'You don't recognize me, do you, Bernie?'

I tried to put his face into a context but I couldn't recognize him. 'No,' I said.

'Well, no reason you should. But I remember seeing you when I used to share an office with Peter Underlet and then Underlet went to Jakarta and I went to Bonn and worked for Joe Brody. Jesus, Bernie. Have you forgotten?'

'No,' I said, although I had forgotten. This man was a stranger to me.

'On vacation huh?'

'I had a few days' leave due.'

'And you came to Salzburg. Sure, screw the sunshine. This is the spot to be if you are looking for a chance to get away from it all. Are you . . .' he paused and delicately added '. . . with anyone?'

'All alone,' I said.

'I wish we could have had dinner together,' said the man regretfully. 'But I have to be back in Vienna tonight. Tomorrow I'm on the flight to Washington DC.'

'Too bad,' I said.

'I just had to make this pilgrimage,' he said. 'Sometimes there are things you just have to do. Know what I mean?'

'Yes,' I said.

'Well, good luck with the stamp collecting. What did you say it was . . . Zeppelinpost?'

'Yes,' I said, but of course I hadn't told him that. I'd just said airmail.

He waved and went back through the doors to the lounge. If he'd been sent by Joe Brody with the task of making me squirm, he'd done rather well. I closed the catalogue and resumed my contemplation of the grim grey walls of Festung Hohensalzburg on the far side of the river. I needed a belly laugh. Perhaps after I'd had a stiff drink, I'd stroll across town, catch the funicular up to the fortress and take a look round the torture chamber.

8

I didn't eat dinner in the hotel. I found a charming little place near the Mozart statue, or it might have been near the Papageno fountain or the Mozart footbridge. I heard the music of an accordion playing a spirited version of 'The Lonely Goatherd' and went in. The interior was done in dark wood panelling with red check tablecloths. It was almost empty. On the walls there were shiny copper pans together with the actual marionettes that had been used to perform the Mozart operas in the world-famous *Marionettentheater*. Or maybe they were plastic replicas. The waiter strongly recommended the breaded pork schnitzel, but as my mother told me, you should never trust a man in lederhosen. It took several glasses of the local Weizengold wheat beer to help me recover. The accordion music was on tape.

I got back to the hotel late. There were men everywhere: standing about in the lobby, others drinking solemnly in the bar and all of them eyeing each other warily. I knew they were stamp dealers, for I could detect the ponderous gravity that so often attends the first evening when men are gathered together for business purposes.

Even the serious drinkers were quiet. A group near the bar were speaking in that stilted German that is usually the sign of the expatriate. One said, 'I don't know why people say the Austrians are venal, it took them more than a century to discover how much money they could make out of Mozart.'

His companion shushed him. Rightly so, for even his quiet voice was audible on the other side of the hotel. Then suddenly there was a loud shuffling and squeaking noise from the revolving doors and into the lobby there came two young couples. They had gleaming complexions and perfect wavy hair. Their clothes were chic and expensive and the women wore glittering jewellery and they all had that boisterous self-confidence with which the wealthy are so often endowed. They were not stamp dealers. Everyone turned to see them, for their sudden entrance into the sombre hotel lobby was unwelcome, like noisy brightly coloured TV advertisements interrupting the soft nostalgia of an old black and white film.

They must have sensed the feelings their unexpected appearance had provoked, for they became quieter and their movements more composed as they made their way across the marble floor. The lift was not working, so they went up the grand staircase to their rooms. The eyes of every man followed the progress of the glamorous people, the women with their long dresses decorously lifted as they ascended the stairs, the young men murmuring together.

I looked around for the mysterious American but there was no sign of him. I had done enough for one day: I went to bed. As I put my head on the pillow a clock began to chime eleven and soon another one joined in.

The auction started exactly on time, as most things do in that part of the world. It was all Zeppelin mail today, starting with the earliest examples, mail of the 'pioneer' airships *Viktoria Luise* and *Schwaben*. Then came one postcard from the airship *Deutschland* which bore the airship company's red stamp, and the bidding just kept going and going until it reached the sky. There were three men after the card and the room went silent as the auctioneer just kept his litany of numbers going with glances from one side to the other. The bidding stopped suddenly as two of the men seemed to decide simultaneously that there was no longer a margin of profit left. Crack, went the hammer, and the reaction was a sudden shuffle of tense muscles and released breaths. They were all writing the price into their catalogues. This would set a higher value for such items and would mean a reappraisal of their stocks.

The room wasn't crowded but there was a continuous flow of people as specialists interested in particular items came in and took part in some spirited bidding and then went to drink coffee in the glassed-in sidewalk café, or out on the terrace to smoke and chat with their colleagues.

They must have been running a bit behind time that morning, for the auctioneer kept glancing at his watch and there seemed to be a general tendency to hurry things along.

As the auction reached 1914, and the wartime Zeppelins, there was something of an exodus that left only a couple of dozen specialists. Whether this was because the First World War items were a neglected part of the stamp collector's world, or because this particular auction contained poor examples, I had no way of knowing. But when the auctioneer announced the beginning of a Hungarian collection of *Graf Zeppelin* mail, sold by order of the executor of the deceased man's estate, almost every chair was taken, and there were some who preferred to remain standing at the very back.

I was ready well before Lot 584 was offered for sale. Face down on the table in front of me there was a large white card printed with a big black number 12. That was my number and when the bidding for 584 began I tipped it up so that it was visible to the auctioneer. For a fraction of a second he met my eyes to tell me that I was in the auction, and increased the bid accordingly. Behind me there must have been a dozen or more bids offered somewhat mechanically. The price kept going up, and it was hard to know whether my raised card made any difference. The auctioneer looked into the distance and deliberately gave no clue as to where the bids were coming from.

The bidding slowed. That first flurry of bids had gone, leaving more serious ones. 'One thousand nine hundred!' he called, and as the total increased each bid was a bigger jump. Suddenly we were into bigger bids. I tipped the card to keep the bidding going but someone behind me was interested too. We were now at double the estimated price and the bids were still coming!

The auctioneer didn't look surprised. That morning there had been other things to surprise him more: items ignored and items fetching three or four times their estimates. I tried to remember how much cash I had in my wallet over and above the money that Hoffmann had left with me. 'Two thousand five hundred!' They were 100-schilling increments now, and still going.

'Two thousand six hundred!' Behind me there were two other people bidding for the damned envelope. I turned but could not see either of my rivals.

'Two thousand nine hundred!' The auctioneer was looking at me now, an eyebrow lifted. I showed my bidding card again and he lifted his eyes to somewhere at the back of the room.

'Three thousand . . .' and even before he said it he was looking over my head and saying 'Three one . . . Three two . . .'

His eyes came back to me. I held the card resolutely upright and his eyes passed discreetly over me and to the room. 'Three three . . . three four . . . three five . . .' He hadn't even brought his eyes back to me. There must be two of them fighting it out. And they weren't slowing. I turned to see the room. One of the auction officials was standing in the corner at a telephone. He lifted his hand. So it was a phone-in customer who was bidding against me plus someone at the back of the room.

'Three thousand seven hundred schillings!'

Some sort of pause had come in the bidding, for the auctioneer's eyes came back to me. 'Three thousand seven hundred schillings at the back of the room,' he said.

I nodded. The auctioneer said, 'Three eight at the front of the room.'

From somewhere behind me I heard a German voice say, 'Three

312

nine,' and then another German voice say, 'Four thousand on the phone.'

'Four thousand one hundred at the back of the room,' said the auctioneer. And then immediately, 'Four two . . . three . . . four, five.' Even the auctioneer was surprised. 'Four thousand six hundred at the back of the room.'

He was looking at me. I nodded. He looked up and said, 'Four . . .' and then said, 'Five thousand one hundred schillings to the back of the room.'

I turned to get a proper look at who was bidding and was in time to see the man at the telephone wave a hand to indicate the bidder had stopped.

'For the second time: five thousand one hundred schillings,' said the auctioneer looking at me quizzically.

I lifted the numbered card. 'Five two at the front.'

For a moment I thought the bidding had stopped. I was relieved. If I turned out all my pockets and persuaded the hotel to take an English cheque I might put together that amount of cash. Then the auctioneer said, 'Five three . . .' and then without looking in my direction at all he said, 'Five four . . . Five five.'

Someone else had joined the bidding and before I could catch my breath the price was at six thousand Austrian schillings.

The auctioneer was tapping his hammer again. 'For the third time . . .' I shook my head. 'Gone!'

Once again the Department had given their orders and then so arranged things that the man in the field could not carry them through. I put the numbered card in my pocket as a souvenir and got to my feet. I wanted to see the man who now owned what I'd been sent here to buy.

He made no attempt to avoid detection. He looked sixtyish; wavy hair, a bit overweight but physically rather trim. He was wearing a Black Watch tartan jacket and dark slacks with a spotted bow tie. His neatly trimmed grey beard and gold-rimmed bifocals all added up to an American college professor on a sabbatical. He was leaning against the edge of a table and as he saw me he smiled and edged his way past the other men to join me. I waited for him.

'Oh boy! I wondered what was happening,' he said in English with a soft American accent. 'I thought you maybe had a buy bid too.'

'No,' I said. 'I had a limit.'

'And am I glad you did. We could have gone through the ceiling. Can I buy you a drink?'

'Thanks,' I said.

'I haven't seen you around before.'

'I work in London,' I said.

As we reached the door he asked one of the auction staff where he could pick up his purchase and was told to go to the cashier's office – a room on the ground floor at the back of the hotel. It was all well-organized, and evident that the same firm held auctions here regularly.

'Jesus, look at that rain and it's becoming hail,' he said as we walked past the bookstall and along the corridor.

There was a line waiting outside the cashier's office when we got there. We joined the line. 'It was a good item but I've seen better,' said the man, continuing with the conversation. 'My name is Johnson, Bart Johnson. I work in Frankfurt but I come from Chicago. Are you a Zeppelinpost expert?'

'No,' I said.

He looked at me and nodded. 'Well Graf Zeppelin is a kind of hero for me. I was always crazy about airships. It started when I was a kid and someone gave me a piece of fabric from the *Shenandoah* that crashed in Ohio in 1925. I've still got it, framed on the wall. Yes, back in my office I keep a file on everything. And I looked up Berezowski's *Handbuch der Luftpostkunde* . . . You know that of course?'

'I'm not sure I do.'

'Jesus, I depend on Berezowski even more than I rely on the *Sieger Katalog*.' In his hands he had a catalogue and a blue folder containing cuttings and handwritten notes. He flipped it open to refer to it.

I sensed that some reaction was expected so I said, 'Do you really?'

'Berezowski's 1930 book is a classic for this kind of reference. It's been reprinted: you can still buy copies. I'll give you an address and you can get one mailed. But in the clippings I came across an article that Dr Max Kronstein wrote in the *Airpost Journal* in January 1970. He says the Paraguay post office refused to accept International Reply Coupons; *that's* why Paraguay mail is so rare. The only mail with Paraguay adhesives came from residents – foreign residents.'

'That's very interesting,' I said.

'Yes, isn't it?' He flipped the file closed and put a gold pencil into his pocket. 'And ever since Sieger listed the mail to Europe as being worth ten per cent more than mail to USA, our customers prefer it. In fact I looked up Kummer: he says that only sixty items went to the USA and about 180 to Europe so I'd say it was the other way around. Mind you, you can never be sure because mail sent to Europe might have been destroyed by the war, while items in American collections remained safe.' He kept a finger in the file, as if it might be necessary for him to prove these contentions to me by references to it.

'Yes,' I said.

'Sure. I know. I mustn't go on so much. You seem kind of disappointed. Was it for your own collection?'

'No, it was just a job.'

'Well, don't take it to heart, fella. There's a whole lot more Zeppelinpost out there waiting to be bought. Right?' I nodded. He stroked his beard and smiled. The line moved forwards as some dealers emerged from the office with their purchases.

'Say, who was that character I saw you talking with on the terrace yesterday?'

'An acquaintance,' I said.

'What's his name?'

'I've been trying to remember,' I said. 'I thought he was with you.'

'Thurkettle,' he supplied. 'He said his name was Ronnie Thurkettle. So he's not a buddy of yours?'

'I hardly know him.' Now I remembered the name but his face was still not familiar to me.

'Say, what kind of work does that guy do? He's not in the stamp business is he? I used to see him in Frankfurt and all around but I never figured what kind of job he has.'

'Works for the State Department,' I said. 'But that's all I know about him.'

'He buttonholed me yesterday. He came on real friendly, but he just wanted to pick my brains about Zeppelinpost. He doesn't know the first thing about airmail. He was expecting me to explain the catalogue to him. I told him to go and get a good book on the subject. I'm not about to give lessons to guys like him: he's not my kind. Know what I mean?'

'How did he take it?'

'Take it? He backed off and changed the subject. He's not a friend of mine. No way. I just used to see him around when I was in public relations. Frankfurt; I'd see him at those little shindigs the contractors give to entertain visitors: cute little weenies on a stick and diluted Martinis. You know. I guessed he was with the government. Washington is printed all over him: right? But I thought maybe he was a civilian with the army.'

'No,' I said. 'State.'

'I stay well away from those guys. They bring trouble and I don't need it.' The line moved again until we were at the front. A soft buzzer sounded and the security man signalled for us to go in. There was not much room in the cashier's office. A morose clerk looked through a small metal grille. Behind him there was a girl with a table piled with philatelic covers and cards in transparent plastic and a cash box full of cheques and money of all denominations. 'Johnson's the name. Johnson, Bartholomew H.,' said my companion. 'Lot 584. Six thousand schillings. I have an account with you.' The room had an unfamiliar smell, like incense. Maybe it was the clerk's after-shave. Or the money.

The man behind the grille turned the pages of the book. 'What number?' he asked.

'Lot 584.' Johnson now had a thick bundle of Austrian money in his hand. He riffled it. It seemed as though all these stamp dealers liked cash.

'There must be a mistake,' said the man behind the grille.

'Johnson Bartholomew H. I have an account. Six thousand schillings. If you want cash, I have it here.' He flip-flopped the wad of money and said, 'I'm not going to spend ten thousand schillings before getting on the plane this afternoon.'

The clerk said, 'Lot 584 went for six thousand two hundred schillings. A telephone bid.'

'No sir!' said Johnson. 'I got it.'

'You have made a mistake, sir,' said the man behind the grille.

'*You've* made the mistake, buddy. Now give me my cover.'

'I'm sorry.'

'I insist. It's mine! Now let me have it.' He was angry.

'I'm afraid it's no longer here,' said the clerk. 'It went off with a lot of other material. It's for a very well-known client.'

'What am I?' said Johnson angrily.

'I'm sorry you are disappointed, sir,' he said. 'But there is really nothing I can do and there are many other customers waiting.'

'How do you like that?' He shouted so loudly that the security man looked around the door, but the steam was going out of him.

'Let's get out of here,' I said, a number one rule amongst the people I work with being never get tangled with the law.

'You haven't heard the last of this!' Johnson said to the man behind the grille.

'I'm very sorry, sir. I really am.'

Once out in the corridor again we both became objects of curiosity for those who had heard Johnson shouting. He brushed the front of his suit self-consciously and said, 'Come on. Let's get a drink.'

'Good idea,' I said.

It took him several minutes to recover his composure. He seemed really rattled. If it was all an act it was an Oscar-worthy performance. Once seated at the counter in the bar he said, 'What the hell was that all about? You were there. You saw me get that damned cover. Or am I going nuts?'

'You're not going nuts,' I said.

'Did you tell me your name?'

'No, I didn't.'

'I'm not going nuts,' said Johnson. 'It's these Austrians who are going nuts. Give me a double scotch,' he called to the barman. He raised his eyes and I nodded. 'Make it two double scotches.'

'Let me pay,' I said. 'I suddenly seem to have a lot of cash.'

'Me too,' he said and laughed. 'I've got to get out of here, these people drive me crazy. Want a ride to the airplane? Or have you got a car?'

'When?'

'I'm catching the seven o'clock plane to Vienna,' he said, and I told him that would suit me just fine. The whisky calmed him down. I let him talk about his stamps while I made appropriate interjections and thought about other things.

Later I walked upstairs with him. His room was near the stairs and mine along the same corridor. As he let himself into his room he said, 'I'll take a bath and maybe grab a sandwich. See you in the lobby about five-thirty?'

'Right,' I said.

Then, as his door closed I heard him say, 'Well, what about that?' and I wondered what he was referring to. But by that time I'd grown used to his spirited disposition and decided that he was talking to himself.

There was plenty of time. I wondered whether to phone London and tell them that someone else had bought the cover but decided to put it off for an hour or two. By that time I'd be speaking to a Duty Officer rather than to Dicky or Stowe.

I went to the window and stared down at the rainswept street. The tourists were indomitable. Buttoned tight in long brightly coloured plastic coats, their feet encased in transparent overshoes, their hoods with drawstrings tightened to reveal small circles of grim red faces, they trekked past like combat-hardened veterans resolutely moving up to the fighting line. I got a glass from the bathroom and poured myself a shot of duty-free scotch. I'd promised Gloria not to touch the hard stuff while I was away this time, but that was not taking into account the

317

fiasco in the auction room and the way in which I would soon have to explain my failure.

I kicked my shoes off, stretched out on the bed and dozed. All day – like an errant poodle tugging its leash – my mind had tried to explore some other time and place. And yet these fugitive memories remained fuzzy grey and unfocused. It was when I closed my eyes and relaxed that my memories sniffed out what had been bothering me all day.

'Deuce' Thurkettle! Jesus Christ, how could I ever have forgotten Deuce Thurkettle, even if he now preferred to be known as Ronnie? I'd never known him but his dossier was something not to be forgotten.

'Deuce' not in the sense of runner-up, quitter or coward, the way the word is sometimes used, nor a 'pair' in a poker game. This man was Deuce because of the barbaric double murder for which he'd gone to prison. Deuce Thurkettle came to Berlin after being released from some high-security prison in Arizona, where he was serving a life sentence for murder in the first degree.

Perhaps it was a long dull afternoon after too much Southern-fried chicken when some bright young fellow sitting behind a desk in Langley, Virginia, had got this brilliant idea of sending a convicted murderer into Berlin on a tourist visa, to get rid of a troublesome KGB agent who had so far eluded all attempts to incriminate him.

I remembered the Deuce Thurkettle file and the way I'd read it all the way through without pause. I suppose to some extent I read it because I was not supposed to see it. It was a CIA document buried deep in the dank dark place where the CIA buried their secrets. Or that's where it should have been. Poor old Peter Underlet had taken it home with him. He had shown it to me one evening after the two of us had dinner – and two bottles of lovely Château Beychevelle 1957 – in his apartment. I could recollect each page of that bizarre insight into the cloistered mentality of the administrator: '. . . and Thurkettle's knowledge of electronic timing devices, sophisticated locks, modern handguns and explosives, added to his proved physical resources, qualify him as an outstanding field agent.'

Underlet had opened the file to that page of a long report from Langley before he slammed the whole thing on to my knees. 'Look at that,' said Underlet bitterly. 'That's what those shits in Washington think about field agents. Without any training or experience this murdering bastard becomes a field agent overnight, an outstanding field agent it says there.'

I remember Underlet slumping back in the armchair and drinking his wine and saying nothing while I read the file through. 'Deuce'

318

Thurkettle; how could I have forgotten him, the first of a trio of hit men who came unbidden and unwelcome to the CIA offices of Europe during that unhappy period?

Afterwards – weeks afterwards – we talked about it again. By that time I had become more indignant about the morality of Washington DC than about what the episode revealed of the desk-man's feelings about field agents.

I was no longer stretched out, I was sitting up in bed fully aware of the racing pulse and tension that comes when the mind is on the verge of remembering some important image. What happened to those three jailbirds? All three were given the elaborate new identities that later became the reward for mafiosi who turned State's evidence. Thurkettle: Thurkettle. There was speculation that he murdered a supermarket tycoon in Cologne: a man with whose wife Thurkettle had a love affair. I wasn't sure that was Thurkettle. Had Thurkettle's name been in any of those 'most wanted – confidential' lists? My memory just could not get hold of it.

By now I was on my feet. I paced the room knowing beyond any doubt that it all added up to a conclusion that would seem obvious when the questions were asked. Obvious, that is to say, to the questioner.

I decided to ask Johnson some more questions: about Thurkettle and anything else that emerged. I put on my shoes and went down the corridor to knock at the door of Johnson's room. There was no response. I turned the knob and found the door unlocked.

Inside, the bedroom was empty. A clean shirt, underclothes and socks were laid out on the bed, in the careful way a valet might arrange clothes for a fastidious employer. From the bathroom there came the sound of water running. The door was closed. Johnson called, 'Put it down on the table. There's a tip there for you.'

'It's not room service: it's me,' I said.

'You're early aren't you?' His voice was distorted like that of a man cleaning his teeth.

'That guy Thurkettle. I remembered something about him.'

'Give me fifteen minutes.' There was a splutter as if the tooth cleaning was proceeding energetically.

Okay, I thought, everything is normal. I went back to my room. I don't know how long I sat there before the sound of the explosion made me jump out of the chair and run for the door. Afterwards the newspapers said the forensic department estimated it at 300 grams of explosive, but that amount would have taken the bathroom door off and maybe the wall and me too.

But it was a loud bang all the same, and that unmistakable stink of explosive came rolling down the corridor to meet me. My mind went blank. Experience said hide under the bed: curiosity made me wonder what had happened.

For better or worse, I hurried along the corridor and into Johnson's room. I went to the bathroom and grabbed the handle as the door fell off its hinges. I don't know what kind of explosive they'd used but the inside of the bathroom was black with soot and dirt. Maybe that had come from something else. The wash-basin was the centre of the damage: the mirror had disappeared, except for a couple of splinters dangling from the fixing screws. Below it, looking like some example of modern sculpture, the blue china pedestal remained in position supporting one elegant slice of basin.

What remained of Johnson was on the floor face up and twisted between the water-closet bowl and the bidet. There were appalling burn marks on the torso and his clothes were scorched. There was very little blood: the heat of the explosion had cauterized the blood vessels. Around him there were hundreds of pieces of broken chinaware. I didn't have to look twice to know what had happened. His hand was only a stump and what was left of him above the neck was wet and shiny and spread all over the marble floor.

It was the electric razor bomb, an old trick but I'd never seen the results of one before. Find out what model of razor your victim uses, fill one with any decent plastic explosive – shaping it for something really directional – and fit a neat little detonator (made in Taiwan – please state on order form whether 110 v. or 220 v.) and he'll obligingly hold it to his head and switch on the electricity!

Poor Johnson. Behind me excited voices indicated that people were crowding into the bedroom now, so I slid back amongst them, vociferously asking everyone what had happened. Johnson. Had there been someone waiting for him when he went into his room? Was that remark, 'Well, what about that?' rhetoric, or had he been talking to a visitor, someone like Deuce Thurkettle whose 'knowledge of electronic timing devices, sophisticated locks, modern handguns and explosives, added to his proved physical resources, qualify him as an outstanding field agent'?

And if Thurkettle was the killer, why? Or, to turn the whole thing on its end; was Thurkettle some sort of deep-cover operator for whom a bizarre background story of a murder conviction had been fabricated? If so who killed Johnson, if Johnson was his real name? And all the time another part of my mind was telling me that London Central would not expect me to phone them now. Not even Stowe would expect me to make contact, not with this mess to extricate myself from, and the likelihood of the Austrian police listening to phone calls. Despite everything, I was somewhat comforted by that reprieve.

9

My plane took off from Salzburg airport in a Wagnerian electric storm that lit up the Alps with great flashes of blue light and thunder that shook the world. Rain beating upon the metal skin was audible over the muzak and the plane slewed and yawed as it fought the gusting winds and climbed through the narrow path between the mountains.

I still had to get the horrific vision of that torn apart body out of my mind. With nothing to read except the flight magazine I took the stamp catalogue from my bag and looked again at the cover I'd failed to get. I studied the picture closely and tried to understand what demon drove men to amass expensive collections of these pretty little artefacts. The colour photo was so realistic that it seemed almost as if I could lift it from the page. Using the scissors of my Swiss army knife I cut out the illustration and put it in my wallet.

It was late when we descended for the landing in Vienna. The storm had passed over and the stars were shining in a moonless sky. The address that Hoffmann had provided for me was in the Inner City. I looked again at the coloured map of Vienna that I'd picked up from the airline counter. It was a brightly coloured depiction of the city – with isometric drawings of such buildings as the Imperial Palace – garlanded with adverts for such diversions as a 'revue-bar', a 'kontakt club sauna', and 'private escort services' all captioned in German, Arabic and Japanese. Close study of the map revealed that my destination was a sidestreet off Kärtner Strasse, a well-known thoroughfare which runs from the Opera Ring – that surrounds the inner city – to St Stephen's Cathedral at its centre.

It was dark when the taxi dropped me outside the huge shape of the State Opera House just after the curtain descended on the final act of *Der Barbier von Sevilla*. Many doors opened simultaneously so that yellow rectangles of light fell out on to the pavement. Then people emerged, not many at first, just a dozen or so, silently exploring the rain-shiny streets with an air of disoriented caution, as inter-galactic voyagers might emerge from a huge stone spaceship. From inside there came the muffled roar of applause. Moments later the ensemble's final bow released a flood of people, and these were clamorous and elated. A swirling press of them swept across the forecourt and the pavement and

322

into the road with no thought of the traffic, laughing and calling to each other, like upper-class felons unexpectedly released from imprisonment.

'Fussgängerzone,' explained the cab driver, executing an illegal U-turn and positioning his cab ready for homegoing crowds who were already raising their arms to hail him. 'You have to walk from here.' By now the street was filled with people dressed in the sort of amazing fur coats and evening clothes that are de rigueur when Germans or Austrians attend a cultural event. A group of such overdressed opera-goers besieged the cab as it came to a stop and began bidding for it in loud voices that quickly became an argument between competing groups.

I paid off the driver and pushed my way through the hordes of people who were still spewing from the Opera House doors. But as I progressed the crowds thinned, for few people were heading into the narrow streets of the city centre. Soon I was alone and my footsteps echoed as I walked past the dark shops and closed cafés. Downtown Vienna goes to sleep early.

The address I wanted was in a narrow ill-lit Gasse, an alley of antique shops, their façades neglected and dilapidated in the way that only the most exclusive antique shops are. Through the gloomy shop windows rich oriental rugs, polished furniture and old glassware gleamed. The door for one shop displayed a brass plate with the discreet legend 'Karl Staiger'. I pushed the bell. It was a long time before there was any response. Even then it was an upstairs window being opened, and closed again shortly afterwards.

I could see through the shop window as eventually a dim light came on at the back of the shop, silhouetting the furniture and the shape of the short plump man who picked his way through the display to the door. It took him some time to release the bolts and security locks on the shop door. He allowed the door to open only to the extent that the security chain permitted. Through the gap he called, 'Yes? What is it?'

'I'm looking for Baron Staiger,' I said. 'I have come from Salzburg.' There was a sigh. The door was closed while the chain was taken off the hook.

When he opened the door to look at me I saw it was Otto Hoffmann himself. I had every excuse for not recognizing him sooner, for this was a more sober fellow than the jolly little man who'd given me three thousand Austrian schillings and a lecture on philately in Salzburg. Now he was dressed up in a stiff shirt and formal bow tie, wearing over it a colourful embroidered smoking jacket. He stared at me for a moment without replying. It was almost as if he was trying to find

323

reasons to send me away. But, grudgingly, he said, 'Hello Samson.' It was not a warm welcome. 'I told you to phone.'

'It wasn't possible to phone.'

'Why not?'

'I had no change,' I said facetiously.

'You'd better come in. Here in Vienna I'm von Staiger.' His accent was the same: pure Viennese, right down to the ih instead of ich. He let me step inside the shop and I waited while he went through the rigmarole of securing the front door again.

He switched out the light in the shop and led the way to the very back and up the narrow wooden staircase. From the basement there came those smells of bonding materials, freshly shaved wood and polish that together distinguish the workshop. The three upper floors were given over to living quarters. On the staircase there were engravings and embroidery in antique frames, and on the landing was a fine oak commode in pristine condition. It seemed that some of these rooms doubled as showrooms. As we got near the top of the house I could hear music, and a smell of cooking – or rather the legacy of some former meal preparation – replaced the more acrylic odours from the basement. 'I have company,' explained Staiger. 'Put your coat on the rack and leave your bag here. We will talk later.'

'Okay.'

At the top of the house two small rooms had been made into one, and there were about a dozen people there. They were all dressed in an extravagant fashion that in London I might have mistaken for fancy costume. The women wore lots of jewellery and décolleté dresses, one of them smoke-coloured silk with tiered flounces, and another spectacular design was trimmed with antique lace. The men were in evening dress suits with vivid cummerbunds, or sashes, and some of the older men wore medals.

This fellow Baron Staiger had none of the merriment I'd seen in Hoffmann in Salzburg. He made no attempt to introduce me to his guests, listlessly addressing those who had noticed our entrance with the words, 'This is Mr Samson, a friend from Salzburg.' I was damp. The heavy rain had penetrated my trenchcoat, and my baggy old suit had creases in all the wrong places. They looked at me without enthusiasm.

In the corner a pianist was wrestling with George Gershwin, and they were both losing. After my entrance he played a few desultory bars of waltztime and then gave a smile as if he knew me. The piano stopped soon after that. I had the feeling that my entrance had spoiled the gemütlich atmosphere.

The waiter bore down. Asked what I'd like to drink, and hearing there was no hard liquor, I took the *Gspritzter* and stood around waiting for everyone to go home. I could not avoid the impression that Staiger wanted to be distanced from me in every way, for after making sure I had a drink in my hand, he moved to a group on the other side of the room.

'So you live in Salzburg now?' asked someone from behind me. I turned and saw it was the piano player, who in the better light I now realized with a shock was someone I knew.

Jesus H. Christ! It was a malevolent reptile named Theodor Kiss, who preferred to be called Dodo. The last time I'd seen him he was threatening to tear me to pieces and was equipped with the means to do so. Now he smiled sweetly, his long white hair giving him a rather august appearance despite the unpressed dinner suit. He was a vicious old man, a Hungarian who'd changed sides when Germany lost the war and carved a new career with the victors. 'No, do you?' I replied.

'Vienna actually. I have a wonderful new apartment. I decided to move . . . the south of France has become so . . . so vulgar.'

'Is that so?' I could see the new red scar tissue across Dodo's scalp: the wound made when Jim Prettyman felled him and probably saved my life.

'And how is my darling Zu?' He was a friend of Gloria's family.

I mumbled something about her being well.

He knew I didn't want to talk with him but he enjoyed persisting. 'I studied in Vienna of course. The city is like a home to me; so many old friends and colleagues.'

I nodded. Yes, indeed: plenty of old colleagues here for a one-time Nazi like Dodo. The waiter offered us a tray with dabs of Liptauer cheese on small shapes of toast. I popped a couple in my mouth. I'd had no food on the plane.

'Vienna is the most beautiful city in the world,' said Dodo. 'And so gemütlich! Do you like the opera?'

I was eventually rescued from the conversation by a man who asked me if I was a newspaper reporter. Dodo moved away. The newcomer was thickset, with a little beard of the sort called a van Dyke, although on him it looked somewhat Mephistophelean. I answered that I wasn't and he seemed content that I shouldn't be. He raised an arm to indicate a large painting: a grotesque arrangement of abstract shapes in primary colours. 'You like it?' he asked.

'What is it?' I said.

'It is modern art,' he said with a patronizing drawl. 'Do you know what that is?'

'Yes. Modern art is what happened when painters stopped looking at girls.'

'Really?' he said coldly. 'Is that not *Kulturbolschewismus*?' It was a low blow. Cultural Bolshevism was the name the Nazis coined to condemn anything other than the state-approved social realist art.

'I'm getting to like it,' I said in my usual cowardly way. 'Are you a painter?'

'Andras Scolik!' He clicked his heels and bowed from the neck. 'I write music,' he said. 'Viennese music.'

'Waltzes?'

'Waltzes!' he said disdainfully. 'Of course not! Real music!'

'Oh, yes,' I said. I caught the attention of a passing waiter and this time I had local champagne. It tasted just like the *Gspritzter*.

'No,' he said, 'I didn't write the famous "Yodeler" or shepherd songs like "In the Salzkammergut folk are gay". I hope that doesn't disappoint you too much.'

'No,' I said.

'It is a battle against history,' he said. 'We Austrians do everything to excess, don't we?'

'No,' I said.

'Yes, we do. Foreigners laugh at us. Our national costume is comic, our version of the German language is incomprehensible, our cuisine indigestible, our bureaucracy indomitable. Even our landscape and our climate are absurd and extreme. Mountains and snow! How I hate it all. Ask a foreigner to name a famous Austrian and he says Julie Andrews.'

I was not expecting to arouse such fervour. I tried to calm him down. 'I was thinking of Mozart,' I said hurriedly.

It seemed only to infuriate him more. 'Don't talk to me of Mozart. This damned country is enslaved by his memory. We musicians are prisoners of Mozart and his wretched eighteenth-century music. Tum-titty-tum-titty-tum-tum-tum. I despise Mozart!'

'I thought everyone liked Mozart,' I said.

'The English like him. That anaemic eighteenth-century music suits the bloodless English temperament.'

'Perhaps that's it,' I said, having given up hope of cooling his temper.

'Dead composers! They only like dead composers. When Mozart was alive they seated him with the servants: one place above the cooks but well below the valets. That's what they do to musicians when they are alive.'

'You don't really despise Mozart, do you?' I asked him.

'Tum-titty-tum-titty-tum-tum-tum.'

326

'Consider,' I said authoritatively, 'the psychological insight, the dramatic integrity and the musical elegance.'

'Rubbish! Why did that foolish boy waste so much time with German operas – toy music – couldn't he see that the future of opera was rooted in the sublime genius of the Italians? Listen to *La Traviata*. You will hear passion . . . profound human feelings as expressed by the lush sound of a full-sized orchestra and scored by a composer of real genius who understood the art of singing in a way that little Mozart never could.'

'Andras!' called someone from the other side of the room. 'Could you settle an argument over here?'

The angry musician bowed stiffly from the neck and, spilling a few drops of his wine, took his leave of me with all the formalities. I sipped my drink and looked round. There was a distinct heightening of atmosphere in the room. Instead of that jaded weariness that so often attends the mourners at a dying party, there was a feeling of expectancy, but what was expected I could not guess.

I examined the room. It would seem to have been cleared of some of its furniture in preparation for this gathering. Some faded rectangles on the wall revealed the places from which large pictures had been removed and replaced with smaller ones. Those few items of furniture remaining were choice antiques, inlaid occasional tables and a sideboard of Hepplewhite style. But my attention went to a set-piece at one end of the room. It had obviously been arranged to captivate some rich client. Three lovely chairs designed in the stark and geometrical Secessionist style, and behind them two superb posters by Schiele. I went to get a closer look at the chairs. My reluctant host must have seen me admiring his wares for he was smiling as he came towards me with a bottle of champagne in his hand.

'I hope Andras was not too abusive,' said Staiger. He filled my glass. He seemed reconciled to my gate-crashing his party.

'He was most informative.'

'Are you with the Diplomatic Corps?' This time there was a smile and a twitch of the nose. 'Or is London Central sending us a more subtle type of man these days?' Staiger was a decade younger than me and yet he could get away with such a remark without inciting anger or resentment. Baron Staiger of Vienna, and Herr Hoffman of Salzburg, and God knows what in the other places he went, was provided with more than his full share of that Viennese *Zauber* that the rest of the world calls schmaltz.

He said, 'Andras has had a disappointing evening, I'm afraid. He has spent ten years trying to get his string quartet performed. Tonight it was. His loyal friends went but there were not enough of us to fill the hall.' He sipped his drink. 'Worse still, I think Andras realized that his composition wasn't really very good.'

'Poor Andras,' I said.

'His parents own the Scolik Konditorei,' said Staiger ironically. 'Know it? Each afternoon old ladies stand in lines to devour that superb Scolik poppy-seed strudel with a big dollop of Schlagobers. It is like owning a gold mine. The strudel will help him survive his crisis of confidence.'

'Is that what he's having?'

'Strudel?' he asked mockingly. 'No, you mean a crisis of confidence. Tomorrow he will face the music critics,' said Staiger. 'And Vienna breeds a savage race of critics.'

'Karl!' said a small sharp-featured woman who soon made it evident from her manner that she was Staiger's wife. Ignoring me she said, 'Anna-Klara has arrived, Karl.' She touched his arm. I wondered if she knew about her husband's other lives. Perhaps she thought I was a part of them.

Staiger smiled in a satisfied way. 'She has? *Kolossal*!' I was later to discover that he considered this lady's visit a social coup of some magnitude. He looked round to make sure that there was no aspect of the room that would disgrace him in the eyes of this renowned visitor, and found only me. For a moment I thought he would hide me in a cupboard, but he swallowed, looked at his wife apologetically and – as if explaining his predicament – said, 'When the guests have gone home, I have some work to do with Herr Doktor Samson.' He smoothed his thinning hair as if checking that it was in place.

The wife looked at me and nodded grimly. She knew I wasn't really a Doktor, a real Doktor would have been called 'Baron' and a real Baron 'Prince'. That's how things worked in Austria. I smiled but she didn't respond. She was a dutiful Austrian wife who let her husband make decisions about his work. But she didn't have to like his down-at-heel work-mates. 'Here comes Anna-Klara,' she said.

The arrival of the guest of honour was what they had all been waiting for. This soprano had been performing at the opera that night, and when she came into the room it was an entrance befitting the reverence that this assembled audience afforded her. She swept in with a flourish of the long flowing skirt. Her yellow hair was piled high and glittering with jewels. Her make-up was slightly overdone, but that was de rigueur for someone who'd hurried from the opera stage.

328

Her fellow guests greeted her with a concerted murmur of awe and devotion. With the Staigers at her side, the *gnädige Frau* went from one to another of them like a general inspecting a guard of honour. Here, bowing low, was a *Doktor Doktor* and a *Frau Doktor*, his wife; the bureaucrat's wife – *Frau Kommerzialrat* – gave a sort of a curtsy; the *Hofrat* – court adviser for a Habsburg Emperor long since dead and gone – kissed her hand. Anna-Klara had gracious words for all of them, and special compliments for Andras Scolik and the string quartet performance she'd missed. Scolik brightened. Anna-Klara had praised him. And, after all, there was always the strudel.

It was a bravura performance, and with impeccable instinct Anna-Klara stayed for only one glass of champagne before departing again. Once she had gone the party broke up quickly.

It was midnight when I sat down with Karl Staiger in his office at the back of the shop. All the church clocks in Vienna were proclaiming the witching hour. The room smelled of varnish, and Staiger opened the window a fraction despite the bitter cold night outside. Then he moved a lot of unopened mail from where it was leaning against an antique carriage clock and compared the time with that on his wristwatch. It was a beautiful clock, its face decorated with dancing ladies. The movement ticked happily inside the glass-sided case. He nodded proudly at me as a father might smile to see his child play the piano for guests. Satisfied, he moved more books and papers to clear a space on his desk where a green-shaded lamp made a perfect circle of light upon a pink blotter.

'What happened?' said Staiger.

'I haven't got it,' I said. I had no intention of talking to him about the death of Johnson, or mentioning Thurkettle and his possible role in the murder.

'Haven't got what?' He had his arms loaded with books.

From my jacket pocket I produced my wallet and I laid the coloured photo of the cover exactly in the centre of the pool of light. 'This,' I said, smoothing it out. 'I haven't got this.'

He put the books on to a cupboard and looked down at the photo. Then, without speaking, he took the bundle of unopened mail propped against the clock. Going quickly through it, he chose a packet that bore the large and impressive-looking labels of a courier company. It was a small padded bag secured with metal staples. He tore it open with an effortless twist and shook the contents from it.

On to the table slid a blue envelope with Paraguay stamps and Zeppelin marks: the same cover as that depicted in the colour photo upon which it fell.

329

'But I've got it,' said Staiger with a satisfied smile.

'What's the story?' I picked up the cover that had caused so much trouble and probably brought about the amiable Johnson's death. I turned it in my hands. It seemed such a useless piece of paper to be sold for such a high price.

'I only know what I can read between the lines,' he said. 'But I think the Americans sent someone to buy it over your head. I had to get on to one of the biggest dealers in Vienna – an old friend – and ask him to get it at all costs.'

'He must have phoned his bids.'

'There was no time for anyone to get to Salzburg.'

'The room bidder was chiselled, the auction was rigged. At least, that bid was.'

'These things happen,' said Staiger. 'I had no idea the Americans would try to intervene or I would have given you more cash. But it turned out all right. I was told to get it; I got it.' He picked up the cover and held it against the light.

'Is there something inside?'

'Usually there is some stiffening to protect such covers, a piece of card, sometimes one that advertises some long-forgotten stamp dealer.' But while saying this he took from the drawer of his desk a beautiful ivory letter opener and tapped it against his hand. 'You know that the best items in the sale were from a private collection put together in the nineteen thirties by a famous Hungarian airpost dealer named Zoltan Szarek. He was the author of the 1935 Szarek Airpost Manual, long out of print. Now that the Szarek collection is broken up it is the end of one of the world's greatest.' He turned the letter opener round. One end of it concealed a tiny penknife blade. He opened the blade and to my surprise cut open the precious Paraguay envelope.

Having seen the sort of passion that these philatelic objects aroused in men like Staiger I was amazed at this vandalism. But there was a surprise to come, for inside the blue envelope there were two passport-sized photos. The photos were obviously recent ones. The people had grown older since the last time I'd seen them and the photos were dull and lacking in true blacks because they were printed on that sort of grey-toned photo-paper that is used in countries that can't afford much silver. He placed them on the blotter in front of me. 'Anyone you know?'

Two people stared back at me: a man and a woman. One was a Russian KGB man who operated under the name of Erich Stinnes. It was a stiffly posed version of the photo Bower had shown me in Berlin. The other was my wife.

330

That was not all. The 'stiffener' was provided by the presence of two small identity cards. They were pink: both printed on a typical example of the coarse stock standard for Eastern Europe's endless flood of official paperwork. Each was a specific journey visa: one person, one journey, one admission to the socialist people's republic, one exit. The rubber stamp was that of the *Statni Tajna Bezpecnost*, Czechoslovakia's Secret Security Organization. One card bore Staiger's photo, the other mine.

10

The region of Czechoslovakia that borders Austria's northern frontier is Moravia. Somewhat surprisingly, it is a short drive from downtown Vienna. Or would have been, had we not run into the Haydn Festival. Once at the border we'd passed through the Austrian controls with no more than a moment's pause while Staiger waved his papers at them. But the Czechoslovak checkpoint was a different matter entirely.

It was a busy place, for it lies on the direct route from Vienna to Prague, and beyond that Berlin. Here, through the gap between Alps and Carpathians, the wind from the Russian steppe brings sudden drops in temperature and bites through even the warmest of clothes to chill the bones. As well as the cars, on this day about twenty or so articulated heavy trucks from all corners of Europe were lined up nose to tail. Inside their vehicles, windows tightly closed, the drivers dozed, chatted and read, patiently waiting their turn in the large grey-painted hut where the cargo manifests and vehicle documentation were slowly read, incessantly queried and reluctantly rubber-stamped by uniformed bureaucrats, beady-eyed men with inky fingers and regularly oiled guns.

Baron Staiger, aka Otto Hoffmann, this morning wearing a wavy brunette toupee, had collected me from the Vienna hotel where I'd spent the night after leaving his home. We were in a white jeep-like Subaru, and somewhat conspicuous amongst the exotic collection of Eastern bloc vehicles. There were mud-spattered Ladas, smelly two-stroke Wartburgs, a Skoda cabriolet repainted bright pink, and a wonderful old Tatraplan with a long fin marking the air ducts of the rear engine compartment. With imperious disregard of the other drivers Staiger drove to the head of the line and parked carelessly alongside the glass-sided box from which half a dozen Czech officials surveyed the landscape with impassive disdain.

Staiger said, 'Wait in the car,' and went over to engage the sentry in animated talk while tapping the pink identity cards. Whatever dialect the sentry spoke Staiger seemed to speak it too, for the response was warm and immediate. The sentry nodded at Staiger and looked up and waved in the direction of a large green car on the Czech side of the border. Two men in civilian clothes hurried over to Staiger. They were tall, bulky men in trenchcoats, the sort of men who want everyone to know they work for the 'First Section' of the STB: that most effective of all the East European secret police services which – significantly perhaps – chose an ancient Prague monastery as its headquarters. The barrier was immediately raised.

'All okay,' said Staiger as he climbed back into the driver's seat bringing with him a breath of chill winter air.

'All okay,' I echoed. 'Well, that's a nice change.'

'What?'

'All that tomfoolery with the stamp auction . . . and at the end it went wrong.'

'It's a regular route for our documents,' he said smugly. 'The Prague office arranged it; usually it goes like clockwork.'

'Maybe someone should tell them that we live in the age of quartz crystals,' I said.

'The Americans were bidding against us. They got wind of what was happening. The Vienna CIA office sent a man with a pocketful of money.'

'And that's not the way we work,' I said bitterly, remembering my inadequate allotment of schillings.

'No one can outbid the Americans,' he said. 'It was lucky that I could fix it.'

The green car was on the road ahead of us as we went through the crossing point and through the frontier zone where trees and bushes have been cleared and mines sowed.

'They'll stay with us.'

'Will they?' I said and tried to sound pleased.

We followed them into the Moravian countryside. Eventually their green car turned off the main Prague road. The track was poorly maintained and to keep behind them Staiger had to engage the four-wheel drive.

This is a strange and baleful landscape: a sinister legacy of history. Until a generation ago some of these border regions were as prosperous as any in the whole land. Since the time of the Empire, German-speaking people lived in these lovely little towns with tree-lined thoroughfares and baroque houses set around grand squares.

But Adolf Hitler used the *Volksdeutsche* as an excuse to add these border lands to his Third Reich. This was the 'far-away country' that Britain's Prime Minister – having contrived the modern world's first summit meeting – would not go to war for. This was where 'appease-ment' got a new pejorative meaning and 'Munich' became a way of

333

saying surrender. Here lived the Czechs who waved swastika flags and welcomed the German invaders in their own language.

But after Hitler was defeated, the Stalinist government in Prague ruthlessly pushed the three and a half million German-speaking Czechs out of the country. Given only a few hours' notice the exiles were permitted to take only what they could carry. They hiked across the border to find a new homeland. The vacated homes were ransacked by authorized officials and looters too. In a gesture more political than practical the houses were eventually turned over to vagrants and gypsies. Now few of even those residents remain.

We drove through villages that reflected the ambivalence the authorities showed towards this old 'German region'. Stop and go; push and pull; here were the fits and starts of a ponderous socialist bureaucracy burdened by its own historical perspective. Old buildings were half demolished and new ones half built. Piles of rubble spewed out into the roadway and abandoned cinder-block frameworks waited for roofs and windows that would never come.

We bumped through a little ghost town, disturbing a slumbering pack of gaunt dogs that slipped away without even barking. There were no people anywhere. The houses on the main square – their regal 'Maria Theresa yellow' stucco faded into a pox of chalky scars – were boarded up. So were the shops.

I pushed at the heating control again. 'For the last time, Staiger. When are you going to tell me what this is all about?' In London I had been told to do whatever he said. I was doing so but I did not enjoy being kept in the dark.

He shifted in the driver's seat as if his spine was becoming stiff. 'I cannot do that,' he said affably, as he'd said it so many times before on this endless and uncomfortable journey. 'My orders are to take you to the place we have to visit: nothing else.'

'And bring me back?'

He smiled. 'Yes. Bring you back too. At four o'clock. That's all I know.'

Until now the few bits of conversation we'd exchanged had been only Viennese gossip, mostly concerning people I knew only slightly or not at all. Even worse, I'd heard Staiger's detailed observations on Vienna's confectionery, in particular its *Torten*. He'd explained exactly why he preferred the single-layer simplicity of the *Linzertorte* to everything else at Sacher. He revealed every last secret of Demel's delicate *Haselnusstorte* and told me which of their vast selection of Torten benefited from the addition of a portion of whipped cream, and which

334

would be spoiled by such a garnish. He even gave me the address of a little café where the extraordinary quality of the apricot filling they put in their *Sachertorte* made it preferable to the one they served at Sacher's.

'What do I have to do at this meeting? Did they tell you that in your orders?'

He wrenched his mind away from the cakes. 'They said you would know.'

'Is it a Russian?'

'I say I don't know. This is the truth; I don't know. Soon we will be there.' He was disappointed that his thesis on pastries had been so coolly received. Perhaps at some other time I would have enjoyed his dissertation, even joined him for a Kaffeeklatsch tour of the city. But not today.

The clouds were dark and in the dull light the distant mountains loomed unnaturally large. Everything was grey: the sky was grey, the mountains were grey, the farm buildings were grey: even the snow was grey. It was like a poorly printed snapshot: no black nor white anywhere. Life in Eastern Europe was like that nowadays. Belief had gone. Communism had faded but capitalism had not arrived: everyone muddled along, complying but not believing.

On and on we went, slower now that the road was bad. We came to a road junction where two khaki-coloured trucks were parked at the roadside. Three men in camouflaged battle smocks and netted helmets stood by the tailboard of the rearmost vehicle. As we got closer I could see one of them was an officer, the other two were NCOs with automatic rifles slung over their shoulders. They turned to watch us pass.

It was at this junction that we turned on to an even worse road. Soon the green car stopped and pulled aside so that we could pass. As we overtook it the men inside stared at us with a curiosity seldom displayed by such people. Staiger seemed undismayed. The road climbed and we bumped and rattled along a pot-holed path where muddy pools were glazed with patterned ice. In the fields, islands of ancient snow had shrivelled to reveal the hard earth. Birds circled in the sky, already deciding where to spend the night. Snow remained everywhere. Alongside this remote and narrow track, drifts of it piled high, its surface shone with tiny diamonds of ice and showed none of the accumulated carbon stains that passing traffic deposits.

'They're there,' said Staiger. 'See the tyre tracks.'

'Yes,' I said.

'Or perhaps it was the debugging team.'

335

'Did you bring anything to eat?' I asked.

'I thought we'd have time to stop on the Austrian side. I didn't expect we'd be this late,' he said with solemn regret. He lifted his hand from the wheel to indicate another farm ahead.

Built in some ancient time when a farmer's life was punctuated with the role of warrior, it was sited to command a field of fire upon the full extent of the wide valley behind us. The cluster of buildings included two enormous barns, their roofs covered with snow. There was an entrance gateway of considerable grandeur, whose sculptured coat of arms had been deliberately chiselled away but not entirely obliterated so that a decapitated lion clung precariously to half a shield. Tucked away from the wind on the lee side of the ruined gate lodge there were two Czech traffic policemen sitting astraddle motorcycles. They watched us pass.

After the gate a long approach road led past wooden troughs, which steamed gently, and corrugated iron pigsties, to what once had been the central building of a fortified farmhouse.

The car only just squeezed through the low narrow archway, bumped over the cobbles into an enclosed yard and stopped at the back door of a farmhouse upon the walls of which the floral patterns of folk-art paintings could barely be discerned. The yard was big, a huge piece of farm machinery was quietly rusting away in the corner, and some chickens – flustered momentarily by the car – resumed their search for sustenance between the stones. There was a smell of rubbish burning or perhaps the stove needed cleaning.

Scrambling about on the roof there were two men, each equipped with powerful binoculars. Two more men, in short leather overcoats and large boots, sat on a bench in the yard. Hats tipped forward over their eyes, they sprawled like drunken sunbathers, but I noted the relaxed postures of men who remained still for long periods. And I noticed the undone top buttons that would make it easy for them to pull something from a shoulder holster in a hurry.

Without moving they watched us from under lowered eyelids. I got out and waited for Staiger as he carefully locked the doors of his car.

Suddenly a large black mongrel dog came flying out from a doorway, barking and snarling. With reckless speed, and suicidal disregard for its leash, the hound threw itself at my throat. But as the long chain reached its fullest extent the dog choked and toppled sideways, its bark strangled. Tugging ferociously at the chain it crouched low and continued to snarl and bare its teeth, making an exaggerated display of aggression as many creatures do when their anger is constrained.

336

The men seated on the bench had hardly moved during this display of canine fury. Now Staiger laughed nervously and made sure his hat was balanced on his toupee. 'Go in,' said Staiger. 'I will be waiting for you.'

By that time I had begun to guess what was to come. Inside, the farmhouse was dark, its tiny windows set low in the thick walls. The floor was rough worn tiles and there was not much furniture except a refectory table, pushed back against the wall because it was so big, and some old chairs with rush seats.

She was standing in the gloom. She spoke in a whisper. 'Bernard!' My first impression was that Fiona was shorter and thinner than I remembered. Then, with a twinge of guilt, I realized that this was because I'd been with Gloria so long.

'What bloody mad game are you up to now?' I said. The words emerged as a mumble, revealing I suppose my confusion. I still loved her but I was wary of her, unable to decide what she wanted of me, and unwilling to provide for her another chance of duping me in some way or other.

'Don't be angry.'

'Don't be angry,' I said wearily. Her deliberate passivity fuelled my rage and suddenly I shouted, 'You stupid devious bitch. What are you up to now? Are you raving mad?'

She looked me up and down and smiled. Who knows what kind of animosity lay concealed within her? If she was equally angry with me, she disclosed no sign of it. She waited for the steam to go out of me, as she knew it would, and smiled again. She still had that wonderful smile that had devastated me the first time I met her. It was a humorous smile, with a trace of mockery in it, but it was an invitation to join her in her view of the world about us, and it was an invitation I never could resist. 'There is nothing to eat here. Nothing at all. I knew you'd be hungry.' Her voice was flat, perhaps deliberately so, and even though she was my wife I could not tell what emotions were in her mind. It had always been so. Sometimes I wondered whether this enigmatic quality was what made her so attractive to me and I wondered to what extent she failed to understand me in return. Not much I think.

'Bernard, darling.' She tried to put her arms round me but I shrank away.

She said, 'How are the children?' and I was burned by the warmth of her body; overwhelmed by a perfume I'd almost forgotten.

'They're fine. They miss you.' I amended it: 'We all miss you.' Her eyes mocked me. 'Billy is so big. As tall as you perhaps. He has a craze for motorcars; posters, models and even a big plastic engine that he keeps taking to pieces and reassembling.'

'Was that your Christmas present?' she asked, demonstrating her remarkable intuition. It was madness to try to keep any secret from her, and yet I still tried.

'Yes. It was labelled "educational toy",' I said. She gave a little laugh recognizing our long-standing joke that I fell prey to anything so labelled. 'Sally has been chosen to play Portia at school. I believe Billy is a bit jealous.'

She smiled. 'Yes, he would be. Billy is the actor. Portia: *The Merchant of Venice?*'

'*Julius Caesar.*'

'Of course.

> *Am I yourself,*
> *But, as it were, in sort, or limitation,*
> *To keep with you at meals, comfort your bed,*
> *And talk to you sometimes? Dwell I but in the suburbs*
> *Of your good pleasure? If it be no more,*
> *Portia is Brutus' harlot, not his wife.'*

'What a memory you have.'

Fiona said, 'You're supposed to reply,

> *You are my true and honourable wife,*
> *As dear to me as are the ruddy drops*
> *That visit my sad heart.*

Didn't you learn any Shakespeare at school?'

'I learned it in German,' I said.

That amused her. 'I read a lot nowadays: Dickens, Jane Austen, Trollope, Thackeray, Shakespeare.'

A note of alarm sounded somewhere deep in my mind. The books were all English ones. Most security people would be alarmed at what smelled awfully like home-sickness. But I didn't say that. I said, 'Portia will have a lovely costume; blue with gold edging.'

She held out her hand to me. I took it. I found an amazing intimacy in this formal gesture. Her hand was small and warm, she'd always had warm hands. She said, 'How absurd that it should be like this,' and then hurriedly, as though to preclude other discussions that she wanted to avoid, she added, 'There were so many difficulties about my leaving Berlin, and then suddenly I had to go to a conference in Prague and it was easy.' There was an unconvincing gaiety in her voice as she said it,

338

the tone I remembered from times when she tried to make a joke about Billy getting the 'flu and spoiling his birthday, or her opening the car door angrily and scratching the paintwork. 'How much have they told you?'

I stood back to look at her. She was as lovely as ever. Her hair was drawn back tight in the severe style she'd adopted since going to the East. She wore a simple dark green suit that was almost Chanel, but I guessed it had been made by some wonderful little woman she'd found round the corner. Fiona could always find some 'treasure' to do things she wanted done. On her finger she had our wedding band. She looked down at our clasped hands as if in some renewed pledge of her vows. This was the ravishing girl I'd married so proudly. But that was a hundred years ago and the changes that the recent stressful years had brought were evident too. I could see within her something I'd never seen before: some weariness, or was it apprehension? Perhaps that's what at first I'd mistaken for smallness of stature.

She turned her hand in mine. I said, 'You've lost our engagement ring.'

'We'll get another.'

I said nothing.

'I was working in Dresden. A man was killed. It was a terrible night. I washed my hands at the infirmary. It was careless of me. I turned the car round and went back but it wasn't there and no one had seen it.'

She was clenching her hands as if telling me about the lost ring had been a fearsome ordeal. But I could also see that Fiona was as undaunted as she'd ever been. I knew the way she contained her fear by means of willpower, as some brilliant actress might play a role and bring an unconvincing character to life. Giving me no time to reply she added, 'They are not the trousers for that suit. The new lady in your life is not looking after you, dearest.' She was cool and relaxed now; the gruesome memories locked away again.

'I'm all right.'

'Does she iron your shirts? You were always so fastidious about your shirts. Sometimes, away from you, I have found myself worrying about the laundry. It's silly isn't it?' There was bitterness there. A trace of the real Fiona showing through. It was all jokes of course: the laundry and these exploratory probes about other women. Everything was a joke until Fiona blew the whistle and joking ended.

'She's decent: she's loyal and she loves me,' I blurted out in the face of Fiona's sarcasm. No sooner was it said than I regretted it, but it was what she wanted. Once I'd revealed my feelings, Fiona was ready to proceed. 'How much have they told you?' she asked again.

'Nothing,' I said. 'They told me nothing.' I thought back to Stowe's furrowed brow and guarded answers. Obviously Stowe had been told nothing either. I wondered who the hell did know exactly what was going on.

'Poor darling, but perhaps it was the best way.'

'You're coming out now,' I said, confirming by my words what my eyes found it hard to believe. 'I was right wasn't I?' Even now I was not unquestionably sure that she'd been working for London all the time.

'Not long now,' she said.

'You're not going back to Berlin?'

'Just for a little while.'

'Why?'

'You know how it is . . . there are other people who would be in danger. I'll have to tidy things up. A few weeks, that's all. Perhaps only days.'

I didn't reply. The dog in the yard barked as if at an approaching stranger. Fiona looked at her watch. I suddenly remembered how much I'd hated the way that Fiona's dedication to the Department came before everything. Competing with her career was worse than having to compete with an irresistible lover. She must have seen those feelings in my face for she said, 'No recriminations, Bernard. Not now anyway.'

I knew then that I had handled the whole thing wrongly. With grotesque misjudgement I had taken her at face value, and all women hate that. Some other kind of man would have swept her off her feet, made love to her here and now, and damn the consequences. Some other kind of woman might have provided the opportunity for me to do so. But we were us: two professionals discussing technique man to man.

She stepped away from me and, while studying her wedding ring, said, 'I'm the only one who can make that sort of decision and I say I must go back.'

'Why come here? Why take the chance?' I said. I'm sure she'd found a convincing excuse for this meeting with the enemy but it was madness for her to risk her life meeting me. I could remember so many good men who had been lost because of such foolishness. Men who had to see a girlfriend for the last time. Men who couldn't resist a meal in a favourite café, or men like old Karl Busch who hid me for three agonizing days in Weimar, then, after we'd got away, went back to get his stamp collection. They were waiting for him. Karl Busch was taken down to the security barracks in Leipzig and was never heard of again.

'Oh Bernard.' There was a sigh.

'Why?'

'Because of you. Don't be so dense.'

'Me?'

'You were raking through everything . . . About me . . .' She made a gesture of despair with her open hand.

'Are you telling me that you've made this reckless sidetrip just to tell me to stop digging out the facts?'

'London Central tried everything to reassure you but you carried on.'

'They tried everything, except simply telling me the truth,' I said emphatically.

'They hinted and advised. Finally they couldn't think of any way to persuade you. I didn't know how far they would go . . . I said you must hear it from me. We put together this official – but off-the-record – meeting. London has already made concessions: I go back looking like a skilful negotiator. It will be all right.'

'The bloody fools! Didn't you tell them how dangerous it is for you sitting out here talking with me?'

'They know it's dangerous but you kept snooping into everything. You were putting together a picture of the whole operation. Leaving a trail too. That was even more dangerous.'

'Of course I was snooping. What did you expect me to do? You are my wife.' I stopped. I was exasperated. Although my theory had been proved correct I could accept the enormity of it: London Central had sent Fiona to be a field agent in the East and decided not to confide in me. 'For God's sake . . .'

'It seemed a clever idea at the time,' said Fiona calmly. Despite the phrase there was nothing in her voice to suggest it wasn't a clever idea now.

'Who thought it was a clever idea?'

'Your surprise, or let's rather say astonishment . . . Your anger, indignation and obvious bewilderment protected me, Bernard.'

'I asked you, "Who thought it was a clever idea?" '

'I wanted to tell you everything, darling. I insisted upon it at first. I wanted you in at the briefings and the preparation. The original idea was that you would be my case officer, but then it became obvious that there couldn't be a case officer in the ordinary sense of that term. There was no question of frequent regular contact.'

'So who decided otherwise?'

'At the beginning the D-G was against the whole scheme. He gave it no more than a twenty-five per cent chance of coming off.'

'I would have given less than that.'

'The D-G made it a condition that you would not be told.'

'The D-G . . . Sir Henry?'

'He has his good days as well as his bad ones.'

'So the more fuss I kicked up the better?'

'At first, yes. And it certainly worked,' said Fiona. 'In the first few weeks Moscow put you under their priority surveillance; they watched you with the greatest interest. They even had one of their psychological behaviour experts write a report on you. Erich Stinnes got hold of a copy and I read it. It said that no actor could have put on a performance like yours. And of course they were right. It was your behaviour that finally convinced them that I was really theirs.'

'Didn't they guess the truth? That you acted without telling me?'

'The Soviet Union may have women fighter pilots and crane operators but marriage is a sacred institution here. Thanks to the millions of war casualties, Marx's views on marriage – like his views on a lot of other things – have been shelved indefinitely. Wives in the USSR do as their husbands say.'

I looked at her without speaking. She smiled. I wondered why I had been surprised by this whole business. Fiona: cultured privileged daughter of philistine nouveau riche father; exceptional Oxford graduate who studied Russian at the Sorbonne. She joins the Department and marries a man who never went to college and whose sole claim to any sort of respect is his reputation as a field agent. Why wouldn't such a person prove to be the ultimate exponent of women's emancipation? Why wouldn't such a woman want to be an even better field agent, at whatever the cost to me and the children and everyone else around her?

'When did all this start?' I asked.

'Long ago,' she replied airily.

'September 1978?' That was the night of one of those 'Baader-Meinhof' panics. The content of a Russian army signals intercept got back to Karlshorst so quickly that everyone thought we had a superspy sitting in Operations. She nodded. 'You leaked that intercepted signal to them? So you were working both sides already.' I took a moment or two to recollect what had happened. 'Joe Brody was called in to handle the subsequent investigation, just in order to calm the anxiety in American hearts. In some way or other you slipped past him. But with you in the clear the blame was put upon Werner Volkmann and he wasn't even given a chance to defend himself. Frank wouldn't use him any more, and Werner took it badly.'

'That's right,' she said and bit her lip. She'd always disliked Werner, or at least dismissed him as something of a simpleton. Had some feeling of guilt, at the part she'd played in framing him, seeded that dislike? She said, 'Then when they opened an orange file on Trent the blame was put on him.'

'Trent was killed,' I said.

She had her answer ready. Her voice was calm and conciliatory. 'Yes, killed by your friend Rolf Mauser. With a gun he borrowed from you. You can't implicate the Department in Trent's death.'

'But how convenient it was. Trent took his secret to the grave, and the secret was that he didn't give that intercept to the Russians.'

She said nothing.

I said, 'Were you approached at Oxford? Was it that long ago?'

'By the Department? Yes.'

So that was it. Those stories of her joining Marxist groups at college were true but it had been done to try her out. Of more personal concern was the way she'd let me recommend her for a job with the Department. That had all been a ruse: a way of covering her previous service. She must have been in regular contact with the KGB by then. Getting the SIS job would have made her case officer feel ecstatic. I could see the long-term planning that had made her so convincing as a Russian agent. It made me feel a damned fool but I controlled my anger. 'Who else knew?' I asked.

'I can't tell you that, darling.'

'Who else?'

'No one else. Not Coordination, not Central Funding, not Internal Security, not even the Deputy.'

'The D-G knew,' I persisted.

'No one working there now,' she said pedantically. 'That was the condition the D-G made. No one!'

'You made my life hell,' I told her gently.

'I thought you'd be proud of me.'

'I am,' I said, trying to put some feeling into my words. 'I really am. But now is the time to pull out. Come back to Vienna with me. Your KGB identification plus my special identity card would get us through the control. We could catch an evening plane to London.'

'I'm not sure that it would, Bernard. The crossing points are all on the computer nowadays. Believe me, it's something I know about.' I knew that tone of voice; there was no arguing with it.

She'd heard me say a million times that field agents have to have the last word in such matters. I'd always used my experience as a field agent to have the final decision. Now my wife had proved to be the most amazing field agent of all. She'd moved into the top echelon of the East's espionage network and fooled them all. I was in no position to argue with her.

Lightly, as if to turn the conversation to trivial matters, she said, 'I will have to make sure the computer gives the okay when I come. London have promised me something special in the way of papers.'

'They have good people here,' I said without really believing it. I wondered if her forged papers were being prepared by Staiger; done by the same crooks whom he got to fake his stamps and covers.

'I know.'

'And Erich Stinnes too?' When the history of the Department is written no fiasco of the recent past will demonstrate its capacity for vacillation and confusion better than the way in which Stinnes was handled. Stinnes was a slippery customer, a real old-time KGB officer. He'd said he wanted to defect to us, then doubts arose on both sides until Stinnes was categorized as hostile and imprisoned by us. He eventually went back to the East as part of an exchange.

'Stinnes is kept entirely separate. That's the way it was planned.' She paused and changed the subject slightly. 'When you got rid of that brute Moskvin you removed my greatest danger. He suspected the truth.'

'He took a Russian bullet too. One of your people shot him. Did you know that?'

She gave a frosty smile.

I didn't want to leave it like that. 'I wish . . .'

She raised a hand to silence any recrimination from me and said, 'We've only got a few minutes. The car must leave at four. I must be back in Prague. There's this damned security conference tomorrow and I have to be briefed.' The dog barked again, more fiercely this time, and the barking stopped with a shrill yelp, as if the dog had been dealt a blow.

'Yes, four o'clock. I understand.'

'So they did tell you something?'

It was a feeble joke but I smiled and apologetically said, 'We left Vienna early but there was the Haydn Festival, and the road . . .'

'I know,' she said. 'It's always like that when it's really important. You used to say that.'

'When I was late?'

'No, I didn't mean that, Bernard.' She took a quick look at her watch. 'There is another thing . . .' she said. 'My fur coat. I left it with my sister Tessa. I'm worried she might sell it, or give it away or something . . .'

I remembered the coat. It was a breathtaking birthday present from her father at a time when he was very keen to establish his love for her, and his wealth and success. The huge silky sable coat must have cost thousands of pounds. Fiona had always been vocally opposed to the wearing of things made of animal fur but once she'd tried on that coat her moral reservations about the fur trade seemed to dwindle. 'What do you want me to do?'

'You must get it back from her.'

'Well . . .' I said hesitantly, 'I can't say I've talked with you.'

'You'll find a way,' she said. Now it was my problem. I could see why she was so good at management.

There was the sort of awkward silence that only an English couple would inflict upon themselves. 'And everything's all right? The children are well?' she asked again.

'Wonderful,' I said. She knew that of course. It would have been part of the deal that she had regular reports on the children. And on me. I wondered if such reports would have included news of my living with Gloria. For one terrible moment it flashed through my mind that Gloria might have been assigned to live with me and monitor everything I did, said and thought. But I dismissed the idea. Gloria was too unconventional to be an informer. 'The children miss you, of course,' I added.

'They haven't grown to hate me, have they, Bernard?'

'No, of course not, darling.'

I said it so glibly and quickly that she must have sensed the reservations I had. It would not be easy for her to rebuild her relationships with the children.

She nodded. 'And you?'

I don't know whether she was asking whether I was all right or whether I'd grown to hate her. 'I'm all right,' I said.

'You've lost weight, Bernard. Are you sure you're quite well?'

'I went on a diet so I can fit into my old suits.'

'I'm glad you're still the same,' she said somewhat ambiguously, and there was more affection in that banal phrase than in anything she'd said up to that time.

I suppose I should have said all the things that were bottled up inside me. I should have told her that she was as beautiful as ever. That she was as brave as anyone I'd ever met. That I was proud of her. But I said, 'Take care of yourself. It's so near the end now.'

'I'll be all right. Don't worry, darling.' I could hear in her voice that her mind was no longer devoted to me or the children. She'd already started thinking of the next stage: it was the way of the professional. The only way to stay alive.

There came the sound of a big V8 engine. Through the window I saw her car moving out from where it had been parked in the barn. A black official car. A big shiny machine like that with official licence plates and motorcycle outriders would attract attention. And surely it was impossible to get it through that archway and down that pot-holed track.

Well, Fiona was good at doing the impossible. She'd proved that over and over.

11

Once back in London it was easy to believe my trip to Central Europe had all been a dream. In fact I suppressed all thought of my meeting with Fiona from my mind. Or I really tried to do so. When Gloria met me at the airport, she gave a whoop of joy that could be heard across the concourse. She grabbed me and kissed me and held me tight. It was only then that I began to see the full extent of the terrible emotional dilemma I had created: or should I say dilemma that Fiona had created for me.

Gloria had left her new car – an orange-coloured Metro – double banked outside Terminal Two, a place where the parking warden charm school invigilates its ferocity finals. But she got away unscathed: I suppose it was tea time.

The car was brand new and she was keen to demonstrate its wonders. I sat back and watched her with delight. The awful truth was that I felt relaxed, and truly at home, here in London with Gloria in my arms. She was young and vital, and she excited me. My feelings for Fiona were different – and more complex. As well as being my wife, my colleague and my rival, she was the mother of my children.

Werner Volkmann's caustic wife Zena once told me that I'd married Fiona because she was everything that I wasn't. By that I suppose she meant educated, sophisticated and moving in the right circles. But I would have claimed otherwise. My education, sophistication, and the circles I moved in too, were radically different to anything Fiona had known, but not inferior. I'd married her because I loved her desperately but perhaps it was a love too coloured by respect. Perhaps we'd both married believing that it was the combination of our talents and experience that really mattered; that we would prove to be an invincible combination and our children would excel in every way. But such reasoning is false; marriages cannot be held together solely by mutual respect. Especially when that respect depends upon inexperience, as respect so often does. Now we knew each other better, and I had discovered that Fiona's love for me was sober and cerebral, like her love of learning and her love of her country. Gloria was not much more than half Fiona's age: Lord, what an oppressing thought that was! But Gloria had an irrepressible energy and excitement and curiosity and contrariness. I loved Gloria as I loved the exhilaration she'd brought to my life and the boundless love she gave both me and the children. But I loved Fiona too.

'Good trip?' She tried to demonstrate the self-seeking radio and the auto-reverse tape player while overtaking a bus on the inside. She was an unrestrained driver as she was an unrestrained lover and an unrestrained everything else.

'The usual routine. Salzburg and Vienna. You know.' I felt no pang of conscience at saying that the trip had been routine. This was not the right time to sit down with Gloria and hear what she thought about Fiona. I hadn't yet worked out what I thought myself.

'I *don't* know! How would I know? Tell me about it.'

'Salzburg: von Karajan held up rehearsals while we had a cup of that awful coffee he brews up under the rostrum. Then on to Vienna: a private view of the Bruegels and a boring little cocktail party reception for me. Then a private dinner with the ambassador and that uncomfortable box the Embassy subscribes to at the Opera. The usual stuff.' She bared her teeth at me. I said, 'Oh yes, and I was attacked by a fierce dog.'

'We're invited to the Cruyers',' Gloria told me as she got to the traffic lights near Hogarth's house. 'Daphne phoned me at home. She was terribly friendly. I was surprised. She's always been rather distant with me. Long dresses would you believe? And black tie.'

'You're joking.'

'No I'm not.'

'Black tie? Long dresses? At the Cruyers'?'

'On Saturday evening. Your sister-in-law Tessa and her husband are going. I don't know who else.'

'And you said "yes"?'

'Dicky knew you were expected back today.'

'Good God.'

'I sent your dinner suit to the cleaners. It will be ready Saturday morning.'

'Do you know these trousers don't match this jacket?' I asked her.

'Of course. I'm always telling you. I thought you did it to annoy Dicky.'

'Why would having mismatched trousers and jacket annoy Dicky?'

'It's no good trying to put the blame on me. You should keep your suits on proper hangers and not leave everything draped around. Of course your trousers get mixed up. Did someone remark on it then?'

'I just noticed.'

348

'I'll bet someone remarked on it, and made you feel a fool.' She laughed. 'What did they say – "Have you got another suit like that at home?" Is that what they said?' She giggled again. Gloria loved her own jokes: they were the only ones she saw the point of. But her laughter was infectious and despite myself I laughed too.

'No one noticed except me,' I insisted.

'It's about time you had a new suit. Or what about grey flannels and a dark blue blazer? You could wear that outfit to the office.'

'I don't want a new suit or blazer and flannels, and if I did buy new clothes I wouldn't buy them for the office.'

'You'd look good in a blazer.'

I never knew when she was serious and when she was goading me. 'Wouldn't I need a badge on the pocket?'

'Alcoholics Anonymous?' she said.

'Very droll.'

'I've bought a lovely dress,' she confessed. 'Lilac with big puff sleeves.' So that was really it. That little preamble about me having a new suit was just to assuage her guilt about spending money on a dress.

'Good,' I said.

That wasn't enough to put her at her ease. 'I didn't have a long dress, and I didn't want to rent one.'

'Good. Good. I said good.'

'You are a pig, darling.'

I kissed her ear and grunted.

'Don't do that when I'm driving.'

The Cruyers' dinner party must have been planned for weeks. At previous dinners his wife Daphne – an unenthusiastic cook – could be seen dashing in and out of the kitchen, sipping champagne between stirring the saucepans, referring to cookery books and hissing instructions to Dicky. But this time they had some gravelly-voiced old fellow to open the door and breathe alcohol fumes upon all arriving guests; and an elderly lady, attired in full chef's outfit, complete with toque, to do whatever was happening in the kitchen. There was a smell of boiled fish as she peered out of the kitchen to see us in the hallway. Whether she was counting the dinner guests or checking on the old man's sobriety was unresolved by the time the doorbell sounded behind us.

There was soft guitar music trickling out of the hi-fi. 'We tried to get Paul Bocuse,' Dicky was saying as we moved into the crowded drawing room, 'but he sent his sous-chef instead.' Dicky turned to greet us and said, 'Gloria, chérie! How spiffing you look!' in the fruity voice he used to tell jokes. He gave her a deferent, stand-off kiss on both cheeks to avoid spoiling her make-up.

'And *Bernard*, old sport!' he said, his tone suggesting that it was an interesting coincidence that Gloria and I should arrive together. 'No need to introduce you to anyone here. Circulate! It's chums only tonight.'

Most of the people must have already consumed a glass or two of wine, for there was that shrill excitement that comes from drinking on an empty head. Daphne Cruyer came across to greet us. I'd always liked Daphne. In a way I shared with her the problem of putting up with Dicky every day. She never said as much, of course, but I sometimes thought I detected that same fellow-feeling for me.

Daphne had been an art student when she first met Dicky. She had never entirely recovered from either experience. Tonight the drawing room was elaborately decorated with Japanese lanterns and paper fish. I guessed it was Daphne's purchase of her amazing rainbow-patterned silk kimono that had prompted this formal gathering. I would hardly think it was prompted by Dicky's new white slubbed-silk dinner jacket. But you could never be sure.

Daphne asked me how I was, with that unusual tone of voice that suggested she really wanted to know. In an effort to reciprocate this kindness I didn't tell her. Instead I admired her kimono and her Madame Butterfly hairdo. She'd bought the kimono on holiday in Tokyo. They'd gone on a ten-day trip to Japan together with their well-travelled neighbours. I would never have guessed how much you pay for a cup of coffee on the Ginza but Daphne had adored every moment of it, even the raw fish. She said Gloria was looking well. I agreed and reflected upon the fact that it had taken over three years for the Cruyers to decide that Gloria and I were socially acceptable as a couple, and that this momentous decision had coincided with the moment I learned that my wife was about to return.

'Dicky said everything in the office got into a terrible muddle when you went away,' said Daphne.

'I think it did,' I agreed.

'Dicky became awfully moody. Awfully withdrawn. I felt sorry for him.'

'I came back,' I said.

'And I'm glad,' said Daphne. She smiled. I wondered how much Dicky had told her about my time on the run in Berlin. Nothing I hoped: but it wouldn't be the first time that Daphne had wormed information out of him. She was awfully clever at handling Dicky. I should get her to give me a few lessons.

'We built on to the attic,' said Daphne. 'I have a little studio upstairs now. You must see it next time you're here.'

'For painting?'

'Still-life pictures: fruit and flowers and so on. Dicky wants me to go back to doing abstracts. But he was always adding blobs of colour to them. I got so angry with him that I finally went back to fruit and flowers. Dicky is such a meddler. I suppose you know that.'

'Yes, I do.'

When Daphne had moved on I said my hellos to everyone including Sir Giles Streeply-Cox – a retired Foreign Office man – and his wife. 'Creepy-Pox' with his sanguine complexion and bushy white sideburns might have been mistaken for a prosperous farmer until one heard that baroque Whitehall accent. Nowadays he grew roses between visits to London where he chaired a Civil Service interview board and prowled around the more languorous latitudes of Whitehall spreading alarm and despondency. Like all such senior officials and politicians he had a prodigious memory. He remembered me from another dinner party not so long before. 'Young Samson isn't it? Saw you at that gathering at that girl Matthews' little place. Nouvelle cuisine wasn't it? Ummm I thought it was. Don't get enough to eat, what?' The Streeply-Coxes certainly got around.

He leaned close to me and said, 'Tell me something, Samson. Do you know the name of this damned tune?'

'It's called "Cordoba",' I said. 'Albeniz; played by Julian Bream.' I answered authoritatively because after purchasing his hi-fi Dicky had played it over and over to demonstrate the track selector.

'Catchy little piece,' said Streeply-Cox. He looked at his wife and nodded before adding, 'My wife said you were a know-all.'

'I try, Sir Giles,' I said and moved away murmuring about getting another glass of wine.

Once clear of the dreaded Streeply-Cox I decided that finding another glass of champagne wouldn't be a bad idea. I waylaid the old man with the drinks and then took a moment or two to look around. The same rather battered painting of Adam and Eve dominated the fireplace. Dicky always called it *naïf* in an attempt to give it class but to my eyes it was just badly drawn. The framed colour photo of Dicky's boat had gone. That rather confirmed the rumours I'd heard about him putting it up for sale. Daphne had never been happy about that boat. She was rather prone to sea-sickness and yet if she didn't join Dicky on his nautical weekends she knew there was a risk that some other female would share the captain's cabin.

The antique cabinet that had once held a collection of matchbox covers now held a Japanese dagger, some netsuke and an assortment of other small oriental artefacts. On the wall behind it there were six framed woodblock prints, including the inevitable 'Breaking Wave'. They'd fitted a fine mesh screen across the artificial coal fire. I suppose too many people threw litter into it. Dicky was always on his knees, clawing cigarette butts and screwed up scraps of paper from the plastic coal.

I reflected that every decoration in the room was new except the Adam and Eve that Daphne had found in a flea market in Amsterdam. It was a sign of the Cruyers' widening horizons and deepening pockets. I wondered how long Adam and Eve would last and what they'd be replaced with. Adam was already looking a bit apprehensive.

It was while trying to decide about the expression upon the face of Eve that I spotted my errant sister-in-law Tessa, and her husband George Kosinski. They were both dressed up to the nines, but even Tessa in her Paris model-gown didn't excel the stupendous Gloria, who looked more enchanting than ever.

Tessa came over. She must have been getting on for forty but she was still vibrantly attractive, with her long fair hair and bright blue eyes, and she still had that breathless way of speaking that made one think that she'd been waiting anxiously to see you again. 'I thought maybe you'd been sent to the bloody moon, poppet,' she said, giving me an uncharacteristically coy kiss. 'I've missed you, darling.'

I confess to a frisson as she kissed me: I'd never noticed before how much like Fiona she could look. Tonight especially so. Perhaps it was just an accident of her dress or make-up. Perhaps it was something to do with Tessa getting older; or Fiona getting older; or me getting older. Whatever it was, for a moment it made me stare at her, deprived of words until she said, 'Fuck! Is my lipstick smudged or something?'

'No, Tessa. You're looking more lovely than ever. Just stunning.'

'Well that's really something coming from you, Bernard. All we girls know that being noticed by Bernard Samson is the ultimate accolade.'

The old fellow – whom I heard Daphne address as 'Jenkins' – came round with a big silver tray of champagne. Tessa selected one unhurriedly and held her glass up to the light as if silently offering a toast but I knew she was trying to identify the champagne from its colour and the bubbles. It was one of her party tricks. Her mastering it must have cost George a fortune.

Having approved of what she saw, but without naming it, she drank some. 'Did you ever see such a darling butler?' said Tessa as Jenkins moved away. 'How sweet of Daphne to find an evening's work for some poor old pensioner.'

I wondered how I was going to persuade Tessa to return Fiona's fur coat. What was I going to use as an excuse? And where was I going to put the damn thing without having to go into a lot of discussion about it with Gloria?

'I was thinking about Fiona's fur coat,' I began.

'Oh, yes, darling. Do tell.'

'I thought perhaps I should put it with all the other things.'

'All what other things?' She swung her hair back from her face.

'Some bits and pieces that Fiona liked especially.'

'It's a beautiful bit of fur, you know. Daddy paid the absolute earth for it.'

'Yes, it's something of a responsibility for you.'

'I'm not wearing it, poppet, if that's what you're on about.'

'No, I'm sure you're not, Tessa, and it's kind of you to look after the damned thing all this time. I just thought that . . .'

'No trouble at all, darling. It's with my own furs and when summer comes . . . if it ever comes, they'll all go into refrigerated storage together.'

'Well, you see, Tessa . . .' I started. She tilted her head as if very interested in what I was going to say but let her fair hair fall forward, so that she could hide behind it. At that moment we were interrupted by an old acquaintance of mine: Posh Harry, a CIA troubleshooter from Washington. A short thickset man of vaguely oriental appearance, he was of that mixed Hawaiian and Caucasian ancestry that in his birthplace is called hapa haoli. He was in his middle thirties, always carefully groomed and of pleasing appearance. It would be easy to imagine him, suitably costumed, singing baritone in *Madame Butterfly*, or more credibly perhaps *South Pacific*.

'And who is this glorious young lady you're talking to, Bernard?' said Harry.

Tessa put an arm through his and said, 'Have you forgotten so soon, Harry? I'm mortified.' Posh Harry smiled, and before he could start an explanation the sonorous voice of Jenkins announced, 'Ladies and gentlemen. Dinner is served.' I caught Tessa's eye and she smiled sardonically.

Tessa's husband was talking to Gloria. He was fortyish. Born in London's East End of impoverished Polish parents, he had become rich selling cars and, later, property. I had the impression that George put himself in the hands of the most expensive tailors, shirtmakers,

353

outfitters and hairdressers he could find. So he was to be seen in a succession of dinner suits cut to ever changing fashions.

This evening George seemed to notice Gloria for the first time, for he fell deep in conversation with her soon after we arrived. I was somewhat surprised by this, for George had always seemed ill at ease with women, except the ones he knew well. Sometimes I wondered how he ever came to get married to Tessa; and why. Fiona used to say that it was Tessa's inexhaustible infidelities that had driven George to making so much money, but George was on the way to riches long before Tessa married him.

George was a man of irreproachable integrity, something I wouldn't have thought of as a prime asset in the second-hand car business. Once I'd said this to him. Characteristically George had given me a short lecture upon the probity and good will of his profession.

George and Gloria were talking when dinner was announced. Because George was very short, she had perched herself on one arm of a sofa so he didn't have to look up to her. George liked her, I could see that in his face, and when others came to join them in conversation he was determined to keep her attention. Jenkins now repeated his announcement in a louder voice. They all looked up.

After a couple of false starts, Jenkins heaved open the doors of the dark, candlelit dining room to reveal the long polished table set with flowers and gleaming tableware. The assembled company paused for a moment to gaze at this spectacle. This I felt was the beginning of a new age of Cruyerdom, a bid for the better life, a home background that would suit a man destined to rub shoulders with the mighty, brilliantly administer the secret dimension of political affairs, and retire with that coveted K. The only question that remained was why had I been invited.

'Daphne! How picturesque!' called Tessa as we moved in. '*Un véritable coup de théâtre*, darling!'

'Shush!' I heard George say to her as we circled around to find our name cards. He said it in a quiet impersonal way, as a member of a theatre audience might react to a latecomer without interrupting the action on the stage. As we sat down, George, with his enviable memory, recalled a meeting with Posh Harry a few years previously when Harry visited George's used motorcar emporium in one of the less salubrious parts of Southwark, south London.

Posh Harry smiled without either confirming or denying it. That was his way. Harry could be inscrutable. He was dressed in a remarkable shiny black dinner suit with a lace-trimmed shirt that Beau Brummel might have worn except that it was a bit too frilly. Harry was always a fancy dresser, and it had to be admitted that he could carry it off. With him, and wearing a strapless satin gown cut very very low, was the same American woman I'd seen him with in Southwark. She was in her middle thirties and would have been pretty except for the rather plump features which gave her a look of unremitting petulance. This impression was heightened by the strident candied-yams and black-eyed peas accent she affected. At dinner she was sitting next to me. Her name turned out to be Jo-Jo.

I was interested to watch the inter-action between Posh Harry and our host. I wondered when it was that they first met, and I wondered if Harry's presence in London signalled some CIA development that I should find out about. I knew that there was a new Station Chief in London: maybe Harry was his trouble-shooter.

'What's your new boss like?' Dicky casually asked Posh Harry once we were all seated and the wine was being poured.

Harry, who sat across the table from me, replied, 'Say Dicky, what does *die neue Sachlichkeit* really mean?'

Dicky said, 'The new realism. It means realistic painting. Isn't that right, Bernard?'

Constitutionally incapable of answering such a question in any way but fully, I said, 'And poetry. It's nineteen twenties jargon . . . a reaction against Impressionism. Also against beauty in favour of functionalism.'

Dicky said, 'You see, Bernard isn't just a pretty face.' He laughed and so did Jo-Jo. I could have banged their heads together.

Posh Harry smiled and said, 'My new boss keeps talking about *die neue Sachlichkeit* like he's going to be a new broom and give everyone hell.'

Dicky smiled. I suppose it was Harry's prepared answer to an expected question. Posh Harry spoke damned good German. I'd be surprised if he really didn't know what it meant.

Posh Harry added, 'Never mind Bernard's "pretty face". I want to know where he's been hiding this gorgeous little girl all this time.' He was sitting next to Gloria, who sipped her wine to conceal her self-satisfied smile.

The first course was a crab soup with garlic bread. While Jenkins ladled it out with studied care there was the usual small-talk. Daphne Cruyer, relieved of her kitchen duties and with Jenkins to serve the food, was for the first time a guest at one of her own dinner parties. She seemed to thrive on it. Dicky too seemed delighted with this chance to play host. He was beaming the whole evening except when Jenkins – offering a second helping of crab soup from a heavy Japanese bowl – poured some of it over him. Even then Dicky only said, 'Steady on, Jenkins man!', albeit rather loudly.

It was at this stage of the proceedings that I overheard Daphne's loud whisper that told the evidently unsteady Jenkins not to try to dish up the salmon. Instead he was to put the whole fish in front of Dicky. It must be said that Jenkins didn't do this with good grace. He slammed the platter down with enough force to make the cutlery jingle.

'I'm totally with Jefferson's interpretation of the Tenth Amendment,' Dicky was saying as the fish arrived so dramatically before him. He'd been treating his end of the table – which is to say me and Harry, for the ladies each side of him were trying to hear Daphne at the other end – to his views on federal government.

Dicky stared at the newly arrived salmon as if bewildered. His confusion might have been partly due to the huge pale green scales the fish wore, although on closer inspection these proved to be wafer-thin slices of cucumber, laboriously arranged in overlapping rows. Dicky looked up and saw Daphne – at the other end of the table – staring at him and making energetic sawing motions with her hand. He looked at Posh Harry, who gave an inscrutable smile and murmured something about his position as a government employee making it inappropriate for him to voice any opinion on states' rights.

Dicky had to be satisfied with this because he was, by that time, struggling to divide up the poached salmon. I don't know what persuaded Dicky to try slicing through it rather than fillet it from the bone; perhaps he took Daphne's mime too literally. But he soon discovered that even an overcooked salmon's spine is not easily severed with a silver serving spoon. Yielding to considerable force, for Dicky was nothing if not strong, the head seemed to slide off the platter, hide under the flowers, and look at Dicky reproachfully.

Daphne, while watching Dicky, got everyone's attention by suddenly beginning to describe a place in north London where she was going for skiing lessons on plastic snow. Everyone turned to face her. There was a certain shrill note in her voice, perhaps because the skiing season was over. As if suddenly remembering this she said she was going to lessons there all through summer and winter so that next year she'd be really good. Only Tessa – sitting on my right – turned to see what had happened when the head came off. She said, 'What a gorgeous fish. Did you land him yourself, Dicky?'

Dicky smiled grimly, and so did the indomitable Jenkins, who I now noticed was leaning slouched against the sideboard and watching Dicky's efforts appreciatively.

'It's not farmed salmon,' said Daphne. 'It's wild.'

'So would I be, darling,' said Tessa turning back to her.

Daphne gave her a frosty smile. Tessa was suspected of a torrid affair with Dicky some years previously and Daphne had not forgotten it.

'Jenkins,' said Daphne in a trilling nursery school voice. 'Would you pour the wine please.' And because Daphne had spent so many years monitoring Dicky, she was able to add in time, 'Not the Chambertin, Jenkins; the white Hermitage.' And this time her voice was less composed.

As Dicky said afterwards, the wonderful beurre blanc sauce completely concealed the broken pieces of fish. But Tessa's stated view was that it was like eating darning needles wrapped in cotton wool. Tessa was one of those ladies who didn't like finding fish bones in their fish. Anyway, there were plenty of second-helpings.

Moreover there was hare cooked in red wine to follow. It came ready-sliced on plates. The little old lady in the kitchen was working miracles. And rhubarb pie followed by a huge Stilton cheese with vintage port.

Fully recovered from his contest with the salmon, Dicky was in top form, which meant attentive and charming. There was never a time when I more easily understood Dicky's success in everything he did. He told jokes – good jokes – and laughed at his guests' stories. He made sure everyone had what he or she wanted, from aperitifs to cigars, and was even cordial with Daphne.

George and Sir Giles were sitting each side of Daphne but I noticed that Tessa had been distanced from Dicky. I wondered if Daphne had chosen the place settings. The cards were in her handwriting. And it was Tessa whom Daphne looked at when she stood up and called upon the ladies to retire. I thought Tessa would make a fuss and say no – as I'd seen her do before when she was feeling bolshie – but she got to her feet meekly and left the room with the rest of them.

As if on cue, Sir Giles then told three rambling anecdotes about his time in Whitehall. Coming near enough to indiscretion to keep our attention, he made sure no beans were spilled.

It was towards the end of this port and cigar session that Dicky got Sir Giles and George into a discussion about interest rates – no fashionable London dinner party being complete without an examination of the Treasury's fiscal policy – and turning aside from it Posh Harry said to me, 'Did you hear about your old buddy Kleindorf?'

'No, what?'

'Dead!' He stopped. He must have seen how much the news affected me.

'What happened?'

'He overdosed. You saw him recently somebody told me.'

'By mistake?'

'Mistake? And followed it with a whole bottle of brandy just to make sure?'

'Brandy?'

'French vintage brandy, the best from his cellar. I suppose he figured he couldn't take it with him.'

'Poor old Rudi.'

'He was old enough to have loyal friends both sides of the Wall. Not many people like that left. "Der Grosse Kleiner" was the last of the Berlin old-timers,' said Posh Harry.

'Damn nearly,' I said.

'Who else is there? Lange you mean? He's American. That old swine Rudi Kleindorf knew where the bodies are buried. And he's taken his secrets to the grave, Bernard.' He chewed a piece of water biscuit: Harry didn't like cheese very much. 'He never got over losing his son. And he went the same way: O.D. Holy cow! Where will all those deadbeats go, now that the Babylon is no more?'

'Poor Rudi,' I said again. 'Why would he do that?'

'I heard he was in trouble with the authorities.'

'He was always in trouble with the authorities,' I said.

'His father was some kind of war hero. Name of Rudolf Freiherr von Kleindorf. Career officer. Made his name in the winter fighting on the Eastern Front. The first Panzer Army was chopping its way out of Tarnopol. One after another he carried three of his wounded joes to safety. Under fire the whole time: the Russkies should have dropped him but a blizzard made visibility tough for them. Recommended for the Knight's Cross with diamonds or some damn trinket but he didn't get one. Maybe that's why the story went around and made him into a legend amongst the other ranks. An aristocratic Prussian officer who risks his life saving enlisted men has got everything going for him.' He grinned. 'Get saddled with a reputation like that and you've got to keep it up, right? I guess he was one of those brass-gutted guys who figure they'll never get killed. We've known a few like that, eh Bernard?'

'And?'

'He was right. They often are, aren't they? Kleindorf senior survived the war, and went to bat for his corps commander who was accused of

358

war crimes. And darn it, he noticed that some desk-bound zombie in the war crimes commission had written "Australian Division" in the indictment instead of "Airborne Division" and Kleindorf senior got the charges thrown out of court on that technicality. A sharp cookie! They say that when Kleindorf attended any of those post-war veterans' gatherings he was cheered to the echo for fifteen minutes. Rudi grew up in his father's shadow: I guess the old man was a tough act to follow. That's why he never mentioned anything about him.'

'You know the devil of a lot about the Kleindorfs,' I said.

'I had to run a check on him a few years back. I went through all the files, including his dad's. It was kind of fascinating.'

'I see why Rudi wanted his son to go into the army.'

'To keep up the family tradition, you mean? Yeah, I guess we are all a little inclined to have other people make up for the things we didn't do for our folks, don't you think?'

'I don't know,' I said.

He didn't press me, but when he next spoke he leaned forward slightly as if to emphasize the importance of what he said. 'These krauts stick together, Bernard. You can't be in Europe ten minutes without noticing that. We could learn from them. Right?'

I didn't know what the hell he was getting at but I said, 'You're right, Harry.' My brother-in-law George was watching Posh Harry with great interest. George was the only complete outsider there, but he knew that Harry had some sort of connection with the CIA. Harry had virtually told him so the first time they met. That was a time when Harry was very pushy; now he'd quietened a lot.

It was then that Dicky took his cigar from his mouth, blew a little smoke, looked at me and said, 'Harry would like you to go for lunch with his people next week, Bernard.'

'Is that so?' I said and wondered why Posh Harry hadn't proposed this culinary rendezvous himself. I looked at Harry. He was looking at Dicky.

Dicky said, 'I said okay.'

'Does that mean you're going to lunch?' I said.

Dicky smiled, 'No, Bernard. They don't want a rubber-stamp wallah like me: they want an ex-field man to sort out their worries.' He ran the tip of a finger along his lips, wondering, I suppose, if I was going to respond in kind.

Perhaps I would have done except that Posh Harry hurriedly said, 'We'd appreciate it, Bernie, we really would.'

Streeply-Cox looked at me and sanctimoniously boomed, 'We've got to cooperate as much as possible. It's the only way; the only way.' He brushed crumbs from his flowing white sideburns.

'You took the words right out of my mouth, Sir Giles,' I said.

'Splendid, splendid,' he replied.

Dicky jumped to his feet and said, 'Methinks 'tis time we joined the ladies.'

When I entered the drawing room Daphne seemed to be demonstrating some dance step, but she stopped awkwardly as Dicky ushered the men in. Gloria was sitting next to Tessa and she looked up and winked as she met my eye. I went across to her as I knew I was expected to do. 'Oh, Bernard,' Gloria whispered. 'Tessa wants us to go on with them to a lovely party. Can we go? Do say we can.'

'When?'

'Now. After this.'

I looked at my watch. 'It will make a very late night by the time we get home.'

'But we're all dressed up aren't we? Do let's go.'

'If you'd like to,' I said.

'They're wonderful,' said Gloria. 'I love George and Tessa is so funny.'

'That depends upon where you're sitting,' I said. 'Do you know where this party is?'

'George says we should go in his Rolls. There's plenty of room.'

'And leave the car here?'

'I'll come back and get it.'

'And how would I get home? Walk?'

'Don't be so mean, Bernard. We can both come back and get it. Or we could get a cab home and come and get it in the morning.'

'The meters start at eight-thirty.'

'Can we go, Bernard, or can't we?'

I looked at her. 'I'd sooner go home right now with the most beautiful woman in the room.'

'Do let's go,' said Gloria, who obviously was not in the mood to be flattered into doing what I wanted.

'It sounds wonderful.'

'I do love you, Bernard.'

'You're a horrible wheedling female,' I said.

'A Bavarian prince and princess!'

Oh my God, I thought, what have I let myself in for? But on the other hand it would provide another chance to talk to Tessa about that damned fur coat.

360

12

The prince and princess had their house in Pimlico, a corner of central London around which the Thames bends before getting to Westminster. When, long ago, Thomas Cubitt had finished selling large stucco-fronted houses with balconies to the rich of Belgravia, he built the same designs on the cheaper land of neighbouring Pimlico. Pimlico was said to be coming up: it still is. For it never became another Belgravia despite the similarity of its gardens, squares and grand-looking houses. It was, and to this day remains, an area of mixed fortunes: a plight not assisted by the local government's seemingly random arrangement of one-way streets and barriers which make the district a notorious maze for motorists.

Cubitt's large houses are now divided into cramped apartments, or as the adverts put it 'studio flats' and 'roof terraces'. Seedy hotels and boarding houses with crudely lettered signs offer accommodation in convenient proximity to London's only cross-country bus station and the busy Victoria railway terminal.

It was in one of the quieter streets of this region that our host had purchased a large house and refurbished it at considerable expense. It was, George explained to me while driving there, a shrewd investment. The sort of investment that he admired so many other German businessmen for making now that the Deutschmark was so highly valued. The prince would use the place for his visits to London, entertain his business associates there and save money on what it would cost him to do those same things in hotels and restaurants. Property prices in that area were certain to keep rising and the chances were that in twenty years he would end up with an excellent profit on his investment. This made me ask George why he himself had bought an apartment in Mayfair – London's most expensive residential area – rather than do the same sort of thing.

'Ah,' replied George, 'because I am the son of poor parents. I want to enjoy the pleasures that money can bring. I want to go home each night and sleep amongst the richest men in England. I need that reassurance.' He chuckled.

'It's not true,' said Tessa. 'It's my fault. We live in Mayfair because I wouldn't go and live in Pimlico.' We laughed. There was an obvious element of fact in what both of them said. But the truth behind the rationale was that childless Tessa and George had no one to make a good investment for. In the silence that followed, I wished I hadn't asked him about house values.

All the nearby parking places were full, but we stayed with George while he parked his Rolls a block or so away. It was a cold night and the street lights tinted the empty streets with a grim blue that made it seem even colder. Entering the house brought a sudden change. The heated exertions of the guests, the bright lights, the crowded rooms, the warmth of the bodies and the noise and excitement were electrifying. And so was the idea of a drink.

It was a big party: perhaps a hundred people were drifting through the house laughing, chatting in loud confident voices and tipping back their drinks. In the largest room there were a dozen or so people dancing to the music of a small band and there was a buffet table with shellfish, smoked salmon and sliced beef being constantly replenished by waiters in white jackets. 'This is how the other half live,' said Gloria as we made our way to where our young and glamorous hostess was standing by the fireplace talking to a well-dressed bearded man who proved to be the caterer.

Gloria was right. Prince Joppi's world was quite different to our more secret world, where, for various reasons, men drank and conversed with studied caution. Neither was this the ordinary world of supply and demand; it was a world of abundance. All around me there were the over-people: over-anxious, over-weight, over-bearing, over-educated, over-rated, over-weening, over-achievers, over-selling, over-spending and over-producing. They ate and drank and noisily celebrated their good fortune. Never mind tomorrow, there would always be people like me and Fiona and Bartholomew H. Johnson to look after that.

The princess gave a welcoming smile as she caught sight of George and Tessa. She was petite and very slim with dark hair that was in that state of rat-tailed disorder that takes very expensive hairdressers many hours to arrange. Her make-up, specifically the way in which her eyes were elaborately painted with green, blue and black shadow, was stagy. Most striking of all was her dark suntan. Germany is a notably sunless land and there is a type of German for whom a sun-darkened skin is an essential status symbol no matter that health warnings advise against it.

The music stopped. The dancers waited to resume but the musicians put down their instruments and departed for refreshments. 'Tessa, darling!' said the princess as we got to her. They embraced in that perfunctory way that women do when they are wearing make-up and jewellery and have their hair done. 'Promise me that you'll never let George take my husband away again.'

'Whatever did they do?' said Tessa, a laugh in her voice as if the answer might be both shocking and entertaining.

'That beastly scuba diving school. Joppi can't talk about anything else, ever since they went there.'

'But that was ages ago,' said Tessa. 'That was in Cannes.'

'I know. I thought it would go the way of the oil painting and the computers: forgotten after a week or two, but Joppi has been absolutely demented . . . He's bought all the equipment: air bottles and . . . I don't know . . . Even books about it. He wants me to do it too but I can't swim.'

'Poor darling Ita,' said Tessa with no hint of sincerity.

Further indicating her distress, the princess fanned herself, a mannerism more that of a schoolgirl than of a grown woman. 'George,' she said. 'Do something to get Joppi out of the billiards room.' To Tessa she petulantly added, 'It's always the same at parties; Joppi hides away in there and doesn't help at all.'

Tessa said, 'How lucky you are, Ita. George helps me and it's absolute hell.' George smiled and then said, 'Let me introduce Gloria and Bernard my brother-in-law.'

'Are you really Tessa's brother?'

'No, I'm married to her sister.'

'And you are Gloria,' said the princess somewhat condescendingly and smiled to show the sort of satisfaction women get from uncovering what might be illicit relationships.

After a few more pleasantries Tessa took Gloria under her wing and they disappeared together upstairs while George took me to meet our host in the billiards room. From George's description I was expecting someone old and fat, a rotund wurst-gobbler likely to be found in a beerhall swaying to the melody of *In München steht ein Hofbräuhaus – eins, szwei, gsuffa!* But the prince turned out to be a tall thin sleek man of about thirty-five. A cosmopolitan tough guy who spoke English with no trace of an accent. Suntanned like his wife, he had unnaturally black hair that was shiny and brushed close to the skull. His dinner suit was conservatively cut by some expensive tailor. Like George and many of the other guests he wore it in the casual manner of men who spend a great deal of time in such costume.

He was standing by the marker drinking wine and studying the position of the cue ball. He looked up as we entered. 'George!' he said with what appeared to be genuine pleasure.

'All alone?' said George. 'Perhaps you'd prefer . . .'

'No, George. I was hoping you would come.' He snapped his cue into the rack with an excess of force, as a well drilled soldier might place his rifle somewhere close at hand.

George said, 'This is Bernard, a very good friend despite being my brother-in-law.'

'Brother-in-law and friend too!' he said, grimacing in mock surprise. 'That's surely a tribute to the grace and generosity in both of you.'

As I went through the formalities the vague feeling of recognition snapped into focus. I'd seen the activities of this 'playboy prince' in some of the less serious German newspapers and magazines.

George said, 'Quite a dressy crowd here tonight, Joppi.'

'Not many real friends. They're people my wife feels we owe favours or hospitality to,' said Joppi, as if his wife was suffering a strange and troubling delusion; an affliction from which he hoped she'd eventually be released.

'Ita tells me you've become an expert diver, Joppi,' said George.

'Yes, next time you'll find I'm even better than you,' said Joppi. 'It is a matter of fitness, George. And practice.' To ask any German to undersell such hard-earned achievements is to ask a great deal. 'We spent Christmas in my brother's beach home near Rio and the water was perfect. Now I'm good, damned good.'

'Lucky man,' said George.

'You're guests, and not drinking,' the prince said. 'We must rectify that immediately.' He smoothed his perfectly smooth jacket and began to move towards the door as if guessing that his wife had asked George to prise him out of the billiards room.

He snapped his fingers, German style, at the nearest waiter and conjured up drinks for us. But before I could get my hands on one Tessa – bright-eyed and smiling – had grabbed my arm. 'First, you dance, Bernard. I insist.'

I hadn't danced for so long that it required all my concentration not to tread on her toes, but soon I was managing well enough to try talking too. 'When can I pop over for that fur coat?'

'Joppi's a lovely dancer isn't he?' Tessa said as if she'd not heard me.

I turned my head to see our host with Gloria gripped tightly in his arms. 'Yes,' I said.

'I knew he would be interested in Gloria. She is just his type.'

'But will Gloria find him interesting?' I asked.

'That doesn't matter half so much,' said Tessa. 'He will find *her* interesting, and that's what attracts any woman.'

I didn't argue with her: probably she was right. I'd never understood women and had given up hope that I might ever do so. Anyway it would do no good to argue with Tessa. She handled her life in her own way and made no concessions to anyone, not even to her husband.

'He's like that,' said Tessa. There was the hint of a joke in her tone. She was being provocative and made no secret of it. 'He has quite a reputation with the ladies. He'll proposition her; you see if he doesn't.'

'How do you know?'

'You silly man!'

I steered her sharply round to avoid bumping into another couple and said, 'When was that?'

'Me and Joppi? He wanted me to leave George but that was just his machismo. He would have left me high and dry after a few months. I knew that.'

'Does George know?'

'There is nothing to know, darling.' We danced without speaking for a little while and then Tessa said, 'Gloria is awfully worried about you, darling.'

'Gloria is worried?'

'You're not looking your best, Bernard. Surely other people have mentioned it to you?'

'No, they haven't.'

'Don't get snotty. You're looking bloody rotten if you want to hear the truth of it. Gloria thinks you should see the doctor and I agree with her.'

'See a doctor? What am I supposed to be suffering from?'

'Stress can do strange things, Bernard. You're probably overworked . . . I don't know. But you're damned jumpy and suspicious all the time. And apart from that you don't look well.'

'I'm one hundred per cent,' I said.

'My man in Harley Street is really wonderful, Bernard. Would you go and let him give you a check-up: as a personal favour to me.'

'I do believe you're serious.'

'Of course I am. And I promised Gloria to talk to you.'

'I'll think about it.'

'No. Say you'll go. I'll make the appointment.'

'I said I'd think about it.'

'I'll phone you next week. I'm going to keep on at you until you go.'

'For God's sake, Tessa.' Then, realizing that I was being inappropriately rude, I gave her a kiss on the cheek. What I didn't tell her was that even a routine check-up like that would have to be reported to the

Department. I didn't want anyone there asking if I was sick. All kinds of complications would follow. They were just looking for an excuse to put me on the shelf.

I saw Joppi again. He was a skilful dancer and Gloria was loving every moment. She gave no sign of thinking that the prince should go and see a doctor. As they went gliding round the floor I regretted that I hadn't made more effort at Frau Brand's dancing classes back in Uhlandstrasse when I was twelve years old. 'And he's a friend of George's?' I said.

'Friend? George can't stand him. George detests Germans; you know that, Bernard. He turned away the offer of a Mercedes agency. He won't even buy a second-hand German car for resale.'

'So why do you come here?'

'Ita is one of my best friends. She's a sweet girl. We go shopping together. And when it's my turn to arrange one of my charity lunches, you'd be amazed how many of those ladies want to meet a princess.'

'I was wondering when I could collect that fur coat,' I said, having given up hope of being able to introduce the subject with more subtlety.

'It was George who first met them,' said Tessa. 'He met Joppi at Mass; George always attends Mass, you know. You'd never guess that's where they met would you?'

'No, I wouldn't have guessed that.' I watched Joppi laughing with Gloria and hugging her as they danced together and said, 'Perhaps you'd like to visit us out in the sticks, and have dinner one evening?'

'We'd love that, Bernard my sweet. But please don't say bring that bloody coat because the answer is no.'

'It's just that–'

'Your Gloria is a nice girl. I don't know her very well but from what I see of her I like her. And I like the way she worries about you: you're a lucky man. But I'm not going to deliver Fiona's fur coat for you to give to her. It's just not on, Bernard. It's wrong and I'm surprised you don't see that.'

'Come to dinner anyway,' I said.

'It's almost summer,' said Tessa.

'Yes,' I said as the music stopped.

'Do look,' said Tessa, her amused voice not concealing the malicious pleasure that coloured her view of the world. 'He's probably propositioning her now. He'll invite her to go to Rome for the weekend, or to the penthouse they keep in New York. It must be very tempting.'

It was no use showing anger. No one was exempt from Tessa's Schadenfreude. 'It's getting late,' I said, 'and I have to be up early tomorrow.'

Generously George insisted upon us going back to his Mayfair apartment for a nightcap. And then, leaving Gloria and Tessa to chat, he drove me back to collect the car near Dicky's house. 'That house of Joppi's,' said George suddenly. 'It's full of rot.'

'Is it?' I said.

'I went upstairs to use the bathroom. My God! You should see the woodwork. And it's established in the walls . . . the plaster. You didn't notice?'

'No,' I said.

'To get rid of that, the whole house will have to be gutted.'

'Did you tell him?'

'And be the bringer of bad news? No. Poor fellow. I couldn't bring myself to spoil his evening.'

'Didn't he have it surveyed?'

'He listened too much to that fancy architect – all stainless steel and indoor plants – I can't stand those fellows.'

'No chance of redress?'

'Suing the builders, you mean? Compensation? No chance at all. They were right cowboys. Those people form a new company for every job, and go bust as soon as they are paid. Those people work like that.'

'Poor Prince Joppi,' I said.

'Yes, poor devil,' said George solemnly. Had Tessa not told me George's real feelings, I might have thought he meant it. He was a good driver, careful, alert and considerate of other road users. When a young fellow in a dented Ford came roaring past him on the wrong side and gave a toot on the horn to reprimand George for driving too safely, George just pulled over and made more room for him.

'Stupid bastard!' I said angrily.

'Perhaps he had a bad day,' said George mildly. Sometimes I wondered whether it was his piety that provided him with such remarkable tolerance. If so, it was a convincing argument for Roman Catholicism. 'You're a man of the world, Bernard,' said George suddenly.

I was about to give a flippant answer but I realized that George had something on his mind. So I grunted and said I would like to think so.

'Any experience of drug addiction? Cocaine, heroin, that kind of thing?'

'I'm not an expert.'

'There's a fellow hanging around Tessa . . . She was talking about drugs the other night, saying that there is a lot of nonsense talked about them, and I don't doubt there is.'

367

George went silent. I said, 'I'd better get this clear, George. You think this fellow is selling drugs to her?'

'Yes, Bernard, I do think so,' he said cautiously.

'Give me his name and address.'

'I don't want to overreact,' said George. 'That could bring about the very thing I'm so anxious to avoid.'

'There's no harm in checking,' I said. 'I know good people who would give you some answers within a couple of days.'

'Calls himself Bill Turton but I wouldn't give too much importance to that. He's a prosperous-looking American, not young.' Having started to confide in me, he stopped and thought about it for a moment. 'It wouldn't be so easy, Bernard. He's one of those people without a fixed address: hotels, clubs, rented places, one country to another. Never stays long anywhere.'

'Is this what Tessa tells you?'

'She invited him up for drinks the other evening. I didn't like him at all. I could see he was charming and friendly and all that but I had an instinctive reaction.'

'You may be worrying unnecessarily.'

'He was there at the Joppis' tonight.'

'Was he?' I was surprised and wished George had brought the matter up when there was an opportunity for me to see the man.

'Always lots of that sort of muck available at the Joppis'. Did you go upstairs?'

'Upstairs? No.'

'One of the rooms upstairs . . . They think it's very smart and sophisticated.'

'I noticed that there was a mood . . . a sort of hysteria.'

'Hysteria. Yes, that's the word isn't it? I can't imagine how people can bear poisoning their own bloodstream with chemicals. Do you know that Tessa won't eat processed food because of the chemical additives? And yet she . . .'

'I'm sorry, George.'

'That's why she wanted to go. Did you notice how animated she became?'

'Not any more than usual. She's always in high spirits, you know that, George.'

'A big fellow: grey wavy hair and glasses.'

'There were a lot of people like that,' I said.

'This fellow has a little rim beard and no moustache. Curious-looking cove.'

'I didn't see him,' I said truthfully. It could have been a description of Mr Bart Johnson, but Bart Johnson was dead.

13

It was the morning after Prince Joppi's party that I was walking along South Audley Street and bumped into Rolf Mauser. Rolf was about seventy years old, a wartime artillery captain who didn't let anyone forget that he'd won the coveted Knight's Cross. He was an un-principled rogue but he had an engaging manner, and when he worked for my father, and later as the barman in Lisl's hotel, I saw a lot of him. It was Rolf Mauser who'd shown me how to pick a lock and how to hold a playing card out of sight while shuffling the rest of the pack. When I was a child I'd been devoted to him and even though I'd long since seen him for what he really was I'd never completely shaken off some of that awe. Although for me Rolf had become an elderly figure of fun, underlying the fun there was something ruthless and frightening.

I was surprised to see him here in London, for the last I'd heard of him he'd settled down to live permanently in East Berlin.

'You're looking well, Rolf. What are you doing in London?' He was a big fellow and wore one of those heavy brown leather overcoats with plenty of straps and buttons. Its tight fit made him look as if he was about to explode out of it. This impression of impending detonation was heightened by the rosiness of his cheeks and nose.

'Bernd! Hello! I'm visiting my relatives. I have a cousin who lives in Luton.'

'Where are you living nowadays?' I asked.

He bent his head and touched his green loden hat as if to ease the constriction of its band, but it would be possible to read into this physical gesture a hint of apology. 'I'm still in the East. When you get to my age, Bernd, you're looking for peace and quiet. And what's more it's cheap.'

'Still in the same apartment?' He'd put me up there once. His apartment was large, comfortable but somewhat neglected, rather like Rolf himself.

'Prenzlauer Berg, yes. Fifty-five marks a month! The rent of my apartment is the same now as it was twenty-five years ago. Can you say that about any apartment in the West?'

'No.'

He lowered his bushy eyebrows and defensively added, 'Sometimes there are shortages: but basic foodstuffs – bread, milk, meat and eggs – are cheap. So are restaurant meals, and fares and theatres and concerts. I'm comfortable in the East, Bernd. Very comfortable.' It sounded like a little speech he'd rehearsed.

'And a little money goes a long way over there,' I said.

His face stiffened. Mauser had worked for the Department and was probably in receipt of some small pension through the good offices of Schneider, von Schild and Weber, the bank which discreetly handled such delicate financial affairs in Berlin. Social security payments for the old – unlike almost all other types of benefit – are not high in the DDR. Only a dedicated cynic like Rolf could be extolling, even to me, the wonders of this regime under which he'd chosen to retire, while he was largely living on the proceeds of the pension he'd got from trying to overthrow it. 'That's what I was saying, isn't it?'

'It's good to see you, Rolf.'

'So I have to line up for groceries and meat sometimes: I don't mind lining up. I have time to spare. And when I walk home from the shops I don't have to worry about being burgled or mugged.'

'You're lucky. Where are you going?'

'Yes, I am lucky,' he asserted as if he wasn't quite sure of my sincerity. 'No matter how tough they are with the youngsters, old fellows like me can come and go as we like. I don't have to climb over the Wall, Bernd.' He grinned.

If I knew anything about Rolf Mauser – and I knew quite a lot – he would never see eye to eye with any socialist regime. He was a rebellious loner. The Communists, like the Nazis and indeed the Church, had always welcomed converts to their cause but it was difficult to imagine Mauser acquiring *sozialistisches Staatsbewusstsein*, that unquestioning enthusiasm for the regime that the DDR expects of its citizens. Mauser was a pragmatist and a self-centred one at that. Long, long ago I'd heard my father describe Rolf Mauser as the sort of arrogant, bellicose German who earned for his race the civilized world's contempt. Calmly my mother had asked him why he went on employing him; because he'll do things no one else will even attempt, replied my father.

'Come and have coffee?' I suggested. I guessed that he would be very short of hard currency, and casual cups of coffee are one of the first things such indigents sacrifice.

'I'd like that, Bernd. That's the one thing I can't get at a reasonable price. Luckily my son sends me a packet every month. I can't live without a cup of good coffee in the morning.'

There was a smart little coffee house nearby and we walked there quickly with Rolf complaining at great length about the weather. 'It gets right into my bones,' he said as we sat down. It was the dampness, of course. Rolf, like most Berliners, found the marginally warmer English climate poor compensation for the penetrating chilly moisture that most natives don't even notice.

The coffee house was a chintzy place that I knew well. I used to have coffee here with Fiona when we worked in a nearby office. That was before we were married. I ordered a big pot of coffee before we found a table. It was the best way to get things moving.

'How is Axel? I haven't seen him for a long time.' I was at school with Mauser's son. At one time we'd been close friends.

'They live in a nice house in Hermsdorf but his marriage is not too smooth. Ever since that wife of his got that wonderful job and started earning big money she's become a monster.' He shrugged and reached for a Danish pastry.

'I'm sorry.'

'Work work work that's all she thinks about. She's a career woman,' he said contemptuously. 'But Axel won't hear a word against her. I don't see the attraction she has for him. He needs a real woman.' I'd heard Rolf railing against his daughter-in-law for many long years. The way he spoke of her you wouldn't think the marriage had lasted a couple of decades and that they had a teenage son.

'Axel was one of the brightest boys in the school,' I said. Rolf had always been smug about the way Axel was consistently top of the class. He especially liked to tell my father that Axel had done better than I had.

He tore the wrapping from a sugar cube. There was a ferocity – if not to say malignity – to everything he did. Hellos, goodbyes, even thank-yous were a part of this belligerent spirit. I wondered if it was a pose he'd cultivated to maintain his authority as a young army officer, a pose that eventually devoured his true nature. 'And now he's working as a clerk in the Polizeipräsidium. I know, it's a waste of a good brain, but he won't listen to me.' He tossed the sugar into his coffee.

'I suppose he's worried about his son.'

'His son? What is there to worry about?'

'I didn't mean that,' I said. 'I meant that Axel probably works hard to keep his marriage going so that his son has a mother and father and a settled home life.'

'Nonsense!' said Rolf Mauser. He chewed his pastry, his mouth moving as if in anger.

'Axel loves the boy,' I said. 'I remember how he assembled a racing bicycle for him. He put it together with such loving care.'

'I know, I know. The kid had an accident: some fool in a Porsche: broke his leg; kept driving, didn't stop. He'd had a few drinks, I suppose. Axel blamed himself. That's stupid isn't it?'

'I don't know,' I said. In fact, of course, most fathers would have felt equally guilty. It was only roughnecks like old Rolf who saw things in such a simplistic light. I suppose it was the war. I remember Rolf telling stories about the last days of the Berlin fighting. Hauptmann Rolf had been sent off on patrol with a 'flying court martial' and they summarily executed anyone on the street who couldn't give a proper account of himself. They shot him there and then and hanged the body in full view with a sign saying 'I deserted my post'. Axel had said he couldn't imagine his father doing such things but I saw Rolf in a different light. I knew that Rolf could be a cold-blooded killer if he thought it necessary.

Perhaps my thinking was communicated to him, but if so it arrived in a distorted form, for he said, 'If Axel had served in the army he might have kept a better sense of proportion.'

'Is that what the army gave you, Rolf?'

He furrowed his brow, his eyebrows bristling so that he looked ferocious. I remembered being frightened of such grimaces when I was a child. 'Ever dream, Bernd?'

'Of being rich, or a film star?' I knew what he meant of course but I couldn't resist jollying him along. The fact was that I didn't want to hear his dreams; I didn't want to hear anyone's dreams. I had enough of my own.

'I don't sleep so well nowadays. I went to the doctor; he said it was my age. Stupid little schlemiel.' He leaned forward. 'I always dream about my time in the army, Bernd. I remember things I haven't thought of for years. And such detail! I got command of a self-propelled artillery battery when the battalion was out of the line. My battery commander went down with some kind of fever, I didn't know you could get fever in the middle of a Russian winter but I learned a lot in Russia. It was Christmas and we were refitting in Krasnograd. Ever heard of Krasnograd?'

'I don't believe I have,' I said.

'A God-forsaken dump in the middle of nowhere. But there were trees; a lot of trees considering that the region had been fought through. The men liked the trees, it reminded them of home. Heavy snow and wooded countryside: with an effort of imagination it could almost have been the homeland. The peasants remained there of course, they always did. Russian peasants would sooner die than leave their village, they were all like that. I couldn't understand it. Then, in the middle of my

373

daily bowl of pea soup – that powdered muck, but the cook had found some ancient potatoes to go into it – the signals lieutenant came back from headquarters and told me that the battery was mine. Wow! Did that soup suddenly taste good!'

He sat back and gave a half smile, but not at me. He didn't even see me at that moment: Rolf Mauser was miles away, and decades back in time, fighting his war in Russia. He rubbed his face. 'Taking command of six huge 15cm heavy howitzers mounted on tank chassis was quite an event in the life of a young man. I took it very seriously. I went round and spoke to every officer and man under my command: two officers, twenty-nine NCOs and ninety-two enlisted men. Most of them were newly arrived replacements: green kids, not long out of school. The other night in my dream I recalled every name and face. I even remembered the equipment I signed for.' He looked at me and wanted me to see how important all this was to him. 'I could even taste that damned *Erbsensuppe*.'

'And when you woke up?'

'Still remembered everything. Twenty-eight lorries, two motor-cycles, sixteen light machine guns, twenty machine pistols, forty-eight handguns and seventy-eight rifles. I even remembered the names and ranks. Every one of their stupid faces.'

For a moment I thought he was about to recite all their names and numbers and give me the specifications of the hardware and its state of readiness. Perhaps the consternation showed on my face, for he said, 'Take my word for it. I can see those men now. Every face, every accented word they spoke. We left most of them deep under the ice and snow. By summer, only half a dozen of those men were still serving with me.'

For the very first time I saw that Rolf Mauser had spent his life entertaining dreams of military glory. An absurd ambition perhaps, but no more absurd than the dreams of most men. And, if the statistics were to be believed, no more unlikely than ending up with a happy marriage and loving family. 'General Rolf Mauser' had an implausible ring to it but the award of a 'tin tie' must have provided new impetus to his hopes of promotion, and certainly he had the necessary ruthlessness.

'Everyone dreams, Rolf,' I said. 'It's nothing to do with getting old.'

'So what do I do?'

'Get another doctor.'

He gave a humourless smile before paying all his attention to the coffee and what remained of his pastry.

For a brief time neither of us spoke. Then, 'Der grosse Kleiner is dead,' said Mauser as he stuffed down the final mouthful of his Danish pastry.

'So I heard. What do you know about it?'

'Don't tell me it was suicide.'

'I don't know anything about it,' I protested.

'Kleindorf wasn't the type.' He used the tip of his tongue to remove a crumb from his teeth.

'So what was it then?'

'He was a dope dealer. He was behind the refining and he was the contact between East and West.'

'Who says?'

'Regular consignments of it were coming through Schönefeld, arriving in the West for re-packaging and then going back there again. There were DDR officials taking a cut. It's all being hushed up. Even the West Berlin authorities are keeping stumm.'

'Why?'

'The official word is that the relationship between the two Germanies must not be threatened by such crimes.'

'And the unofficial word?'

Rolf let a slow smile spread across his big round face. 'That officials on both sides are deeply implicated. Big shots, I mean.'

'Sounds a bit far-fetched,' I said doubtfully.

'Does it, Bernd? We've known each other a long time, haven't we? Are you seriously telling me that you've never heard rumours or stories about such dealings?'

'Rumours, yes.' I wondered if he'd heard the sort of stories Larry Bower had got from Valeri the double agent. 'Even so . . .'

'Kleindorf had a massive dose of heroin; that's what he died of. You know that?'

'I thought it was sleeping tablets.'

'Yes. That's the story that's being put around.' He nodded. 'Do you happen to have a cigarette on you, Bernd?'

Having stopped smoking for a long period I'd lately been accepting offered cigarettes. This morning my nerve had cracked and I'd bought a packet of cheroots. But I suddenly resolved to try harder. I handed the unopened packet to him. I said, 'Isn't that more to your taste?'

'It's very kind of you, Bernd. Are you sure?'

'I've stopped smoking.'

He lit one immediately and continued. 'But the real story is that Kleindorf died while in bed with one of his young dancing girls, a woman with a strong Silesian accent who disappeared long before the police arrived and has never been traced.'

'What are you getting at?'

'She'd worked for him for only a few days. The name and address she gave to his secretary at the Babylon were false.' He blew smoke.

'Do you think the woman murdered him?'

'She arrived in town with an American. They flew out together: two first class tickets to Rome. There were no needle marks on Kleindorf. Except for the marks of the needle that killed him.' He waited for me to absorb that fact and then said, 'He'd never take hard drugs: he was a health freak. Jogged every morning without fail.'

'What did the autopsy say?'

'No autopsy. The certificate said death was due to an overdose of sleeping tablets. An accident. Hurried burial; a demand for an inquest summarily refused.'

'I heard he'd drunk a whole bottle of vintage brandy.'

'There was an empty bottle in the bedroom. Who can say how much he'd drunk unless they open the stomach? Probably he'd had a drink with the girl. Did you ever see Kleindorf drunk?'

'No,' I said.

'Exactly. It's a cover-up. It sounds perfectly credible unless you know what Kleindorf was really like.'

'Okay,' I said. 'The stuff comes from Asia. They bring it into East Berlin. The Schönefeld airport customs let it go through because it's official policy to help the decadent West mainline its way to oblivion. Okay. What I don't get is why it does a turn-around and makes a journey back East again.'

'The consignments they are tapping into are brown, raw stuff. You have to be pretty desperate to float that shit into your bloodstream. None of the people at that end of the dealing has the know-how, the resources or the equipment to refine it, or the guts to risk it. That was Kleindorf's contribution to their game.'

'Have another coffee, Rolf.' I signalled to the waitress.

'This is a good place for coffee,' said Mauser appreciatively. 'I'm glad I met you, Bernd.'

'What sort of people in the East would be buying this stuff?' I said. 'And where would the money come from?'

Rolf Mauser knew he was being pushed, but that was better than admitting to not knowing. 'You know how these things work, Bernd. The transaction was drugs for paper-work.'

He paused as if he'd said something self-evidently significant.

Perhaps he had but I wasn't going to let him stop there. 'Would you enlarge on that notion?'

'Permissions. Imports. Contracts. A signature and a rubber stamp on a desk over there can mean a lot of money over here. You know that, Bernd. So does your friend Werner Volkmann.' He puffed smoke. It was a subdued gesture of aggression. He looked at me and waited for a reply.

'You're not saying Werner was implicated?' Before taking over the running of Lisl's hotel Werner had made a lot of money from avalizing: putting together import and export deals so that the DDR didn't have to part with hard currency. In that respect Werner's livelihood had depended upon East Berlin signatures and rubber stamps.

'I don't know.' He waved a hand. 'But if he was, he got out of that business at exactly the right time. He doesn't go over there any more.'

'He's busy with Lisl's,' I said. I watched Rolf tap ash from the cheroot. All my desire to smoke had gone: the smoke, the smell, the ash, the very idea disgusted me.

'Of course he is,' said Mauser. 'And if I were you, Bernd, I'd find myself something to be busy with.' A meaningful look. 'Because there are a lot of people on both sides of the Wall who are looking for someone to lay the blame on. You would fit the role nicely.'

'As a drug courier?'

'With evidence from both sides? It would be overwhelming. Who would believe anyone protesting his innocence if East and West put together a story?'

'How do you know all this, Rolf?'

'I know a lot of people and I keep my ears open.'

I chatted with him for almost another half an hour, but Rolf had decided to say no more, or perhaps knew no more, and the conversation turned to chatter about his family and other people we both knew. His aforementioned relative in London was not amongst the people he talked of. I wondered whether his cousin was not just a cover to hide the real reason for his visit. There were several chair-bound Departmental officials not so far away from here who would be pleased to have someone like Rolf Mauser to amplify their long, tedious and tendentious reports about the DDR: writing which bore little resemblance to the reality. It would be rash of him to continue to work for us, but given, on the one hand, the pressure the Department was always ready to apply to anyone who could be useful, and on the other hand Rolf Mauser's appetite for both risk and extra spending money, I guessed that he might be doing exactly that. An added dimension was provided by the possibility that he was playing a double game reporting everything back to the other side. I hoped any Departmental person dealing with him had considered that and kept it in mind constantly.

When I left Mauser I found myself disturbed by the conversation we'd had. There was something about his words that unsettled me. I'd known that same feeling since I was a child. Mauser enjoyed alarming people.

14

I dismissed Rolf Mauser from my mind as I walked up to Oxford Street and went into Selfridges hardware department to get a new hinge for the garage door. It had to be big, for the door's timber was not in first-class condition. Eventually I'd have to fit metal doors, but that was not an outlay I wanted to face in my present circumstances. And when Gloria went to study at Cambridge I might decide to sell the place. One of the store assistants went into a stock room and found the sort of long hinge I needed. I was carrying it with me – wrapped in brown paper – when I went to the address in Upper Brook Street, behind the American Embassy, to meet Posh Harry for his promised lunch.

'No need to have brought your Kalashnikov, Bernard,' said Harry when he saw the parcel. 'Strictly no rough stuff; I promised Dicky that.' He laughed in that restrained naughty-boy way that oriental people sometimes do. 'Come and have a drink,' he said and led the way up to a first floor room. As always he was neatly dressed in somewhat English-style clothes: grey flannels and a dark blazer with ornate metal buttons and, on its pocket, the gold wire badge of a Los Angeles golf club.

Mayfair is an exclusive district of elegant residences most of which are offices in disguise. It is a place of high rents and short leases, of private banks and property developers, art dealers and investment managers all discreetly hidden behind simple brass nameplates. These houses are small, and the cramped, over-furnished upstairs room into which he showed me was designed for rich transients. The house had been given the sort of refurbishment that my brother-in-law called 'the gold tap treatment'. There were lots of table lamps made from big robust jars and sturdy shades, sofas with loose covers of glazed chintz, and the sort of carpet that wine doesn't stain.

However any effect of gracious eighteenth-century living was marred by the 'refreshment centre' in the corner: a plastic-topped table held a hot-plate with two big glass jugs of coffee, mugs, paper cups and biscuits, and a handwritten notice about putting ten pence into the cash box and not using mugs with names on them.

'Take the weight off your feet,' said Harry as he unlocked a reproduction terrestrial globe the upper hemisphere of which hinged at the equator to reveal a core of drink. 'A Martini or name your poison.'

'A Martini will do nicely.' I watched him select the bottles: Beefeater and Noilly Prat.

'I'll tell you this, Bernard,' he said as he went across the room and pulled at a bookcase. 'You can keep California.' His exertions bore fruit as a section of antique leather books and shelving came loose in his hand to give access to a small refrigerator that was concealed behind it. 'Yes, sir!' With a commendable dexterity he threw ice-cubes into a jug and held two chilled glasses while gripping the gin bottle under his arm.

He removed the stopper from the gin bottle and mixed the cocktails with careless skill. 'Take it easy on the gin,' I said.

'I never had you figured for a guy who was heavily into vermouth,' he said, ignoring my strictures. He held up the glasses as if judging the colour of the concentration and then handed one of them to me. 'Only one thing I can't tolerate, Bernard . . . a vermouth addict. Pass that across your tonsils – the perfect Martini.'

'I like California,' I said.

'Not working for my outfit you wouldn't like it,' he said. He went to the window and looked down at the traffic. It came from Hyde Park and into this one-way street like close-packed herds of shiny migrating animals, thudding past without respite. 'They let me go. Can you believe it?'

I smiled and tasted my drink. Whatever failings Posh Harry had exhibited in California, mixing Martinis could not be amongst them.

Harry said, 'There are a couple of files I want to ask your advice about before lunch.' He looked at his watch. 'Our table is booked for one o'clock. Okay?'

'Sure.'

'Am I glad we had this meeting today, Bernard. You don't know what a favour you're doing me.'

'I am?'

'Providing me with an excuse to stay clear of the office. Joe Brody is in town and kicking ass like there is no tomorrow.'

'Joe Brody?'

I suppose he saw my antenna wobbling. He said, 'Yeah, Joe Brody! Joe Brody has flown in from Vienna and is lunching with the Ambassador today, but that didn't stop him from coming in to the office and raising hell with just about everyone working there.'

'Is Brody such a tough guy?'

'He can be: unless you know how to handle him.' He gave a foxy smile. 'He needs the velvet touch, if you know what I mean. You must know Brody?'

380

'We've met in Berlin.'

'Brody is itchy for a big promotion. The buzz is that he will go into Operations at a senior level.'

'Brody is too old.'

'In the CIA, old buddy, no one is ever too old. That's what keeps us all bright-eyed and bushy-tailed and breathing down the necks of our bosses.'

'Brody?'

'And he's making sure Washington knows he's alive and kicking. Get the picture?'

'I thought Brody was in Vienna.'

'Forget Brody. I can handle Brody. Let me show you these files. You tick some boxes and tell me anything we're getting wrong, then we go and write off the rest of this month's expenses in the Connaught. What about that?'

'It's a deal,' I said.

'Look through this while I go and get the rest of the stuff from the safe upstairs.' He handed me a coloured file and a felt-tip pen.

I looked through the file. It had the expected pink addendum sheet at the back, arranged with a question and answer format that the CIA designed for 'day by day turn-around' of urgent material. There was nothing very difficult about the framed questions, even though I was depending entirely upon my memory. But there were a lot of them.

Harry came back with two more files and slammed them on to my knees. Noticing that my glass was empty he went and mixed two more of his 'perfect' Martinis.

'There's another file but I can't find it. One of the clerks says it went to Grosvenor Square. Could be Brody wanted it. It might arrive with the messenger at noon. Anyway do what you can and then we'll go and eat. Leave your parcel here. We'll come back after lunch and if that damned file's arrived maybe you'd take a look at that one too.'

'Okay.'

My work done, we walked to the Connaught Hotel in Carlos Place, the cold air only partially undoing the effect of Harry's Martinis.

He'd reserved a seat by the window and Posh Harry did everything he'd promised. We struck into the à la carte side of the menu and the wines he selected were appropriately excellent. It was the first time I'd ever had such a friendly conversation with Posh Harry. I'd known him for many years but met him only in the line of business.

If an agent's competence was measured by his personal cover then Posh Harry was one of the most proficient I'd known. For years no one seemed quite certain if he was linked to the CIA. Even now I was not sure if he worked for them on a permanent basis. Harry's brother – much older than Harry – had died miserably on a CIA mission in Vietnam, and the way I heard it Harry blamed the Company for his death. But that wasn't anything I'd ever mentioned to him, and if any trace of bitterness remained from that ancient episode there would be little chance of him revealing his feelings.

Harry, no less assertive and no less devious than Rolf Mauser, was everything the old man wasn't. Mauser was a bully who enjoyed the rough-and-tumble process of getting his own way. For Harry the end result was all that mattered. It was I suppose the fundamental difference between Europe and the Orient, between the visible and the concealed, between force and stealth, boxing and judo.

It would have been wiser of me to have given more weight to such reflections before lunch, for by the time I got back to the house in Brook Street I was unprepared for the furious reception that awaited us.

'Do you know what time it is?' yelled Joe Brody, whose lunch with the Ambassador had apparently been a briefer and more austere refreshment than ours.

'I'm sorry, Joe,' replied Harry, caught halfway up the stairs with a red-faced Joe Brody shouting at him from the upper landing. I looked at Brody with interest. Until now I'd never seen him in anything but a relaxed and gentle mood.

Brody was wearing a striped blue three-piece suit appropriate for lunch with the Ambassador. He was old, a bald man with circular gold-rimmed glasses that fitted tight into his face like coins that have grown into the trunk of a gnarled tree. At other times I'd seen him smiling sagely while holding a drink and listening indulgently to those around him. But here was a frenzied little fellow who could even plough furrows across Posh Harry's calm features. 'You're sorry. Goddamnit, you should be. Who's this? Oh, it's you Samson, I almost forgot you were coming over here. Have you finished?'

By that time we were at the upper landing. Joe Brody ushered the two of us back into the room we'd been in before lunch. He strode across the room, took off his jacket and tossed it on to a chair. Slowly, like some aroused reptile, the jacket uncoiled and slid to the floor. Brody gave no sign of noticing it.

I didn't answer. Brody looked at me and then at Harry. I felt embarrassed, as one feels when accidentally witnessing a blissfully married couple suddenly transformed by a savage domestic rift. In the silence one became aware of the traffic noise which provided an unending roar, like distant thunder.

When Harry realized that I had decided not to tell Brody whether we had finished, he said, 'Not quite, Joe.'

'Jesus Christ!' And then even more furiously, 'Jesus Christ!'

'Just one more file,' said Harry repentantly.

'Did you ask him about Salzburg?' Brody said, talking about me as if I wasn't present.

'I wasn't sure if you wanted me to bring that up,' said Harry.

'Sit down, Bernard,' said Joe Brody. He gave a nervous fleeting smile as if trying to reassure me that I was not a part of his row with Harry, but some of his wrath spilled over.

'Do you want a drink, Joe?' said Harry, still trying to assuage Brody's wrath.

'No I don't want a goddamned drink. I want to see some work done around here.' Brody grabbed his nose as if about to take a dose of nasty medicine. Harry muttered something about needing a glass of club soda and went and poured one for himself. I'd never known Posh Harry even slightly discomposed but now his hands were trembling.

Brody sank down into the armchair facing me and sighed. Suddenly he looked exhausted. His tie knot had loosened, his waistcoat was partly unbuttoned and a lot of his shirt had become a rumpled lifebelt round his waist. His bad temper had made demands upon his attire and his stamina. But any expectations I had about his temper moderating were not encouraged by the harshness of his voice as he continued. 'One of our people was blown away: in Salzburg. You hear about that?'

'I was there,' I said.

'Sure you were there. What exactly happened, Bernard?'

'So that was one of your people?'

'I asked you what exactly happened.'

'I don't know what exactly happened,' I said.

'Now don't snow me, Bernard. I haven't got a lot of time and I'm not in the mood.'

'I can't tell you anything that the police investigation hasn't already revealed.'

'You saw the police report?'

'No,' I admitted.

'So how the hell would you know?' He grabbed his nose again, then finished the gesture by rubbing his mouth fiercely with the flat of his hand. I decided it was a gesture of self-restraint by a man who was on the verge of a real tantrum.

'Take it easy, Mr Brody,' I said. 'It was an explosive charge triggered by mains electricity. Your man Johnson died. That's about all I can tell you.'

'Would you please describe Johnson.'

'Pleasant manner. Tallish, in good physical shape but slightly overweight. Grey wavy hair; rim beard, no moustache. Gold-rimmed bifocals—'

'That's enough. Who set it up, kid?'

'I've no idea.'

'I think you have,' said Brody, letting his voice go a bit nasty.

'Then give me a clue,' I said.

'I'm asking the questions,' said Brody. 'Think again.'

'I've told you all I can tell you, Mr Brody.'

He sat there glowering at me.

'I'm going to ask you again, Bernard. I want to put this on a formal footing.'

'You can put it on any kind of footing you choose,' I said. 'I've told you once and I'll tell you again. I don't know.'

'Our guy,' he said and paused. I'd forgotten the way senior CIA men always said 'our guy'. When he continued he spoke in that disjointed way that people do when they are upset. 'Our guy was named Bart Johnson. He was a good man . . . worked out of Frankfurt. I've known Bart twenty years. We were together in Moscow: a long time back. Toughed out some bad ones. I lunched with the Ambassador today. I wanted him to know that Washington has authorized me to follow this one up as forcibly as my resources permit.'

'I'm gratified to hear that, Mr Brody, because if I should get blown away like your friend Johnson, I'd like to be up there knowing that someone is following me up as forcibly as resources permit.'

'Okay, Bernard, we know you were in contact with Bart Johnson. No one is saying that you were implicated in the killing but I want to know exactly what was going on in that damned hotel right up to that explosion.'

'The only thing I can tell you that was going on in that hotel up until the explosion was a stamp auction.' I was trying to keep my voice calm and polite but not entirely managing it.

'Try harder.'

'Try easier questions.'

'Okay. Here's an easier question: why are you being such an asshole?'

I got to my feet and went across the room. Inconspicuously fitted into the oak panelling, and flanked by two horse-racing prints, there was a door. In front of the door there was an occasional table with an inlaid chequered top upon which chess pieces had been arranged by some interior decorator. I turned. Brody was standing up. I kicked the table aside, chess pieces and all, and tried to open the door. It was locked. 'Will you open the door, Mr Brody? Or shall I do it?'

Perhaps without that bottle of Château Talbot and the double measure of malt whisky with which my meal had ended I would have had neither the rashness nor the force to do what I did next. I raised my boot and kicked the door almost off its hinges. It swung into the next room with a noise like thunder.

For a moment I thought I'd made a terrible miscalculation, but I hadn't. Standing up blinking in the sudden light were two shirt-sleeved men with headphones clamped over their ears. Their faces were set in an expression of horror. Beyond them there were some TV monitoring screens shining in the gloom. The operators had jumped to their feet. One of them leapt back so that his headphones' lead pulled a piece of equipment from the table. It fell to the floor with a crash. Then the heavy door, with a prolonged squeaking noise, twisted on its remaining hinge and sank slowly to the floor, landing finally with a resounding bang. Neither operator said anything: perhaps it happened to them frequently.

They were of course putting me on videotape. I suppose it would have been stupid of them to hear what I knew without having some sort of record of it, but that didn't mean that I had to sit there and cheerfully confess to anything that might later be construed as making me an accessory to a murder.

'Okay, smart ass, you've made your point,' said Brody calmly. It was a different sort of voice now. I still don't know how much of his former bad temper was feigned. And if it was feigned to what extent it was a device to intimidate me or to intimidate Posh Harry. 'Come and sit down again. We'll talk off the record if that's what you want.' To the two video operators he said, 'Take off you guys. We'll cut the crowd scene,' and he smiled at his own joke.

Posh Harry hadn't moved. He was still standing near the refrigerator sipping his soda water.

'Could we go downstairs and talk in another room?' I asked. 'The kitchen for instance?'

'With the water running and the fluorescent light on?' offered Brody sarcastically. He went and picked up his jacket from the floor, frisking it to make sure his wallet was still in place. 'Sure. Anything that will make you feel good, Bernard.' His manner was warmer now, as if he preferred the idea of talking about his friend Johnson's death to someone who could kick doors in.

We went downstairs to the tiny kitchen in the basement. It had the same well-preserved look that the rest of the house had. Here was a kitchen where no meal was ever cooked. There were wet cups and saucers in the sink and some glasses on the draining board. On the shelf above it there were packets of coffee and a huge box of tea bags and a big transparent plastic container marked sugar. A grey slatted blind obscured the window.

Joe Brody opened a refrigerator filled with canned drinks. He helped himself to a Pepsi, snapped the top open and drank it from the can. He didn't offer anyone else one: he appeared to be lost in thought.

I sat with Harry at the circular kitchen table. Brody gripped an empty chair, rested his foot on a bar of it and said, 'Were there two Americans, or just the one?'

'Two,' I said, and described Thurkettle and the way he'd come out on to the terrace and talked about sharing an office with Peter Underlet, and the way in which Johnson had approached me after the auction. I didn't say that I'd bid in the auction and I left out any mention of my wanting the cover.

Brody sat down and said, 'We know about the auction.'

'Why don't you tell me what you know, Mr Brody? I'll try and fill in the spaces.'

'Thurkettle, you mean?'

'That's what I mean,' I said.

'Well, now you see why I wanted to leave a few of the details out,' said Brody. 'We're trying to establish that both men were there at the time of the explosion.'

'I heard Johnson speak to Thurkettle as he went into his room. At the time I thought he was talking to himself. Afterwards . . . well, I don't know.'

'When was that?' said Brody. He up-ended his Pepsi and drained the last of it with obvious relish. I suppose he needed the sugar.

'Maybe half an hour before the explosion,' I replied.

'What did he say?' Carelessly Brody tossed the empty can across the room. It landed with a clatter in the rubbish bin.

When Brody's eyes came back to me I said, 'I think he said "What about that?" It was the sort of remark a man might make to himself. But it might have been a greeting.'

'To someone already in his room?'

'He knew Thurkettle was there the previous day.'

386

'How do you know that?'

'He talked about it. He asked me if I knew who he was.'

'He asked you that?'

'He said he'd met Thurkettle before but didn't know who he worked for or what he did.'

'Do you know who Thurkettle is? Really know?'

'I do now,' I said.

'Let me ask you a speculative question,' said Brody. 'Why would Thurkettle go back to the hotel and go to that room? The bomb was already in the razor. Why didn't he keep going?'

'Ummm,' I said.

'Don't umm me. You must have thought about it,' said Brody. 'Why didn't he keep going?'

'I don't know,' I said. 'But when I went back to warn him who Thurkettle was . . .'

'Hold the phone,' said Brody. 'Are you expecting me to believe you were going to tip Johnson off about Thurkettle? You? The guy who sits there stonewalling all questions about the death? No sir, I don't buy that.'

'I'm not sure what I was going to do. I went along to his room to find out what the hell was going on.'

'Okay, keep talking.'

Posh Harry got up and went to the refrigerator and after looking at everything on offer, and selecting a tumbler from the cupboard, poured himself a drink of soda. Harry must have been very fond of soda. Or perhaps he was trying to sober up. Brody glared at him to show that such movement disturbed his concentration. Harry sipped his soda and didn't look at Brody.

I said, 'I went into his room and spoke with him just before the explosion. He said I was to come back in fifteen minutes. Right after that the damned thing exploded.'

'Let me get this straight. You spoke with Johnson in his room a few minutes before he died?'

'He called from the bathroom.'

Brody said, 'The bathroom door was closed? You didn't see him?' He tugged his nose as if in deep thought.

'That's right.' I began to understand what was going on in Brody's mind. He waited a long time. I suppose he was deciding how much to tell me.

Eventually Brody said, 'When that voice told you to come back in fifteen minutes there were two men in the bathroom. Johnson was probably just about to be murdered.'

'I see,' I said.

'I don't think you see at all,' said Brody.

'Who was Thurkettle working for?'

'He's a renegade. He's been a KGB hit man for two years. We've lost at least four men to him but this is the first time he's come so close to home. Johnson and Thurkettle knew each other well. They'd worked together back in the old days.'

'That's rough,' I said.

Brody couldn't keep still. He suddenly stood up and tucked his shirt back in to his trousers. 'Damn right it is. I'll get that bastard if it's the last thing I do.'

'So he didn't die as the result of the explosion?'

'You worked that out did you?' said Brody sarcastically. He went over to the sink and turned to look at me, leaning his back against the draining board.

'Thurkettle murdered Johnson and after that blew his head off with explosive. Why? To destroy evidence? Or was Johnson too smart to go for the razor bomb? Was Thurkettle caught switching razors? Did he kill Johnson then use the bomb with a timing device?' Brody still staring at me gave a contemptuous little smile. 'That way he wouldn't get spattered with brains and blood.'

Posh Harry had regained his customary composure by this time. Still holding his glass of fizzy water he went over to where Joe Brody was lounging against the kitchen unit and said, 'You'd better level with him, Joe.'

Brody looked at me but said nothing.

Harry said, 'If you want the Brits to help they have to know the way it really happened.'

Brody, speaking very slowly and deliberately, said, 'We think Thurkettle killed Johnson and then blew his head off to destroy evidence. But the guy who told you he was Johnson was really Thurkettle.'

'The hell it was!' I said softly as the implications hit me.

Brody enjoying my consternation added, 'The dead body you saw in the bathroom was the man who spoke with you on the terrace.'

'I see.'

'You don't see much, Samson old buddy,' said Brody. I'd earned that rebuke: I should have looked more closely at the dead body on the floor.

Posh Harry said, 'Thurkettle changed identity with his victim on a previous occasion. It had us real puzzled for ages.'

'So what are you going to do about it, Bernard?' said Brody.

'I'll stick with the soap and water shaves,' I said. Brody scowled. I got to my feet to show them that I wanted to leave. He turned away and leaned across the sink to prise open the slatted blind and look out of the window. There was a minuscule yard and a white-washed wall and large flower-pots in which some leafless stalks struggled for survival. From the front of the house, through the double-glazing, came the traffic noise: worse now that the end of the working day was so close.

'Don't forget the Kalashnikov,' said Posh Harry.

Joe Brody was still looking at the yard. He seemed not to have heard.

I went upstairs to get my parcel. Harry came with me and added a few snippets to what I knew about Thurkettle. Other US government departments, resentful at the way the CIA had got Thurkettle released from prison and provided with false documentation, had proved singularly uncooperative now that he had in Harry's words 'run amok'. The CIA had sought a secret indictment from a federal grand jury in the District of Columbia and had it thrown out of court on the grounds of lack of identification. An application to the Justice Department had also failed and so had the attempt to have Thurkettle's citizenship revoked. Harry explained that there was now a desperate need to link Thurkettle with a crime. Everyone – by which I suppose he meant Brody – had been hoping that my evidence would supply the needed link. Until it was obtained Thurkettle was thumbing his nose at them and walking free.

'I still don't get it,' I said. 'If you find out why Thurkettle blew Johnson away things might become clearer.'

'We know why,' said Posh Harry smoothly. 'Johnson had the goods on him.'

'On Thurkettle?'

'That was Johnson's assignment. They were buddies. Joe Brody told Johnson to find him and get pally. Last week Johnson phoned Brody and confirmed that Thurkettle was peddling narcotics. He couldn't say much on the phone but he said he had enough evidence to put Thurkettle in front of a grand jury.'

'But Thurkettle was a jump ahead of all concerned.'

'Joe Brody blames himself.'

'Narcotics.'

'The prevailing theory in Grosvenor Square,' said Harry, 'is that Thurkettle blew poor old Kleindorf away too.'

'Why would he do that?'

'I was hoping you'd tell me. We think Thurkettle is doing business with London Central.' He laughed in a way that said it might be a joke. I decided not to get angry: I was too old to get angry twice in one day.

I nodded and thanked him for lunch and felt pleased that I hadn't mentioned Tessa's new friend with his rim beard and no moustache. They would have been all over George and Tessa. Anyway by now he might have shaved it off.

We talked for a few minutes more and then I said goodbye to Posh Harry, and went home. I hadn't brought the car into town that day, I was using the train. Standing all the way in the shabby compartment I had a chance to reflect on what had happened. Had I been set up, I wondered? Brody's fury had been all too convincing and Posh Harry's reaction to it could not have been entirely feigned. But had the powerful Martinis, and the big lunch with lots to drink, been a way of getting me softened up for Brody's grilling? And to what extent had Dicky guessed what I was walking into?

15

I'd known 'Uncle' Silas all my life. He'd been my father's boss from a time before I was born. I remembered him in Berlin when I was a child. He was young Billy's godfather and distantly related to my mother-in-law.

He had long since retired from the Department and he now lived at his farm in the Cotswold hills. He was old and becoming more exasperating every time I saw him but I knew there had been times when I'd exasperated him more than he ever had me. To look truth right in the eye I suppose I'd only kept my job this long because my father had made good friends; and Uncle Silas was one of them.

So when I had a phone call from an agitated Mrs Porter, his house-keeper, and was told that Silas Gaunt was seriously ill and asking for me, I went to him. I didn't ask for permission, or tell Dicky I needed a day off, or even send a message to the office. I went to him.

The day began with unabating heavy rain and the wet roads persuaded me to drive cautiously. It was a long drive and so I had plenty of time to reflect upon this precipitate action during the journey. As I got to the Cotswolds the hills were lost in grey silken skeins of mist, and the trees on the estate were entangled in it. 'Whitelands' consisted of about six hundred acres of fine agricultural land and an incongruous clutter of small buildings. There was a magnificent tithe barn, large enough to hold the parson's tribute of corn, and stabling for six horses. The tan-coloured stone farmhouse itself had suffered a couple of hundred years of depredations by philistine occupiers, so that there was a neo-Gothic tower and an incongruous wing that housed the large billiards room.

I was used to arriving here to find a dozen cars scattered in the front drive and – on sunny days – parked in the shade of the three tall elms that marked the limits of the lawn. On such days the house was noisy with appreciative guests. It was not like that today. The front drive was empty except for a muddy Land-Rover from which three young men in faded denim were unloading equipment including, I noticed, three bright red hard-hats and three sets of earmuffs. The rain had stopped but the water dripped from the drenched trees and the lawn squelched underfoot.

As I stepped on the metal grating in the porch it rattled reminding me to scrape the mud from my shoes. I pushed open the front door and went in to the hallway. The house was silent, and like all such farmhouses, dark. The tiny windows, set in the thick stone walls, allowed only small rectangles of daylight to cut coloured rugs out of the oriental carpet. Suddenly from the drawing room, through several closed doors, Lohengrin began singing 'In fernem Land'.

Mrs Porter, his ever-cheerful, ever-dependable cook, house-keeper and general factotum, came from the kitchen to say hello and take my coat. Still holding it she went past me to look out of the front door. She sniffed the air with relish, as a submarine commander might savour the night after a long spell submerged. Over her shoulder I saw that one of the forestry men had donned a red helmet and ear covers and was climbing one of the trees. He was getting very wet.

She came back to me. 'Yes, I thought I heard your car,' she said. 'I'm so pleased you are here, Mr Samson. I was worried . . . I still am. He becomes so listless when he is ill.'

'Really?' I said. I didn't find it easy to visualize a listless Uncle Silas.

'He got up and dressed when he heard that you were coming. I phoned the doctor about it but he said it would be all right as long as he stayed indoors, rested and kept warm.'

'That sounds like the doctor,' I said.

She smiled uncertainly. Women like Mrs Porter become alarmed if their faith in medicine comes under attack. 'The doctor said that Mr Gaunt could be taken from us any time,' she said in a voice that seemed intended to remind me of the leading role Silas' physician played in a drama where I was no more than a walk-on. I assumed a suitably sober face and she said, 'He's writing his memoirs. Poor soul! He seems to know his time is coming.'

His memoirs! Political careers would be ended; reputations in shreds. It was unthinkable that Silas would ever get permission to write such a book, but I didn't contradict her.

'He puts it away when I go in there. I'm supposed not to know about it but I guessed when he smuggled the little typewriter downstairs. Before the last bad turn I would hear him tapping away in the music room every day. That's where he is now. Go in, I'll bring you tea.'

The 'music room' was the drawing room into which Silas had installed his hi-fi and his record collection. It was where he sat each evening listening to music. He didn't care much for television. I was reluctant to interrupt his opera but Mrs Porter came up to the door and said, 'Do go in,' and added with an almost soundless whisper which her exaggerated lip movement helped me understand, 'He's probably asleep, it's the pills.'

At Mrs Porter's insistence I barged into the room. I didn't see him at first, for his back was to me as he faced the log fire. He wore a dark shirt and a plum-coloured velvet smoking jacket, complete with cream silk handkerchief flopping from the top pocket. It was the sort of outfit an Edwardian actor might have chosen to go to the Café Royal. A tartan car rug was beside him on the floor. It had fallen from his knees or perhaps he'd pushed it aside when he heard me arrive. His feet – in bright red carpet slippers – were resting amongst the fire irons. The music was loud and there was a smell of wood smoke. As if in response to a draught from the doorway the fire burned bright so that yellow shapes ran across the low ceiling. 'Who's that?' he growled. He wasn't asleep.

People who knew Silas Gaunt well, amongst whom my father was certainly numbered, spoke of his exquisite courtesy, old-world manners and compelling charm. My mother had once described him as a boulevardier: it was the first time I'd ever heard the word used. To hear them speak of Gaunt you would have expected to meet one of those English eccentrics in the mould of Henry Fielding's Squire Allworthy. But the Silas Gaunt I knew was a devious old devil who paradoxically demonstrated the skin of a rhino and the sensitivity of a butterfly, according to his long-term plans.

'I hope I'm not intruding,' I said very quietly.

'I'm listening to *Lohengrin*, damn it!' he said. I was somewhat relieved to find, whatever his corporeal condition, that his bellicose spirit was alive and well. Then as he turned his head to see me, and the fire flickered brighter, he said, 'Oh, it's you, Bernard. I thought it was Mrs Porter again. She keeps pestering me.'

During my childhood Silas had always shown affection for me, but now he was old and he'd withdrawn into his own concerns with ageing, sickness and death. There was less affection in him now. 'She's concerned about you, Silas,' I said.

'She's in league with that damned pill-pusher,' he said. He switched off the record-player in a way that simply lifted the stylus. The record under the transparent lid kept turning.

I found a place to sit. He'd lost a lot of weight. His clothes were loose so that his wrinkled neck craned from his oversized shirt collar. The shadowy room was cluttered with his bric-à-brac, antiquarian curios and mementoes from far places: scarabs, an African carving, a battered toy locomotive, a banderilla, an alpenstock carved with the names of formidable climbs, a tiny ivory Buddha and a broken crucifix. Once

Silas had told me that he didn't want to be buried in the earth. He didn't want to be in a tomb or consecrated ground. He'd like to be put in a museum surrounded by his possessions, just as so many of Egypt's kings were now to be found.

'We're all concerned about you,' I said. It was a somewhat feeble response and he just glared at me.

'That damned doctor wants my grandfather clock,' said Silas.

'Does he?'

'That's all he comes here for. Never takes his eyes off it when he's here. The other day I told him to go and put his bloody stethoscope on its movement since he was so interested in asking me if it kept good time.'

'Perhaps he just wanted to make polite conversation.'

'That marquetry work is what attracts him but he's got central heating. It would dry out and crack in six months in his place.'

'It's a lovely clock, Silas.'

'Eighteenth-century. It was my father's. The front panel has warped a fraction. Some of the inlay work projects just a shade. It has to be polished very carefully by someone who understands. Mrs Porter doesn't let anyone else touch it. She winds it too.'

'You're fortunate to have her looking after you, Silas.'

'That damned quack wants to have it before I die. I know what he's after: a written statement about the clock's condition and history. That sort of provenance affects the price in auction. He told me that.'

'I'm pleased to see you looking so well,' I said.

'His house is filled with clocks. Skeleton clocks, carriage clocks, balloon clocks, clocks riding on elephants, clocks in eagles' bellies. I don't want my lovely clock added to a collection like that. It would be like sending a child to an orphanage, or Mrs Porter to the workhouse. He's a clock maniac. He should go and see a psychologist, there's something wrong with a man who wants to live in a house filled with clocks. I couldn't hear myself speak for all the ding-donging and carry-on.'

There came a light tap at the door. Silas said, 'Come in!' in the jovial booming tone he used for Mrs Porter. But it proved to be one of the young men. 'All ready to go, Mr Gaunt,' he said, his voice enriched with the local accent.

'Very well,' said Silas without turning to see him.

The man looked at him as if expecting some more earnest response. 'We'll go ahead then.'

'I said yes,' said Silas irritably.

The man looked at the back of Silas' head, looked at me, rolled his eyes and then withdrew. I waited to see if Silas would account for the interruption but he just said, 'I've rediscovered Wagner in my old age.'

'That's gratifying.'

After a long pause he said, 'I'm losing the elms. They've got that damned disease.'

'All of them?'

'The ones at the front.' He bit his lip. 'They've always been here: my father loved them. I suppose I shouldn't let myself become upset about those stupid trees but . . .'

'You can put in others,' I said.

'Yes, I'm going to put in six oaks.' He smiled. It was understandable that he identified so closely with the trees that had always framed the house from the drive. There would be more trees, and more people too, but Silas Gaunt would have been felled, fired and forgotten by the time they matured. He brought out a bright red cotton handkerchief, dabbed his eyes and blew his nose. 'Is it too smoky for you? Open the window if it is.'

'I'm fine.'

'Fledermaus went well? You saw Fiona?' Outside there came the sound of the chainsaw being started up. His face stiffened but he pretended not to hear it.

'I saw her,' I said.

'It's clear to you now?'

It was still far from clear but there was little or nothing to be gained from saying so. 'So we're pulling her out?' I said, wanting him to confirm it.

'In due time.'

'It's a miracle she's lasted so long.'

'She's a damned good girl,' said Silas. 'A wonderful woman.'

'And Erich Stinnes is coming too?'

Silas looked at me blankly. He must have been momentarily diverted by the racket of the chainsaw. The sound of it came in longer and longer bursts as they severed larger and larger branches prior to the felling. A tree is like a network of course, and that's how the old wartime training manuals always depicted it. And like a tree, a network is destroyed beginning with a twig. Then a small branch, until it's uprooted and eradicated. 'Stinnes . . .' said Silas. 'Yes, I suppose so. Does Stinnes matter?'

'Matter?' I said. I was as puzzled as he seemed to be.

'Enrolling Stinnes . . . getting him to go back there and work for us was brilliant. It was the master touch,' said Silas. His eyes were bright and alert now. 'If Stinnes eventually comes back intact the Department will break every rule in the book to get a K for Bret Rensselaer.'

I looked at him carefully. So Stinnes *was* working for us. But surely what he really meant was if *Fiona* eventually comes back intact, but he didn't want to be that candid with me. 'Was that Bret's doing?'

'No. But sending Stinnes back was originally Bret's idea. Bret pushed and pushed for it.'

'It was madness,' I said. 'Maybe Stinnes pulled it off; maybe they are playing with him. Who can be sure? Either way sending him back was reckless. It endangered Fiona.'

'Can't you see it, even now?' said Silas. He shook his head at my slowness. 'We didn't care a jot what happened to Erich Stinnes, and we still don't. Stinnes was sent back there for one reason, and for one reason only: to reinforce the story that Fiona was a genuine defector.'

'Not to work alongside Fiona?'

'No, no, no. That was the beauty of it. No one revealed to Stinnes that Fiona went back to work for us; because virtually no one there knows. Every one of our people believes that Fiona's defection was the worst blow the Department ever suffered, and whatever suspicions passed through his mind Stinnes went back believing that too.'

I said, 'Do you mean Stinnes was told to report and defuse what Fiona was supposedly doing to us?' It was beautiful. It had the symmetry that distinguishes art from nature.

Silas smiled contentedly as he watched me thinking about it. 'Yes, "Operation Damage Control", that's what Bret told Stinnes he was. Stinnes was just a means to an end.'

'And so was I,' I said bitterly. 'I've been made a fool of, right from the start.' The revelation that my wife was a heroine, rather than a traitor, should have made me rejoice. In some ways it did, but on a personal level I felt bitter at the way I'd been used. My anger extended to everyone who knew about Fiona's long-term commitment, and had kept it from me. Everyone included Fiona. From outside, the sound of the chainsaw was now continuous. They must have been cutting through the trunk.

'You mustn't look at it like that,' said Silas. He sighed. It wasn't one of the histrionic sighs he'd used in the old days. It was the sigh of a sick old man who finds the effort of living too much for him. 'You played a vital role in what happened. What sense was there in having you worry about the operational side?'

'That's what Fiona said. Was this what you wanted to see me about?' I asked.

'That damned quack says I could go any time.'

I nodded. He looked ill. Mrs Porter wasn't worrying unnecessarily.

'I suppose Mrs Porter told you that. She tells everyone. I can see from the look in their faces when they come in here to talk to me.'

'She's very discreet,' I said to calm his anger.

'What will happen when I go, I've been asking myself. Bret is sick, and anyway Bret doesn't know the whole story. The D-G knows but no one will listen to him because they say he's batty. What do you think about him?'

These were dangerous waters and I navigated away. 'I haven't seen him for a long time,' I said.

'The rumour is that he has Alzheimer's, but my quack says the only way they can confirm Alzheimer's is by means of a post-mortem.' There was a sudden silence and then a soft thud and a muddle of voices as the felled tree hit the wet lawn. The sound of its death saddened me. Silas gave no sign of having heard it but I knew he had. 'Do you know what I think?' He shifted restlessly. A man as big and powerful as Silas was apt to resent infirmity in a way that other men did not. He eyed me to make sure I was giving him my full attention. Then he said, 'The old man's deaf.'

'Yes,' I said. 'Everyone knows that.'

'Even more deaf than he admits,' said Silas. 'They all think he's crazy because he's too damned vain to get himself a modern hearing aid. I think the D-G is as smart as you and I.'

'I'd like to think you are right,' I said, and then tried to get back to the point. 'So you, Bret and the D-G are the only ones who know that Fiona is one of ours?'

'That's exactly right. Even the Vienna team who arranged the meeting for you last week think she was acting for Moscow.'

'I'm relieved to hear it.'

'If all three of us – me, Bret and the D-G – go at once, and that's not beyond the bounds of credibility, you and Fiona will be the only ones who know the true story. Even the case officer processing her report is not really a case officer; he doesn't know where they come from.'

'And so I'd have little chance of convincing anyone that she's one of ours.'

'And Fiona won't dare try.' He gave a little cough to clear his throat. 'Yes, that's the position, Bernard. That's why I sent for you.'

'What do you propose we do?' I said.

'Wait.' I looked at him. His face was white and bloated but ill or not, it still displayed the fierce determination that he'd always shown. 'We can't pull Fiona out until the time is right.'

'Don't wait too long, Silas,' I said. 'Agents get over-confident, we both know that. She'll have to be ordered out. I wanted her to come back with me.'

'And undo everything she's worked for? Bernard your wife is a perfectionist. Surely you must have realized that during your married life with her?'

'No,' I said. All I'd discovered during my married life with Fiona was that, although I'd shared with her just about every idea, thought and emotion I had, she'd guarded her own secrets with a discipline that was no less than obsessional. I felt as if I'd been swindled. Not bilked, burned or ripped off for a short-term loss but systematically deceived for years and years by the person who had vowed to love me and care for me. Fiona Kimber-Hutchinson, do you take this bachelor? Yes, I was taken.

'She wants to stage her own death, so that they won't be alerted to what she's been doing over there. Stage her death and then go to ground somewhere for six months or so. We could continue using her material for ages if they are not alerted to what she's been doing.'

I followed the reasoning but the implications made my head swim. If Fiona was to be hidden away somewhere, would I be there with her? And what reason could Gloria be given for my sudden disappearance; telling her the whole truth would be out of the question. And what about the children?

Silas added, 'She's given us all sorts of wonderful stuff that we haven't used for fear of endangering her. Once she was safe we could really pull all the stops out.'

He might have said more but Mrs Porter came and set out tea for us. She had excelled herself today: homemade sausage rolls and a Kugelhopf; a sweet bread she'd learned to make after discovering that it brought back to Silas happy memories of times long ago.

'I can't eat all that, woman,' said Silas fiercely.

'Don't fuss! Mr Samson will eat it. It's a long drive; he must be hungry.'

Silas reached in his pocket for the keys that were on a ring at the end of a gold chain. He held one key up. 'You see this fellow, Mrs Porter? If anything should happen to me, you take this little item and you give it to Mr Samson. You phone him and tell him to come here, and you give it to him and to no one else. You understand that, don't you, Mrs Porter?'

In a carefree gesture, worthy of a boulevardier, he swung the keys round on the end of the chain before tucking them back into his pocket. Outside the chainsaw noise began again.

'I can't bear to think of such a thing, Mr Gaunt.'

'You'll do as I say now. I can depend upon you, can't I?'

'You know you can, sir.'

'That's good. Now toddle along. I don't want you weeping all over me.'

Mrs Porter arranged the cups and lifted the lid on the vacuum jug to show me it was filled with hot water. Silas grunted to indicate his impatience. She gave me a brave smile, sniffed and withdrew.

'I saw that fellow Dodo in Vienna,' I told Silas casually as I poured tea from the magnificent silver tea pot. There was a date engraved on it. Silas had been given it by his staff when he left Berlin.

'Ah, yes. We had to do something about him,' said Silas vaguely.

'So what happened?'

'They gave him an MBE or something and supplemented his pension.'

'They did what?'

'Don't get excited, Bernard. It was probably the best way of handling it. He was getting to be rather disgruntled and he knows too much for us to let him go around talking his head off. He got the stick and carrot routine.'

'He's a drunk.'

'He's settled down, Bernard. He knows what's good for him.'

'An MBE was the carrot?' Even a cynic like me was appalled.

'No citation, nothing like that. For services rendered to the intelligence community. All very vague. An MBE will disqualify his revelations. That award will make Moscow think we're pleased – that he is acting on our orders.' His compressed lips moved in what might have been a fleeting artful smile to celebrate the cunning of it. 'It doesn't cost anything, Bernard, and it's Fiona's safety we have to think about.'

'Yes.' How very English! When the peasants became troublesome, throw a title to them.

'Give me that big brown packet.' I took it from the table and passed it to him. From it he got a legal document: the curiously ornate sort of thing that – along with wigs and gowns, and the world's most autocratic trade union – English lawyers find indispensable to practising the law. It consisted of about forty pages of typed material bound together with green tape that passed through eyelet holes punched in each sheet.

'Here's a complete description of everything I know concerning Fiona's assignments. Names, dates and so on. It's all here.'

Thinking he was about to give it to me I held out my hand, but he ignored it. 'Have you got a pen that works?' He opened it to the back page and said, 'I want you to witness my signature. The solicitor johnny comes round tomorrow for me to sign and swear in his presence. I want you as a witness too. You don't mind I hope.'

'No,' I said. 'Of course not.'

He signed his name and then showed me where he wanted me to sign, pedantically insisting that my address was written in block capitals in the appropriate space. 'I want to make sure that it is legally valid,' he said. Where it said Occupation, I wrote civil servant. He inspected what I'd done, blew on the ink to help dry it and pronounced it satisfactory.

'Can I read it now?' I asked.

'No need for you to read it, Bernard. This is just for insurance purposes. I have every reason to hope I'll be alive and well when Fiona returns.'

'Of course.'

He heaved himself from his chair and went over to an antique military chest. Using a key on his key chain he locked the document away. He held up the key before putting it back in his pocket. 'Understand, Bernard?'

I nodded. 'She was recruited at Oxford was she?' I asked.

'Let's rather say she was noticed there. It was a cousin of mine – a history professor – who recruited for us. He'd never put forward a female student before. Fiona was to speak at a debate and he suggested that we both went over there to hear her. I'll never forget that evening. She was supporting the motion that Einstein's theory of relativity was a hoax. I wish you'd heard her: it was an impressive performance, Bernard.'

'But Fiona doesn't know anything about mathematics,' I said.

'That's perfectly true, but not many of the audience did either. She was clever enough to exploit that. The other speakers bored everyone with rational argument. When it came to Fiona she was attractive and amusing. She made fun of her opponents and put together a loose but reasoned and coherent argument. She couldn't win of course, everyone knew that – but she demonstrated some fast thinking. She assembled a few well researched facts, a few half-truths and a lot of absolute bosh and cobbled together a convincing whole picture from it all.'

'I thought that's what everyone did at university.'

'You're not far wrong, Bernard. But in Fiona I saw someone who could keep her own mind crystal-clear and far removed from the material she was handling. That is the essence of the work we do, Bernard. Failure in the art of intelligence comes to those who cannot distinguish between what they know to be facts, and what they wish were true.'

'Or will not distinguish,' I said feelingly.

'Precisely. And your wife is a realist, Bernard. No flights of fancy for her, no romanticism, no wishful thinking.'

'No,' I said. 'None at all.'

'She was never recruited. I kept her to myself. It was the way things were done at that time. We all had our own agents: your dad, me, Lange, ran our own people by means of Central Funding's unregistered transfers. The sort of money you hounded Bret Rensselaer about not too long ago: remember?'

'Yes,' I said.

'When Sir Henry became Director-General I told him that Fiona was in deep cover. When she pressed for a chance at this big one I brought Bret in too. We decided to keep it to that. Her name was never written down.'

He relapsed into silence. I poured more tea for myself but he didn't touch his. Staring into the fire, he seemed to be lost in thoughts that he was reluctant to share. 'I miss your dad,' he said finally. 'Your father always had an answer for everything that came along. He hadn't had his brain pickled by bloody university lecturers. I don't think he ever sat an examination in his life.' Silas looked at me; I didn't respond. Silas said, 'Self-educated people such as your father – auto-didacts I hear them called nowadays – don't read in order to find accord with the answers predetermined by half-baked examining boards, they find an individual point of view.' He sat back in his chair. 'My word, Bernard, I've laughed to see your father demolish some of those young lads they sent us. He could quote from such diverse sources as to leave them gasping: Jung, Nietzsche, Suetonius, Saint Paul, Hitler, George Washington, statistics from Speer's confidential records, Schiller and Einstein. It was all at your father's command. I remember him explaining to a scholarly old SS general that his great hero Arminius – who valiantly defeated the Romans in a way that the Britons, Celts and the rest of them had failed to do – deprived Germany of the benefits of civilization, kept her in a state of barbaric chaos so that for centuries they didn't even use stone for building. "You Germans have a couple of centuries of civilization to catch up with," said your father patiently. It was difficult to know how much of it was to be taken seriously.' Silas chuckled. 'We had such good times together, your dad and I.' For a few moments Silas was his old self again, but then, as if coming to terms once more with the fact of my father's death, he relapsed into a solemn silence.

'What happened at Berchtesgaden, Silas? What happened there that seemed to destroy my dad's career?'

'And cast a shadow on my career too,' said Silas. 'Ever wonder why I didn't get my K?'

'No,' I said, but in fact it was a question that I'd heard asked many times.

'How much do you know?'

'A German, a man named Winter, was shot. Dad was blamed. That's all.'

'Two Germans: a prisoner in the direct custody of your dad and the fellow's brother who, technically at least, had a US army commission. It was the American Zone. The war had ended. The men involved were all waiting to go home. They weren't front-line soldiers. They were middle-aged family men, supply clerks, warehouse men, misfits in low medical categories; not used to handling weapons: nervous, drunk, trigger-happy . . . Who knows how it actually happened? Your father was the only Englishman there and he'd ruffled a lot of feathers. The Yanks dumped all the blame on him. Max was sorry afterwards. He told me so more than once.'

'Max?'

'Max Busby. Lange's man.' Seeing my blank look he added, 'The one who was killed when you came over the Wall with him. He had been a captain in the American army. He was in charge of a search party, that night when the Germans were shot. You didn't know that? Max didn't ever tell you?'

It took me a little time to get over my astonishment. 'No, Max never told me that. He was a damned good friend.' It was a mealy-mouthed description of a man who had been shot dead while giving me a chance to get home safe and sound. But I didn't have to say more: Silas knew the story.

'To you he always was. Max liked you, Bernard, of course he did. But I often wondered to what extent he was trying to make up for the injustice he helped to bring upon your dad. It was Max's evidence that convinced the inquiry that your dad accidentally fired the shots. That story suited them. It enabled the soldiers to go back to civilian life almost immediately and it deprived the US newspapers of a story that they were planning to make into headlines. But your father's reputation

402

never recovered from it. They were going to get rid of him to some rotten liaison job but I insisted that he stayed with me.'

'So that's why Dad hated Max,' I said.

'Max: yes, and Lange too. He didn't have much time for any American after that. It was a childish reaction but he felt bitter and frustrated.'

'Didn't he want the inquiry reopened?'

'Of course he did. Your father wanted that verdict quashed more than anything in his life. But the Department couldn't permit the publicity that would have come with it. And the official policy, of both us and the Americans, was to avoid anything that might engender bad feelings between the Allies.' He sat back. The memories had invigorated him for a moment but now their ghosts had invaded the room and he seemed not to know that I was there. I drank some of my lukewarm tea.

When Silas spoke his voice was strained. He said, 'I think I'd better have some of that damned medicine. Mrs Porter knows how much to give me.'

'I'll go now, Silas,' I said finally. 'You must get some rest.'

'Stay to lunch, Bernard.'

'I must get back,' I said.

He didn't put up much argument. Now that his task was done all the energy was sapped from him, he wanted to be left alone.

'I'm sorry about the elms, Silas.'

'The oaks will look fine,' he said.

I declined Mrs Porter's invitations to stay for something to eat. I had the feeling that Silas wanted me to leave the house and go away, rather than have something by myself in the kitchen. Or was that my paranoia? Whatever the truth of it, I wanted to get away and think my thoughts to myself. At the quiet little church, on the narrow road that goes from Whitelands gates to the village, a line of parked cars gave notice of a service in progress. It was a funeral. Perhaps two dozen dark-garbed people were standing around an open grave, huddled under their umbrellas while the priest braved the elements, his vestment whipped by the wind and his face radiant with rain.

Crawling along behind a tractor, I was given a chance to study this solemn little ceremony. It depressed me further, reminding me that soon – very soon – Silas and Whitelands and all they meant would have vanished from my life. My mother was old and sick. Soon Lisl would be gone, and the hotel would be unrecognizable. When that happened I would no longer have any connections with the times that meant so much to me.

Perhaps Silas was right: perhaps a shelf in a museum, with all the rubbish of our lives surrounding us, would be the best end of us all.

Suffering from this somewhat irrational melancholy I stopped at the next little town for a drink. No pubs were open and the only restaurant was full of noisy housewives eating salads. I went into the grocery store and bought a half-bottle of Johnnie Walker and a packet of paper cups.

I drove down the road until I reached the main road and a lay-by where I could pull off the road and park. The rain continued. It was the ideal sort of day and place and time to commit suicide.

As soon as the windscreen wipers were switched off the glass became a confusion of dribbling rain and there was the steady patter of it on the roof. I reached for the bottle, but before I took a drink from it I relaxed back upon the head-rest and must have gone straight to sleep. I'd known such instant sleep before, but always until now it had accompanied danger or great stress.

I don't know how long I slept. I was awakened by the sound of a car pulling up alongside me. There was the buzz and slap of windscreen wipers and the resonant babble of a two-way radio. I opened my eyes. It was a police car. The uniformed cop lowered his window and I did the same.

'Are you all right, sir?' The suspicious look on his weathered face belied the courtesy of his address. I pushed the whisky bottle down between the seats but I couldn't get it completely out of sight.

'Yes, I'm all right.'

'Mechanical trouble of any kind? Shall I call the breakdown service?' The rain continued, the cop didn't get out of his car.

'I just thought I'd look at the map.'

'Very well, sir, if you're fit and well, and able to drive.' They pulled away.

When the police car was out of sight I got out of the car and stood in the rain. It refreshed me. Soon I felt better. I got back into the car and switched on the heater and the radio. It was tuned to the Third Programme: Brendel playing Schubert. I listened. After a few minutes I tossed the unopened whisky into the ditch.

I wondered if the policemen had been told to keep an eye on me but decided it was unlikely. Yet even the doubt was a measure of my distress; in the old days I would never have given it a moment's thought. Perhaps there was something wrong with me. Maybe all these people who kept telling me I looked ill were right.

I thought about everything Silas had said. I was particularly disturbed by the idea of Fiona going to ground, so that the KGB would not realize that she had been working for us all the time. It would be difficult to arrange such a deception.

There was another way for the Department to achieve the same objective; by killing Fiona while she was still working over there. It would be simple enough to arrange, there were plenty of Thurkettles around, and it would be complete and effective. Even if the KGB detected the hand of the Department in such a killing, that would only 'prove' that Fiona's defection was genuine. Expedient demise. Such a ruthless solution would be unthinkable and unprecedented but Fiona's unique position was just as unthinkable and just as unprecedented.

16

I didn't go in to the office that day. As I drove back from Silas Gaunt's farm the weather got worse until, near London, I found myself driving through a spectacular electrical storm that lit the sky with blue flashes, made the car radio erupt static noises and provided long drumrolls of thunder. I went straight home. It was early evening. The house was cold, empty and dark, a chastening reminder of what it would be like to live alone. The children were eating with friends. I lit the gas fire and sat down in the armchair and watched the flame changing colour until the whole grid was red. I dozed off.

I was wakened by Gloria's arrival. She switched on the light and, although she must have noticed the car outside, she raised a hand and gave a little start of surprise at seeing me sitting there. It was a very feminine action, contrived perhaps, but by some magic she could get away with such childish posturing. She was very wet. I suppose I should have gone to the station and collected her but she didn't complain. 'There's only frozen *Székelygulyás*,' she said as she took off her soaking wet raincoat and got a towel to dry her hair.

'Only frozen *Székelygulyás*,' I said reflectively. 'What a colourful life we live.'

'I didn't get to the shops,' said Gloria. I heard the warning note in her voice.

'We can go to Alfonso's or the little Chinese place,' I offered.

'What has made you growly tonight, teddy bear?'

'I'm not growly,' I said and managed a convincing smile to prove it.

'A soft-boiled egg will do me,' she said.

'Me too,' I agreed.

She was standing in front of the mirror combing her wet hair. She looked at me and said, 'You say that, Bernard, but when I give you just an egg you always end up at bedtime rummaging through the larder and opening tins or having Shredded Wheat.'

'Let's have the frozen *Székelygulyás*,' I said, having suddenly remembered that it wasn't some new packaged line from the supermarket; it was her mother's Hungarian home cooking. Criticizing such a meal could lead to a tangle in the psyche that only a Freudian gourmet could hope to unravel. 'It's my very favourite! Is that the chicken in sour cream?'

'It's pork with pickled cabbage,' she said angrily, but when I pulled a face at her she grinned. 'You are a bastard! You really are.'

'I knew it was pork and cabbage,' I said.

'Or there's the new fish and chip shop, the one we haven't tried.'

'What kind of wine goes with *Székelygulyás*?'

'You hate Hungarian food.'

'No I don't.'

'You said the caraway seeds got in your teeth.'

'That was my other teeth.'

She knelt down beside my chair and put her arms round me. 'Please try, Bernard. Please try and really love me. I can make you happy, I know I can, but you must try too.'

'I really love you, Gloria,' I said.

'Is Silas very ill?'

'I'm not sure,' I said. 'One moment he seems on the point of collapse and the next moment he's shouting and laying down the law.'

'I know he means a lot to you.'

'He's old,' I said. 'We all have to go sooner or later. He's had a good innings.'

'Is it something I've done then?'

'No, darling. You're perfect. I give you my word on that.' I meant it.

'It's this house isn't it? You've hated this house ever since we moved here. Is it the journey? Your other house was so central.'

She kissed my ear. I held her. 'The house is fine. It's just that I'm trying to work out a few problems at work. You'll have to make allowances for the growly factor.'

'Dicky Cruyer, you mean?'

'No. Dicky is the least of my worries. Without me to do ninety per cent of his work, he'd probably be shifted off somewhere where he could do less damage.'

'But?'

'A lot of people would like to see Dicky booted out of the German Desk. Deputy Europe for instance. He detests Dicky. If getting rid of me meant getting rid of Dicky too, Gus Stowe would do it and throw a party to celebrate.'

Gloria laughed. The idea of a celebratory party given by Gus Stowe was not easy to imagine. 'Let me put the food into the microwave,' she said. The way she chose to say let me, instead of using some more assertive syntax, was the essence of our relationship. Despite what others may think, my love for her was not of any paternal sort: but what was the nature of her love for me? 'And I'll bring you a glass of wine.'

'I'll get it.'

'You sit there and take it easy. When dinner is ready, I'll tell you the latest about Dicky. It will make your eyes pop.'

'Nothing Dicky could do would surprise me,' I said.

She brought me a glass of chilled wine. There was no scotch. No gin, vodka or anything else. We'd run out of such stuff and she'd never bought more. She wanted to rescue me from hard booze. I sat back and drank the wine and took it easy while listening to the electronic squeaks of the timer on the microwave. The oven was her newest toy. I'd overheard her talking to the cleaning lady about it. She'd boasted of cooking delicious braised liver in it, although in fact the liver had exploded and covered the inside of the oven with a garlicky film of pulverized goo. She'd ended up in tears.

But now I could hear her singing quietly to herself and I knew I'd done the right thing in choosing her mother's Hungarian cooking, prepared by Gloria in her new machine. It gave her a chance to play at housekeeping. The particular pleasure she got from it was demonstrated by the elaborate way she'd arranged on the table our tête-à-tête meal. There were candles and even a long-stemmed rose, albeit an artificial one.

'How wonderful you are,' I said when I was permitted into the kitchen to eat.

'I've forgotten the pepper mill,' she said, reaching for it hurriedly. There was a nervousness in her voice, an anxiety, so that sometimes her earnest desire to please me made me uneasy. It made me feel like a tyrant.

'Tell me your news about Dicky.'

'I don't know how Daphne puts up with him,' said Gloria. She liked to begin with a preamble that set the mood. 'Daphne is such a clever woman. You know she's painting leather jackets?'

'Painting leather jackets? Daphne?'

'She's an artist, Bernard.'

'I know she went to art school.'

'Same thing.'

'On leather jackets?'

'Dragons and psychedelic nudes. You haven't seen them? I know you'd love to have one, darling.'

'Having a psychedelic nude, even on a leather jacket, might prove a bit too much for me these days.'

'They take hours.'

'I would imagine.'

'Stop it!'

'What?'

'I'm serious. Daphne works very hard and Dicky doesn't understand her.'

'Did he tell you that?'

'Of course not. I wish you'd listen instead of trying to be so smart.'

'I like this pork and cabbage. A bit too much salt but it's very good.'

'Last time you said it was tasteless. I put the extra salt in.'

'It's delicious. So what about Dicky?'

'He's going to Berlin on Friday. He's booked a suite at Kempinski's; he's taking a girl with him. Poor Daphne. If she ever finds out . . .'

'What girl? Someone from the office?'

'I don't know,' she said.

'Where did you hear these rumours?'

'They are not just rumours. He's got the suite booked.'

'Did Dicky's secretary tell you?'

Gloria took a moment to swallow her cabbage and then drank some wine too. It gave her time to consider her reply. 'No, of course not.'

'She has no right to be gossiping about such things.'

'You wouldn't tell Dicky?'

'No,' I said, 'of course not. But it's stupid of her to gossip like that.'

'Don't be stuffy, teddy bear,' she said pouring more wine.

'Suppose there was no woman,' I said. 'Suppose Dicky was waiting for an agent coming through the wire? Suppose that agent's safety depended upon everyone keeping their mouth shut.'

'Yes.' She thought about it and said, 'Suppose it *was* a woman; suppose it was your wife?'

'Impossible,' I said.

'Why impossible?'

'Because Fiona is one of theirs! Damn you, I wish you'd get that simple fact into your thick blonde Hungarian head!' I saw the sudden alarm in her face and only then realized that I was shouting and banging on the table.

She said nothing. I could have bitten my tongue off as soon as I'd said it. But once it was said, there was no way ever to unsay such a stupid gratuitous insult.

'I'm sorry, Gloria. Forgive me, please. I didn't mean it.'

She was crying now, the tears running down her flushed cheeks as if they'd never stop. But she managed a hint of a smile and said, 'You did mean it, Bernard. And there's nothing I can do to make you see me any other way.'

409

'Let's go and sit in the other room,' I suggested. I poured the last of the wine.

'No. It's almost time for me to go and collect the children, and I must throw some clothes into the spin-drier before I go.'

'Let me collect them,' I said.

'You don't know where it is, Bernard. It's all ill-lit one-way streets: you'll get lost.'

She was right. She usually is.

17

It was easy to know when Dicky was having a new love affair. I suppose it is easy for the casual observer to know when any husband is having a new love affair. There was that tiger look in his eye, that stiffened sinew and summoned-up blood that Shakespeare associated with Mars rather than Venus. His detailed evaluation of expensive restaurants had become even more rigorous. The plats du jour of some of the favoured ones were sent to him each morning on the fax. And there were jokes.

'Ye Gods, Bernard! As far as ethnic food goes – the less authentic the better!' He looked at the fingernail he'd been biting and gave it another brief nibble.

He'd been striding around his office, pausing sometimes to look out of the window. He was jacketless, with his waistcoat unbuttoned, a dark blue shirt and a white silk bow tie. His shoes were black patent leather of a design that simulated alligator hide.

Dicky had mentioned his planned weekend in Berlin several times. He said he was 'mixing business with pleasure' but then immediately changed the topic of conversation by asking me if it would be a good idea if Pinky came to work here in London. I found the idea appalling but I didn't say so. Answering that sort of question in London Central was fraught with dangers. Almost everyone here was related to, or at school with, someone else in the building. It could easily turn out that Pinky was Dicky's distant cousin or shared nannies with the D-G's son-in-law, or some such connection. 'Fiona said she couldn't spell,' I told him.

'Spell!' said Dicky, and gave one of those little hoots of laughter that indicated how ingenuous I was. 'Even I can't spell properly,' he said, as if that clinched the matter for all time.

I felt like saying, well, you can't bloody well do anything properly, but I just smiled and inquired whether Pinky was asking for a transfer.

'Not officially, but she was at school with your sister-in-law.' A tiny smile. 'It was Tessa who mentioned it to me, actually.' When I didn't react Dicky added, 'At my dinner party.'

'It's a small world,' I said.

'It is,' said Dicky. There was an audible sigh of relief in his voice as if he'd been trying to make me admit to that fact all the morning. 'And strictly between the two of us, Tessa is also going to be in Berlin next weekend.'

'Is she?'

'Yes,' he ran a fingertip around his mouth as if showing me where it was. 'As a matter of fact, she . . .' He looked at his watch. 'Look here, can you hang on for a cup of coffee?'

'Yes, thanks.' I'd enjoyed many cups of coffee with Dicky in his office but that didn't mean that the Kaffeeklatsch was part of his everyday routine. Dicky usually cloistered himself away from the hurly-burly to have his coffee. It was, he said, a time for him to wrestle with his thoughts, to struggle with difficult ideas, a time to confront his innermost self. Invitations to join him in his spiritual mêlée were not extended lightly or without thought of recoupment. I can truly say that most of the worst experiences of my life sprang from some notion, order, favour or plan that I first encountered over a cup of Dicky's wonderful coffee.

With coffee Dicky smoked a cheroot. It was a bad habit, smoking – a poison really – he was trying to cut himself down to three a day. I suppose that's why he didn't offer one to me.

'The fact is . . .' started Dicky, sitting back in his swing-chair, coffee in one hand and cigar in the other, 'that is to say, an important detail of next week's trip is that I need your help and cooperation.'

'Oh, yes?' I said. This was an entirely new line for Dicky, who had always denied his need for anyone's help or cooperation.

'You know how much I depend upon you, Bernard.' He swivelled an inch or two from side to side but didn't spill his coffee. 'Always could: always can.'

I found myself looking for the fire escape. 'No,' I said, 'I didn't realize that.'

Delicately Dicky placed his cigar in the cut-glass ashtray and used his free hand to tug at one end of his bow tie so that it came unknotted. On the wall behind him there was a framed colour photo of Dicky and the D-G in Calcutta. They were standing at a stall offering a huge array of crude portrait posters. Lithographs of famous people from the Ayatollah and all the Marxes to Jesus Christ and Laurel and Hardy surrounded Dicky and his boss. They were all looking straight ahead: except Dicky. He was looking at the D-G.

'I don't want to hurt Daphne,' said Dicky, as if suddenly deciding upon a new approach. 'You understand . . .'

He left it there and looked at me. By now I was beginning to guess what was coming, but I wasn't going to make it easy for him. And I wanted time to think. 'What is it, Dicky?' I said, sipping my coffee and pretending not to be giving him my whole attention.

'Man to man, Bernard, old sport. You see what I mean?'

'You want me to go instead?'

'For God's sake, Bernard. You can be dense at times.' He puffed at his cigar. 'No, I'm taking Tessa.' A pause. 'I've promised and I'll have to go through with it.' He added this rider woefully as if a call of duty prevailed over his personal wishes. But then he fixed his eye on me, and, with a quick glance towards the door to be sure he wasn't overheard, he said, 'For the weekend!' He said it fiercely, through almost gritted teeth, as if my failure to understand was about to cause him to run amok.

'We all go? Gloria too?'

He shot to his feet as if scalded and came round to where I was sitting. 'No, Bernard; no, Bernard; no, Bernard. No!'

'What then?'

'You come along. You stay at Tante Lisl's but for all practical purposes you are in the hotel suite with Tessa.'

'For all *practical* purposes? Surely for all *practical* purposes *you* will be there with Tessa.'

'I'm not in the mood for your bloody comedy,' he barked. But then, remembering that I was designated to fulfil an indispensable role in his curious scenario, he became calm and friendly again. 'You check into the hotel. Okay?' He was standing by the lion's skin rug and now he gave the head of it an affectionate little kick with the toe of his shiny patent leather shoe. He'd always been an animal lover.

I said, 'If it's just the propriety of it, why don't you check in under an assumed name?'

He became huffy. 'Because I don't care to do that,' he said.

'Or get Werner to let you have a room at Lisl's?'

I watched his face with interest. I don't think even Lisl herself would put the hotel high on a list of Berlin accommodation suitable for a lovers' tryst.

'Jesus Christ! Are you mad?' I saw then that he was nervous. He was frightened that the desk clerk at some big hotel would challenge him in some way and he'd be revealed not just as an adulterer but as a bungling adulterer. Certainly Tessa in such a situation would not make it easy for him. She'd revel in it and make the most of it. 'Lisl's,' he said. 'What a thought.'

He chewed a nail. I suppose I shouldn't have been surprised at this aspect of Dicky. I'd discovered long ago that womanizers like him are often uneasy and incapable when faced with the minor logistics of such adventures: hotel bookings, plane tickets, car rentals. The sort of man who will boast of his doings to all comers at his club will go to absurd lengths in attempts to deceive the concierge, the waiters or the room maid. Perhaps that's why they do it.

'Well,' I said. 'You won't . . .'

He cut me short. He wasn't going to let me give him a negative reply. Dicky was a grandmaster at squeezing the right sort of replies from people. Now would come the softening up: a barrage of incontrovertible platitudes. 'Your sister-in-law is one of the most remarkable women I've ever met, Bernard. Glorious!'

'Yes,' I said.

He poured more coffee for me without asking if I wanted it. Cream too. 'And your wife of course,' he added. 'Two truly extraordinary women: brainy, beautiful and with compelling charm.'

'Yes,' I said.

'Fiona took the wrong road of course. But that can happen to anyone.' By Dicky's standards this was an astonishingly indulgent attitude to human frailty. Perhaps he saw that in my face, for he immediately added, 'Or almost anyone.'

'Yes, almost anyone.'

'Daphne is astonishing too,' said Dicky, delivering this accolade with distinctly less emphasis. 'Creative, artistic.'

'And hard-working,' I said.

He was less sure of that. 'Well, yes, I suppose she is.'

'Daphne was in good form the other night,' I said. 'Did I thank you for dinner?'

'Gloria wrote.'

'Oh, good.'

'I only wish I could give Daphne the sort of support and encouragement she needs,' said Dicky. 'But she lives on a mountain top.' He looked at me. I nodded. He said, 'Artists are all like that: creative people. They live in harmony with nature. But it's not so easy for those around them.'

'Oh, really? What form does this take? In Daphne's case, I mean?'

'She's only truly happy when she's painting. She told me that. She has to have time to herself. She spends hours up in her studio. I encourage her, of course. It's the least I can do for her.'

'You won't find Tessa needs any time to herself,' I said.

He smiled nervously. 'No. Tessa is like me: very much a social animal.'

'May I ask why you are going to Berlin?'

'Why *we* are going,' Dicky corrected me. 'You'll have to come along, Bernard. No matter what reservations you may nurture about my peccadilloes . . . No, no.' He raised a hand as if warding off my interjections but in fact I had not moved. 'No, I understand your reservations. Far be it from me to persuade any man to do something against his conscience. You know how I feel about that kind of thing.'

'I didn't say it was against my conscience.'

'Ahh!'

'It's not against my conscience, it's against the German legal code. The old German law, that made incest a crime, still applies in the case of a man committing adultery with his sister-in-law.'

'I've never heard of that,' said Dicky, suspecting, rightly, that I was inventing this historic clause on the spur of the moment. 'Are you sure?'

I turned slightly towards the phone on his table and said, 'I can get someone in the legal department to look it up for you.'

'No,' said Dicky. 'Don't do that for the moment. I might go downstairs and look it up myself.'

I said, 'You didn't explain why I had to go.'

'To Berlin? It has been ordained that you, me and Frank Harrington have a pow-wow in Big B to go through some damned stuff the Americans want.'

'Can't it wait?'

'Written instructions from the D-G himself. No way to wriggle out of that one, Gunga Din.'

'And you're taking Tessa?'

'Yes. She has these bonus tickets that airlines give to first-class passengers who fly a great deal. She has to use up the free mileage.'

'So you don't have to pay Tessa's fare?'

'It was too good an opportunity to turn away.'

'I suppose it was.'

'I should have married someone like Tessa, I suppose,' said Dicky.

I noticed it wasn't Tessa's unique attractions he wanted but only someone in her category. Whether this left Daphne wanting in brains, wealth, beauty, chic, charm or sexual performance was left unspecified. 'Tessa is already married,' I said.

'Don't be so priggish, Bernard. Tessa is a grown-up woman. She's sensible enough to decide these things for herself.'

'When is this meeting?'

'Frank is being difficult about precise times. We have to fit in around his golf and bridge and his jaunts with his army cronies.'

'You've booked the hotel?'

'They get so full at this time of year,' said Dicky.

I heard a defensive tone in his voice. On a hunch I said, 'Have you booked it in my name?'

'Yes . . .' Momentarily he was flustered, but he recovered quickly. 'I told the hotel that we are not yet sure who will be using the suite. They think we are a company.'

I was damned angry but Dicky had played his cards with customary finesse. I couldn't see anything specific that I could complain about that Dicky wouldn't be able to explain away. 'When do we leave?'

'Friday. Tessa insists on going to some bloody opera that's only on that night. Pinky is arranging the tickets. I'm hoping for a preliminary meeting with Frank and his people on Friday afternoon. We should be through by Monday evening. Tuesday evening at the latest.'

There goes my weekend with Gloria and the children. Dicky saw my face and said, 'You'll have days off to make up for the loss of the weekend.'

'Yes, of course,' I said, although it wasn't much fun to be monitoring the weeds in the garden, and fixing my own lunch, while the children were at school and Gloria was slaving in the office.

'You're getting to be very surly lately,' Dicky observed while he was pouring the last of the coffee for himself. 'Don't fly off the handle: I'm just telling you that for your own good.'

'You're very considerate, Dicky.'

'I can't understand you,' Dicky persisted. 'You've got that gorgeous creature doting on you and still you go around with a long face. What's the problem? Tell me, Bernard, what is the problem?' Although the words were arranged like questions, Dicky made it quite clear from his tone and delivery that he didn't want an answer.

I nodded. It was best to nod with Dicky. Like the Japanese he framed his questions in the expectation of affirmative responses.

'Brooding won't bring Fiona back. You must pull yourself together, Bernard.' He gave me a 'chins up' smile.

I felt like telling Dicky exactly what I thought about him and his plan to implement me in the cuckolding of George but he wouldn't have understood the reasons for my anger. I nodded and left.

At the end of the working day I drove homeward with Gloria but we didn't go directly to number thirteen Balaklava Road. She said she wanted to collect some clothes from her parents' home. The actual reason for the visit was that she'd promised to look in and see the house

416

was safe while they were away on holiday. They lived in a smart, burglar-afflicted suburb near Epsom, a few stations beyond us on the Southern Railway's commuter routes.

The Kents – her parents had changed their name after escaping from Hungary – lived in a four-bedroom double-glazed neo-Tudor house with a gravel 'in and out' front drive on which their two cars could be parked and still leave room enough for the tanker that delivered their heating oil.

This evening the front drive was empty, the cars locked away. Her parents were spending ten days at their holiday villa in Spain. Gloria went through an elaborate routine of unlocking doors and switching off burglar alarms within the prescribed sixty seconds. Then we went inside.

The house smelled of a syrupy perfume resembling violets. Gloria said their cleaning woman was coming in every morning and systematically 'shampooing' the carpets. 'I'll make you a cup of coffee,' she suggested. I agreed. It was interesting to watch her in her parents' home. She became a different person: not a more diffident or childlike one, but vicariously proprietorial, as if she were a real estate clerk showing the house to a prospective purchaser.

We sat in the kitchen. It was a designer kitchen: Marie-Antoinette at her most rustic. We sat on uncomfortable stools at a plastic Louis Seize counter and watched the coffee dripping through the machine. The overhead light – bleak and blue – came from two long fluorescent tubes which buzzed.

It gave me a chance to look at her. All day she'd been her usual warm and good-natured self. It was almost as if she'd forgotten yesterday's clash. But she hadn't. She didn't forget anything. How beautiful she was, with all that energy and radiance that is the prerogative of youth. No wonder people such as Dicky envied me. Had they realized that Fiona would soon be returning perhaps they would have envied me even more. But for me it was a miserable dilemma. I couldn't look at Gloria without wondering if I was going to be able to handle the personal crisis that Fiona's return would bring. The idea of Fiona being kept in deep cover for six months made it even more irresolvable. And what about the children?

'I don't think you've been listening to a word of what I've said,' I suddenly heard Gloria say.

'Of course I have,' and with an inspired evasion tactic I added, 'Did I tell you who Dicky is going to Berlin with?'

'No.' Her eyes were wide open. She swung her blonde hair back and held it as she leaned very close so that I was conscious of the warmth of her body. She was wearing a crimson shirt dress. On most women it would have looked awful but she brought a dash to such cheap bright clothes, just as small children so often do.

'Tessa,' I said.

'Your Tessa?'

'My sister-in-law. Yes.'

'So Tessa is up to her old tricks. I thought the affair with Dicky was over long ago.'

'Yes. That's been puzzling me too.'

'It's hardly a puzzle, darling. People like Dicky, and Tessa too, are capricious.'

'But Dicky was warned off last time.'

'Warned off seeing Tessa? By Daphne, you mean?'

'No. The Department didn't like it. Clandestine meetings with the sister of a defector looked like a potential security risk.'

'I'm surprised Dicky took any notice.'

'You shouldn't be. Dicky may wear funny bow ties and play the Bohemian student, but he knows exactly how far to go. When the bugle sounds and the medals are being awarded he toes the line and salutes.'

'Except when it comes to Tessa you mean. Perhaps it's love.'

'Not Dicky.'

'So perhaps he's had official permission to bed Tessa,' she joked.

'That's what it must be,' I agreed, and not long afterwards I was to reflect upon her joke. 'Perhaps what Dicky found irresistible was not having to pay her fare.'

'What a swine he is. Poor Daphne.' She poured the coffee and, in a dented biscuit tin, discovered a secret supply of chocolate biscuits.

'And he's booked his hotel in my name. What about that?'

She took it very calmly. 'Why?'

'I suppose he's going to tell Daphne some story about me going off with Tessa.'

'But you're not going?'

'I'm afraid I am.'

'The weekend?' I nodded. She said, 'I told the Pomeroys to come to dinner on Saturday.'

'Who the hell are the Pomeroys?'

'The parents of Billy's friends. The children were eating with them last night. They are terribly kind.'

'You'll have to put them off,' I said.

'I've put them off twice before when you went on trips.'

'It's an order from the D-G. You know what that means. There's no way I can get out of it.'

'The weekend?'

'I go on Friday morning; back on Monday or Tuesday. Dicky's secretary will know what's happening over there.'

'And on Sunday there's Billy's car club meeting. I said you'd take him.'

'Look! It's not my idea, darling.'

For a long time she drank her coffee without speaking. Then she said, 'I know it's not,' as if responding to some other question that only she knew about. 'But you said there was going to be a party at Werner's hotel. I know you wanted to go.'

'It's just to promote the hotel. We'll go some other time. They are always having parties, and anyway it would be no fun without you.'

After the coffee I went with her to the room she had when living here with her parents. They kept it for her as if they were expecting her every night. Toys, teddy bear, dolls, children's books, school books, a Beatles poster on the wall. The bed had been made up with freshly laundered linen. Taking her away from them was my doing and there were times when I felt bad about it. And I hadn't even married her. How would I feel if some time my daughter Sally disappeared with some middle-aged married man? Sometimes I wondered how I would be able to deal with the inevitable separation from the children. Would I find myself keeping their bedrooms as shrines at which I could pray for a return of their childhood days with me?

Looking out from the bedroom window I could see the flat roof of a large single-story building that had been added to the house. Seeing me looking at it, Gloria said, 'I cried when they ruined my view of the garden. There was a lovely chestnut tree there and a rhododendron.'

'Why did you need extra space?'

'It's a surgery and workshop for Daddy.'

'I thought he had a surgery in town.'

'This is for special jobs. Didn't you know?'

'Why would I know?'

'Want to see? It's where he does work for the Department.'

'What kind of work?'

'Come and see.'

She got the big bunch of keys that her father had left with her and we went down into the neat little dental surgery. She opened the door, and while she searched for the light switches the room was only lit from a glass box in the corner where tropical flowers appeared under

419

ultraviolet lights. When she switched on the light, apart from seeming unusually cramped with apparatus, it was like any other dentist's workplace: a modern fully adjustable chair and elaborate drill facing a large window. There was a big ceramic spittoon, a swivelling cold-light and many glass-fronted instrument cabinets, packed with rows and rows of curiously shaped drills, forceps, scalers and other spiky implements.

Gloria went round the room naming the equipment and describing what it was for. She seemed to know a lot about dentistry despite having resisted her father's wish that she should become one. This she said was her father's secret sanctum.

'Who comes here for treatment?' I asked.

'Not so many nowadays, but I can remember a time when Daddy worked more hours here than at his proper surgery. I remember one poor Polish boy who was in the chair for at least six hours. He was so exhausted that Daddy let him come and sit in the drawing room with Mummy and me, to take his mind off things.'

'Agents?'

'Yes, of course. At university, Daddy wrote a thesis on the history of European dentistry. After that he began his collection of old dental tools. Now he can look into anyone's mouth and know where they had their teeth fixed, and when. Look at that.' She held up a particularly barbarous-looking instrument. 'It's very old . . . from Russia.'

'I was lucky,' I said. 'My teeth were always fixed by a Berlin dentist and my cover story was always German. I didn't have to have any of my dental work changed.'

'I've known my father to completely eliminate all previous dentistry to give an agent a completely new mouth: Russian, Polish, Greek . . . Once he did old-fashioned Spanish dental work for a man who was going to be using the identity of a Civil War veteran.

'Come and look at the workshop.' She unlocked the door of an adjoining room and we went inside. This was even more cramped, with filing cabinets and racks of tools and equipment. There was a tiny lathe, a bench drill and even a small electric kiln. On a large table near the window there was the work in progress. A desk light was centred upon something concealed under a cloth. Gloria removed the cotton dust-cloth and gave a little shriek as a human skull was revealed. 'Alas, poor Yorick! We mustn't touch it. It's probably a demonstration piece that will be photographed for a textbook. He does replicas of old dentistry and sends them as examples to police pathologists and coroner's departments all over the world. This one must be a special job, from the way he's covered it over so carefully.'

I went closer to look at the skull. It was shiny, like plastic, and there were gold inlays and porcelain crowns fitted into it. 'Did you never want to be a dentist?'

'Never. And Daddy was always so considerate that he never really pressed the idea on to me. It was only recently that I realized how much he'd always hoped I'd become interested in his practice, and his collection. Sometimes he had students work with him. Once I remember he brought a young newly qualified dentist home for dinner. I've often wondered if he was hoping that a romance would blossom.'

'Let's lock up and go home,' I said. 'Shall we take some fish and chips back for everyone?'

'Do let's.'

'I'm sorry if I've been a bit bad-tempered lately, darling.'

'I haven't noticed any difference,' she said.

18

Afterwards I looked back and saw that weekend in Berlin as the beginning of the end, but I don't know how much of that view was hindsight. At the time, it seemed unusual simply because of the hectic way in which meeting followed meeting and the way Frank Harrington – always something of a mother hen – became so flustered that he was phoning me in the middle of the night, and then admitting that he'd forgotten what he was calling about.

Not that any of the meetings decided anything very much. They were typically casual Berlin Field Unit conferences at which Frank presided in his inimitably avuncular style and smoked his foul-smelling pipe and indulged in long rambling asides about me or my father or the old days or all three together.

It was on Sunday morning that Frank first gave me an inkling of what was happening. Dicky was not there. He had left a message to say he was showing Tessa 'round the town', although what Dicky knew about Berlin could be written on the head of a pin and still leave plenty of room for the Lord's Prayer.

It was just me and Frank. We were in his study in the big house at Grunewald. He had a secretary there and some of the top secret material was filed there. It gave Frank an excuse for a day at home now and again. That incredible and unforgettable study! Although I could not identify any single object as having its origins in the sub-continent, this room could have been the Punjab bungalow of some pukka regimental officer, some hero of the Mutiny just back from hunting the nimble blackbuck with cheetahs. Shuttered against the daylight, the dim lamps revealed a fine military chest with magnificent brass fittings, the mounted horns of some unidentified species of antelope, a big leather-buttoned sofa and rattan furniture; all of it bleached, creaky or worn, as such things become in the tropics. Even the sepia portrait of the sovereign seemed to have been selected for her resemblance to the young Victoria. The room expressed all Frank's secret longings, and like most people's secret longings they had no basis in reality.

Even Frank was at his most regimental, with a khaki safari shirt, slacks and plain brown tie. He'd been tapping the map with his fountain pen and asking me questions of a sort that usually were the concern of other technical grades. 'What do you know about the East Berlin Autobahn entrances?' he said.

He indicated the wall upon which two large maps had been fixed. They were a new addition and rather spoiled the 'great days of the Raj' décor. One was a map of east Germany, or the German Democratic Republic, the rather Orwellian name its rulers prefer. Like an island in this communist sea, our Sectors of Berlin were bridged to the West by three long Autobahnen. Used by motorists of both East and West, these highways were a favoured place for clandestine meetings. Smugglers, spies, journalists and lovers all arranged brief and dangerous rendez-vous at the roadside. And consequently the DDR made sure the roads were policed constantly night and day.

The second map – the one Frank was tapping upon – was a Berlin street map. The whole city, not just the West. It was remarkably up to date, for I immediately noticed the projected changes to the Autobahn entrances, including the yet to be built turn-off which would – some time in the dim and distant future – provide the West with a new control point on the south side of the city. Rumours said the East Germans wanted the West to pay a great deal of money for it. That was the usual way that anything got done.

'I don't use them,' I said. 'I always fly nowadays.'

'Pity.' He looked at the street map and with his pen showed me the old Berliner Ring and the route that East Berliners took when joining the Autobahn from their side of the city.

'There was a general directive about us using the Autobahn,' I reminded him gently. There was a fear that departmental employees, with heads full of secrets, might be kidnapped on the Autobahnen. It was not a groundless fear. There was a whole filing case full of unsolved mysteries: motorists who started out on the long drive to the Federal Republic and were never seen again. There was no way for the West's authorities to investigate such mysteries. We had to grin and bear it. Meanwhile, those who could fly, flew.

'I want you to drive back down the Autobahn this time,' said Frank.

'When?'

'I'm waiting to hear.' His pipe stem was tapped against his nose in what I suppose was a gesture of confidentiality. 'Someone is coming out.'

'Through Charlie?' That would mean a non-German.

'No. You'll pick them up on the Autobahn,' said Frank. I waited for some explanation or expansion but he gave neither. He continued to look at the street map and then said, 'Ever heard of a man named Thurkettle? American.'

'Yes,' I said.

'You have?' Unless Frank had been attending drama lessons since our previous meeting, he was completely taken aback by this revelation. Clearly he'd not heard about my escapade in Salzburg. 'Tell me about him.'

I briefly told Frank about Thurkettle without going into detail about my task in Salzburg.

'He's here,' said Frank.

'Thurkettle?' It was my turn to be surprised.

'Arrived by air last night. I told London but I got only an "acknowledgement and no further action" signal. I'm wondering if London knows all this you've just told me.'

'Yes, they do,' I said.

Frank frowned. 'We both know how signals get spiked and forgotten,' he said. 'They should at least let me tell the Americans and the police.'

'You can tell them off the record,' I said.

'That might bounce and get me into hot water.' Frank was something of an expert at finding reasons for inaction. 'If Thurkettle has come here on some secret mission for the Yanks, and London has been informed in the usual way, well! . . .' He shrugged. 'They might be displeased to find I've told all and sundry.'

'On the other hand,' I said, 'if Thurkettle has come to town to blow away one of the CIA's golden boys, they might feel that one routine signal to London was an under-reaction.'

'It was a confidential,' said Frank. 'My informant was someone who I can absolutely not name. If London, or the CIA office, demand details of the identification I will find myself having one of those wretched arguments that I hate so much.' He looked at me and I nodded. 'What do you think this fellow's here for, Bernard?'

'No one seems to be sure who Thurkettle works for. The prevailing wisdom – if Joe Brody is anyone to go by – is that he's a hit man who works for anyone, that is to say anyone who comes up with the right target for the right price. Brody says the KGB have used him over the past two years. If Thurkettle was on his way to see our friends in Normannenstrasse, he'd fly into Schönefeld.'

'You mean he's targeting someone here in the West?' Frank screwed his face up. 'I can't put a tail on him. I don't know where he's gone, and even if I did know I simply haven't got the resources.'

'West Berlin isn't on the way to anywhere,' I said. 'No one comes here en route to anywhere; they come here and go back again.'

'You're right. Perhaps I should send London a reminder.' He used his clenched fist to brush up the ends of his moustache. To the casual observer it looked as if he was giving himself two quick punches on the nose: perhaps that's what he thought London was likely to give him if he persisted. 'I'll leave it for the weekend; they might respond again.'

Good old Frank: never hesitate to do nothing. 'Phone the old man,' I suggested.

'The D-G? He hates being disturbed at home.' He scratched his cheek and said, 'No, I'll leave it for the time being. But I'm disturbed by what you told me, Bernard.'

I realized that my description of Thurkettle's activities had put Frank into a difficult position. Until talking with me he still had the chance to plead ignorance of anything concerning the man or the danger that he might present to Allied personnel here. I wondered if I should suggest that we both forget what I'd said but Frank could be very formal at times. Despite the friendship that went back to my childhood – or even because of it – he might consider such a suggestion treasonable and insulting. I decided not to take a chance on it.

'One thing I still haven't got clear, Frank,' I said. He raised an eyebrow. 'You sent Teacher to get me, and had me sit in on Larry Bower and the old apparatchik. Why?'

Frank smiled. 'Didn't Larry explain that?'

'No,' I said. 'Larry didn't explain anything.'

'I thought it might be something that would interest you. I remembered that you were handling Stinnes at one time.'

'Why not simply show me the transcript?'

'Of the debriefing?' Pursed lips and a nod, as if this was a novel and most interesting suggestion. 'We could have done that; yes.'

'Would you like to hear what I think?' I said.

'Of course I would,' said Frank with that suppressed irony with which a doting parent might indulge a precocious child. 'Tell me.'

'I kept thinking about it. I wondered why you would give me a close look at a still active agent. That's not the way the training manual says it's done.'

'I don't always go by the training manual,' said Frank.

'You are not contrary or perverse, Frank,' I said. 'What you do, you do with a purpose.'

'What's eating you, Bernard?'

'You didn't invite me to that safe house in Charlottenburg to hear the debriefing and see Valeri,' I said. 'You brought me over there so that Valeri could see me. See me close up!'

425

'Why would I have done that, Bernard?' He found a stray thread on his sleeve, plucked it off and dropped it into an ashtray.

'To find out if Valeri could identify me as one of the people mixed up in the narcotics racket?'

'There is such a thing as being too sceptical,' said Frank gently.

'Not in this business there isn't.'

He smiled. He didn't deny the allegation.

'You need a holiday, Bernard.'

'You're right,' I said. 'Meanwhile, when do I start my trip down the Autobahn?'

'Not for a few days,' said Frank. 'Tuesday at the earliest.' I suppose he thought I would welcome a few days idling around in Berlin but I wanted to get back and he must have seen that in my face. 'Look on the bright side. You'll be able to enjoy Werner's costume party tonight.' When I didn't respond to this he added, 'It's out of my control, Bernard. We just have to wait for the message.'

'When am I to be briefed?'

'There won't be a briefing. We're keeping it all very low-key. But Jeremy Teacher will be with you. He's waiting downstairs. I'll get him up here now and he'll tell you his plans.' Frank picked up his internal phone and said, 'Send Mr Teacher up here, would you.'

I wasn't delighted at the idea of having Teacher tell me his plans. 'Let's get this straight, Frank,' I said. 'Is Teacher running this show, or am I?'

'No need to designate a boss,' said Frank. 'Teacher is easy to get along with. And it's a simple enough job.'

'Never mind all that smooth London Central talk, Frank,' I said. 'If I'm picking up a DDR national on DDR territory and bringing him out, that's Operational. When did Teacher ever work in Operations?'

'He didn't,' admitted Frank. 'And he's never been a field agent either. I suppose that's the real thrust of what you're saying.'

'You're damn right it's the real thrust of what I'm saying. I'll go alone. I don't want to be playing nanny to some pen-pusher who wants a glimpse of life at the sharp end.'

'You can't do it alone. You'll have a passenger. Someone will have to drive. Who knows what unexpected things might happen? We can't risk it.'

'Teacher?'

'He's the best man I've got.'

'Let me take Werner,' I said.

'Werner is a German national cleared only for non-critical employment,' said Frank primly.

'And that bloody Teacher is . . .'

There was a knock at the door and Teacher came in. Losing his wife did not seem to have done anything to improve his miserable demeanour. He brought a sulking broodiness into the room. The smile he gave as he shook hands was sour, and although the grip of his hand was firm there was something listless in the gesture. Perhaps he'd heard me before he came in.

'Tell Bernard what you've arranged,' said Frank.

'Volkswagen van. Diplomatic plates. We meet the other car at a pull-off near the Brandenburg exit. It should be very straightforward. They don't stop diplomatic vans.'

'Bernard says when will you go?'

'I'm waiting for diplomatic passports for all three of us. We can't expect those to come through until after the weekend.'

'No,' I said. 'Don't let's ruin anyone's weekend.'

Teacher looked at me and looked at Frank.

Frank said, 'Are you armed, Bernard?'

'No,' I said.

'Jeremy will have a non-ferrous pistol,' said Frank, unable to conceal his distaste. Frank had a dislike of firearms that ill fitted his romantic notions of the army.

'That's nice,' I said. Teacher pretended I wasn't there.

'It won't come to that,' said Frank. 'It's a straightforward little job. A drive down the Autobahn, that's all.' I didn't respond and neither did Teacher. If it was so bloody simple, I thought, why wasn't Frank doing it? 'But there is one more thing . . . I've been through this with Jeremy.' A pause revealed that Frank was having difficulty; that's probably why he'd left it to last. 'There must be no question of the field agent going into custody over there. You understand?'

'No,' I said. 'I don't understand. We'll be in a diplomatic vehicle you said.'

'That's not one hundred per cent, Bernard. Remember poor little Fischbein? They dragged him out of that car right in the Alex.'

'I've been briefed,' said Teacher.

But I wasn't going to let Teacher get Frank off the hook. 'Then brief me, Frank.'

'If the worst came to the worst, Bernard. The agent would have to be . . . eliminated.'

'Killed?'

'Yes, killed.' Frank looked again at the map, as if searching for something, but I think he was trying to avoid my eyes. 'Jeremy has the gun for that purpose.'

'Poor bloody agent,' I said.

'All concerned are aware of what's at stake,' said Frank stiffly. 'Including the agent.'

Frank turned and looked at me now. His blunt-ended moustache was completely grey these days. Frank was too old to be involved with Operations. Too old, too squeamish, too weary, too good-hearted. Whatever it was, the strain on him showed in his face.

'It's all right, sir,' said the ever-helpful Teacher. 'We'll do whatever has to be done.'

Teacher's face was lined too, but Teacher was not old nor weary. Teacher was a tough little bastard in a way that I'd not recognized before. They'd chosen him well for this job.

Frank seemed not to hear Teacher. It was as if it were just me and Frank in the room. 'Okay, Bernard?' he just said softly. I looked Frank in the eyes and I knew, beyond any shadow of a doubt, that it was Fiona who was going to be picked up on the Autobahn. It was Fiona who knew what might have to be done to prevent her being interrogated by the professional torturers at Normannenstrasse. And Teacher was there in case I hesitated when it was time to pull the trigger.

'Yes, Frank,' I said. 'It's okay.'

On the Sunday evening there was a big party at Lisl's. The printed invitations said it was to celebrate the opening of the newly refurbished premises. On this pretext Werner had obtained the support of a number of his suppliers, and the invitations, like the paper napkins and some of the other objects in evidence, bore the trademarks of breweries and distillers.

Now that it was almost summer, and the evenings had lengthened, Werner's plan was to hold the party in a huge tent he'd had erected in the courtyard at the back of the hotel. But all afternoon the sky had darkened and by evening there was torrential rain falling from an endless overcast. Only the most intrepid guests ventured into the chilly tent, and the inauguration was celebrated indoors.

But it was something more than the official reopening of the hotel. And it was Frank's presence at the party at Lisl's on Sunday evening that told me that he felt the same way. Frank was past retirement, soon he would be gone. Looking back on it afterwards, I saw that he regarded it as his very own gala finale. Frank had never shared my love

428

for Lisl, and despite all evidence to the contrary, he persisted in blaming Werner for that old 'Baader Meinhof' fiasco for which Frank had taken a share of criticism. But even Frank knew that Lisl's was the only place in Berlin to celebrate, and having decided that, he was at his most ebullient and charming. He even wore fancy costume: the Duke of Wellington!

'It's the end of an era,' said Lisl. We were sitting in her little study. This was the room in which Lisl spent so much of her life now that walking had become so painful for her. Here she had breakfast, and played bridge and looked at the account books and gave favoured residents a measured glass of sherry when they came to pay their bills. On the wall there was a picture of Kaiser Wilhelm, on the mantelpiece a hideous ormolu clock, and around the table where she took breakfast four carved Venetian-style figure-of-eight dining chairs, all that remained of her parents' grand dining room.

Now she never sat in her beloved chairs; she was in a functional steel wheelchair that she could manoeuvre at such high speed that Werner had fixed a small bulbhorn to it.

The noise of the party came loudly through the tightly closed door. I don't know whose idea it was to use Lisl's wind-up gramophone and her collection of ancient 78s to provide the music, but it had been hailed as the ultimate in chic, and now Marlene was purring 'Falling in Love Again' against a honky-tonk piano for what must have been the fifth consecutive time. Werner had predicted that it wouldn't be loud enough but it was loud enough.

Even Lisl had sought refuge from the dedicated and unrelenting playfulness that Berliners bring to their parties. Open on the floor there was a very old suitcase that had belonged to my father. It dated from the days before designer labels, when such things were properly made. The outside was pale green canvas with leather for the handle, the binding and the corners. The lining was calico. Inside it there were his papers: bills, accounts, newspaper clippings, a couple of diaries, a silk scarf, even the British army uniform tunic that he so seldom wore. I was rummaging through it while Lisl sat in her wheelchair, sipped her sherry and watched me. 'Even his gun,' she said. 'Be careful with it, Bernd. I hate guns.'

'I noticed it,' I said. I took it from its leather holster. It was a Webley Mark VI, a gigantic revolver that weighed about two and a half pounds, the sort of weapon that the British Army had been hanging on its officers since the First World War. It was blue and perfect, I doubt if my father had ever fired it. There was a box of ammunition too. Nickel jacket .455 inch rounds 'for service use'. The label was dated 1943 and the seal was unbroken.

'That's everything. Klara made sure that all your father's things were packed in his case. So that's all apart from the footstool, the mattress and the set of Dickens.'

'Thank you, Lisl.'

'The end of an era,' she mused sadly. 'Werner taking over the hotel. The changes to the rooms. You taking your father's things. I'm a stranger here now, a stranger in my own home.'

'Don't be silly, Lisl. Werner loves you. He's only done it all for you.'

'He's a good boy,' she said sadly, not grudging him her affection but reluctant to abandon the self-pity she so relished.

There was a sudden increase in the noise of the party as Werner came in and shut the door behind him. Werner was dressed as a knight in full armour. Expediently the armour was fashioned entirely of fabric cunningly embroidered with gold and silver wire to reproduce the intricate decoration on etched and gilt metal. He looked magnificent, even Lisl thought so. Lisl looked equally splendid in a long brightly patterned dress that – acording to the rental company's label – was that of a thirteenth-century noblewoman, and was based upon the stained glass figures of Augsburg Cathedral. It included diadem and wimple and a light but voluminous cloak. Whatever the integrity of the design she made a fine figure alongside Werner, the wheelchair providing her with an imposing throne. I thought he might have chosen his costume and hers with filial congruity in mind but he later confided that it was the only garment he could find in her size that was also bright crimson. Lisl loved vivid colours.

'It's a madhouse out there,' said Werner as he stood against the door and caught his breath. His face was pink with excitement and exertion. 'I brought you some more champagne.' He had the bottle in his hand and he poured some for both of us. 'Absolutely ghastly.'

'It sounds ghastly,' I said, although I had long grown used to the way in which Werner organized this sort of frenzied fancy dress party, and then went around all evening saying how much he hated it.

He looked at me. 'I wish you'd put on your costume,' he said. He'd selected an amazing mid-nineteenth-century costume for me that was called 'the Biedermeier gentleman' on the box. It came complete with a frock coat and high hat. I suspected that Werner had chosen it with a certain sardonic glee that I had no intention of sustaining.

'I'm all right like this,' I said. I was wearing a battered grey suit, my only concession to the party being one of Werner's more colourful bow ties.

'You're so bloody English,' said Werner, not unkindly.

'Sometimes I am,' I admitted.

'There must be a hundred and fifty people out there,' he told me. 'Half of them gatecrashers. The word got around I suppose; they're all in costume.' It was typical of him that he should show a trace of pride that so many should want to gatecrash his party. 'Do you want the Duchess to tell your fortune, Lisl?'

'No, I don't,' said Lisl.

'They say she's a witch,' said Werner as if that was a recommendation.

'I don't want to know the future,' said Lisl. 'When you get to my age the future holds nothing but heartbreak and pain.'

'Don't be a misery, Lisl,' said Werner, who dared to go much further with her than I would ever do. 'I'm going to make sure you meet people.'

'Go away!' said Lisl. 'I'm talking to Bernd.'

Werner looked at me and gave a tiny grin. 'I'll be back,' he promised and returned to the party which was getting louder every minute. He stood in the open doorway for long enough for me to see the crowded dance floor. There was a frenzied crowd of dancers all elaborately costumed – Germans take fancy dress parties as seriously as they take every other social activity from opera-going to getting drunk – and waving their arms in the air more or less in time with the music. Sequined chorus girls, a Roman Senator, Karl May's Old Shatterhand and two squaws danced past wriggling and smiling. Jeremy Teacher – dressed as a thin elegant curly-haired gorilla – was dancing with Tessa, who was in a long diaphanous yellow dress with long antenna bobbing above her head. Teacher was holding her tight and talking: Tessa was wide-eyed and nodding energetically. It seemed an unlikely combination. The door closed.

'What time will they go home?' Lisl asked me.

'It won't go on very late, Lisl,' I promised, knowing full well that it would go on very late indeed.

'I hate parties,' said Lisl.

'Yes,' I said, although I could see she had already decided to go and circulate. She preferred to be pushed round in her wheelchair. It gave her an added sense of majesty. I supposed I'd have to do it but I knew she'd find a way of making me look a bloody fool while doing so.

I locked up the suitcase. 'Come on, Lisl,' I said. 'Let's go and look round.'

'Must we?' she said, and was already looking in the mirror to inspect her make-up. Then the door opened again. There was a short smiling man standing there.

At first I thought he was in a specially elaborate costume that included face-black. Then I recognized Johnny the Tamil. He looked different; he was wearing gold-rimmed glasses. He laughed. 'How wonderful!' he said. 'How wonderful!' I thought he must be referring to the party but he seemed almost not to notice that the party was going on at all. Perhaps he was stoned. 'Wonderful to find you, Bernard,' he said. 'I've looked all over town.'

'I heard the cops got you,' I said.

He looked at me over his glasses. 'I was lucky. There was the cruise missiles demonstration. Three hundred arrests. They needed the space in the cells. They threw me out.' His German had not improved but I'd got used to his accent.

'I'll get you a drink,' I offered. Behind him, through the open door I spotted the Duke of Wellington holding tight to a rather gorgeous geisha. For a fleeting moment I thought it was Daphne Cruyer, but as she turned her head and smiled at Frank I knew it wasn't.

'No. I must go. I brought this for you.' He gave me a large dog-eared envelope. I opened it. There was a plastic box that looked a bit like a small radio. 'It's Spengler's . . .' said Johnny. 'He wanted you to have it. It's his chess computer.'

'Thanks.'

'He always said that if anything happened to him I could have his glasses and you could have his computer. That's all he had,' Johnny added unnecessarily. 'The cops took his passport.'

'For me? Are you sure?'

'I'm sure. Spengler liked you. I put new batteries in.'

'Thanks, Johnny. Do the glasses suit you?' He looked quite different in the glasses.

'No, they make everything blurred. But they are stylish, aren't they?'

'Yes, they are,' I said. 'This is Tante Lisl. Have a drink?'

'Hello, Tante Lisl.' He seemed baffled at the idea that Lisl might really be my aunt but he didn't question it. 'No. I must go, Bernard.'

'Did they find out who killed Spengler?' I asked.

'They haven't even found out his real name or where he came from. No one cares about him, except us.'

He waved and was gone. Lisl had made no attempt to follow the conversation. 'You should be careful who you mix with in this town,' she said. 'It's not like London.'

Lisl, who, as far as I knew, had never been to London, had been saying that to me since I was six years old, and brought Axel Mauser back to see my Nazi medal collection.

Johnny's visit was over so quickly that I forgot to give him some cash. With people like Johnny a few marks go a long way. Goodness knows what time and trouble he'd spent in tracking me down. He'd even stolen new batteries for me: long-life batteries, the very best. I suppose he got them from Wertheim. He liked stealing from Wertheim: he said it was a quality shop.

In the event it was Werner who trundled Lisl around the party as she bowed graciously, offered her hand to be kissed or gave a regal wave, according to the degree of approval she extended to these merry-making guests.

I took my father's suitcase down to the cellar but when I got there I sat down for a few minutes. I was aware of the absurdity of hiding away from Werner's party, aware too of the derision I'd face from Werner if he found me down here.

But I didn't want to be upstairs with a hundred and fifty exhilarated people most of whom I didn't know, in disguises I couldn't penetrate, celebrating the end of something I didn't want to say goodbye to.

I went and sat in the little hideaway next to the boiler room, a place I used to come to do my homework when I was a child. There was always a bright light and a tall pile of old newspapers and magazines in here. Reading them, instead of doing my homework, was one of the reasons I'd become so good at German that I could often beat all the German kids in vocabulary tests and essay writing.

I did the same thing now. I took a newspaper from the top of the big pile and sat down on the bench to read it. There was a story about the discovery of buried nerve gas at Spandau. It had been there since the Second World War.

'Bernard, darling! What are you doing here? Are you ill?'

'No, Tessa. I just wanted to get away from it all.'

'You really are the limit, Bernard. The limit. The limit.' She repeated the words as if she found some pleasure in saying them. Her eyes were wide and moist. I realized that she was stoned. Not drunk on alcohol. She was on something more powerful than that. 'Really the limit,' she said again. She extended her arms. The almost transparent yellow cloth was attached to her wrists so that she became a butterfly. The bright light made her a whirling shadow on the whitewashed wall.

'What is it, Tessa?'

'Your friend Jeremy is looking for you.' She twirled around to enjoy again the fleeting shadows she made.

'Who is Jeremy?'

'You mean, Jeremy who, darling.' She laughed shrilly at her joke. 'Jeremy thing!' She clicked her fingers. 'Jeremy the cultivated ape. Know you not the couplet: *He doth like the ape, that the higher he climbs the more he shows his ars.* Francis Bacon. You think I'm an untutored wanton, but I went to school and I can quote Francis Bacon with the best of you.'

'Of course you can, Tessa. But you seem a little high yourself.'

'And the more I show my arse? Is that what you mean, Bernard, you rude sod?'

'No, Tessa, of course not. But I think it might be a good idea to get you back to your hotel. Where's Dicky?'

'Are you listening to me, Bernard? Jeremy the ape is desperate to find you. He is going mad. He is in fact going ape!' More laughter; soft but shriller, and a suggestion that hysteria was not far away. 'The signal has come and you must go.'

'Is that what Jeremy the ape said?'

'The signal has come and you must away.'

'Tessa!' I shook her. 'Listen to me, Tessa. Get a hold of yourself. Where is the ape now?'

'He was trying to get into one of Werner's three-piece lounge suits – blue with a pin stripe – but Werner got angry and wouldn't let him borrow any clothes. They were both shouting. Werner doesn't like him.' She smiled. 'And Werner's suits are too big.'

I said it slowly. 'Where is Jeremy the ape now?'

'You're not going without me. The car's here. Van. Ford van, a lovely shade of blue. Diplomatic plates. Outside in the rain. Jeremy the ape is driving. They make good drivers, apes. My father employed one for years. Then he started wanting extra bananas all the time. They can be awfully tiresome, apes. Did I tell you that?'

Outside, the rain was falling in great steel sheets, hammering the road and pounding upon the roof of the Ford van. Jeremy Teacher, still in gorilla costume, was in the driver's seat. He was soaking wet. I asked him what was happening and had to shout to make myself heard above the sound of the rain and thunder. 'Get in,' he said.

'What's happening?' I said for maybe the fourth time.

'What the hell do you think is happening?' he said furiously. 'The bloody signal came through three and a half hours ago!'

'You said a VW van.' He shot me a poisonous look. 'I haven't got my

434

passport,' I said, my mind racing as I thought of all the other things I didn't have.

'Get in! I've got the passports here.' The prospect of going through the checkpoints dressed as a gorilla had obviously put him in a foul temper.

It was then that I noticed that Tessa was dancing about in the rain. She was drenched but she seemed oblivious of the arresting sight she offered as the thin material clung tightly to her body.

It was Tessa dancing round the Ford Transit – added to the sight of a gorilla gunning it while arguing volubly with a civilian who might have been his keeper – that brought other revellers out into the street. They made an astonishing sight in their costumes, and although some of them had umbrellas, many were as indifferent to the downpour as Tessa was.

Werner came too, struggling under the weight of my father's suitcase. He opened the rear door to put it inside and as he was doing so Tessa pushed him aside and climbed into the van, slamming the door with a crash that made the metal body-work sing.

'Let's go!' shouted Teacher.

'Tessa's in the back,' I said.

He looked round and shouted, 'Get out of there, Tessa.'

'I'm coming with you,' she cooed.

'Don't be silly. You haven't got a passport,' said Teacher with a calm politeness that was commendable under the circumstances.

'Oh yes I have,' she said triumphantly. She had produced it from somewhere and was holding it up in front of her to show him. 'Dicky said I was to carry it everywhere while I was here.'

'Get out, you stupid bitch!' He revved the engine as if hoping that would persuade her but it didn't. It simply confirmed that the engine was not firing properly. I had doubts that it would ever complete the journey.

'I won't. I won't.'

'For Christ's sake get her out of there,' shouted Teacher to me.

'Who the hell do you think you are,' I said. 'You get her out.' I recognized one of Tessa's bloody-minded moods and decided to let the intrepid Mr Teacher earn his pay.

He looked at his watch. 'We must go.' With a string of curses he opened his door and got out, but as the rain hit him and soaked his hairy gorilla outfit he changed his mind and climbed back into the driver's seat again.

'Come on, Tessa. We're leaving.'

'I'm coming too,' she said.

'No, you're bloody not!' said Teacher. He switched the heater on to full. His damp costume was obviously chilly.

Then Dicky arrived on the scene. He was dressed as Harlequin, the carefully decorated face, chequered costume and imposing hat a favourite for Germany's Fasching celebrations. He spotted Tessa and dutifully told us that she was in the back of the van. Teacher gave a loud and angry sigh. 'Then get her out of it,' he said, abandoning his usual respectful attitude to those set in authority over him.

By now there seemed to be dozens of people in bizarre costumes milling around the van, although in the darkness and the relentless rain it was difficult to be sure who they really were. But they formed such a crush that getting through them, getting the door open and getting Tessa out would be physically difficult even if no one objected to Tessa being manhandled. And if I knew anything about the effects of alcohol on the male psyche, any sort of struggle with Tessa would be enough to start a riot.

There was a flash of lightning. Hordes – in ever more amazing garb – spilled into the street. The commotion round the van had become the party's new attraction. A rain-soaked Frederick the Great was waving both hands in glee, while Barbarossa, his false beard bedraggled, offered his hat to a Roman maiden to protect her coiffure.

I saw the Duchess. She was dressed as a witch, in a pointed hat and a long black gown with occult symbols on the skirt of it. That damned cat was with her despite the heavy rain, its eyes glowing angrily in the darkness. The Duchess was standing in front of the van and began making solemn gestures with her wand. A roll of thunder came in on cue.

'What's that old cow doing?' Teacher asked.

'I think she's casting a spell,' I replied.

'Jesus Christ!' said Teacher, aggravated beyond control. 'Has everyone gone insane?'

Before the Duchess had finished her incantation Harlequin stuck his painted face through the window of the van and said, 'Teacher is in charge. Remember that, Bernard.' I ignored him. He grabbed my shoulder and in the voice of an exasperated parent talking to a naughty child, he said, 'Look here, Bernard! Do you hear what I said?'

I looked at Dicky's elaborately made up face and his cold little eyes. Years and years of repressed resentment welled up in me. The way in which he'd been promoted over my head, the pompous things he said, his pretentious lifestyle, his readiness to cuckold poor old George and make jokes about it. Now emotion took precedence over common sense. Whatever the consequences, now was the time to react. I pulled my fist back and gave him a solid punch on the rouged nose. Not hard, but it was enough to send him reeling back into the roadway just as another car came past. With incredibly quick response the driver swerved with a sharp squeal of brakes and avoided him. I turned to see him through the window. Dicky still staggered back, hat askew, feet splayed wide apart. His arms were flailing to keep balance, but he fell backwards into the road and his big cocked hat came off.

'Go! Go! We'll sort it out at the checkpoint,' I yelled.

Teacher let in the clutch and there was a squeak of rubber and a sickening bump followed by a woman's scream. I knew immediately what had happened. That bloody cat 'Jackdaw' had gone under the van to shelter from the downpour. Now it was flattened under the rear wheels. We might have hit the Duchess too, but Teacher spun the wheel and narrowly missed her and we sped out into the traffic of the Ku-Damm.

The wet streets shone with the coloured light of the neon signs that summoned tourists to meet the junkies, winos and dropouts who had made the Europa Centre their home. 'Is she still in the back?' said Teacher as we passed the Gedächtniskirche, preserved to remind the nostalgia-prone that old Berlin had its fair share of ugly buildings. Even at this time of night there was plenty of traffic. Teacher gunned the motor a couple of times and after that the engine began firing more efficiently. I suppose the rain must have been afflicting it.

'I'm here, darling,' said a voice from the back. 'I can guess who you are going to meet. If you dare to try throwing me out at the checkpoint I'll scream it aloud to the whole world. You wouldn't like that, would you?'

'No we wouldn't like that,' I said.

'This bloody heater's not working,' said Teacher and slapped it with his hairy hand.

'That's a damned convincing costume, Jeremy,' I said admiringly. Tessa giggled softly but Teacher didn't answer.

19

Traffic leaving West Berlin for the Autobahn to West Germany goes through the Border Control point at Drewitz in the south-west corner of the city.

The procedures are efficient and, for a car with Diplomatic plates, minimal. On the DDR side of the controls it is customary for the drivers and passengers of vehicles so marked to flatten their identity papers against the glass of the window, where they are examined by the flashlights of the communist officials who work with that studied slowness that in the West is usually the modus operandi of trade unionists in dispute.

Eventually the guards grudgingly waved us through. They gave no sign of noticing that one of us was a gorilla. Teacher tossed the diplomatic passports into the glove compartment and we began the long and monotonous journey to the West. In keeping with the DDR's siege mentality, there are no cafés or restaurants on this road. There's nowhere to savour those sixty-eight different flavours of icecream that punctuate long wide American freeways, none of the bifteck aux pommes frites avec Château Vinaigre that mark the expensive kilometres of France's autoroutes, not even the toxic waste and strong tea so readily available on Britain's motorways.

At first there was a great deal of traffic on the road. Lovers and husbands returning from blissful weekends passed each other on the way home. Trucks starting out at the stroke of midnight after the weekend embargo on heavy vehicles slowly and laboriously overtook other heavyweights. In the fast lane Germans roared past us at top speed, flashing their lights lest they be inconvenienced in their public demonstration of German mechanical superiority. '*Deutschland über alles*,' said Teacher as one such Mercedes driver, who'd come tailgating close behind us, pointed his finger to his head as he overtook, and sprayed us with dirty water.

'Tessa's gone to sleep,' I said.

'Something good had to happen,' said Teacher. 'It's the law of averages.'

'Don't bet on it,' I said. The wipers squeaked and squealed at the rain. Teacher reached for the radio switch but seemed to have second thoughts about it.

We came up behind a line of heavy trucks, the wind whipping the covers of the rearmost vehicle, and stayed there for a bit. 'Keep awake. We'll check *all* the exits,' said Teacher. 'The message may have got it wrong.'

'No comment,' I said.

These East German Autobahnen were in poor condition. Little had been done on this stretch since it was first built in Hitler's time. Subsidence here and there had caused wide cracks, and hasty patches of shoddy maintenance had failed to cure the underlying fractures. All over Europe the motorways were poxed with signs, and littered with the equipment of construction gangs, as the Continent's roads succumbed to an arterio-sclerosis that had every sign of proving fatal.

There had been roadworks at several places along the route, but after the turn-off for Brandenburg – a town that forms the centre of a complex of lakes to the west of Berlin – the westbound side of the Autobahn was reduced to single-lane working. Teacher slowed as our headlights picked out the double row of plastic cones, some of them overturned by the gusts of wind that accompanied ceaseless heavy rain.

The road curved gently to the left and began a downward gradient. From here I saw ahead of us the ribbon of highway marked by pinpoints of light that climbed like a file of insects and disappeared suddenly over the distant hill only just visible against the purple horizon.

This section of the Autobahn was being widened. Lining the road were colossal machines: bulldozers and towering power shovels, spreaders, graders and rollers, the bizarre toys of a Gargantuan world.

'Look there!' I said as I spotted a car parked amongst the machines, its parking lights just visible through the downpour.

'That's them,' said Teacher, the relief audible in his voice. He swung the wheel. We bumped off the edge of the roadway and down on to the mud, picking the way carefully past metal drums, steel reinforcements, abandoned materials, broken wooden fencing and other undefinable debris. We were about fifty yards from the other car when Teacher judged us close enough. He stopped and turned off the engine: the lights died. The noise of the rainstorm was suddenly very loud. It was dark except when passing cars, coming round the curve, swept the site with their headlight beams. The light came swinging across it like the revolving rays of a lighthouse. There was no movement anywhere.

'Careful,' I said. 'When you open the door we'll be lit up by the interior light. We'll be sitting targets.' I slid into the back of the van, opened the suitcase and rummaged to find the ammunition and the pistol. I loaded it carefully. It wasn't the sort of thing you could tuck into the waistband of a pair of cheap trousers so I kept it in my hand.

'I'm getting out,' said Teacher. 'You two stay here.'

'Whatever you say.'

It was no time to start a row, but as he opened the door and got out of the driver's seat I slid out the back and into the darkness and pouring rain. Outside there was the sort of stink that roadworks always exude, the smell of disturbed earth, faeces and fuel oil. But the road here runs through a tall forest and the felling of the trees had added sap to the medley of odours. The rain soaked me to the skin before I'd taken more than two steps through the sticky mud. I kept the gun under my coat and out of sight, and watched the dim figure of Teacher walking cautiously towards the car. Some traffic swung past, driving carefully along the prescribed lane, their beams dulled by the steady rain.

While Teacher moved forward, someone got out of the car which I could now recognize as a Wartburg. The other side had taken the precaution of taping up the interior light switch. The Wartburg's interior remained dark, and the glare of the parking lights was enough to make it impossible to see whether it was a man or a woman standing there. Nearer to me – and directly behind the nearest of the big yellow machines – there was a barrier. It fenced off the deep excavations where the foundations were being extended.

'Please walk forward, one at the time,' I heard Teacher call, his uncertain German evident from only those few words.

Suddenly the full beams of the Wartburg came on. This light was hard and brilliant. It came cutting through rain that shone like glass beads, and exposed Teacher as an absurd and soaking wet gorilla. Teacher was alarmed and jumped aside into the darkness but I could still see his outline.

From the bulldozer closest to me I heard a movement, a soft metallic click that might have been the safety catch of a gun. A figure had shifted position from behind the bulldozer's tracks in order to see where Teacher had gone. I moved closer to the line of earth-moving machinery which would provide me with the sort of cover that the other side had taken advantage of. Now I could see more clearly in the darkness. There seemed to be a woman standing by the Wartburg and possibly others still inside it. The metallic sound I'd heard had come from someone standing near the barrier. It was a man holding a gun with a long silencer attached. All their attention was on Teacher.

It was like watching a performance on a fully lighted stage, its backdrop the tall trees of the immense forest while to one side there were the twin lines of traffic – one red one white – flickering away into the far distance. Now I could see Teacher, but he couldn't see the figure with the gun who was silhouetted against the mud and puddles which shone like silver in the beams of the Wartburg's headlights.

I heard a shout – almost a scream – a woman's voice, and there was someone running through the squelching mud behind me. I turned to see but our Transit van was in my field of view. Then came the first shot: the sort of soft plop you only get the first time from a gun with a brand-new silencer. It wasn't Teacher. The woman called again. She was shouting, 'Do as you were told!' In German, Berlin German.

Then came another shot, a loud report from an unsilenced gun and the smashing of glass. It was a single shot from somewhere to the left of me. Now came a confusion of darkness, pierced by pistol shots and the sudden beams of passing headlights. Traffic rumbling past gave light enough to show that the Wartburg had suffered a broken windscreen, its shattered glass scattered around like hail. In that brief flicker of light I saw Teacher standing crouched with a pistol held at arm's length, the way actors stand in TV movies about cops. I couldn't be sure whether he'd fired the shot. Had he I wondered tried to hit someone inside the car, and if so had he succeeded?

Then something came fluttering out to make a glowing pattern between me and the light of the Wartburg headlights. Until that moment I thought Tessa was still in the back of the Transit van, but there could be only one person who would go whirling through the mud, twisting and turning, oblivious to the rain and the gunfire.

Whoever shot her was standing near the front nearside wheel of the Wartburg. She was very close to the gunman when she was hit and lifted in the air. Bang. Bang. Two rounds from a shotgun floated her through the headlight beams with her skirt and draped sleeve shining and translucent yellow. As she fell back to earth she metamorphosed to crimson and the cloth wrapped round her like some beautiful flying insect that in fast playback becomes a twitching chrysalis. Illuminated by the headlights she lay full-length in the mud. The rain beat down. She moved again and then was still.

'You bastard!' said someone in English. It must have been Teacher. And then he fired, I recognized the pump-pump sound of the 9mm Browning I'd seen him carrying. Two shots very loud and very close together. One of them hit the steel frame of a big earth-moving machine, and was deflected into the sky with the piteous little cry that spent rounds give. But the other shot hit the Wartburg's near-side headlight and it went out with a secondary explosion and much hissing as the rain found the hot metal of the light.

Bang. Bang. Bang. Bang. Bang. There were men with guns in the darkness over beyond Teacher. No silencers. They returned the fire immediately. Several shots, so close together in time that they sounded almost like one. Teacher ran, stumbled and then went down with a loud scream. I could just see him in the gloom beyond the light provided by the Wartburg's solitary beam. He writhed and shouted, hugging himself with both arms like a man trying to escape from a straitjacket of pain.

But under cover of the attention he was getting I was able to slide round the back of the bulldozer and scramble up on to the wide track. The blade was elevated and I used it for cover as I climbed as high as I could.

I was rewarded with a view of the whole site. More traffic moving slowly past in single file provided light to see the wide trench of the excavations, the line of earth-moving machines and at the end of it the Wartburg. In the centre of the stage there was the Transit van parked askew and to the left of it Teacher's body. Two men came from the direction of the shots and stood over Teacher. One of them prodded the body with the toe of a shoe. There was no sign of life. 'It's all safe now,' he said. I recognized the voice of Erich Stinnes.

From behind the Wartburg there came the woman. She walked carefully so as not to put her shoes into the worst of the muddy pools. It was Fiona, my wife.

'How many did they send?' said one of the men.

'A man and a woman,' said Stinnes. 'They are both dead.' Fiona walked past Tessa's body and looked down at Teacher without giving any sign of recognizing him. I realized then that she'd not recognized her sister either. Stinnes turned to look at the Transit van. He was probably considering the smashed windscreen of the Wartburg and what it would be like to be behind it driving through the rain that was still falling.

At that moment I had many alternatives. I suppose the textbook would have wanted me to negotiate with them, but I wasn't a dedicated reader of textbooks and training manuals, which is the principal reason that I was still alive. So I raised my big revolver and resting the barrel on the dozer's heavy steel blade – the sort of position considered unsporting by the instructors supervising the Department's outdoor firing range – I fired at the one who was farthest away, aiming for the centre of the body. The heavy Webley round hit him like a sledge-

442

hammer slamming him into the darkness where he remained still and silent. The second man – the one called Stinnes – stepped back in alarm but his training overcame his fear and, without seeing me, he raised his gun and fired three times, aiming in my general direction. The bullets buzzed past my head and one plucked at my coat. It was the right thing to do: the prevailing theory being that your adversary stops shooting and seeks cover. But my reactions were far too slow for such theories and by that time I'd hit him with my second round. It struck him in the neck.

It was a sight that was to interrupt my sleep, a finale to nightmares that awoke me sweating in the middle of so many dark nights. For Erich Stinnes spurted blood like a fountain, high in the air. And with blood spurting – hands to his throat – he stumbled backwards with a gasping noise and went slipping and sliding along in the mud until he hit the barrier around the excavation. There he stayed for a moment and then slowly he toppled and went head-first down into the waterlogged trench with a loud splash.

Fiona, frozen in fear, and spattered with fresh blood stayed where she was. I waited. There was no sound from anywhere. There was a pause in the passing traffic and the forest absorbed the sounds of the wind and rain.

Then Fiona ran back to the Wartburg. As she did so the heel of her shoe broke and she twisted her ankle, stumbling so that as she reached the car she was down on one knee and sobbing with the pain of it. From the assumed security that the darkness gave her – and unaware of how close I was – she called, 'Who is it? Who is there?'

I didn't reply, make a sound or even move. There was someone with a silenced gun somewhere out there, and until I settled with him it wasn't safe to climb down to the mud.

I waited a long time. Then Fiona hobbled to the Wartburg, leaned in and doused the headlight beam. Now the site was entirely in darkness except for the occasional lights from passing traffic as it swept round the bend and started down the hill.

Fiona tried to start the car but the bullet that had smashed the headlight must have done some other damage, for the starter motor screamed but didn't turn the engine over. In the silence of the forest I heard her curse to herself, gently and softly. There was desperation in her voice.

It was then that I saw the other one. He was creeping very slowly along the line of the barrier. I caught only a glimpse of him but I could see he was wearing a trenchcoat and the sort of waterproof hat that Americans wear when golfing. I guessed who it was: Thurkettle.

443

For a long long time I saw and heard nothing except the sounds and light of the passing traffic. Then I heard a man's voice call, 'Are we going to wait here all night, Samson?'

It was Thurkettle's voice. I remained silent.

Thurkettle called again, 'You can take the woman and take the Ford and go. Take your gorilla too. I don't want any of you.'

I didn't respond.

'Do you hear me?' he said. 'I'm working your side of the street. Get going. I've got work to do.'

I called, 'Fiona! Do you hear me?'

She looked around but couldn't spot me.

'Get to the Ford, start up the engine and roll forward a yard or two. Then keep it ticking over.'

Fiona stepped forward and then kicked both shoes off and went squelching through the mud. Nervously, and pained by her twisted ankle, she made her way slowly to the van. She got into it and started up the engine. After a moment finding the controls she drove forward a little way and cut the engine to idling softly.

'Now you owe me one, Bernie,' called Thurkettle.

'Give my regards to Count Zeppelin,' I said. I still had the edge on him. I knew where he was but he hadn't located me. I clambered down to the ground and estimated how many paces I would need to get to the other side of the van. If Thurkettle started shooting I'd have the van as cover.

I waited for a few minutes so that Thurkettle would start looking round to see if I'd got away. Then I ran across to the van. A heavy truck came crawling round the curve and caught me in its headlight beams. I kept running and threw myself down into the mud just as I reached the rear of the van. I stayed there for a moment to catch my breath. No shots came. I moved to the front and put a hand to the glass to get Fiona's attention. 'Can you see him?' I whispered.

'He's behind the Wartburg.'

'Is he one of yours?'

'I know nothing about him.'

'Didn't he come with you?' I asked her.

'No. He's on a motorcycle.'

'Are you fit to drive?'

'Yes, of course,' she said; her voice was firm and determined.

'We'll get out of here and leave him to it. Slide down low in the seat, in case he shoots. I'm going to climb in. When I say "Go" start driving. Not too fast in case you stall.'

444

I slid my hand around the door seating until I found the light switch and then I pushed it to keep the light off. I opened the door and scrambled inside. 'Go!' I said softly. Fiona revved the engine and we went bumping forward over the rough ground. There were no shots.

In the darkness the van bumped over some planks of wood and then we rolled up over a high ledge and on to the Autobahn. It was very dark: no traffic in sight either way. We started westwards. We were about half a mile down the road when there was a great red ball of light behind us.

'My God!' said Fiona. 'Whatever's that?'

'Your Wartburg going up in flames, unless I miss my guess.'

'In flames?'

'Someone is destroying the evidence.'

'Evidence of what?' she said.

'Let's not go back and ask.'

The flames were fierce. We could still see them from miles away. Then as we went over the brow of a hill the light on the horizon vanished suddenly. Very little forensic evidence would be salvaged from such a blaze.

I asked Fiona if she wanted me to drive. She shook her head without answering. I tried in other ways to start a conversation but her replies were monosyllabic. Driving along the Autobahn that night gave her something to concentrate upon. She was determined not to think about what she'd done, and in no mood to talk about what we'd have to do.

My arm began to throb. I touched it and found my sleeve was sticky with blood. One of the bullets had come closer than I'd realized. It was not a real wound, just a bad extended graze and an enormous bruise, of the sort that bullets make when they brush the flesh. I wadded a handkerchief and held it pressed against my arm to stanch the dribbling blood. It was nothing that would put me in hospital, but more than enough to ruin my suit.

'Are you all right?' There was no tenderness in her voice. It was as much admonitory as concerned, the voice of a schoolteacher herding a class of kids across a busy street.

'I'm all right.' We should have been talking and embracing and laughing and loving. We were together again and she was coming home to me and the children. But it wasn't like that. We weren't the same carefree couple who'd honeymooned on a bank overdraft and got hysterically drunk in the registry office on one half bottle of champagne shared amongst four people. We sat silent in the darkness. We watched the traffic crawling to Berlin, and saw the Porsches scream past us. And

I dribbled blood and the unspoken dreams that keep marriages going bled away too.

The rain stopped or perhaps we drove out of it. I switched on the car radio. There was a babble of Arabic, Radio Moscow's news in German and then that powerful German transmitter that during the night effectively overwhelms all opposition throughout Central Europe. A big schmaltzy band: *Only make-believe I love you. Only make-believe that you love me. Others find peace of mind in pretending, couldn't you, couldn't I, couldn't we?*

Behind us a strip of sky gradually lightened and coloured to become a contused mass of mauves and purples.

'All right, darling?' I asked. Still she didn't respond to my overtures. She just concentrated on the road, her lips pressed together and her knuckles white.

The unbearable uncertainties that gave me severe stomach pains as we got nearer and nearer to the frontier proved unfounded. When we stopped she looked in the driving mirror and wiped some spots of blood from her face with a handkerchief moistened with spittle. Her expression was unchanging.

'All all right?'

'Yes,' I replied.

She drove forward. A bored border guard, seeing the Diplomatic registration plates, gave us no more than a glance before going back to reading his newspaper.

'We made it,' I said. She didn't answer.

There was a reception committee waiting for us on the other side of the control point. It was dawn, with the uncertain light that soldiers use to start their battles. Some army vehicles were parked by the roadside: an armoured personnel carrier, a staff car and an ambulance: the complete panoply of war. From the empty roadside two soldiers suddenly materialized. One was middle-aged, the other in his twenties. Then came a cheerful young colonel of some unidentifiable unit with his khaki beret pulled tight upon his broad skull and a battle smock with no badges other than parachute wings and his rank stencilled in black.

'We have a helicopter here,' said the colonel. He affected a short swagger-stick, wielding it to give Fiona a mock salute. 'Are you fit enough to travel to Cologne?' His voice was loud, his manner almost jubilant. He was clean and freshly shaved and seemed oblivious to the hour.

'I'm all right,' said Fiona. The colonel opened the door to let her out of the driver's seat. But Fiona sat tight and didn't even look at him to

446

explain why. She held the steering wheel very tight and, looking straight ahead, she gave a little sniff. She sniffed again, loudly, like a child with a runny nose. Then she began to laugh. At first it was the natural charming laugh that you might expect from a beautiful young woman who had just won the world championship in espionage and double-dealing. But as her laughter continued the colonel began to frown. Her face became flushed. Her laughing became shrill and she trembled and shook until her whole body was racked with her hysterical laughter, as it might be afflicted with a cough or choking fit.

The laughing still didn't stop. I became alarmed but the colonel seemed to have encountered it before. He looked at the blood spots that covered her, and then at me. 'It's the reaction. From what I can see, she's had a rough time.' Over his shoulder he said, 'You'd better help her, Doc.'

As he stood aside, the younger man behind him stepped forward. The middle-aged soldier handed him something. Then the boyish-looking doctor reached in through the window, grabbed her and with a minimum of fuss – in fact with no fuss at all – he put a hypodermic needle into her upper arm, right through her sleeve. The army is like that. He kept hold of her arm and watched her while she quietened down. Then he felt her pulse. 'That should do it,' he said. 'A sedative. No alcohol. Better if she doesn't eat for an hour or two. There will be an RAF doctor waiting for you at Cologne airport, I'll give you a message for him. He'll go with you all the way.'

'All the way to where?' I asked.

The young doctor looked at the colonel, who said, 'Didn't they tell you? It's always the same isn't it? They never tell the people at the sharp end. You're transferring to a transatlantic flight. It's a long journey but the air force will look after you.'

Fiona was relaxing. The laughter had completely stopped and she looked around her as if waking from a deep sleep. She let the colonel help her down from the car. 'Where are your shoes?' he asked her gallantly and tried to find them.

'I've lost my shoes,' she said flatly and pushed back her hair as if becoming aware of her scruffy appearance.

'That doesn't matter a bit,' said the colonel. 'They have lovely shoes in America.'

447

20

Summer is not the best time to be in southern California. Even 'La Buona Nova', the big hillside spread in Ventura County where Fiona was hidden away for her official debriefing, had long energy-sapping days when there was not a breeze off the Pacific. Bret Rensselaer was in charge. Some people – including me – had said he was too old ever to become a full-time Departmental employee again. But Bret was officially considered as Fiona's case officer. Bret had been a party to Fiona's long-term plan to defect to Moscow since that time when she first confided it to him. He'd monitored her progress. There was really no one else who could debrief her.

Bret Rensselaer was determined to make a big success of what would obviously be the last job he'd ever do. The prospect of a knighthood was never mentioned but you didn't have to be a mind-reader to know what Bret thought would be an appropriate thank-you from a grateful sovereign. No worries about Bret bowing the head for that one: he'd walk coast to coast on his knees for a K.

No one ever mentioned any kind of thank-you for me. When my salary cheque was paid I noticed that all the allowances and extras had been trimmed off it. I was down to the bare bones. When I mentioned this to Bret he said that I should remember that I wasn't having to pay for my food and keep. Good grief I said, what about the way I'm being deprived of contact with my children? I didn't mention Gloria for obvious reasons. It was Bret who brought Gloria into our conversation. He said that she had been told that I was on a special mission too secret for details to be revealed. The Department was making sure my children were happy and well cared for. He said it as if his words contained some not very veiled threat for me: I had the feeling that what Gloria was told would depend upon my good behaviour.

One day I noticed amongst the papers on Bret's marble-topped table a coloured postcard. It was van Gogh's portrait of a blue-uniformed postman, a picture of which Gloria was inordinately fond. 'Could that card be for me?' I asked him.

'No,' he said immediately and without hesitation.

'You're sure?'

'It's my private correspondence,' said Bret.

I felt like grabbing it to see but the table was big and Bret reached it before I did. He put it in a drawer. I knew it was a card from Gloria to me. I just knew it.

After that I was seldom allowed into Bret's 'office', and when I did go in there his table was always cleared. And in all that time the only correspondence that was forwarded to me was a picture of Paul Bocuse. It was postmarked Lyon and was from Tante Lisl describing the meal she'd eaten.

They put me and Fiona into a comfortable guest house set apart from the main buildings. It was complete with kitchen, dining room and a young Mexican girl to make breakfast and clean and tidy. Fiona spent four – sometimes five – hours almost every day with Bret. Neither of them emerged to eat a proper lunch. Sandwiches, fruit and coffee were sent into them and they carried right on talking. Bret had a part-time secretary but she wasn't with them during these sessions. His large and very comfortable office, with its window grilles and security locks, had maps and reference books and a computer that would feed into his screen and/or print out anything he required from all sorts of data banks. Everything Fiona said was recorded on tape and locked away in a huge safe. But there were no transcripts – all that would come later. This was the first run-through so that Bret could alert London and Washington to anything urgent.

Sometimes I went in and listened, but after a few days Fiona asked me to stay away. My presence made her too selfconscious, she said. I was hurt and offended at the time, but one-to-one was the usual form for such debriefings, and I'd never much liked having someone 'sit in' when I was doing one of these deep analysis stunts.

So I swam in the blue outdoor pool, caught up on my reading and listened to the 24 hours a day classical music on KSCA-FM or to cassettes on the big hi-fi. Most days I swam with Mrs O'Raffety, the artistic old lady who owned the place, and who had to swim on account of her bad back. And most days we took lunch together too.

I would have liked to go into Los Angeles, or, failing that, go for a beer in Santa Barbara which was much nearer. Walk along the beach, drive up the Pacific Coast Highway, do the tour of the Hearst Mansion – anything to break the monotony. But Bret was unyielding: both of us were confined inside La Buona Nova compound surrounded by the chain-link fences, the armed Mexican guards and the dogs. It was a prison, a nice comfortable prison but we were sentenced to stay there for as long as the Department decreed. I had the nasty feeling that that

449

would turn out to be a very long term indeed. But what could I do? It was for Fiona's safety, said Bret. There was no arguing with that.

One night, soon after arriving, I'd tried to talk to Fiona about her time with Stinnes and his merry men. We were preparing for bed. She answered normally at first but then she grunted shorter replies and I could see she was getting very upset. She didn't weep or anything as traumatic as that. Perhaps it would have been better for all concerned if she'd done so: it might have helped her. But she didn't weep; she climbed into bed and curled up small and pulled the bedsheet over herself.

Each evening we'd eat dinner with Bret, our hostess and her son-in-law, an amiable lawyer. They were dull affairs at which the Mexican servants hovered all the time and the rest of us made small-talk. Sometimes I'd see Bret Rensselaer at the pool and exchange pleasantries with him. His only response to anything I said about Fiona seeming unwell, was bland reassurances. The doctor had given her a physical the day following her arrival and she had lots of vitamin pills and sleeping pills if she required them. And he told me that she'd been through a tough time and generally treated me like a neurotic mother worrying about a child with a grazed knee. But the changes I saw in Fiona were perhaps not evident to those who didn't know her so well. The changes were all small ones. She seemed shrunken and her face was drawn, and she didn't walk absolutely upright in the attractive way that I remembered so well. There was the soft and hesitant way she spoke and the diffidence she showed to everyone from me and Bret right through to the Mexican house servants.

One evening at dinner she spilled a couple of drips of barbecue sauce on the tablecloth – the kind of thing I do all the time – and she slumped back in her chair and closed her eyes. No one round the table gave any sign of noticing it but I knew she was close to screaming, close perhaps to breaking point. The trouble was that she'd confide nothing to me, no matter how I tried to get her to talk. Finally she accused me of harassing her, so then I stopped and left it all to Bret.

Two days later Bret asked me to sit in with them for the morning session. 'There are a few things unexplained,' said Bret.

'From where I'm sitting there are a lot of things unexplained,' I said.

Fiona sat slumped in a big armchair. Bret was behind a table – an elaborate modern design of pink marble with polished steel legs – with his back to the tinted window. The garden was packed with colour. Against the whitewashed wall of the yard there were orange and lemon trees, jasmine, roses and bougainvillaea. There was no perfume from them, for the window was tightly closed and the air-conditioning fully on. Bret looked at me for a long time and finally said, 'For instance?'

'The traces of heroin in the Ford van.' It was a bluff and it didn't work.

'Let's not get side-tracked,' Bret said. 'We're supposed to be establishing the identities of the other people there.'

'Fiona can tell you that,' I said. 'She was in the car with them.'

'Erich Stinnes,' said Fiona somewhat mechanically. 'Plus a Russian liaison man. And there was a man I had never seen before. He arrived on a motor cycle.'

'Good! Good!' murmured Bret as he laboriously wrote it down in case he forgot. He looked up. 'Three men,' he said and gave a quick nervous smile. Bret Rensselaer was one of those slim elegant Americans who, whether sick or healthy, always look well cared for: like a vintage Bugatti or a fifty-carat diamond. Sitting behind his desk, golden pen in hand, he looked like a carefully posed photo in a society magazine. He was wearing tailored white designer slacks and a white tennis shirt with a red stripe at the collar. It all went well with his white hair and made his tanned face seem very brown.

I wondered if the mysterious 'extra man' was going to be identified as Thurkettle. I didn't volunteer that idea, and I noticed that Fiona said nothing of his American accent.

'Have the monitors picked up anything?' Fiona asked.

'Nothing in any of the newspapers or periodicals and certainly nothing on the radio.' He gave another of his crisp little smiles and fidgeted with his signet ring. 'It would be surprising if there was.'

'And even more surprising if you told us about it,' I said.

Bret wasted no more than a moment on that one. He grunted and turned to Fiona again. 'Why would they burn the car, Fiona?'

'Bernard says it was to destroy the evidence,' she replied.

'I was asking you, Fiona.'

'I really have no idea. It might have been an accident. There was still one man there.'

'Ah! The man on the bike?'

'Yes,' she said.

'I wish you could tell me more about him.' He waited in case Fiona said something. When she didn't he said, 'And you didn't talk with Stinnes or this liaison guy during the car journey?'

'No, I didn't.'

'Did they talk together?'

'I don't think there's much to be gained in this line,' said Fiona. 'I've told you all I know about them.'

Bret nodded sympathetically. He looked at his yellow legal pad and said, 'This "other man" came by motorcycle? Unusual that, don't you think?'

'I really don't know how unusual it was, Bret.'

'But if the car was set on fire after you left, it has to be the biker who did it?'

'I assume so,' said Fiona.

'So do I,' said Bret. 'Now we come to the final stage of this strange business – him letting you get away so easily.'

Fiona nodded and wet her lip as if she was distressed to think about it. 'Strange, yes.'

'What would be the motive for that? Bernie here had just shot his two buddies. Then he let you go. Does that sound a little crazy?'

Fiona said, 'It was a stalemate. He couldn't move without getting shot. He knew Bernard couldn't get to the van without offering a target. Some kind of compromise had to be reached.'

'No, it didn't, honey,' said Bret. 'These people were in their own country. Let's say Mr X holds out until it's daylight. Passing traffic will see what's happening. The construction workers will arrive. Just about anything that happens will resolve things his way. Right?'

'I don't know who he was,' said Fiona, as if she hadn't listened to Bret's question.

'What does that mean?' said Bret.

Fiona looked at me needing support. I said, 'Fiona means that if some CIA agent was in a shoot-out on the Pacific Coast Highway, along the road from here, how keen would he be to have himself discovered by the local cops and passers-by when daylight comes?'

'Well, okay,' said Bret in a voice that conceded nothing. 'But this is the U.S. of A. Liberal newspapers who are looking for ways to take a swipe at the government, crackpot Senators ditto. In a situation like that, maybe some CIA agent might want to keep a low profile at whatever cost. But in the DDR . . . I don't see it.'

'Why don't you just tell us what you want us to say, Bret?' I said.

'Come again,' said Bret, the frayed edge of his temper showing through.

'We all know you're writing a fairy story,' I said. 'It's a scenario that was probably all settled months, maybe years, ago. You don't want to know what really happened: you just want to find excuses for saying everything went as planned. I know what the report will be: fifty pages patting all the desk men on the back, and saying what a wonderful job they did. The only decisions still to be made are who gets the knighthood and who will have to make do with an MBE or a CBE.'

'You're a rude bastard, Bernard,' he said softly.

'Yes. I know. Everyone tells me the same thing. But what I say is true, all the same.'

He looked at me and conceded just a fraction. 'Wasn't it Goethe who said, *Der Ausgang giebt den Taten ihre Titel* – how's that? The outcome decides what the title will be? Sure. This is a phenomenal success story. It's Fiona's success. She won't ever get a proper credit for it because that's not the way the Department handles these things: we all know that. What she will get is the report. Would you rather I write it up as some kind of turkey? You want me to say she screwed up?'

'No,' I said. Bret could always find a way of putting his opponents in the wrong.

Fiona said nothing. Her contribution to the talking was minimal and yet she was not uncooperative: she was like a sleep-walker. She knew her sister was dead – Bret had told her – but she avoided mention of Tessa. It was as if Tessa had never been there, and Bret left it like that. There were a lot of things that Fiona would not talk about, she seldom even mentioned the children. I didn't envy Bret his task.

Bret looked at his watch. 'Well, let's move on to a few easier questions. We'll get some of those rare roast beef sandwiches sent in, and break early. How about that?'

The sandwiches were lousy too.

A couple of days later we had a visitor. James Prettyman was an Americanized Englishman who used to work alongside me. Since then London Central had sent him to Washington in some deep cover plan that enabled him to do things for them at arm's length. At one time we'd been close friends. Now I wasn't so sure, although I suppose I owed him a favour or two.

Jim was in his early thirties. He had the wiry form and presence of mind that are associated with the pushier type of door-to-door salesmen. His complexion was pale and bloodless. His head was domelike and he was losing his silky hair but sometimes a strand of it fell across his eyes. I think he was glad to see it.

It was early in the morning when he arrived. He was wearing a blue striped suit, the lightweight cotton you need in Washington DC at this sweaty time of the year. There was a paisley silk square in the top pocket and the trousers were very rumpled, as if he'd been strapped in to his seat for a few hours.

'Good to see you, Bernie,' he said and gave me a sincere handshake and fixed me with his eyes, in that way that Americans do when they are trying to recall your name. 'I'm sitting in.' He looked at his watch. 'Later this morning. You, me and Bret: okay?'

'Good,' I said, uncertain of what was expected of me. I thought he must have come to talk with Fiona but she was taking breakfast in bed having been given a morning of 'free activity'.

Bret Rensselaer went into secret session with Jim Prettyman and I was summoned to join them at ten o'clock. The remains of their breakfast were still distributed around the room. Bret couldn't think without striding round the room so there were plates of half-eaten corn muffins, cups and unfinished glasses of orange juice on every side. I poured myself coffee from the vacuum jug and sat down. I reached for the cream jug but when I poured from it only a drip or two remained.

Bret Rensselaer said, 'Jim would like to hear your version of what happened.'

I looked at Bret and he added, 'On the Autobahn.'

'Oh,' I said. 'On the Autobahn.'

'Who was this man on the motor cycle?' said Prettyman.

'No one seems to know,' I said.

'I told Jim you had theories,' said Bret. 'And I told him you wouldn't open up.'

Jim said, 'Off the record, Bernie.'

'It was a dark night, Jim,' I said.

He leaned forward and switched off the tape recorder and said, 'Off the record.'

'Oh, that kind of off the record,' I said. I drank some coffee. It was cold. 'I think your vacuum flask is on the blink,' I said. 'Yes, well . . . He had an American accent.'

'They've all got American accents,' said Bret. 'It's the teaching machines.'

'So I hear,' I said.

'Did you recognize the voice?' said Prettyman.

'Are you putting me on?' I asked. 'Do we have to go through with this nonsense?'

'Who was it?'

'Jesus, Jim! You know who it was. It was a thug named Thurkettle, a renegade American. A hit man the Department brought in to make sure Tessa Kosinski was blown away.'

454

'Why you dumb . . .' started Bret, but Prettyman waved a hand that silenced him.

'Tell me more,' said Prettyman. 'Why would the Department want to kill Fiona's sister?' It was casually put, but in his voice there was that specially kindly tone with which psychiatrists coax maniacs.

'The car burned,' I said. 'Tessa Kosinski's remains – no more than a few bone fragments and ashes – will be identified as her sister Fiona. Fiona is hidden here: Moscow won't know that she is alive and well and spilling everything to you guys.'

'You're forgetting the teeth,' said Bret. 'They are sure to find some jawbone. Fiona had dentistry – a crown and a filling – while she was over there in East Berlin.' If anything was needed to convince me that my theory was right, it was Bret's remarkable knowledge of Fiona's dental chart.

Prettyman looked at Bret and then at me and then sneaked a quick look at his wristwatch.

'I'm forgetting nothing,' I said. 'Let's suppose a skull, sufficiently like Fiona's, was fitted with dental work that exactly matched hers. That would have been put into the car.'

'Two women's skulls in the car?'

'That's why you need a madman like Thurkettle. Hacking a head from a body is covered by his all-inclusive fee.'

'Thurkettle is the one who wasted the CIA man in Salzburg,' said Prettyman, as if remembering the name from something in the dim and distant past. Then he said, 'It would need a lot of planning . . . a lot of cooperation. Who would put him in position and so on?'

'There was drug trafficking: officials on both sides. A scapegoat was needed. All concerned were desperate to close the file. That spot, with the construction work on the highway, would provide a chance to bury any inconvenient evidence.'

'Where did you get all this?' said Prettyman.

I said, 'It's the only feasible explanation.'

'You'll have to do better than that, Bernie,' said Prettyman in a voice that seemed truly friendly. 'I'll listen to anything you have to say. I learned what I know from you: all of it. But you'll have to do a rewrite for that cockeyed script.'

'So what in hell was Tessa doing there?'

It was Bret's turn to speak. 'Isn't that a question for you to answer, Bernard? You took her there with you. Remember?'

'Will you go and see Gloria?' I asked Prettyman on a sudden and desperate impulse. 'Tell the children I'm well and that I love them?'

Bret said nothing.

Prettyman calmly said, 'There's not much chance of me getting a trip to London anytime in the foreseeable future, Bernie.'

I drank my tepid black coffee and didn't answer.

'I'll be back,' Prettyman told me like a dutiful son visiting a difficult octogenarian. 'But I have to be at Camarillo Municipal Airport by two. Next month maybe . . . Good to see you, Bernie. Really good! I mean that sincerely.'

'Get stuffed!' I said.

Prettyman looked at Bret. Bret responded with a tiny shrug as he was showing Prettyman out. I remained where I was but I could hear them in the next room. As they parted I heard Prettyman say, 'What a tragedy. Both of them.'

I heard Bret reply, 'It's not too late. Let's see what happens.'

It was a week afterwards that I learned that Camarillo Municipal Airport used to be a fully equipped US Air Force operational base and that the runways are still in good order. So when Prettyman went there he hopped back into the supersonic military jet that had brought him, and he was in Washington for happy hour. I suppose it was something that Fiona had said to Bret and Washington had to be told double quick.

We'd been at the house for over a month before Fiona began to open up to me. Even then what she said was fairly banal stuff about her day-to-day work in Berlin, but it was a start. Then each evening it became routine for us to talk for half an hour or so. Sometimes we'd talk over a drink in our sitting room, and sometimes we'd take a walk around the perimeter fence. Then one evening Fiona almost trod upon a big grey rattlesnake, and after that we kept to the paths and the terrace. It was a big property, and high enough so that on a pitch-black night like this the California coastline shone like a diamond necklace laid out all the way to Los Angeles.

'What really happened?' she said one night as we were standing there looking at the view and listening to the ocean.

'They got you out,' I said. 'That's what happened.'

'What was Tessa doing there? That's what I can't understand. What was Tessa doing there, Bernard?'

'I told you,' I said. 'She was having an affair with Dicky. She thought it would be fun, I suppose.'

'I loved you so much when I married you, Bernard. I loved you because you were the only man I'd ever met who had a real respect for the truth. You never lied to me, Bernard. I wanted my children to be like you.'

I was holding her hand, staring into the darkness and trying to recognize the distant coastline.

She said, 'You wouldn't be working against me, would you, Bernard? You wouldn't do that?'

'What do you mean?'

'They haven't even told George that Tessa is dead.'

'Why not?'

'Poor George. He'd never do harm to anyone.'

'Why haven't they told him?'

She turned to look at me. 'He's been sworn to secrecy and told that Tessa went to Berlin with you and that you've run away together . . . run away somewhere where no one can find you.'

'So that's the story,' I said. It fitted so neatly: the hotel room that Dicky had shared with Tessa was registered in my name.

'They want Moscow to believe that Tessa is alive. The story is that it was me who was killed at the Brandenburg exit.'

'The burning car. Yes, that would be it.'

'Could they get away with such a deception, Bernard?'

'There was trade in heroin. Could Erich Stinnes have been involved?'

'Erich? No!'

'A lot of people think he was,' I persisted. 'And he was working for the Department. Do you see how he could have been set up?'

'Stop worrying about Erich.'

'Who says I'm worrying about him?'

'You identify with him . . . the way he grew up in Berlin with a father in the army . . . you identify with him.'

I didn't deny it: she knew. I suppose I'd been shouting in my sleep. I'd had a couple of nightmares. 'I killed him.'

'It's all over, darling. Stop torturing yourself. Why was Tessa there? That's what I want to find out.'

'Tessa was an addict, you know.'

'That's what Bret said.'

'That might have been the reason she went to Berlin. There was a man named Thurkettle who probably supplied her. I think he might have cut off her supply to make her follow him there. There were a lot of people involved. A scapegoat was needed. You can bet the official explanation is that you were bringing it in.'

'That I was bringing it? Heroin? Whose explanation? East or West?'

'Everyone. It was a chance to close the file,' I said.

'How far would the Department go with that?'

'This is an unprecedented situation. We can't be guided by past examples.'

'Uncle Silas knew what I was really doing.'

'Yes, I know, I talked to him. Uncle Silas said they needed six months with Moscow still believing you remained loyal. They'll be using all the material that they were frightened of using before in case you were compromised.'

'You're saying someone deliberately planned it so that Tessa would die?'

'I don't know.' My answer came too pat and she thought I was not telling her all I knew. 'I really don't know, Fi.'

She put her arm round me. 'I have no one to trust any more. Sometimes that frightens me.'

'I understand.'

'Was it like that for you?'

'Sometimes.'

'Who would plan such a terrible thing?'

'Perhaps I've got it all wrong,' I said.

'Bret?'

'I wouldn't start going through the possibilities. Probably it was a mixture of planning and opportunity. Maybe it's nothing like that. As I say: maybe I've got it all wrong.'

'I suppose Tessa did look like me. Daddy always said so.'

'I have no evidence one way or the other,' I said. 'The most important thing is to give Bret the sort of answers he wants. We have to get out of here. The children need us.'

'I abandoned them,' said Fiona. 'They must hate me.'

'Of course they don't.'

'Why wasn't it me? Tessa so loved life, and you and the children can manage without me. Why wasn't it me?'

'You've got to start again, Fi,' I said.

'I didn't even recognize her,' said Fiona. 'I left her there in the mud.'

I could hear the ocean but I couldn't see anything there but darkness. I said, 'Why don't we see if Bret would let the children come here for the final three or four weeks?'

'Bret says we'll be here for a long time,' she said casually, as if she didn't care.

I shivered. I was right. We were imprisoned here. Maybe for years. Maybe indefinitely. I knew of defectors, needing protection, who were tucked away out of sight for a decade or more. 'Tell Bret you insist upon seeing the children,' I suggested.

She didn't reply immediately, and when she did her voice was listless. 'I love the children and I desperately want to see them. But not here.'

'Whatever you say, Fi.'

'I need time, Bernard. I'll be that lucky joyful girl you married, and the good times will come round again. We'll live happily ever after. But I need time.'

From the Pacific Ocean there came that smell of salt and putrefaction that is called fresh air. The sky was very dark that night: no stars, no glimmer of moonlight. Even the lights along the waterfront were being extinguished.

SPY SINKER

1

'Bret Rensselaer, you are a ruthless bastard.' It was his wife's voice. She spoke softly but with considerable force, as if it was a conclusion arrived at after long and difficult reasoning.

Bret half opened his eyes. He was in that hedonistic drowsy half sleep that makes awakening so irksome. But Bret Rensselaer was not a hedonist, he was a puritan; he saw himself as a direct descendant of those God-fearing, unyielding nonconformists who had colonized New England. He opened his eyes. 'What was that?' He looked at the bedside clock.

It was very early still. The room was flooded with sunlight coloured deep yellow by the holland blinds. He could see his wife sitting up in bed, one hand clutching her knee and the other holding a cigarette. She wasn't looking at him. It was as if she didn't know he was there beside her. Staring into the distance she puffed at the cigarette, not letting it go far from her mouth, holding it ready even as she exhaled. The curls of drifting smoke were yellow like the ceiling, and like his wife's face.

'You're utterly cold-blooded,' she said. 'You're in the right job.' She hadn't looked down to see whether he was awake. She didn't care. She was saying the things she was determined to say, things she'd thought a lot about, but never dared say before. Whether her husband heard her or not seemed unimportant.

Without a word of reply, he pushed back the bedclothes and got out of bed. It was not a violent movement. He did it gently so as not to disturb her. She turned her head to watch him go across the carpet. Naked he looked thin, if not to say skinny – that was why he looked so elegant in his carefully cut suits. She wished she was skinny too.

Bret went into the bathroom, drew back the curtains and opened the window. It was a glorious autumnal morning. The sunlit trees made long shadows across the gold-tipped grass. He'd not seen the flower-beds so crowded with blooms. At the end of his garden, where the fidgeting boughs of weeping willows fingered the water, the slow-moving river looked almost blue. Two rowing boats tied up at the pier bobbed gently up and down amid a flotilla of dead leaves. He loved this house.

463

Since the eighteenth century, many wealthy Londoners have favoured such upstream Thameside houses. With grounds that reach the water's edge they are hidden behind anonymous brick walls all the way from Chiswick to Reading. They come in all shapes, sizes and styles from palatial mansions in the Venetian manner to modest three-bedroom residences like this one.

Bret Rensselaer breathed deeply ten times, the way he did before doing his exercises. The view of the garden had reassured him. It always did. He had not always been an Anglophile but once he'd arrived in this bewitching land, he knew there was no escape from the obsessive love he had for everything connected with it. The river that ran at the foot of his garden was not an ordinary little stream; it was the Thames! The Thames with its associations of old London Bridge, Westminster Palace, the Tower, and of course Shakespeare's Globe. Still, after living here for years, he could hardly believe his good fortune. He wished his American wife could share his pleasure but she said England was 'backward' and could only see the bad side of living here.

He stared at himself in the mirror as he combed his hair. He had the same jutting chin and blond hair that his mother had passed on to him and his brother. The same good health too, and that was a priceless legacy. He put on his red silk dressing gown. Through the bathroom door he heard a movement and a clink of glass, and knew it was his wife taking a drink of bottled water. She didn't sleep well. He'd grown used to her chronic insomnia. He was no longer surprised to wake in the night and find her drinking water, smoking a cigarette or reading a chapter of one of her romantic novels.

When he returned to the bedroom she was still there: sitting cross-legged on the bed, her silk nightdress disarranged to expose her thighs, and its lacy shoulder trimming making a ruff behind her head. Her skin was pale – she avoided the sun – her figure full but not overweight, and her hair tousled. She felt him examining her and she raised her eyes to glare at him. In the past such a pose, that fierce look on her face, and a cigarette in her mouth, had aroused him. Perhaps it was a shameless wanton that he had hoped to discover. If so his hopes had soon been dashed.

He stepped into the alcove that he used as a dressing room and slid open the mirrored wardrobe door to select a suit from the two dozen hanging there, each one in its tissue paper and plastic bag as it had arrived from the cleaners.

'You have no feelings!' she said.

'Don't, Nikki,' he said. Her name was Nicola. She didn't like being called Nikki but it was too late now to tell him so.

'I mean it,' she said. 'You send men out to die as if you were sending out junk mail. You are heartless. I never loved you; no one could.'

What nonsense she spoke. Bret Rensselaer's position at SIS was Deputy Controller of European Economics. Yet it was a shrewd guess, there were times when he had to give the final okay on dangerous jobs. And when those tough decisions were to be made Bret did not shy from making them. 'You left it a darn long time before telling me,' he said reasonably, while hanging a lightweight wool and mohair suit near the light of the window and attaching the braces to the trousers. He screwed up the blue tissue wrapping and tossed it into the linen basket. Then he selected shirt and underclothes. He was worried. In this quarrelsome mood Nikki might blurt out some melodramatic yarn of that kind to the first stranger she came across. She hadn't done such a thing before but he'd never known her in this frame of mind before.

'I've been thinking about it lately,' she replied. 'Thinking about it a lot.'

'And did this thought process of yours begin before or after last Wednesday's lunch?'

She looked at him coolly and blew smoke before saying, 'Joppi has nothing to do with it. Do you think I would discuss you with Joppi?'

'You have before.' The way she referred to that Bavarian four-flusher by that silly diminutive name made him mad. No matter that just about everyone else did the same.

'That was different. That was years ago. You ran out on me.'

'Joppi is a jerk,' said Bret and was angry with himself for betraying his feelings. He looked at her and knew, not for the first time, murderous anger. He could have strangled her without a remnant of remorse. No matter: he would have the last laugh.

'Joppi is a real live prince,' she said provocatively.

'Princes are ten a penny in Bavaria.'

'And you are jealous of him,' she said, and didn't bother to conceal her pleasure at the idea of it.

'For making a play for my wife?'

'Don't be ridiculous. Joppi has a wife already.'

'One a day, from what I hear.'

'You can be very childish sometimes, Bret.'

He didn't respond except to look at her with fierce resentment. He deplored the way that Americans like his wife revered these two-bit European aristocrats. They'd met Joppi at Ascot the previous June. Joppi had a horse running in the Coronation Stakes and was there with a big party of German friends. Subsequently he'd invited the Rensselaers for a weekend at a house he'd leased near Paris. They had stayed with him there but Bret had not enjoyed it. He'd watched the unctuous Joppi looking at Nikki in a way that Bret did not like men to look at his wife. And Nikki had not even noticed it: or so she said when Bret complained of it afterwards. Now Joppi had invited Nikki to lunch without going through the formality of inviting Bret along. It made Bret sizzle.

'Prince Joppi,' said Bret with just enough emphasis upon the first word to show his contempt, 'is a two-bit racketeer.'

'Have you had him investigated?'

'I ran him through the computer,' he said. 'He's into all kinds of crooked deals. That's why we're going to stay clear of him.'

'I don't work for your goddamned secret intelligence outfit,' she said. 'Just in case you forgot, I'm a free citizen, and I choose my own friends and I say anything I want to say to them.'

He knew that she was trying to provoke him but still he wondered if he should phone the night duty officer. He'd have a phone contact for Internal Security. But Bret didn't relish the idea of describing the nuances of his married life to some young subordinate who would write it down and put it on file somewhere.

He went and ran the bath: both taps fully on gave him the temperature he preferred. He squirted bath oil into the rushing water and it foamed furiously. While the bath was filling he returned to Nikki. Under the circumstances, reasoning with her seemed the wiser course. 'Have I done something?' he asked with studied mildness. He sat down on the bed.

'Oh, no!' said his wife sarcastically. 'Not you.' She could hear the water beating against the bath with a roar like thunder.

She was tense, her arms clamped round her knees, the cigarette forgotten for a moment. He looked at her, trying to see something in her face that would give him a hint about the origin of her anger. Failing to see anything that enlightened him he said, 'Then what. . . ?' And then more briskly but with a conciliatory tone, 'For goodness sake, Nikki. I have to go to the office.'

'I have to go to the office.' She attempted to mimic the Englishness that he'd acquired since living here. She was not a good mimic and her twanging accent, that had so intrigued him when they first met, was still strong. How foolish he'd been to hope that eventually she would embrace England and everything English as lovingly as he had. 'That's all that's important to you, isn't it? Never mind me. Never mind if I go stir-crazy in this Godforsaken dump.' She tossed her head to throw her hair back but when it fell forward again she raked her fingers through it to get it from her face.

He sat at the end of the bed smiling at her and said, 'Now, now, Nikki, darling. Just tell me what's wrong.'

It was the patronizing 'just' that irritated her. There was something invulnerable about his resolute coldness. Her sister had called him 'the shy desperado' and giggled when he called. But Nikki had found it easy to fall in love with Bret Rensselaer. How clearly she remembered it. She'd never had a suitor like him: slim, handsome, soft-spoken and considerate. And there was his lifestyle too. Bret's suits fitted in the way that only expensive tailoring could contrive and his cars were waxed shiny in the way that only chauffeur-driven cars were, and his mother's house was cared for by loyal servants. She loved him of course but her love had always been mingled with a touch of awe, or perhaps it was fear. Now she didn't care. Just for a moment, she was able to tell him everything she felt. 'Look here, Bret,' she said confidently. 'When I married you I thought you were going to . . .'

He held up his hand and said, 'Let me turn off the bath, darling. We don't want it flooding the study downstairs.' He went back into the bathroom; the roar of water stopped. A draught was coming through the window to make steam that tumbled out through the door. He emerged tightening the knot of his dressing gown: a very tight knot, there was something neurotic in that gesture. He raised his eyes to her and she knew that the moment had passed. She was tongue-tied again: he knew how to make her feel like a child and he liked that. 'What were you saying, dear?'

She bit her lip and tried again, differently this time. 'That night, when you first admitted that you were working in secret intelligence, I didn't believe you. I thought it was another of your romantic stories.'

'Another?' He was amused enough to smile.

'You were always an ace bullshitter, Bret. I thought you were making it all up as some kind of compensation for your dull job at the bank.'

His eyes narrowed: it was the only sign he gave of being angry. He looked down at the carpet. He had been about to do his exercises but she'd hammer at him all the time and he didn't want that. Better to do them at the office.

'You were going to bleed them white. I remember you saying that: bleed them white. You told me one day you'd have a man working in the Kremlin.' She wanted to remind him how close they had been. 'Remember?' Her mouth was dry; she sipped more water. 'You said the Brits could do it because they hadn't grown too big. You said they could do it but they didn't know they could do it. That's where you came in, you said.'

Bret stood with his fists in the pockets of the red dressing gown. He wasn't really listening to her; he wanted to get on, to bathe and shave and dress and spend the extra time sitting with a newspaper and toast and coffee in the garden before his driver came round to collect him. But he knew that if he turned away, or ended the conversation abruptly, her anger would be reaffirmed. 'Maybe they will,' he said and hoped she'd drop it.

He lifted his eyes to the small painting that hung above the bed. He had many fine pictures – all by modern British painters – but this was Bret Rensselaer's proudest possession. Stanley Spencer: buxom English villagers frolicking in an orchard. Bret could study it for hours, he could smell the fresh grass and the apple blossom. He'd paid far too much for the painting but he had desperately wanted to possess that English scene for ever. Nikki didn't appreciate having a masterpiece enshrined in the bedroom, to love and to cherish. She preferred photographs; she'd admitted as much once, during a savage argument about the bills she'd run up with the dressmaker.

'You said that running an agent into the Kremlin was your greatest ambition.'

'Did I?' He looked at her and blinked, discomposed both by the extent of his indiscretion and the naïveté of it. 'I was kidding you.'

'Don't say that, Bret!' She was angry that he should airily dismiss the only truly intimate conversation she could remember having with him. 'You were serious. Dammit, you were serious.'

'Perhaps you're right.' He looked at her and at the bedside table to see what she'd been drinking, but there was no alcohol there, only a litre-size bottle of Malvern water. She'd stuck to her rigorous diet – no bread, butter, sugar, potatoes, pasta or alcohol – for three weeks. She was amazingly disciplined about her dieting and Nikki had never been much of a drinker: it went straight to her waistline. When Internal Security had first vetted her they'd remarked on her abstinence and Bret had been proud.

He got up and went round to her side of the bed to give her a kiss. She offered her cheek. It was a sort of armistice but his fury was not allayed: just repressed. 'It's a glorious sunny day again. I'm going to have coffee in the garden. Shall I bring some up?'

She pulled the bedside clock round to see it. 'Jesus Christ! The help won't be there for an hour yet.'

'I'm perfectly capable of fixing my own toast and coffee.'

468

'It's too early for me. I'll call for it when I'm ready.'

He looked at her eyes. She was close to tears. As soon as he left the room she would begin weeping. 'Go back to sleep, Nikki. Do you want an aspirin?'

'No I don't want a goddamned aspirin. Anytime I bug you, you ask me if I want an aspirin: as if talking out of turn was some kind of feminine malady.'

He had often accused her of being a dreamer, which by extension was his claim to be a practical realist. The truth was that he was even more of a romantic dreamer than she was. This craving he had for everything English was ridiculous. He'd even talked of renouncing his US citizenship and was hoping to get one of these knighthoods the British handed out instead of money. An obsession of that kind could bring him only trouble.

There was enough work in the office to keep Bret Rensselaer busy for the first hour or more. It was a wonderful room on the top floor of a modern block. Large by the standards of modern accommodation, his office had been decorated according to his own ideas, as interpreted by one of the best interior decorators in London. He sat behind his big glass-topped desk. The colour scheme – walls, carpet and long leather chesterfield – was entirely grey and black except for his white phone. Bret had intended that the room should be in harmony with this prospect of the slate roofs of central London.

He buzzed for his secretary and started work. Halfway through the morning, his tray emptied by the messenger, he decided to switch off his phone and take twenty minutes to catch up with his physical exercises. It was a part of his puritanical nature and upbringing that he would not make a confrontation with his wife an excuse to miss his work or his exercises.

He was in his shirt-sleeves, doing his thirty pressups, when Dicky Cruyer – a contender for the soon to become vacant chair of the German Stations Controller – put his head round the door and said, 'Bret, your wife has been trying to get through to you.'

Bret continued to do his pressups slowly and methodically. 'And?' he said, trying not to puff.

'She sounded upset,' said Dicky. 'She said something like, "Tell him, you get your man in Moscow and I'll go get my man in Paris." I asked her to tell me again but she rang off.' He watched while Bret finished a couple more pressups.

'I'll talk to her later,' grunted Bret.

'She was at the airport, getting on the plane. She said to say goodbye. "Goodbye for ever," she said.'

'So you've said it,' Bret told him, head twisted, smiling pleasantly from his position full length on the floor. 'Message received and understood.'

Dicky muttered something about it being a bad phone line, nodded and withdrew with the feeling that he'd been unwise to bring the ugly news. He'd heard rumours that all was not going well with the Rensselaer marriage, but no matter how much a man might want to leave his wife it does not mean that he wants her to leave him. Dicky had the feeling that Bret Rensselaer wouldn't forget who it was who had brought news of his wife's desertion, and it would leave a residual antipathy that would taint their relationship for ever after. In this assumption Dicky was correct. He began to hope that the appointment of the German Stations Controller would not be entirely in Bret's gift.

The door clicked shut. Bret began the pressups over again. He had inflicted that mortifying rule on himself: if he stopped during exercises he did them all over again.

When his exercises were done Bret opened the door that concealed a small sink. He washed his face and hands and as he did so he recalled in detail the conversation he'd had with his wife that morning. He told himself not to waste time pondering the rift between them: what was gone was gone, and good riddance. Bret Rensselaer had always claimed that he never wasted time upon recriminations or regrets, but he felt hurt and deeply resentful.

To get his mind on other matters he began to think about those days long ago when he'd wanted to get into Operations. He'd drafted out some ideas about undermining the East German economy but no one had taken him seriously. The Director-General's reaction to the big pile of research he'd done was to give him the European Economics desk. That wasn't really something to complain about; Bret had built the desk into a formidable empire. But the economic desk work had been processing intelligence. He always regretted that they hadn't taken up the more important idea: the idea of promoting change in East Germany.

Bret's idea had never been to get an effective agent into the top of the Moscow KGB. He would prefer having a really brilliant agent, with a long-term disruptive and informative role, in East Berlin, the capital of the German Democratic Republic. It would take a long time: it was not something that could be hurried in the way that so many SIS operations were.

The Department probably had dozens of sleepers who'd established themselves, in one capacity or another, as long-time loyal agents of the various communist regimes of East Europe. Now Bret had to find such a person, and it had to be the right one. But the long and meticulous process of selection had to be done with such discretion and finesse that no one would be aware of what he was doing. And when he found that man, he'd have the task of persuading him to risk his neck in a way that sleepers were not normally asked to do. A lot of sleepers assigned to deep cover just took the money and relied upon the good chance that they'd never be asked to do anything at all.

It would not be simple. Neither would it be happy. At the beginning there would be little or no cooperation, for the simple reason that no one around him could be told what he was doing. Afterwards there would be the clamour for recognition and rewards. The Department was very concerned about such things. It was natural these men, who laboured so secretly, should strive so vigorously and desperately for the admiration and respect of their peers when things went well. And if things did not go well there would be the savage recriminations that accompanied post-mortems.

Lastly there was the effect that an operation like this would have upon the man who went off to do the dirty work. They did not come back. Or if they did come back they were never fit to work again. Of the survivors Bret had seen, few returned able to do anything but sit with a rug over their knees, talk to the officially approved departmental shrink, and try vainly to put together ruptured nerves and shattered relationships.

It was easy to see why they couldn't recover. You ask a man to leave all that he holds most dear, to spy in a strange country. Then, years later, you snatch him back again – God willing – to live out his remaining life in peace and contentment. But there is no peace and no contentment either. The poor devil can't remember anyone he hasn't betrayed or abandoned at some time or another. Such people are destroyed as surely as if they'd faced a firing squad.

On the other hand it was necessary to balance the destruction of one man – plus perhaps a few members of his family – with what could be achieved by such a coup. It was a matter of the greater good of the community at large. They were fighting against a system which killed hundreds of thousands in labour camps, which used torture as a normal part of its police interrogation, which put dissenters into mental asylums. It would be absurd to be squeamish when the stakes were so high.

Bret Rensselaer closed the door that hid his sink and went to the window and looked out. Despite the haze, you could see it all from here: the Gothic spike of the Palace of Westminster, the spire of St Martin's in the Fields, Nelson balancing gingerly on his column. There was a unity to it. Even the incongruous Post Office tower would perhaps look all right given a century or so of weathering. Bret pushed his face close to the glass in order to see Wren's dome of St Paul's. The Director-General's room had a fine view northwards and Bret envied him that. One day perhaps he would occupy that room. Nikki had made jokes about that and he'd pretended to laugh at them but he'd not given up hopes that one day . . .

Then he remembered the notes he'd made about the whole project. A great idea struck him: now that he had more time, and a staff of economists and analysts, he'd have it all up-dated. Maps, bar charts, pie charts, graphs and easy to understand figures that even the Director-General would understand could all be done on the computer. Why hadn't he thought of it before? Thank you, Nikki.

And that brought him back to his wife. Once again he told himself to be resolute. She had left him. It was all over. He told himself he'd seen it coming for ages but in fact he hadn't seen it coming at all. He'd always taken it for granted that Nikki would put up with all the things of which she complained – just as he put up with her – in order to have a marriage. He would miss her, there was no getting away from that fact, but he vowed he wouldn't go chasing after her.

It simply wasn't fair: he'd never been unfaithful to her all the time they'd been married. He sighed. Now he would have to start all over again: dating, courting, persuading, cajoling, being the extra man at parties. He'd have to learn how to suffer rejection when he asked younger women out to dinner. Rejection had never been easy for him. It was all too awful to contemplate. Perhaps he'd get his secretary to dine with him one evening next week. She'd told him it was all off with her fiancé.

He sat down at his desk and picked up some papers but the words floated before his eyes as his mind went back to Nikki. What had started the breakdown of his marriage? What had gone wrong? What had Nikki called him: a ruthless bastard? She'd been so cool and lucid, that's what had really shaken him. Thinking about it again he decided that Nikki's cool and lucid manner had all been a sham. Ruthless bastard? He told himself that women were apt to say absurd things when they were incoherently angry. That helped.

2

East Germany. January 1978.

'Bring me the mirror,' said Max Busby. He hadn't intended that his voice should come out as a croak. Bernard Samson went and got the mirror and placed it on the table so Max could see his arm without twisting inside out. 'Now take the dressing off,' said Max.

The sleeve of Max's filthy old shirt had been torn back as far as the shoulder. Now Bernard unbound the arm, finally peeling back a pad that was caked with pus and dried blood. It was a shock. Bernard gave an involuntary hiss and Max saw the look of horror on his face. 'Not too bad,' said Bernard, trying to hide his real feelings.

'I've seen worse,' said Busby, looking at it and trying to sound unruffled. It was a big wound: deep and inflamed and oozing pus. Bernard had stitched it up with a sewing needle and fishing line from a survival kit but some of his stitches had torn through the soft flesh. The skin around it was mottled every colour of the rainbow and so tender that even to look at it made it hurt more. Bernard was pinching it together tight so it didn't break right open again. The dressing – an old handkerchief – had got dirty. The side that had been against the wound was dark brown and completely saturated with blood. More blood had crusted in patches all down his arm. 'It might have been my gun hand.'

Max bent his head until, by the light of the lamp, he could see his pale face in the mirror. He knew about wounds. He knew the way that loss of blood makes the heart pound as it tries to keep supplying oxygen and glucose to the brain. His face had whitened due to the blood vessels contracting as they tried to help the heart do its job. And the heart pumped more furiously as the plasma was lost and the blood thickened. Max tried to take his own pulse. He couldn't manage it but he knew what he would find: irregular pulse and low body temperature. These were all the signs: bad signs.

'Put something on the fire and then bind it up tight with the strip of towel. I'll wrap paper round it before we leave. Don't want to leave a trail of blood spots.' He managed a smile. 'We'll give them another hour.' Max Busby was frightened. They were in a mountain hut, it was winter and he was no longer young.

473

A one-time NYPD cop, he'd come to Europe in 1944, wearing the bars of a US Army lieutenant, and he'd never gone back across the Atlantic except for an attempted reconciliation with his ex-wife in Chicago and a couple of visits to his mother in Atlantic City.

After Bernard had replaced the mirror and put something on to the fire, Max stood up and Bernard helped him with his coat. Then he watched as Max settled down carefully in his chair. Max was badly hurt. Bernard wondered if they would both make it as far as the border.

Max read his thoughts and smiled. Now neither wife nor mother would have recognized Max in his filthy overcoat with battered jeans and the torn shirt under it. There was a certain mad formality to the way that he balanced a greasy trilby hat on his knees. His papers said he was a railway worker but his papers, and a lot of other things he needed, were at the railway station and a Soviet arrest team was there too.

Max Busby was short and squat without being fat. His sparse hair was black and his face was heavily lined. His eyes were reddened by tiredness. He had heavy brows and a large straggly black moustache that was lop-sided because of the way he kept tugging at one end of it.

Older, wiser, wounded and sick, but despite all that and the change in environment and costume, Max Busby did not feel very different to that green policeman who'd patrolled the dark and dangerous Manhattan streets and alleys. Then, as now, he was his own man: the wrongos didn't all wear black hats. Some of them were to be found spooning their beluga with the police commissioner. It was the same here: no black and white, just shades of grey. Max Busby disdained communism – or 'socialism' in the preferred terminology of its practitioners – and all it stood for, with a zeal that was unusual even in the ranks of the men who fought it, but he wasn't a simplistic crusader.

'Two hours,' suggested Bernard Samson. Bernard was big and strong, with wavy hair and spectacles. He wore a scuffed leather zip-front jacket, and baggy corduroy trousers, held up by a wide leather belt decorated with a collection of metal communist Parteitag badges. On his head there was a close-fitting peaked cap of the design forever associated with the ill-fated Afrika Korps. It was a sensible choice of headgear thought Max as he looked at it. A man could go to sleep in a cap like that, or fight without losing it. Max looked at his companion: Bernard was still in one piece, and young enough to wait it out without his nerves fraying and his mouth going dry. Perhaps it would be better to let him go on alone. But would Bernard make it alone? Max was not at all sure he would. 'They have to get through Schwerin,' Bernard reminded him. 'They may be delayed by one of the mobile patrols.'

Max nodded and wet his lips. The loss of blood had sapped his strength: the idea of his contacts being challenged by a Russian army patrol made his stomach heave. Their papers were not good enough to withstand any scrutiny more careful than a cop's casual flashlight beam. Few false papers are.

He knew that Bernard wouldn't see the nod, the little room was in darkness except for the faint glimmer from an evil-smelling oil-lamp, its wick turned as low as possible, and from the stove a rosy glow that gave satin toecaps to their boots, but *Qui tacet, consentire videtur*, silence means consent. Max, like many a NY cop before him, had slaved at night school to study law. Even now he remembered a few basic essentials. More pertinent to his ready consent was the fact that Max knew what it was like to be crossing a hundred and fifty kilometres of moonlit Saxon countryside when there was a triple A alert and a Moscow stop-and-detain order that would absolve any trigger-happy cop or soldier from the consequences of shooting strangers on sight.

Bernard tapped the cylindrical iron stove with his heavy boot and was startled when the door flipped open and red-hot cinders fell out upon the hearth. For a few moments there was a flare of golden light as the draught fed the fire. He could see the wads of brown-edged newspaper packed into the cracks around the door frame and a chipped enamel wash-basin and the ruck-sacks that had been positioned near the door in case they had to leave in a hurry. And he could see Max as white as a sheet and looking . . . well, looking like any old man would look who'd lost so much blood and who should be in an intensive-care ward but was trudging across northern Germany in winter. Then it went dull again and the room darkened.

'Two hours then?' Bernard asked.

'I won't argue.' Max was carefully chewing the final mouthful of rye bread. It was delicious but he had to chew carefully and swallow it bit by bit. They grew the best rye in the world in Mecklenburg, and made the finest bread with it. But that was the last of it and both men were hungry.

'That makes a change,' said Bernard good-naturedly. They seldom truly argued. Max liked the younger man to feel he had a say in what happened. Especially now.

'I'll not make an enemy with the guy who's going to get the German Desk,' said Max very softly, and twisted one end of his moustache. He tried not to think of his pain.

'Is that what you think?'

'Don't kid around, Bernard. Who else is there?'

475

'Dicky Cruyer.'

Max said, 'Oh, so that's it. You really resent Dicky, don't you?' Bernard always rose to such bait and Max liked to tease him.

'He could do it.'

'Well, he hasn't got a ghost of a chance. He's too young and too inexperienced. You're in line; and after this one you'll get anything you ask for.'

Bernard didn't reply. It was a welcome thought. He was in his middle thirties and, despite his contempt for desk men, he didn't want to end up like poor old Max. Max was neither one thing nor the other. He was too old for shooting matches, climbing into other people's houses and running away from frontier guards, but there was nothing else that he could do. Nothing, that is, that would pay him anything like a living wage. Bernard's attempts to persuade his father to get Max a job in the training school had been met with spiteful derision. He'd made enemies in all the wrong places. Bernard's father never got along with him. Poor Max, Bernard admired him immensely, and Bernard had seen Max doing the job as no one else could do it. But heaven only knew how he'd end his days. Yes, a job behind a desk in London would come at exactly the right stage of Bernard's career.

Neither man spoke for a little while after that. For the last few miles Bernard had been carrying everything. They were both exhausted, and like combat soldiers they had learned never to miss an opportunity for rest. They both dozed into a controlled half sleep. That was all they would allow themselves until they were back across the border and out of danger.

It was about thirty minutes later that the thump thump thump of a helicopter brought them back to wide-eyed awakening. It was a medium-sized chopper, not transport size, and it was flying slowly and at no more than a thousand feet, judging from the sound it made. It all added up to bad news. The German Democratic Republic was not rich enough to supply such expensive gas-guzzling machines for anything but serious business.

'Shit!' said Max. 'The bastards are looking for us.' Despite the urgency in his voice he spoke quietly, as if the men in the chopper might hear him.

The two men sat in the dark room neither moving nor speaking: they were listening. The tension was almost unbearable as they concentrated. The helicopter was not flying in a straight line and that was an especially bad sign: it meant it had reached its search area. Its course meandered as if it was pin-pointing the neighbouring villages. It was

476

looking for movement: any kind of movement. Outside the snow was deep. When daylight came nothing could move without leaving a conspicuous trail.

In this part of the world, to go outdoors was enough to excite suspicion. There was nowhere to visit after dark, the local residents were simple people, peasants in fact. They didn't eat the sort of elaborate evening meal that provides an excuse for dinner parties and they had no money for restaurants. As to hotels, who would want to spend even one night here when they had the means to move on?

The sound of the helicopter was abruptly muted as it passed behind the forested hills, and for the time being the night was silent.

'Let's get out of here,' said Max. Such a sudden departure would be going against everything they had planned but Max, even more than Bernard, was a creature of impulse. He had his 'hunches'. He wrapped folded newspaper round his arm in case the blood came through the towel. Then he put string round the arm of the overcoat and Bernard tied it very tight.

'Okay.' Bernard had long ago decided that Max – notwithstanding his inability to find domestic happiness or turn his professional skills into anything resembling a success story – had an uncanny instinct for the approach of danger. Without hesitation and without getting up from his chair, Bernard leaned forward and picked up the big kettle. Opening the stove ring with the metal lifting tool, he poured water into the fire. He did it very carefully and gently, but even so there was a lot of steam.

Max was about to stop him but the kid was right. Better to do it now. At least that lousy chopper was out of sight of the chimney. When the fire was out Bernard put some dead ashes into the stove. It wouldn't help much if they got here. They'd see the blood on the floorboards, and it would require many gallons of water to cool the stove, but it might make it seem as if they'd left earlier and save them if they had to hide nearby.

'Let's go.' Max took out his pistol. It was a Sauer Model 38, a small automatic dating from the Nazi period, when they were used by high-ranking army officers. It was a lovely gun, obtained by Bernard from some underworld acquaintance in London, where Bernard's array of shady friends rivalled those he knew in Berlin.

Bernard watched Max as he tried to move the slide back to inject a round into the chamber. He had to change hands to do it and his face was contorted with pain. It was distressing to watch him but Bernard said nothing. Once done, Max pressed on the exposed cocking lever to

477

lower the hammer so the gun was ready for instant use but with little risk of accident. Max pushed the gun into his inside breast pocket. 'Have you got a gun?' he asked.

'We left it at the house. You said Siggi might need it.' Bernard swung the rucksack over his shoulder. It was heavy, containing the contents of both packs. There was a grappling hook and nylon rope as well as a small digging implement and a formidable bolt-cutter.

'So I did. Damn. Well, you take the glasses.' Bernard took them from round Max's neck, careful not to jar his arm. 'Stare them to death, Bernard. You can do it!' A grim little laugh. Silently Bernard took the field-glasses – rubber-clad Zeiss 7×40s, like the ones the Grenzpolizei used – and put his head and arm through the strap. It made them uncomfortably tight, but if they had to run for it he didn't want the glasses floating around and banging him in the face.

Max tapped the snuffer that extinguished the flame of the oil-lamp. Everything was pitch black until he opened the door and let in a trace of blue starlight and the bitterly cold night air. 'Attaboy!'

Max was expecting trouble and Bernard did not find the prospect cheering. Bernard had never learned to face the occasional violent episodes that his job provided in the way that the old-timers like Max accepted them even when injured. Was it, he wondered, something to do with the army or the war, or both?

The timber cabin was isolated. If only it would snow again, that would help to cover their tracks, but there was no sign of snow. Once outside Max sniffed the air, anxious to know if the smoke from the stove would carry far enough to alert a search party. Well at least choosing this remote shelter had proved right. It was a hut for the cowherds when in summer the cattle moved to the higher grazing. From this elevated position they could see the valley along which they had come. Here and there, lights indicated a cluster of houses in this dark and lonely landscape. It was good country for moving at night but when daylight came it would work against them: they'd be too damned conspicuous. Max cursed the bad luck that had dogged the whole movement. By this time they should have all been across the border, skin intact and sound asleep after warm baths and a big meal and lots to drink.

Max looked up. A few stars were sprinkled to the east but most of the sky was dark. If the thick overcast remained there, blotting out the sun, it would help, but it wasn't low enough to inconvenience the helicopters. The chopper would be back.

'We'll keep to the high ground,' said Max. 'These paths usually make good going. They keep them marked and maintained for summertime walkers.' He set off at a good pace to show Bernard that he was fit and strong, but after a little while he slowed.

For several kilometres the beech forest blocked off their view of the valley. It was dark walking under the trees, like being in a long tunnel. The undergrowth was dead and crisp brown fern crunched under their feet. As the trail climbed the snow was harder. Trees shielded the footpath and upon the hard going they made reasonably good speed. They had walked for about an hour and a half, and were into the evergreens, when Max called a halt. They were higher now, and through a firebreak in the regimented plantations they could see the twist of the next valley ahead of them. Beyond that, through a dip in the hills, a lake shone faintly in the starlight, its water heady with foam, like good German beer. It was difficult to guess how far away it was. There were no houses in sight, no roads, no power lines, nothing to give the landscape a scale. Trees were no help: these fir trees came in all shapes and sizes.

'Five minutes,' said Max. He sank down in a way that revealed his true condition and wedged his backside into the roots of a tree. Alongside him there was a bin for feeding the deer: the herds were cosseted for the benefit of the hunters. Resting against the bin, Max's head slumped to one side. His face was shiny with exertion and he looked all in. Blood had seeped through the paper and there was a patch of it on the sleeve of the thick overcoat. Better to press on than to try to fix it here.

Bernard took out the field-glasses, snapped the protective covers from the lenses, and looked more carefully at the lake. It was the haze upon the water that produced the boiling effect and softened its outline.

'How are your feet?' said Max.

'Okay, Max.'

'I have spare socks.'

'Don't mother me, Max.'

'Do you know where we are?'

'Yes, we're in Germany,' he said, still staring through the glasses.

'Are you sure?'

'But that's our lake, Max,' Bernard affirmed. 'Mouse Lake.'

'Or Moulting Lake,' suggested Max.

'Or even Turncoat Lake,' said Bernard, suggesting a third possible translation.

Max regretted his attempt at levity. 'Something like that,' he said. He resolved to stop treating Bernard like a child. It was not so easy: He'd known him so long it was difficult to remember that he was a grown man with a wife and children. And what a wife! Fiona Samson was one of the rising stars of the Department. Some of the more excitable employees were saying that she was likely to wind up as the first woman to hold the Director-General's post. Max found it an unlikely prospect. The higher echelons of the Department were reserved for a certain sort of Englishman, all of whom seemed to have been at school together.

Max Busby often wondered why Fiona had married Bernard. He was no great prize. If he got the German Desk in London it would be largely due to his father's influence, and he'd go no further. Whoever got the German Desk would come under Bret Rensselaer's direction, and Bret wanted a stooge there. Max wondered if Bernard would adapt to a yes-man role.

Max took the offered field-glasses to have a closer look at the lake. Holding them with only one hand meant resting against the tree. Even holding his arm up made him tremble. He wondered if it was septic: he'd seen wounds go septic very quickly but he put the thought to the back of his mind and concentrated on what he could see. Yes, that was the Mause See: exactly as he remembered it from the map. Maps had always been a fetish with him, sometimes he sat looking at them for hours on end, as other men read books. They were not only maps of places he knew, or places he'd been or places he might have to visit, but maps of every kind. When someone had given him the *Times Atlas of the Moon*, Max took it on vacation and it was his sole reading matter.

'We must come in along the southern shore,' said Bernard, 'and not too close to the water or we'll find ourselves in some Central Committee member's country cottage.'

'A boat might be the best way,' Max suggested, handing the glasses back.

'Let's get closer,' said Bernard, who didn't like the idea of a boat. Too risky from every point of view. Bernard was not very skilled with a set of oars and Max certainly couldn't row. In winter a boat might be missed from its moorings, and even if the water was glassy smooth – which it wouldn't be – he didn't fancy being exposed to view like that. It was an idea typical of Max, who liked such brazen methods and had proved them in the past. Bernard hoped Max would forget that idea by the time they'd covered the intervening countryside. It was a long hike. It looked like rough going and soon it would be dawn.

Bernard felt like saying something about the two men with whom they had been supposed to rendezvous yesterday afternoon, but he kept silent. There was nothing to be said; they had gone into the bag. Max and Bernard had been lucky to get away. Now the only important thing was for them to get back. If they didn't, the whole operation – 'Reisezug' – would have proved useless: more than three months of planning, risks and hard work wasted. Bernard's father was running the operation, and he would be desolated. To some extent, his father's reputation depended upon him.

Bernard got up and dusted the soil from his trousers. It was sandy and had a strange musty smell.

'It stinks, right?' said Max, somehow reading his thoughts. 'The North German Plain. Goddamned hilly for a plain, I'd say.'

'German Polish Plain they called it when I was at school,' said Bernard.

'Yeah, well, Poland has moved a whole lot closer to here since I did high school geography,' said Max, and smiled at his little joke. 'My wife Helma was born not far from here. Ex-wife that is. Once she got that little old US passport she went off to live in Chicago with her cousin.'

As Bernard helped Max to his feet he saw the animal. It was lying full-length in a bare patch of ground behind the tree against which he'd rested. Its fur was caked with mud and it was frozen hard. He peered more closely at it. It was a fully grown hare, its foot tight in a primitive wire snare. The poor creature had died in agony, gnawing its trapped foot down to the bone but lacking either the energy or the desperate determination required for such a sacrifice.

Max came to look too. Neither man spoke. For Max it seemed like a bad omen and Max had always been a great believer in signs. Still without speaking they both trudged on. They were tired now and the five minutes' break that had helped their lungs had stiffened their muscles. Max found it difficult to hold his arm up, but if he let it hang it throbbed and bled more.

'Why didn't he go back?' said Max as the path widened and Bernard came up alongside him.

'Who?'

'The poacher. Why didn't he go back and look at his snares?'

'You mean we are already in the *Sperrzone*? There was no fence, no signs.'

'Locals know where it is,' said Max. 'Strangers blunder onwards.' He unbuttoned his coat and touched the gun. There was no practical reason for doing so except that Max wanted to make it clear to Bernard that he hadn't come all this way in order to turn himself in to the first person who challenged them. Max had shot his way out of trouble before: twice. Some people said those two remarkable instances of good luck had given him a false idea of what could be done when facing capture;

Max thought the British with whom he worked were too damned ready to let their people put their hands up.

He stopped for a moment to look at the lake again. It would be so much easier and quicker to be walking along the valley instead of along this high path. But there would be villages and farms and dogs that barked down there. These high paths were less likely to have such dangers but the ice on the northern aspects meant they were sometimes slower going and the two men didn't have time to spare.

The next hill was higher and after that the path would descend to cross the Besen valley. Perhaps it would be better to cross it somewhere else. If the local police were alerted they were sure to put a man at the stone bridge where the footpath met the valley road. He looked at the summit of the hill on the far side of the river. They'd never do it. The local people called these hills 'mountains', as people do in regions where no mountains exist. Well, he was beginning to understand why. After you walked these hills they became mountains. Everything was relative: the older he got the more mountainous the world became.

'We'll try to get over the Besen at that wide place where the stones are,' said Max.

Bernard grunted unenthusiastically. If they'd had more time Max would have made it into more of a discussion. He would have let Bernard feel he'd had a say in the decisions, but there was no time for such niceties.

Scrambling down through the dead bracken and the loose stones caused both men to lose their balance now and again. Once Max slid so far he almost fell. He knocked his wounded arm when recovering himself, and the pain was so great that he gave a little whimper. Bernard helped him up. Max said nothing. He didn't say thanks, there was no energy to spare.

Max had chosen this place with care. Everywhere on its east side the Wall occupied a wide band of communist territory. Even to get within five kilometres of the Wall itself required a permit. This well guarded and constantly patrolled prohibited region, or *Sperrzone*, was cleared of trees and any shrubs or growth that could conceal a man or child. Any agricultural work permitted in the *Sperrzone* was done only in daylight and under the constant surveillance of the guards in their watchtowers. Artfully the towers were different in height and design, varying from the lower 'observation bunkers' to the tall modernistic concrete constructions that resembled airport control towers.

But in the *Sperrzone* of that section of the frontier that NATO codenames 'piecemeal', good or bad fortune has called upon the DDR to contend with the lake. It was the presence of a lake at a part of the Wall that was undergoing extensive repair work that caught Max Busby's attention in the so-called Secret Room.

For the regime it was a difficult section: the Elbe and the little river Besen that feeds into it, plus the effect of the Mause See, all contributed to the marshiness of the flat land. The Wall was always giving them problems here no matter what they did about waterproofing the foundations. Now a stretch almost three kilometres long was under repair at seven different places. It must be bad or they would have waited until summer.

Getting through the *Sperrzone* was only the beginning. The real frontier was marked by a tall fence, too flimsy to climb but rigged with alarms, flares and automatic guns. After that came the *Schutzstreifen*, the security strip, about five hundred metres deep, where attack-trained dogs on *Hundelaufleine* ran between the minefields. Then came the concrete ditches, followed by an eight-metre strip of dense barbed wire and a variety of devices arranged differently from sector to sector to provide surprises for the newcomer.

To what extent this bizarre playground had been dismantled for the benefit of the repair gangs, remained to be discovered. It was difficult to forget the helicopter. The whole military region would be alerted now. It wouldn't be hard to guess where the fugitives were heading.

When they reached the lake it was not anything like the obstruction that either of them had anticipated. They'd been soaked to the knees wading across the slow-moving Besen. The necessary excursion into the Mause See – to get around the red marker-buoys which Max thought might mark underwater obstacles – did no more than repeat the soaking up to the waist. But there was a difference: the hard muscular legs had been brought back to tingling life by brisk walking, but the icy cold water of the lake up to his waist drained from Max some measure of his resolution. His arm hurt, his guts hurt and the arctic water pierced through his belly like cold steel.

The snow began with just a few flakes spinning down from nowhere and then became a steady fall. 'What a beautiful sight,' said Bernard and Max grunted his agreement.

There was just a faint tinge of light in the eastern sky as they cut through the first wire fence. 'Just go!' said Max, his teeth chattering. 'There's no time for all the training school tricks. Screw the alarms, just cut!'

Bernard handled the big bolt-cutters quickly and expertly. The only noise they heard for the first few minutes was the clang of the cut wire. But after that the dogs began to bark.

★

Frank Harrington, the SIS Berlin 'resident', would not normally have been at the reception point in the Bundesrepublik waiting, in the most lonely hours of the night, for two agents breaking through the Wall, but this operation was special. And Frank had promised Bernard's father that he would look after him, a promise which Frank Harrington interpreted in the most solemn fashion.

He was in a small subterranean room under some four metres of concrete and lit by fluorescent blue lights, but Frank's vigil was not too onerous. Although such forward command bunkers were somewhat austere – it being NATO's assumption that the Warsaw Pact armies would roll over these border defences in the first hours of any undeclared war – it was warm and dry and he was sitting in a soft seat with a glass of decent whisky in his fist.

This was the commanding officer's private office, or at least it was assigned to that purpose in the event of a war emergency. Among Frank's companions were a corpulent young officer of the Bundesgrenzschutz – a force of West German riot police who guard airports, embassies and the border – and an elderly Englishman in a curious nautical uniform worn by the British Frontier Service, which acts as guides for all British army patrols on land, air and river. The German was lolling against a radiator and the Englishman perched on the edge of a desk.

'How long before sun-up?' said Frank. He'd kept his tan trenchcoat on over his brown tweed suit. His shirt was khaki, his tie a faded sort of yellow. To the casual eye he might have been an army officer in uniform.

'An hour and eight minutes,' said the Englishman after consulting his watch. He didn't trust clocks, not even the synchronized and constantly monitored clocks in the control bunker.

Hunched in a chair in the corner – Melton overcoat over his Savile Row worsted – there was a fourth man, Bret Rensselaer. He'd come from London Central on a watching brief and he was taking it literally. Now he checked his watch. Bret had already committed the time of sunrise to memory; he wondered why Frank hadn't bothered to do so.

The two men had worked together for a long time and their relationship was firmly established. Frank Harrington regarded Bret's patrician deportment and high-handed East Coast bullshit as typical of the CIA top brass he used to know in Washington. Bret saw in Frank a minimally efficient although congenial time-server, of the sort that yeoman farmers had supplied to Britain's Civil Service since the days of

484

Empire. These descriptions, suitably amended, would have been acknowledged by both men and it was thus that a modus vivendi had been reached.

'Germans who live near the border get a special pass and can go across nine times a year to see friends and relatives,' said Frank, suddenly impelled for the sake of good manners to include Bret in the conversation. 'One of them came through yesterday evening – they are not permitted to stay overnight – and told us that everything looked normal. The work on the Wall and so on . . .'

Bret nodded. The hum of the air-conditioning seemed loud in the silence.

'It was a good spot to choose,' Frank added.

'There are no good spots,' interposed the BGS officer loudly. He looked like a ruffian, thought Frank, with his scarred face and beer belly. Perhaps riot policemen had to be like that. Meeting no response from either of the strange foreigners, the German officer drank what remained of his whisky, wiped his mouth, belched, nodded his leave-taking and went out.

The phone in the next room rang and they listened while the operator grunted, hung up and then called loudly, 'Dogs barking and some sort of movement over there now.'

Bret looked at Frank. Frank winked but otherwise didn't move.

The English guide swallowed the last of his whisky hurriedly and slid off the desk. 'I'd better be off too,' he said. 'I might be needed. I understand two of your freebooters might be going in to try to help.'

'Perhaps,' said Frank.

'It won't work,' said the Englishman. 'In effect it's an invasion of their soil.'

Frank stared at him and didn't reply. He didn't like people to refer to his men as freebooters, especially not strangers. The guide, forgetting his glass was empty, tried to drink more from it. Then he set it down on the desk where he'd been sitting and departed.

Left to themselves, Bret said, 'If young Samson pulls this one off I'm going to recommend him for the German Desk.' He was sitting well back in the chair, elbows on its rests, hands together like a tutor delivering a homily to an erring student.

'Yes, so you said.'

'Can he do it, Frank?' Although framed as a query, he said it as if he was testing Frank with an exam question, rather than asking help with a difficult decision.

'He's not stupid.'

'Just headstrong,' supplied Bret. 'Is that what you mean?'

'Are you sure you wouldn't like a drink?' asked Frank, holding up the bottle of scotch which was on the floor near his chair. Bret had bought it in the duty-free shop at London airport but he hadn't touched a drop.

Bret shook his head. 'And the wife?' said Bret, adding in a voice that was half joking, half serious, 'Is Mrs Samson going to be the first female Director-General?'

'Too fixed in her viewpoint. All women are. She's not flexible enough to do what the old man does, is she?'

'A lead pipe is flexible,' said Bret.

'Resilient I mean.'

'Elastic,' said Bret, 'is the only word I can think of for the capacity to return to former shape and state.'

'Is that the primary requirement for a D-G?' asked Frank coldly. He'd trained with Sir Henry Clevemore back in wartime and been a personal friend ever since. He wasn't keen on discussing his possible successors with Bret.

'Primary requirement for a lot of things,' said Bret dismissively. He didn't want to talk but he added, 'Too many people in this business get permanently crippled.'

'Only field agents surely?'

'It's sometimes worse for the ones who send them out.'

'Is that what you're worried about in the case of Bernard Samson? That too much rough stuff might leave a permanent mark? Is that why you asked me?'

'No. Not at all.'

'Bernard would do a good job in London. Give him a chance at it, Bret. I'll support it.'

'I might take you up on that, Frank.'

'Freebooters!' said Frank. 'Confounded nerve of the man. He was talking about my reception team.'

From the next room the operator called, 'They've put the search-lights on!'

Frank said, 'Tell them to put the big radar jammer on. I don't want any arguments: the Piranha!' The army hated using the Piranhas because they jammed the radars on both sides of the line. 'Now!' said Frank.

The first searchlight came on, spluttering and hissing, and its beam went sweeping across the carefully smoothed soft earth ahead of them.

Now neither Max nor Bernard could hope that they'd get right through undetected.

Bernard went flat on the ground but Max was a tough old veteran and he went running on into the darkness behind the searchlight beam, confident that the region round the beam was darkest to the eyes of the guards.

The Grenzpolizei up in the tower were caught by surprise. They were both young conscripts, sent here from the far side of the country and recommended for this special job after their good service in the Free German Youth. There had been an alert, two in fact. Their sergeant had read the teleprinter message aloud to them to be sure they understood. But alerts were commonplace. None of the Grepos took them too seriously. Since the boys had arrived here six months ago, there had been nine emergencies and every one of them had turned out to be birds or rabbits tripping the wires. No one tried to get through nowadays: no one with any sense.

On the Western side of the Wall, Frank's reception team – Tom Cutts and 'Gabby' Green – had come up very close by that time. They weren't directly in Frank's employ, they were specialists. Despite being in their middle thirties, they were, according to their papers, junior officers of the Signal Corps. With them was a genuine soldier, Sergeant Powell, who was a radar technician. His job was to make sure nothing went wrong with their equipment, although, as he'd told them quite frankly, if something did go wrong with it, it was unlikely that he'd be able to repair it there in the slit trench. It would have to go back to the workshop, and then probably to the manufacturer.

These 'freebooters' had been dug in there a long time, dressed in their camouflaged battle-smocks, faces darkened with paint, brown knitted hats pulled down over the tops of their ears. Helmets were too heavy, and, if you dropped them, dangerously noisy. It was a curious fact that they were safer dressed as soldiers than as civilians. Those Grepos over there were cautious about shooting soldiers; and soldiers on both sides of the Wall were garbed almost identically.

They didn't speak very often: every sound carried a long way at night and they'd worked together often enough to know what had to be done. They'd manhandled the little radar set forward and got the antenna into a favourable position ahead of them as soon as darkness came the previous evening, and then spent all night with the set, watching the movements of the vehicles and the guards. Both men were wearing headphones over their knitted hats, and Gabby, whose taciturn disposition had earned him his nickname, had his eye to the big Hawklite image-intensifying scope.

'Yes,' he said suddenly, the rubber-sided microphone clamped tight to his mouth. 'One! No: two of them. One running . . . the other on the ground. Jesus!'

The searchlight had come on by that time, but it provided no help for anyone trying to see what was happening.

'And there go the infra-red lights too. My, my, they are getting serious,' said Gabby calmly. 'Can we jam?' Tom had already tuned the jammer to the required wavelength, but it was a lower-power machine that would only affect the small sets. 'I'll have to go forward. I can't get it from here.'

Tom said nothing. They'd both hoped that it wouldn't be necessary for either of them to cross into DDR territory. Over the last year they'd had a couple of close shaves, and their opposite numbers – the two-man team who were responsible for the stretch of Wall to the north – had both been killed after one of them stepped on a mine that had been 'accidentally' left on the West side of the Wall when DDR repair parties had finished work.

Tom Cutts's misgivings would have been confirmed had he had a chance to see into the Russian Electronic Warfare Support Vehicle that was parked out of sight behind the dog kennels. Inside its darkened interior a senior KGB officer named Erich Stinnes could just about fit between the collection of electronic equipment. His face was tense and the lenses of his glasses reflected the screen of a battlefield radar far more sophisticated than the 'man-portable' infantry model that the two 'freebooters' had placed into position.

'One of them is moving forward,' the Russian army operator told Stinnes. The blip that was Gabby glowed brighter as he scrambled from his trench and exposed more of his body to the radar.

The EW support vehicle provided more than one indication of what was happening in the sector. There was a thermal imager rendering the warmth of human bodies into revealing white blobs, and now that the infra-red lights were on, the automatic IR cameras were taking a picture every five seconds. If it came to an inquiry there would be no chance of proving the DDR was in the wrong.

'Let him come,' said Stinnes. 'Perhaps the other fellow will come too. Then we'll have both of them.'

'If we wait too long the two spies will escape,' said the Grepo officer who'd been assigned to give Stinnes all the help and assistance he required.

'We'll get them all, never fear. I've followed them a long way. I'll not miss them now.' They didn't realize how circumscribed he was by the rules and regulations. But without breaking any applicable rules Stinnes had supervised what can only be described as an exemplary operation. The two agents arrested in Schwerin had yielded the details of their rendezvous after only two hours of interrogation. Furthermore the methods used to get this 'confession' were by KGB standards only moderately severe. They had detected the two 'Englishmen' at the log cabin and kept them under observation all the way here. Apart from the misrouteing of a helicopter by some imbecilic air traffic controller it was a textbook operation.

'The second man is coming forward,' said the operator.

'Kolossal!' said Stinnes. 'When he gets to the wire you can shoot.' The unrepaired gap in the Wall had enabled them to plan the fields of fire. It was like a shooting gallery: four men trapped inside the enclosure formed by the Wall, the wire and the builders' materials.

It was Gabby who shot the searchlight out. Afterwards Bernard said it was Max, but that was because Bernard wanted to believe it was Max. The death of Max distressed Bernard in a way that few other losses had ever done. And of course Bernard never shook off the guilt that came from his being the only survivor.

He saw the other three die. Max, Tom and Gabby. They were cut to pieces by a heavy machine gun: an old reliable 12.7mm Degtyarev. The noise of the machine gun sounded very loud in the night air. Everyone for miles around heard it. That would teach the English a lesson.

'Where's the other one?' said Stinnes, still watching the radar screen.

'He tripped and fell down. Damn! Damn! Damn! They're putting the big jammer on now!' As the two men watched, electronic clutter came swirling up from the bottom of the screen: major interference like a snowstorm.

'Where is he?' Stinnes slapped his hand upon the blinded radar and its useless screen and shouted, 'Where?' The men in the bunker with him jumped to their feet, stared straight ahead, standing stiff and upright as a good Russian soldier is taught to stand when a senior officer shouts at him.

Thus it was that Bernard Samson drowned in the clutter and scrambled away unhurt, running like he'd never run before, eventually to fall into the arms of Sergeant Powell.

'Shit!' said Powell. 'Where did you come from, laddie?' For one wild moment Sergeant Powell thought he'd captured a prisoner. When he realized that it was only an escaper from the East he was disappointed. 'They said there'd be two. Where's the other fellow?'

3

Cambridgeshire, England. February 1978.

Sir Henry Clevemore was not renowned for his hospitality, and rightly so. As the Director-General of the Secret Intelligence Service, he carefully chose the people he met and where he met them. The chosen venue was unlikely to be his own home, a magnificent old timber and stone mansion, a large part of which dated from the sixteenth century. In any case Lady Clevemore did not enjoy entertaining, she never had. If her husband wanted to entertain he could use the Cavalry Club in Piccadilly. It was more convenient in every way.

So it was a flattering exception when on a chilly February evening he invited Bret Rensselaer – a senior Departmental employee – to drive out to Cambridgeshire for dinner.

Sir Henry appeared to have overlooked the fact that Rensselaer was the sort of American who liked to wear formal clothes. Bret had agonized about whether to wear a tuxedo but had finally decided upon a charcoal suit, tailored in that waisted style so beloved of Savile Row craftsmen, lightly starched white shirt and grey silk tie. Sir Henry was wearing a blue lounge suit that had seen better days, a soft collared shirt with a missing button and highly polished scuffed black brogues that needed new laces.

'For God's sake, why a woman?' said Bret Rensselaer more calmly than his choice of words suggested. 'Why ever did you choose a woman?' This was not the way Departmental staff usually addressed Sir Henry Clevemore, but Bret Rensselaer had 'a special relationship' with the Director-General. It was a relationship based to some extent upon Bret Rensselaer's birthplace, his influential friends in the State Department, and to some extent upon the fact that Bret's income made him financially independent of the Secret Intelligence Service, and of most other things.

'Do smoke if you want to. Can I offer you a cigar?'

'No thank you, Sir Henry.'

Sir Henry Clevemore sat back in his armchair and sipped his whisky. They were in the drawing room staring at a blazing log fire, having been served a grilled lobster dinner and the last bottle of a particularly good

Montrachet that Sir Henry had been given by the Permanent Under-Secretary.

'It doesn't work like that, Bret,' said Sir Henry. He was being very conciliatory: they both knew how the Department worked but the D-G was determined to be charming. Charm was the D-G's style unless he was in a hurry. 'I wasn't looking for a female,' said Sir Henry. 'Of that you can be quite sure. We have a number of people . . . I know you wouldn't expect me to go into details . . . but several. Men and women we have been patiently playing to the Russians for years and years, in the hope that one day we'd be able to do something spectacular with one of them.'

'And for her that day has come?' said Bret. He extended an open hand towards the fire to sample its heat. He hadn't been really warm since getting out of his car. That was the trouble with these stately old homes, they could never be efficiently heated. Bret wished he'd taken a chance on what sort of evening it would be, and worn warmer, more casual clothes: a tweed jacket perhaps. Sir Henry probably wouldn't have cared or even noticed.

The D-G looked at Bret to see if there was an element of sarcasm there. There wasn't: it was just another example of the American directness of approach which made Bret the best candidate for looking after a really promising double agent. He turned on the charm. 'You started this thing rolling, Bret. When, a few weeks back, you floated this idea I didn't think much of it, to tell you the truth. But I began looking at possible candidates, and then other things happened that made it seem more and more possible. Let's just say that the float has twitched and that may be a sign the other side is ready to bite. It may be, that's all.'

Bret suppressed a temptation to say that in too many such situations the Russians had devoured the bait so that the Department had reeled in an empty hook. Everything indicated that the Russians knew more about turning agents than their enemies did about running them. 'But a woman . . .' said Bret to remind the D-G of his other reservation.

'An extraordinary woman, a brilliant and beautiful woman,' said the D-G.

'Enter Miss X.' Bret's feelings were bruised by the D-G's stubborn reluctance to provide more details of this candidate. He'd expected to be having a say in the final selection process.

'*Mrs* X, to be precise.'

'All the more reason that the Russkies will not want her over there. It's a male-dominated society and the KGB is the last place we'll ever see change.'

491

'I'm not sure I agree with you there, Bret.' The D-G permitted himself a little grin. 'They are changing their ways. So are we all, I suppose.' He couldn't hide the regret in his voice. 'But my feeling is that we'll gain from their old-fashioned entrenched attitudes. They will never suspect that we would try to plant a woman into the Committee.'

'No. I guess you're right, Sir Henry.' It was Bret's turn to wonder. He liked the way the old man's mind worked. There were people who said the D-G was past it – and the D-G sometimes seemed to go to great lengths to encourage that misreading – but Bret knew from first-hand experience that, for the overall strategy, the old man had an acute mind that was tortuous and sometimes devious. That was why Bret had taken his idea about 'getting a man into the Kremlin' to Sir Henry in person.

The old man leaned forward. The polite preliminaries, like the evening itself, were coming to an end. Now they were talking as man and master. 'We both know the dangers and difficulties of working with doubles, Bret. The Department is littered with the dead bodies of people who have misread their minds.'

'It goes with the job,' said Bret. 'As the years go by, a double agent finds it more and more difficult to be sure which side he's committed to.'

'They forget which side is which,' said the D-G feelingly. He reached forward for a chocolate-covered mint and unwrapped it carefully. It was the very devil trying to do without a cigar after dinner. 'That's why someone has to hold their hand, and get inside their head, and keep them politically motivated. We learned that from the Russians, Bret, and I'm sure it's right.'

'But it was never my idea to become the case officer,' said Bret. 'I have no experience.' He said it casually, without the emphasis that would have been there had he been determined not to take on this new task the D-G was giving him. That softening of attitude was not lost upon the D-G. That was the first hurdle.

'I could give you a million reasons why we don't want an experienced case officer on this job.'

'Yes,' said Bret. The sight of a known case officer in regular contact with an agent would ring every alarm bell in the KGB.

But the D-G did not put that argument. He said, 'I'm talking about an agent whose position and opportunity may be unique. So this is a job for someone very senior, Bret. Someone who knows the whole picture, someone whose judgement I can trust completely.' He put the mint in his mouth and screwed the wrapper up very tight before placing it in the ashtray.

492

'Well, I don't know if I fit that picture, Sir Henry,' said Bret, awkwardly adopting the role that Englishmen are expected to assume when such compliments are paid.

'Yes, Bret. You fit it very well,' said the old man. 'Tell me, Bret, what do you see as our most serious shortcomings?'

'Shortcomings? Of the British? Of the Department?' Bret didn't want to answer any questions of that sort and his face showed it.

'You're too damned polite to say, of course. But a fellow less inhibited than you, speaking recently of British shortcomings, told me that we British worship amateurism without having intuitive Yankee know-how; result disaster.'

Bret said nothing.

Sir Henry went on, 'Whatever the truth of that assessment, I am determined that this operation is going to be one hundred per cent professional, and it's going to have the benefit of that "can do" improvisation for which your countrymen are noted.' He raised his hand in caution. 'I will still need to go through the details of your plan. There are a number of points you raise that are somewhat contentious. But you realize that, of course.'

'It's a ten-year plan,' said Bret. 'They are in a bad way over there. A well-planned attack on their economy and the whole damned communist house of cards will collapse.'

'Collapse? What does that mean?'

'I think we could force the East German government into allowing opposition parties and free emigration.'

'Do you?' The idea seemed preposterous to the old man, but he was too experienced in the strategies of Whitehall to go on record as a disbeliever. 'The Wall comes down in 1988? Is that what you are saying?' The old man smiled grimly.

'I don't want to be too specific but look at it this way. In World War Two RAF Bomber Command went out at night and dropped bombs on big cities. Subsequent research discovered that few of the bombers had found their way to the assigned targets, and the few that did bombed lakes, parks, churches and wasteland so that only one bomb in ten was likely to hit anything worthwhile.'

Sir Henry was fingering the coloured cards upon which there were graphs and charts showing various statistics mostly concerned with the skilled and unskilled working population of the German Democratic Republic. 'Go on, Bret.'

'When Spaatz and Jimmy Doolittle took the US Eighth Air Force into the bombing campaign they went in daylight with the Norden

493

bombsight. Precision bombing and they had a plan. They bombed only synthetic-oil plants and aircraft factories. No wasted effort and the effect was mortal.'

'Weren't they called panacea targets?'

'Only by the ones who were proved wrong,' said Bret sharply.

'I seem to remember some other aspects of the strategic bombing campaign,' pondered the old man, who hadn't missed the point that the RAF got it wrong and the Americans got it right. Neither did he miss the implication that the efforts of the SIS had up till now been ninety per cent futile.

'I wouldn't want to labour the comparison,' said Bret, who belatedly saw that this example of the RAF's wartime inferiority to US bombing performance might be less compelling to an English audience. He tried another approach. 'That "Health and Hospitalization" chart you are holding shows how many physicians between the ages of twenty-five and thirty-five are holding their health scheme together. I estimate that the loss of twenty-five per cent of that labour force – that's the red sector on the chart – would make the regime start closing hospitals, or hospital departments, at a rate that would be politically unacceptable. Or take civil engineering: look at the chart I see on the table there . . .'

'I've looked at the charts,' said Sir Henry, who had never liked visual presentations.

'We must target the highly skilled labour force. It will put acute strain upon the communist society because the regime tells its people that they endure low wages and a drab life to get job security and good social services: health care, urban transportation and so on. And a brain-drain is something they can't counter. It takes seven years to train a physician, an engineer or a chemist: even then you need a bright kid to start with.'

'You mentioned political opposition,' said the D-G, and put Bret's charts aside.

Bret said, 'Yes. We also have to change our disdainful attitude to these small East German opposition groups. We must show a little sympathy: help and advise the Church groups and political reformers. Help them get together. Did you see my figures for Church denominations? The encouraging thing the figures demonstrate is that we can forget the rural areas: Protestants in the large cities will give us enough of the sort of people we want and we can reach townspeople more easily.'

'Strategic bombing. Ummm,' said the D-G. Even the Cabinet Secretary might see the logic of that approach when he was being told about all the extra money that would be needed.

'And the people we want are the people in demand in the West. We don't have to invent any fancy high-paid jobs for the people we entice away. The jobs are here already.' Bret pulled out another sheet. 'And see how the birth-rate figures help us?' Bret held up the graph and pointed to the curving years of the early Eighties.

'How do we get them here?'

Bret grabbed another chart. 'These are people leaving East Germany for vacations abroad. I have broken them down according to the country they vacation in. Under the West German constitution every one of those East Germans is entitled to a West German passport on demand.'

The D-G stopped Bret's flow with a gesture of his hand. 'You are proposing to offer a crowd of East German holiday-makers getting off a bus in Morocco a chance to swap their passports? What will the Moroccan immigration authorities say about that?'

Bret gave a fixed smile. It was typical of the old man that he should take a country at random and then start nit-picking. 'At this stage it would be better not to get bogged down in detail,' he replied. 'There are many ways for East German citizens to get permission to travel, and the numbers have been going up each year. The West German government press for a little more freedom every time they fork out donations to that lousy regime over there. And remember we are after the middle classes – respectable family men and college-educated working wives – not blue denim, long-haired hippy Wall-jumpers. And this is exactly why we need Mrs X over there looking at the secret police files and telling us where the effective opposition is; who to see, where to go and how to apply the pressure.'

'Tell me again. She's to. . . ?'

'She must get access to the KGB files on opposition groups – who they are and how they operate – Church groups, democrats, liberals, fascists, even communist reformers. That's the best way that we can evaluate who we should team up with and prepare them for real opposition. And we need to know how the Russian army would react to widespread political dissent.'

'You are the right man for Mrs X,' said Sir Henry. He remembered the PM saying that every Russian is at heart a chess-player, and every American at heart a public-relations man. Well, Bret Rensselaer's zeal did nothing to disprove that one. The sheer audacity of the scheme plus Bret's enthusiasm was enough to persuade him that it was worth a try.

Bret nodded to acknowledge the compliment. He knew there were other things that had influenced the old man's decision. Bret was

American. And if Sir Henry was persuaded by Bret's projections for the East German economy then Bret must be the prime choice to run the agent too. He had a roomful of experts in statistics, banking, economics, and even an expert in 'group and permutation theory' he'd raided from the cryptanalysts. Bret's economic analysis department was a success story. It would make perfect deep cover for a case officer. And since a woman was involved there was another advantage: now that he was separated from his wife, Bret could be seen in the company of a 'brilliant and beautiful woman' without anyone thinking they were discussing their work.

'I take it that Mrs X has managed without a case officer for a long time,' said Bret.

'Yes, because Silas Gaunt was involved. You know what Gaunt is like. He squeezed a promise from me that nothing would be on paper and that he would be the only contact.'

'Literally the only contact?' said Bret, without dreaming for a moment that the answer would be in the affirmative.

'Literally.'

'Good God! So why. . . ?'

'Bring someone else in now? Well, I'll tell you. Gaunt only comes up to town once a month and I'm not sure that even that isn't too much for him.'

And of course Silas Gaunt was a dedicated exponent of the sort of public school amateurism that the D-G apparently had rejected. 'Has something happened?'

Bret's reaction confirmed the D-G's belief that this was the right man for the job: Bret had instinct. 'Yes, Bret. Something has happened. Some wretched Russian wants to defect.'

'And?'

The D-G sipped some whisky before saying, 'And he's made the approach to Mrs X. He took her aside at one of those unacknowledged meetings those Foreign Office fellows like to arrange with our Russian friends. I have never known anything good to come from them yet.'

'A KGB man wants to defect.' Bret laughed.

'Yes, it is a good joke,' said the D-G bitterly. 'I wish I were in a position to join in the merriment.'

'I'm sorry, sir,' said Brett. 'Was this a high-grade Russian?'

'Pretty good,' said the D-G guardedly. 'His name is Blum: described as third secretary: working in the service attaché's office: almost certainly KGB. The contact was made in watertight circumstances,' he added.

'She'll have to tell them,' said Bret without hesitation. 'Watertight or not, she'll have to turn him in.'

'Ummm.' Bret Rensselaer was completely cold-blooded, thought the D-G. It wasn't an attractive characteristic, but for this job it was just the ticket.

'Unless you want to throw away all those years of good work.'

'You haven't heard all the circumstances, Bret.'

'I don't have to hear all the circumstances,' said Bret. 'If you don't turn in that Russkie, you will erode the confidence of your agent.'

'This particular Mrs X . . .'

'Never mind the psychologist's report,' said Bret. 'She'll know that you measured the risk, that you put her in the scales, with this Russian defector in the other pan.'

'I don't see it that way.'

'Never mind how *you* see it. In fact never mind the way it really is. We are sitting here talking about an agent whom you call "unique". Right?'

'Whose position and opportunity may be unique.'

'May be unique. Okay. Well I'm telling you that if you compromise her, in even the slightest degree, in order to play footsie with a Russian agent, Mrs X will never deliver one hundred per cent.'

'It might go the other way. Perhaps she'll feel distressed that we sacrificed this Blum fellow,' said the D-G gently. 'Already she's expressed her concern. Remember it's a woman.'

'I'm remembering that. She must contact them right away and reveal Blum's approach to her. If you show any hesitation in telling her that, she'll deeply resent your inaction for ever after. A woman may express her concern but she doesn't want to be neglected in favour of a rival. In hindsight it will infuriate her. Yes, I'm remembering it's a woman, Sir Henry.'

'This fellow Blum might be bringing us something very good,' said the D-G.

'Never mind if he's bringing an inside line to the Politburo. You'll have to choose one or the other: not both.' The two men looked at each other. Bret said, 'I take it that Mrs X is separated from her husband?'

The D-G didn't answer the question. He sat back and sniffed. After a moment's thought he said, 'You're probably right, Bret.'

'On this one, I am, sir. Never mind that I don't know Mrs X; I know that much about women.'

'Oh, but you do.'

'Do?'

'You *do* know Mrs X. You know her very well.'

The two men looked at each other, both knowing that the old man would only divulge the name if Bret Rensselaer agreed to take on the job of running her. 'If you think I'm the right person for the job,' said Bret, yielding to the inevitable. They'd both known he'd have to say yes right from the very beginning. This wasn't the sort of job you advertised on the notice-board.

'Capital!' said the D-G in the firm bass tone that was the nearest he ever got to expressing his enthusiasm. He looked at his watch. 'My goodness, it's been such a splendid evening that the time has flown.'

Bret was still waiting to hear the name but he responded to his cue. He got to his feet and said, 'Yes, I must be going.'

'I believe your driver is in the kitchen, Bret.'

'Eating? That's very civil of you, Sir Henry.'

'There's nowhere round here for a chap to get a meal.' Sir Henry pulled the silk cord and a bell jangled somewhere in a distant part of the house. 'We're in the wilds here. Even the village shop has closed down. I don't know how on earth we'll manage in future,' he said, without any sign that the problem was causing him great stress.

'It's a magnificent old house.'

'You must come in summer,' said Sir Henry. 'The garden is splendid.'

'I would like that,' Bret responded.

'Come in August. We have an open day for the local church.'

'That sounds most enjoyable.' His enthusiasm dampened as he realized that the D-G was inviting him to be marshalled around the garden with a crowd of gawking tourists.

'Do you fish?' said the D-G, shepherding him towards the door.

'I never seem to have enough time,' said Bret. He heard his driver at the door. In a moment the servants would be in earshot and it would be too late. 'Who is it, sir? Who is Mrs X?'

The D-G looked at him, relishing those last few moments and anticipating Bret's astonishment. 'Mrs Samson is the person in question.'

The door opened. 'Mr Rensselaer's car is here, sir.' Sir Henry's butler saw the look of dismay on Bret's face and wondered if he was not well. Perhaps it was something about the food or the wine. He'd wondered about that Montrachet: in the same case he'd come upon a couple of corked bottles.

'I see,' said Bret Rensselaer, who didn't see at all, and was even more surprised than Sir Henry thought he would be. All sorts of thoughts and consequences were whirling round in his mind. Mrs Bernard Samson.

My God! Mrs Samson had a husband and young children. How the hell could it be Mrs Samson?

'Goodnight, Bret. Look at all those stars . . . It will freeze hard tonight unless we get that rain those idiots on the TV keep forecasting.'

Bret almost got back out of the car. He felt like insisting that he should have another half an hour to discuss it all. Instead he dutifully said, 'Yes, I'm afraid so. Look here, sir, we can't possibly give Bernard Samson the German Desk in view of what you've told me.'

'You think not? Samson was the only one to get across alive the other night, wasn't he?'

'Yes, that's right.'

'What bad luck. It was the other one – Busby – we needed to talk to. Yes, that's right: Samson. No proper schooling of course, but he has flair and deserves a shot at the German Desk.'

'I was going to make it official tomorrow.'

'Whatever you say, Bret, old chap.'

'It's unthinkable with this other business on the cards. From every point of view . . . unthinkable. We'd better give the desk to Cruyer.'

'Can he cope?'

'With Samson as an assistant he'll manage.' Bret shifted position on the car seat. He began to think that the D-G had planned all this, knowing that Bernard Samson was about to be promoted. He'd invited Bret out here to dinner just to prevent him appointing Samson and thus threatening the prospect of the big one: putting Mrs Samson into 'The Kremlin'. The cunning old bastard.

'I'll leave it with you,' said the D-G.

'Very well, sir. Thank you. Goodnight, Sir Henry.'

The D-G leaned into the car and said, 'Oh, yes. On that matter we discussed: not a word to Silas Gaunt. For the time being it's better he doesn't know you're a party to it.'

'Is that wise, sir?' said Bret, piqued that the D-G had obviously passed it off as his own idea when talking to 'Uncle' Silas.

The D-G knew what was going through Bret's mind. He touched the side of his nose. 'You can't dance at two weddings with one bottle of wine. Ever hear that little proverb?'

'No, sir.'

'Hungarian.'

'Yes, sir.'

'Or Romanian, or Croatian. One of those damned countries where they dance at weddings. Get started, old chap. You've got a long journey and I'm getting cold.'

Sir Henry slammed the door and tapped the roof of the car. The car moved away, its tyres making loud crunching noises on the gravel roadway. He didn't go back into the house, he watched the car until it disappeared round the bend of the long drive.

Sir Henry rubbed his hands together briskly as he turned back and went indoors. All had gone well. It would need a lot of tough talking to get it all approved, but Sir Henry had always been good at tough talking. Bret Rensselaer could do it if anyone could do it. The projections were convincing: this was the way to tackle the German Democratic Republic. And it was Bret's idea, Bret's baby. Bret had the right disposition for it: secretive, obsessional, patriotic, resourceful and quick-witted. He cottoned on to the fact that we couldn't have Samson running the German Desk while his wife was defecting: that would be a bit too much. Yes, Bret would do it.

So why did the Director-General still have reservations about what he'd set in motion? It was because Bret Rensselaer was too damned efficient. Given an order, Bret would carry it out at all costs. The D-G had seen that determination before in rich men's sons; over-compensation or guilt or something. They never knew where to stop. The D-G shivered. It was cold tonight.

As the car turned on to the main road Bret Rensselaer sank back into the soft leather and closed his eyes to think more clearly. So Mrs Bernard Samson had been playing out the role of double agent for God knows how many years and no one had got even a sniff of it. Could it be true? It was absolutely incredible but he believed it. As far as Mrs Samson was concerned, Bret would believe anything. Fiona Samson was the most radiant and wonderful woman in the whole world. He had been secretly in love with her ever since the day he first met her.

4

Kent, England. March 1978.

'We live in a society full of preventable disorders, preventable diseases and preventable pain, of harshness and stupid unpremeditated cruelties.' His accent was Welsh. He paused: Fiona said nothing. 'They are not my words, they are the words of Mr H. G. Wells.' He sat by the window. A caged canary above his head seemed to be asleep. It was almost April: the daylight was fading fast. The children playing in the garden next door were being called in to bed, only the most restless of the birds were still fidgeting in the trees. The sea, out of sight behind the rise, could be faintly heard. The man named Martin Euan Pryce-Hughes was a profile against the cheap net curtains. His almost completely white hair, long and inclined to waviness at the ends, framed his head like a helmet. Only when he drew on his curly pipe was his old, tightly lined face lit up.

'I thought I recognized the words,' said Fiona Samson.

'The Fabian movement: fine people. Wells the theorist, the great George Bernard! . . . The Webbs, God bless their memory. Laski and Tawney. My father knew them all. I remember many of them coming to the house. Dreamers, of course. They thought the world could be changed by writers and poets and printed pamphlets.' Without looking at her he smiled at the idea, and she could hear his disdain in the way he said it. His voice was low and attractive with the sonorous call of the Welsh Valleys. It was the same accent that she'd heard in the voice of his niece Dilwys, with whom she'd shared rooms at Oxford. The Department had instructed her to encourage that friendship and through her she'd met Martin.

On the bookshelf there was a photo of Martin's father. She could see why so many women had thrown themselves at him. Perhaps free love was a part of the Fabian philosophy he'd so vigorously embraced when young. Like father like son? Within Martin too there was a violent and ruthless determination. And when he tried he could provide a fair imitation of his father's famous charm. It was a combination that made both men irresistible to a certain sort of young woman. And it was a

501

combination that brought Martin to the attention of the Russian spy apparatus even before it was called the KGB.

'Some people are able to do something,' said Fiona, giving the sort of answer that seemed to be expected of her. 'Others talk and write. The world has always been like that. The dreamers are no less valuable, Martin.'

'Yes, I knew you'd say that,' he said. The way he said it scared her. There often seemed to be a double meaning – a warning – in the things he said. It could have meant that he'd known she'd say it because it was the right kind of banality: the sort of thing a class-enemy would say. She infinitely preferred to deal with the Russians. She could understand the Russians – they were tough professionals – but this embittered idealist, who was prepared to do their dirty work for them, was beyond her comprehension. And yet she didn't hate him.

'You know everything, Martin,' she said.

'What I don't know,' he admitted, 'is why you married that husband of yours.'

'Bernard is a wonderful man, Martin. He is brave and determined and clever.'

He puffed his pipe before replying. 'Brave, perhaps. Determined: undoubtedly. But not even his most foolish friends could possibly call him clever, Fiona.'

She sighed. They had been through such exchanges before. Even though he was twice her age he felt he must compete for her. At first he'd made sexual advances, but that was a long time ago: he seemed to have given up on that score. But he had to establish his own superiority. He'd even shown a bitter sort of jealousy for her father when she'd mentioned the amazing fur coat he'd given her. Any fool can make money, Martin had growled. And she'd agreed with that in order to soothe his ego and pacify him.

Only lately had she come to understand that she was as important to him as he was to her. When the KGB man from the Trade Delegation appointed Martin to be her father-figure, factotum and cut-out, they'd never in their wildest dreams hoped that she would wind up employed by the British Secret Intelligence Service. This amazing development had proceeded with Martin monitoring and advising her on each and every step. Now that she was senior staff in London Central, Martin could look back on the previous ten years with great satisfaction. From being no more than a dogsbody for the Russians he'd become the trustee of their most precious investment. There was talk of giving him some award or KGB rank. He affected to be uninterested in such things but the thought of it gave him a warm glow of pleasure: and it might prove an advantage when dealing with the people at the London end. The Russians respected such distinctions.

She looked at her watch. How much longer before the courier came? He was already ten minutes late. That was unusual. In her rare dealings with KGB contacts they'd always been on time. She hoped there wasn't trouble.

Fiona was a double agent but she never felt frightened. True, Moscow Centre had arranged the execution of several men over the previous eighteen months – one of them on the top deck of a bus in Fulham; killed with a poison dart – but they had all been native Russians. Should her duplicity be detected, the chances of them killing her were not great but they would get her to tell them all she knew, and the prospect of the KGB interrogation was terrifying. But for a woman of Fiona's motivation it was even worse to contemplate the ruin of years and years of hard work. Years of preparation, years of establishing her bona fides. Years of deceiving her husband, children and her friends. And years of enduring the poisonous darts that came from the minds of men like Martin Euan Pryce-Hughes.

'No,' Martin repeated as if relishing the words. 'Not even his best friends could call Mr Bernard Samson clever. We are lucky you married him, darling girl. A really clever man would have realized what you are up to.'

'A suspicious husband, yes. Bernard trusts me. He loves me.'

Martin grunted. It was not an answer that pleased him. 'I see him, you know?' he said.

'Bernard? You see Bernard?'

'It's necessary. For your sake, Fiona. Checking. We make contact now and again. Not only me but other people too.'

The self-important old bastard. She hadn't reckoned on that, but of course the KGB would be checking up on her and Bernard would be one of the people they'd be watching. Thank God she'd never confided anything to him. It wasn't that Bernard couldn't keep a secret. His head buzzed with them. But this was too close to home. It was something that she had to do herself without Bernard's help.

'I suppose you know that they have given me this direct emergency link with a case officer?' She said it in a soft and suggestive voice that would have well suited the beginning of a fairy story told to a wide-eyed and attentive audience of five-year-olds.

'I do,' he said. He turned and gave her a patronizing smile. The sort of smile he gave all women who aspired to be his comrades. 'And it's a fine idea.'

'Yes, it is. And I shall use that contact. If you or Chesty or any of those other blundering incompetents in the Trade Delegation contact any of the people round me with a view to checking, or any other stupid tricks, they'll have their balls ripped off. Do you understand that, Martin?'

She almost laughed to see his face: mouth open, pipe in hand, eyes popping. He'd not seen much of that side of her: for him she usually played the docile housewife.

'Do you?' she said, and this time her voice was hard and spiteful. She was determined that he'd answer, for that would remove any last idea that she might have been joking.

'Yes, Fiona,' he said meekly. He must have been instructed not to upset her. Or perhaps he knew what the Centre would do to him if Fiona complained. Lose her and he'd lose everything he cherished.

'And I do mean stay away from Bernard. You're amateurs; you're not in Bernard's league. He's been in the real agent-running business from the time when he was a child. He'd eat people like you and Chesty for breakfast. We'll be lucky if he's not alerted already.'

'I'll stay away from him.'

'Bernard likes people to take him for a fool. It's the way he leads them on. If Bernard ever suspected . . . I'd be done for. He'd take me to pieces.' She paused. 'And the Centre would ask why.'

'Perhaps you're right.' Pretending indifference, the man got to his feet, sighed loudly and looked out of the window over the net curtain as if trying to see the road down which the messenger would come.

It was possible to feel sorry for the old man. Brilliant son of a father who had been able to reconcile effortlessly his loudly espoused socialist beliefs with a lifetime of high living and political honours, Martin had never reconciled himself to the fact that his father was an unscrupulous and entertaining rogue blessed with unnatural luck. Martin was doggedly sincere in his political beliefs: diligent but uninspired in his studies, and humourless and demanding in his friendships. When his father died, in a luxury hotel in Cannes in bed with a wealthy socialite lady who ran back to her husband, he'd left Martin, his only child, a small legacy. Martin immediately gave up his job in a public library to stay at home and study political history and economics. It was difficult to eke out his tiny private income. It would have been even more difficult except that, at a political meeting, he encountered a Swedish scholar who persuaded him that helping the

USSR was in the best interest of the proletariat, international socialism and world peace.

Perhaps the cruellest jest that fate had played upon him was that after seeing his father thrive in the upper middle-class circles into which he'd shoved his way, Martin – educated regardless of expense – had to find a way of living with those working classes from which his father had emerged. His rebellion had been a quiet one: the Russians gave him a chance to work unobserved for the destruction of a society for which he felt nothing. It was his secret knowledge which provided for him the strength to endure his austere life. The secret Russians and, of course, the secret women. It was all part of the same desire really, for unless there was a husband or lover to be deceived the affairs gave him little satisfaction, sexual or otherwise.

From the household next door there came the sudden sound of a piano. These were tiny cottages built a century ago for agricultural workers in the Kent fields, and the walls were thin. At first there came the sort of grandiose strumming that pub pianists affect as an overture for their recitals, then the melody resolved into a First World War song: 'The Roses of Picardy'. The relaxed jangle of the piano completed the curious sensation Fiona already had of going back in time, waiting, trapped in the past. This was the long peaceful and promising Edwardian Springtime that everyone thought would never turn cold. There was nothing anywhere in sight to suggest they were not sitting in this parlour some time at the century's beginning, perhaps 1904, when Europe was still young and innocent, London's buses were horse-drawn, HMS *Dreadnought* unbuilt and Russia's permanent October still to come.

'They're never late,' she said, looking at her watch and trying to decide upon an explanation which would satisfy her husband if he arrived home before her.

'You seldom deal with them,' he said. 'You deal with me, and I'm never late.'

She didn't contradict him. He was right. She very seldom saw the Russians: they were all too likely to be tailed by MI5 people.

'And when you do contact them, this is the sort of thing that happens.' He was pleased to show how important he was in the contact with the Russians.

She couldn't help worrying about this Russian who'd tried to defect. He'd seen that she was alone and approached her in what seemed to be an impulsive decision. Had it all been a KGB plot? She'd seen him only that once, but he'd seemed such a genuine decent man. 'It must be difficult for someone like Blum,' she said.

505

'Difficult in what way?'

'Working in a foreign country. Young, missing his wife, lonely. Perhaps shunned because he is Jewish.'

'I doubt that very much,' he said. 'He was a third secretary in the attaché's office: he was trusted and well paid. The little swine was determined to prove how important he was.'

'A Russian Jew with a German name,' said Fiona. 'I wonder what motivated him.'

'He won't try that stunt again,' said Martin. 'And the attaché's office will get a rocket from Moscow.' He smiled with satisfaction at the idea. 'Everything will go through me, as it was always done before Blum.'

'Could it have been a trick?'

'To see if you are loyal to them? To see if you are really a double: working for your SIS masters?'

'Yes,' she said. 'As a test for me.' She watched Martin carefully. Bret Rensselaer, her case officer, who was master-minding this double life of hers, said he was certain that Blum was acting on orders from Moscow. Even if he wasn't, Rensselaer had explained, it's better we lose this chance of a highly placed agent than endanger you. Sometimes she wished she could look at life with the same cold-blooded detachment that Bret Rensselaer displayed. In any case, there was no way she could defy him, and she wasn't sure she wanted to. But what would happen now?

Martin gave a cunning smile as he reflected upon this possibility. 'Well if it was a test, you came through with flying colours,' he said proudly.

She realized then, for the first time, what a stalwart supporter she had in him. Martin was committed to her: she was his investment and he'd do anything rather than face the idea that his protégée was not the most influential Soviet agent of modern history.

'It's getting late.'

'There there. We'll get you to the train on time. Bernard's coming back from Berlin today, isn't he?'

She didn't answer. Martin had no business asking such things even in a friendly conversational way.

Martin said, 'I'm watching the time. Don't fret.'

She smiled. She regretted now the way that she had snapped at him. The Russians had decided that the two of them were joined by a strong bond of affection: that Martin's avuncular manner, as well as his unwavering political belief, was an essential part of her dedication. She didn't want to give them any reason to re-examine their theory.

She looked round the tiny room and wondered if Martin lived here all

506

the time or whether it was just a safe house used for other meetings of this sort. It seemed lived-in: food in the kitchen, coal by the fireplace, open mail stuffed behind the clock that ticked away on the mantelpiece, a well-fed cat prowling through a well-kept garden. A clipper ship in full sail on the wall behind spotless glass. There were lots of books here: Lenin and Marx and even Trotsky stared down from the shelves, along with his revered Fabians, an encyclopedia of socialism, and Rousseau and John Stuart Mill. Even the tedious works of his father. It was an artful touch. Even a trained security man was unlikely to recognize a KGB agent who was so openly familiar with the philosophies of the dissidents, revisionists and traitors. That was Martin's cover: a cranky, old-fashioned and essentially British left-wing theorist, out of touch with modern international political events.

'It's my son Billy. His throat was swollen this morning,' said Fiona and looked at her watch again. 'Nanny should be taking him to see the doctor about now. Nanny is a sensible girl.'

'Of course she is.' He didn't approve of nannies and other domestic slaves. It took him back to his own childhood and muddled emotions about his father that he found so difficult to think about. 'He'll be all right.'

'I do hope it's not mumps.'

'I'm watching the time,' he said again.

'Good reliable Martin,' she said.

He smiled and puffed his pipe. It was what he wanted to hear.

It was a long-haired youth who arrived on a bicycle. He propped it against the fence and came down the garden to rat-a-tat on the front door. The canary awoke and jumped from perch to perch so that the cage danced on its spring. Martin answered the door and came back with a piece of paper he'd taken from a sealed envelope. He gave it to her. It was the printed invoice of a local florist. Written across it in felt-tip pen it said: 'The wreath you ordered has been sent as requested.' It bore the mark of a large oval red rubber stamp: 'PAID'.

'I don't understand,' she said.

'Blum is dead!' he announced softly.

'My God!' said Fiona.

He looked at her. Her face had gone completely white.

'Don't worry,' he said soothingly. 'You've come out of it as pure as the driven snow.' Then he realized that it was the news of Blum's death that had shocked her. In a desperate attempt to comfort her he said, 'Our comrades are inclined to somewhat operatic gestures. They have probably just sent him home to Moscow.'

'Then why. . . ?'

'To reassure you. To make you feel important.' He took a cloth from the shelf and wrapped it carefully round the bird cage to provide darkness.

She looked at him, trying to see what he really believed, but she couldn't be sure.

'Believe me,' he added. 'I know them.'

She decided to believe him. Perhaps it was a feminine response but she couldn't shoulder the burden of Blum's death. She wasn't brave about the sufferings that were inflicted upon others, and yet that was what this job was all about.

She got home after half-past eight, and it was only about ten minutes later that Bret Rensselaer phoned with a laconic, 'All okay?'

'Yes, all okay,' she said.

'What's wrong?'

Bret had heard something in her voice. He was so tuned to her emotions that it frightened her. Bernard would never have guessed she was upset. 'Nothing's wrong,' she said carefully, keeping her voice under control. 'Nothing we can speak about.'

'Are you alone?'

'Yes.'

'Usual time: usual place.'

'Bernard's not here yet. He was due back.'

'I arranged something . . . delayed his baggage at the airport. I wanted to be sure you were home and it was all okay . . .'

'Yes, goodnight, Bret.' She hung up. Bret was doing it for her sake but she knew that he enjoyed showing her how easy it was for him to control her husband in that way. He was another of these men who felt bound to demonstrate some aspect of their power to her. There was also an underlying sexual implication that she didn't like.

5

Somerset, England. Summer 1978.

The Director-General was an enigmatic figure who was the subject of much discussion amongst the staff. Take, for instance, that Christmas when a neat panel bearing the poker-work motto 'Only ignorance is invincible' was hung in a prominent position on the wall beside his desk. The questions arising from that item were not stilled by the news that it was a Christmas present from his wife.

His office was a scene of incomparable chaos into which the cleaning ladies made only tentative forays. Books were piled everywhere. Most of them were garlanded with coloured slips of paper indicating rich veins of research that had never been pursued beyond the initial claims staked out for him by his long-suffering assistant.

Sir Henry Clevemore provided a fruitful source for Bret Rensselaer's long-term anthropological study of the English race. Bret had categorized the D-G as a typical member of the upper classes. This tall shambling figure, whose expensive suits looked like baggy overalls, was entirely different to anyone Bret knew in the USA. Apart from his other eccentricities the D-G encouraged his staff to believe that he was frail, deaf and absent-minded. This contrived role certainly seemed to provide for him a warm loyalty that many a tougher leader would have envied.

One of the disagreeable aspects of working in close cooperation with Sir Henry was the way he moved about the country in such a disorganized and unplanned style that Bret found himself chasing after him to rendezvous after rendezvous in places both remote and uncomfortable. Today they were in Somerset. In the interests of privacy the D-G had taken him to a small wooden hut. It overlooked the sports field of a minor public school of which the D-G was a conscientious governor. The D-G had made a speech to the whole school and had lunch with the headmaster. Bret at short notice had had to be driven down at breakneck speed. There had been no time for lunch. No matter, on a hot day like this Bret could miss lunch without feeling deprived.

The school's surroundings provided a wonderful view of mighty trees, rolling hills and farmland. This was the English countryside that had inspired her great landscape painters: it was brooding and mysterious despite the bright colours. The newly cut grass left a pungent smell on the air. Although not normally prone to hay fever, Bret found his sinuses affected. Of course it was an affliction aggravated by stress and it would be unwise to conclude that the prospect of this meeting with the Director-General had played no part in bringing on the attack.

Through the cobwebbed window two teams of white-clad teenagers could be seen going through the arcane gymnastics that constitute a cricket match. Entering into the spirit of this event, the D-G had changed into white trousers, a linen jacket that had yellowed with age, and a panama hat. He had seated himself in a chair from which he could see the game. The D-G had wiped his piece of window clear but Bret saw the scene through the grimy glass. Bret was standing, having declined to sit upon the cushioned oil drum that the D-G had indicated. Bret kept half an eye on the game, for the D-G referred to it at intervals seeking Bret's opinions about the way it was being played.

'Tell the husband,' said the D-G, shaking his head sadly, 'and it's no longer a secret.'

Bret didn't answer immediately. He watched the left-handed batsman thumping his bat into the ground and waiting for the ball to come. The fielders were well spread out anticipating some heavy swings. Bret turned to the D-G. He'd already made it clear that in his opinion Fiona Samson's husband would have to be told everything: that she was a double agent and was being briefed to go over there. 'I will see her later today,' Bret said. He'd hoped to get the D-G's okay and then he would brief Bernard Samson too. By tonight it would all have been done.

'What are you doing with her at present?' the D-G asked.

Bret walked away a couple of paces and then turned. From that characteristic movement the D-G knew that unless he nipped it in the bud he was going to get one of Bret's renowned lectures. He settled back in his chair and waited for an opportunity to interrupt. Bret had no one else he could explain things to. The D-G knew that providing Bret with a sounding board at frequent intervals was something he could not delegate. 'If we are going to place her in the sort of role where she will pull off the sort of coup we're both hoping for, we can't just leave things to chance.'

'Bravo!' said the D-G, reacting to a stroke that sent the ball to the far boundary. He turned to Bret and smiled. 'We haven't got too much time, Bret.'

'We need ten years, Director, maybe twelve.'

'Is that your considered opinion?'

Bret looked at the old man. They both knew what he was thinking. He wanted Fiona Samson in place before he came up for retirement. Forget the modest, self-effacing manner that was his modus operandi, he wanted glory. 'It is, Sir Henry.'

'I was hoping for something earlier than that.'

'Sir Henry, Fiona Samson is nothing more than an agent in place as far as Moscow is concerned. She has never done anything. She has never delivered.'

'What do you have in mind?'

'She should be posted to Berlin. I want them to have a closer look at her.'

'That would speed things up. They would start thinking of getting her over there quickly.'

'No, they want her in London where the big stuff is hidden.' Bret got out his handkerchief and selfconsciously blew his nose, making as little noise as possible. 'Forgive me, Sir Henry. I think the newly cut grass . . .'

'Then why Berlin?'

'She will have to do something for them.'

The D-G looked at him and pulled a face. He didn't like these stunts which required that the KGB were given things. They were always given good things, convincing things, and that meant things that the Department should keep to itself. 'What?'

'I haven't got as far as that, Director, but we'll have to do it, and do it before the end of the year.'

'Would you acquaint me with a little of your thinking? Wait one moment, this fellow is their fast bowler.'

Bret waited. It was a hot day: the grass was bright green and the boys in their cricket clothes made it the sort of English spectacle that under other circumstances Bret might have relished. The ball came very fast but bounced and went wide. Bret said, 'Mrs Samson goes to Berlin. During her time there she gives them something substantial . . .' Bret paused while the D-G winced at the thought, '. . . so that we have a big inquiry from which she emerges safe. Preferably with their help.'

'You mean they arrange that one of their agents takes the blame?'

'Well, yes. That, of course, would be ideal,' said Bret.

The D-G was still watching the match. 'I like it,' he said without turning round.

Bret smiled grimly. It was an uphill struggle, but that was something of an accolade coming from Sir Henry Clevemore, although it could of course have been prompted by some cricketing accomplishment that Bret had failed to understand. He said, 'Mrs Samson comes back here to London and they tell her to keep still and quiet.'

'That's one year,' the D-G reminded him.

Bret said, 'Look, sir. We can deliver Mrs Samson to them right away, of course we can. She's like a box of nuts and bolts: an all-purpose agent they can use anywhere. But that's not good enough.'

'No,' said the D-G, watching the cricketers and wondering what was coming.

'We must take this woman and clear her mind of everything she knows.'

'Classified material?'

'I'm already making sure she sees nothing that would affect the Department.'

'How did she take that?'

'We have to make our plans as if she will be interrogated . . . interrogated in the cellars at Normannenstrasse.' In the silence that followed a big fly buzzed angrily against the window glass.

'It's a nasty thought.'

'The stakes are high, Sir Henry. But we're playing to win.' He looked around the hut. It was insufferably hot and the air was perfumed with linseed oil and weedkillers for the lawn. Bret opened the door to let a little air in.

The D-G looked at Bret and said, 'A good thunderstorm would clear the air,' as if this was something he could arrange. Then he added, 'You're making me wonder whether a woman is right after all.'

'It's too late to change the plan now.'

'Surely not?' Even the D-G was feeling the heat. He mopped his brow with a red silk handkerchief that had been protruding from his top pocket.

'Mrs Samson knows what we intend. If we change to another agent our plan is known to her. I have shown her the figures and the graphs. She knows that the skilled and professional labour force is our target. She knows that we want to bleed their essential people and she knows the sort of opposition groups we intend to support over there.'

'Wasn't that a little premature, Bret?'

'It will all depend upon her once she's there. She must understand our strategy so well that she can improvise her responses.'

'I suppose you're right. I wish it was you explaining it all to the Cabinet Secretary next week. All your charts and mumbo-jumbo . . .

You see Bret, if we don't persuade him to go along with the fundamental idea . . . Do you have an operational name yet?'

'I thought it was better not to ask the Department for an operational name.'

'No, no, no, of course not. We'll think of one. Something that suggests the weakening of the economy without prejudicing the security of our operation. Any ideas?'

'I thought Operation Haemorrhage? Or Operation Bleeder?'

'Blood; casualties. No. And bleeder is an English expletive. What else?'

'Leaker?'

'Vulgarism with connotations of urinating. But Sinker might do.'

'Sinker then. Yes, of course, Sir Henry.'

'Oh, my God, this fellow is useless. Left-handed and look at the way he's holding the bat.' He turned to Bret. 'You understand what I mean about persuading him to the basic idea?'

Bret understood exactly. If the Cabinet Secretary didn't go for the economic target then they'd start having second thoughts about using Bret. Mrs Samson would be provided with a different case officer.

The D-G said, 'There still remains the problem of the Soviets engaging her for operational service over there. We can't leave that to chance.'

'Agent X has to be created from scratch,' said Bret, having decided that naming Mrs Samson might be creating doubts in the D-G's mind. 'I must deliver to them an agent who is so knowledgeable and experienced in one specific field of activity that they will have to put her in the place we want.'

'You've lost me now,' said the D-G without taking his eyes from the cricket.

'I shall spend this year studying the Russian links with the East German security police, particularly the KGB-Stasi operational command in Berlin. I'll come to you with a complete picture of their strengths and weaknesses.'

'Can you do that?'

'I spent most of last week reading Operational Briefs. Give me a closer look at the command structure over there, and my analysts could build a detailed picture. It will take time but we'll get what we need.'

'Their security is good,' said the D-G.

'We will be trying to discover what they need . . . the things they *don't* know. I have good people in my section. They are used to sifting through figures and building a picture of what is going on.'

'For economics, yes. It's possible to do that with statistics of banking, exports, imports and credit and so on because you're dealing with hard facts. But this is far more complex.'

'With respect, Sir Henry, I think you're wrong,' said Bret Rensselaer with a slight rasp to his voice that betrayed his tension.

The D-G forgot the cricket and looked at him. Bret's eyes were wide, his smile fixed, and a wavy lock of his blond hair had fallen out of place. Until this very moment he hadn't realized to what extent Bret Rensselaer had become consumed with his new task.

For the first time the D-G began to feel that this mad scheme might actually work. What a staggering coup it would be if Bret really did it: planting Mrs Samson into the East Berlin command structure where she could use their own secret records on protest groups, dissidents and other anti-communists to guide the Department as they planned the economic destruction of the communist regime. 'Time will tell, Bret.'

'Yes, indeed, sir.'

The D-G nodded to Bret. Was it the prospect of moving from a vitally important, but somewhat wearisome, world of committees into the more dashing excitement of operations that had so animated him? Or had the departure of his wife, now seemingly a permanent separation, provided him with more time? Or had the loss of his spouse to another man made it necessary for Bret to prove himself? Perhaps all of those. And yet the D-G had not allowed for Mrs Fiona Samson and the influence her participation had had upon Bret Rensselaer's strength and determination.

'Give me a free hand, sir.'

'But ten years . . .'

'Perhaps I shouldn't have given a time frame.' His sinuses hurt: he felt an overwhelming need to blow his nose again and did so.

The D-G watched him with interest. He didn't know Bret had sinus problems. 'Let's see how it goes. What about finance?' He turned back to the cricket. The left-handed batsman had hit a superb catch – up up up it went and curved down like a mortar bomb – but luckily for him there was no fielder able to reach it. One fellow ran in for it but was unable to judge where it would land. The ball hit the ground and there was a concerted groan.

'I'll need money and it must not be routed through Central Funding.'

'There are many ways.'

'I have a company.'

'Do it any way you like, Bret. I know you won't waste it. What are we talking about? Roughly?'

'A million sterling in the first year. Double that in the second and all subsequent years, adjusted for inflation and the exchange rate. No vouchers, no receipts, no accounts.'

'Very well. We'll have to concoct a route for the money.' The D-G shielded his eyes with a folded newspaper. The sun had come round to shine through the window. 'Have I forgotten anything?'

'No, sir.'

'I'll not keep you then. I'm sure you have things to do. Look at this: the captain has put another fast bowler on. And he's rather good. What do you think, Bret?'

'Very good indeed, sir. Very fast. A problem will arise when we send Mrs Samson to work in Berlin. Will they continue to use this Welsh socialist as the contact? If not we'll have to be very careful setting up the new one. Berlin is quite different to London: everyone knows everyone.'

'And everyone hates everyone,' said the D-G. 'You'd better have her float the possibility before them and see what reaction she gets.'

'The Welshman is very supportive,' said Bret. 'He's determined to believe that she's the KGB superspy. She's his protégée. She could make a terrible blunder and he'd still hold on to his trust in her. But when she goes to Berlin they'll be more suspicious. You know how it is when someone's treasure is scrutinized by a rival: the KGB will turn her over.'

The D-G frowned. 'Is this some narrative form of second thinking?' he said tartly.

'No, sir. I am sure the Berlin tour is an essential part of the plan. I'm simply saying that she will be under a lot of stress.'

'Out with it then.' The D-G stood tall and bent his head to see Bret over his glasses.

'We're asking her to give up her husband and children. Her colleagues will despise her . . .'

'When did she say all this to you?'

'She hasn't said it.'

'She hasn't expressed doubts at all?'

'Not to me. She's a patriot: she has a wonderful sense of purpose.'

The D-G sniffed. 'We've seen patriots change their minds, haven't we, Bret?'

'She won't,' said Bret firmly and certainly.

'Then what is it?'

'The husband. He should be told. He will be able to give her the sort of help and encouragement she'll need. She'd go East knowing that her

515

husband will be keeping her family intact. It would be something for her to hang on to.'

'Oh, don't let's go through that again, Bret.' The D-G turned away.

'You said I'd have a free hand.'

He swung round, and when he spoke there was a hard note in his voice. 'I don't remember saying any such thing, Bret. You asked for a free hand: almost everyone in the Department asks for a free hand at some time or another. It makes me wonder what they think I am paid to do. I will of course give you as much freedom as possible. I'll guard you from the slings and arrows of outrageous officialdom. I'll give you non-voucher funds and I'll listen to any crackpot idea you bring me. But a secret is a secret, Bret. The only chance she has of coming out of this in one piece is to have her husband overwhelmed and horrified when she goes over there. That will be the ace card that saves her. Never mind help and encouragement, I want Bernard Samson to become demented with rage.' He used the newspaper to slam at the buzzing fly and after a couple of swipes the fly fell to the floor. 'Demented with rage!'

'Very well, sir. I'm sure you know best.' Bret's tone did nothing to make the D-G think he'd changed his opinion.

'Yes, I do, Bret. I do know best.' They both watched as the batsman swung and then seemed to leap backwards, blundering into the wicket so that the stumps were knocked asunder. A fast ball had hit him in the belly. He went down clutching his stomach and rolled about in agony. 'Left-handed,' pronounced the D-G without emotion. The other cricketers gathered around the fallen boy but no one did anything: they just looked down at him.

'Yes, sir,' said Bret. 'Well, I'll be off.'

'She might waver, Bret. Agents do when the time gets close. If she does you'd better make sure she toes the line. There is too much at stake now for a last-minute change of cast.'

Bret stood there in case the D-G had more to say. But the D-G flicked his fingers to dismiss him.

Once outside Bret blew his nose again. Damn this grass: he'd keep away from cricket matches on freshly mowed grass in future. Well, the old man could still provide a surprise or two, thought Bret. What a tough old bastard he was. Bernard must not be told under any circumstances. So that was what 'Only ignorance is invincible' meant. By the time he got to his car Bret's sinus problem was entirely gone. It was the stress that brought it on.

6

Fiona Samson, a thirty-one-year-old careerist, was a woman of many secrets and always had been. At first that had made her relish her demanding job in London Central – the most secret of all the government's secret departments – but as her role as a double agent developed and became more complex she found there were times when it all became too much for her. It had always been said that double agents eventually lose their own sense of direction and fail to distinguish which side they really work for, but for Fiona it was different. Fiona could not envisage ever becoming a supporter of communist regimes: her patriotism was a deeply rooted aspect of her upper middle-class upbringing. Fiona's torment came not from political doubts: she worried that she would not be able to cope with the overwhelming task that she'd been given. Bernard would have been perfect for such a double agent role; like most men he could compartmentalize his brain and keep his family concerns quite separate from his work. Fiona could not. She knew that her task would become so demanding that she would have to neglect her husband and children more and more and finally – with no possible warning – leave them to fend for themselves. She would be branded a traitor and they would be spattered with the dirt. The thought of that distressed her.

Had she been able to discuss it with Bernard it might have been different, but authority had decreed that her husband should not know the plan. In any case she was not good at talking with Bernard. No less spirited than her extrovert sister Tessa, Fiona's fires were damped down and seldom showed a flicker. Sometimes, or even often, Fiona would have enjoyed being like Tessa. She would have got great and immediate relief and satisfaction from the sort of public performance – displays of anger or exhilarated madness – for which her sister was famous, but there was no choice for her.

Fiona was beautiful in a way that had sometimes separated her from other women. Fiona's beauty was a cold perfect radiance of the sort that is to be seen in the unapproachable models posing with such assurance in glossy magazines. Her brain was cold and perfect too; her mind had

517

been bent by pedantic university teachers to think in terms of male priorities and had sacrificed many of the unbridled joys of femininity in order to become a successful surrogate male. Fiona's miseries, her tensions and her times of great happiness were shared only reluctantly –grudgingly sometimes – with those around her. Emotion of any sort was always to be hidden, her father had taught her that. Her father was an insensitive and opinionated man who had wanted sons, something he explained to his two children – both daughters – at every opportunity, and told them that boys didn't cry.

Fiona's marriage to Bernard Samson had changed her life forever. It was love at first sight. She'd never met anyone like Bernard before. A big bear-like man, Bernard was the most masculine person she'd ever met. At least he had the qualities that she thought of as being masculine. Bernard was practical. He could fix any sort of machine and deal with any sort of people. He was of course a male chauvinist: categorical and opinionated. He never thought of helping in the house and couldn't even boil an egg successfully. On the other hand he was constantly cheerful, almost never moody and quite without malevolence. Inclined to be untidy he gave no thought to his clothes or his appearance, never put on airs or graces and while enjoying art and music he was in no way 'intellectual' or 'artistic' in the way that so many of her male acquaintances were determined to be.

Fiona's husband was the only person she'd ever met who completely disregarded other people's evaluation of him. Bernard was a devoted father, more devoted to the children than Fiona was if the truth was faced. And yet he was not the unmotivated drifter that her father had warned her about. Bernard was driven by some force or thought or belief in the way that great artists are said to be, and woe betide anyone who got in his way. Bernard was not an easy man to live with. He'd been brought up in post-war Berlin – his father a senior intelligence officer – in an atmosphere of violence and betrayal. He was by nature tough and undemonstrative. Bernard had killed men in the course of duty and done it without qualms. He was well adjusted and enjoyed a self-confidence that Fiona could only wonder at and envy.

The burden of their marriage came from the fact that Bernard was far too much like Fiona: neither of them found it easy to say the things that wives and husbands have to say to keep a marriage going. Even 'I love you' did not come easily from Bernard's lips. Bernard really needed as a wife some noisy extrovert like Fiona's sister Tessa. She might have found a way of getting him out of his shell. If only Bernard could be foolish and trivial now and again. If only he could express doubts or fears and come to her for comfort. Fiona didn't need a strong silent man: she was strong and silent herself. It was difficult for a man like Bernard to be really sympathetic to a woman's point of view and Bernard would never understand the way that women would cry for 'nothing'.

Lately, there had been many occasions when the complex tangle of Fiona's working life became too much for her. She was using tranquillizers and sleeping tablets with a regularity that she'd never needed before. Bernard had found her crying several times when he'd come into the house unexpectedly. She had told him she was under treatment from her gynaecologist; embarrassed dear old Bernard had not pursued it further.

When she found herself weighed down by her thoughts, and the worries would not go away, Fiona found an excuse to leave the office and walked to the Waterloo mainline railway station. She'd come to like it. Its size suggested permanence while its austere design and girder construction gave it anonymity: a vast waiting room made from a construction kit. Coming through the dirty glass of its roof the daylight was grey, dusty and mysterious. Today – despite the rain – she had benefited from the walk from the office. Now she sat on a bench near number one platform and quietly cried her heart out. No one seemed to notice these emotional outbursts, except once when a lady from the Salvation Army offered her a chance for prayer at an address in Lambeth. Sobbing was not so unusual on Waterloo Station. Separations were common here and nowadays it was a place where the homeless and hungry were apt to congregate. London Airport was probably just as good a place to go for the purpose of weeping, but that provided too great a chance of seeing someone she knew. Or, more exactly, of someone she knew seeing her. And Waterloo Station was near the office, and there were tea and newspapers, taxi-cabs and metered parking available. So she went to number one platform and cried.

It was the prospect of leaving Bernard and the children, of course. They would end up hating her. Even if she did everything that was expected of her, and returned a heroine, they would hate her for leaving them. Her father would hate her too. And her sister Tessa. And what would happen to the children? She had asked Bret that, but he had dismissed her fears. The children would be cared for in the manner that her sacrifice and heroism deserved, he'd said in that theatrical style that Bret could get away with because he was so damn certain. But how sincere was he? That worried her sometimes. Sincere or not she couldn't help thinking that her children would be forgotten once she was working in the East. Billy would survive boarding school – and perhaps even flourish there – but Sally would find such an environment unendurable. Fiona had resolved not to put her children through the sort of childhood that she had hated so much.

Bret told her that the only thing that frightened her more than the prospect of finding that her husband and children wouldn't be able to manage without her, was the prospect of finding that they could. Bastard! But perhaps there was a glimmer of truth there. Perhaps that was the permanent crippling dilemma that motherhood brought.

She had never been a very good mother and that knowledge plagued her. She'd never wanted motherhood in the way that her sister Tessa so desperately did. Fiona had never liked babies: her friends' babies had appalled her with their endless demands and the way that they completely upset the households. Babies cried very loudly; babies vomited very frequently and dirtied their nappies very stenchfully. Even when hugging her own babies she had always been uneasy in case her dress was soiled. The children's nurse had seen that right from the start, and Fiona still remembered the accusing look in her eyes. That look said, I am their real mother: you are not fit to look after them.

Fiona was useless with children but she didn't want to be barren either. She wanted to tick motherhood off the list. She worried about them always, and wanted them to be clever at school, and most of all she looked forward to sharing their lives with them when they grew up. But it was now that they needed her so much. Perhaps it was not too late. Perhaps she should walk out of London Central and apply herself to the children as she had applied herself to her studies and her work.

Never a day went past but she told herself that she should go to Bret and tell him she had changed her mind. But each time she spoke to him – long before she could bring the conversation to the point she wanted – he persuaded her that her first duty was to her country and the Department. Even the Director-General had spoken with unusual gravity about this scheme to get her into position as a field agent, a field agent of prime importance. It would, of course, show that women could bring off an intelligence coup as well as any man. That, more than anything else, had helped her keep going when her spirits were low.

Since the beginning of the year her tiffs and differences with Bernard had multiplied. It wasn't all Bernard's fault, things had been difficult for him too. Operation 'Reisezug' had been something of a disaster: three of their own people killed, or so the rumour said. Max Busby was carrying a lot of the material in his memory and Max never came back.

Bernard didn't talk about it but anyone who knew him could see how shaken he was.

Bernard was now officially 'rested' from field work and, in what might have been an effort to comfort her, Bret Rensselaer had let slip the fact that the Department had decided that Bernard should spend the rest of his life behind a desk. Not the German Desk. Dicky Cruyer – a vain and shallow man – had got the German Desk. Bernard was in line for it and would have done it with more skill and intelligence, but Dicky had the administrative experience as well as the personality and background that the Department favoured for top jobs. Bernard said that all Dicky had was the right old school tie, but Bernard could be a bit touchy about such things. She'd wondered if Bret decided against Bernard's promotion because of her assignment, but Bret insisted that it was a decision made at the top.

She was sure that her painful domestic life could be transformed if Bret would let her confide in her husband. As it was she couldn't always account for her movements. It had been bad enough when she'd only had to have the odd meeting with Martin Euan Pryce-Hughes. Now there were countless covert briefings by Bret and a lot of studying to do. And the studying was of material that she mustn't let Bernard catch sight of. Bernard was smart and quick. She wouldn't have to make many mistakes for him to guess what was happening, and the D-G had taken it upon himself to tell her that if Bernard discovered what was planned the whole thing was off.

Poor Bernard; poor Billy; poor Sally. She sat on the bench at Waterloo and thought about them all. She felt drained and ill. Crying released the tension within her but it did nothing to alleviate the pain. She cried some more in the constrained, unobtrusive and dignified way she'd learned to cry at boarding school, and stared across the concourse where people were hurrying for their commuter trains or saying their farewells. She told herself that their troubles might be worse than hers but that did nothing to help: in fact it made her feel even more dejected.

The weather did nothing to cheer her. It was one of those miserably cold and rainy days that so often punctuate an English summer. Everyone was bundled into coats and scarves and the cold damp air contributed to Fiona's chilly gloom. Trains arrived; trains departed. A young woman wanted to know the time, and an elderly couple walked past arguing vociferously. Pigeons and sparrows came gliding down from the girders of the roof, encouraged by a bearded man on a bench nearby who threw crumbs to them. She sat there watching the birds for what seemed a long time.

'Pardon me, madam.' Fiona looked up to see two men: a uniformed railway policeman and a man in civilian clothes. 'You were talking to a young woman a few minutes back?' It was the policeman who spoke.

At first she thought they were going to tell her to move on, or arrest her for soliciting, or make some other sort of fuss, but then she realized that the man in civilian clothes was not a policeman. 'Yes?'

'In a dark blue coat, with a red silk scarf? Dark hair. Pretty girl.' It was the man in the camel-hair coat speaking. He'd taken his hat off in a courteous gesture that surprised her, and she noticed the way he gripped it in his suntanned hand. He seemed nervous.

'She just asked me the time. She caught the train for Southampton,' said Fiona. A train announcement, resonant and unintelligible, interrupted her and she waited for it to finish. 'At least, that's what she said she was going to do.'

'She had a big green plastic bag with a shoulder strap,' said the man.

It was, she decided, a question. 'She had a bag,' said Fiona. 'I didn't notice anything about it.'

'Are you all right, madam?' said the policeman. He'd noticed her reddened, tear-filled eyes.

'I'm quite all right,' she said firmly. She looked at her watch and got to her feet to show that she was about to leave.

The policeman nodded. He wanted to believe her; he wasn't looking for more trouble. 'It's the gentleman's daughter,' explained the policeman.

'My name's Lindner. Adam Lindner. Yeah, she's only sixteen,' said the man. 'She ran away from home. She looks older.' He had a soft transatlantic accent that she couldn't place.

'We'll phone Southampton,' said the policeman briskly. 'They'll pick her up when the train gets there.'

'Was there anyone with her?' asked the father authoritatively.

Fiona looked at him. He was tall and athletic; in his late thirties perhaps. His moustache was full but carefully trimmed. He had doleful eyebrows and a somewhat squashed nose in a weather-beaten face. He was handsome in a seemingly uncontrived way, like the tough-guy film-stars whose photos she'd pinned above her bed at school. His clothes were expensive and too perfect, the style that foreigners selected when they wanted to look English: a magnificent camel-hair overcoat, a paisley-patterned tie, its knot supported by a gold pin through the shirt collar, and the shiny Oxford shoes. 'Yes,' she said, 'there was a man with her.'

'A black man?'

'Perhaps. I didn't notice. Yes, I believe so.'

'It makes it easier from our point of view,' said the policeman.

A gust of wind lifted discarded newspapers and other litter so that it moved enough to scare the birds. Conversation faltered as English conversations do when minds turn to the delicate and devious rituals of leave-taking.

'We have your phone number, Mr Lindner,' said the policeman. 'As soon as we hear from Southampton the desk sergeant will phone.' It ended there. The policeman had other work to do.

'If that's all?' said Fiona, moving away. 'I have to get a taxi.'

'I'm going to Maida Vale,' the man said to Fiona. 'Can I drop you off anywhere?' She still couldn't recognize the accent. She decided he was a merchant seaman, or oil worker, paid off after a long contract and enjoying a spending spree.

'It's all right,' she said.

'No, please. It's pouring with rain again and I would appreciate company.'

Both men were looking at her quizzically. She resented the way that men expected women to explain themselves, as if they were second-class citizens. But she invented an explanation. 'I was seeing someone off. I live in Marylebone. I'll get a cab.'

'Marylebone: I go right through it.' And then, 'Thank you, constable, you've been most helpful.'

'Children do funny things,' said the policeman as he took his leave. 'It will be all right. You'll see.'

'It was bad luck,' said the man. 'Another fifteen minutes and we would have stopped her.' Fiona walked towards the cab rank and he fell into step alongside her. 'Will you look at that rain! You'd better ride with me.' There were about fifty people standing in line for taxis and no taxis in sight.

'Very well. Thank you.'

They walked to his car, talking about the treacherous English weather. His manner now was ultra-considerate and his voice was different in some way she could not define. She smiled at him. He opened the door for her and helped her into the seat. It was a Jaguar XJS convertible: grey, shiny and very new. 'I suppose Mrs Lindner is worried,' said Fiona. As the engine started with a throaty roar the stereo played a bar or two of a Strauss waltz before he switched it off, twisted his neck and carefully backed out of the parking place.

'There is no Mrs Lindner,' he said while craning to see behind the car. 'I was divorced five years back. And anyway this girl is not my daughter: she's my niece.'

'I see.'

Down the ramp and through the cars and buses he went with no hesitation: he didn't drive like a man unaccustomed to London traffic. 'Yeah, well I didn't want to say it was my niece; the cops would immediately think it was some bimbo I was shacked up with.'

'Would they?'

'Sure they would. Cops think like that. And anyway I am a Canadian and I'm here without a work permit.' He bit his lip. 'I can't get tangled up with cops.'

'Did you give them a false name?'

He looked round at her and grinned admiringly. 'Yeah. As a matter of fact I did.'

She nodded.

'Oh boy! Now you are going to turn out to be a cop from the Immigration Department. That would be just my sort of lousy luck.'

'Would it?'

'Yeah. It would.' A pause. 'You're not a cop. I mean, you're not going to turn me in, are you?'

'Are you serious?'

'You're damn right, I'm serious. I was working in Sydney, Australia, and the hall porter turned me in. Two heavies from Immigration were waiting in my suite when I got back that night. They'd gone through my mail and even cut the lining out of my suits. Those Aussies are rough. Mind you, in Uruguay in the old days it was worse. They'd shake you down for everything you had.'

'It sounds as if you make a study of illegal immigration.' She smiled.

'Hey that's better! I thought maybe you'd given up smiling for Lent. Immigration? Yeah well my cousin buys and sells airplanes. Now and again I take time off to deliver one of them. Then maybe I get tempted to take on a few local charters to make a little extra dough.'

'Is that what you are doing in London?'

'Airplanes? No, that's just my playtime. I learned to fly in the air force, and kept it up. In real life I'm a psychiatrist.'

'This niece of yours . . . was she another invention?' asked Fiona.

'Now, I'm not completely off my trolley. She is the daughter of my cousin Greg and I was supposed to be looking after her in London. I guess I will have to phone Winnipeg and tell Greg she's jumped ship.'

'Will he be angry?'

'Sure he'll be angry but he won't be surprised. He knows she can be a pretty wild little girl.'

'How come you. . . ?'

'Greg was in the air force with me and he owns a big slice of the airplane brokerage outfit.'

'I see.'

'Because I'm a psychiatrist, he thinks that I can straighten her out. Her local quack's treatment was just to keep doping her with amitriptyline and junk like that.'

'But you can't straighten her out either?'

'Girls who . . .' The flippant answer he was about to give died on his lips. 'You really want to know? It could be she has a schizophrenic reaction to puberty, but it will need someone with a whole lot more specialized experience to diagnose that one.'

'Does her father know you think that?'

'I don't know what made me tell you . . . No, it's too early to tell Greg. It's a heavy one to lay on parents. I want to talk to someone about her. I was trying to arrange for a specialist to look at her without letting her catch on to it.' He stole another glance at Fiona. 'Now it's my turn to guess about you. I'll bet you are a student of philosophy. Am I right, Miss. . . ?' he said with a big grin.

'Mrs Samson. I am married and I have two children.'

'No fooling? That can't be true! Two children: they must be very young. My real name is Harry Kennedy. Good to know you, Mrs Samson. Yeah, the girl will maybe come out okay. I've seen cases like this before. No call to worry her folks. It's not drugs. At least I hope to God it's not drugs. She doesn't get along very well at school. She is not the academic sort of kid. She likes parties and music and dancing: she's always been like that from the time when she was tiny. She doesn't like reading. Me, I couldn't live without books.'

'Me too.'

'You weren't seeing anyone off, were you?' he said suddenly without looking away from the road.

'No.'

'Why were you at the station then?'

'Does it matter?'

'I am being very nosy. But it was my good fortune that Patsy spoke with you. I couldn't help wondering about you.'

'I wanted to think.'

'Sad thoughts?'

'Everything is relative. I have a good life: no complaints.'

525

'You need a drink.'

She laughed. 'Perhaps I do,' she said.

He drove right through Marylebone. The traffic was light. She should have said something, made him take her directly home, but she said nothing. She watched the traffic and the rain, the grim-faced drivers and the endless crowds of drenched people. He pulled into the parking lot behind a well-kept block of flats in Maida Vale. 'Come up and have a drink,' he said.

'I don't think so,' she said and didn't move.

'There is no need to be afraid. Like I told you, my name is Harry Kennedy. I have an allergic reaction to work permits but other than that I am quite harmless. I work in the psychiatric department of the St Basil Clinic in Fulham. Eventually they will get me a work permit and I will live happily ever after.'

'Or perhaps move on to pastures new?'

'Could be.'

'And you really are a psychiatrist?'

'It's not something I'd invent, is it?'

'Why not?'

'It's the ultimate deterrent to all social relationships. Look at the effect it's already having on you.'

'One drink.'

'And then home to husband and children,' he promised.

'Yes,' she said, although the children were being looked after by a competent nanny and Bernard was in Berlin for a job that would take three days.

Kennedy's flat was on the second floor. She followed him up the stairs. This block had been built in the nineteen thirties and, apart from a few chunks of granite chiselled from the façade by bomb fragments, it had survived the war intact.

'I'm renting this place from a rich E.N.T. man at the clinic. He's in New York at Bellevue until next April. If they renew his contract he'll want to sell it.' The apartment was big; in the Thirties architects knew the difference between a bedroom and a cupboard. He took her damp raincoat and hung it on a bentwood rack in the hall. Then he removed his own coat and tossed his hat on to a pile of unopened mail that had been placed alongside a bowl of artificial flowers on the hallstand. 'I keep meaning to forward all that mail to him but it's mostly opportunities to purchase vacations and encyclopedias from the credit card companies.'

His three-piece suit – a chalk stripe, dark grey worsted – was cut in a boxy American style that made him look slimmer than he really was. On his waistcoat there was a gold watch-chain with some tiny gold ornament suspended from it.

He ushered her into the drawing room. It was spacious enough to take a baby grand piano, a couple of sofas and a coffee table without seeming cramped. 'Come right in. Welcome to Disneyland. Take a seat. Gin, whisky, vodka, vermouth . . . a Martini? Name it.' She looked around at the furnishings. Someone had gone to a lot of trouble to keep everything in sympathy with the art deco that had been in style when the block was built.

'A Martini. Do you play the piano?'

He went into the kitchen and she heard him open the refrigerator. He returned with two frosted Martini glasses, chilled gin and chilled vermouth. Under his arm there was a box of snacks. He poured two drinks carefully. 'I'm fresh out of olives,' he said as he carried the drinks across to her. 'The help eats them as fast as I buy them. She's Spanish. Yeah, I play a little.'

'A quick drink and then I must go.'

'Have no fear. I will drive you home.'

'It's an attractive room.' She took the glass by its stem and held it against her face, enjoying the feel of its icy coldness.

'You like this art deco junk?' He drank some of his Martini and then put the glass down, carefully placing it on a coaster. 'The E.N.T. man inherited it. His parents were refugees from Vienna. Doctors. They got out early and brought their furniture with them. I had to take an oath about not leaving Coca-Cola glasses on the polished tables, and not smoking. He's going to ship it to New York if he stays there.'

'It's lovely.'

'He's a sentimental kind of guy. It's okay I guess but I prefer something I can relate to. Have one of these.' He indicated the snacks; tiny cheesy mouthfuls in a freshly opened red box bearing a picture of an antique steamship on the Rhine.

'I'm not hungry.'

'Would it help to talk about it?'

'No, I don't think so.'

'You're a beautiful woman, Mrs Samson. Your husband is a lucky man.' He said it artlessly and was not selfconscious: no Englishman she'd met could deliver such compliments without bluster and embarrassment.

'I am lucky too,' she said quietly. She wished he wouldn't look at her: her hair was a mess and her eyes were red.

527

'I'm sure you are. Is your drink all right? Too much gin?'

'No, it's just the way I like it.' She drank some to show him that it was true. She was uneasy. After a few minutes of small-talk – Kennedy had been discovering the pleasures of the opera – she said, 'Perhaps you could ring for a taxi? They sometimes take ages to come at this time.'

'I'll drive you.'

'You must wait for the phone call from the police.'

'You are right. But must you go so soon?'

'Yes, I must.'

'Could I see you again?'

'That would be less wise.'

'I'm delivering a Cessna to Nice next week – Friday, maybe Saturday – and collecting a Learjet. It's a sweet job: not many like that come along. There's a really good restaurant twenty minutes along the highway from Nice airport. I'll have you back in central London by six p.m. Now don't say no, right away. Maybe you'd like to bring your husband or your children. It's a four-seater.'

'I don't think so.'

'Think it over. It could make just the sort of break that would do you good.'

'Is that a medical opinion?'

'It sure is.'

'It's better not.'

'Let me give you my phone number,' said Kennedy. Without waiting to hear what she decided he gave her a printed card. 'This lousy weather keeps up and maybe you'll feel like a spot of Riviera sunshine.' She looked at the card: Dr H. R. Kennedy and the Maida Vale address and phone number. 'I had them done last month at one of these fast print shops. I was going to see patients here but I decided not to.'

'I see.'

'It was against the terms of the lease and I could see there would be arguments if my patients started using the car park spaces.' He went to the phone and asked for a taxi. 'They are usually very prompt,' he said. 'I have an account with them.' Then he added thoughtfully, 'And seeing patients here might have set the immigration guys on my tail.'

'I hope your niece returns soon.'

'She will be okay.'

'Do you know the man she's with?'

Kennedy paused. 'He is a patient. At the clinic. He met her when she was waiting for me one afternoon.'

528

'Oh.'

'He can be violent. That's why the police were so good about it.'

'I see.'

'You helped me, Mrs Samson. And I appreciate your keeping me company, I really do.' The phone rang to say the cab was waiting outside. He helped her on with her coat, carefully making sure that her long hair was not trapped under the collar. 'I would like to help you,' he said. In bidding her a decorous goodbye his hand held hers.

'I don't need help.'

'You go to railway stations in order to hide your unhappiness. Don't you think that a marriage in which a wife is frightened to be unhappy in the presence of her husband might leave something to be desired?'

Fiona found his apparent simplicity and honesty disarming. She had no great faith in psychiatry and in general distrusted its practitioners, but she felt attracted to this amusing and unusual man. He was obviously attracted to her, but that had not made him fawn. And she appreciated the way that Kennedy so readily confided his fears of the Immigration Department and the trust he'd shown in her. It made her feel like a partner in his lawless activities. 'Is that the sort of dilemma patients like me bring along to you?'

'Believe me, I have no patients who in any way resemble you, Mrs Samson, and I never have had.'

She gently pulled her hand away from his and went through the door. He didn't follow her but when she glanced up, before getting into the taxi, she could see his face at the window.

She looked at her watch. It was late. Bernard tried to phone about this time each evening.

'Hello, sweetheart.' To her astonishment she arrived home to find Bernard, Nanny and the two children sitting round the little kitchen table. The scene was printed upon her memory for ever after. They were all laughing and talking and eating. The table displayed the chaos she had seen at Bernard's mother's house: tea in cups without saucers, teapot standing on a chipped plate, tin-foil frozen food containers on the tablecloth, sugar in its packet, a slab of cake sitting on the bag in which it was sold. The laughter stopped when she came in.

'We wondered where you'd got to,' said Bernard. He was wearing corduroy trousers and an old blue roll-neck sweater that she had twice thrown away.

'Mr Samson said the children could eat down here,' said the nanny nervously.

'It's all right, Nanny,' said Fiona and went and kissed the children. They were newly bathed and smelled of talcum powder.

'You've got a cold nose,' said Billy accusingly and then chuckled. He looked so like Bernard.

'You're rude,' his little sister told him. She had been raised to the level of the table by sitting upon a blue silk cushion from the drawing room sofa. Fiona noticed that a dollop of tomato sauce had fallen upon it but kept smiling as she gave her daughter a kiss and a hug. She had a special love for little Sally, who sometimes seemed to need Fiona in a way that no one else had ever done.

Fiona embraced Bernard. 'What a wonderful surprise. I didn't expect you until the weekend.'

'I slipped away.' Bernard put an arm round her, but there was a reluctance to his embrace. For some other wives such a hesitation might have been a danger signal. Fiona knew that it was a sign that something had gone wrong in Berlin. A shooting? A killing? She looked at him to make sure he was not injured. She wouldn't ask him what had happened, they didn't talk about departmental matters unless they concerned the both of them, but she knew it would take a little time before Bernard would be capable of physical contact with her.

'You're all right?'

'Of course I'm all right.' A smile did not hide the hint of irritation. He did not like her to show her concern.

'Will you have to go back?' The children were watching them both with great interest.

'We'll see.' He contrived a cheerfulness. 'Nothing will happen for a few days. They think I'm chasing around Bavaria.'

She gave him another decorous kiss. She wished Bernard would not be so intractable. Deliberately disobeying instructions in order to come home early was flattering but it was the sort of behaviour that the Department found inexcusable. This was not the time to say that. 'It's a lovely surprise,' she said.

'Eat some dinner, Mummy,' said Sally. 'There's plenty.'

'Mummy doesn't eat frozen meals, do you Mummy?' said her brother.

Nanny, who had no doubt purchased the 'delicious ready-to-eat country farmhouse dinner', looked embarrassed. Fiona said, 'It depends.'

'It's not meaty,' said Billy, as if that was a recommendation. 'It's all sauce and pasta.' He pushed a spoon into the remains to show her.

'It's very salty,' said Sally. 'I don't like it.'

The nanny took the spoon away from Billy and then went to get a cup and saucer for Fiona to have tea with them.

Fiona took off her coat and hat. Then she grabbed a piece of kitchen paper in order to see what could be done to remove the sauce from the silk cushion. She knew that in doing so she would be spoiling the gemütlich atmosphere into which she had intruded but she simply could not sit down and laugh and talk and forget it. She couldn't. Perhaps that was what was wrong with her and with her marriage.

Before she could get started, Nanny poured tea for her and then began clearing the table. Bernard leaned over and said to the children. 'Now who's my first passenger on the slow train to Dreamland?'

'Me, Daddy, me!' They both yelled together.

Soon Fiona was left alone, dabbing at the stain on the cushion. From somewhere above she could hear the excited calls of the children as Bernard carried them up to bed. 'Choo-choo! Choo-choo!'

Darling, darling, Bernard. How she wished he could be a wonderful father without making her feel like an inadequate mother.

7

Sylvester Bernstein was a fifty-year-old American. Together with his
wife he lived in a Victorian red brick terrace house in Battersea. One
small room on each of three floors with a kitchen and bathroom that had
been added at the back by a previous owner in the early Seventies. Now
that this south side of the river had been invaded by affluent young
couples – who'd discovered how close it was to central London – the
whole street was undergoing a transformation. There were yellow
coloured front doors, and even pink ones with brass knockers, and
nowadays more and more of the cars parked nose to tail along the street
were without rust. The local 'planning department' regulations prohibited the use of these houses as offices but Bernstein was confident
that no one would complain about the way he'd made his garret room
into an office with a typewriter, a couple of desks, two phone lines and a
telex machine. Private investigators didn't spend much time in offices:
at least Sylvester Bernstein didn't.

Bernstein had been a CIA man for twenty-one years. He took
retirement after the wounds in his leg refused to heal. He'd married a
girl he'd met in Saigon, an English nurse working for Christian Aid,
and she suddenly decided that they must live in England. At that time
the dollar was high against sterling, so his retirement pay gave him
enough to live well in London. When the dollar weakened, Bernstein
was forced to go back to work. His contacts in Grosvenor Square helped
him to get that elusive work permit and he set up in business as
Sylvester Bernstein, private investigator. But truth to tell, most of his
clients came to him because of his long career as a CIA man. Some of
those clients were still in the twilight world of 'security'; people who
wanted a job done while they remained at arm's length from it. The job
Bernstein was doing for Bret Rensselaer was typical of the work he did,
and because he'd known Bret a long time, and because Bret was a
demanding client, Bernstein did not have one of his sub-contractors do
the job for him. He did most of it personally.

They were sitting in the downstairs room. On the walls hung cheap
Victorian prints of scenes from Walter Scott novels. The elaborate

532

fireplace was complete with lily-patterned tiles and polished brass fender and all the fire-irons. The iron grate however held not coal but an arrangement of dried flowers. Virtually everything, even the furniture, had come with the house. Only his wife's china collection, the beige wall-to-wall carpet, the American-style bathroom and such things as the large-screen TV on a smart trolley were new. It was a diminutive room, but panelled wooden connecting doors were open to reveal an even smaller dining room, and through its window a view of the tiny back garden. Bret lounged on the sofa, the papers Bernstein had prepared for him fanned out so that he could refer to them.

'Is Martin Euan Pryce-Hughes his real name?' asked Bret, who was unfamiliar with Welsh names. He had to look down at the papers to remember it.

'His old man was Hugh Pryce-Hughes.' Bernstein was a short pot-bellied man wearing a grey three-piece suit that he'd been heard to describe as 'native costume'. It was more or less like the suit that Bret Rensselaer wore – and which gave him the urbanity one expected of a diplomat or surgeon – but the suit looked wrong on Bernstein, for his features, complexion and demeanour suggested a manual labourer, or maybe an infantryman. He was not now, however, in the right physical shape to be either; his face was red, the sort of complexion that comes with high blood-pressure, and he had a wheeze that smoking aggravated. Enough grey hair remained to see that it had once been brown and curly, and his hands were strong with short thick fingers upon one of which he wore a fraternity ring and upon another a flashy diamond. With ramrod spine, he sat splayfooted on a little bentwood chair. One black sock had sagged to reveal a section of bare leg. He was aware of his stiff unnatural pose but it reconciled his legs with the fragments of Vietnamese metal embedded in them. His voice was low and firm; unmistakably American but not stridently so. 'The famous Pryce-Hughes.'

Bret looked down and furrowed his brow.

'The writer,' said Bernstein. 'Internationally famous . . . the one who wrote those books about the Fabian Society. His memoirs created all the fuss about Wells and Shaw. You must have heard of him.' Bernstein was a great reader. The bookcase held Dreiser, Stendhal, Joyce, Conrad and Zola – he was not too fond of the Russian novels – and he'd read them all not once but several times. He was proud to be a graduate of Princeton but he was also aware that Bret, and others like him, regarded Bernstein as reassuring proof that an Ivy League education did not guarantee success in what Bret called 'the real world'.

'No, Sylvy, I've never heard of him,' said Bret. 'For these Brits, internationally famous means known in England, Scotland, Ireland and Wales. How many books?'

Bernstein smiled briefly. 'Maybe half a dozen.'

'You'd better get them for me.'

'His father's books? What for? You're not going to read them?'

'Of course I am.' Bret was thorough, and he wanted Bernstein to be reminded of that.

'As long as you don't ask *me* to read them,' said Bernstein.

'No,' said Bret. 'There is no call for *you* to read them, Sylvy.'

'You haven't suddenly taken against smoking, have you?' When Bret shook his head Bernstein took out a packet of Lucky Strike and shook one loose.

Bret said, 'Could you initiate a file for me?'

Bernstein flicked open a well-worn Zippo lighter with an inscription that read 'Rung Sat Special Zone', a souvenir of an unhealthy trip into a mangrove swamp southeast of Saigon during the Vietnam war. He kept it to remind himself, and anyone else who had to be reminded, that he'd had another sort of life not so long ago. He took his time lighting a cigarette and then said, 'What's on your mind?'

'A secret file, recording meetings, reports and payments and so on. A file of stuff coming in from one of our own people.'

'We don't work like that. No one works like that. No one keeps all the information from one agent in the same file. The Coordination people take it and distribute it. They make damn sure no name, nor any clue to the source, is on it.'

'I didn't ask you how we work,' said Bret.

Bernstein blew smoke while looking at Bret. Bret stared back. 'Oh, I see what you mean. A bogus file.' Bret nodded. 'A file to prove that someone *was* one of our people when actually he *wasn't* one of our people.'

'Don't let's get too deeply into existentialism,' said Bret.

'A file with real names?'

'A few real names.'

'You want to frame Martin Pryce-Hughes? You want to make someone think he's reporting to us?'

'That's what I want.'

Sylvy blew more smoke. 'Sure. It can be done; anything can be done. How far back would you want to go?'

'Ten years?'

'That would take us back to the days of mechanical typewriters.'

'Maybe.'

'You're not thinking of something they could take back to Moscow and put under the microscope?'

'No. Something to show someone briefly.'

''Cause real good forgeries cost. We'd need real letterheads and authentic department names.'

'Not that ambitious.'

'And I get it back?'

'What for?'

'To feed it into the shredder.'

'Oh, sure,' said Bret.

'Why don't I throw something together then? I'll sort out some photocopies and provide a sequence of material the way it would be if we filed it that way. It will give us something to look at and talk about. When we get that the way you want it, I'll find someone good to do the forgeries.'

'Great,' said Bret. He wished Bernstein wouldn't use words such as forgeries, it made him feel uneasy. 'Keep it very circumstantial. We're not trying to produce exhibit A for Perry Mason.'

'A subtle, tasteful kind of frame-up. Sure, why not? But I'd need to know more.'

'You take it and show it to this creep and lean on him.'

'How's that?'

'Lean on him. Say you're from a newspaper. Say you're from the CIA, say anything but scare the shit out of him.'

'Why?'

'I want to see which way he jumps.'

'I don't see your purpose. He'll know it's a fake.'

'Do it.'

Bernstein looked at him. He knew Bret because he knew other men like him. Bret didn't have any operational purpose for frightening the old man: he just felt vindictive. 'It would be cheaper just to beat him up,' said Bernstein.

Bret scowled. He knew exactly what Bernstein was thinking. 'Just do it, Sylvy. Don't second-guess me.'

'Whatever you say, doc.'

Bret smiled politely. 'Anything more on the woman?'

'No. She hasn't seen the boyfriend for a week. Maybe they had a fight.'

'Boyfriend? Is that it?' said Bret as casually as he could.

'Oh, sure. She doesn't go along to his fancy apartment in Maida Vale to play chess.'

'He's a psychiatrist,' said Bret.

'I'll bet he is.'

Bret found that offensive. He didn't want that kind of wisecrack; this was strictly business. 'Just four beats to the bar, Sylvy,' he said. It was the nearest he got to a reprimand.

Bernstein smoked and didn't reply. So this wasn't just a job, there was more to it. Was this guy Kennedy a relative of Bret Rensselaer, or what? 'If she wanted to consult him, why wouldn't she go and consult him at the hospital?'

'She would have to report any kind of medical treatment, especially a visit to a psychiatrist,' said Bret. 'Remember the way it goes?'

'So this might be a way of seeing a shrink in secret? Is that what you mean?'

'She's under a lot of strain.'

Bernstein took a quick drag at his cigarette. 'Yeah, well, I'm not asking you too many questions about this one, Bret, because you told me it's touchy, but . . .'

'But what?'

'Kennedy isn't that kind of shrink. Not any more he's not. At the clinic he's doing work on crowd hysteria and hallucination. He doesn't see patients; he analyses figures, gives lectures and writes dissertations on the herd instinct and that kind of junk. The clinic is paid by some big US foundation and the work they publish is studied by various police departments.'

'So tell me your theory,' said Bret.

'What can I tell you: he's a good-looking guy. An airplane freak. Canadian. Soft-spoken, well-heeled, smartly dressed, very, very bright and muy simpatico. You get the picture? This Samson lady . . . she's a very attractive woman.' He stopped. A conversation with Bret, when he was in a touchy mood like this, was like a stroll through a minefield. He smoked his cigarette as if trying to decide what to say next. 'Maybe that kind of soft shoulder, and the Canadian charm this guy Kennedy peddles, is just what she's short of.'

'A good-looker, is he?'

'You saw the photos, Bret.'

'Looked like he was assembled from a plastic kit.'

'He's a natty dresser, I said that. But even people who don't like him admit he's brilliant. Good flyer, good doctor and good lover too maybe. He's one of those people who always come out on top in exams: fluent, adaptable and sophisticated.'

536

'And on the down side?'

'My guess is: neurotic, restless and unhappy. He can't settle down anywhere. But lots of women go for guys like that, they figure they can help them. And look at her husband. I've met him a few times. He's a really rough diamond, isn't he?'

'You said . . .'

'That I liked him. And I do up to a point. He's dead straight: I wouldn't like to cross him.' It was quite an accolade coming from Bernstein. 'He's a man's man: not the sort you'd expect to find hitched to a twin-set and pearls lady like that.'

Bret bit his lip and was silent for a moment before saying, 'Sometimes things are not . . .'

'Oh, I know what you're going to say. But I've been doing this kind of work for a long time now. Two people like that . . . She goes to his apartment: alone, never with her husband . . . He never goes to her place. And you only have to see them together to know he's crazy about her.' He flicked ash into an ancient ceramic ashtray around the rim of which the words 'Long May They Reign. Coronation 1937' were faintly visible. It was part of his wife's collection of commemorative china-ware. He moved it, so there was no danger of it being knocked and broken, and waited for Rensselaer to react.

'It's improbable,' pronounced Bret.

'You say it's improbable. Okay, you're the boss. But do *my* job for a little while, and maybe you'd start thinking you can't use that word improbable, because when boys and girls get together, *nothing* is improbable.'

Bret smiled but he felt sick at heart. In his own futile way he loved and cherished Fiona Samson, and didn't want to believe she was having a casual affair. 'Okay, Sylvy. You usually get it right.'

'There's always a first time. Maybe they just drink tea, look at pictures of his airplanes and talk about the meaning of life. But really I don't think so, Bret.'

Bret Rensselaer got up, overcome with anger. He looked around angrily, as if an escape from the room would bring with it escape from the facts he didn't want to face. He couldn't get out of his mind the wonderful relationship that he believed had developed between him and Fiona Samson over the weeks and months since he'd started preparing her for what would undoubtedly be the intelligence coup of the century. Fiona was the perfect pupil. 'Pupil' perhaps wasn't the right word and it certainly wasn't a word he would use to her about their relationship. Protégée, perhaps; although that wasn't the right word either. In a grimmer truth the relationship was more like the one a prizefighter has with a trainer, a manager, or a promoter.

She needed his support nowadays. The strain was beginning to tell on her, but that was only to be expected. He liked to help her, and of course Bret would not have denied that there was a certain frisson to the way that they had to meet covertly, in such a way that her husband wouldn't start suspecting. For by now Bret had reluctantly come round to the D-G's idea that advantages could be obtained from Bernard Samson's dismay at his wife's defection.

'How could she?' It was only when he stole a glance at Bernstein that Bret realized that he'd asked the question aloud. He turned away and went across to the dining table to lean upon it with both arms outstretched; he had to think.

Bret and Fiona, they had become so close that lately he'd dared to start believing that she was becoming fond of him. He'd arranged fresh flowers whenever she came, and she'd remarked on it. Her rare but wonderful smiles, the curiously fastidious way she poured drinks for both of them, and sometimes she brought silly little presents for him, like the automatic corkscrew which replaced the one he'd broken. There was the birthday card too: it came in a bright green envelope and said 'With all my love, Fiona'. Bad security, as he told her at their next meeting, but he'd placed it by his bedside clock; it was the first thing he saw when he woke up each morning. Bret closed his eyes.

Bernstein watched him twisting and turning but said nothing. Bernstein waited. He wasn't puzzled; he didn't puzzle about things he wasn't paid to puzzle about. He'd discovered over the years how mysterious could be the ways of men and women, and Bret Rensselaer's wild pacing and unrestrained mutterings didn't alarm him or even surprise him.

Bret hammered a fist into his palm. It was inconceivable that Fiona was having an affair with this man Kennedy. There must be some other explanation. Bret had come to terms with the fact that, when she said goodbye to him, Fiona Samson went home to her husband and children. That was right and proper. Bret liked Bernard. But who the hell was Kennedy? Did Fiona smile and make jokes with Kennedy? Even more awful to think about, did she go to bed with this man?

It was at that point that Bret Rensselaer steadied himself on the mantelpiece, drew back his foot and kicked the brass fender as hard as he could. The matching fire-irons crashed against the fireplace with such force that the grate sang like a tuning fork, and one of the tiles of the hearth was hit hard enough to crack.

'Take it easy, Bret!' said Bernstein in a voice that, for the first time, betrayed his alarm. He found himself standing up, holding, for safety, the two Queen Victoria Diamond Jubilee plates that were his wife's most treasured items.

This displacement activity seemed to release some of Bret's anger, for the desperate nature of his movements subsided, and he stepped more carefully about the room and pretended to look at the books and then out of the window to where his car was parked. It was not often that Bret was lost for words but he simply could not get his thoughts in order. 'Jesus Christ!' he said to himself, and resolved to get Fiona Samson assigned to Berlin right away, perhaps by the weekend.

When Bret sat down again both men remained silent for a while and listened to the dustmen collecting the garbage: they banged the bins and yelled to each other and the truck gave a plaintive little hooting noise whenever it backed up.

'Give me a butt, Sylvy.'

Bernstein let him take one and flicked the Zippo open. He noticed that Bret was trembling but the cigarette seemed to calm him down.

Bret said, 'What would you say to a regular job?'

'With your people?'

'I just might be able to fix it.'

'Are you getting tee'd off with paying me out of your own pocket?'

'Is that what I'm doing?' said Bret calmly.

'You never ask for vouchers.'

'Well, what do you say?'

'I wouldn't fit into a British setup.'

'Sure you would.'

'The truth is, Bret, that I wouldn't trust the British to look after me.'

'Look after you how?'

'If I was in trouble. I'm a Yank. If I was in a jam, they'd feed me to the sharks.' He stubbed out his cigarette very hard.

'Why do you say that?' Bret asked.

'I know I'm stepping out of line, Bret, but I think you're crazy to trust them. If they have to choose between you and one of their own, what do you think they are going to do?'

'Well, let me know if you change your mind, Sylvy.'

'I won't change my mind, Bret.'

'I didn't know you disliked the Brits so much, Sylvy. Why do you live here?'

'I don't dislike them; I said I don't trust them. London is a real nice place to live. But I don't like their self-righteous attitude and their total

539

disregard for other people's feelings and for other people's property. Do you know something Bret, there is not an Englishman living who hasn't at some time or other boasted of stealing something: at school or in the army, at their college or on a drunken spree. All of them, at some time or other, steal things and then tell about it, as if it was the biggest joke you ever heard.'

Bret stood up. Bernstein could be sanctimonious at times, he thought. 'I'll leave all this material. I've read it all through. I don't want it in the office.'

'Anything you say, Bret.'

Bret brought out his wallet and counted out twenty fifty-pound notes. Bernstein wrote 'one thousand pounds sterling' on a slip of paper without adding date or signature or even the word 'received'. It was the way they did business.

Bret noticed the freshly cut leather on the toe of his shoe and touched it as if hoping it would heal of its own accord. He sighed, got up and put on his hat and coat and began thinking of Fiona Samson again. He would have to face her with it, there was no alternative. But he wouldn't do that today, or even tomorrow. Much better to get her off to Berlin.

'This guy Pryce-Hughes,' said Bret very casually as he stood near the door. 'What do you make of him, Sylvy?'

Bernstein was not sure what Bret wanted to hear. 'He's very old,' he said finally.

Bret nodded.

8

The afternoon was yellowing like ancient newspaper, and on the heavy air there came the pervasive smell of the lime trees. Berlin's streets were crowded with visitors, column upon column, equipped with maps, cameras and heavy rucksacks, less hurried now as the long day's parading took its toll. The summer was stretching into autumn, and still there were Westies here, some of them fond parents using their vacations to visit draft-dodging sons.

Her day's work done, Fiona sighed with relief to be back in their new 'home'. There was a bunch of flowers, still wrapped in paper and cellophane, on the hall table. It was typical of Bernard that he'd not bothered to put them into a vase of water, but she didn't touch them. She took off her hat and coat, checked to be sure there was no mail in the cage behind the letter-box nor on the hall table, and then examined herself in the mirror for long enough to decide that her make-up was satisfactory. She had aged, and even the make-up could not completely hide the darkened eyes and lines round her mouth. She flicked her fingers through her hair, which had been crushed under the close-fitting hat, then took a breath and put on a cheerful smile before going into the drawing room of her rented apartment.

Bernard was already home. He'd taken off his jacket and loosened his tie. Shirt wrinkled, red braces visible, he was lolling on the sofa with a big drink in his hand. 'What a mess you look, darling. A bit early for boozing, isn't it?' She said it loudly and cheerfully before seeing that Bernard's father was sitting opposite him, also drinking.

Despite her flippant tone, Mr Brian Samson, still technically her superior in the office, frowned. He came forward and gave her a kiss on the cheek. 'Hello, Fiona,' he said. 'I was just telling Bernard all about it.' If it did anything, the kiss confirmed her father-in-law's feelings about upper-class wives who came home and reprimanded their husbands for making themselves comfortable in their own homes.

'All about it?' she said, going to one of the display shelves above the TV where by common consent the mail was placed until both of them had read it. There was only a bill from the wine shop and an elaborate engraved invitation to her sister's birthday party. She'd seen both pieces of mail but examined them again before turning round and smiling. Since neither man offered to get her a drink she said, 'I think I'll make some tea. Would anyone like tea?' She noticed some spilled drink and took a paper napkin to mop it up and then tidied the drinks tray before she said, 'All about what, Brian?'

It was Bernard who answered: 'The Baader–Meinhof panic, as they are now calling it.'

'Oh, that. How boring. You were lucky to miss it, darling.'

'Boring?' said her father-in-law, his voice rising slightly.

'Much ado about nothing,' said Fiona.

'I don't know,' said her father-in-law. 'If the Baader–Meinhof people had hijacked the airliner and flown it to Prague . . .' Ominously he left the rest unsaid.

'Well that would have been impossible, father-in-law,' she said cheerfully. 'The signal that came back from Bonn said that Andreas Baader committed suicide in Stammheim maximum security prison a year ago and the rest of them are in other prisons in the Bundesrepublik.'

'I know that,' said the elder Samson with exaggerated clarity, 'but terrorists come in many shapes, sizes and colours; and not all of them are behind bars. It was an emergency. My God, Fiona, have you been to Bonn lately? They have barbed wire and armed guards on the government buildings. The streets are patrolled by armoured cars. It's not boring, Fiona, whatever else it may be.'

Fiona made no concession to her father-in-law. 'So you don't want tea?' she said.

'The world is going mad,' said Samson senior. 'One poor devil was murdered when his own godchild led the killers into the house carrying red roses. Every politician and industrialist in the country is guarded night and day.'

'And complaining because they can't visit their mistresses, or so it said on the confidential report,' said Fiona. 'Did you read that?'

'What I can't understand,' said her father-in-law, ignoring her question and holding Fiona personally responsible for any delinquency attributed to the younger generation, 'is the way in which we have people demonstrating in favour of the terrorists! Bombs in German car showrooms in Turin, Leghorn and Bologna. Street demonstrations in London, Vienna and Athens. *In favour of the terrorists*. Are these people mad?'

Fiona shrugged and picked up the tray.

Bernard watched but said nothing. Throughout the world 1977 had seen an upsurge in the terrorist activities of religious fanatics and assorted crooks and maniacs. People everywhere were expressing their bewilderment. The older generation were blaming everything upon their children, while younger people saw the mindless violence as a legacy they had inherited. Bernard's wife and his father provided a typical example of this. Any conversation was likely to degenerate into an exchange in which they both assumed archetypal roles. Bernard's father thought that Fiona had too many airs and graces: too rich, too educated and too damned opinionated, he'd told Bernard once after a difference of opinion with her.

As Fiona went to the kitchen she delivered a Parthian shot: 'In any case, hardly a suitable cue for panic, father-in-law.'

Bernard wished she wouldn't say 'father-in-law' in that tripping way. It irritated his father, but of course Fiona knew that only too well. Bernard tried to intercede. 'Dad says it was the Russian message ordering the Czechs to keep their airfield open all night that did it. We put two and two together and made five.'

Fiona was amused. 'At this time of the year hundreds of East Bloc military airfields are working round the clock. This, darling, is the time of their combined exercises. Or hasn't that military secret filtered back to London Central yet?'

She wasn't in view but they could hear her pouring the hot water into the teapot and putting cups and saucers on a tray. Neither man spoke. The animated discussion they'd been having before Fiona's arrival had been killed stone dead. Brian looked at his son and smiled. Bernard smiled back.

Fiona came in and set the tray down on the table where Bernard had been resting his feet. Then she knelt on the carpet to pour the tea. 'Are you both sure. . . ?' she said. She had arranged cups and saucers for all three of them, and a sugar bowl because her father-in-law took sugar in his tea.

'No thank you, darling,' said Bernard.

She looked at Bernard. She loved him very much. The hurried assignment to Berlin had not been wonderful for either of them but it had given her a chance to break away from the foolish relationship with Kennedy. These brushes with Samson senior were upsetting, but he was old, and in fact she'd found that the more she disliked the old man, the more she came to appreciate Bernard. He was always the peacemaker but never showed weakness either to her or to his father. Bernard, what a wonderful man she'd found. Now she'd had a chance to see things in perspective, she knew that he was the only man for her. The perilous relationship with Harry Kennedy was behind her. She still didn't comprehend how that frenzied affair could have happened except that it disclosed some alarming sexual vulnerability of which she'd never been aware.

Even so, she couldn't help but wonder why he hadn't sent the postcard. One was forwarded here every week: a coloured advertising card from a 'hair and beauty salon' off Sloane Street. Some friend of his owned it: a woman friend no doubt.

'No mail?' she asked as she measured milk into her tea and stirred it to see the colour of it.

'Only that same crimpers,' said Bernard.

'Where did you put it?'

'You didn't want it, did you?'

'If I take the card they said I could get a price reduction,' said Fiona.

'It's in the waste bin. Sorry.'

She could see it now. From where she knelt on the floor she could almost have reached it. It was in the basket together with an empty Schweppes tonic bottle and a crumpled Players cigarette packet that must have been Brian's. The postcard was torn into small pieces, almost as if Bernard had sensed the danger it held. Fiona resolved not to touch it, although her first impulse was to go and get it and piece it together.

'Anyway,' added Bernard, 'you won't be in London for a bit, will you?'

'No, that's right.' She sat back on her heels and sipped her tea as if unconcerned. 'I was forgetting that.'

'I told Dad that you are going out tonight. He wants me to go to some little farewell party at the Club and have dinner with him afterwards. Is that okay?'

She could have laughed. After all the trouble she'd gone to to arrange the secret meeting with Bret Rensselaer this evening, she now found that her husband was completely uninterested in her movements. She told him anyway. 'I'm at a familiarization briefing. Someone is coming from London.'

Bernard was hardly listening to her. To his father he said, 'If Frank will be there, I'll return some books I borrowed from him.'

'Frank will be there,' said his father. 'Frank loves parties.'

'Too bad you're not free, darling,' Bernard told his wife.

'Farewell parties are usually more fun without wives,' said Fiona knowingly.

'Another drink, Dad?' said Bernard and got to his feet.

His father shook his head.

'Where will you have dinner?' she asked.

'Tante Lisl's,' announced Bernard with great pleasure. 'She is cooking venison specially for us.' Tante Lisl owned a hotel that had once been her home. Brian Samson, and his family, had been billeted upon her when the war ended. It had become a sort of second home for Bernard, and old Tante Lisl a surrogate mother. Bernard's undisguised delight in the old house sometimes gave Fiona a feeling of insecurity. She felt that now.

Bernard came over and gave her a kiss on the top of her head. 'Goodbye, love. I might be late.' As he went out with his father he said, as if to himself. 'I mustn't forget to take those flowers for Lisl. She loves flowers.'

As she heard the front door close behind the two men Fiona closed her eyes and rested her head back in the armchair. Of course the flowers were not for her: how could she have imagined they were? The flowers were for that dreadful old woman against whom Bernard would hear no word said.

Bernard could sometimes be the archetypal selfish male. He took her for granted. He was delighted at the prospect of spending an evening with his father and his cronies, drinking and telling their stories. Stories of secret agents and daring deeds, exaggerated in the course of time and in the course of the evening's drinking.

It said a great deal about their relationship that Bernard would have been uncomfortable with her at such a gathering. Bernard respected her, but if he really loved her he would have wanted her with him whatever the company he was in. Secretly she lived for the day when he would be forced to see her for what she was: someone who could play the agent game as well as he could play it. Perhaps then he would treat her as she wanted to be treated: as an equal. And if meantime she'd used the same sort of secrecy to steal a little happiness for herself, could she be blamed? No one had been hurt.

She looked round the room at the mess that Bernard had left for her to tidy up. Was it any wonder that she had found such happiness in the short and foolish love affair with Harry Kennedy? He had given her a new lease of life at a time when she was almost in despair. During the time she'd had with Harry she had stopped the tablets and felt like a different person. Harry treated her with care and consideration and yet he was so wonderfully outgoing. He wasn't frightened to tell her how much he adored her. For him she was a complex and interesting human being whose opinions counted, and with him she found herself exchanging personal feelings that she had never shared with Bernard. When it came down to hard facts: she loved Bernard and put up with him, but Harry loved her desperately and he made her feel deeply feminine in a way she'd never experienced before.

Now that was all over and finished with, she told herself. She could look back soberly and see the affair with Harry for what it was: the most glorious luxury; a release in time of stress, a course of treatment.

She looked at the time. She must have a bath and change her clothes. Thank heavens she'd brought with her some really good clothes. For this evening's meeting she would need to look her best as well as have her wits about her.

Fiona Samson's appointment was in Kessler's, a family restaurant in Gatower Strasse, Berlin-Spandau. Its premises occupied the whole house, so that there were dining rooms on every floor. Downstairs old Klaus Kessler liked to supervise his dining room waiters in person. He stood there in his long apron amid dark green paintwork, red checked gingham table-cloths and the menu written on small slates. Kessler described it as a 'typical French bistro', but in fact its décor, and the menu too, showed little change from the Berlin Weinstube where the family had been serving good simple food since his grandfather's time.

Up the narrow creaking stairs there was a second dining room, and above that three upper rooms were more elaborately furnished, and with better cutlery and glass, linen cloths and handwritten menus without prices. These were booked for small and very discreet dinners. It was in one of them that Fiona had dinner with Bret Rensselaer that evening.

'You got away all right?' Bret said politely. She offered her cheek and he gave her a perfunctory kiss. There was champagne in an ice bucket: Bret was already drinking some.

The waiter took her coat, poured her a glass of champagne and put a menu into her hands.

'There was no problem,' said Fiona. 'Bernard is at a party with his father.'

'I hear the venison is good,' said Bret, looking at the menu.

'I don't like venison,' said Fiona more forcefully than she intended. She sipped her champagne. 'In fact I'm not very hungry.'

'Kessler says he'll do a cheese soufflé for us.'

'That sounds delicious.'

'And a little Westphalian ham to start?' Anticipating her approval he put down the menu and whipped off the stylish glasses that he wore when reading. He was vain enough to hate wearing them but his attempts to wear contact lenses had not worked out well.

'Perfect.' Neither of them were interested enough in the food to read the menu all through. It was a relief, thought Fiona. Bernard could never sit down in a restaurant without cross-examining the waiter about the cooking in its most minute details. What was worse, he was always trying to persuade Fiona to try such things as smoked eel, tongue or – what was that other dish he liked so much? – *Marinierter Hering*.

'How are you enjoying Berlin?' Bret asked.

'Having Bernard with me makes a difference.'

'Of course. His mother went to England to look after the children?'

'It was sweet of her but I miss them awfully,' she said. A platter of ham arrived garnished with tomatoes and pickles, and there was a lot of fussing about as the waiter offered them a selection of bread rolls and three different types of mustard. When the waiter had departed she said, 'I suppose at heart I'm a housewife.' She spread butter on her black bread but she watched Bret's reaction. Exactly a week ago she'd decided that she would not be able to go through with this mad project of defecting to the KGB as some sort of superspy.

Fiona's life had become too complex for her. The clandestine meetings with Martin Euan Pryce-Hughes had not been too stressful. She was a sleeper: they met rarely. Her assignment had provided her with a smug feeling of serving her country, and the Department, while demanding little or nothing from her. Then had come the bombshell from Bret Rensselaer that the Prime Minister had asked the D-G for a long-term commitment to getting someone into the top echelons of the enemy intelligence service. Of course she hadn't entirely dismissed the thought that Bret had exaggerated the way it had happened, especially now that she saw the gain in prestige – and self-esteem too – that her planned mission brought to Bret.

Perhaps she could have handled the secret meetings with Martin and Bret, especially since at first Bret had been so understanding and sensitive about the strain on her. But that totally unexpected coup de foudre that had smitten her after the chance meeting with Harry Kennedy was the last straw. And while the meetings with Martin and with Bret could be kept to a minimum, cancelled at short notice with no questions asked, and no recriminations, the meetings with Harry were something quite different. She sometimes ached to see him. On the days when they were to meet, she became so consumed by the prospect that she could think of nothing else. It was amazing that no one – not Bernard, not Bret nor her sister Tessa – had seen the turbulence within her. Well, it all had to stop. No more Martin, no more Bret and no more Harry. She was even considering resigning from the Department. If Bret put up any sort of resistance to letting her go free she would do exactly that. She had enough money from her father to tell them all to go to hell. Bret would argue, whine and maybe yell, but she only had one life and what she did with it was going to be her decision.

When a woman reaches her thirties, she starts to ask herself some demanding questions. What was she doing with her life that was more important than having a real home and looking after her husband and her children? How could she contemplate prolonged separation from them? Let them send some other agent to the East. There must be dozens who wanted to make their name by such an operation. But not she.

She ate some ham and a piece of the warm bread roll. Since Bret had not spoken, she said it again. 'I suppose at heart I'm a housewife.'

If Bret guessed what was in store he gave no immediate sign of it. 'We're changing the name of my department. Instead of the European Economics Desk it's officially to be the Economics Intelligence Section and I am named "Department Head". Rather grand, isn't it?' It came as no surprise to either of them. When Bret had told her about his master plan – Sinker – for bringing down the German Democratic Republic by targeting the respectable middle class, she knew it was right. Anyone who'd read a history book could see that Hitler gained power by wooing the German middle classes while the communists disdained them.

'So congratulations are in order?' she asked.

'They surely are,' he said and they raised their glasses and drank. She smiled; how proud Bret was of his new appointment. She would never really understand him; she wondered if anyone did. He was so perfect and yet so contrived, right down to that perfect suntan. His navy blue cashmere jacket and grey slacks were probably chosen to show her how informal he could be but, together with the silk bow tie and starched shirt complete with cuffs long enough to reveal onyx links, he looked like a fashion plate. He was highly intelligent, charming, and, although no longer young, handsome; and yet he remained completely devoid of any sort of sexual attraction.

'Have you seen Frank?' she asked.

'About the big panic? Yes, I spent this afternoon with him.'

'Is there going to be a row?'

'Maybe but I don't think so. For us, in fact, it provides a perfect opportunity.'

'To fire Frank?' It was a mischievous and provocative question that she knew Bret would let pass.

Impassively Bret asked, 'Were you there when the intercept came in?' She nodded. 'Tell me about it.'

'It was in the small hours of the morning – I can look it up in the log if you want it timed exactly. The duty cipher clerk brought it, they'd deciphered it very quickly. It came through the Russian Army transmitter at Karlshorst with the authorization of the commanding general's office. It was an order that some military airfield in southwest Czecho be kept on a twenty-four-hour operational status.'

'Did Frank see it?'

'It was handed to him. Frank pooh-poohed it at first and then did his usual sitting on the fence routine.'

'Who was in charge of communications room security?'

'You must have got all this from Frank.'

'Who was in charge?'

'Werner Volkmann.'

'Bernard's German buddy?'

'Yes, that's him.'

'Good. It will all work nicely.'

'What will?'

'You're going to take a copy of that intercept and give it to Pryce-Hughes.'

'Give it to Martin?'

'That's what I said. Be precise. I've written down exactly what I want you to say.'

She drank some champagne. 'You know what will happen?'

'Tell me what will happen, Fiona.'

'Moscow will tell Karlshorst immediately, they're very touchy about military signals. No matter what I stipulate about secrecy, they'll send an intercepted traffic warning to the commanding general's office and change everything.'

'Yes, they'll change the codes and ciphers. We could live with that,' said Bret.

'I'm not an expert on signals,' said Fiona. 'But surely they change the codes and ciphers three or four times a week anyway? For a penetration like this they will change the system.'

'Whoever gave approval must know what they'll do,' said Bret, without concern for anything but his own plans.

'What is this all about?'

'I'm going to make you a star,' said Bret. 'I'm going to get the Soviets to sprinkle you with stardust and start thinking of you as a potential big-shot.'

'I don't like it, Bret.'

She was expecting him to ask why but he dismissed her reservations with a wave of his hand. 'I had to get the D-G's authority for this one, Fiona. It's a big concession and it shows that the old man is really convinced.'

'Won't NATO make a fuss? Moscow will change everything. Everything.'

'There is no question of confiding our secrets to NATO,' said Bret. 'You know what we decided.'

'Yes, I know.' She was about to tell him of her decision to pull out when there was the sound of heavy footsteps on the stairs and Kessler himself came with the soufflé. It was magnificent, a great yellow dome of beaten egg, with flecks of browned cheese making a pattern all over it.

Fiona made the appreciative ohhs and ahhs that old Kessler expected and Bret added his compliments in hesitant German. Kessler served the soufflé and the side salad and offered bread rolls and butter and topped up their glasses until Fiona wanted to scream.

Once the old man had gone she tried again. 'I've been thinking of the whole operation: thinking hard and very carefully.'

'And now you want out?' He looked at her and nodded before probing into the soufflé on his plate. 'It's exactly right. Look at that, soft in the middle but not raw.'

She didn't know how to react. 'Yes, I do, Bret. How did you guess?'

'I know you well, Fiona. Sometimes I think I understand you even better than your husband does.'

She drank, nodded nervously but didn't answer. That had always been Bret's angle. He understood her: it was the style that any sensible case officer adopted to the agent he ran. She'd seen it all from the other side so she knew the way it was done. She needed a drink and emptied her glass of champagne greedily.

Bret took her glass to refill it. He brought the bottle from its ice bucket, holding it fastidiously as the water dripped from it. Then he poured carefully so that it didn't foam too much. 'Yes, I understand,' he said without looking up from the glass.

'I'm serious, Bret.'

'Of course you are. It's a strain, I know that. I worry about you. You surely must know I worry.'

'I can't do it, Bret. For all sorts of reasons . . . if you want me to

550

explain . . .' She was angry at herself. She had decided before coming here that she wouldn't put herself in the position of a supplicant. She had nothing to apologize for. Circumstances had changed. She simply couldn't continue with it.

'There is nothing to explain, Fiona. I know what you're going through.'

'I won't change my mind, Bret.'

He looked up at her and nodded with an affectionate, paternal indifference.

'Bret! I won't change my mind. I can't go.'

'It's the build-up,' he said. 'That's what makes it so stressful, this long time of preparation.'

'Bret. Don't think you can just let it go and that I'll reconsider it and eventually it will all be on again.'

'Ummm.' He looked at her and nodded. 'Maybe a big glass of champagne is what I need too.' He poured more for himself. It gave him something to do while she fretted. 'Every agent goes through this crisis, Fiona. It's not any failure of nerve, everyone gets the jitters sometime or other.' He reached across and touched the back of her hand. His fingers were icy cold from holding the champagne bottle and she shivered as he touched her. 'Just hang on: it will be all right. I promise you: it will be all right.'

It was anger that restored to her the calm she required to answer him. 'Don't patronize me, Bret. I'm not frightened. I am not on the verge of a nervous break-down, neither am I suffering from premenstrual tension or any other weakness you may believe that women are prey to.' She stopped.

'Get mad! Better you blow a valve than a gasket,' said Bret, smiling in that condescending way he had. 'Let me have it. Say what you have to say.'

'I've worked in the Department a long time, Bret. I know the score. The reason that I'm not going ahead with the plan – your plan I suppose I should say – is that I no longer feel ready to sacrifice my husband and my children in order to make a name for myself.'

'I never, for one moment, thought you might be motivated by the prospect of making a name for yourself, Fiona.'

The way he maintained his gentle and conciliatory tone moderated her anger. 'I suppose not,' she said.

'I knew it to be a matter of patriotism.'

'No,' she said.

'No? Is this the same woman who told me,

"There is but one task for all –
One life for each to give.
Who stands if Freedom fall?
Who dies if England live?"'

She wet her lips. A favourite quote from Kipling was not going to divert her from what she had to say. 'You talk of a year or two. My children are very young. I love them: I need them and they need me. You are asking too much. How long will I be away? What will happen to the children? What will happen to Bernard? And my marriage? Use someone without a family. It's madness for me to go.'

She had kept her voice low but the expression on his face, as he feigned interest and sympathy, made her want to scream at him. Who stands if Freedom fall? Yes, Bret's words had scored a point with her and she was shaken by being suddenly brought face to face with the resolute young woman she'd been not so long ago. Was it marriage and motherhood that had made her so damnably bovine?

'It is madness. And that is exactly what will make you so secure. Bernard will be distraught and the Soviets will give you their trust.'

'I simply can't cope, Bret. I need a rest.'

'Or you could look at it another way,' said Bret amiably. 'A couple of years over there might be just the sort of challenge you need.'

'The last thing I need right now is another challenge,' she said feelingly.

'Sometimes relationships come to an end and there is nothing to be done but formally recognize what has happened.'

'What do you mean?'

'That's the way it was with me and Nikki,' he said, his voice low and sincere. 'She said she needed to find herself again. Looking back on it, our marriage had diminished to a point where it was nothing but a sham.'

'My marriage isn't a sham.'

'Maybe not; but sometimes you have to look closely in order to see. That's the way it was for me.'

'I love Bernard and he loves me. And we have two adorable children. We are a happy family.'

'Maybe you think it's none of my business,' said Bret, 'but this sudden instability – this ring down the curtain and send the orchestra home, I can't go on, nonsense – hasn't resulted from your work but from your personal life. So you need to take a look at your personal affairs to find the answer.'

Bret's words acted upon her like an emetic. She closed her eyes in

552

case the sight of the plate of food caused her to vomit. When finally she opened her eyes she looked at Bret, seeking in his face an indication of what he was thinking. Failing to find anything there but his contrived warmth, she said, 'My personal affairs are personal, Bret.'

'Not when I find you in an emotional state and you tell me to abandon the most important operation the Department has ever contemplated.'

'Can you never see anything except from your own viewpoint?'

Bret touched his shirt cuff, fingering the cuff-link as if to be sure it was still there. But Fiona recognized in the gesture, and in the set of his shoulders and the tilt of his head, something more. It was that preparation for something special seen in the nervous circular movement of the pen before a vital document is signed, or the quick limbering up movements of an athlete before the start of a record-breaking contest. 'You are not in a position to accuse anyone of selfishness, Fiona.'

She bit her lip. It was a direct challenge: to let it go without responding would be to admit guilt. And yet to react might bring down upon her the grim avalanche that loomed over her in nightmares. 'Am I selfish?' she asked as timorously as possible, and hoped he'd laugh it off.

'Fiona, you've got to keep to the arrangements. There's a hell of a lot riding on this operation. You'll do something for your country the equal of which few men or women ever get a chance at. In just a year or two over there, you could provide London Central with something that in historical terms might be compared with a military victory, a mighty victory.'

'A mighty victory?' she said mechanically.

'I told you before; the economic projections suggest that we could make them knock the Wall down, Fiona. A revolution without bloodshed. That would go into the history books. Literally, into the history books. Our personal affairs count for nothing against that.'

He knew everything she wanted to hide; she could see it in his eyes. 'Are you blackmailing me, Bret?'

'You are not yourself tonight, Fiona.' He feigned concern but without putting his heart into it.

'Are you?'

'I can't think what you mean. What is there to blackmail you about?'

'I don't respond to threats; I never have.'

'Are you going to tell me what I'm supposed to be threatening you about? Or do I have to start guessing?' Fiona could see he was loving it; what a sadist he was. She hated him and yet for the first time ever she saw within him some resolute determination that in other circumstances might make a woman love him. He would fight like this on her behalf too; there was no doubt about that. It was his nature.

'Answer one question, Bret: are you having me followed?'

He put down his fork, leaned back in his chair, clasped his hands with interlocked fingers, and stared at her. 'We are all subject to surveillance, Fiona. It's a part of the job.'

He smiled. She took her glass of champagne and tossed it full into his face.

'Jesus Christ!' He leapt to his feet spluttering and fluttering and dancing about to dab his face and shirt-front with the napkin. 'Have you gone ape?'

She looked at him with horror. He went across the room to get more napkins from a side table. He dabbed his suit and the chair and as his anger subsided he sat down again.

She hadn't moved. She hated to lose control of herself, and rather than look at him she picked up her fork and used it to follow a blob of soufflé across her plate. 'But Bernard doesn't know?' she said without looking up. She didn't eat the piece of soufflé: the idea of eating was repugnant now.

He ran a finger round inside his collar. The champagne had made it stick to the skin. 'Such housekeeping is done outside the Department. It would be bad security to use our own people.'

'Promise me that Bernard won't know.'

'I could promise that he won't be told by me. But Bernard is a shrewd and resourceful man . . . I don't have to tell you that.' He looked at his watch. He wanted to go and change.

'It's all finished anyway.'

'I'm glad.' He looked at her and – despite the wet stains on his shirt and his disarranged hair – he gave her his most charming smile.

'You know what I'm talking about?' she asked.

'Of course not,' he said, and kept smiling.

'It's clearly understood that I'm over there for only a year and then I must be pulled out?'

'A year. Yes, that was always the plan,' said Bret. 'Have you got a purse? I'll give you the details of the intercept. Phone the contact number for Pryce-Hughes first thing tomorrow. It's his morning for being at the office number he gave you.' Even being doused with champagne had not unnerved him.

'You're a cold-blooded bastard,' she told him.

'It never was a job suited to hot-blooded people,' said Bret.

9

London. April 1983.

For Bret Rensselaer that long long ago dinner in Berlin was a hiccup in the lengthy preparation that Fiona Samson had undergone for her task. Looking back, it was just a chance for him to provide some of the comfort and reassurance that become necessary to agents when traumatic indecision attacks them. It had been, he told the D-G, in one of the reviews Bret liked to provide, an inevitable stage in the briefing and preparation period of any long-term agent placement. 'It was a role change for her. Some would call it the "schizothymic period", for we had to inflict upon a normal personality the task of becoming two separate ones.'

The D-G was about to challenge both the terminology and the scientific basis of what sounded like a distorted over-simplification, but just in time he remembered a previous discussion in which Bret – who had been psychoanalysed – buried him under a barrage of psychological doctrine which had included extensive notes, statistics and references to 'the fundamentally important work of James and Lange'. So the D-G nodded.

Bret reminded him that in this case the agent was a woman, a highly intelligent woman with young children. Thus the attack had been more acute than usual. On the other hand, these factors which made her vulnerable to doubts and worries were the same elements which would make her less suspect when she went to bat for them. Fiona Samson was a stable personality, and Bret's subtle conditioning had reinforced her behaviour, so that by the time she was 'put into play' Bret was confident that the 'transference' would be complete. Since that awful champagne throwing scene an emotional dependence upon Bret, and thus upon the decisions made in London Central, had provided her with the necessary motivation and internal strength of mind.

'You know far more about these things than I do,' declared the D-G with a genial conviction that did not reflect his true feeling. 'But my understanding was that in a scientific context "transference" sometimes means the unconscious shifting of hatred, rather than love and respect.'

'Entirely true!' said Bret. Jolted, not for the first time, by the old man's sharpness, he recovered quickly enough to add, 'And that's an aspect of the work that I have already taken into account.'

'Well, I'm sure you have everything under control,' said the D-G, looking at his watch.

'I do, Director. Depend upon it.'

Bret Rensselaer was not basing these conclusions upon his personal experiences with field agents; he'd had little personal contact with those strange animals in the course of his career (although of course the day-to-day decisions he'd made had had an effect upon the whole service). The Director-General was well aware of Bret's purely administrative background. He'd chosen him largely because he had no taint of Operations on him – and no one had guessed that a dedicated desk man like Bret could function as a case officer – and thus Fiona's role of double agent would be more secure.

But Bret Rensselaer, and Fiona Samson, were not the only ones coping with the problems of the role change. For if Fiona had never been an agent before, and Bret had never been a case officer, it was also true that the D-G had never before faced the harrowing experience of sending into enemy territory someone he knew as well as he knew Fiona Samson. However it was too late now to change his mind. The D-G allowed himself to be comforted by Bret's optimistic reassurances because he could think of no possible course of action if he became anxious.

If that long ago dinner at Kessler's was remembered by Bret as no more than a temporary failure of Fiona's resolution, it was burned into her memory as a program is burned into a micro-chip. She remembered that horrifying evening in every last humiliating detail. The condescension with which Bret Rensselaer had treated her desire to pull out of the operation, the insolent way he had so smoothly blackmailed her into continuing. The contempt he'd shown for her when she'd thrown the champagne: humouring her as one might the infant daughter of a respected friend. And, most shaming of all, the way in which she had done exactly what he told her to do. For, like so many humiliations, hers was measured by the success of the opposing party: and Bret's dominance by the end of that dinner had been absolute.

From that dire confrontation onwards, she had never again expressed any desire to withdraw from the task ahead. After those first few agonizing weeks during which she desperately hoped that Bret Rensselaer would leave the Department, be transferred or suffer a fatal accident, no idea of being released from her contract entered her head. It was inevitable.

Like most women – and here Fiona evidenced women customs and immigration officers, women police officers and secretaries in her own office – she was more conscientious and painstaking than her male peers. Her detached contempt for Bret, and other men like him, was best demonstrated by doing her job with more care and skill than he did his. She would become this damned 'superspy' they wanted her to be. She would show them how well it could be done.

Fiona's meetings with Martin Euan Pryce-Hughes continued as before, except that Bret made sure that the little titbits she was able to throw to him, and the responses to his requests for specific information, were better than the *Spielmaterial* he'd been given before. Pryce-Hughes was pleased. Reacting to a broad hint from him Fiona asked for more money: not much more but enough to assert her worth. Moscow responded promptly and generously and this pleased Bret, and pleased Pryce-Hughes too. And yet, as month after month became a year, and time went on and on, she began to hope that the Department's long-term plan to place her in the enemy camp would be abandoned. Bret continued with their regular briefing sessions, and her duties were arranged to that purpose. Her use of the computers was strictly defined and she never handled very sensitive papers. But the D-G appeared to have forgotten about her, and forgotten about Bret Rensselaer too. Once or twice she came near to asking the D-G outright, but decided to let things continue. Bernard said the D-G was becoming eccentric to the point of disability but Bernard always inclined to overstatement.

Typically it was her younger sister, Tessa, who made the whole thing erupt again. 'Darling, Fi! You are always there when I need you.'

'You have such good champagne,' said Fiona, in an effort to reduce the tension that was evident in her sister's face, and in the way she constantly twisted the rings on her fingers.

'It's my diet: caviar, champagne and oysters. You can't get fat on it.'

'No. Only poor,' said Fiona.

'That's more or less what Daddy said. He disapproves.' As if in contravention Tessa picked up her glass, looked at the bubbles and then drank some champagne.

Tessa had always shown a constitutional spirit that bent towards trouble. The relationship between Fiona and her younger sister provided a typical example of sibling rivalry – it was a psychological phenomenon to which Bret referred many times during their sessions together. Their father, a single-minded man, had his favourite motto ('What I want are results not excuses') embroidered on a cushion displayed on the visitor's chair in his office. He believed that any form of forgiveness was likely to undermine his daughters' strength and his own.

Tessa had discovered how undemanding and convenient it was to play the established role of younger child, and let Fiona fulfil, or sometimes fail to fulfil, her father's expectations. Tessa was always the one of whom little was expected. Fiona went to Oxford and read Modern Greats; Tessa stayed at home and read Harold Robbins. Temperamental, imaginative and affectionate, Tessa could turn anything into a joke: it was her way of avoiding matters that were demanding. Her own boundless generosity made her vulnerable to a world in which people were so cold, loveless and judgemental. In such a world did it matter too much if she indulged in so many frivolous little love affairs? She always went back to her husband and gave him her prodigious love. And what if, one casual night in bed with this silly drunken lover, he should confide to her that he was spying for the Russians? It was probably only a joke.

'Describe him again,' said Fiona.

'You know him,' said Tessa. 'At least he knows all about you.'

'Miles Brent?'

'Giles Trent, darling. Giles Trent.'

'If you'd stop eating those damned nuts I might be able to understand what you are saying,' she said irritably. 'Yes, Giles Trent. Of course I remember him.'

'Handsome brute: tall, handsome, grey wavy hair.'

'But he's as old as Methuselah, Tessa. I always thought he was queer.'

'Oh, no. Not queer,' said Tessa and giggled. She'd had a lot of champagne.

Fiona sighed. She was sitting in Tessa Kosinski's elaborately furnished apartment in Hampstead, London's leafy northwestern suburb, watching the blood-red sun drip gore into the ruddy clouds. When, long ago, London's wealthy merchants and minor aristocracy went to take the waters at regal and fashionable Bath, the less wealthy sipped their spa water in this hilly region that was now the habitat of successful advertising men and rich publishers.

Tessa's husband was in property and motor cars and a diversity of other precarious enterprises. But George Kosinski had an unfailing talent for commercial success. When George bought an ailing company it immediately recovered its strength. Should he wager a little money on unwanted stock his investment flourished. Even when he obliged a local antique dealer by taking off his hands a painting that no one else wanted, the picture – dull, dark and allegorical – was spotted by one of George's guests as the work of a pupil of Ingres. Although many nonentities can be so described, Ingres' pupils included the men who taught Seurat and Degas. This, the coarse canvas and the use of white paint so typical of the Ingres technique, was what persuaded the trustees of an American museum to offer George a remarkable price for it. He shipped it the next day. George loved to do business.

'And you told Daddy all this: Trent saying he was a Russian spy and so on?'

'Daddy said I was just to forget it.' Idly Tessa picked up a glossy magazine from the table in front of her. It fell open at a pageful of wide-eyed people cavorting at some social function of the sort that the Kosinskis frequently attended.

'Daddy can be very stupid at times,' said Fiona with unmistakable contempt. Tessa looked at her with great respect. Fiona really meant it: while Tessa – who also called her father stupid, and worse, from time to time – had never completely shed the bonds of childhood.

'Perhaps Giles was just making a joke,' said Tessa, who now felt guilty at the concern her elder sister was showing.

'You said it *wasn't* a joke,' snapped Fiona.

'Yes,' said Tessa.

'Yes or no?'

Tessa looked at her, surprised by the emotions she had stirred up. 'It wasn't a joke. I told you: I went all through it with him . . . about the Russian and so on.'

'Exactly,' said Fiona. 'How could it have been a joke?'

'What will happen to him?' Tessa tossed the magazine on to a pile of other such periodicals.

'I can't say.' Fiona's mind processed and reprocessed the complications this would bring into her life. She looked at her younger sister, sitting there on the yellow silk sofa, in an emerald-green Givenchy sheath dress that Fiona – although the same size – could never have got away with, and wondered whether to tell her that she might be in physical danger. If Trent told his Soviet contact about this perilous indiscretion it was possible that Moscow would have her killed. She opened her mouth as she tried to think of some way to put it but, when Tessa looked at her expectantly, only said, 'It's a gorgeous dress.'

Tessa smiled. 'You were always so different to me, Fi.'

'Not very different.'

'The Chanel type.'

'Whatever does that mean?'

Teasingly Tessa said, '*Tailleur*, with a jacket lined to match the blouse, chain belt and gardenia; everyone knows what a Chanel type looks like.'

'What else?' Sometimes Tessa's manner could be trying.

'I knew you would end up doing something important . . . something in a man's world,' said Tessa very quietly as she waited for her sister to pronounce on what might happen next. When Fiona made no reply, Tessa added, 'I didn't ask Giles what he did: he just came out with it.'

'Yes. He works in the Department,' said Fiona.

'I'm sorry about all this, Fi, darling. Perhaps I shouldn't have troubled you with it.'

'You did right to tell me.'

'Sometimes he can be so adorable,' said Tessa.

'Why did you ever get married?' said Fiona.

'For the same reason as you, I suppose. It was a way of making Daddy angry.'

'Making Daddy what?' said Fiona.

'Don't pretend you didn't know that marrying your pigheaded tough-guy would make Daddy throw a fit.'

'I thought you liked Bernard,' said Fiona amiably. 'You kept telling me to marry him.'

'I adore him, you know I do. One day I'll run off with him.'

'And was marrying George *your* way of persecuting Daddy?'

She didn't answer for a moment. 'George is such a lovely man . . . a saint.' And then, realizing that it wasn't the accolade a husband would most wish for, added, 'Only a saint would put up with me.'

'Perhaps George needs the opportunity to forgive.'

Tessa gave no heed to that idea. 'I thought a second-hand car dealer would lead an exciting life. It's silly I know, but in the films they are always in the underworld with gangsters and their molls,' she grinned.

'Really, Tess!' Delivered wearily it was an admonition.

'It's rather gruelling, darling, living with a man who gets upset when ladies use naughty words, and who gets up at six o'clock to make sure he doesn't miss Mass. Sometimes I think he would like to see me slaving in the kitchen all day, the way his mother did.'

'You're a complete fool, Tessa.'

'I know. It's all my fault.' She got to her feet suddenly and excitedly said, 'I know! Why don't we go and have dinner at Annabel's?' She stroked her beautiful dress. 'Just the two of us.'

'Sit down, Tessa. Sit down and calm down. I don't want to go to Annabel's. I want to think.'

'Or I've got a home-made chicken stew in the freezer; I'll put it in the oven while we go on talking.'

'No, no. I'll have to eat something with Bernard.'

Tessa dropped back into the sofa, grabbed her glass and drank some champagne. 'You're lucky not to live in Hampstead: it's full of eggheads. My bloody cleaning woman phoned up and said she couldn't come today: she has a conference with her script editor! Script editor; Jesus Christ! Do have some more booze, Fi. I hate drinking alone.'

'No thanks, Tess. And I think you've had enough for one night.'

Tessa put the glass down and didn't refill it. Being in her sister's bad books made her feel wretched. Fiona was the only one she had, after George her husband, and she couldn't go to George with all her troubles. Most of her troubles came from these silly little love affairs she was always becoming caught up in: she couldn't expect George to help her with those.

'Can I use your phone?' said Fiona.

Tessa made an extravagant gesture with both hands. 'Use the one in the bedroom if you want privacy.'

Fiona went into the bedroom. Upon the big four-poster bed, an antique lace bedspread was spread over a dark red cover to show it off. The bedside table held a smart new phone and an assortment of expensive perfumes, pill bottles and paperback books. An aspirin bottle had been left open and tablets were scattered about. Fiona picked up the phone but hesitated before dialling.

Despite Bret Rensselaer's sanguine theories, Fiona Samson was not a person who readily turned to other people – male or female – for advice or instruction. She was self-sufficient, and self-critical too, in a way that an eldest child so often can be. But now she felt the need of a second opinion. She looked at her watch. Having carefully rehearsed the story in her mind, she dialled Bret's number. His phone rang for a long time but there was no reply. She tried again: it was always possible that she had misdialled, but again the ringing was unanswered. This frustration put her off balance, and it was then that she was suddenly struck with the idea of phoning Uncle Silas.

Silas Gaunt's career was little short of a legend in the unwritten story of the Department. Uncle Silas could not be compared to other men: he was virtually unique. Every now and again, the British establishment decorously embraces a rogue, if not to say a rogue elephant, a man who breaks every rule and delights in doing so. One who recognizes no master and few equals. Gaunt's career was marked by controversy, and he began his time as Berlin Resident by having a vociferous argument with the Director-General. It was an indication of both his diplomacy and his ruthlessness when he emerged with no enemies in high places.

Gaunt, a distant relative of Fiona's mother, was the man who had so energetically protected Brian Samson, and then his son Bernard, against well-placed people who believed that the senior ranks of the Secret Intelligence Service were the exclusive province of a certain sort of upper-class Englishman quite unlike Samson and his son. The Samsons survived: the opposition didn't reckon on Gaunt's ingenuity, devious games, or rage. But when Gaunt finally retired, the collective sighs of relief were heard throughout the service. Gaunt, however, was not out of the game. The Director-General knew and respected him, and his regard could be measured by the way that Sir Henry handled the Fiona Samson operation. Only Bret Rensselaer, who'd come to him with the idea, Silas Gaunt and himself were party to the secret.

Now, on impulse, Fiona dialled the number of the Whitelands farm in the Cotswolds. Finding it was Silas himself who answered, Fiona didn't hesitate nor waste time with pleasantries; she didn't even give her name. Relying upon him to recognize her voice, she said, 'Silas. I must see you. I must. It's urgent.'

There was a long silence. 'Where are you? Can you talk?'

'At my sister's flat. No, I can't.'

'Next weekend soon enough?'

'Perfect,' she said.

Another long silence. 'Leave it to me, darling. Bernard will be invited, plus you and the children.'

'Thank you, Silas.'

'Think nothing of it. It's a pleasure.'

She replaced the phone. When she looked down to see what was crunching underfoot she found she'd crushed aspirins and other pills into the gold-coloured carpet. She looked at the mess; she worried about Tessa. To what extent had she made her sister into the sort of woman she'd become? Fiona had always been the 'eldest son', with effortless top marks and a relationship with her father that Tessa never knew.

Despite being her father's favourite she was never taken into his confidence, for he kept his financial affairs secret: to the extent of employing several different accountants and lawyers so that no one would know the full picture of his investments and interests. But Fiona was taken to his office to meet the staff and there seemed to be a tacit agreement that eventually Fiona would replace her father.

It never happened of course. Fiona went to University, and

flourished. She enjoyed being in a man's world and while there she was recruited into the most masculine preserve of all: that mystic and exclusive British brotherhood that enjoys a duality of name and profoundly secret purpose. The obsessional secrecy that her father had maintained prepared her for the Secret Intelligence Service, but nothing her father showed her of his business world could compete with it.

And when, within this brotherhood, she found a man unlike any other she had ever met, she wanted him, and got him. Bernard Samson had grown up in this secret world of physical hardship and brutality. A kill or be killed world. Many of her father's friends had seen service in the war – some had been decorated as heroes – but Bernard Samson was fundamentally different to any of them: for his war was a dark, dirty, private war. Here at last was a man her father could not fathom, and heartily detested. But if, as Chandler said, 'down these mean streets a man must go who is not himself mean, who is neither tarnished nor afraid . . . Complete man, common man and yet an unusual man,' then Bernard Samson was such a man. The day she first saw him she knew that it would be unendurable to lose him to another.

Fiona married. Tessa, neglected and insecure, floated away; a victim of Fiona's career-making and her father's indifference. Poor Tessa, what might she have been if Fiona had guarded her and advised her and given to her according to her need?

'Are you all right?' Tessa called from the next room.

'I'm coming, Tessa. It will all be all right. I promise you, I'll sort it out.'

Tessa came to her. 'I knew you would, Fi.' She threw her arms round Fiona's neck and kissed her. 'Dearest, darling, wonderful Fi, I knew you would.'

Such displays of affection embarrassed Fiona, but she stood stiff and still and put up with it.

Had the invitation to see Silas come in other circumstances, Fiona Samson would have enjoyed every minute of the weekend she spent with her husband and children at Whitelands, the farming estate to which Silas Gaunt had retired. His six hundred acres of the Cotswolds provided superlative walks and breath-taking views across the mighty limestone plateau that borders the shining River Severn.

But in this context everything was fraught with worries and dangers. Dicky Cruyer, the enterprising German Desk Controller, and his arty wife Daphne were there. Bret Rensselaer had brought a young blonde girl. Diffident in the company of so many strangers, she clung tight to him; so tight in fact that they'd arranged to have the only two bedrooms with a connecting door. Fiona guessed that Bret had requested those two rooms when she asked Silas if she could have the two children next to her, and Silas had replied that there were other needs greater than hers, and laughed.

Silas was a pirate, or at least he looked the part. A huge pot-bellied ruffian with a jowly face surmounted by a huge forehead and bald head. His baggy clothes were of high quality but he preferred old garments – as he preferred old wine and old friends – and displayed the faded patches and neat darns that were the work of his faithful housekeeper Mrs Porter, as an old warrior his medals.

The house itself was made of local stone, a lovely tan colour, and the furnishings – like the family portraits obscured behind murky coach varnish and the superb early eighteenth-century dresser – were in appropriate style. Silas Gaunt liked the dining room, especially when it was crowded, as it was this Saturday lunchtime. Gaunt stood at the head of the lovely Georgian mahogany table, carving an impressive beef sirloin for his professional cronies: the Samsons, Tessa, the Cruyers, Bret Rensselaer, and dominating them by the force of his personality.

Fiona Samson watched it all with a feeling of detachment. Even when her son Billy spilled gravy down his shirt, she only smiled contentedly, as if it was an incident depicted in an old home movie.

She watched the Cruyers with interest. Fiona had been at Oxford at the same time as Dicky. She remembered seeing him being cheered to victory at the debating society, and his making a pass at her that day when he was celebrating his cricket blue. One of the brightest of the bright boys at Balliol, he'd got the German Desk for which Bernard had been shortlisted and there was talk that he'd get the Europe job when the time came. Now she wondered if Silas Gaunt was going to propose that he was made a party to her secret. She hoped not: already enough people knew, and if Dicky was to be told while Bernard was kept in ignorance she would find it intolerable. Dicky noticed her looking at him and smiled at her in that shy manner that he'd found so effective with the Oxford girls.

She looked too at Tessa. Her husband George Kosinski was away. It was typical of Silas, and his luck and intuition, to guess that Tessa was connected with the phone call and to go to the trouble of inviting her in case he needed to know more.

When, after lunch, Silas took the men into the billiards room with a trayful of cigars and brandy, Fiona took Billy and Sally upstairs to do their homework.

'In leap year, Mummy, do ladies ask men to marry them?' said Sally.

'I don't think so,' said Fiona.

'My teacher said they do,' said Sally, and Fiona realized she had walked into the sort of trap Sally was fond of setting for her.

'Then teacher is no doubt right,' she said.

'It was Miss Jenkins,' said Sally. 'Daddy said she is a fool.'

'Perhaps you misheard Daddy.'

'I was there,' said Billy, joining in the conversation. 'He *actually* said that Miss Jenkins was a bloody fool. It was when she told him not to leave our car in the headmaster's car space.'

'It was a Saturday,' said Sally in defence of her father.

'That's quite enough,' said Fiona sharply. 'Let's start the maths homework.'

There was a knock and then Tessa looked round the door. 'Yes?' said Fiona.

'I wondered if the children would like to go to the stables.'

'They must do their homework.'

'There's a foal: born last week . . . just for half an hour, Fi.'

'They have a test on Monday,' said Fiona.

'Leave them with me, Fi. I'll see they do their homework. Go for that long walk to Ringstone, you are always saying you enjoy that.' Tessa was keen to be rid of her: she loved to be with the children and they seemed to respond to her. Tessa was a born rebel and they sensed it and were intrigued.

Fiona looked at them. 'Very well. Thirty minutes and then you must do your homework.' She turned. 'I'm relying on you, Tess.'

There was a happy chorus as they declared their intention to work hard under their aunt's direction. Sally came round and squeezed her mother's hand as if asserting her love. Billy wasted no time before getting into raincoat and scarf. As Tessa took the children off, Fiona heard Billy telling her, 'If the Russians restore the monarch, he will have to be a commie Tsar.' It was his favourite joke since Silas had laughed at it.

Tessa was right, Fiona needed a little time to herself. There was so much to think about. She found an old raincoat and a man's hat in the hall and, wearing the walking shoes she kept in the back of her beloved red Porsche, she slipped away. Alone, striding through the misty rain, she made for the summit of Ringstone Hill above Singlebury. It was about six miles and she walked with the brisk determination with which she did so many other things.

She knew the way, she had done it many times, sometimes with the family and sometimes just with Bernard. She was gratified by the sight of accustomed gates, streams and hedgerows, as familiar as the faces of old friends: varying sometimes with fresh patches of soft mud, a shiny new brass padlock, or the rusting frame of an abandoned bike. The boundary of Whitelands was marked by six fallen firs, casualties of the winter gales. Shallow-rooted trees, like their human counterparts, were always the first to go. She looked at one. From its rotting bark came primroses uncurling their canary heads. She counted their petals as she had when a child: five petals, six petals, some with eight petals. All different; like people. She'd grown up believing that four-petalled primroses were lucky: no four-petalled ones in sight today. It was Bernard who explained that four-petalled primroses were a necessity of cross-fertilization: she wished he'd not told her. She strode on and waded through a vast rippling lake of bluebells before starting to climb again. No surprises; just the expectation before each grand view.

The light changed constantly. The wet fields became ever more radiant under the drizzling dark grey sky and the bright yellow gorse left its scent on the air. She scrambled up to the bare hilltop – for the stone is a stone in name only – and stopped to catch her breath. She'd not been aware of the wind but now it sent the light rain to sting her face, and crooned gently through the wire fence. She turned slowly to survey the whole horizon. Her kingdom: three hundred and sixty degrees and not a person, nor even a house in sight, just the distant clamour of a rookery settling down for the night. To the north the sky was buttressed by black columns of heavy rain. The exertion of the climb had driven from her mind all thoughts of what disturbing conclusions tomorrow's dialogue with Silas Gaunt might bring. But now her mind raced forward again.

She was not an explorer nor an experimenter; Fiona's brain was at its best when evaluating material and planning its use. It was a capacity that provided her with an excellent chance to judge her own potential as a field agent. Secrecy she had in abundance, but she didn't have many of the qualities she saw in Bernard. She didn't have his street-wise skill at fast thinking and fast moving. Fiona could be mean, stubborn and cold-hearted, but these for her were long-term emotions: Bernard had that mysterious masculine ability to switch on cold-blooded hostility at a moment's notice and switch it off a split-second later. She pulled the hat down over her ears. The sky blackened and the rain was getting worse. She must get back in time to bathe and change for dinner. Saturday night dinners were dress-up affairs when you stayed with Uncle Silas. She would have to do something with her hair and borrow the iron to smooth her dress. Tessa and the other women would have been preparing themselves all afternoon. She looked at her watch and at the route back. Even the friendly rolling Cotswolds could become hostile when darkness fell.

'You looked very glamorous last night, my dear,' said Uncle Silas.

'Thank you, Silas. But to tell you the truth I can't keep up with the smart chatter these days.'

'And why should you want to? I like you when you are serious: it suits you.'

'Does it?'

'All beautiful women look their best when sad. It's different for men. Handsome men can be a little merry but jolly women look like hockey captains. Could any man fall in love with a female comic?'

'You talk such rubbish, Silas.'

'Was it that dreadful architect's prattle that pissed you off?'

'No. It was a wonderful evening.'

'Swimming pools and kitchens; I don't think he can talk about anything else. I had to invite him though, he's the only blighter who knows how to repair my boiler.'

He laughed. It was some complicated joke that only he appreciated. He'd grown accustomed to his own company and remarks like this were solely for his own satisfaction. They were sitting in the 'music room', a tiny study where Silas Gaunt had installed his hi-fi and his collection of opera recordings. There was a log fire burning and Silas was smoking a large Havana cigar. He was dressed in a magnificent knitted cardigan. It had an intricate Fair Isle pattern and was coming unravelled faster than Mrs Porter could repair it, so that woollen threads trailed from his elbows and cuffs.

'Now tell me what's troubling you, Fiona.' From the next room there was the measured and intricate sound of a piano: it was Bret playing 'Night and Day'.

Fiona told Silas about Tessa's exchanges with Giles Trent, and when she had finished he went and looked out of the window. The gravel drive made a loop around the front lawn where three majestic elms framed the house. Tessa's racing-green Rolls-Royce was parked outside the window. 'I don't know how your sister manages that car,' he said. 'Does her husband know she uses it when he's away?'

'Don't be such a pig. Of course he does.'

He looked at her. 'Then it sounds as if we've got an orange file on our hands, Fiona.'

'Yes, it does.' An orange file meant an official inquiry.

'Giles Trent: the treacherous swine. Why do these people do it?' She didn't answer. 'What would you have done if Tessa had put this to you but without the special situation that you are in?'

Without hesitation Fiona said, 'I'd have taken it to Internal Security. The Command Rules spell it out.'

'Of course you would.' He scratched his head. 'Well we can't have the IS people in on this one, can we?' Another pause. 'You wouldn't have mentioned it to your husband first?'

'No.'

'You seem very sure of that, Fiona.'

'It would be the same for him, wouldn't it?'

'I'm not sure it would.'

'Uncle Silas! Why?'

He turned and looked at her. 'How can I put it to you . . . You and I belong to a social class obsessed by the notion of conduct. At our best public schools, we have always taught young men that "service" is the highest calling, and I'm proud that it should be so. Service to God, service to our sovereign, service to our country.'

'You're not saying that because Bernard wasn't at public school –'

He held up a hand to stop her. 'Hear me out, Fiona. We all respect your husband. Me more than anyone, you know that. I cherish him. He's the only one out there who knows what it's like to be in the firing line. I'm simply saying that Bernard's background, the boys he grew up with and his family, have another priority. For them – and who is to say they are in error? – loyalty to the family comes before everything. I really do mean before *everything*. I know, I've spent my life commanding men. If you don't understand that aspect of your husband's psyche you might get into a lot of trouble, my dear.'

'Working-class boys, you mean?'

'Yes. I'm not frightened to say working-class. I'm too old to care about taboos of that sort.'

'Are you saying that if Tessa had taken her problem to Bernard he would have hushed it up?'

'Why don't we put it to the test? Sit your husband down next week and have Tessa tell him her story.'

'And what do you think he'll do?'

'More to the point, what do *you* think he'll do?' said Silas.

'I can't see that any benefit could come of such speculation,' said Fiona. Silas laughed at the evasion. Fiona was irritated and said, 'You are the one making the allegations, Silas.'

'Now, now, Fiona. You know I'm doing nothing of the kind. Put it to Bernard, and he'll find some ingenious solution that will keep you and Tessa out of it.' He smiled artfully. The word ingenious implied Bernard's flagrant disregard, if not to say contempt, for the rule book, and that was something Silas shared with him.

'Bernard has a lot on his mind right now,' said Fiona.

'Make sure you ask him to keep Tessa out of it.' He found a loose thread, tugged it off and dropped it carefully into the fire.

'How?' said Fiona.

'I don't know how. Ask him.' He smoked his cigar. 'A far more important thing for the moment is that Giles Trent has obviously been used to monitor everything you've been telling them.' He blew smoke, making sure it went towards the fire. Whenever Mrs Porter smelled cigar smoke she nagged him: the doctor had told him not to smoke. 'You must have thought about that. Any worries there?'

'Nothing that I can think of.'

'No, I think not. We've kept you very very secret and given them only strictly kosher material. Whatever Trent has been reporting to them, his reports will have only increased your status with Moscow.'

'I hope so.'

'Cheer up, Fiona. Everything is going beautifully. This will suit our book. In fact I'll get permission for you to visit the Data Centre again. That should make your masters prick their ears, what?'

'Will you tell Bret about Tessa?' She didn't want to face Bret with it herself: it would become an interrogation.

'Let's tell him now.' Having hidden his cigar in the fireplace he pressed a bellpush. Seeing the look of alarm on Fiona's face he said, 'Trust your Uncle Silas.' 'Night and Day' continued in the next room.

When Mrs Porter put her head round the door he said, 'Ask Mr Rensselaer if he can spare a moment. I think I heard him playing the piano.'

'Yes, sir. I'll tell him right away.'

When Bret came – eyebrows raised at seeing Fiona with Silas in what was obviously some kind of discourse – Silas said, 'It's good to hear the piano again, Bret. I keep it tuned but nowadays no one plays.' Bret nodded without replying. Silas said, 'Bret, we seem to be having another problem with our playmates.'

Bret looked from one to the other of them and got the idea instantly.

'This is getting to be a habit, Fiona,' he said. Bret was huffed that she'd taken her story to Silas Gaunt and didn't disguise his feelings.

'We are all targeted,' said Silas. 'They focus on London Central. It's natural that they should.'

'We are talking KGB?'

'Yes,' said Silas, tapping ash into the fire. 'This wretched Pryce-Hughes fellow has been rather indiscreet. He's let drop the word to Fiona that they have someone else working in London Central.'

'Jesus H. Christ!' said Bret.

'From the context Fiona inclines to the view that it's a fellow called Giles Trent.' Silas took a poker and stabbed at the burning log, which bled grey smoke. He carefully rolled it to the very back of the hearth.

'Training,' said Bret, after racking his brains to remember who Trent was.

'Yes. He was shunted off to the training school two years ago, but that doesn't make him any less dangerous.'

'Does anyone else know?' asked Bret.

'The three of us,' said Silas, still brandishing the poker. 'Fiona wasn't sure how to handle it. She was going directly to Internal Security. It was, of course, better that she brought it to me, off the record.'

Bret's hurt feelings were somewhat soothed by this explanation. 'We don't want Internal Security involved,' he said.

'No. Better like this,' said Silas. 'Off duty: off the record, all unofficial.'

'What next?' Bret asked.

'Leave it with me,' said Silas. 'I've worked out a way of doing it. No need for you to know, Bret. What the eye doesn't see . . . Are you all right, Bret?'

'This year my sinuses are playing merry hell with me.'

'It's that damned log fire, is it? Let me open the window a fraction.'

'If there's nothing else I'll just go out in the garden for a moment.'

'Of course, Bret, of course. Are you sure you'll be all right?'

Bret stumbled out of the room holding a handkerchief to his face. 'Poor Bret,' said Silas.

'I won't tell Bernard that I've spoken with you,' said Fiona, still unsure of exactly what was expected of her.

'That's right. Now stop worrying. Can you persuade Tessa to tell her story to your husband?'

'Probably.'

'Do that.'

'Suppose Bernard goes to Internal Security?'

'It's a risk we'll have to take,' said Silas. 'But I want you kept out of it. If push comes to shove, you'll just have to deny Tessa ever told you. I'll see you are protected.'

'That smoke is affecting me now,' said Fiona.

'Get back to the others, or they'll start thinking we have a love affair or something.'

'You won't want to talk to Tessa?'

'Stop playing the elder sister. If I want to talk to her I'll fix it.'

'She gets very nervous, Silas.'

'Go and walk about in the garden and get the smoke out of your eyes,' he said.

When she'd gone he sank down on to his favourite armchair and let out a groan. He leaned close to the fire and prodded it again. 'Why do these things happen to me?' he complained to the log. As if in response the smoking log burst into a flicker of flame.

If Fiona had seen him now she would have been less confident of Silas Gaunt's ability to make her troubles disappear. 'We'll have to put you into the bag neatly and quickly, Mr Giles Trent,' he muttered, and tried to visualize the reactions of Trent's controller when he found his man was uncovered. Would they try to pull him out and save him? Or would Moscow perceive another spy trial, in the very heart of London Central, as a triumph worth sacrificing a piece for? This might be one of those cases where both Moscow and London would agree that a favourable outcome was a permanently silent Trent. If it came to that, Silas had better make sure there was someone available to do the deed. He called to mind a tough old German war veteran who'd once worked as a barman at Lisl's hotel, and while there had done all sorts of nasty jobs for Silas. He went over to live in the East: perfect! Who'd link such a man with London Central? What was the fellow's name – oh yes, Rolf Mauser, a wonderful ruffian. Just the fellow for a job like this. He wouldn't contact him directly of course, it would be imperative to keep it at arm's length.

10

Maida Vale, London. April 1983.

'Have you gone to sleep, honey?' Fiona buried her head in the pillow and didn't answer. The mattress heaved as he slid out of bed and went into the bathroom. It was a sunny spring day. Being in bed in broad daylight, behind closed curtains, made her feel guilty. What had happened to her? At least a thousand times, over the years, she had vowed never again to see Harry Kennedy, but he was so charming and amusing that he intrigued her. And then she would find herself thinking of him, or a bunch of flowers would arrive, or an advert from the 'hair and beauty salon', and her resolution invariably weakened and she came back to him.

Sometimes it was no more than a quick drink at some pub near the clinic or a few words over the phone, but there were times when she needed him. Now and again it was a meeting like this and she relished every moment of it.

She watched him walk naked across the room and open the wardrobe. He was muscular and tanned except the buttocks left pale by his shorts. Lately he'd done three delivery trips to Saudi Arabia. Across his shoulders, like a bandoleer, there were livid scars from a forced landing in Mexico ten years ago. He felt her looking at him and leered at her.

This illicit relationship had transformed Fiona. It had thrown a bombshell into the routine of her married life. Being with Harry was exciting, and he made her feel glamorous and desirable in a way that Bernard had never been able to do. Sex had come to play an important part in it but it was something even more fundamental than that. She couldn't explain it. All she knew was that the pressure upon her in her working life would have been unendurable without the prospect of seeing him if only for a brief moment. Just to hear his voice on the telephone was both disturbing and invigorating. She was now understanding something she'd never known, the kind of teenage love she'd only heard other girls talk about, the kind they sang about in pop tunes she couldn't stand. Of course she felt guilty about deceiving Bernard, but she needed Harry. Sometimes she thought she might be able to eliminate some of the guilt that plagued her if they could continue their friendship on a different, platonic, basis. But as soon as she was with him any such resolve quickly faded.

'Ah, so you are awake. How about a champagne cocktail? I've got everything right here.'

She laughed.

'Is that funny?' he said. He put on his chequered silk dressing gown while looking at himself in the mirror and smoothing it and adjusting the knot in the belt.

'Yes, darling, very funny. Tea would be even better.'

'Tea? You got it.'

After Harry went out she reached over to the bedside table and picked up the lunchtime edition of the evening paper. There on the front page a headline proclaimed the 'Chelsea Bathroom Shooting'. An intruder had broken into Giles Trent's house and shot him in the shower. The killer had used the plastic shower curtain to avoid being splashed with blood and washed his hands before leaving. A conveniently unnamed Scotland Yard spokesman called it 'very professional indeed', and one of those experts who are always ready to speak to newspapers said it had 'all the signs of a typical New York Mafia execution'. The reporter seemed to imply that narcotics were involved. There was a blurred photo, one column wide, of a very young Giles Trent in bathing trunks, arms akimbo and broad smile. On an inside page there was a large photo of the house in Chelsea with a policeman on duty outside it.

Thank God Bernard had kept Tessa and Fiona out of the whole business. Uncle Silas had been entirely right about Bernard. It was disconcerting that certain of his male friends understood him in a way that she had never been able to. He was so secretive. Without any discussion or explanation to her, he'd got Giles Trent to confess, and confess without mentioning Tessa. Now Trent was dead, and however ugly his death she couldn't help but feel a measure of relief.

There were other portentous signs. Bret had asked her to copy out a long secret document about Bank of England support for sterling. It was all in her handwriting and she never handed it over to Martin. As far as Fiona could see that meant only one thing: Bret was going to pass that to the KGB through some other agent. Why her handwriting? Only a complete fool would produce a document so incriminating unless this was going to be concrete evidence of her personal work for the other side. There was something ominous about the way Bret brushed her questions aside.

Another forewarning came from the amount of material she'd handed over to Martin in recent weeks. Bret said that none of it was of vital importance but there was such a lot of it. London Central just wouldn't want to keep passing it through at this rate, and yet what excuse would she be able to provide for lessening the flow? It all added up to one thing: they intended that she should go East, and go soon. She dreaded it, but in some ways the waiting was even worse.

Every day now she looked at her husband and the children with love and with longing. Each time she saw her sister she wanted to warn her that they would soon be separated, but any sort of hint or preparation was out of the question. To make it more painful, Fiona had become convinced that she'd never return. There was no logical reason, nor any evidence to support her failure of confidence. The premonition was purely instinctive and purely feminine. It was a calm fatalism that a matriarch might feel, surrounded by her family, on her deathbed.

If only it was possible to settle some of the vital things that would now be decided without her. She kept worrying about Billy and his school. She'd always hoped that eventually Bernard would come to see the advantages that little Billy would enjoy from going to a good public school. She could get him in: her father had promised her that. But with her absent, there was no chance at all that Bernard would do anything about it. Bernard had a phobia about public schools – 'beating, buggery and bad manners' – and about those who'd ever attended one, or so it seemed.

Harry came in with a tray of tea. 'You've read that newspaper story at least three times, darling. Does it have some special significance?' He leaned over and kissed her.

'The eternal psychologist,' she said and, throwing the paper aside as casually as she could manage, she took the tray on to her knees. A tiny vase contained what must have been the very last violets of the year. How delicate they looked. Lovely transparent china, silver teaspoons and two slices of the rich English fruit cake she adored. He must have had it all prepared. 'How splendid!' She held the tray steady as he climbed back into bed alongside her. 'Harry, what do you know about the English public school system?'

'You don't take milk with Earl Grey tea, do you, honey-child?'

'No. I drink it plain.'

'Public schools? What oddball things go round in that brain of yours. Most of the guys at the clinic seem to have survived them without visible damage. But then how can I tell? And mind you, there are not many of them I'd want to be in the shower with if the lights went out. What's on your mind?'

'I have close friends . . . Her husband is being sent abroad by his company. They are thinking of putting the boy into a boarding school.'

'And you're asking me if that's a good idea.' He set the cups on their saucers. 'My opinion as a psychiatrist, is that it? How can I tell you without seeing the kid? And the husband and wife too.'

'I suppose you are right.'

'If the husband doesn't want it done that way, the wife would be dumb to defy him, wouldn't she?' He poured some tea. 'Is that strong enough?'

'He hates all public schools. Yes, it's perfect.'

'Why's that?'

'Snobbery, bullying, privilege: the instilling into certain sorts of children that they are an élite. He thinks it contributes to British class hatreds.'

'Yeah and he is probably right, but you could say the same about shopping in Knightsbridge.'

'Bullying too?' she laughed.

'You bet. You mean you never tackled those determined old ladies with their sharpened umbrellas?'

'Were you at a boarding school?' She drank some tea and before he answered said, 'We don't really know each other, do we?'

'That's why we should get married,' he said.

'I wish you would stop saying that.'

'I mean it.'

'It upsets me.'

'Listen, I'm crazy about you. I'm free, white and over twenty-one. I'm in good shape at the gym and pretty good shape at the bank. I now have a twenty-year lease on this place and you chose most of the furniture. I love you more than I knew I could love anyone. I think of you day and night; I only come alive when we are together.'

'Stop it. You know nothing about me.'

'Then tell me about yourself.'

'Harry, we both know that this relationship is stupid and selfish. The only way we preserve it is by keeping our other lives to ourselves.'

'Non-sense!' he always said it in two syllables. 'I don't want to keep anything from you.'

'I don't know anything about you: your politics, your parents, your wife . . . or wives. I don't even know how many you've had.'

He held up the teaspoon. 'My parents are dead. I have no politics and I no longer have any wife. My divorce is finalized. No children. My ex-wife is French-Canadian and lives in Montreal. She was always dunning me for more money. That's why I skedaddled and had to keep moving. Now she has remarried and I'm really free.' He drank tea. 'Like I told you, my niece Patsy is back with her father in Winnipeg and the guy she ran away with is in jail for shop-lifting. That's all ancient history. What else would you like to know?'

'Nothing. I'm saying that it's better that we don't know too much about each other.'

'Or?'

'Or we'll start discussing our problems.'

'Would that be so awful? What problems do you have, honey?'

Poor Harry: the probability was that she'd soon be moving away to the East. When that happened the SIS would stage a full-scale inquiry just for the look of the thing. It would be foolish to rule out the possibility that Special Branch would find out about her relationship with Harry. Should they come to talk to him it was vital that everyone was left with the idea that she was a long-term Marxist. Anything else could spell danger. 'Only silly things, I suppose.'

'For instance?' He leaned over and kissed her on the cheek.

'Perhaps you'd no longer love me if you knew,' she said, and ruffled his hair in what she hoped was the appropriate patronizing gesture of a Marxist spy.

'I'll tell you something,' he said impulsively. 'I'm thinking of giving up the shrink business.'

'You're always saying that.'

'But this time for real, baby! For a hundred thousand dollars my cousin Greg will sell me a quarter share in his airplane brokerage. If I worked with him full-time we could let one of the pilots go. He needs the extra hundred thousand to buy a new lease on the Winnipeg hangar and buildings.'

'You said it was a risky business,' said Fiona.

'And it is. But no more risk than I can handle. And I've had about as much psychiatry as I can stomach.' He stopped but she said nothing. 'It's all office politics at the clinic: who gets this and who gets that.'

'But you have a work permit. You could go anywhere and get a job.'

'No I couldn't. It's not that sort of permit. And what kind of job could I get? I only went into the crowd hysteria research at the clinic to get away from neurotic housewives going into menopause. I've got to get away, Fiona. I've got to.'

'I didn't realize that you were so unhappy.' At moments like this she loved him more than she could say.

'Having you is all that keeps me going. There is nothing more important to me than you are,' said Harry, and, growing more serious added, 'No matter how long you live I want you always to remember this moment. I want you to remember that my life is yours.'

'Darling Harry.' She kissed him.

'I don't ask you to say the same. Your circumstances are different. I make no demands of you: I love you with everything I've got.'

She laughed again. The hours she spent with Harry were the only time she was able to forget what was in store for her.

11

London. May 1983.

'My God, Bret, how I wish you wouldn't suddenly appear un-announced, like an emissary from the underworld.' It was a silly expression from her schooldays, hardly an appropriate way to greet Bret Rensselaer even if he had walked into her home unannounced. Yet, as she said it, Fiona realized that nowadays she was beginning to think of him as some svelte messenger from another darker world.

The idea amused Bret. He was standing in the kitchen with his hat in his hand, smiling. A summer shower glittered as sequins all over his black raincoat. He said, 'Is that how you rate me, Fiona, a go-between for Old Nick? And what form does he assume when he is not the Director-General?'

Fiona was in her apron, her hair a complete mess, emptying the dishwasher. Cutlery in hand, she smiled, a nervous twitch of the lips, and said, 'I'm sorry, Bret.' She picked up a cloth and wiped a knife blade. 'The cutlery never comes out without marks,' she said. 'Sometimes I think it would be quicker to wash everything in the sink.' She spoke mechanically as her mind rushed on to Bernard.

'Your lovely au pair let me in; she seemed to be in a hurry.' Bret unbuttoned his black raincoat to reveal black suit and black tie. 'I am looking a bit sombre I'm afraid. I've been to the service for Giles Trent.'

She didn't offer to take his coat nor ask him to sit down. 'You startled me. I was waiting for a phone call from Bernard.'

'That might be a long wait, Fiona. Bernard went over there to sort out the Brahms Four fiasco. No one knows where he's got to.'

Over there, those awful words. She went cold. 'What was the last contact?'

'Relax, Fiona. Relax.' She was standing as if frozen, ashen faced, with knives and forks in one hand and a cloth in the other. 'There is absolutely no reason to think he's run into trouble.'

'He should never have gone; they know him too well. I pleaded with him. When did he make contact?'

'You know how Bernard likes to operate; no documents, no

preparations, no emergency link, no local back-up, nothing! He insists it be done that way. I was there when he said it.'

'Yes, I know.'

'Bernard likes to play the technocrat, but when he hits the road he's strictly horse and buggy.' Bret touched her arm for a moment to comfort her. 'And his track record says he's right.'

She said nothing. He watched her. Mechanically, with quick movements of the cloth, she polished the cutlery and continued to put it into the drawer, knives, forks and spoons each in their separate compartments. When the last one was done, she took the damp cloth and carefully draped it along the edge of the table to dry. Then she sat down and closed her eyes.

Bret hadn't reckoned on her being so jumpy but he had to tell her: it was the reason he'd come. So after what seemed an appropriate time, he said, 'Everything points to the notion that they will take you over there some time over the next seventy-two hours.'

'Me?'

'If they are smart, they will. They think you're blown. You'd better be ready.'

'But if they arrest Bernard . . .'

'Forget Bernard! He went because he's the most experienced Berlin agent we have. He'll be all right. Start thinking of yourself.'

'But if he's arrested?'

Bret stayed calm. In a measured voice he said, 'If Bernard is held, you can do more for him over there than you can sitting here waiting for the phone.'

'You're right, of course.'

'Don't try playing it by ear yourself. Leave that to Bernard. Sit down right now and make sure you have everything committed to memory: out of contact devices, the "commentary" and your own goodbye codes in case things go wrong. We'll get you home, Fiona, don't worry about that.' A cat strolled in, and standing on the doormat, looked first at Bret and then at Fiona. With her foot Fiona pushed the plastic bowl of food nearer to the door, but after sniffing it very closely the cat walked out again.

'I've learned it all and destroyed my notes.'

'Once there, you won't be contacted for several weeks. They'll be watching you at first.'

'I know, Bret.'

She sounded listless and he tried to snap her out of that. 'They will try to trick you. You must be ready for them.'

579

'I'm not frightened.'

He looked at her with admiration. 'I know you're not, and I think you're an extraordinary woman.'

This compliment surprised her. It was delivered with warmth. 'Thank you, Bret.' Perhaps somewhere under that smooth silky exterior there was a heart beating.

'Is there anything we've forgotten, Fiona? I keep going over it again and again. Try to imagine that you really are the agent they think you are . . .' He snapped his fingers. 'Money! Wouldn't you want to leave some money – maybe money for the children – and instructions of some kind? A final letter?'

'My father arranged a trust fund for the children. Letter? No, that's too complicated. Bernard would find some way of reading between the lines.'

'My God!' said Bret in real alarm. 'You think he could?'

'I've lived with Bernard many years, Bret. We know each other. Quite honestly, I don't know how we've been able to keep everything secret from him for so long.'

'I know it's been rugged at times,' said Bret, 'but you came through.' He looked at his watch. 'I'll leave you now. I know you well enough to know you'll want a little time alone, to think. Take time out to rest and get ready. We'll monitor your journey right up to the time we can't stay with you.'

She looked at him, wondering what would happen at the point he wouldn't be able to stay with her, but didn't ask. 'Shall I let you know if Bernard phones?'

'No need. I have someone tapping into your phone.' He looked at his watch. 'As from an hour back. If you want me I'll be at home.'

He buttoned his raincoat. 'If my guess is right, this is where it all begins.'

She smiled ruefully.

'Good luck, Fiona. And see you soon.' He was going to kiss her but she didn't look as if she wanted to be embraced, so he winked and she responded with a smile.

'Goodbye, Bret.'

'Suppose it's all a KGB caper? Suppose the Russkies grab her and keep her husband too; suppose they then ask you to do a deal?' Sylvester Bernstein was wearing a raincoat with a wool lining: the sort of garment a man buys soon after he starts surveillance duties.

'We'll worry about that when it happens,' said Bret. He shivered. He wasn't expecting it to be so cold, even in Scotland at night.

'You'd sure be behind the eight ball, old buddy. Two agents down the tube.'

'We have others.'

'Is that official policy?'

'Once deposited an agent is dead,' said Bret. 'There are no second chances or retirement plans.'

'Does Mrs Samson know that?' said Bernstein.

'Of course she does; unless she is stupid. We can't count on getting her back in one piece. Even if we do, she won't be in good shape. Even getting her set up for this task has taken a lot out of her. She used to be sweet, gentle and trusting: now she's learned to be tough and cynical.'

'Nice going, Bret,' said Bernstein. So Bret was taking it badly. This kind of nonsense was Bret's way of dealing with his worries about Fiona Samson. Sylvy had seen other case officers in similar circumstances. They often formed an emotional attachment to the agent they were running.

Bret didn't reply. He huddled closer to the wall of the ruined building in which the two men had found shelter from the cold rainy wind off the sea. It was a wild night, a Götterdämmerung that you had to be on this lonely piece of coastline to appreciate. The sea was black, but a can-opener, inexpertly used, had torn open the horizon to reveal a raging tumult of reds and mauves lit with the livid flashes of an electrical storm. What a night to bid goodbye to your homeland. What a night to be out of doors.

'This is some desolate place,' said Bernstein, who had known many desolate places in his life.

'Once it was a submarine base,' said Bret. 'The last time I was here that anchorage was full of ships of the Home Fleet: some big battle wagons too.'

Bernstein grunted and pulled up the collar of his coat and leaned into it to light a cigarette.

Bret said, 'The Royal Navy called this place HMS Peafowl, the sailors called it HMS Piss-up. That jetty went all the way out in those days. And there were so many depot ships and subs that you could have walked on them right across the bay.'

'How long ago was that?' said Bernstein. He blew smoke and spat a shred of tobacco that had stuck to his lip.

'The end of the war. There were subs everywhere you looked. The flat piece of tarmac was the drill field that the Limeys called "the quarter deck". The British are quite obsessed with marching and drilling and saluting: they do it to celebrate, they do it for punishment,

581

they do it to pray, they do it for chow. They do it in the rain, in the sunshine and in the snow; morning and afternoon, even on Sunday. This . . . where we are now, was the movie theatre. Those concrete blocks along the roads are the foundations for the Quonset huts, row upon row of them.'

'And stoves maybe?' said Bernstein. He clamped the cigarette between his lips while he used his night-glasses to study the water of the bay.

'I can hardly believe that it's all gone. When the war was on, there must have been eight thousand servicemen stationed here, counting the engineering facilities on the other side of the bay.'

'I never had you figured for a sailor, Bret.'

'I was only a sailor for twenty-five minutes,' said Bret. He was always selfconscious about being invalided out of the service. Angry at having to divert and land him, his submarine captain told him he was a Jonah. Bret, who had falsified his age to volunteer, never forgot that Jonah label and never entirely freed himself from it.

'Twenty-five minutes. Yes, like me with Buddhism. Maybe it was long enough.'

'I didn't lose faith,' said Bret.

'You were in the US Navy?' said Bernstein, wondering if Bret had been with the British so long ago.

'No, I was in U-boats,' said Bret sourly. 'I won the Iron Cross, first class.'

'Pig boats eh?' said Bernstein, feigning interest in an attempt to pacify the older man.

'Submarines. Not pig boats: submarines.'

'Well, now you've got yourself another submarine, and it belongs to the Russkies,' said Bernstein. He looked at his watch. It was an antiquated design with green luminescent hands; another item acquired when he began surveillance work.

To the unspoken question, Bret said, 'They're late but they'll turn up. This is the way they always do it.'

'Here? Always here?'

'It's not so easy to find a place where you can bring a sub in close to the shore; somewhere some landlubber can launch an inflatable boat without getting swamped. Somewhere away from shipping lanes and people.'

'They sure are late. What kind of car are they in?' Bernstein asked with the glasses still to his eyes. 'A Lada? One of those two-stroke jobs maybe?'

'Deep water too,' explained Bret. 'And sand and fine gravel; it's got to have a sea bed that won't rip the belly out of you. Yes, they'll come here. It's one of the few landing spots the Soviets would dare risk a sub at night.'

'Take the glasses. I think I saw a movement on the water.' He offered them. 'Beyond the end of the jetty.'

'Forget it! You won't see anything. They won't surface until they get a signal, and they won't get a signal until their passengers are here.'

'Don't the Brits track them on the ASW . . . the sonar or radar or whatever they got?'

'No way. It can be done but there's the chance that the Russkie counter-measures will reveal they are being tracked. Better they don't know that we are on to them.'

'I suppose.'

'I could have asked the navy to track them with a warship but that might have scared them away. Don't fret, they will come.'

'Why not a plane, Bret? Submarines! Jesus, that's *Riddle of the Sands* stuff.'

'Planes? This is not Nam. Planes are noisy and conspicuous and too risky for anything this important.'

'And where do they go from here?'

'Somewhere close; East Germany, Sassnitz has submarine facilities. From there the train ferry could take her to Stockholm. Plane to Berlin.'

'A long way round. Why not take a train from Sassnitz to Berlin?'

'They are devious folk. They like to route their people via the West. It looks better that way,' said Bret. 'I'm going back to the car to phone. There was a car following them right from the time they left London.'

Bernstein pulled a face. His confidence in the British security and intelligence organizations, right down to their ability to follow a car, was very limited.

Bret Rensselaer walked back along the road and climbed the broken steps to where they'd left the car. It was out of sight behind the last remaining wall of the Sick Bay where, in 1945, Bret had been ignominiously deposited by his submarine captain after falling down a ladder during an Atlantic patrol.

Before getting into the car he took a look at the bay. The water was like black syrup and the horizon was getting brighter as the storm headed their way. He sighed, shut the door and phoned the other car. 'Johnson?'

It answered immediately. 'Johnson here.'

'Boswell. Where the hell have you got to?'

'A spot of trouble, Boswell. Our friends had a little collision with another car.'

'Anyone hurt?'

'No, but a lot of arguments about who was drunk. They've sent for the police.'

'How far away are you?'

'About an hour's drive.'

'Get them back on the road, Johnson. I don't care how you do it. You've got a police officer with you?'

'Yes, he's here.'

'Get him to sort it out. And do it quick.'

'Will do, Boswell.'

'And phone me when they are on their way. I'll stay in the car.'

'Will do.'

The phone gave the disengaged tone and Bret put it back in its slot. He looked up to find Bernstein standing by the car. 'Get inside and warm up,' said Bret. 'Another hour. At least another hour.'

Bernstein got into the car and settled back. 'Is it all okay? It's beginning to rain.'

Bret said, 'I figured I might sometimes be wiping the backsides of the Brits, but I didn't figure I'd be doing it for the Russkies too.'

'You're really master-minding this one, Bret. I hope you know what you're doing.'

'If I do,' said Bret, 'I'm the only one who does.' He started the engine and switched on the heater.

'Who owns this spread nowadays?' said Bernstein, looking down upon the abandoned brick buildings that had once been the administration block.

'The British Admiralty hung on to it.'

'Some chutzpah, those Russkies.' He reached into his pocket.

'It suits us,' said Bret. 'We know where to find them.' He raised his hand in warning. 'Don't smoke please, Sylvy. It affects my sinuses.'

Bernstein sat fidgeting with his hands as he tried to decide whether it was better to smoke outside in the freezing cold or sit desperately deprived in the warm. Bret watched him clasping his hands together and after five minutes or more of stillness and silence said, 'Are you all right?'

Bernstein said, 'I was meditating.'

'I'm sorry.'

'It's okay.'

Bret said, 'Did you really get into Buddhism?'

'Yeah. In Nam: Zen Buddhism. I was living with a beautiful Cambodian girl who taught me about meditation. I was really taken with it.'

'You're a Jew.'

'The beliefs are not mutually exclusive,' said Bernstein. 'Meditation helped me when I was captured.'

'Captured by the Viet Cong?'

'Only for about twelve hours. They questioned me.' He was silent for a moment, as if just saying it caused him pain. 'It was dark when I came conscious again and I got loose and escaped, crawling away into the jungle.'

'I didn't know that, Sylvy.'

'So who wants to know about Nam? The guys who fought there were shafted by everyone, from the White House down to the liberal newspapers; and that's pretty damn low. That's why I came and lived in Europe.'

'Look at that lightning. It's going to be rough out there. How would you like to be putting out to sea tonight?'

'She was still seeing that guy Kennedy, right up to the end.'

Bret swung his head round with an abrupt movement that betrayed his surprise. 'She swore it was all over.'

'How many husbands send their wife a dozen dark red long-stem roses with a note inviting them to come to tea?'

'You're sure?'

'Florists are a must.'

'What do you mean?'

'Bret, for a spell, when times were tough, I took divorce jobs. I can probably get the bill for the roses if you want to see it.'

'We'll have to turn Kennedy over,' said Bret.

'We found nothing last time. We checked his medical qualification and his military service. The clinic where he works say he's hard working and reliable. Anyway it's a bit late now, isn't it?' said Bernstein. 'She's on her way.'

Bret looked at him. He'd told him only as much as he had to be told, but Sylvy Bernstein had spent a lifetime in the intelligence world. He knew what was happening. 'We still need to know,' said Bret.

'It was kind of fortuitous, the way Kennedy picked her up at Waterloo Station, wasn't it?' Bernstein rubbed his chin. He had a tough beard and he needed a shave. 'Serendipitous is the word: I read it in a book.'

'She's a very attractive woman,' said Bret, repeating what Bernstein had said many times, and dismissed the idea of it being an enticement.

'And he's a real smooth shrink. But is he the kind of guy who picks up ladies in railroad stations?'

Bret still couldn't face it. 'It was a special situation, Sylvy. Kennedy's daughter ran away. You talked to the railway cop. You said . . .'

'Okay, okay. It was really his cousin's daughter and Kennedy is a Canadian. It won't be easy to do a complete vetting job on him. And a guy who gives a false name to a cop is likely to have given a few false names to a lot of other people. But why should I talk myself out of an assignment? I need the money.'

'We'd better turn him right over, Sylvy,' said Bret, as if saying it for the first time. The preliminary check on Kennedy had turned up nothing incriminating but foreign nationals – especially those who moved around a lot – were sometimes difficult to investigate. Perhaps he should have been more thorough right from the start, but he'd been so shocked at the idea of Fiona being unfaithful to her husband that he'd not given proper consideration to a full investigation of the man. And yet what could be more obvious? If the KGB were going to use her in a top job it would be standard procedure to place someone close to her: very close to her. A lover! That was the way the minds of the KGB always worked. Bret said, 'Do a complete vetting job: birth record, the Canadian police computer, Washington too. Check his medical school and military service. Have someone talk to his neighbours, colleagues, friends and family: the full procedure. Your way of doing things is faster than if I do it through official channels.'

'What am I looking for?'

'Jesus, Sylvy! Suppose this guy Kennedy turns out to be a KGB fink?'

'Okay. I'll work as fast as I can, Bret, but you can't hurry these things without showing your hand, and I know you want the lid kept on it.'

'A dozen red roses,' said Bret. 'Well, maybe we'll find they were from her sister or her father.'

'I think I'll stretch my legs,' said Bernstein. He felt as if he'd expire unless he smoked a cigarette.

12

Fiona's defection – despite the way in which the Department made sure no word of it leaked to press or TV – caused a sensation amongst her immediate circle.

Of those working in the Department that day, Bret Rensselaer was the only person who knew the whole story of Fiona Samson's going. Temporarily assigned to him as a secretary, there was a nineteen-year-old blonde 'executive officer' called Gloria Kent. Bret had contrived to have this strikingly attractive trainee working with him, and her presence helped to straighten an ego bent after his wife's departure. Alone in Bret's office, it was Gloria who was the first to hear that Bernard Samson had been arrested in East Berlin. She was appalled.

Gloria Kent had had a schoolgirl crush on Bernard Samson ever since she had first seen him in the office. Perhaps her feelings showed on her face when she brought the bad news to Bret Rensselaer, for after a muttered curse he told her, 'Mr Samson will be all right.'

'Who will tell his wife?' said Gloria.

'Sit down,' said Bret. Gloria sat. Bret said, 'According to our latest information Mrs Samson is also in East Germany.'

'His car is on a meter and covered in parking tickets.'

Bret disregarded this complication. 'I don't want this to go all round the office, Miss Kent. I'm telling you because I will need you to work with me to allay fears and stop silly rumours.' He looked at her: she nodded. 'We will have to assume that Mrs Samson has defected, but I have no reason to believe that her husband was a party to her activities.'

'What will happen to her children?'

Bret nodded. Miss Kent was quick: that was one of the problems on Bret's mind. 'There is a nanny with them. I have been trying to phone Mrs Samson's sister, Tessa Kosinski – but there is no reply.'

'Do you want me to go and knock on the door?'

'No, we have people to do that kind of thing. Here's the phone number. Keep trying it. And the office number for her husband is in my leather notebook under Kosinski International Holdings. See if he knows where his wife might be. Don't tell him anything other than that

587

both Samsons are delayed on duty overseas. I'm going to the Samsons' house. Ring me there and tell me what's happening. And tell the duty armourer I'm coming down to collect a gun.'

'Yes, sir.' She went back to the office and started phoning. The idea of Fiona Samson defecting to the communists was too overwhelming for her to properly consider the consequences. Everyone in the Department had watched the steady rise of Fiona Samson. She was a paragon, one of those amazingly lucky people who never put a foot wrong. It was impossible not to envy her: a beautiful woman from a rich family who had left her mark on Oxford. Cordon Bleu cook, charming hostess, with two children and a wonderfully unconventional husband whom Gloria secretly coveted.

'Yes?' came a slurred and sleepy voice. 'Ahhhh. What's the time? Who's there?'

It was Tessa, who liked to sleep until eleven o'clock, awakened by the phone. Gloria told her that Mr and Mrs Samson had been unavoidably detained abroad. Would it be possible for Mrs Kosinski to go to the Samsons' house and take charge of the children? She tried to sound very casual.

It took a few moments to allay Tessa's fears that her sister had been hurt in an accident, but Gloria's charm was well up to the situation and Tessa soon decided that the best way to find out more was to go to the Samson house and ask Bret Rensselaer.

In record time Tessa bathed, put on her make-up, found the Chanel beret with camellia that she always wore when her hair was a mess, and threw a plaid car coat round her shoulders. She looked into the study where her husband was studying share prices on his computer and told him what little she knew.

'Both of them? What's it all about?' he said.

'Neither of them said anything about going anywhere,' said Tessa.

'They don't tell you everything.' George had grown used to the secretiveness of his wife's family.

'I don't like the sound of it,' said Tessa. 'I thought there was something odd going on when Fiona asked me to look after her fur coat.'

'Is there anything for lunch?' asked George.

'There's a home-made chicken stew in the freezer.'

'Is that still all right? It's dated 1981.'

'I spent hours on that stew,' said Tessa, aggrieved that such rare forays into domesticity were not appreciated.

By the time that Tessa arrived at the Samson house, two heavily built men who answered to Bret were rolling up the overalls they had worn to probe between the floorboards and investigate every inch of the dusty attic. Bret Rensselaer was standing before the fireplace wearing a black trenchcoat. He finished the coffee he was drinking.

He'd recently seen Tessa at Whitelands, and without preliminaries said, 'Mrs Samson has taken a trip to the East.' He put his cup on the mantelshelf. 'For the time being the children need someone to reassure them . . . The nanny seems to be taking it very calmly but your presence could make all the difference.' Bret had insisted that Fiona engage a reliable girl who could survive a proper security vetting. The present nanny was the daughter of a police inspector. Now and again Fiona had complained that she was not a very good nanny but now Bret's caution was paying off.

'Of course,' said Tessa. 'I'll do anything I can.'

'We're very much in the dark at present,' Bret told her, 'but whatever the truth of it there will be no official comment. If you get any calls from the Press, or any other kind of oddball, say you are the housekeeper, take their number and call my office.' He didn't tell Tessa that every call to this phone was being monitored and two armed men were watching the house to make sure that Moscow didn't try to kidnap the children.

One of the children – Billy – came from the kitchen where Nanny was frying eggs and sausages for lunch. 'Hello, Auntie Tess. Mummy is on holiday.'

'Yes, isn't that fun?' said Tessa, leaning down to kiss him. 'We are going to have a wonderful time too.'

Billy stood there looking at Bret for a moment and then summoned up the courage to say, 'Can I look at your gun?'

'What's that?' said Bret, uncharacteristically flustered.

'Nanny says you have a gun in your pocket. She says that's why you won't take your raincoat off.'

Bret wet his lips nervously, but long before he could think of any reply, seven-year-old Sally appeared and grabbed Billy by the arm. 'Nanny says you are to come to the kitchen and have your lunch.'

'Come along children,' said Tessa. 'We'll all have lunch together. Then I'll take you somewhere lovely for tea.' She smiled at Bret and Bret nodded his approval and appreciation.

'I'll slip away soon,' said Bret. He'd heard somewhere that Tessa Kosinski had been using hard drugs, but she seemed very normal today, thank heavens.

In the dining room, Nanny was dishing up the food. She had set the big polished table for four, as if guessing that Tessa would eat with them.

After the two technicians had packed away their detection apparatus and left, Bret took a quick look round on his own account. Upstairs on Fiona's side of the double bed a nightdress was folded neatly and placed on the pillow ready for her. On the bedside table he saw a book from the Department's library. He picked it up and looked at it: a coloured postcard – advertising a 'hair and beauty salon' off Sloane Street – was being used as a bookmark. He stood there for a moment relishing the intimacy of being in her bedroom. From a security point of view there was nothing to worry him anywhere. The Samsons had worked for the Department a long time: they were careful people.

As he let himself out of the front door, Bret heard Billy insisting, 'Well, I'll bet he's shot lots of people.'

Bernard Samson had been arrested in a Biergarten near Müggelheimer Damm. It was a forest that stretched down to the water of the Müggelsee. A thousand or so inebriated men celebrating Himmelfahrt – Ascension Day – had provided the congestion and confusion in which Bernard, and his closest friend Werner Wolkmann, had helped two elderly refugees to escape westwards. It was not a simple act of philanthropy: one of the escapees was an agent of the Department.

Werner and the others had got away when Bernard created a diversion. It was a brave thing to do but Bernard had had ample time to regret his rash gesture. They had locked him in an office room on the top floor of the State Security Ministry's huge office block on Frankfurter Allee.

This office was not like the cells in the basement – from which some prisoners never emerged – but its heavy door and barred window, plus the difficulty of moving from floor to floor in a building where every corridor was surveyed by both cameras and armed guards, was enough to hold anyone but a maniac.

Bernard had been interrogated by an amiable KGB officer named Erich Stinnes. He spoke the same sort of Berlin German that Bernard had grown up with, and in many things the two men saw eye to eye. 'Who gets the promotions and the big wages – desk-bound Party bastards,' said Stinnes bitterly. 'How lucky you are not having the Party system working against you all the time.'

'We have got it,' said Bernard. 'It's called Eton and Oxbridge.'

'What kind of workers' state is that?' said Stinnes.

'Are you recording this conversation?' asked Bernard.

'So they can put me in prison with you? Do you think I'm crazy?'

It was the sort of soft treatment that was usually followed up by browbeating from a ferocious tough guy partner, but Stinnes was waiting for a 'KGB Colonel from Moscow', who turned out to be Fiona Samson from London.

By that time Bernard Samson had begun to suspect what was about to happen. Some of the clues that Bret Rensselaer had so artfully supplied to the other side had become evident to the ever more worried Bernard.

The desperate realization that his wife was a KGB Colonel was a betrayal of such magnitude that Bernard felt physically ill. But the effect upon him – and the agony of it – was not greater than many men have suffered when discovering that their wife has been unfaithful to them with another man. For each individual there is a threshold beyond which pain does not increase.

For Fiona the pain was made worse by the guilt of inflicting it upon a man who loved her. She was very tired – and the journey had left her with a splitting headache – that morning when they brought Bernard in to face her. It was a test – perhaps the toughest one she would face – of her ability, her conviction and her resolution to pursue her role even in the face of Bernard's contempt and hatred.

Brought in by a guard he was dirty and unshaven. His eyes stared at her in a way she had never seen before. It was a horrible hateful exchange but she played her part determined that Bernard would see no glimmer of hope. Only his despair would protect her.

There was a tray with coffee pot and cups on the desk but Bernard didn't want any. 'Is there anything to drink in this office?' he demanded.

She found a bottle of vodka and gave it to him. He poured it into a cup and drank a large measure in one gulp. Poor Bernard: she suddenly became afraid that this would be the beginning of a long drunken bout. 'You should cut down on the drinking,' she said.

'You don't make it easy to do,' he said. He smiled grimly and poured more for himself.

'The D-G will send for you, of course,' she said more calmly than she felt. 'You can tell him that the official policy at this end will be one of no publicity about my defection. I imagine that will suit him all right, after all the scandals the service has suffered in the past year.'

'I'll tell him.'

She watched him: he'd gone green. 'You never could handle spirits on an empty stomach,' said Fiona. 'Are you all right? Do you need a doctor?'

'It's you I'm sick of,' he said.

It was as much as she could bear. She pressed the floor button and the guard came to take her husband away. Against her training, and her better judgement, she blurted out, 'Goodbye then, darling. Do I get one final kiss?'

But Bernard thought she was gloating. 'No,' he said and turned away.

As soon as Bernard had been taken through Check-point Charlie and released, Fiona pleaded tiredness and went back to the hotel suite they had provided as temporary accommodation. She took a long hot bath, two sleeping pills and went to bed. She slept the clock round. When she finally awoke there was a moment in which she believed that it was all a terrible dream, that she was at home in London with no complications to her life. She pulled the bedclothes over her head and stayed there unmoving while she slowly came to terms with the bizarre world in which she found herself.

After that terrible encounter with her husband, Fiona's arrival and installation in East Berlin was more endurable. The debriefing seemed to go on forever, but Bret Rensselaer had thought of just about everything and her prepared answers seemed to satisfy the men who asked the questions.

The KGB personnel chief had gone to a lot of trouble to make her as comfortable as possible, and the minuscule apartment with its hard bed and outdated kitchen had to be compared with the crowded rooms and shared kitchens and bathrooms that were a normal part of living in the capital of the DDR.

Her office in the KGB/Stasi operational command building was light, and it had a new sheepskin rug and a pinewood desk, imported from Finland. These were considered status symbols. More important, they'd assigned to her a fifty-year-old male secretary named Hubert Renn, who spoke fluent Russian, some French, a little English and could take shorthand. Renn was a hard-line communist of a kind which only Berlin produced, and which was now almost extinct. He was the son of a stone mason, and together with his fifteen brothers and sisters had grown up in a dark three-room tenement in a cobbled alley in Wedding. During the nineteen twenties *das rote Wedding* was so solidly communist that the block was run on communal lines by appointed Party officials. Renn's mother had been a member of the ISK –*Internationaler Sozialistischer Kampfbund* – a political sect so strict that its members rejected alcohol, tobacco and meat. She left the ISK upon marriage, since only full-time workers were permitted membership.

Short, agile, undernourished and eternally combative in spirit, Renn was also efficient. It was typical of his frugality and practicality that when he turned back the lapel of his jacket he revealed a selection of pins, safety-pins and even a needle.

When Fiona first came face to face with her newly appointed secretary she thought that they'd met before. This mistaken familiarity came from her memories of people depicted in old photos of Berlin streets. Despite this feeling she was to discover that Renn was like no other person she'd ever met. With his thick neck, truculent ruddy face, neglected teeth and the short hair that responded to neither brush nor comb, here was a character straight out of Brecht.

Little Hubert Renn had been exposed to Leninism and Marxism while in the dented tin bath that doubled as a cradle. Essentially militant, the ISK rejected Marx's theory about the inevitable collapse of capitalism. The necessity of violent struggle was something he had heard his mother and father endlessly debating. After such an upbringing no one could teach Renn anything about the phraseology of left-wing politics. Even Pavel Moskvin, a Moscow-backed bully with whom Fiona had that morning crossed swords, could not best him in political argument. But Renn didn't mince words about 'the German road to socialism' or spend much time discussing why, at the vital Parteitag in April 1946, the party's declared aspirations had been based upon Marx and Engels and not Lenin and Stalin. Renn – who had been present at that historic congress – preferred to ask, somewhat archly, why it had taken place in the Admiralspalast theatre, noted otherwise for 'top comedy routines'.

My father was an anarchist, he told Fiona once when they were discussing some of the heresies, and that was the key to Renn's character, for Renn too was an anarchist in his soul. Fiona wondered if he realized it; perhaps he simply didn't give a damn any more. Some who'd waited too long for the millennium became like that. Renn's description of Pavel Moskvin – a 'Moscow-backed bully' – was freely offered to Fiona that morning before she'd met the man. And Renn was just as ready to be outspoken about everyone else in the building.

For the first couple of weeks Fiona had suspected that this outlandish old fellow had been put into her office as some sort of agent provocateur, or because no one else in the building would put up with such an oddball, but it didn't take her long to understand that in the DDR the bureaucratic process didn't work like that. It wasn't so easy, for even the most senior staff, to arrange to get the secretary that they wanted, and old Renn would not be an agent provocateur easy to run. The truth was that staff were assigned according to a rota in the personnel office. Her grade was eligible for a clerk of Renn's seniority and his previous boss had retired the week before she arrived.

Fiona and her secretary had spent all of Wednesday in a small conference centre in Köpenick Altstadt, in the wooded outskirts of Berlin. She had witnessed lengthy and sometimes acrimonious exchanges between her colleagues. There had been senior security men from Poland, Czechoslovakia and Hungary meeting to discuss the still somewhat muddled and disorganized political reform groups, and religious groups, in the East Bloc. Agreeing upon a concerted policy of dealing with them was not so easy. Fiona was pleased at the material she was gathering. It was exactly the sort of intelligence that Bret Rensselaer was so keen on, and the anxiety the communist security men had revealed at this meeting in every way supported Bret's projections. When contact was eventually established with London she would have a policy formulated.

She was going through the meeting in her mind while they waited for the car that would take them back to the Mitte. The others had been collected by a bus from the transport pool but Fiona was entitled to her own car. Cars, more than any other perquisite or privilege, were a sign of status, and establishing status was all-important in the DDR. So they waited.

Fiona walked down to the river, admiring the cobbled streets and the crooked old buildings. Surrounded with trees, Köpenick's church and Rathaus huddled upon a tiny island at a place where the River Spree divided. On the adjacent island – *Schlossinsel* –there was a richly decorated seventeenth-century palace. In its magnificent *Wappensaal* Frederick the Great had stood trial for desertion. From where they were standing it was possible to raise a loud cheer for the dilatory rate at which East Berlin was being rebuilt. From this view it was easy to visualize Köpenick on the day that renowned bogus captain marched in to discover how devoutly the Germans revere a military uniform, no matter who wears it.

She had hoped that the fresh air would help rid her of her headache: she'd been having too many of these racking headaches lately. It was stress, of course, but that didn't make the pain any easier to endure.

'Herr Renn,' said Fiona: she never called him by his first name.

Renn had been looking at the traffic crossing the bridge. Soon the East would be clogged with cars just as the West already was. He looked at her. 'Did I forget something, Frau Direktor?'

'No. You never forget anything. You are the most efficient clerk in the building.'

He nodded. What she said was right and he acknowledged the truth of it.

'Do you trust me, Herr Renn?' It was a deliberate way of shocking him.

'I don't understand, Frau Direktor.' He glanced round but there was no one else standing along the riverfront: just workers and shoppers going home.

'I never get the minutes of the morning meetings until late in the afternoon of the following day. Is there a reason for that?'

'Everyone receives the minutes by the same delivery.' He gave a sly smile. 'We are slow; that is the only reason.' A large air-conditioned bus came crawling over the bridge. Pale Japanese faces pressed against its grey smoked glass. From inside it came the shrill commentary of the tour guide of which only the words 'Hauptmanns von Köpenick' could be easily distinguished. The bus moved slowly on and was lost behind the trees. 'They never go and see the Schloss or the Art Museum,' said Renn sadly. 'They just want to see the town hall. The tour guide will tell them about the bootmaker who bought an army captain's uniform from a pawn shop, assumed command of some off-duty grenadiers and arrested the mayor and the city treasurer. Then they will all laugh and say what fools we Germans are.'

'Yes,' said Fiona. Despite the Schloss and the dark green woodland and the clear blue lakes and the rivers, the only thing anyone ever remembered about Köpenick was its captain.

'The sad thing is,' said Renn, 'that poor old Wilhelm Voigt, the bootmaker, didn't want the city funds; he wanted a residence permit, and Köpenick had no department authorized to issue one. He wasn't a Berliner, you see, and his escapade was a fiasco.'

'I am not a Berliner, nor even a German by birth . . .' She did not finish.

'But you speak the most beautiful German,' said Renn, interrupting her. 'Everyone remarks upon it: wonderful Hochdeutsch. When I hear it, I feel selfconscious about my miserable accent.' He looked at her. 'Do you have a headache?'

She shook her head. 'Do you not sometimes wonder if I am a class enemy, Herr Renn?'

He pursed his lips. 'Vladimir Ilyich Lenin was born into a bourgeois family,' said Renn in what was a typically ambivalent reply.

'Leaving the birth of Comrade Lenin aside for the moment,' said

Fiona. 'If there was an attempt to have me removed from this job, what would be your attitude?'

His already contorted face became agitated as he wet his lips and frowned to indicate deep thought. 'I would have to consider the facts,' he said finally.

'Consider the facts?'

'I have a wife and family,' said Renn. 'It is them that I have to consider.' He turned to see the river, slow and unctuous now; once it had been fast, clear and fresh. Not so long ago anglers had landed big fish here, but there was no sign of any now. He stared down into the water and hoped the Frau Direktor would be satisfied.

'Are you saying that you would throw me to the wolves?' said Fiona.

'Wolves? No!' He turned to her. 'I am not a thrower, Frau Direktor. I am one of the people who are thrown.' The church clock struck six. His working day was over and done. He opened his overcoat in order to reach into his back pocket for a flask. 'About this time I sometimes take a small glass of schnapps . . . If the Frau Direktor would permit.'

'Go ahead,' said Fiona. She was surprised. She didn't know that the old man was such a dedicated drinker but it explained a lot of things.

He unscrewed the top to use it as a cup, and poured a sizeable measure. He offered it to her. 'Would the Frau Direktor . . . ?'

'No, thank you, Herr Renn.'

He brought it up towards his mouth carefully, so as not to spill it, bending his head to meet it. He drank half of it in one gulp, looked at her as it warmed his veins, and said, 'I'm too old to get into vendettas.' A pause. 'But that doesn't mean I have no guts for it.' A street-car went past, its wheels screaming protest on the rails as it turned the corner. 'Is the Frau Direktor quite sure . . . ?'

'Quite sure, thank you, Herr Renn.'

He held the drink and stared across the river as if she wasn't there, and when he spoke it was as if he was talking to himself. 'Most of the people on our floor are Germans, time-serving officials like me. None of them are looking for a battle: they are waiting for their pension. The eight "friends" are another matter.' He drank the rest of the schnapps from the metal cup.

Fiona nodded. Since 1945 Russians were always called 'friends', even when some German war veteran found himself recounting the way in which such 'friends' had jumped into his trench and bayoneted his comrades. 'Perhaps I will have a drink,' said Fiona.

Renn wiped the rim of the cup with his fingers and poured one for

596

her. 'Six of those friends are in other departments, and would not be promoted whatever happened to you.'

Fiona took a tiny sip of schnapps. It was damned strong stuff: she nearly choked on it. No wonder the old man had a red-veined face. 'I see what you mean,' she said. It left the two Russians, both German specialists: Pavel Moskvin and the one who affected the operating name of Stinnes (as Lenin and Stalin had assumed theirs). These were the two men she had clashed with during the conference that afternoon. Tough professionals who had let her know that working for a woman was not a relationship to which they would gladly accede. The argument had come about because of a proposed operational journey to Mexico City. She suspected that the whole thing was chosen simply as a way of showing her how formidable their combined strengths could be against her.

Renn said, 'The big man – Moskvin – is the dangerous one. He has considerable influence within the Party machine. At present he is in disgrace with Moscow – some black-market scandal which was never made public – and such men will go to absurd lengths to prove their worth. He is emotional and violent; and well-adjusted people fall victim to action that is sudden and unpremeditated. The other man – Erich Stinnes – with his convincing Berlin German, complete with all the slang and expletives, is an intellectual: icy cold and calculating. He will always think in the long term. For someone as clever as you, he will prove easier to deal with.'

'I hope so,' said Fiona.

'We must drive a wedge between them,' said Renn.

'How?'

'We will find a way. Moskvin is a skilful administrator but Stinnes has been a field agent. Field agents never really settle down to the self-discipline and cooperation that our work demands.'

'That's true,' said Fiona, and for a moment thought of her husband and his endless difficulties at the London office.

'Don't allow your authority to be undermined. Moscow has put you here because they want to see changes. If there is resistance, Moscow will support change and whoever is making the changes. Therefore you must be sure you are the one making the changes.'

'You are something of a philosopher, Herr Renn.'

'No, Frau Direktor, I am an apparatchik.'

'Whatever you are, I am grateful to you, Herr Renn.' She looked in her handbag, found some aspirins and swallowed two of them without water.

'It is nothing,' said the old man as he watched her gulp the pills, although of course they both knew he'd stuck his neck out. Even more important, he'd indicated to her that under other circumstances he'd probably yield more. Fiona wondered whether he was already calculating what she could do for him in return. She dismissed the idea; better to wait and see. Meanwhile he might prove an invaluable ally.

'To you, perhaps, but a friendly word goes a long way in a new job.'

Renn, who'd been watching the bridge, touched his hat as if in salutation but in fact he eased the hat because the band was too tight. 'From each according to ability; to each according to need,' quoted the old man, stuffing the flask back into his pocket. 'And here comes our Volvo.' Not car, she noted, but Volvo. He was proud that she rated an imported car. He smiled at her.

In a year or so she would scuttle off back to the West and Hubert Renn would be left to face the music: Stasi interrogations were not gentle. They would be bound to suspect that he was in league with her. She hated the thought of what she was doing to him. It made her feel like a Judas, but that of course is exactly what she was. Bret had warned her that these conflicting loyalties were stressful but that didn't make them any easier to bear.

When she got home, to one of the coveted apartments in the wedding cake blocks that line Frankfurter Allee, she sat down and thought about the conversation for a long time. Finally she began to understand something of Renn's motivation. Just as the Russians could not fathom the way in which some Europeans could be staunch capitalists but rabidly anti-American, Fiona had not understood the deeply felt anti-Russian feelings that were a part of Hubert Renn's psyche. Renn, she was later to discover, had seen his mother raped by Russian soldiers and his father beaten unconscious during those memorable days of 1945 when the commander's Order of the Day told the Red Army 'Berlin is Yours'. And later she was to hear Hubert Renn refer to his Russian 'friends' by the archaic and less friendly word 'Panje'.

She washed a lettuce and cut thin slices from a Bockwurst. It was the fresh fruit she missed so much: she still couldn't understand why such things were so scarce. She had found a privately owned baker near the office and the bread was good. She'd have to be careful not to put on weight – everything plentiful was fattening.

It was an austere little room well suited to reflection and work. The walls were painted light grey and there were only three pictures: an engraving of a Roman emperor, a sepia photo of fashionable ladies circa 1910 and a coloured print of Kirchner's *Pariser Platz*. The frames, their

598

neglected condition, as well as the subject matter, suggested that they had been selected at random from some government storage depot. She was grateful for that human touch just the same. Her bedroom was no more than an alcove with a hinged screen. The old tubular-framed bed was painted cream and reminiscent of the one she'd slept in at her boarding school. There were many aspects of life in the DDR – from the endless petty restrictions to the dull diet – that reminded her of boarding school. But she told herself over and over that she had survived boarding school and so she would survive this.

When she went to bed that night she was unable to sleep. She hadn't had one night of sound natural sleep since coming over here. That terrible encounter with Bernard had been a ghastly way to start her new life. Now every night she found herself thinking about him and the children. She found herself asking why she'd been born with a lack of the true maternal urge. Why had she never delighted in the babies and wanted to hug them night and day as so many mothers do? And was she now being acutely tortured by their absence because of the way she had squandered those early years with them? She would have given anything for a chance to go back and see them as babies again, to cuddle them and feed them and read to them and play with them the nonsense games that Bernard's mother was so good at.

Sometimes, during the daytime, the chronic ache of being separated from her family was slightly subdued as she tried to cope with the overwhelming demands made upon her. The intellectual demands – the lies and false loyalties – she could cope with, but she hadn't realized how vulnerable she would be to the emotional stress. She remembered some little joke that Bret had made about women adapting to a double life more easily than a man. Every woman, he said, was expected to be a hooker or matron, companion, mother, servant or friend at a moment's notice. Being two people was a simple task for any woman. It was typical Rensselaer bullshit. She switched on the light and reached for the sleeping tablets. In fact she knew that she would never return to being that person she'd been such a short time ago. She had already been stretched beyond the stage of return.

13

Whitelands, England. June 1983.

'No, Dicky, I can hear you perfectly,' said Bret Rensselaer as he pressed the phone to his ear and shrugged at Silas Gaunt, who was standing opposite him with the extension earpiece. Dicky Cruyer, German Stations Controller, was phoning from Mexico City and the connection was not good. 'You've made it all perfectly clear. I can't see any point in going through it again. Yes, I'll talk to the Director-General and tell him what you said. Yes. Yes. Good to talk to *you*, Dicky. I'll see what I can do. Goodbye. Goodbye.' He replaced the handset and sighed deeply.

Silas Gaunt put the earpiece in the slot and said, 'Dicky Cruyer tracked you down.'

'Yes, he did,' said Bret Rensselaer, although there had been little difficulty about it. The Director-General had told Bret to visit Silas and 'put him in the picture'. Bret had left the Whitelands telephone number as his contact, and Mrs Porter – Gaunt's housekeeper – had put the call from Mexico through to the farm manager's office.

Having thanked the greenhouse boy who'd run to get them, Silas, wearing an old anorak, muddy boots and corduroy trousers tied with string at the ankles, led the way – ducking under the low door – out to the cobbled yard. Bret was being shown round the farm.

'I don't encourage guns any more,' said Silas. 'Too damned hearty. Those gigantic early breakfasts and mud all through the house. It became too much for Mrs Porter and to tell you the truth, too much for me too. Anglers are not so much trouble: quieter, and they're gone all day with a packet of cheese sandwiches.'

Silas swung open the yard gate and fastened it again after Bret. The fields stretched away into the distance. The harvest would be gathered early. The field behind the barn would be the first one cut and flocks of sparrows, warned by the sound of the nearby machinery that the banquet would not be there forever, were having a feed that made their flight uncertain as they swooped and fluttered amongst the pale ears.

It was a lovely day: silky cirrus torn and trailed carelessly across the deep blue sky. The sun was as high as it could get, and, like a ball thrown into the air, it paused and the world stood still, waiting for the afternoon to begin.

As they walked along they kept close to the hedge so that Silas could be sure it had been properly trimmed and weeded. He grabbed ears of unripe wheat, and with the careless insolence of the nomad, crushed them in his hand, scattering chaff, husk and seed through his splayed fingers. Bret, who had no interest in farms or farming, plodded awkwardly behind in the rubber boots that Silas had found for him, with a stained old windbreaker to protect his elegant dark blue suit. They went through a door set in the tall walls that surrounded the kitchen garden. It was a wonderful wall, light and dark bricks making big diamond patterns that were just visible under the espaliered fruit trees.

'I am not convinced that it was a wise move to send both Dicky Cruyer and Bernard Samson to Mexico City,' said Bret, to resume the conversation. 'It leaves us somewhat depleted, and those two seem to fight all the time.'

Silas pointed to various vegetables and said he was going to start a little rose garden next year and reduce the ground given to swedes, turnips and beetroots. Then he said, 'How is Bernard taking it?'

'His wife's defection? Not too well. I was thinking of making him take a physical, but in his present paranoid state he'd resent it. I guess he'll pull out of it. Meanwhile, I'll keep an eye on him.'

'I have no experience as an agent in the field,' said Silas. 'Neither have you. I can think of very few people in your building who know what's involved. In that respect, we are like First World War generals, sitting back in our château and sipping our brandy, and subjecting the troops to nastiness that we don't comprehend.'

Bret, not knowing exactly what was coming, and never ready to state his views without time to think, made a sound that indicated measured agreement.

'But I have seen a lot of them,' said Silas, 'and I know something of what makes such fellows tick. Fiona Samson will not wind down slowly like a neglected clock. She'll keep going at full power until she has nothing more to give. Then, like a light bulb, she'll glow extra bright before going out.'

It sounded too melodramatic to Bret. He looked at Silas wondering if this same little speech, with other names, had been used many times before, like next-of-kin letters when the unthinkable happened. He couldn't decide. He nodded. 'When the question of her going over there was first discussed, I was in favour of taking the husband into our confidence.'

601

'I know you were. But his ignorance has proved a great asset to us, and to his wife. It's given her a good start. Now it's up to her.' Silas looked around him in a proprietorial manner and crushed a clod of earth with the toe of his heavy boot. It was good fertile soil, dark and rich with leafmould.

Bret undid his borrowed windcheater and fingered a bundle of computer printout to be sure he hadn't dropped it during his walk.

It was hot in the garden, everything silent and still, protected by the high garden walls. This was the culmination of the gardener's year. There was billowing greenery everywhere but all too soon the summer would be over; the leaves withered; the earth cold and hard. 'Look at these maincrop carrots,' said Silas. He bent over to grab the feathery leaves. For a moment he seemed on the point of uprooting one but then he changed his mind and let go. 'Carrots are tricky,' said Silas. 'They grow to maturity and you have to decide whether to lift them and store them or leave them in the earth.'

Bret nodded.

'Leave them in the earth and you get a sweeter-tasting carrot but if there is a really severe frost, you lose them.' He found a carrot and pulled it up. It was small and thin but of a beautiful colour. 'On the other hand if you lift them, you can be sure that they haven't been got at by the worms and slugs. See what I mean, Bret?'

'So how do you decide when to pull them?'

'I consult,' said Silas. 'I talk to the experts.'

Bret decided to ignore the wider implications of Silas's agricultural nostrums and return to the subject of Bernard Samson. 'But once that decision was taken, it might have been wiser to move Bernard Samson out of Operations. He's too damned curious about what exactly happened.'

'That's natural enough,' said Silas.

'He pries and asks questions. On that account, and a few others too, Samson was not the man to send to talk to a potential KGB defector in Mexico City, or anywhere else.'

'Why?' asked Silas sardonically. 'Because he hasn't been to University?'

'This KGB fellow: Stinnes – whatever his motives or intentions – will be expecting an Oxbridge man. Sending a blue-collar type like Samson will make him think he doesn't rate.'

'You're a dedicated Anglophile, Bret. No disrespect, I'm delighted that you should be. But it sometimes leads you into an exaggerated regard for our old British institutions.'

Bret stiffened. 'I have always supported Samson, even when he was at his most intractable. But Oxford and Cambridge attract the most competitive students, and will always be the Department's finest source of recruits. I'd hate to see the day come when that policy changed.'

Silas ran his hand lovingly over the outdoor tomatoes. One of them, full size and deep red, he picked and weighed in his hand. 'Oxford and Cambridge provide an excellent opportunity to learn, although not better than any well-motivated student can find in a first-class library. But an Oxbridge education can make graduates feel that they are members of some privileged élite, destined to lead and make decisions that will be inflicted upon lesser beings. Such élitism must of necessity be based upon expectations that are often unfulfilled. Thus Oxbridge has not only provided Britain with its most notable politicians and civil servants but its most embittered traitors too.' Silas smiled sadly, as if the traitors had played a long-forgiven and half-forgotten prank upon him.

'Elite?' said Bret. 'You'd search a long way to find someone more arrogant than Bernard Samson.'

'Bernard's arrogance comes from something inside him: some vitality, force and a seemingly inexhaustible fund of courage. Our great universities will never be able to furnish inner strength, no one can. What teachers provide is always superimposed upon the person that already exists. Education is a carapace, a cloak laid upon the soul: a protection, a coloration or something to hide inside.'

To get the conversation back on to a more practical plane Bret said, 'And Samson drinks too much.'

'That's rather judgemental,' said Silas. 'Few of us would be absolved from that one, truth be told.' Silas took a clasp-knife and cut the tomato in half to study it before biting a piece out of it.

'You're right, of course,' said Bret deferentially, and added, 'Remember I recommended Samson for the German Desk.'

Silas swallowed the piece of tomato but some of the juice dribbled down his chin. He wiped his mouth with the back of his hand and said, 'Indeed you did. But you didn't do it with enough vigour and follow-through to get it for him.'

'I plead the Fifth, Silas.' Bret decided not to explain that his decision was deliberate and reasoned: it would take too long. 'But let's not argue. Samson and Cruyer are both in Mexico. We have a lot riding on this one; a careless move now could set us back severely.'

'Yes, we must move with great caution,' said Silas. 'We have the woman installed in the East and now we must hope that all continues to go well for her. No contact yet?' He offered the remaining half of tomato to Bret, but Bret shook his head. Silas threw the tomato on to the rubbish.

'No, Silas, no contact. I'm leaving her alone for as long as possible. It's not primarily an intelligence-gathering operation at this stage of the game. I think you and the D-G both agreed that it shouldn't be. We said that right at the start.'

'Yes, Bret, we did. She has enough problems, I'm sure.'

'For the time being, let her masters digest the material she's providing them with.' Bret had been moving restlessly, looking round to be sure that they were not observed or overheard. Now he fixed his eyes on Silas. 'But before too long we must provide the Soviets with some really solid affirmation of Mrs Samson's creed. It's going well but we must exploit and reinforce success.' These final words were spoken with fervour.

Silas looked blankly at Bret. The words Bret had emphasized were the sort of axiom to be found in the works of Sun-tzu, Vegetius, Napoleon or some wretch of that ilk. Silas did not believe that such teachings embodied truths of any relevance to the craft of espionage, but decided that this was not the right time to take that up with Bret.

Thinking that Silas might not have heard, Bret said it again. 'We must exploit and reinforce success.'

Silas looked at him and nodded. Despite that glacial personality there was a certain boyish enthusiasm in Bret, a quality not unusual in Americans of any class. Bret combined it with another American characteristic: the self-righteous passion of the crusader. Silas had always thought of him as warrior prince: hand-woven silk under the heavy armour, marching through the desert behind the True Cross. Austere and calculating, Bret would have made an invincible Richard the Lionheart but an equally convincing Saladin.

Silas said, 'I hope you're not thinking of anything costly, Bret. The other evening I calculated that the code and cipher changes and so on that the D-G ordered after Mrs Samson went over there must have cost the Department nearly a million sterling. Add in the costs that we don't shoulder, I'd say there was a worldwide bill for three million. And that's without the incalculable loss of face we suffered at losing her.'

'I'm watching the bottom line, Silas.'

'Good. And what did you conclude about this fellow in Mexico City, Bret? Animal, vegetable or mineral?' Silas bent over and fingered the spinach like a child dabbling a hand in the water.

'That's what I want to talk about. He's real enough; a forty-year-old

KGB major of considerable experience.' Bret put on the speed-cop style glasses that he used when reading, and, reaching inside the stained waterproof that Silas had loaned him, he produced a concertina of computer printout. 'No need to tell you that our records don't normally extend down to KGB majors, but this fellow has a high profile so we know something of his background.' Bret looked down and read from the paperwork. 'Sadoff. Uses the name Stinnes. Born 1943. Regular officer as father. Raised in Berlin. Assigned to KGB, Section 44, the Religious Affairs Bureau. With Security Police in Cuba . . .'

'For God's sake, Bret. I can read all that piffle for myself. I'm asking you who he is.'

'And whether he really wants to come over to us. Yes, of course you're asking that, but it's too early yet.' He passed the computer printout to Silas, who held it without looking at it.

'What does Cruyer say about him?'

'I'm not sure that Cruyer has actually seen him yet.'

'Then what the devil are those two idiots doing out there?'

'You'll be pleased to hear that it was Samson who saw Stinnes.'

'And?'

'This one is worth having, Silas. We could get a lot out of him if he's properly handled. But we must go very slowly. For safety's sake we must assume he is approaching us under orders from Moscow.'

Silas sniffed and handed the printout back unread. A corpulent pirate, scruffy in that self-assured manner that is often the style of such establishment figures, he shuffled along the line of tall stakes up which the broad beans had grown. Long since shunned by the kitchen there were, amongst the leaves, a few beans that had grown huge and pale. He plucked one and broke the pod open to get the seeds inside. He ate one. When he turned round to Bret he said, 'So: two possibilities. Either he will go back to Moscow and tell them what he discovered, or he is genuine and will do as we say.'

'Yes, Silas.'

'Then why don't we play the same game? Let's welcome the fellow. Give him money and show him our secrets. What?'

'I'm not sure I follow you, Silas.'

'Abduct the bastard. Moscow screams in anger. We offer Stinnes a chance to go back and work for us. He goes back there.'

'And they execute him,' said Bret.

'Not if we abduct him. He is blameless.'

'Moscow might not see it that way.'

'Don't break my heart; this is a little KGB shit.'

'I suppose so, yes.'

'Romance him, turn him round, and send him back to Moscow. Who cares if he betrays us, or betrays them . . . You don't see it?'

'I'm not sure I do,' said Bret.

'Damn it, Bret. He finds us in total disarray after the loss of Mrs Samson. We're distraught. We give him a briefing designed to limit the damage we've suffered from her defection. He goes back believing that. Who cares which side he thinks he's working for? Even if they execute him, they'll squeeze him first. Come to think of it, that would suit us best.'

'It's brilliant, Silas.'

'Well, don't sound so bloody woeful.'

'It will require a lot of preparation.' Bret was beginning to discover that a secret operation shared only between himself, the Director and Silas Gaunt meant that he himself did virtually all the hard work. 'It will be a very time-consuming and difficult job.'

'Look at it as a wonderful opportunity,' said Silas. 'The one thing we must be sure about is that this KGB fellow doesn't cotton on to Sinker. I don't want him to even get a hint that our strategy is now directed towards the economy.'

'Is that what it's directed at?'

'Don't be bitter, Bret. You've got just about everything you've asked for. We can't go one hundred per cent manpower and economy: the military and political considerations are still valid.'

'It's a matter of definition, Silas. Rearmament can be described in economic terms or political ones without bending the figures.'

Silas took another bean from its pod and examined it. 'We'll huff and we'll puff and we'll blow their Wall down.' He offered Bret a bean. Bret didn't want one.

'I'm not the big bad wolf,' said Bret.

14

Fiona Samson was surprised when her secretary, Hubert Renn, invited her to his birthday party and she spent an hour or so thinking about it. She knew that Germans liked to celebrate birthdays, but now that she had got to know him better she had found him to be a pugnaciously independent personality, so set in his ways that it was hard to imagine him going to the trouble of arranging a birthday party, let alone one to which his superior was to be invited.

Fiona had come to terms with him but she knew that Renn did not easily adapt to taking orders from a young person or from a woman, let alone a young foreign woman. But Renn was German and he did not make his feelings evident in any way that would affect his work.

And there was the problem of what present to give him, and what to wear. The first was quickly solved by a visit to the *valuta* shop where Fiona, as a privilege that went with her job, was permitted to spend a proportion of her salary on goods of Western manufacture. She bought a Black and Decker electric drill, always one of the most sought-after imports in a country where repairs and construction were constant problems. She wrapped it carefully and added a fancy bow.

What to wear was not so easily decided. She wondered what sort of event it was to be. Would it be a small informal dinner, or a big family gathering, or a smart affair with dancing to live music? She rummaged through the clothes she'd brought with her – all of them selected for banality of design and sombre colours – and decided upon a short afternoon dress she'd bought long ago at Liberty in Regent Street: narrow stripes of black and crimson with pleated skirt and high buttoned collar. She had bought it for a holiday with Bernard and the children. They had stayed at a farm in western Scotland and it had rained almost every day. She had brought the dress home again still unworn. She looked at herself in the mirror and decided that, now she had at last discovered a reasonably good hairdresser, it would do.

The dinner party, for such it turned out to be, was given in a private room in an elaborate sports club complex near Grünau. Although she

607

could have asked for the use of a car, Fiona went on the S-Bahn to Grünau Station, and then caught a street-car.

Here in this attractive suburb southeast of the city, the River Spree has become the Dahme and there is extensive forest on both banks. The club's main entrance, around which the new premises had been built, dated from the 1936 Olympics. Along this 2,000 metres of swastika-bedecked Berlin river, thirty thousand spectators had seen the amazing triumphs of physically perfect German youth using radically new designs of lightweight sculls and shells. Hitler's Olympics were transmitted on the world's first public TV service and Leni Riefenstahl made her world-acclaimed film *Olympiad*. The golden successes resulting from selection, dedicated training and German technology – and the way in which the propaganda machine used them – provided the Third Reich with a political triumph. The 1936 Olympics afforded a glimpse of the Nazi war machine in mufti. It had been, in all its aspects, a taste of things to come.

Fiona was in the lobby looking at the Tenth Olympiad photos, and some of the old awards, displayed in a big glass case, when Hubert Renn saw her. She offered him her best wishes and he bowed. 'Are you interested in sport, Frau Direktor?'

'At college I was on the swimming team. And you, Herr Renn?'

'No. Apart from hockey I was never able to do very much. I was not tall enough.' Renn was dressed in a suit she hadn't seen before, with a red bow tie and matching kerchief in his top pocket. 'I am so glad you were able to honour us with your presence, Frau Direktor. It will be only a small gathering and it won't go on too late. We are simple people.'

The day of the celebration was not his saint's day, of course; Renn's father, a dedicated atheist, could never have sanctioned a baptism. But there were candles in abundance, for in Germany – where the pre-Christian heritage is evident in every old festival and custom – no revelry is complete without the flame of the candle.

It was a small gathering, held in the Gisela Mauemayer room, named in honour of Germany's 1936 world discus champion. Her portrait was painted on the wall, a beautiful sad-eyed girl with long blonde hair worn in a bun. The table was laid out with wines and water already to hand. At the head of the table a few small presents had been placed next to Hubert's plate. Renn's wife, Gretel, was wearing a wonderful dress. When Fiona admired it she admitted that it had belonged to her grandmother and she hadn't had a chance to wear it for over eight years. Gretel was a shy slim woman, aged about fifty, with greying hair that had obviously been specially tinted and waved for this evening.

The meal was excellent. Some hunter friend of the Renns always provided venison as a birthday gift. Marinated in wine, spices and herbs, it made a delicious pot roast at this time of the year when the Berlin evenings were becoming chilly.

It was a curious party, marked by a certain stiffness that was in no way accounted for by any shortcoming in Fiona's grasp of the language. Yet the birthday rituals seemed rehearsed, and even when the drink had been consumed, Fiona noticed no substantial relaxation amongst the guests. It was as if they were all on their best behaviour for her.

Among those seated round the table there was Renn's daughter Käthe, noticeably pregnant, and her dutiful husband who worked in one of the lignite-burning power stations that polluted the Berlin air. Hubert Renn's bearded brother Felix was a retired airline pilot, seventy years old and a veteran of Spain's civil war. There were also a man and his wife who worked as clerks in the same building as Fiona and Renn, and, seated next to Fiona, a cordial Englishwoman named Miranda. She was, like Fiona, in her middle thirties and spoke with the brisk accent affected by smart Londoners, and those who wish to be mistaken for them.

'It's an unusual name,' said Fiona. 'Is that a tedious thing to say?'

'I chose it. I was an actress before I married. It was my stage name. I discovered it when I was in *The Tempest* at school. I was a terrible little snob. It stuck.'

'It's a lovely name.'

'No one over here thinks it's very unusual, of course, and I've got used to it.'

'Were you an actress in England?'

'Yes. I was quite good. I should have kept to it but I was getting on for thirty years old and I'd never had a decent West End part. My agent had decided to retire. A man fell in love with me and I married him. You know how it happens.'

'And he was German?'

'Very German . . . young and sexy and masterful, just what I needed at the time, I suppose. He was on holiday in England and staying with people I knew.'

'And he brought you to Berlin?'

'I'd been a member of the party since I was eighteen so I couldn't yield to the capitalist lures of Hollywood, right? And my mister-right had friends at the Babelsberg film studios. Babelsberg, I thought, the

UFA studios; Josef von Sternberg, Emil Jannings, Greta Garbo, Marlene Dietrich. Wow! And this Wunderkind guaranteed that there would be plenty of acting work over here.'

'And was there?'

'I don't know, I promptly became pregnant, so after a few one-day jobs playing Englishwomen and American women for TV, I looked for other work. I did ghastly little jobs translating for various government departments: travel adverts and that sort of garbage. And then my husband died.'

'Oh, I'm sorry. What did your husband do?'

'He got fall-down drunk.'

'Oh,' said Fiona.

'Little Klaus was born. I managed. I had the apartment and there was a decent pension. I suppose the DDR is the best place to be if you have to find yourself a widow with a baby.'

'I suppose it is.'

'You're married?'

'I left my husband to come here,' said Fiona. It had become her standard reply to such questions but it still hurt her to say it. Into her mind there immediately came the picture of Bernard and the two children sitting round the table eating a frozen dinner the night she first met Harry Kennedy. How she yearned for them now.

'Yes, Hubert told me that you'd given up everything for your beliefs. That was a wonderful thing to do. Your perfume is heavenly. Sometimes I think good make-up and perfume are the only things I miss. What is it . . . if you don't mind me asking?'

'No, of course not. Arpège. I haven't graduated to any of the new ones. Was your husband related to the Renns?'

'Arpège, yes, of course it is. Hubert is the Godfather to my little Klaus.'

'I see.'

'Not really a Godfather, of course; this ersatz arrangement they have over here.'

'*Namengebung*,' said Fiona. It was the secular ceremony permitted by the communist regime.

'Your German is fantastic,' said Miranda. 'Fancy your knowing that. I wish my German was half as good. When I hear you gabbing away, I envy you.'

'Your German sounded excellent to me,' said Fiona.

'Yes, it's very fluent, but I don't know what I'm saying half the time.'

She laughed. 'I suppose that's how I got myself into trouble in the first place.'

It was then that Hubert's brother Felix stood up to propose a toast. The Sekt was poured, and the cake was cut. Cakes are to German-speaking people what soufflés, spaghetti and smoked salmon are to their European neighbours. Hubert Renn's birthday cake in no way challenged this doctrine. The beautifully decorated multi-layered cake was so big that even one thin slice proved too much for Fiona.

Feix, a tall bony old fellow with a closely trimmed beard, proved to be a good speaker and he kept the company amused for five minutes before toasting the Renns.

When the celebration ended they came outside to find a brilliant moon. A light wind moved the trees and there was no sound other than a distant plane. Felix Renn said it was the late flight heading out of Berlin for Warsaw.

Declining offers of a car ride, Fiona walked back to Grünau Station. She had discovered walking to be one of the compensations of her life here. A woman could walk in these empty streets without fear of being attacked or accosted, and even this urban neighbourhood, so near the centre of town, was green and rural.

Living alone in a strange town had not been good for Fiona. She kept telling herself that it provided her with a chance to collect her thoughts in a way she could never do before. In fact the loneliness had slowly given way to bouts of depression: black and morbid moods, not that state of low spirits that is called depression by those who have never known the real thing. Fiona had the black bouts of despair and self-disgust from which recovery comes slowly. And like most psychological illness her fears were rooted in actuality. It was crippling to be without Bernard and the children – and painful to think how much they must hate her. Only with great difficulty was she able to endure her miseries.

Work was the medicine she took. When she wearied of the work provided by her job, she read German history and improved her spoken and written German: she still got the cases wrong sometimes. She never thought about how long she might be here. Like a committed combat soldier she adjusted her mind to the idea of being dead. Fortunately Renn, and the others, had not known her in her normal frame of mind and assumed that this moody woman with her unexplained silences and flashes of bad temper was the person she had always been.

As she walked along under the trees, the moonlight bright enough to throw her shadow on the grass verge, she speculated about Renn's birthday party, and his choice of guests, and could not help wondering if there was to be another birthday party that would better reflect the relatives, friends and neighbours that he clearly had in abundance. Were the people present the ones closest to him and his wife after a lifetime spent here in the city? If not why not?

And if such an elegant little dinner – extravagant by the standards of life in the DDR – was a normal event in the life of the Renns, why had his wife Gretel not worn that dress for eight years?

What of the forthright Miranda? In this puzzling town, with all its half-truths and double-meanings, there was nothing more enigmatic than candour. She still hadn't worked it out by the time she reached Grünau. The grandiose nineteenth-century Stadtbahn station was bleak and neglected, a puddle of rain under the arch, cracked paving and its shiny brickwork, and enamel signs, stained with dribbles of rust. And yet the platforms were swept and tidy and the litter bins emptied. To Fiona a lot of the East sector of the city was like this; like the dilapidated mansion of some impoverished duchess who will not admit defeat. The other people waiting for the train were quietly spoken and respectably dressed. Even the mandatory drunk was sitting on a trolley humming softly to himself.

The train came in and the guard, in a smart uniform, watched the drunk stumble safely aboard before giving the go-ahead.

As the train rattled along, elevated above the city on its elaborate iron support, Fiona thought again about the guests. Felix, Hubert's eloquent brother: she wondered which side he'd fought for in the civil war in Spain. If for the communists how did he survive the Nazi years, and if for Franco how did he endure the ones following? And yet it was the presence of Miranda that puzzled Fiona most. She wondered why Hubert Renn had never mentioned that the mother of his 'Godchild' was a Londoner born and bred, and why he'd not told Fiona that another Englishwoman was to be with them tonight. Had it been the birthday party of some other person, none of these things might have merited comment, but Fiona knew Renn by now and she knew this birthday dinner was not the sort of function he enjoyed.

Fiona's curiosity would have been satisfied by the scene in the same Gisela Mauemayer room at ten-thirty the next morning. Miranda was there together with two Russians and a black girl. She had described the previous evening in great detail.

Fiona's bellicose colleague Pavel Moskvin was also there. He was about fifty years old and weighed over 200 pounds. He had the build of an American football player. His hair was closely cropped and his eyes set a little too close to the squashed nose that made his large head look as if it had been bowled along the ground until its protuberances broke off, and then stuck upon his shoulders without a neck.

Sitting calmly in a corner, occasionally reading from a book, there was Erich Stinnes, a wiry man with a pointed face and hair thinning enough to show his scalp. His metal-rim spectacles, of the most utilitarian design, brown corduroy suit and heavy boots made up an ensemble that well-paid communists sometimes found irresistible.

Opposite Stinnes sat a tall lively Jamaican woman in her late twenties. Her fake leopard-skin coat was thrown across a chair and she was dressed in a tight white sweater and red pants. She sat toying with a red apple, rolling it across the table from hand to hand. Miranda looked at the black girl: quite apart from her clothes and make-up, there was something about her manner that had immediately identified her as being from the West.

Staring at Miranda, Moskvin, restless with the contained anger which boiled continually within him, said, 'Tell me about her.' His voice was hoarse, like that of a man who shouts too much.

'I've told you,' said Miranda softly. She stood at the other end of the table. She refused to sit down and was determined not to be intimidated by him. She'd seen his type of Russian before; many of them.

'Tell me again, damn you.' He went and studied the painting of the discus thrower with unseeing eyes.

Miranda spoke to his back. 'Frau Samson is an inch or so taller than I am. She has longer legs.'

Without turning round he said, 'That doesn't matter.'

'You know nothing,' said Miranda, contemptuous now that she was on the firm ground of her own expertise. 'If I am to imitate her walk, it will make a difference.'

The black girl took a noisy bite out of the apple. Moskvin glared at her: she smiled. They all disliked him, Moskvin knew that. He'd grown up amongst such hostility; it was not something that had ever troubled him.

'We'll arrange it so that you won't have to imitate the walk,' said Moskvin, still looking at the black girl. Then he turned and fixed those eyes on Miranda. 'Can you do her voice?'

'Her voice is easy,' said Miranda.

The black girl took another bite of the apple. 'Keep quiet,' said Moskvin.

'I gotta eat, buddy,' said the black girl.

613

Moskvin went to the table and switched on the tape recorder. Fiona's voice came from it, saying, 'It's a lovely name.' (pause) 'Were you an actress in England?' (pause) 'And he brought you to Berlin?' (pause) 'Oh, I'm sorry.' (pause) 'What did your husband do?'

Moskvin switched off the machine. 'Now you,' he said.

Miranda hesitated only a moment, and then stiff and formal, and holding her hands together as if about to sing Lieder, she recited the same words: 'It's a lovely name.' She took a breath. 'Were you an actress in England?' She wet her lips and, completely relaxed now, she delivered the last three without pausing. 'And he brought you to Berlin? Oh, I'm sorry. What did your husband do?' Then she smiled. It was an impressive performance and she knew it. She'd always had this ability to mimic voices. Sometimes she found herself copying the voices of people she was speaking with, and it could cause annoyance.

'Good,' said Moskvin.

'Remarkable,' said Stinnes. The black girl clapped her hands very softly. Miranda still couldn't decide whether the girl was hostile to all of them or only to Moskvin.

'But will you be able to do it without the recording to prompt you?' said Moskvin.

'I'd need to see her again.'

'That will be arranged, and we'll have lots and lots of recordings for you.'

'The recordings are a help but I must see her speak too. I have to watch her mouth. So much depends upon the tongue if I am to make conversation. And I need to hear more of her vocabulary.'

'You will be told exactly what to say. There is no need for you to be sidetracked into any conversation other than the words we want spoken. It's simply a matter of making the voice sound natural, and imitating it accurately.'

'Good,' said Miranda.

'The element of surprise will be on your side,' said Moskvin. 'You will have spoken to the husband and to the sister before they recover from their amazement.'

'The phone is easy but . . .'

'I have solved the other problem,' said Moskvin. 'Her husband will be in a car, the driver's seat, and he'll be prevented from turning around. That will be Harmony's job and she's an expert, aren't you, Harmony?'

'You bet your ass I am, boss,' said Harmony, in a tone of self-mockery that Moskvin seemed not to register.

Still looking at Miranda, Moskvin said, 'You'll get into the back seat. You'll be close but he won't see you.'

'Good. I'll use the Arpège perfume she likes. He'll recognize the scent of it.'

'He'll smell you but he won't see you,' said Moskvin.

'I could never make myself look like her,' said Miranda. 'Just one glimpse of me and he'd . . .'

'I have thought of that too,' said Moskvin. 'No need to make you look anything like her. On the contrary we'll give you a black wig, dark glasses and heavy make-up. They will not be surprised that she would disguise herself to visit England. For them it will make better sense that way.'

'That's a load off my mind. I could never pass myself off as her. She's very beautiful.' She looked at the two Russians. 'In fact I like her.'

'We all do,' said Stinnes. 'We are doing this to help her.'

'I didn't know that,' said Miranda doubtfully.

'But she mustn't know,' added Stinnes.

'Under no circumstance must she guess,' said Moskvin, and he slammed his hand down on the table. 'Or you'll wish you'd never been born.'

'Okay,' said Miranda more calmly than she felt. She hated to admit it but Moskvin did frighten her, and she was not a person easy to frighten.

'She gets the message,' said Harmony. 'Can I eat my apple now, boss man?'

15

Bosham, Sussex, England. October 1983.

Few actions within the law can provide more joy than the dispassionate evaluation of a colleague's failure. And so it happened that the field operation that Pavel Moskvin planned against London Central became celebrated in speech and writing, and perhaps in song too, for long after Moskvin was dead and buried.

Some blamed the failure entirely upon Moskvin. He was a desk man, without the practical experience that service in the field provides (it was field agents in particular who inclined to this view). Moskvin was, undeniably, a bully; he was always in a hurry and he failed to understand the English. But then, many of his peers were bullies, very few of them were not in a hurry and even in England it was difficult to find anyone who claimed to understand the English.

A more convincing explanation of the fiasco came from less passionate observers, who located the flaw in the duality of the leadership: Pavel Moskvin, a career KGB officer too dependent upon his influence in Moscow, in partnership with Erich Stinnes, experienced field agent who, although senior to Moskvin, had no reason to expect benefit from the operation's success.

Others looked at the two women in the team: the black Jamaican woman who had never responded to KGB discipline in all the years of her service, and the Englishwoman who had been bullied into a vital part in the operation simply because she could imitate voices. Some said the women were truculent, others that their English mother-tongue bonded the two of them and created a potential rebellion. Others, all of them men, believed that no women were suited to such jobs.

'First prize for booboos, shit-face,' said Harmony Jones to Moskvin. They were in a small cottage in Bosham, near the south coast of England, where Moskvin was laying his trap for Bernard Samson. 'London to Berlin, then back to London again. This is the dumbest operation I was ever on, honey.'

Moskvin was not used to such defiance. He controlled his terrible anger and said, 'It is all part of the plan.'

Erich Stinnes looked up from his guidebook: *Chichester and the South*

616

Downs. He watched them dispassionately. It was not his operation, and even if the British caught him he'd already put out feelers to them about defection. He'd told Moscow that the first approaches came from the other side and got permission to continue his contacts, so he would survive come what may.

Pavel Moskvin had reasoned along lines of equal infallibility. This operation was going to make his name, so it had to be dramatic. He was going to entice Bernard Samson into a trap, interrogate him to the point of death and then leave his mutilated body in an SIS safe house in England! If Samson's interrogation revealed something to question or destroy the reputation of his new superior, Fiona Samson, so much the better. Even the safe house had been chosen because Fiona Samson had revealed its existence during one of her initial debriefing sessions. Should the location prove compromised it would be Fiona Samson's treachery, not his failure.

Miranda looked at her three colleagues and shivered. She had never expected it to be like this. Miranda had played her part exactly as briefed.

Miranda had been standing on a grass verge, on a section of road near Terminal 3 at London Airport, when she saw Bernard Samson driving a car with Harmony sitting in the seat next to him. The car stopped very near her and then she had climbed into the back seat and mimicked the voice of Fiona Samson.

There had been a moment, when she got into the car behind this man Bernard Samson, when she thought she was going to faint. But it was just like being on the stage: at that final moment her professionalism took over and it all went smoothly.

'It's me, darling. I hope I didn't terrify you.' That sweet and careful upper-class voice with just a hint of taunting in it.

'Fiona, are you mad?' said Samson. He didn't look round and in any case the driving mirror had been twisted away from him. It went just as Harmony said it would. Bernard Samson, Harmony told her, was a professional; pros don't do and die, they reason why.

Samson was convinced. It was the most successful performance of Miranda's career: what a pity that there were only two people in the audience. But an allowance had to be made for the fact that fifty per cent of the audience was startled out of his senses and being threatened by a very nasty-looking hypodermic syringe held close against his thigh.

Miranda continued, 'To come here? There is no warrant for my arrest. I have changed my appearance and my name . . . no, don't look round. I don't want you unconscious.' She had rehearsed every syllable of it so many times that it was automatic. The poor devil was completely fooled. Miranda felt sorry for him. Of course he would try to follow Harmony afterwards, what husband wouldn't?

When Miranda returned to this fisherman's cottage, from her performance at London Heathrow, Moskvin had given no word of appreciation. Miranda hated him.

'Suppose Bernard Samson *doesn't* track Harmony's movements?' said Miranda. 'Suppose he doesn't come? Suppose he tells the police?'

'He'll come,' said Moskvin. 'He doesn't get paid to send for the police; it's his job to find people. He'll trace Harmony's movements. He'll think his wife is here and he'll come.'

'Then what?' said Miranda. She was still wearing the expensive wig and make-up that Moskvin had chosen for her. She hoped to keep the wig.

Harmony smiled sourly. She had been the one who had laid the trail for Samson, asking the way three times before buying the tickets, doing the stupid things that mere common sense would have avoided. Moskvin's final obvious vulgarity had been to choose a beautiful black girl just in case anyone should miss her. What kind of jerk wouldn't be suspicious following that brass band parade to get here? And her brief confrontation with Bernard Samson gave her reason to suspect that he wasn't a jerk. She didn't want to be here when he arrived.

'Who cares?' said Harmony. 'Us girls are getting out of here, Miranda baby! Go upstairs and scrub that damned make-up off your face, and then we'll scram. A day in Rome is what we both need after three long days with this fat fart.' She got to her feet.

'Give me thirty minutes,' said Miranda.

Moskvin was annoyed at the way that Harmony Jones had sweet-talked him into routeing the two women through Rome. She'd given him persuasive operational reasons at the time but now it was clear that she just wanted to enjoy a sidetrip.

'I might need you,' said Moskvin, but his former ability to terrify the two women had gone, largely due to the insolence with which the black woman treated every order he gave her.

'What you need, boss man . . .' she began but then decided not to provoke him further. She took Miranda's make-up box and went to the stairs. Miranda followed.

'And don't call me shit-face,' said Moskvin solemnly as the two women went through the low door that led to the stairs.

Harmony made an obscene gesture but did it out of Moskvin's sight. As they went upstairs Miranda began to giggle.

It was a wonderful old house: the crude staircase, confined between white painted plank walls, echoed with the footsteps of the two women. At the top, the narrow latched door had a corner lopped off to accommodate the pitch of the roof. Its essential Englishness produced in Miranda a sudden but not entirely unexpected yearning to live in England again.

As the sound of the footsteps overhead revealed the movements of the women, Erich Stinnes looked up from his guidebook. 'Did you know that Bosham village is depicted on the Bayeux Tapestry?' he asked. 'This is where King Canute ordered the incoming tide to go back.'

Moskvin knew that Stinnes was only trying to provoke him into a fit of anger, so he didn't reply. He got up and went to the window. Bosham is on a tiny peninsula between two tidal creeks. From here he could see the water and the boats: motor boats and sailing boats of all shapes and sizes. When Samson was dead and finished with, they would leave by boat. Stinnes was a skilful yachtsman. Under cover of darkness they would slip away as if they had never been here. The perfect conclusion to a perfect operation.

'I wouldn't stand too near the window,' said Stinnes helpfully. 'It's an elementary principle on this sort of operation.'

Moskvin moved away. Stinnes was right of course: he hated Stinnes.

'The back-up team should be here by now.'

Stinnes looked at him and displayed surprise. 'They arrived half an hour ago.'

'Then where are they?'

'You didn't expect them to come and knock on the door, did you? They have a mattress: they'll sleep in the van until they're needed. It's parked near the pub.'

'How do you know all this?'

'I arranged it, didn't I? Why do you think I've been visiting the bathroom: did you think I had diarrhoea? From upstairs you can see the pub car park.'

'Do you have a gun?'

Stinnes shook his head.

'I brought a gun,' said Moskvin. He put it on the table. It was a Smith and Wesson .44 Magnum, a truly enormous pistol that Moskvin had gone to great trouble to have waiting here for him.

Stinnes looked at the colossal pistol and at Moskvin. 'That should be enough gun for both of us,' said Stinnes.

'Then there is nothing to do but wait,' said Moskvin.

Stinnes put a marker into a page of his guidebook and closed it.

'Remember, this place – Bosham – is where King Canute ordered the tide to go back.'

'What happened?' said Moskvin, who had never heard of King Canute.

'The tide kept coming in.' Stinnes picked up his shoulder bag and said, 'I'll be in the way here. I'd better go down and check that the boat is gassed up and ready to sail. You know the phone number.'

'Yes, I know it,' said Moskvin. He'd been counting on help from Stinnes but he was determined not to ask for it.

Upstairs Miranda was wiping the make-up off her face, using lots of cold cream and peering closely at herself in the mirror.

Harmony, who was packing her case, said, 'That bastard. I cleared everything out of the car, just the way I've been trained to do, and he yells at me for being late. Most of the trash belonged to Moskvin anyway. He's an untidy swine.' She produced a clear plastic sandwich bag into which she had carefully put everything from the rented car. There were two maps of southern England, bits of scrap paper, a broken ballpoint pen, an old lipstick, three pennies and a watch crystal. 'Any of this junk yours, honey?' she asked Miranda.

'No,' said Miranda.

'These rental companies never clean out the cars right: a quick wipe of the ashtray and that's it.' She emptied the contents of the bag, to use it for her make-up.

'I'm almost ready,' said Miranda. 'I think I'll have a day or two in England. I'll join you in Rome the day after tomorrow. Would that be all right?'

'Suit yourself, baby,' said Harmony Jones. 'I have a lot of catching up to do in Rome.'

Stinnes slept on the boat that night. There were three double cabins and he made himself comfortable in one of them. He had the generator going and stayed up late reading: *The White Company*. He was a dedicated Sherlock Holmes fan and was persevering with his favourite author's excursion into medievalism. The weather was good and Stinnes enjoyed the sounds and motion of the anchored boat and the smells of the wet timber and the salt water.

It was five o'clock the next morning when Moskvin called him on the phone. 'Come immediately,' said Moskvin, and Stinnes hurried out into the brittle pinkness of early morning and reached the cottage within eight minutes.

'What's happening?' asked Stinnes.

'He's here,' said Moskvin. 'Bernard Samson arrived about midnight. The back-up team in the van spotted him. We brought him inside as easily as anything.'

'Where is he now?'

'Upstairs. Don't worry, he's tied up. I let the back-up team go. Maybe that was a mistake.'

'What do you want me for?' asked Stinnes.

'I'm not getting anywhere with my questions,' admitted Moskvin. 'I think it's time he faced another interrogator.'

'What have you asked him?'

Moskvin smashed his fist against his open hand in frustration. 'I know that Samson woman is a British spy. I know it and I'll squeeze it out of her husband if it's the last thing I do.'

'Oh, so that's the line of questioning,' said Stinnes. To him it seemed the stupid obsession of a man who had repeatedly told him how much he objected to taking orders from any woman.

There was no way that Moskvin could miss the ridicule in his colleague's voice, but he'd become used to the superior attitude that Stinnes always showed towards him. 'Go up and talk to him. Play mister nice guy.'

When Stinnes went upstairs, Moskvin followed him. Moskvin was not able to sit still downstairs and wait for results: he had to see what was happening. He stood in the doorway behind Stinnes.

The front upstairs room was very small and much of the space was taken up by a small bed. It was pushed against the wall and there were cushions on it so it could be used as a sofa. In the corner there was a dressing table with a large mirror in which the captive was reflected.

'I'm going to undo this gag and I want you to . . .' Stinnes started and then stopped abruptly. He looked round at Moskvin and back to the captive. 'This is not Bernard Samson,' he told Moskvin.

The man tied to the chair was named Julian MacKenzie. He was a probationer who worked for the Department. Bernard Samson had told him to trace the movements of the black girl. He'd done so all too efficiently. MacKenzie was fully conscious and his eyes showed his fear as Moskvin waved the pistol in the air.

'What do you mean?' said Moskvin angrily. He grabbed Stinnes's arm in his huge hand and dragged him back into the narrow corridor. Then he closed the door. It was dark. The only glimmer of light was that escaping from the room downstairs.

'I mean it's not Bernard Samson,' said Stinnes quietly.

'Who is it?' said Moskvin, shaking him roughly.

621

'How the hell would I know who it is?'

'Are you positive?'

'Of course I am. Samson is about fifteen years older than this kid. I've seen Samson close-to. I know him well. Of course I'm positive.'

'Wait downstairs. I'll find out who this one is.'

As Stinnes went downstairs he heard Moskvin shouting and there were replies from the young man that were too quiet to hear properly. Stinnes sat down in the armchair and took *The White Company* from his pocket but found he just kept reading the same paragraph over and over. Suddenly there was the loud bang of the .44 Magnum. A scream. More shots. Stinnes leapt to his feet, worried that the noise would wake up the whole neighbourhood. His first instinct was simply to clear out, but he was enough of a professional to wait for the other man.

Moskvin came down the stairs so slowly that Stinnes was beginning to wonder if he'd shot himself or been injured by a ricochet. Then Moskvin lurched into the room. His face was absolutely white, even his lips were bloodless. He dumped his pistol on the dresser and put out a hand to steady himself on the edge of the kitchen table. Then he leaned over and vomited into the sink.

Stinnes watched him but kept well back. Moskvin pushed the gun aside and retched again and again. Finally, slowly and carefully, he wiped his face on a towel and then ran the water into the sink. 'That's done,' said Moskvin, trying to put on a show of bravado.

'Are you sure he's dead?' said Stinnes. Taking his time he looked out of both windows. There was no sign that the noise of the shot had attracted any interest from the neighbouring cottages.

'I'm sure.'

'Then let's get out of here,' said Stinnes. 'Can you make it to the boat?'

'Damn your stupid smiling face,' said Moskvin. 'I'll have the last laugh: you just wait.'

But Stinnes wasn't smiling: he was wondering how much longer he could endure the stupid antics of this brutal peasant.

In Berlin that evening, Fiona went to the State Opera. The indispensable Hubert Renn could always produce an opera or concert ticket for her at short notice, and this afternoon she'd suddenly noticed that it would be the last chance to catch the much-discussed avant-garde production of *Der Freischütz*.

She sat entranced. It was one of her favourite operas. This extraordinary selection of simple folk melodies and complex romanticism gave her a brief respite from work. For a brief moment it even enabled her to forget her worries and loneliness.

The interval came. Still engrossed with the music, she couldn't endure the scrum around the bar and there were a lot of West Berliners here tonight, easily distinguished by their jewellery and flamboyant clothes. She turned away to wander through the lobby and look at the exhibition – 'Electricity for tomorrow' – atmospheric photos of power-generating stations in the German Democratic Republic. She was looking at the colour print of a large concrete building reflected in a lake when someone behind her said, 'There you go, sweetheart! How about a glass of white wine?'

She turned and was astounded to see Harry Kennedy standing there with two glasses of wine in his hands and a satisfied smile on his face. 'The show really starts in the intermission, doesn't it?'

Her first reaction was not pleasure. She had been dreading an encounter with some old friend, colleague or acquaintance on the street, who would recognize her. Now it had happened and she felt as if she was going to faint. Rooted to the spot, her heart beat furiously. She felt the blood rush to her face and looked down so that he wouldn't see the flush of her cheeks.

He saw the effect he'd had. 'Are you all right? I'm sorry . . . I should have . . .'

'It's all right,' she said. She was quite likely to be under surveillance. If so, her reaction to this meeting would be noted and recorded.

Harry spoke hurriedly to save her from speaking. 'I knew you wouldn't miss *Der Freischütz*, I just knew. Oh boy, what a production, the pits, isn't it? And what about those trees! But what a great voice he has.'

'What are you doing here, Harry?' she said carefully and calmly.

'Looking for you, honey-child.' He handed the wine to her and she took it. 'I'm sorry to leap on you this way.'

'I don't understand you . . .'

'I live here,' he said.

'In the East?' She drank some wine without tasting it. She hardly knew what she was doing. She didn't know whether to keep talking or cut him dead and walk away.

'I'm here for a year now. A professor from the Charité Hospital was in London and came to see the work we were doing at the clinic. They invited me to spend a year working here. They are not paying me but I finagled a little grant . . . Enough to keep me going for the year. I was glad to escape from those jerks in London and I suspect the clinic was glad to get rid of me.'

'Here in East Berlin?' She drank more wine. She needed a drink and it gave her a chance to study him. He looked even younger than she remembered him: his wavy hair more wavy, and the battered face looking even more battered as he worried how she would react.

'Yeah. At the Charité. And I knew you wouldn't miss *Der Freischütz*. I have been here for every performance . . . I love you, Fiona sweetheart. I had to find you.' Again he stopped.

'You came for every performance?'

'You once said it was your favourite opera.'

'I suppose it is,' she said. She was no longer sure; she was no longer sure about anything.

'Are you mad at me?' he asked. He looked like a West Berliner in his black suit and bow tie. Here was a different Harry Kennedy to the one she'd last seen in London: cautious and diffident. But superimposed upon this diffidence, and almost prevailing over it, there was the pride and pleasure of finding her again.

'No, of course not,' she said.

Her distant manner made him suddenly anxious. 'Is there someone else?'

'Only my husband in London.'

It was as if a load was lifted from his shoulders. 'When I realized that you'd left him, I knew I had to find you. You're the only one I've ever loved, Fiona. You know that.' It wasn't a communication; it was a declaration.

'It's not like London,' she said awkwardly, trying to adjust to the idea of him being here.

'Say you love me.' He'd taken so much trouble; he was expecting more of her.

'Don't. It's not as easy as that, Harry. I work for the government here.'

'Who cares who you work for?'

Why wouldn't he understand? 'I defected, Harry.'

'I don't care what you did. We are together again; that's all that matters to me.'

'Please try and understand what is involved.'

Now, for the first time, he calmed down enough to look at her and say, 'What are you trying to tell me, baby?'

'If you see me on a regular basis, your career will be ruined. You won't be able to go back to London and take up your life at the place you left it.'

'I don't care, as long as I have you.'

'Harry. You haven't got me.'

'I love you . . . I'll do anything, I'll live anywhere; I'll wait forever. I'm a desperate man.'

She looked at him and smiled but she knew it was an unconvincing smile. She felt one of her bad headaches coming on and she wanted to scream. 'I can't be responsible, Harry. Everything has changed, and I have changed too.'

'You said you loved me,' he said in that reproachful way that only lovers do.

If only he would go away. 'Perhaps I did. Perhaps I still do. I don't know.' She spoke slowly. 'All I'm sure about is that right now I can't take on all the complications of a relationship.'

'Then promise nothing. I ask nothing. I'll wait. But don't ask me to stop telling you that I love you. That would be an unbearable restriction.'

The opera bell started to ring. With German orderliness the crowd immediately began to move back towards the auditorium. 'I can't go back to the performance,' she said. 'My head is whirling. I need to think.'

'So let's go to the Palast and eat dinner.'

'You'll miss the opera.'

'I've seen it nine times,' he said grimly.

She smiled and looked at her watch. 'Will they serve dinner as late as this?' she said. 'Things finish so early on this side of the city.'

'The ever-practical Fiona. Yes, they will serve as late as this. I was there two nights ago. Give me the ticket, and I'll collect your coat.'

It is not far from the State Opera on Unter den Linden to the Palast Hotel, and despite Berlin's everpresent smell of brown coal the walk was good for her. By the time they were seated in the hotel dining room she was restored to something approaching her normal calm. It wasn't like her to be so shattered, even by surprises. But meeting Harry at the opera house had not simply been a surprise: it had shown her what a fragile hold she had upon herself. She had been physically affected by the encounter. Her heart was still beating fast.

She watched him as he read the menu. Was she in love with him? Was that the explanation of the shock? Or was it more fundamental, was she becoming unbalanced?

Any feeling she had for Harry was not like the stable and enduring love she had for her home, her children and her husband. Harry's absence from her life had not caused her the heart-rending agony that separation from her family had brought, an agony from which she never escaped. That old love for Harry was something quite different, separate and not in conflict with it. But she could not help recalling that the love she'd once had for Harry was electrifying. It had been illicit and more physical than anything she'd known with Bernard. Sitting here across the table from Harry made her remember vividly the way that not so long ago even a glance from him could be arousing. 'I beg your pardon?' she said absently as she realized he was expecting an answer from her.

'I had it the other night,' he said. 'It was rather good.'

'I'm sorry. My mind was wandering.'

'The Kabinett is always the driest, at least I've learned that in the time I've been here.'

'Wonderful,' she said vaguely and was relieved when he waved to the waiter and ordered a bottle of some wine he'd discovered and liked. His German was adequate and even his accent was not too grating upon her ear. She looked around the restaurant to be sure there was no one there she recognized. It was crowded with foreigners: the only ones who had access to the sort of foreign money with which the bill had to be paid.

'My money comes in Western currency. I eat here all the time,' he told her.

Could he, by any chance, be an emissary from London Central? No. This was not a man whom Bret or Sir Henry would regard as right for the tricky job of intermediary. And yet a paramour would make the perfect cover for a London contact. If that was his role, he'd reveal it soon: that was how such things were done. She'd wait and see what happened: meanwhile she would be the perfect communist. 'So what do you suggest we eat?' she asked.

He looked up and smiled. He was so happy that his elation affected her. 'Steak, trout or schnitzel is all I ever order.'

'Trout then; nothing to start.' And then another thought struck her like a bombshell: could he be Moscow's man? Very very unlikely. At that first encounter in London he'd admitted having no work permit. Had she phoned Immigration they would have pounced on him. Wait a minute, think about it. It was his vulnerability to officialdom that made her decide not to have him officially investigated. That and the fact that Bernard might have started asking questions about him. She lived again through that first encounter on the railway station, step by step, word for word. His 'niece' talked to Fiona and then ran away. It could have been a set-up. There was nothing in that meeting that could not have been previously arranged.

'Fiona,' he said.

'Yes, Harry?'

'I love you desperately.' He did love her: no one could feign adoration in the way that she saw it in his eyes. But, said the neurotic, suspicious and logical side of her, being in love did not mean that he couldn't have been sent by Moscow. 'I know everything about you,' he said suddenly, and she was alarmed again. 'Except why you like *Der Freischütz*. I know every mini-quaver of it by now. I can take Schoenberg and Hindemith, but can you find me ten minutes of real melody in that whole darn opera?'

'Germans like it because it is about a completely unified Germany.'

'Is that what you want: a unified Germany?' he asked.

Red lights flashed. What was the official line on unification? 'Only on the right terms,' she said guardedly. 'What about you?'

'Who was it who said that he liked Germany so much that he preferred there to be two of them?'

'I'm not sure.'

He leaned forward and confidentially said, 'Forget what I said: I'm just crazy about *Der Freischütz*; every little demi-semi-quaver.'

16

London. October 1983.

It was two o'clock in the morning. Bret was in his Thameside house, sitting up in bed reading the final few pages of Zola's *Nana*. Influenced by Sylvester Bernstein, Bret had discovered the joy of reading novels. First Sylvy had lent him *Germinal* and now Bret – always subject to deep and sudden passions – had decided to read every volume of Zola's twenty-volume cycle. The phone rang. He let it ring for a long time, but when the caller persisted he reached for it. 'Hello?' Bret always said hello; he didn't believe in identifying himself.

'Bret, my dear fellow. I do hope I didn't wake you.'

'I'm reading a superb and moving book, Sir Henry.'

'As long as you're not in the middle of anything important,' said the D-G imperturbably. 'I know you are something of a night owl. Anyway this won't wait, I'm afraid.'

'I understand.' Bret put the book aside and closed it regretfully.

'Special Branch liaison came through to me at home a few minutes ago. Apparently a young woman, English by all accounts, walked into the police station in Chichester and said she wanted to talk to someone in our line of business.'

'Oh, yes, sir,' said Bret.

'You're yawning already, of course. Yes, we've seen a lot of those in our time, haven't we? But this lady says she wants to tell us something about one of our people in London. She's mentioned a man whose wife recently left him. Furthermore she met that wife recently in Berlin. You're still with me, are you Bret?'

'Very much with you, Sir Henry. Met her? By name? Mentioned her by name?'

'Apparently: but things usually become a bit vague by the time reports come word of mouth all the way to me. Very very urgent she said it was: someone was about to be killed: that kind of thing. But yes the name was given. Special Branch thought they should check to see if the name rang a bell with us. The night duty officer decided it was important enough to wake me up. I think he was right.'

'Yes, indeed, sir.'

'A Special Branch inspector is bringing this lady up to London. She gave her name as Mrs Miranda Keller, née Dobbs. No joy there of course, the German telephone books are full of Kellers. I wonder if you would be so kind as to talk to her? See what it's all about.'

'Yes, sir.'

'Special Branch have that estate agent's office in Kensington. The house behind the Sainsbury supermarket. You know it, I'm sure.'

'Yes, sir.'

'They will be there in under the hour.'

'I'll get going immediately, sir.'

'Would you really, Bret. I'd be so grateful. I'll be in the office tomorrow. We can talk about it then.'

'Yes, sir.'

'Of course it may be nothing at all. Nothing at all.'

'Well, I'd better hurry.'

'Or it could be our old pals getting up to naughty tricks. Don't take any chances, Bret.'

'I won't, sir. I'd better get started.'

'Yes, of course. Goodnight, old chap. Although for you I suppose it would be good morning.' The D-G chuckled and rang off. It was all right for him; he was going back to sleep.

Mrs Miranda Keller was thirty-six years old, and the wig she was wearing did not make her look younger. It was almost four o'clock in the morning and she'd endured a long car ride through the pouring rain to this grand old house in Kensington, a shabby residential part of central London. Miranda let her head rest back upon the frayed moquette of the armchair. Under the pitiless blue glare of the overhead lighting – which buzzed constantly – she did not look her best.

'As I told you, we have no one of that name working for us,' said Bret. He was behind a desk drinking stale black coffee from the delicate sort of chinaware that is de rigueur in the offices of earnest young men who sell real estate. With it on the antique tray there was a bowl of sugar and a pierced tin of Carnation milk.

'S.A.M.S.O.N.,' she spelled it out.

'Yes, I know what you said. No one of that name,' said Bret.

'They are going to kill him,' said Miranda doggedly. 'Have you sent someone to the house in Bosham?'

'That's not something I'm permitted to discuss,' said Bret. 'Even if I knew,' he added.

629

'Well, these men will kill him if he goes there. I know the sort of men they are.' Wind rattled the windows.

'Russians, you say?'

'You wrote their names down,' she said. She picked up her cup, looked at the coffee, and set it aside.

'Of course I did. And you said there was another woman there too.'

'I don't know anything about her.'

'Ah, yes. That's what you said,' murmured Bret, looking down at his notes. 'My writing is not very elegant, Mrs Keller, but I think it is clear enough. I want you to read through the notes I've made. Start here: the conversation you had in the car at London airport, when you were imitating the voice of this woman you met in Berlin-Grünau.' He gave the sheet to her.

She read it quickly, nodded and offered it back. The wind made a roaring noise in the chimney and the electric fire rattled on its mounting. On the window there was the constant hammering of heavy rain.

Bret didn't take the papers from her. 'Take your time, Mrs Keller. Maybe read it twice.'

She looked at his notes again. 'What's wrong? Don't you believe me?'

'It sounds like a mighty banal conversation, Mrs Keller. Was it worth having you go to all that trouble, when in the final confrontation you simply say things about the children and about laying off this fellow Stinnes?'

'It was just to jolt him: so that he would follow the black girl to find his wife again.'

'Yes,' said Bret Rensselaer doubtfully. He took the sheets of notes and tapped them on the desk-top to get them tidy. Outside a car door slammed and an engine was started. A man yelled goodnight and a woman screamed 'Good riddance!': it was that kind of place.

'And I've asked for nothing.'

'I was wondering about that,' said Bret.

'There's no need to be sarcastic.'

'Forgive me. I didn't intend to be.'

'Could you switch off some of these lights? The glare is giving me a headache.'

'You said it! I hate fluorescent lighting but this place is used as an office. They are all on the same switch.'

'I want nothing for what I've told you. Nothing at all.'

'But?'

'But if you want me to go back there, it's only fair that I get something in return.'

'What do you have in mind?'

'A passport for my five-year-old son.'

'Ahhh!' said Bret in what was unmistakably a groan of agony as he envisaged the arguments that he would have to endure to get a passport for someone not entitled to one. Those professional obstructionists he dealt with in Whitehall would work overtime producing excuses to say no to that one.

'It will cost you nothing,' said Miranda.

'I know,' said Bret in a soft warm voice. 'It's a modest enough request, Mrs Keller. I'll probably be able to do it.'

'If I don't go to Rome tomorrow, or next day at the latest, I'll have a lot of explaining to do.'

'You're British. I would have thought that your son could claim British nationality.'

'I was born in Austria. My father was on a five-year contract there. My son was born in Berlin: I can't pass my citizenship on to him.'

'That's a lousy break,' said Bret. 'I'll do what I can.' He brightened as a sudden solution came to mind. Maybe a counterfeit passport would do: he wouldn't say it was counterfeit of course. 'I suppose any Western passport would serve to get him out of there: Irish Republic, Brazil, Guatemala, Belize or Paraguay.'

The woman looked at him suspiciously. 'Providing I got a certificated right to reside in Great Britain, but I don't want some Mickey Mouse passport that I have to renew every two or three years and bribe some embassy official every time I do it.'

Bret nodded assent. 'Do you have suitable photos of your son?'

'Yes.' From her handbag she took three passport pictures and passed them to him together with a piece of paper upon which she had written the other necessary description.

'So you had this planned before you left Berlin?'

'These Russian pigs are intolerable,' said Miranda. 'I always carry passport pictures.'

How enterprising, thought Bret. 'That's about all we can do right now,' he said. 'Leave it all with me. How can I contact you in East Berlin?'

'I'll need the passport,' said Miranda. 'Until I have the passport in my hand I'll do nothing for you.'

Bret looked at her. She was an intelligent woman. She must have realized that if she went back to the East she was delivering herself into his hands. But she gave no sign of that: she was one of those people who expected everyone to act fairly. It was good to know that such people still existed: Bret would not disabuse her at this stage. 'Would you accept a small payment?'

'I just want the passport for my son.'

'Okay, Mrs Keller. I'll do everything I can to get it for you.'

'I'm sure you will,' she said.

'One last, and vitally important thing, Mrs Keller. The woman you met in Berlin, Mrs Fiona Samson, is a KGB officer. She is a very smart woman. Don't underestimate her.'

'Are you saying she works for Russian intelligence?'

'Very much so. Mean, I should have said: a mean and dangerous woman. Under no circumstances should you confide anything to her.'

'No, I won't.'

'So it wasn't a complete waste of time, Bret?' The D-G was making one of his rare visits to Bret Rensselaer's magnificent monochrome office. He sat on the black leather chesterfield picking at the buttons and determined not to smoke.

There were times when the D-G's distant joviality reminded Bret of Sassoon's World War One general: ' *"He's a cheery old card," grunted Harry to Jack . . . But he did for them both with his plan of attack.*'

'No, sir. Very instructive,' said Bret, who was sitting behind his glass-topped desk wearing a white shirt and spotted bow tie.

'It was a plan to kill Bernard Samson?'

'That is her story.'

'And this other young man was killed instead?'

'Yes, but she doesn't know that. And of course I didn't tell her.'

'Did Samson report being approached by this black girl?'

'No, sir, he did not.' Bret tidied the papers on his desk, although they didn't need tidying.

'And what else did the house in Bosham reveal? Have your chaps reported back to you?'

'I have done nothing about the house in Bosham, and I intend to do nothing.'

After a deliberately audible intake of breath, the Director-General stared at him, thought about it, and finally said, 'Very prudent, Bret.'

'I'm glad you approve, Sir Henry.'

'Where is Samson?'

'Samson is alive and well.'

'You didn't warn him?'

'No sir. I sent him away on a job.'

'Yes, that was wise.' He sniffed. 'So they acted on Mrs Samson's

632

information about the Bosham safe house. They were quick off the mark on that one. Ummm.'

'We come out of it very well, sir.'

'I wish you wouldn't keep saying that, Bret. We're not out of it yet. I don't like the fact that Samson didn't report back that approach. Do you think he believed it was his wife in the back of that car?'

'Yes, probably. But Samson thinks before he acts. All these ex-field people become ultra-cautious: that's why we have to retire them.'

'You'd better make sure Mrs Samson knows about this impersonation.' He sniffed. 'So Bernard Samson didn't report any of it. I don't like that, Bret.'

'No, sir, but there is no reason to think that Samson is in any way disloyal. Or contemplating disloyalty.'

'This Mrs Keller, is she a potential agent for us?'

'No, sir. Out of the question.'

'But we can use her?'

'I don't see how. Not at present anyway.'

'Did you get photos of her?'

'Yes, the Kensington office is good from that point of view. Lots of good clear pictures.'

The D-G tapped his fingers on the leather arm of the chesterfield. 'On the matter of safe houses, Bret. When we agreed that Mrs Samson should reveal the existence of the Bosham safe house, I understood that it was to be kept under surveillance.'

Bret pursed his lips, feeling that he was being admonished for something outside his frame of reference. He said, 'At present my hands are tied . . . but when it becomes safe to do so, disciplinary action will be taken.'

'I do hope so, Bret. But the scheme is to just wait until the housekeeping people go into the Bosham safe house on a routine check-up and find the body?'

'That's right, sir.'

'Good.' He produced an encouraging smile, albeit humourless. 'And now this KGB fellow Stinnes. Silas is pestering me about him. He says we mustn't let his approach grow cold.'

'I thought that might be what you wanted to talk about, sir,' said Bret, diving down into a document case. From it he brought a red cardboard file which he opened to display a concertina of that grey angular computer printout that the D-G found difficult to read. And then he found four 10×8 inch shiny photos of Stinnes. Reaching across he placed them on the glass-topped desk where the D-G could see them, but the D-G didn't crane his neck to look closely.

The photos were arranged side by side with finicky care. It was so typical of Bret Rensselaer, with his boundless faith in charts, graphs, graphics and projections, that he should bring photos of this damned Russian out at this meeting as if that would help them towards a sound decision. 'Has he provided any evidence of good faith?' asked the D-G.

'He told Samson that Moscow have broken the new diplomatic code. That's why we did everything "by hand of messenger".'

The D-G extended a finger and touched one of the photos as though it might have been impregnated with some contagious disease. 'You believe him?'

'You probably spoke with Silas Gaunt,' said Bret, who wanted to know the lie of the land before committing himself to an opinion.

'Silas has got a bee in his bonnet about this one. I was looking for a more sober assessment.'

Bret did not want to say something that would afterwards be quoted against him. Slowly he said, 'If Stinnes and his offer to defect is a Moscow stunt . . .'

The D-G finished the sentence for him. 'The way we have reacted will make those chaps in Moscow feel very good, eh Bret?'

'I try to disregard any personal feelings of triumph or disaster when making decisions of that sort, Sir Henry.'

'And quite right too.'

'If Stinnes is doing this on Moscow's orders, he'd be more likely to bring us some secret document that we'd be tempted to transmit verbatim, or at least in sequence.'

'So that they could compare it and break our code? Yes, I suppose so. So you think he's genuine?'

'Silas thinks it doesn't matter; Silas thinks we should work on him, and send him back believing what we want them to believe over there.' Bret waited for the reaction and was still ready to jump either way. But he could tell that the D-G was attracted by this idea.

After a moment's pause for thought, the D-G said, 'I don't want you to discuss this with Silas for the time being.'

'Very well, Sir Henry.'

'And in course of time, separate Stinnes from Cruyer and Samson and everyone else. This is for you to do alone, Bret. One to one, you and Stinnes. We have to have one person who understands the whole game and all its minutiae and ramifications. One person is enough, and that person must be you.'

Bret put the photos and the printout back into his case. The D-G made agitated movements that indicated he was about to terminate the meeting. 'Before I go, Bret, one aspect of this . . .'

'Yes?'

'Would you say that Bernard Samson has ever killed a man?'

Bret was surprised, and for a moment he allowed it to show. 'I imagine he has, sir. In fact . . . well, I know . . . Yes, many times.'

'Exactly, Bret. And now we are subjecting him to a considerable burden of anxiety, aren't we?'

Bret nodded.

'A man like Samson might not have the resilience that you would be able to show in such circumstances. He might take things into his own hands.'

'I suppose he might.' Bret was doubtful.

'I saw Samson the other day. He's taking it badly.'

'Do you want me to give him sick leave, or a vacation?'

'Certainly not: that would be the worst thing you could do for the poor fellow. It would give him time to sit and think. I don't want him to sit and think, Bret.'

'Would you give me some idea of what . . . ?'

'Suppose he came to the conclusion that his wife had betrayed him, and betrayed his country. That she'd abandoned his children and made a fool of him? Might he not then decide to do to her what he's done to so many others?'

'Kill her? But wait a minute, Sir Henry. In fact she hasn't done that, has she?'

'And that leads us on to another aspect of the horrible position that Samson now finds himself in.' The D-G heaved himself up out of the low seat. Bret got to his feet and watched but decided against offering him assistance. The D-G said, 'Samson is asking a lot of questions. Suppose he discovers the truth? Might it not seem to him that we have played a cruel prank on him? And done it with callous indifference? He discovers that we have not confided in him: he feels rejected and humiliated. He is a man trained to respond violently to his opponents. Might he not decide to wreak vengeance upon us?'

'I don't think so, Sir Henry. Samson is a civilized man.' Bret went across the office and held the door open for him.

'Is he?' said the D-G in that cheery way he could summon so readily. 'Then he hasn't been properly trained.'

17

East Berlin. November 1983.

To the façade of the building in Karl Liebknecht Strasse a dozen workmen were affixing a huge red banner, 'Long Live Our Socialist Fatherland'. The previous one that had promised both prosperity and peace was faded to light pink by the sun.

From the window of Fiona Samson's office there were only the tassels to be glimpsed, but part of the framework for the new banner cut across the window and reduced the daylight. 'I've always wanted to go to America,' admitted Hubert Renn as he picked up the papers from her desk.

'Have you, Herr Renn? Why?' She drank her tea. She must not leave it for it was real Indian tea, not the tasteless USSR stuff from the Georgian crop. She wondered where Renn had found it but she didn't ask.

'Curiosity, Frau Direktor. It is a land of contradictions.'

'It is a repressive society,' said Fiona, dutiful to the line she always took. 'A land where workers are enslaved.'

'But they are such an enigmatic people,' said Renn. He replaced the cap on his fountain-pen and put it in his pocket. 'Do you know, Frau Direktor, when, during the war against Hitler, the Americans began to drop secret agents into Germany, the very first of those parachutists were members of the ISK?'

'*Der Internationaler Sozialistischer Kampfbund?*' She had never heard of that organization until Renn had mentioned that his mother had been a member, and then she'd looked it up in the reference library.

'Yes, ISK, the most radical of all the parties. Why would the Americans select such people? It was as if our friends in Moscow had sent to us, as Stalin's emissaries, White Russian nobility.'

She laughed. Renn gave a skimpy selfconscious grin. There had been a time when such remarks by Renn would have suggested to her that he might be sympathetic to the USA, but now she knew better. If there was anything of his attitude to be deduced from his remarks it was a criticism of Russia rather than praise for the US. Renn was a dedicated disciple of Marx and his theories. As Renn saw it, Karl Marx the incomparable prophet and source of all true enlightenment was a German sage. Any small inconsistencies and imperfections that might be encountered in the practice of socialism – and Renn had never admitted to there being any – were due to the essentially Russian failures of Lenin and Stalin.

But Fiona had learned to live with Hubert Renn's blind devotion to Marxist socialism, and there was no doubt that daily contact with him had opened up to her a world that she had never truly perceived.

There were for instance the regular letters that arrived from Renn's twenty-two-year-old daughter Lisa, her father's great pride. Lisa had taken the learning of the Russian language in her stride and gone on to postgraduate work in marine biology – one of the postgraduate courses the regime permitted to female students – in the University at Irkutsk, near Lake Baikal. The deepest lake in the world, it contains more fresh water than all the North American lakes put together. This region supported flora and fauna not found anywhere else. And yet until Renn had showed her the letter from his daughter she'd not even known where Lake Baikal was! How much more was there to know?

'I will confide a secret,' Renn announced when she gave him back the chatty letter he'd just received from his daughter.

'What is it, Herr Renn?'

'You are to get an award, Frau Direktor.'

'An award? I've heard nothing of it.'

'The nature of the award has still to be decided but your heroic years in England working for the revolution will be marked by an award. Moscow has said yes and now there might also be a medal from the DDR too.'

'I am overwhelmed, Herr Renn.'

'It is overdue, Frau Direktor Samson.'

Renn had been surprised at the way in which Fiona had settled in to her Berlin job. He didn't realize to what extent Fiona's English background had prepared her for the communist regime. Her boarding school had very quickly taught her to hide every human feeling: triumph, disappointment, glee, love or shame. Her authoritarian father had demonstrated the art of temporizing and the value of the soft reply. Her English middle-class background – with its cruel double-meanings, oblique questions and humiliating indifference – had provided the final graduation that amply fitted her for East Berlin's dangers. And of course Renn had no inkling of Fiona's bouts of depression, her ache for her children and the hours of suicidal despair and loneliness.

Hair drawn back in a style that was severe and yet not unbecoming, her face scrubbed and with very little make-up, Fiona, with the slight Berlin accent that she now applied to her everyday speech, had become accepted as a regular member of the KGB/Stasi team. Her office was not in the main building in Normannenstrasse, Berlin-Lichtenberg. As Renn had pointed out, to be one of the horde coming out of that big Stasi building at the end of the day's work, to fight your way down into the Magdalenenstrasse U-Bahn and wait for a train, was not something to yearn for.

There were many advantages to being in Karl Liebknecht Strasse. It was in the Mitte, only a stone's throw from the shops, bars and theatres, and Unter den Linden ran right into it. What the cunning old Hubert Renn really meant of course was that it was near the other government offices to which he had to go on foot, and convenient to the Alexanderplatz S-Bahn which took him home.

'I ordered a car for fourteen-thirty,' said Renn. He stopped to admire the fur-lined coat that Fiona had just bought. Not wanting to attract too much speculation about her finances, Fiona had debated about what sort of winter coat she should wear. Hubert Renn had solved the problem by getting permission for her to buy, with DDR currency, one of the fancy coats normally only on sale to foreign visitors. 'You have a meeting at the clinic for nervous diseases at fifteen hundred,' said Renn. 'I'll make sure the driver knows where to go. Pankow: near where the Autobahn ends. It's a maze of little streets: easy to get lost.'

'Thank you, Herr Renn. Do we have an agenda?'

Renn looked at her with an expression she didn't recognize. 'No agenda, Frau Direktor. Familiarization visit. You are meeting with Doktor Wieczorek.'

'Can't the doctor come here?'

Renn busied himself with some papers that were on the filing cabinet. 'It is usual to go there,' he said stiffly and without turning to look at her.

She was about to say that it all sounded very mysterious and make a joke of it, but she had learned that jokes of that sort did not go down well in the East. So she said, 'Do I need to take papers or files with me?'

'Only a notebook, Frau Direktor.'

'Will you not be there to take notes?' She was surprised by this development.

'I am not permitted to attend the meetings with Doktor Wieczorek.'

She looked at him but he didn't turn round to meet her eyes. 'In that case,' she said, 'perhaps I'll take an early lunch. By the way, Herr Renn . . .'

'Yes, Frau Direktor?'

'There is a doctor, Henry Kennedy . . . Here, I'll write that down for you.' She passed him the slip of paper and he read it carefully as if he might discover some hidden meaning in the name. 'He is from London; working at the Charité on a year's contract . . .'

'Yes, Frau Direktor?'

'For a year's residence he would have been screened, wouldn't he?'

'Yes, Frau Direktor.'

She wanted the next bit to sound as casual as possible. 'Could you let me see the file?'

'It wouldn't be kept in this building, Frau Direktor.' She looked at him. 'But I could look it up.'

'I don't really need the file or even a copy.'

'You just need to know that there are no complications,' offered Renn.

'Exactly, Herr Renn. He is someone I know socially; I will have to see him from time to time.'

'All is clear, Frau Direktor.'

Pankow has long been one of the most desirable residential districts of the central part of Berlin. This was where smartly dressed East Germans arrived to dinner parties in imported cars! And here, Fiona had discovered to her great surprise, there were households that boasted live-in domestic help.

But the clinic was not in the most salubrious part of Berlin-Pankow. It was a three-storey building in imitation marble. Its bleak neo-Renaissance style, monumental proportion and the pockmarks of wartime artillery damage suggested that it was a surviving example of Berlin's Third Reich architecture.

She was glad of her beautiful fur-lined coat. It was snowing: large flakes that came spinning down like discs and made loud crunching noises underfoot. The temperature had dropped with a suddenness that caught even the residents off guard, and the streets were quiet.

The driver found the clinic without any trouble. There was a wall around the building and a tall gate that opened for her car. The ornamental entrance doors surmounted a wide flight of stone steps with a relief, suggesting columns, on each side of it.

The lobby was lit by soft grey light that came from clerestory windows, set deep into the wall above the entrance. Its floor was an intricate mosaic, depicting Roman maidens broadcasting flowers, and the doors on every side were closed. Doktor Wieczorek's name was painted on a wooden plaque and inserted, together with those of other senior medical staff on duty that day, into a large board on the wall behind the reception desk.

'Yes?' The receptionist was a young man with black hair upon which he'd used a generous amount of hair cream. He wore a washable grey linen jacket, a white shirt and black tie. It was a kind of uniform. He was writing something in a ledger and didn't look up.

'Doktor Samson,' said Fiona. The profound trust that Germans showed for doctorates of any sort had persuaded her to start using her academic qualification.

'Your business?' The young man still didn't look up.

'Stand up when you talk to me!' said Fiona. She didn't raise her voice but the tone was enough to remind the young man that a visitor from the Stasi was expected this afternoon.

He leapt to his feet as if scalded and clicked his heels. 'Ja, Frau Doktor.'

'Take me to Doktor Wieczorek.'

'Doktor Wieczorek . . . Herr Dok Dok Dok . . .' said the young man, stuttering and red-faced.

'Immediately. I am on State business,' said Fiona.

'Immediately, Frau Doktor. Yes, immediately.'

Doktor Wieczorek was an elegant forty-year-old specialist who had spent time in the Serbsky Institute of Forensic Psychiatry in Moscow and at the well-known mental hospital which was a part of the Chernyakhovsk prison. He had wavy hair that was beginning to grey at the temples, and a manner that suggested consummate medical expertise. Under his white jacket he wore a smart shirt and silk tie. His firm voice and avuncular manner relaxed her immediately, and so did his readiness to make little jokes about the bureaucracy that he constantly faced and so seldom defeated. 'Coffee?'

'No thank you,' said Fiona. There had been an attempt to make the austere little office look homely with the addition of an oriental carpet and an antique clock that chimed the hours.

'Tea? Tea with milk?' He smiled. 'That was the only thing I could remember about the British when I was a child: the way they poured cold milk into their tea and ruined it. No? Well we'll get on with this "familiarization visit". There is not a great deal to see in the building. At present we have twenty-three patients, one of whom I expect to be able to send home in a month or two. Some, I'm afraid, will never go home, but in the matter of clinical psychiatry I am always reluctant to say there is no hope.' He smiled at her. 'Do you know what we do here?'

'No,' she said.

He turned far enough to get from the shelf a large glass jar inside which a brain was to be seen in murky formalin. 'Look at that,' he said, putting it on the desk. 'That's the brain of "Der Grosse Gustaf", who was a music hall performer of the nineteen thirties. Anyone in the audience could ask him such questions as who fought Max Schmeling in 1933. He'd immediately tell them it was Max Baer who won on a technical knockout in the tenth round in New York City.'

'That's impressive,' said Fiona.

'I'm interested in boxing,' explained Wieczorek. He tapped the jar. 'But "The Great Gustaf" could answer any sort of question: he had a brain like an encyclopedia.'

'Why is it here?'

'There remains in the Soviet Union a small but influential group of medical men who think that slicing up the human brain will reveal some of nature's secrets. Lenin's brain was sliced up and studied under the microscope. So was Stalin's. So were a lot of lesser brains before and since.'

'What did they find?'

'That seems to be a State secret.'

'They discovered nothing, you mean?'

'I didn't say that, did I?' He tapped the jar again. 'But I saved Gustaf from such indignity. Gustaf has his brain intact.'

'Where did you get such a thing?'

'It came from the Charité Hospital at the end of the war. All hospitals have a roomful of such stuff. When the Red Army infantry got into the Charité during the fighting in 1945 they found the generals, and other high-ups who'd been hanged for trying to assassinate Hitler. Their bodies were still preserved in the post-mortem room refrigerators there. The cadavers had been sent from the Plötzensee prison and no one had been told what to do with them. And there was the medical museum, with all sorts of other stuff, over there too but the Red Army high command disapproved and the exhibits were sent to other institutions. We got Gustaf's brain.' He shook the jar so that the brain moved. 'The distribution of the exhibits started a lot of silly rumours. They said that Ernst Röhm's heart had been sent to the University Hospital in Leipzig and it had been contained in a test tube.' He put the jar back on the shelf. 'You must forgive me: physicians are inclined to develop a macabre sense of humour.'

'What sort of success rate do you have, Doctor?'

'They are all failures when they come here,' said Wieczorek. 'We

641

only get patients for whom some other institution can do no more. For most of them we can merely keep the fires under control. It is like the job of your security service, isn't it? Are we drawn to such work, do you think?'

'Surely you are better equipped to answer that question,' said Fiona.

'I cannot answer on your behalf, but for me and many of my colleagues I suspect that dealing in failure provides an excuse for a lack of success. And like you perhaps, I enjoy the challenge of such fragile, complicated and deceptive disciplines. Can you ever be sure that you are right?' He paused. 'Right about anything at all?'

'Sometimes,' said Fiona. 'You still haven't told me about your methods.'

'Carl Jung once said, "Show me a sane man and I will cure him for you." I think about that a lot. Methods? What can I tell you?' He looked at her with polite interest. 'The treatment of seriously disturbed patients has changed radically over the years. First and foremost there remains the old-fashioned analytical session in which patients are encouraged to delve into their own minds. As Freud discovered, it is a lengthy process. So along came the neuro-surgeons who drilled holes into the skull and destroyed brain cells and nerve fibres with surgical instruments.' He waited while the horror of that became clear to her. 'Then came a time when it seemed as if electric shocks through the brain could provide lasting improvement, and that seemed to be the panacea everyone had awaited. It wasn't the answer we had hoped for. But the chemists were waiting their turn, and patients were given massive doses of Dexedrine followed by Seconal and whatever new drug the West German chemical companies were anxious to sell. Now I suppose many specialists are beginning to think that amid his claptrap, Freud may have had a few worthwhile ideas after all. But analysis on the couch is a very long process: we'll never have enough analysts to fight mental illness in that laborious way.'

'And where do you stand?'

'In the matter of treatment? I am a senior consultant here but my staff are permitted considerable freedom to choose what is best for their patients. We have mostly depressives and schizophrenics, some of them catatonics demanding a lot of skill and close attention. However it is in the nature of our function, as a garbage can into which patients are discarded, that we treat a wide variety of illness. After many years of practice I have become reluctant to forbid any kind of treatment that a doctor, after a proper study of a patient, thinks will be beneficial.'

'You forbid nothing?'

642

'That is my stated position.'

'Including lobotomy?'

'A seriously disturbed patient who becomes violent can sometimes be returned to something approaching normal life.' He got up. 'Let me show you the wards.'

The clinic was hushed but not entirely silent. Most of the patients were in bed, sleeping with that impassive calm that medicine provides. One small ward was in semi-darkness. It held six sleepers who had been sedated for a week. It was, explained Doktor Wieczorek, the preliminary part of the treatment for most new arrivals. Underlying the smell of disinfectant there were all the disagreeable odours that warm bodies provide when crowded together in a closed room. He went to the window and raised the blind a fraction so that they could see the sleeping patients. Outside, she saw that the snow was falling much more heavily, the trees were rimed with it and passing cars left black lines in the road. Doktor Wieczorek adjusted the disarranged bedclothes. Sometimes, he joked, it took a week or two for their documentation to catch up with them.

The rooms were all lined with white tiles from floor to ceiling. There was something pitiless about the shiny hardness as it reflected the grey blankets. An ashen-faced patient stared at her but didn't register any emotion. Fiona had that guilty feeling of intrusion that afflicts all fit people in the presence of the sick. Wieczorek pulled down the blind and it was dark. As if in response to the darkness, one of the patients gave a muffled cry but then went quiet again.

Downstairs there was a large 'association room' where half a dozen patients were sitting in metal chairs with blankets over their knees. Two of them, both middle-aged men, were wearing woolly hats. There was no sign of books or newspapers and the patients were either asleep or staring into space. A TV set in the corner was showing a cartoon film, in which a hatchet-wielding mouse was chasing a cat, but the sound was switched off and no one was watching it.

'There is one patient you must meet,' said Doktor Wieczorek. 'Franz: he is our oldest inhabitant. When we got him, in 1978, his memory had completely gone but we are proud to have made a little progress.' He showed her into a bare room with a big square-shaped sink equipped for washing bed-pans. There was a man sitting there in a wheelchair. His body had run to fat as a consequence of his confinement. His complexion was yellowish and his lips were pressed tightly together as if he was trying not to yell. 'Come along, Franz. What about a cup of coffee?'

The man in the wheelchair said nothing, and made no move, except that he rolled his eyes as if trying to see the doctor's face without moving his head. 'I've brought a lady to see you, Franz. It's a long time since you had a visitor, isn't it?' To Fiona Doktor Wieczorek said, 'With patients of this sort the condition varies greatly from day to day.'

'Hello, Franz,' said Fiona, uncertain of what was expected of her.

'Say, hello, Franz,' said Doktor Wieczorek, and added, 'He hears everything but perhaps today he doesn't want to talk to us.' He took the wheelchair and tipped it back to lift the front wheels clear over the step.

Wieczorek took Franz in his wheelchair along the corridor, continuing his small talk and seeming not to notice that Franz didn't answer. Fiona followed. When the chair was positioned in a small room with 'Treatment Room No. 2' on its door it was placed so that Fiona and the doctor could sit down and face the patient. Although he still hadn't moved his head Franz had become agitated at coming into the room. He was looking at a small grey enamel cabinet in the corner. Its dial was calibrated in volts and there was a mechanical timer and wires ending in what looked like headphones. Franz stared at the machine and then at Doktor Wieczorek and then back at the machine again.

'He doesn't like the electric shock treatment,' said the doctor. 'No one does.' He put out a hand and touched Franz in a reassuring gesture. 'It's all right, Franz. No treatment today, old friend. Coffee, just coffee.'

As if by prearrangement a woman in a blue overall came in carrying a tray with cups, saucers and a jug of coffee. The chinaware was thick and clumsy: the sort which didn't readily break if dropped. 'I'll change my mind, if I may?' said Fiona as the doctor began pouring the coffee.

'Good. Changing people's minds is our speciality here. Isn't that right, Franz?' Doktor Wieczorek chuckled.

Franz moved his eyes and stared at Fiona. It seemed as if he could hear and understand everything that was said. Looking into his face, she wondered if there was something faintly familiar about him, but then she dismissed the thought.

'Poor Franz Blum was a hard-working young third secretary working in the attaché's office in London. Then one day he had a complete breakdown. I suppose it was the strain of being without his family in a strange country for the first time. Some people find it very difficult to adapt. The Embassy shipped him back to Moscow as soon as it was realized that he was sick. Everything was tried and although there were times when he seemed to get better, in the long term he just got worse and worse. It's a sad case. In a way he provides us with a constant reminder of the limitations of our science.'

644

Fiona watched Blum as he reached for his coffee, extending two hands and picking it up with very great care.

'One confidential KGB report from London said that Franz was a spy for the British,' said Doktor Wieczorek. 'But apparently there is no hard evidence to support the allegation. There was never any question of him going on trial but we were told the background, in case it could help in diagnosis. There was an inquiry, but even your Stasi interrogators got nothing out of him.'

She kept calm, very calm, but she turned her eyes away from Franz. 'But you did?' Then this was the man she had reported to Martin Pryce-Hughes, the one she had betrayed and consigned to a living death. Was Doktor Wieczorek in on that whole story, or was it all just need-to-know?

'We have that sort of patient sometimes. Franz wasn't easy to deal with. It's a long time ago now but I remember it all so clearly. When he didn't respond to the pills and injections it became clear that electric shock would be the only way to help him. Not just the little sessions that are given to help depressed patients; we tried a new idea, really massive shocks.'

Franz spilled a dribble of coffee down his chin. Wieczorek took a handkerchief and wiped it. Then he gently removed Franz's woollen hat and indicated for Fiona the shaved patches where the electrodes were applied.

'Shock,' said Franz suddenly and loudly as the doctor fingered the bare skin.

'Good,' said Doktor Wieczorek proudly. 'Did you hear that? As clear as anything. Keep up the good work, Franz, and we'll soon be sending you home.' He replaced the knitted hat on the man's head but it remained askew, giving Franz Blum an inappropriately jaunty air. As if the demonstration was over, Doktor Wieczorek stood up and grabbed the wheelchair. He pushed it back into the corridor, where a nurse was waiting to take it from him. 'You didn't have your coffee,' Wieczorek said to Fiona as if suddenly remembering it.

'Is there much more of the clinic to see?' she asked.

'Nothing of consequence. Sit down and drink the coffee. I hope Franz didn't upset you.'

'Of course not,' said Fiona.

'He'll never go home, he'll never go anywhere,' said Doktor Wieczorek. 'He's institutionalized for life, I'm afraid. Poor Franz.'

'Yes, poor Franz,' said Fiona. 'But if the KGB report was true, he was an enemy of the State, wasn't he?'

'An enemy of the people,' Wieczorek corrected her sardonically. 'That's far worse.'

She looked at him: he was smiling. She knew then beyond any doubt that this was a charade, a charade acted out for her to guess the word. The word was 'treachery', and the pathetic zombie they had made of Franz Blum was an example of what would be done to her if she should betray her KGB masters. Is that why he'd quoted Carl Jung: 'Show me a sane man and I will cure him for you'?

'It's good coffee, isn't it?' said Doktor Wieczorek. 'I have a special source.'

'You're lucky,' said Fiona. Perhaps this terrifying warning was a procedure that all senior Stasi staff were subjected to. There was no way to be sure; that was how the country was run. Stick and carrot: award in the morning and warning in the afternoon. This topsyturvy clinic where the 'sane' were cured was just how she saw this 'workers' state' where the leaders lived in ostentatious grandeur in fenced compounds paced by armed guards.

'Yes, I am lucky,' said Doktor Wieczorek, savouring his coffee. 'You're lucky too: we all are.'

18

Bret Rensselaer was overplaying his hand. In trying to make Fiona Samson secure he'd even thrown suspicion on to Bernard Samson, suggesting that he might have been an accomplice to his wife's treachery. It was an effective device, for the Department was just as vulnerable to rumours, and whispered half-truths, as any other organized assembly of competitive humans. The trouble came because opinions were divided about Bernard Samson's integrity, and so a rumour started that another 'mole' was at work within the Department. An unhealthy atmosphere of mistrust and suspicion was developing.

The discovery of the murdered Julian MacKenzie in a Department safe house in Bosham gave further impetus to the gossip. Thanks to what Miranda Keller had told him, Bret knew that it was a case of mistaken identity: the KGB had been after Bernard Samson. But Bret took no action in the matter before getting Samson into the number 3 conference room and admonishing him in the presence of suitable witnesses. Samson shouted back, as Bret knew he would, and Bret ended up by telling everyone who would listen that Bernard Samson was 'beyond suspicion'.

But spinning the web of deceit that he deemed necessary for Fiona's safety was taking its toll of Bret Rensselaer. He was by nature an administrator: brutal sometimes, but sustained always by self-righteousness. Running the Economics Intelligence Section had been a task for which he was ideally fitted. But Sinker was different. His original plan to target the East German economy by draining away skilled workers and professional people was not as easy as it once seemed. Fiona had supplied him with regular information about the East German opposition and other reform groups but they could not unite. His overall problem was that keeping Sinker such a close secret meant telling ever more complex lies to his friends and colleagues. It was vital that none of them could see the whole plan. This was demanding in a way he did not relish. It was like playing tennis against himself: criss-crossing the centre line, leaping the net, wrong-footing

647

himself and delivering ever more strenuous volleys that would be impossible to return.

And this double life left him very little time for relaxation or pleasure. Now, at lunchtime on Saturday, a time when he might have snatched a few hours relaxing with friends at the sort of weekend house-party he most enjoyed, he was sitting bickering with his wife about the divorce and her wretched alimony.

It was typical of Nicola that she should insist upon having lunch at Roma Locuta Est, a cramped Italian restaurant in Knightsbridge. Even the name affronted him: 'Rome has spoken' was a way of saying no complaints would be listened to, and that was exactly the way Pina ran her restaurant. Pina was a formidable Italian matron who welcomed the rich and famous while ruthlessly pruning from her clientele those of lesser appeal. It had become a meeting place for the noisy Belgravia jet-set, a group which Bret assiduously shunned. This being Saturday they were at their most insufferable: table-hopping and shouting loudly to each other, ordering their Anglicized food in execrable Italian. Bret's lunch was not made more enjoyable by discovering that just about everyone here seemed to be on first-name terms with his wife Nicola.

'You really believe it,' she was saying. 'Jesus Christ, Bret. You say you're poor; and you really believe it. If it wasn't so goddamned sneaky, it would make me laugh.' Nicola had obviously taken a lot of trouble with her clothes and make-up, but she was out of his past and he felt no attraction to her.

'You don't have to tell everyone in the room, darling,' said Bret softly. Knowing the sort of place it was, Bret had made appropriate sartorial concessions. He was wearing a suede jacket and tan-coloured silk roll-neck. His normal attire, a good suit, would have looked out of place here on a Saturday lunchtime.

'I don't care if all the world knows. I'll shout it from the house-tops.'

'We've been through all this, before we were married. You saw the lawyers. You signed the forms of agreement.'

'I didn't read what I was signing.' She drank some of her Campari and soda.

'Why the hell didn't you?'

'Because I was in love with you, that's why I didn't.'

'You thought separating would be like it was in old Hollywood movies. You thought I would go to stay in my club and you'd have the house, and the furniture and the paintings and the Bentley and every other damn thing.'

'I thought I might own half of my own home. I didn't know my home was owned by a corporation.'

'Not a corporation: it's owned by a trust.'

'I don't care if it's owned by The Boy Scouts of America: you let me think it was my home, and now I find it never was.'

'Please don't tell me that you gave me the best years of your life,' said Bret.

'I gave you everything.' She stirred her drink so that the ice rattled.

'You gave me hell.' He looked round the dining room, 'I can't think why that woman Pina allows dogs in here: it's unhygienic.' He took out a handkerchief and blew his nose. 'And animal hair affects my sinus.'

'It doesn't affect your sinus,' said his wife. 'You get your sinus and then you look round for something to blame it on.'

Bret noticed that the demonstrative Pina was making her rounds. She liked to take her customers in a bear hug and scream endearments into their ear before discussing their food. 'Yes, you gave me hell,' said Bret.

'I told you the truth, and you found it hell.' With quick agitated movements Nicola opened her handbag to get her cigarettes. Under the handbag there was a copy of *Vogue* and a book called *Somebody Stole My Spy*. On the cover it said 'Better than Ludlum' in letters bigger than the author's name. Bret wondered whether she was really reading the book, or had brought it here as some kind of provocation. She liked to make jokes about his 'career as a spy'.

When Bret leaned forward and lit the cigarette for her, he noticed that she was trembling. He wondered why. He found it difficult to believe that he could cause anyone to become so distressed. 'Jesus!' said Nicola and blew smoke high into the air so that it made little clouds in the plastic vines that hung from the ceiling.

Out of the corner of his eye he saw Pina coming. Bret detested her and decided to flee to the toilet but he was too late. 'And you know my husband,' Nicola was already saying, her voice strangled as she was enveloped in Pina's beefy arms, and drowned by a babble of Italian chatter.

Bret stood up and edged sideways to keep the table between them and nodded deferentially. Pina looked at him, rolled her eyes and yelled in Italian. Bret smiled and gave a little bow to acknowledge what he thought was some flowery Roman compliment but it turned out to be Pina shouting for more menus.

When they'd ordered lunch, or more accurately when they had agreed to the meal that Pina decreed they should have, Nicola went back to talking about the settlement.

'Your lawyer is a bastard,' she said.

'Other people's lawyers are always bastards. That comes with the job.'

Nikki shifted her attack. 'They do what you tell them.'

'I don't tell them anything. There's nothing to tell. The law is explicit.'

'I'm going to California. I'm going to sue you.'

'That won't get you anywhere,' said Bret. 'I don't live in California and I don't own anything in California. You might as well go to Greenland.'

'I'm going to take up residence there. They have communal property laws in California. My brother-in-law says I'd do better there.'

'I wish you'd start using your brains, Nikki. The money my father left me is in a trust. We're not really a part of the Rensselaer family. My grandmother married into it late in life: she changed her children's name to Rensselaer. We never inherited the Rensselaer millions. I just have an allowance from a small trust fund. I told you all that before we were married.'

She waggled a manicured finger at him. 'You're not going to get away with this, Bret. I'll break that damned trust fund if it's the last thing I do. I want what I'm entitled to.'

'Dammit, Nikki. You left me. You went off with Joppi.'

'Leave Joppi out of this,' she said.

'How can we leave him out of it? He's the third party.'

'He's not.'

'Nikki, dear. We both know he is.'

'Well, you prove it. You just try and prove it, that's all.'

'Don't drag it all through the courts, Nikki. All you'll do is make lawyers rich.'

'Who's having the *insalata frutti di mare*?' yelled the waiter into their ears as he bent over the table.

'I am,' said Bret.

'You want the sole off the bone, madam?' the waiter asked Nicola.

'Yes, please,' she said.

Bret looked down at the mangled lettuce upon which sat four cold damp shrimps and some white rubber rings of inkfish, and he looked at Nicola's delicious filleted sole. 'Melted butter?' said the waiter, 'and a little Parmesan cheese?' Nikki always knew what to order: was it skill or was it luck? Or was it Pina?

Bret noticed that the bejewelled woman at the next table was feeding pieces of her veal escalope to a perfectly brushed and combed terrier at her feet. 'It's like a damned zoo in here,' he muttered, but his wife pretended not to hear him.

Nikki abandoned her sole fillets and put down her knife and fork. 'I gave you everything,' she said again, having thought about it carefully. 'I even came to live in this lousy country with you, didn't I? And what did I get for it?'

'What did you get? You lived high on the hog, and in one of the most beautiful homes in England.'

'It wasn't a home, Bret, it was just a beautiful house. But when did I ever see my husband? I'd go for days and days with no one to talk to but the servants.'

'You should be able to cope with being alone,' said Bret.

'Well, old buddy. Now you'll be able to find out what it means to be alone. Because I won't be there when you get home, and no other woman will put up with you. You'll soon discover that.'

'I'm not afraid of being alone,' said Bret smugly. He pushed the shrimp salad aside. His wife was always complaining of being alone and today he had an answer ready: 'Lots of people have been: Descartes, Kierkegaard, Locke, Newton, Nietzsche, Pascal, Spinoza and Wittgenstein were alone for most of their lives.'

She laughed. 'I saw that in the letters column of the *Daily Telegraph*. But those people are all geniuses. You're not a thinker . . . not a philosopher.'

'My work is important,' said Bret. He was put out. 'It's not like working for a biscuit factory. A government job is a government job.'

'Oh, sure, and we all know what governments do.'

'What do you mean by that?' said Bret, with an uncertainty that was almost comic.

'They make the rules for you, and break them themselves. They hike your taxes and give themselves a raise in pay. They take your money away and shower it on all kinds of lousy foreign governments. They send your kids to Vietnam and get them killed. They fly in choppers while you're stuck in a traffic jam. They let the banks and insurance companies shaft you in exchange for political campaign money.'

'Is that what you really think, Nikki?' Bret was shocked. She'd never said anything like that before. He wondered if she had been drinking all morning.

'You're damn right it's what I think. It's what everybody thinks who hasn't got a hand in the pork barrel.'

Alarm bells rang. 'I didn't know you were a liberal.' He wondered what the security vetting people had made of her. Thank goodness he was getting rid of her; but had any of this gone down on his file?

'I'm not a goddamned Democrat or a Liberal or a Red or anything else. It's just that smug guys like you doing your "important work for governments" make me puke.'

'There's nothing to be gained from a slanging match,' said Bret. 'I know you must be disappointed about the house but that's outside my control.'

'Damn you, Bret. I must have somewhere to live!'

He guessed that Joppi was getting rid of her: suddenly he felt sorry for her but he didn't want her back. 'That apartment in Monte Carlo is empty. You could lease it from the trustees for a nominal payment.'

'Lease it from the trustees for a nominal payment,' she repeated sarcastically. 'How nominal can you get? Like a dollar a year, do you mean?'

'If it would end all this needless wrangling, a dollar a year would be just fine. Shall we agree on that?' He waved a hand to attract a waiter, but it was no use. The staff were all standing round a table in the corner smiling at a TV newsreader who was being photographed cuddling a smooth-coated chihuahua. 'Do you want coffee?'

'Yes,' she said. 'Yes to both questions: but I want furniture – good furniture – in the first, and cream and sugar in the second.'

'You've got a deal,' said Bret. He was relieved. Had Nikki resolutely pressed for the Thameside house it would have put him in a difficult position. He would have had to resign. There was no way that the Department would have tolerated him getting into a divorce action, and the risk of its attendant publicity. And yet if he resigned, where would that leave Fiona Samson? He was the only person who knew the whole story, and he felt personally responsible for her mission. There were many times when he worried about her.

Bret looked up to see his chauffeur Albert Bingham easing his way through the crowded dining room. 'What now?' said Bret. Nicola turned round to see what he was looking at.

'Good afternoon, Mrs Rensselaer,' said Albert politely. He reasoned that ex-wives sometimes resumed their authority as employers, and should not be slighted. 'I'm sorry to interrupt you, sir, but the hospital came through on the car phone.'

'What did they say?' Bret was already on his feet. Albert wouldn't interrupt the lunch unless it was something very important.

'Could you be early?'

'Could I be early?' repeated Bret. He found his credit card in his wallet.

'They said you would know what it was,' said Albert.

'I'll have to go,' said Bret to his wife. 'It's an old friend.' He flicked the plastic card with his fingernail so that it made a snapping noise. She remembered it as one of his many irritating habits.

'That's all right,' said Nicola, in the brisk voice that proclaimed her annoyance.

'Let's do it again,' said Bret. He bent forward – the hand holding his credit card extended like a stage magician palming something from the air – and kissed his wife on the cheek. 'Now it's all settled, let's do it again.' He heard the terrier growl as he trod too near its food.

She nodded. He didn't want to have lunch with her again, she could see that as clearly as anything. She saw how relieved he was at this opportunity to escape from her. She felt like crying. She was pleased to be separating from Bret Rensselaer but she found it humiliating that he seemed pleased about it too. She got out her compact and flipped up the mirror to look at her eye make-up. She could see Bret reflected in it. She watched him while he paid the bill.

Bret's original appointment with the Director-General had been for drinks at six o'clock at his house in the country. Now the Director-General had phoned to suggest that they meet at Rensselaer's mews house in London. That was the call on the car phone that Albert had reported. The Department's calls were always described by Albert as being calls from an anonymous hospital, school or club, according to Bret's company and the circumstances in which the message was delivered.

'Are you sure he said the mews house?' Bret asked his driver.

'Quite sure,' said Albert.

'What a memory he has,' said Bret with grudging admiration.

Back at the turn of the century, the mews house had been the stables and coach house for Cyrus Rensselaer's grand London home. The first time Bret saw the big house in the square it was an Officers' Club run by the American Red Cross. After the war it had been sold but the uncomfortable little mews house had been retained. Just a couple of rooms with kitchen, bathroom and garage, it was used by various members of the Rensselaer family, and sometimes by lawyers and agents coming to London on the family's behalf. But because Bret lived in England, he had a key and, by the generous consent of other members of the family, he could use it when he wanted. In return Bret kept an eye on the place and had the leaky roof fixed from time to time. He hadn't slept there for years.

Bret was surprised that the D-G should remember that he had access to the house and was annoyed that he should suggest it for their meeting. He had no consideration; the place was terribly neglected now that there was no permanent tenant to maintain it. 'Go to the mews right away,' Bret told his driver. 'We'll try and get it straightened out before Sir Henry arrives.'

'We'll have half an hour or so,' said Albert, 'and Sir Henry might be late: he said that.'

'It's just as well I remained in London,' said Bret. 'You never know where Sir Henry will turn up.'

'No, sir,' said Albert Bingham.

Bret settled back in the leather seat of his Bentley. He had been tempted to spend the weekend with some horsy friends near Newmarket, and make a sidetrip to the D-G's house in Cambridge-shire. Then his wife had insisted that they met for Saturday lunch and he'd stayed in town. It was just as well. A sudden dash back to London at short notice, just to satisfy the old man's whim, was the kind of thing that gave Bret indigestion pains.

'I'm sorry if this was an inconvenient meeting place,' said Sir Henry Clevemore when he arrived in the tiny upstairs room above the garage. He had knocked his head against the door frame but now, having fitted his huge bulk into a big, somewhat dilapidated armchair, he seemed quite content. 'But it was a matter of some urgency.'

'I'm sorry that it's not more comfortable here,' said Bret. The room was dusty and damp. There were fingermarks on the mirror, unwashed milk bottles in the sink and dead flowers on the bookcase. The only festive note was provided by the carpet, which was rolled up, stitched into canvas and garnished with bright red plastic packets of moth repellant. Used by transients as a place to sleep, the house was sadly lacking in any sort of comfort. Even the electric kettle was not working. What a shame that Nikki was so difficult. This place would really benefit from a woman's touch.

Bret reached down to see if there was hot air coming from the convection heater. He'd put on the electric heating as soon as he arrived, but the air was musty. He resolved to do something drastic about refurbishing the place. He'd write to the lawyers about it. He opened a cupboard to reveal some bottles. 'There is a bottle of whisky . . .'

'Stop fussing, Bret. We needed somewhere to talk in private. This is ideal. No, I don't want a drink. My news is that Erich Stinnes is flying here from Mexico City together with young Bernard Samson. I think we've done it.'

654

'That's good news, sir.' He looked down to see where the D-G's black Labrador was sprawled. Why had the old man brought that senile and smelly creature up into this little room?

'It's going to be your show, Bret. Let Samson do the talking but keep a tight control on what's really happening. We must turn Stinnes round and get him back there.'

'Yes, sir.'

'But it occurred to me, Bret . . .' He paused. 'I don't want to interfere . . . It's your show. Entirely your show.'

'Please go on, sir.' Bret flicked the dust from a chintz-covered chair and sat down very carefully. He didn't want to get his clothes dirty.

The D-G was lolling back with his legs crossed, oblivious of the shabbiness of the room. The gloomy winter light coming through the dusty window was just enough to describe the old man's profile and make spots of light on the toes of his highly polished shoes. 'Should we collar this damned fellow Martin Pryce-Hughes?'

'The communist. Ummm.'

Bret's tone was too mild to satisfy the D-G. 'That little tick who was the contact between Mrs Samson and the KGB hoodlums,' he said forcibly. 'Shall we collar him? Don't say you haven't given it any thought.'

'I've given it a lot of thought,' said Bret in the strangled voice that was his response to unjust criticism.

'You cautioned against pulling him in too soon after Mrs Samson went over. But how long are we going to wait?'

Bret said, 'You see, sir . . .'

The D-G interrupted him. 'Now with this fellow Stinnes arriving here, we have to consider to what extent we want Moscow to link Stinnes and Pryce-Hughes. If Stinnes is to go back there, we don't want them to think that he betrayed Pryce-Hughes to us, do we?'

'No, sir, we don't.'

'Well, for the Lord's sake, man. Spit it out! What is on your mind? Shall we grab Pryce-Hughes and grill him or not? It's your decision. You know I don't want to interfere.'

'You are always very considerate,' said Bret, while really thinking how much he would like to kick the D-G down the narrow creaking stairs and watch to see which way he bounced off the greasy garage floor.

'I try to be,' said the D-G, mollified by Bret's subservient tone.

'But another dimension has emerged. It is something I didn't want to bother you with.'

'Bother me with it now,' said Sir Henry.

'In the summer of 1978 . . .' Bret paused, deciding how much he should reveal, and how he should say it. 'Mrs Samson . . . formed a relationship with a Dr Harry Kennedy.'

When Bret paused again, the D-G said, 'Formed a relationship? What the devil does that mean? I'm not going to sue you for defamation, Bret. For God's sake, say what you mean. Say what you mean.'

'I mean,' said Bret, speaking slowly and deliberately, 'that from about that time, until she went over there, she was having a love affair with this man.'

'Oh my God!' said the D-G with a gasp of surprise upon which he almost choked. 'Mrs Samson? Are you quite sure, Bret?' He waited until Bret nodded. 'My God.' The black Labrador, sensing its master's dismay, got to its feet and shook itself. Now the air was full of dust from the dog's coat: Bret could see motes of it buoyant on the draught coming from the heater.

Bret got his handkerchief to his nose just in time before sneezing. When he recovered he dabbed his face again and said, 'I'm quite sure, Sir Henry, but that's not all. When I started digging into this fellow Kennedy's past, I discovered that he has been a party member since the time he was a medical student.'

'Party member? Communist Party member? This fellow she was having it off with? Bret, why the hell didn't you tell me all this? Am I going mad?' He was straining forward in his chair as if trying to get up and his dog was looking angrily at Bret.

'I appreciate your concern, sir,' said Bret in the gravelly American accent that he could summon when he needed it. 'Kennedy is a Canadian. His father was a Ukrainian with a name that couldn't be written on an English typewriter so it became Kennedy.'

'I don't like the smell of that one, Bret. Are we really dealing with a Russian national wielding a Canadian birth certificate? We've seen a lot of those, haven't we?'

'Ottawa RCMP have nothing on him. Served in the air force with an exemplary record. Medical school: postgraduate and so on. The only thing they could turn up was an ex-wife chasing him for alimony. No political activity except for a few meetings of the party at college.' Bret stopped. The fact that the fellow was being chased for alimony payments made Bret sympathize.

'Well, don't leave it like that, Bret. You're not trying to break it to me that Mrs Samson might have been . . .' The D-G's voice trailed away as he considered the terrifying complexities that would follow upon any doubts about Fiona Samson's loyalties.

656

'No, no worries on that account, Sir Henry. In fact they are both clear. I have no evidence that Dr Kennedy has been active in any way – in any way at all – during the time he was seeing Mrs Samson or afterwards.'

'How do you know?'

'I've been keeping an eye on him.'

'You personally?'

'No, of course not, Sir Henry. I have had someone keeping an eye on him.'

'Someone? What someone? A Department someone?'

'No, of course not, sir. I arranged it privately.'

'Yes, but not paid for it privately, eh? It's gone on the dockets. Perhaps you didn't think of that. Oh, my God.'

'It's not on any dockets, Sir Henry. I paid personally and I paid in cash.'

'Are you insane, Bret? You paid personally? Out of your own pocket? What are you up to?'

'It had to be kept secret,' said Bret.

'Of course it did. You don't have to tell me that! My God. I've never heard of such a thing.' The D-G slumped back in the chair as if in collapse. 'What kind of whisky have you got?' he said finally.

Bret reached for a bottle of Bell's, poured a stiff one into a tumbler for the D-G and gave it to him. After sipping it, the D-G said, 'Confound you, Bret. Tell me the worst. Come along. I'm prepared now.'

'There is no "worst",' said Bret. 'It is as I told you. There is nothing to show any contact between Kennedy and the Soviets.'

'You don't fool me, Bret. If it was as simple as that you would have told me long ago, not waited until I faced you with collaring Pryce-Hughes.'

Bret was still standing near the bottles. He had never been a drinker, but he poured himself a tiny one to be sociable, took it to the window and nursed it. He wanted to get as far away from the dog as he possibly could. The smell of the drink was repulsive and he put it down. He pressed his fingers against the cold window-pane. How well he knew this little house. Glenn Rensselaer had brought him here while still wearing the uniform of a US Army general. Glenn had been someone Bret had loved more than he could ever love the pathetic alcoholic who was his father.

'It's no more than a hunch,' said Bret, after a long time of just looking down at the cobbled mews and the shiny cars parked there. 'But I just know Kennedy is a part of it. I just know he is. I'm sure they put

Kennedy in to run a check on Mrs Samson. They met at a railway station; I'm sure it was contrived.' He let a little whisky touch his lips. 'She must have got through whatever test he gave her, because the signs are that Dr Kennedy is in love with her and continues to be. But Kennedy is a bomb, ticking away, and I don't like it. I kept an eye on Pryce-Hughes because I hoped there would be some contact. But it's a long time ago: I guess I was wrong.'

'Too much guessing, Bret.'

'Yes, Sir Henry.'

'Facts trump the ace of hunches, right?'

'Yes, of course, sir.'

'You'll collar Pryce-Hughes?'

'I'd rather leave that a little longer, Director. I tried to provoke him into a response a few years back. I had someone produce an elaborate file that "proved" Pryce-Hughes was working for London Central. It was a magnificent job – documents, photos and all sorts of stuff – and it cost an arm and a leg. I went along when it was shown to him.'

'And?'

'He just laughed in our faces, sir. Literally. I was there. He laughed.'

'I'm glad we had this little chat, Bret,' said the D-G. It was a rebuke.

'But the file I compiled to incriminate Pryce-Hughes could be very useful to us now, sir.'

'I'm listening, Bret.'

'I want to have the whole file revised so it will incriminate this KGB Colonel Pavel Moskvin.'

'The thug who murdered that lad in the Bosham safe house?'

'I believe he's a danger to Fiona Samson.'

'Are you sure this is not just a way of using that damned file?'

'It will cost very little, sir. We can plant it into the KGB network very easily. That Miranda Keller woman would be perfect in the role of Moskvin's contact.'

'It would be a bit rough on her, wouldn't it?' said the D-G.

'It's Fiona Samson we have to think of,' said Bret.

'Very well, Bret. If you put it like that I can't stop you.'

19

England. Christmas 1983.

Gloria Kent felt miserable. She had brought Bernard Samson's two young children to spend Christmas with her parents. She was tall and blonde and very beautiful and she was wearing the low-cut green dress she had bought specially to impress Bernard.

'Why isn't he with his children?' Gloria's mother asked for the umpteenth time. She was putting the Christmas lunch dishes into the dishwasher as Gloria brought them from the table.

'He was given Christmas duty at the last minute,' said Gloria. 'And the nanny had already gone home.'

'You are a fool, Gloria,' said her mother.

'What do you mean?'

'You know what I mean,' said her mother. 'He'll go back to his wife, they always do.' She dropped a handful of knives and forks into the plastic basket. 'A man can't have two wives.'

Gloria handed over the dessert plates and then put clingfilm over the remains of the Christmas pudding before putting it into the refrigerator.

Ten-year-old Billy Samson came into the kitchen. He was still wearing the paper hat and a plastic bangle that he'd got from a Christmas cracker. 'Sally is going to be sick,' he announced, without bothering to conceal his joy at the prospect.

'No she's not, Billy. I just spoke to her, she's doing the jigsaw. Is the video finished?'

'I've seen it before.'

'Has Grandad seen it before?' asked Gloria. It had been established that Gloria's father was Grandad.

'He's asleep,' said Billy. 'He snores.'

'Why don't you help Sally with the jigsaw?' said Gloria.

'Can I have some more custard?'

'I think you've had enough, Billy,' said Gloria firmly. 'I've never seen anyone eat so much.'

Billy looked at her for a moment before agreeing and wandering off to the drawing room. Mrs Kent watched him go. The little boy was so like

659

the photos of his father. She was sorry for the poor motherless mite but was convinced that her daughter would know only pain from her reckless affair with 'a married man at the office'.

'I know everything you want to say, Mummy,' said Gloria, 'but I love Bernard desperately.'

'I know you do, my sweetheart.' She was going to say more but she saw her daughter's eyes already brimming with tears. That was the heart-wrenching part of it, Gloria knew that only misery was in store for her.

'He didn't want to go,' said Gloria. 'This awful man at the office sent him. I planned everything so carefully. I wanted to make him and the children really happy.'

'What does he say about it?' her mother asked, emboldened by the wine she'd had with lunch.

'He says the same things you say,' said Gloria. 'He keeps telling me he's twenty years older than I am. He keeps saying I should be with someone else, someone younger.'

'Then he can't love you,' declared her mother emphatically.

Gloria managed a little laugh. 'Oh, Mummy. Whatever he does he's wrong in your eyes.'

'When you first told us your father couldn't talk about it for weeks.'

'It's my life, Mummy.'

'You are so young. You trust everyone and the world is so cruel.' She packed the last dirty plate into the dishwasher, closed its door and straightened up. 'What is he doing today that is so important? Or should I not ask?'

'He's in Berlin, identifying a body.'

'I'll be glad when you go to Cambridge.'

'Yes,' said Gloria without enthusiasm.

'Isn't his wife in Berlin?' said her mother suddenly.

'He won't be seeing her,' said Gloria.

In the next room Billy pulled a chair up to the card table where Sally was working at the jigsaw – 'A Devon Scene' – which was a present from Nanny. Sally had got two edges of it complete. Without saying anything Billy began to help with the puzzle.

'I miss Mummy,' said Sally. 'I wonder why she didn't visit us for Christmas.'

'Gloria is nice,' said Billy, who had rather fallen for her. 'What is separated?' He had heard that his parents were separated but he was not sure exactly what this meant.

Sally said, 'Nanny said Mummy and Daddy have to live in different countries so that they can find themselves.'

'Can't they find themselves?' said Billy. He chuckled, 'It must be terrible if you can't find yourself.'

Sally didn't find this funny at all. 'When she finds herself Mummy will come back.'

'Does it take long?'

'I'll ask Nanny,' said Sally, who was clever at wheedling things out of the quiet girl from Devon.

'Is Daddy finding himself too?' And then, before Sally could reply, he found a piece of sky and fitted it into the puzzle.

'I saw that bit first,' said Sally.

'No you didn't! No you didn't!'

Sally said, 'Perhaps Daddy could marry Mummy and marry Gloria too.'

'No,' said Billy authoritatively. 'A man can't have two wives.'

Sally looked at him with admiration. Billy always knew everything. But there was a look she recognized in his face. 'Are you all right?' she said fearfully.

'I think I'm going to be sick,' said Billy.

20

Hubert Renn seldom voiced his innermost thoughts, but had he done so in respect of working for Fiona Samson, he would have said that the relationship had proved far better than he'd dared hope. And when, in the first week of January 1984, he was offered a chance to change jobs and work at the Normannenstrasse Stasi headquarters, Renn declined and went to considerable trouble to provide reasons why not.

Hubert Renn preferred the atmosphere of the small KGB/Stasi command unit on Karl Liebknecht Strasse. And, like many of the administrative staff, he enjoyed the feeling of importance and the day-to-day urgency that 'operational' work bestowed. Also he'd adopted a paternal responsibility for Fiona Samson without it ever becoming evident from the stern and formal way in which he insisted that the office must be run. Neither did Fiona Samson ever demand, or seemingly expect, anything other than Renn's total dedication to his work.

Renn did not find it difficult to understand Fiona Samson, or at least to come to terms with her. This mutual understanding was helped by the way in which Fiona had suppressed and reformed her femininity. The uncertainties and the misgivings that child-bearing and marriage had given her no longer influenced her thoughts. She was not masculine – men and their reasonings were no less puzzling now than they'd ever been – but she was simplistic and determined in the way that men are. Even at her most feminine, she had never fallen into the role of victim the way she'd watched her mother and her sister and countless other women readily play that part. Nowadays, whenever something came up that she was unable to deal with on her own terms, she asked herself what Bernard would do in the same situation, and that often helped her to solve the problem. And solve it without delay.

Had she been perfectly fit, things would have been entirely endurable. But Berlin had got to her. For Bernard it was a second home and he loved it but for Fiona it was a city of bad dreams. She had come to the conclusion that her bouts of depression and the nightmares from which she so often awoke sweating and trembling were not solely brought on by loneliness, or even by the guilt she felt at having abandoned her husband and children. Berlin was the villain. Berlin was eating her heart away so that she would not ever recover. It was nonsense of course, but she was becoming unbalanced and she was aware of it.

In the privacy of her Frankfurter Allee apartment, when she was not slaving over work or trying to improve her German and her Russian, she did sometimes find time to reflect upon the reasons why she found herself in this desperate situation. She dismissed the narrative analysis, the sort of reasoning beloved of psychologists and novelists, that would undoubtedly draw a straight cause-and-effect line through her authoritarian father, the boarding school, her secret government work and its apotheosis in this assumption of another life. It hadn't happened like that. The ability to play out this role was something she'd worked hard to perfect: that part of her illness wasn't a manifestation of some flaw in her personality.

She'd liberated herself from being that little girl who'd gone to boarding school shivering with apprehension, not by marching or shouting slogans but by stealth. That was why the transformation was so complete. She had actually become another person! Although she would never admit it to a living soul, she had even given a name to this tough employee who came to work in the Karl Liebknecht Strasse every day, and slaved hard for the German socialist state: the person was Stefan Mittelberg – a name she'd compiled when perusing a directory – a man's name of course, for in the office she had to be a man. 'Come along, Stefan,' she'd tell herself each morning, 'it's time to get out of bed.' And when she was brushing her hair in front of the mirror, as she always did at the start of each day, she would see hard-eyed Stefan looking back at her. Was 'Stefan' a manifestation of emotional change? Of hardening? Of liberation? Or was 'Stefan' the one who'd had the spontaneous love affair with Harry Kennedy? How else would one explain an act so totally out of character? Well, 'Stefan' was a success story; the trouble was, she loathed 'Stefan'. No matter, perhaps in time she would learn to love this new tougher self.

In the office she concentrated upon becoming the perfect apparatchik, the sort of boss that a man such as Renn would want to work for. But she was a foreigner and she was a woman, and sometimes she needed help and advice when dealing with the devious intrigues of the office.

'How long will the new man be working here?' Fiona asked Renn one day when they were tidying away boxes of papers and celebrating a completely clear desk.

Renn looked at her, amazed that she could be so innocent and ill-informed. Especially since Fiona's Russian award had now come through. She'd been given it at a little ceremony in the hall at Normannenstrasse. Renn had enjoyed a share of the glory. 'New man?' he said. He never rushed into such conversations.

'The young one . . . yellow wavy hair . . .' She paused. 'What have I said?'

Renn found her ignorance both appalling and endearing. Everyone else in the building had learned how to recognize an officer of the political security service in Moscow. 'Lieutenant Bakushin, do you mean?' he asked her.

'Yes. What is he here for?'

'He was one of the executive officers on the Moskvin inquiry.'

'Moskvin inquiry? Pavel Moskvin?'

'But yes. It was held in Moscow last week.'

'Inquiry into what?'

'Conduct.'

'Conduct?'

'That is the usual style. Such inquiries are secret, of course.'

'And is the verdict announced or is that secret too?'

'Lieutenant Bakushin is collecting further evidence. He will probably want to talk to you, Frau Direktor.'

'But Moskvin has just been promoted to Colonel,' said Fiona. She still didn't understand what Renn was trying to tell her.

'That was simply to make it easier for him to give instructions to the Embassy people while he is in London. Here rank does not count for as much as it does in the West. It is a man's appointment that decides his authority.'

'And Lieutenant Bakushin's appointment is a high one?'

'Lieutenant Bakushin could arrest and imprison anyone in the building, without reference to Moscow,' said Renn simply. It made Fiona's blood run cold.

'Have you any idea what Colonel Moskvin was accused of?'

'Serious crimes,' said Renn.

'What sort of crimes are serious crimes?'

'The charges against Colonel Moskvin are something it is better we did not discuss.'

'I heard that the Colonel has many influential enemies in Moscow,' said Fiona.

Renn stood still. For a moment Fiona thought he would murmur some excuse and leave the office – he'd done that before when she had persisted with questions he would not answer – but he didn't do that. Renn went round the desk and stood by her side. 'Major Erich Stinnes is in London leading the English secret service by the nose and creating the sort of havoc I could not even guess at; Colonel Moskvin is also in England supporting the operation. Moscow was very unhappy at the death of the Englishman in the house in Bosham: Colonel Moskvin overstepped his authority. It is because he is unavailable that the inquiry has been staged at this time. The problem the Colonel faces is that if the London operation goes well, Major Stinnes will get the credit for his courage, skill and ingenuity. If anything goes wrong Colonel Moskvin's support will be blamed.' Renn looked at her then hurried on, 'And so meanwhile you are left the most powerful officer in the section.' Renn looked at her; she still hadn't fully understood, so he went on. 'Lieutenant Bakushin sees that. He will take evidence from you on the understanding that you see it too.'

'You mean Bakushin will expect me to give evidence that will help to convict Colonel Moskvin of whatever it is he's accused of so that I take command?'

'Frau Direktor, wild rumours are going round. Some say Colonel Moskvin has been a long-term agent for the British. Mrs Keller is also accused: perhaps you remember her from my birthday party. She fled to the West with her son, using what are believed to be forged United Kingdom passports.' Renn smiled to relieve the tension he felt. 'I am confident that the Moscow inquiry will find Colonel Moskvin innocent; he has friends and relatives highly placed in Moscow. I know how the system works. The Lieutenant is simply collecting evidence for the inquiry. It will be expedient to show caution when you talk with him.'

Fiona took a deep breath. 'Have you ever read *Alice in Wonderland*, Herr Renn?'

'It's an English book? No, I think I have not read it.' He dismissed discussion of the book politely but hurriedly. 'But Frau Direktor, this means you must decide about the meeting in Holland. There is no one else who can sign the orders. With both Colonel Moskvin and Major Stinnes unavailable we need someone senior with fluent English. I hope it won't mean getting someone from another unit.'

'Not if we can avoid it,' said Fiona. 'But surely, Herr Renn, you understand my hesitation.'

'You will go?' said Renn.

'I don't think so,' said Fiona. She wanted to go; a trip to the West – just to breathe the air for twenty-four hours – would give her a new lease of life.

'If it's the risk of arrest, I can arrange for you to travel on diplomatic papers.'

'No.'

'Who else is there?'

She looked at him. She'd thought about it and been tempted, but now that Renn asked the direct question she had no answer ready. 'I would have to clear it with Normannenstrasse. They would have to know.'

Renn picked up a plastic box of floppy disks that was on Fiona's desk waiting for the messenger and toyed with it. 'I really would advise against that, Frau Direktor,' said Renn, his eyes averted and his face red with the embarrassment of such direct rebellion.

'Checking with them,' explained Fiona. 'Technically we all come under their orders.'

'Frau Direktor, to seek instruction from Normannenstrasse, and on a matter which is entirely operational, would be creating a very important precedent. A dangerous precedent.' He shook the box of floppy disks: it rattled. 'Whatever happens in the career of Colonel Moskvin and Major Stinnes this department will I hope continue to function in the way it has done for twelve years or more. But if you ask Normannenstrasse to give you permission for something as normal as the trip to Holland, you'll be virtually putting us under their authority. What would happen in the future? No one here will enjoy anything like independence in any of the work we do. We might as well talk of closing the unit down and going to work in Normannenstrasse.'

She took the box of disks from his fingers and put it back on her desk. Then she looked down at her notepad as if returning to her work. 'I wouldn't want to do that, Herr Renn. You've already told me how much you hate that mad scramble for the Magdalenenstrasse U-Bahn.'

Hubert Renn stiffened and his lips were compressed. By now Fiona should have learned that the sort of joshing that is a normal part of the conversational exchanges in British or American offices did not go down well in Germany. 'But, Frau Direktor . . .'

'Just a joke, a silly joke,' said Fiona. 'I will of course do exactly as you advise, Herr Renn.'

'I'll prepare your papers?'

'Yes, I'll go.' She watched him as he collected together the work he'd done. Hubert Renn was, despite his protestations to the contrary, a complex personality. She'd not yet got over the way in which he was able to reconcile his anti-Russian prejudices with his uncritical dedication to Marx and all his works.

Was Renn's advice – to assume authority beyond what was really hers and use it to make the journey abroad – the bait in some new and nasty trap that her enemies were setting for her? She thought not but she couldn't be sure. Careful, Stefan! No one could be quite sure of anything over here. That was the most important thing she'd learned.

She stood up. 'And there remains the matter of the doctor at the Charité Hospital?'

'Yes, Frau Direktor. These things always take a long time. There is a note on your desk.'

'The note says only that it was all in order.'

Renn came to her side and said, 'Yes, good news, Frau Direktor. Herr Doktor Kennedy is completely clear. Even more than clear: a fellow-traveller. We have used him for some minor tasks in London. He would probably have been used for more important work, except that he'd joined the party when he was a medical student.'

Fiona felt ill. She sat down in her chair again. For a moment she couldn't get her breath. Then she was able to mutter, 'The Communist Party?' Thank God she'd never confided in Kennedy; more than once she'd felt like doing so. He seemed such a dedicated capitalist with his airplane sales and deliveries, but that of course would be a good cover and, as she knew from her day-to-day work, the KGB financed thousands of such businesses to provide cover for agents.

'Yes. What a shame that no one saw his potential and warned him from doing that. Party members cannot, of course, be used for important tasks.'

'Any dates?'

'Nothing since July 1978. Mind you, we have both seen recently how slack the clerks can be when filing the amendments.'

Her head began to throb and she felt sick. 'What did he do for us?'

'Details of that sort are not entered on our files. London Residency would have filed that directly to Moscow. I would guess it to have been surveillance or providing accommodation or arranging references: that's the sort of job such men are used for.'

So that was it: July 1978, a month before the 'accidental' meeting on Waterloo Station. She'd warned Martin off and so Moscow had simply found another way to monitor her. Yes, that would be time enough for Harry to be briefed and prepared. So Harry Kennedy had been assigned by Moscow to check up on her. Was that to be his role in Berlin too? 'Nothing since 1978?'

'Shall I ask Moscow if he is still under instructions?'

'No, Herr Renn, I don't think that would be wise.'

He looked at her and saw that she was not feeling well. 'Whatever you say, Frau Direktor.' He picked up some papers and tactfully left the room.

She swallowed three aspirin tablets: she had packets of them everywhere but they seldom did more than reduce the intensity of the pain. She held her hands over her eyes. By concentrating her mind upon old memories she could sometimes get over these attacks by will-power alone. Pictures of her husband and children flickered in the mind's eye, as blurred and jerky as old film clips. For a long time she sat very still, as someone might recompose themselves after stepping out of a wrecked car unscratched.

21

Berlin. March 1984.

The Director-General – restless and demanding – was on one of his unofficial flying visits to Berlin. Frank Harrington, Berlin supremo, cursed at having his daily schedule turned upside-down at short notice, but the old man was like that. He'd always been like that and lately he was getting worse. Not only did he have sudden inconvenient inspirations that everyone was expected to adapt to without question, but Sir Henry was a terrible time-waster. Ensconced in the most comfortable armchair, with a glass of vintage Hine in his hand, Sir Henry Clevemore would talk and talk, periodically interjecting that he must depart as if he was being detained against his will.

That's how it had been that afternoon. The message from the D-G's office had requested 'a German lunch'. Tarrant, the old valet who had been with Frank longer than anyone could remember, arranged everything. They ate in the dining room of the lovely old Grunewald mansion that came with the job of Berlin resident. Frank's cook did a Hasenpfeffer that had become renowned over the years, and the maid wore her best starched apron and even a lace hat. The old silver cutlery was polished and out came the antique Meissen china; the table had looked quite extraordinary. The D-G had remarked on it in Tarrant's hearing: Tarrant had permitted himself a smug little grin.

After lunch the two men had gone into the drawing room for coffee. That was hours ago, and still the D-G showed no signs of departing. Frank wished he'd asked about the return flight, but to do so now would seem impolite. So he nodded at the old man and listened and desperately wanted to light up his pipe. The old man hated pipe tobacco – particularly the brand which Frank smoked – and Frank knew it was out of the question.

'Well, I must be going,' said the D-G, as he'd said it so many times that afternoon, but this time he actually showed signs of moving. Thank goodness, thought Frank. If he could get rid of the old man by seven he'd still be in time for an evening of bridge with his army chums. 'Yes,' said the D-G, looking at his watch, 'I really must be getting along.'

There was a chap Frank Harrington had known at Eton who went on to be a doctor with a practice serving a prosperous part of agricultural Yorkshire. He said that he'd grown used to the way in which a patient coming to him with a problem would spend half an hour chatting about everything under the sun, get up to go and then, while actually standing at the door saying goodbye, tell him in a very casual aside what was really worrying him. So it was with the Director-General. He'd been sitting there exchanging pleasantries with Frank all the afternoon when he picked up his glass, swirled the last mouthful round to make a whirlpool and finished it in a gulp. Then he put the glass down, got to his feet and said once again that he would have to be going. Only then did he say, 'Have you seen Bret Rensselaer lately?'

Frank nodded. 'Last week. Bret asked my advice about the report on the shooting in Hampstead.' Frank got to his feet and made a not very emphatic gesture with the brandy bottle but the old man waved it away.

'May I ask what you advised?'

'I told him not to make a report, not in writing anyway. I told him to go through it with you and then file a memorandum to record that he'd done so.'

'What did Bret say?'

Frank went across the room to put the bottle away. He remained slim and athletic in appearance. In his Bedford cord suit he could easily have been mistaken for an officer of the Berlin garrison, in his mid-forties. It was difficult to believe that Frank and the D-G had trained together and that Frank was coming up to retirement. 'I remember exactly. He said, "You mean cover my arse?" '

'And is that what you meant?'

Frank stopped where he was, in the middle of the Persian rug, and chose his words carefully. 'I knew you would file a written version of his verbal report to you.'

'Did you?' A slight lift on the second word.

'If that was an appropriate action,' said Frank.

The D-G nodded soberly. 'Bret was nearly killed. Two Soviets were shot by Bernard Samson.'

'So Bret told me. It was lucky that our people were well away before the police arrived.'

'We're not out of the woods yet, Frank,' said the D-G.

Frank wondered whether he was expected to pursue it further but decided that the D-G would tell him in his own time. Frank said, 'From what I hear in Berlin, a KGB heavy named Moskvin was behind it. The same ruffian who killed the young fellow in the Bosham safe house.'

'Research and Briefing take the same line, so it looks that way.' The D-G turned and came back to where he'd been sitting. Looking at Frank he said, 'There will have to be an inquiry.'

'Into Bret's future?'

'No, it hasn't quite come to that, but the Cabinet Office are going through one of those periods when they dread any sort of complaint from the Russians.'

'Two dead KGB thugs? Armed thugs? Hardly likely that Moscow are going to declare an interest in such antics, Sir Henry.'

'Is that a considered opinion based on your Berlin experience?'

'Yes, it is.'

'It's my own opinion too, but the Cabinet Office do not respond to expert opinions; they are too concerned about the politicians they serve.' The D-G said it without resentment or even displeasure. 'I knew that, of course, when I took the job. Our department's strategy, like that of every other government department, must be influenced by the varying political climate.'

'The last time you told me that,' said Frank, 'you added, "but the tactics they leave to me".'

'The tactics are left to me until tactical blunders are spread across the front pages of the tabloids. Did you see the photos of that launderette?'

'I did indeed, sir.' Big front-page photos of the launderette, with the sprawled dead men and blood splashed everywhere, had made a memorable impression upon the newspaper-reading public. But whatever was being said about the shooting in London's bars and editorial offices, the story printed was that it was another gangster killing, with speculation about drugs being offered for sale in all-night shops and launderettes.

' "Five" are pressing for an inquiry and the Cabinet Secretary is convinced that their added expertise would be valuable.'

'A combined inquiry?'

'I can't defy the Cabinet Office, Frank. I will bring it up in committee, and look to you for support.'

'If you are sure that's the right way to do it,' said Frank, with only the slightest intonation to suggest that he didn't think it was.

'It's a matter of retrenching before I get a direct order. In this way I will set up the committee and be able to give Bret the chair,' said the D-G.

'You think Bret will need that sort of help and protection?'

'Yes, I do. But what I want you to tell me is, will Bret have the stamina to see it through? Think before you answer, Frank. This is important to me.'

671

'Stamina? I can't give a quick yes or no on that one, Sir Henry. You must have seen what has been happening to the Department since Fiona Samson defected.'

'In terms of morale?'

'In terms of morale and a lot of other things. If you are thinking of the psychological pressure, you might look at young Samson. He's under tremendous strain, and to make it worse there are people in the Department saying he must have known what his wife was up to all along.'

'Yes, I've even had members of the staff confiding their fears about it,' said the D-G sadly.

'When a chap is having a difficult time with his wife he can get away to work; a chap having a hard time in the office can look forward to a break when he gets home to his family. Bernard Samson is under continual pressure.'

'I understood that he has formed some kind of liaison with one of the junior female staff,' said the D-G.

'Samson is a desperate man,' said Frank with simple truth. He didn't want to talk about Samson's private life: do to all men as I would they should do unto me, was Frank's policy.

'I asked you about Rensselaer,' said the D-G.

'Samson is a desperate man,' said Frank, 'but he can withstand a great deal of criticism. He is a born rebel so he can fight back when called a traitor or a lecher or anything else. Bret is a quite different personality. He loves England as only the foreign-born romantic can. To such people the merest breath of suspicion comes like a gale and is likely to blow them away.'

'Well done, Frank! Was it Literae Humaniores you read at Wadham?'

Frank smiled ruefully but didn't answer. He'd known the D-G ever since they were very young and shared a billet in the war. The D-G knew all about Frank Harrington's mastery of the Greek and Roman classics, and – Frank suspected – was still somewhat envious of it.

The D-G said, 'Will Bret crack up? If the committee turn upon him – as committees in our part of the world have a habit of turning upon a vulnerable chairman – will Bret stand firm?'

'Has this inquiry been given a name?' asked Frank.

The D-G smiled. 'It's an inquiry into Erich Stinnes, and the way he's been handled since coming over to us.'

'Bret will take a battering,' pronounced Frank.

'Is that what you think?'

'The Department is awash with rumours, Sir Henry. You must know that or you wouldn't be here asking me these questions.'

'What is the thrust of the rumours?'

'Well, it's commonly thought that Erich Stinnes has made a complete fool of Bret Rensselaer, and of the Department.'

'Bret was not experienced enough to handle a wily fellow like Stinnes. I thought Samson would keep Bret on the straight and narrow but I was wrong. It now seems that Stinnes was sent to us on a disinformation mission.'

'Is that official?' Frank asked.

'No, I'm still not sure what sort of game Stinnes is playing.'

'A senior official like Stinnes sent on a disinformation mission can do whatever he likes and damn the consequences. He might well decide to come over to us.'

'I share that view.' The D-G took out his cigar case and for a moment was going to light a cigar. Then he decided against it. The doctor had told him to stop smoking altogether, but he always carried a couple of cigars with him so that he didn't become too desperate. Perhaps it was a silly idea to do that: sometimes it was torture. 'You said that some of the staff were of the opinion that Bret had been made a fool of. What do the rest think?'

'Most of the staff know that Bret is reliable and resourceful.'

'You know what I mean, Frank.'

'Yes, I know what you mean. Well, there are some hotheads who think perhaps Bret was working with Fiona Samson.'

'Working with her? They think Bret Rensselaer and Fiona Samson have both been under Moscow's orders for that long?'

'It's an extreme view, Sir Henry, but they spent a lot of time together. There are stories of them having a love affair – a couple of sightings in the wrong hotels, you know the sort of thing. Even young Samson is not entirely certain that it's not true.'

'I didn't realize that such absurd stories were going around.'

'People wonder what motivated Bret, after a lifetime behind a desk, to grab a gun, rush into that launderette and try his hand at the sharp end. We have people trained to do that sort of thing.'

'It wasn't quite like that,' said the D-G.

'The gunfight at the OK Corral was how one of the newspapers described it. I'm afraid that description has provided the basis for a lot of doubtful jokes.'

The D-G sniffed audibly and then again. 'Berlin smells of beer, have you ever noticed that, Frank? Of course it's not the only German town with that odour but I notice it in Berlin more than anywhere else. Hops or malt or something . . .' he added vaguely, as if wanting to declare his unfamiliarity with that plebeian beverage.

'You'll have to support him, Sir Henry. Visibly and unequivocally.'

'I won't be able to do that, Frank. He must take his chances.'

'What do you mean, sir?'

'There are good reasons why I can give him no support; no support whatsoever.'

Frank was stunned. Despite the unwavering good manners for which he was famed, Frank was on the point of asking what the hell the Director-General was there to do, if it wasn't to support his staff when they were in trouble. 'Are those reasons operational or political?'

It was as near as Frank had ever gone to open rebellion, but the D-G accepted the reproach. On the other hand, the decision not to confide the truth about Fiona Samson to Frank was a sound one. Stinnes had to go back to Moscow firmly believing that Fiona Samson was a traitor. To say there were operational reasons for not supporting Bret Rensselaer was only a step away from revealing the whole story of Fiona Samson's mission. 'I can't go into that, Frank,' said the D-G in a voice that drew the line across Frank's toes. If Bret Rensselaer was suspected of being Fiona's co-conspirator, so be it.

'One supplementary, Director,' said Frank, his voice and form of address making it an official question. 'Is Rensselaer to be left to die of exposure? Is he to wither on the vine? Is that the purpose of the inquiry? I have to know in order to formulate my own responses.'

'My God, no! The last thing I want to see is Bret Rensselaer thrown to the sharks, especially the sharks of Whitehall. I want Rensselaer to come out of this on top. But I can't go in and rescue him.'

'I'm glad you made that clear, Sir Henry.'

The exchange of views had produced a stalemate, and the D-G recognized it as such. 'I still have a great deal of work for Rensselaer to do, and he's the only one equipped to do it.'

Frank nodded and thought it was some sort of reference to Bret's Washington contacts, which had always been important to the Department.

The story of that shooting in the Hampstead launderette that had worried the D-G and which the newspapers, and Frank Harrington, were pleased to call 'The Gunfight at the OK Corral' starts a week or so before the D-G's visit to Berlin.

Had Bret Rensselaer displayed his usual common sense he would have kept well out of it. It was a job for the Department's field agents. But Bret was not himself.

Bret Rensselaer missed Fiona Samson, he missed her terribly. Over the time when they had been working together they had met regularly and furtively, like lovers, and this had added to the zest. Bret could not, of course, tell anyone of this feeling he had, and his passion was not assuaged by seeing Bernard Samson, deprived of that perfect woman, going about his business in his usual carefree way. No matter what some people said about Samson's anguish Bret could only see the Bernard it suited him to see. He was especially outraged to discover that Bernard was now living with a gorgeous young girl from the office. Heaven knows how the children were reacting. Bret was appalled by this but took great care to disguise his feelings in the matter. He could see no way to influence what happened to the Samson children. He hoped that Fiona wasn't going to accuse him of bad faith at some future time.

Bret's participation in the shooting in the launderette changed a lot of things. For him it was nothing less than traumatic. Traumatic in the literal sense that the violent events of that night inflicted upon Bret a mental wound from which he never completely recovered.

For Bret everything suggested that the contact with the KGB team in the launderette would be mere routine. There had been no warning that things would go as they did. One minute he was sitting next to Bernard in an all-night launderette in Hampstead, and the next minute he was in the middle of one of the most horrifying nightmares of his entire life.

They were watching Samson's shirts revolving in the suds. Samson insisted that both of them brought laundry and had even produced a plastic bag of detergent; he said he didn't like the stuff they had in the shop. Bret wondered whether it was a mark of Samson's meticulous attention to detail or some sort of joke. Now Samson was intermittently reading a newspaper that was on his knee. He'd given Bret no indication at all that he had a damn great gun – with silencer attached – wrapped inside the *Daily Telegraph*. Samson had been chatting away about his father as if he had not a care in the world.

Bernard Samson could be an amusing companion if he was in a good mood. His caustic comments on his superiors, the government and indeed the world around him were partly his defence against a system that had never given him a proper chance in life, but they sometimes contained more than a grain of truth. Bernard's reputation was of being lucky, but his luck came from a professional attitude and a lot of hard work. Bernard was a tough guy and there can be no doubt that Bret's

675

willingness to involve himself in this caper was largely due to the fact that he felt safe with Bernard.

Bret was wearing an old coat and hat he'd bought at the Oxfam shop specially for this evening's excursion. In the bag, under Bret's soiled laundry, there was a heavy manila envelope containing forty one-hundred-dollar bills. It was funding. The money was to be given to a KGB courier when he used the code word 'Bingo'. Positioned in the street outside the launderette there were enough men to warn Bret of their approach and – should Bret decide that they must be arrested – enough men to hold them. To Bret it seemed very straightforward, but it didn't turn out like that.

Things began with no warning from the men in the street. One of the KGB men had been hiding upstairs, in a room above the launderette, and when he came in unexpectedly he was brandishing a sawn-off shotgun. Then a second man entered; he too had a shotgun. One of the men said 'Bingo', the code word. Bret remained completely calm, or that was how he remembered it afterwards, and reached for the money to show them.

The sequence of the events that followed was disputed, although certainly everything happened in rapid succession. Samson said that this was when the car exploded in the street outside, but as Bret remembered it Samson took the initiative before that.

Samson did not stand up and fire his gun, he remained seated. He used Bret as a shield, and the rage that Bret felt when he realized that, stayed with him for the rest of his life. Leaning forward far enough to see the intruders – there were now two of them – Samson calmly took aim and fired. He didn't even take the gun out of the newspaper that concealed it. The gun was silenced. Bret heard two thuds and was astounded to see one of the KGB men reel back, drop his gun, clutch at his belly and fall over the washing machines spewing blood.

Samson was suddenly up and away. Bret remembered Samson pushing him roughly aside and seeing him stumble over the discarded gun on the floor, although in Samson's version he pushed Bret down to safety and then kicked the gun in Bret's direction. Samson had even reproached him for not picking up the gun and following him through the back door to chase the others.

Bret was suddenly left in the launderette watching the young KGB man die, vomiting and bleeding and mewling like a baby. Bret had never seen anything like this: it was brutal and loathsome. From upstairs somewhere there came more shots – Samson killed another man – and then it was all over and Bret found himself pushed roughly into a car and was speeding away into the night, and passing the police as they were arriving. To Bret's amazement Bernard Samson chose that moment to tell Bret he'd saved his life.

'Saving my life, you son of a bitch?' said Bret shrilly. 'First you shoot, using me as a shield. Then you run out, leaving me to face the music.'

Samson laughed. To some extent the laugh was a nervous reaction to the stress he had just been through, but it was a laugh that Bret would never forget. 'That's the way it is being a field agent, Bret,' he said. 'If you'd had experience or training, you would have hit the deck. Better still, you would have taken out that second bastard instead of leaving me to deal with all of them.'

Bret had hardly listened; he couldn't forget the sight of the dying KGB man bent over, holding tight to one of the washing machines, while his frothy blood streamed out of him to mix with the soapy water on the floor.

'You could have winged him,' croaked Bret.

Bernard scoffed at such naïve talk. 'That's just for the movies, Bret. That's for Wyatt Earp and Jesse James. In the real world, no one is shooting guns out of people's hands or giving them flesh wounds in the upper arm. In the real world you hit them or you miss them. It's difficult enough to hit a moving target without selecting tricky bits of anatomy. So don't give me all that crap.'

It was no use arguing with him, Bret decided, but bad feeling remained. Bret resented the way that Bernard Samson made quick decisions with such firm conviction and seemed to have no misgivings afterwards. Women admired such traits, or seemed to, but Bret was finding every decision he had to make more and more difficult.

Bret was beginning to see that his own planning would have to entail ruthlessness at least the equal of Bernard's. But Bret's present state of mind didn't make things easy. Sometimes he sat staring at his desk for half an hour unable to conclude even self-evident matters. Perhaps Bret should not have gone to the doctor and asked his advice. The Department's doctor was competent and helpful – everything one wanted from a physician, in fact – but he did dutifully report back to the Department.

It began with no more than a slight loss of his usual power of concentration, and a tendency to wake up in the small hours of the morning unable to get back to sleep. Then Bret began to notice that he was being treated like an outsider. He was aware of being treated in a wary and distant manner even when he was chairing the committee. Substance was given to his suspicions when two subcommittees were formed and Bret was deliberately excluded from them. It meant that about three-quarters of the people on the committee were able to have meetings to which he was denied access.

What Bret didn't know was the way in which his downfall was being master-minded by Moscow. Bret had not been targeted because Moscow suspected that Fiona Samson had been planted in Berlin, or for any reason except that he was suddenly vulnerable to the sort of sting operation that they had proved so expert at many times in the past. Not only was Moscow able to blow upon the embers and help the rumours but as the operation proceeded there was false evidence planted. Some of it was crude enough to convince the real experts – like Ladbrook, the senior interrogator – that Moscow was trying to discredit Rensselaer, but that did not mean that the experts could afford to ignore it.

The Director-General had a rough idea of what was happening and decided to go to Berlin and talk to Frank Harrington. Frank was an old friend as well as a well-established member of the senior staff. That lunch and the subsequent afternoon of chatting with Frank did not set the D-G's mind at rest. What Frank told him was little more than washroom gossip but it prepared the D-G for the phone call from Internal Security that said that Ladbrook and Tiptree would like an appointment urgently. The caller boldly told Morgan – the D-G's assistant – that tomorrow would not be soon enough.

They were all waiting for the D-G in the number 2 conference room. There was Ladbrook, the senior interrogator, a decent quiet fifty-year-old who never got ruffled, and Harry Strang, a weather-beaten veteran of Operations. With them was Henry Tiptree, the young fellow whom Internal Security rated as one of their brightest stars. And, sitting unobtrusively in the corner, the Deputy D-G, Sir Percy Babcock.

The table had been arranged with notepads and pencils and water jug and glasses. 'Who else is expected?' asked the D-G, having counted them.

'We couldn't get hold of Cruyer,' said Strang, 'but I've left a message with his secretary.'

'Are we expecting a long session, Percy?' the D-G asked his Deputy.

'No, very short, Director. Internal Security has something to put before you.'

'Quite a crowd,' remarked the D-G. He was well over six feet tall and broad-shouldered too. He towered over them.

'We'll need five signatures,' said the Deputy gently.

'Um,' said the D-G and his heart sank. They all knew what sort of form needed five signatures; one from Internal Security. 'And no one taking notes?'

'That's correct, Director.' Well that was it then. The only way to save Bret from this humiliating investigation was to reveal the secret of Fiona Samson. That was out of the question. Bret would have to take his chance.

They all sat down. The Deputy clicked his gold ballpoint while Harry Strang took out his cigarettes and then remembering the presence of the D-G put them away again. Tiptree, a tall thin fellow with well-brushed red hair and ruddy complexion, poured himself a glass of water and drank it with elegant precision.

Ladbrook looked round the table. They were looking at him expectantly, except for Tiptree who was now drawing circles on the notepad. 'Would you like to start, Sir Percy?' asked Ladbrook diffidently.

'Tell the Director just what you told me,' said the Deputy.

'I'm afraid it concerns senior staff,' said Ladbrook. The D-G looked at him without a flicker of emotion showing on his face.

'Bret Rensselaer,' supplied Tiptree, looking up from his pad. A lock of hair fell forward across his face and he flicked it back with his hand.

'A leak?' said the D-G, but he knew what was coming.

'More serious than that,' said Ladbrook.

'I have the file,' said Tiptree, indicating a box file that he'd put on a side table.

'I don't want to look at files,' said the D-G with a weary despair that came out like irritation. Everyone waited for the D-G to speak again but he settled back in his seat and sighed.

Sir Percy clicked his ballpoint and said, 'Since Bret often takes his orders directly from you, I thought you might want to interpose.'

'Has anyone spoken with Bret?' the D-G asked.

'With your permission,' said Ladbrook, 'I propose a preliminary "talk-through" as soon as it's made official.'

'That's the usual way, is it?'

'Yes, Sir Henry, that's the usual way.'

The Deputy said, 'The interrogator wanted to be quite sure that Bret didn't cite you as a reason for not answering.'

'On this sort of inquiry,' added Ladbrook, 'a loss of momentum like that can be difficult to make up afterwards.'

'I understand,' said the D-G. He noticed Harry Strang get a pen from his waistcoat. So Harry knew how it had to end.

'He'll probably want to speak with you on the phone,' said

Ladbrook. 'When I first tackle him, I mean. He'll probably want to put a call through to you.'

'And you want me not to take the call?' said the D-G.

'Whatever you think best, Sir Henry,' said Ladbrook.

'But I'll bugger up your interrogation if I do take it; is that what you mean?'

Ladbrook smiled politely but didn't answer.

'Give me the form,' said the D-G. 'Let's get it over as quickly as possible.' The Deputy handed his ballpoint to him and slid the papers across the polished table.

'I can do the rest of the paperwork,' said the Deputy gently. 'Morgan can counter-sign the chit on your behalf.'

'It will be a nonsense,' said the D-G as he put his signature on the form. 'I can tell you that here and now. I've known Bret Rensselaer for years; salt of the earth, Bret Rensselaer.'

Harry Strang smiled. He was old enough to remember someone using the almost identical words about Kim Philby.

22

England. April 1984.

How far can you run into a wood? asks the ancient schoolboy joke.
Halfway: after that you're running out. A missile stops in the air and
begins to fall back to the ground, a sportsman's career reaches a
physical peak at which it begins decline. A flower in full bloom falls,
water at its most exuberant disappears into vapour. For most things in
nature there comes a moment when triumph is doom in disguise. So it
was for Pavel Moskvin that lovely day in Berlin when, fittingly
enough, the first growths of spring marked the end of winter.

Erich Stinnes was also riding high. Everything had gone as he'd
predicted. The British seemed to have accepted him at face value
because they found it so difficult to believe that anyone could resist
their way of life. Stinnes had played his role to perfection.
Tropfenweise, drip by drip, he had worn away the hard diamond face
of Rensselaer's reputation until, in front of the committee, he
shattered it completely.

The culmination of all that Stinnes had worked for came on what
had promised to be a routine visit of the 'Stinnes committee' to
Berwick House, where he was being held. An eighteenth-century
manor set in seven acres of attractive English countryside, its fifteen-
foot-high stone wall and ancient moat had made it easy to adapt into a
detention centre. The Whitehall clerks, who had seized house and
contents from its owners by means of some catch-all legislation, had
done little to repair the damage caused by the Luftwaffe's bombs.
There was a musty smell in the house, and if you looked closely
enough at the rotting structure you'd find the woodworms were
working harder than anyone.

The committee travelled together in a bus except for Bret. He
arrived in his chauffeur-driven Bentley having used the lunch hour to
squeeze in an appointment with the doctor. He looked drawn, and the
skin under his eyes had blackened so that the eternally youthful Bret
was suddenly aged.

There was such a crowd that they all sat round the big polished
table in what at one time had been the dining room. On the panelled

wall there was a huge oil painting. A family posed stiffly on a hill near the newly built Berwick House, and stared at the painter as he extended to Gainsborough what is reputed to be the sincerest form of flattery.

The committee were all trying to show how knowledgeable and important they were. Bret Rensselaer sat at one end, and thus established his authority as chairman. Stinnes faced him at the far end, an adversary's positioning that Bret afterwards thought might have contributed to the subsequent fiasco. Bret looked at his watch frequently, but otherwise sat with that look of attention that people who sit on too many committees master, to conceal the fact that they are half asleep. He had heard it all before. Well, thought Stinnes, I'll see if I can wake you up, Mr Rensselaer.

In a committee like that, there would always be a couple of know-alls. It was exactly the same in Moscow: Stinnes could have named their counterparts. The worst bore was Billy Slinger from MI5, a scrawny fellow with a thin, carefully trimmed moustache and a restrained Tyneside accent that Stinnes found challenging. He had been attached to the committee to advise on communications. Of course he felt he must prove to them all how clever he was.

Erich Stinnes had endured the ups and downs of his detention with little change, but there was not much to change. Stinnes was a tough middle-aged man with a sallow face, and hair that he liked to keep as short as possible. When he took off his metal-rimmed glasses – which he did frequently – he blinked like an owl and looked round at the committee as if he preferred to see them slightly out of focus.

Stinnes fielded the questions artfully and let Slinger demonstrate his technical knowledge until he got on to signals procedures. This was something that Moscow had agreed he could disclose, so, quietly and conversationally, he went through the Embassy routines. He started with the day-to-day domestics and went on to a few KGB encoding styles. These were technical developments that Slinger was unlikely to be familiar with, and thus he was unlikely to know that they had already been superseded or were used only for mundane traffic.

Out of the corner of his eye he watched Rensselaer uncoil like a serpent disturbed by the approach of heavy footsteps. 'This is all new to me,' said Slinger repeatedly, his accent more pronounced as he filled sheets of paper with notes scribbled so fast and so excitedly that his pencil broke and he had to grab another and ask Stinnes to slow down.

The other members of the committee became enthusiastic too. Between eager questions from Slinger, one of the committee asked him why he hadn't disclosed these gems earlier. Stinnes didn't answer immediately. He looked at Bret Rensselaer and then looked away and took a long time lighting up a cheroot.

'Well?' said Bret finally. 'Let's hear it.'

'I did,' said Stinnes finally. 'I told you during the first days but I thought it must be stuff you knew already.'

Bret jumped up as if he was going to start shouting. They all looked at him. And then Bret realized that an argument with Stinnes in front of the committee was only going to make him look ridiculous. He sat down again and said, 'Carry on, Slinger. Let's get it down on paper.'

Stinnes inhaled on his cheroot and looked from one to the other like a social worker in the presence of a combative family. Then he started to give them even more material: Foreign Country routeings, Embassy signals room times and procedures and even Embassy contact lists.

It took about an hour, and included some long silences while Stinnes racked his brains, and a few little Stinnes jokes which – due to the tension in the room – everyone laughed at. By the end, the committee was intoxicated with success. Satisfaction flushed their faces and circulated through their veins like freshly sugared blood. And not the least of their triumph was the warm feeling they got from knowing that Bret Rensselaer, so cold and patrician, so efficient and patriotic, was going to get his rightful comeuppance.

As Stinnes left the room to be taken upstairs he looked at Bret Rensselaer. Neither man registered any change of facial expression and yet there was in that exchange of looks the recognition that a contest had been fought and won.

But Bret Rensselaer was not the sort of man who would lie down and play dead to oblige an enemy. Bret Rensselaer was an American: pragmatic, resourceful and without that capacity for long-term rancour that the European is born with. When Bret faced the wall of opposition which Moskvin and Stinnes had between them constructed brick by brick, he did something that neither of the Russians had provided for. Rensselaer went to Berlin and pleaded for the aid of Bernard Samson, a man he'd come to dislike, reasoning that Samson was even less conventional than he was, and certainly far more savage.

'What do we do now?' Bret asked. Stampeded by Stinnes and faced with the prospect of arrest, Bret ran. He was a fugitive and looked like one: frightened and dishevelled and lacking all that smooth Rensselaer confidence.

'What do we do?' echoed Samson. This was Bernard's town and both of them knew it. 'We scare the shit out of them, that's what we do.'

'How?'

'Suppose we tell them we are pulling out Stinnes's toenails one by one?'

Bret shivered. He wasn't in the mood for jokes. 'Be sensible, Bernard. They are holding your friend Volkmann over there. Can't you see what that means?'

'They won't touch Werner.'

'Why not?'

'Because they know that for anything they dream up to do to Werner I'll do it twice to Stinnes, and do it slowly.'

'Is that a risk worth taking?' asked Bret. 'I thought Volkmann was your closest friend.'

'What difference does that make?' asked Bernard.

Alarmed, Bret said, 'Don't get this one wrong, Bernard. There is too much riding on it.' Samson had always been a hard-nosed gambler, but was this escalating response the way to go? Or had Bernard gone mad?

'I know the way these people think, Bret. Moscow has an obsession about getting agents out of trouble. That is the Moscow law: KGB men ignore it at their peril.'

'So we offer to trade Stinnes for Werner Volkmann?'

'But not before letting them know that Stinnes is going to go through the wringer.'

'Jesus! I don't like it. Will Fiona be one of the people making the decision?' asked Bret.

Bernard looked at him, trying to see into his mind, but Bret's mind was not so easy to see into. 'I should think so,' said Bernard.

'Frau Samson,' said Moskvin with exaggerated courtesy and an unctuous smile. 'Have you prepared charges against this West German national Volkmann?'

'I am in the process of doing so,' Fiona Samson fielded the question. She'd learned a lot about Moskvin in the time she'd been working here. Some people thought Moskvin was a fool but they were wrong: Moskvin had a quick and cunning mind. He was pushy and gauche but he was not stupid. Neither was he clumsy, at least not in the physical sense. Every day he was in the basement: weight-lifting in the gym, swimming in the pool, shooting on the range or doing some other sort of physical exercise. He was no longer young, but still he had that overabundance of energy that is usually confined to childhood.

'Do you have another file on him, Comrade Colonel?' he asked sweetly.

Fiona was disconcerted by this question. She had created the

Volkmann file that was open on her desk. 'No more than what you've seen already.'

'No more than this?' said Moskvin, and was able to make it into a very unfavourable pronouncement.

'I know . . .' she stopped.

'Yes? What do you know?'

'In the past he has worked for the SIS office in Berlin.'

Moskvin looked at her. 'Suppose Moscow wanted to see the file on Volkmann? Is this what we'd send?' He flipped the card cover of the file so that his fingernails made a click. It sounded empty.

'Yes,' said Fiona.

Moskvin looked at her and made no secret of the extent of his contempt. Intimidation was a part of his working method. By now she'd recognized him for what he really was. She'd known plenty of other men like Moskvin. She'd known them at Oxford: rowdy sportsmen, keenly aware of their physical strength, and relishing the latent violence that was within them.

'I know Volkmann,' she said. 'I've known him for years. Of course he works for SIS Berlin. SIS London too.'

'And yet you've done nothing about it?' Moskvin looked at her with contempt.

'Not yet,' said Fiona.

'Not yet,' he said. 'Well, now we'll do something, shall we?' He was patronizing her, smiling as tyrants do with small children. 'We'll talk to Volkmann . . . perhaps scare him a little.'

'How?'

'You might learn something, Frau Samson. He hasn't been told that he's being released in exchange for Major Stinnes. We must make him sweat.'

'Volkmann gets his money from doing business in our Republic. Without that he would be penniless. He might be persuaded to work for us.'

Moskvin eyed her. 'Why would he do that?'

'He's back and forth all the time. That's why he was so easy to pick up. Why shouldn't he tell us what happens over there?'

'You could do that?'

'I could try. You say he's being held in Babelsberg?'

'You'll need a car.'

'I'll drive myself.'

'Bring him back here. I'll want to see him too,' said Moskvin.

685

She smiled coldly at him. 'Of course, Colonel Moskvin. But if we frighten him too much he won't come back.'

It had happened before. That was the trouble with agents: you sent them to the West and sometimes they simply stayed there and thumbed their noses at you. 'He has no relatives here, does he?'

'He'll work for us, Colonel Moskvin. He is the sort of man who loves a good secret.'

Now that she had equated Moskvin with those Oxford hearties, she found herself remembering her college days. How she'd hated it: the good times she'd had were now forgotten. She recalled the men she'd known, and those long evenings in town, watching boorish under-graduates drinking too much and making fools of themselves. Keen always to make the women students feel like inferior beings. Boys with uncertain sexual preferences, truly happy only in male society, arms interlinked, singing together very loudly and staggering away to piss against the wall.

She went to Babelsberg in the southwest of Berlin to get Werner Volkmann. It was not very far as the crow flies, but crows flew across the Western sector of the city while good communists had to journey round its perimeter. This was just outside the city limits and not a part of Berlin: it was Potsdam in the DDR, and so the British and American 'protecting powers' did not have the legal right to come poking around here. Volkmann was in the Ausland Block, some buildings that had started out as administration offices of the famous UFA film studios.

Behind the empty film library building, and the workshops, there was an old backlot where the remains of an eighteenth-century village street built originally for the wartime film *Münchhausen* could be seen. 'That was Marlene Dietrich's dressing room,' said the elderly police-man who took her to the interview room. He indicated a store room with a padlock on the door.

'Yes,' said Fiona. The same policeman had said the same thing to her the last time she was here. The interview room had a barred window through which she could see the cobbled yard where she'd parked her car.

'Shall I bring the prisoner?'

'Bring him.'

Werner Volkmann looked bewildered when he was brought in. Hands cuffed behind his back, he was wearing a scuffed leather overcoat upon which there were streaks of white paint. His hair was uncombed and he was unshaven.

'Do you recognize me, Werner?'

'Of course I recognize you, Frau Samson.' He was angry and sullen.

'I'm taking you to my office in Karl Liebknecht Strasse. Do I need an armed police officer to keep you under observation?'

'I'm not going to run away, if that's what you mean.'

'Have they told you what you are charged with?'

'I want a lawyer, a lawyer from the West.'

'That's a silly thing to ask, Werner.'

'Why is it?'

It was extraordinary that Werner, a German who came here regularly, still did not understand. Well, perhaps the best way to start was to make him realize what he was up against. 'This is the DDR, Werner, and it is 1984. We have a socialist system. The people . . .'

'The government.'

'The people,' she repeated, 'don't just control the politics and the economy, they control the courts, the lawyers and the judges. They control the newspapers, the youth leagues and the women's associations and chess clubs and anglers' societies. The privilege of writing books, collecting stamps, singing at the opera or working at a lathe – in fact the right to work anywhere – can be withdrawn at any time.'

'So don't ask for a lawyer from the West.'

'So don't ask for a lawyer from the West,' agreed Fiona. 'You'll have to sit in the back of the car. I can't remove the handcuffs. I can't even carry the key. It's a regulation.'

'Can I wash and shave?'

'At the other end. Do you have any personal possessions here?'

Werner shrugged and didn't answer.

'Let's go.'

'Why you?' asked Werner as they were walking across the cobbled courtyard to her Wartburg car.

'*Machtpolitik*,' said Fiona. It meant negotiations under the threat of violence and was a uniquely German word.

None of the long-dead city officials who drew the outlandish shape of the old boundaries could have guessed that one day Berlin would be thus circumscribed and divided. Jutting southwards, Lichtenrade – where the S-Bahn line is chopped off to become a terminal, and where Mozart, Beethoven and Brahms are streets that end at the Wall – provides an obstacle around which Fiona had to drive to get back to her office in central Berlin.

The normal route back kept to the main road through Mahlow, but Fiona went on to back streets that might have saved her a few minutes in

687

travelling time, except that when she got beyond Mahlow she turned off to a sleepy little neighbourhood beyond Ziethen. Here the pre-war housing of a 'Gartenstadt' had spilled over the Wall into the Democratic Republic. Bordered on three sides by the West, these wide tree-lined roads were empty, and the neighbourhood quiet.

'Werner,' said Fiona as she stopped the car under the trees of a small urban park and switched off the engine. She turned to look back at him. 'You are just a card in a poker game. You know that, I'm sure.'

'What happens to a card in a poker game?' asked Werner.

'At the end of the game you are shuffled and put away for another day.'

'Does it hurt?'

'Within a few days you'll be back in the West. I guarantee it.' A car came very slowly up the street. It passed them and, when it was about a hundred yards ahead, stopped. Werner said nothing and neither did Fiona. The car turned as if to do a U-turn but stopped halfway and then reversed. Finally it went past them again and turned to follow the sign that pointed to Selchow. 'It was a car from a driving school,' said Fiona.

'Why are you telling me this?' said Werner. The car had made him jumpy.

'I want you to take a message.'

'A written message?'

Good old Werner. So he wasn't so simple. 'No, Werner, a verbal message.'

'To Bernard?'

'No. In fact you'd have to promise that Bernard will know nothing of it.'

'What sort of game is this?'

'You come through regularly, Werner. You could be the perfect go-between.'

'Are you asking me to work for Moscow?'

'No I'm not.'

'I see.' Werner sat back, uncomfortable with his hands cuffed behind him. Having thought about it he smiled at her. 'But how can I be sure?' It was a worried smile.

'I can't do anything about the handcuffs, Werner. It is not permitted to have keys together with prisoners in transit.'

'How can I be sure of you?' he said again.

'I want you to go and talk with Sir Henry Clevemore. Would that satisfy your doubts?'

'I don't know him. I've never even seen him.'

'At his home, not in the office. I'll give you a private phone number. You'll leave a message on the answering machine.'

'I'm not sure.'

'Jesus Christ, Werner! Pull yourself together and decide!' she yelled. She closed her eyes. She had lost control of herself. The driving school car had done it.

Werner looked at her with amazement and suddenly understood the panic she had shown. 'Why me? Why now? What about your regular contact?'

'I have no regular contact. I have been finding my way around, using dumps. London would probably have sent someone in a month or so. But this is a perfect opportunity. I will enrol you as a Stasi agent. You'll report to me personally and each time you do I will give you the material to take back.'

'That would work,' said Werner, thinking about it. 'Would Sir Henry arrange material for me to bring?'

'All my reports must be committed to memory,' said Fiona. She had done it now: she had put herself at Werner's mercy. It would be all right. Later she would get Werner to tell her about her husband and her children but not now. One thing at a time.

Now he was beginning to believe. His face lit up and his eyes widened. He was to participate in something really tremendous. 'What a coup!' he said softly and with ardent admiration. In that moment he had become her devoted slave.

'Bernard must not know,' said Fiona.

'Why?'

'For all kinds of reasons: he'll worry and give the game away. He's not good at concealing his emotions. You must know that.'

He looked out of the window. Fiona had chosen her man well. Werner had always wanted to be a secret agent. He yearned for it as other people crave to be a film star or score goals for their country or host a chat show on TV. Werner knew about espionage. He read books about it, clipped newspapers and memorized its ups and downs with a dedication that bordered on the obsessional. There was no need for him to say yes; they both knew that he couldn't resist it. 'I still can't believe it,' he said.

The driving school car came into sight as it turned the corner. It slowed and stopped, the driver carefully indicating his intentions with unnecessary signals. 'I think we should go,' said Fiona.

'I'll do it,' said Werner quietly.

'I knew you would,' said Fiona as she started the engine.

689

She overtook the driving school car and turned as if heading back towards Mahlow. It was a silly precaution that meant nothing. 'You're a brave woman, Fiona,' said Werner suddenly.

'No one,' said Fiona. 'Sir Henry and no one else unless he authorizes it to you personally.'

'How long will it go on?' said Werner.

'One year; perhaps two,' said Fiona.

'I thought they might make me persona non grata,' said Werner. 'I was worried about my work.'

'You'll be all right now,' said Fiona. 'It will be a perfect set-up.'

'Bernard must not know,' said Werner. The idea of having a secret from his best friend appealed to Werner. One day he'd surprise Bernard. It would be worth waiting for.

'Let me tell you what to say when we get back to the office. You'll see a Russian KGB colonel named Moskvin. Don't let him bluff you or bully you. I'll make sure you are okay.'

'Moskvin.'

'He's not a long-term problem,' said Fiona.

'Why not?'

'He's not a long-term problem,' said Fiona. 'He is being got rid of. Just believe me. Now let me tell you how we're going to handle this business of your reporting to me.'

Two days later the exchange took place: Erich Stinnes went East to resume his work for the KGB while Werner Volkmann was freed and came West. The KGB inquiry into the treason of Pavel Moskvin sentenced him to death. The court decreed that verdict, sentence and execution must all remain secret: it was the KGB way of dealing with its own senior personnel. The local KGB commander – a general who had been a close friend of Moskvin's father – decided that 'killed in action in the West' would be merciful and expedient, and so arranged matters. But Moskvin did not accept his fate readily. He tried to escape. The resulting exchange of fire took place on the abandoned Nollendorfplatz S-Bahn station in West Berlin, now converted to a flea market. Moskvin died. Bret Rensselaer, demonstrating his loyalty to the Crown, led the chase after Moskvin and was shot and hurt so seriously that he never resumed his duties in London.

The official British version of the events is very short. It was drafted by Silas Gaunt, who omitted any mention of the exchange of men because neither was a British national. It says that Pavel Moskvin – a KGB colonel on official duties in the West sector of Berlin – ran amok in

690

the flea market. He fired his pistol indiscriminately until the Berlin municipal police were able to subdue him. Two passers-by were shot dead, four were injured, two seriously. Moskvin turned his own pistol on himself at the moment of arrest.

The secret file compiled by the West German government in Bonn had the advantage of detailed reports from both the West Berlin police and their intelligence service. It says that Moskvin was part of a KGB party who'd come West to arrange the exchange of a West German and a Soviet national held by the British SIS. This account says that Moskvin's death was an execution carried out by a KGB team which used two motor bikes to follow Moskvin's car. While it was halted on Tauentzienstrasse, near the KaDeWe department store, an accomplice threw a plastic bag filled with white paint over its windscreen. Moskvin left the car and ran to the S-Bahn station, shooting at his pursuers. At this time civilians were injured by gunshot wounds. When Moskvin jumped down from the platform to the train tracks, perhaps believing he could run along the railway and across the Wall, he was shot dead by a round fired from a Russian Army sniper's rifle. The perpetrator was never found but is believed to have been one of the KGB hit team who'd been seen coming through a checkpoint earlier that day. In support of this theory it is pointed out that there was never a request for Moskvin's body to be returned to the East.

A few days after the shooting, an unofficial mention of the body by British contacts brought from the Soviets only puzzled denials that any Colonel Pavel Moskvin had ever existed. There was no post-mortem. The body was buried at the small cemetery in Berlin-Rudow, very near the Wall. It was at this time that the Russians spontaneously offered to return to the West the remains of Max Busby, an American shot while crossing the Wall in 1978. Some inferred that it was part of a secret deal. Both bodies were buried at night in adjoining plots. It was at the time when the new drainage was being installed at the cemetery, and the burials were unattended except for workmen, a city official and two unidentified representatives of the Protecting Powers. The graves were not marked.

There were other versions too: some less bizarre, some considerably more so. One report, neatly bound and complete with photos of Kleiststrasse, Nollendorfplatz, the S-Bahn station, the U-Bahn station and a coloured street plan showing Moskvin's path in red broken line, had been assembled by the CIA office in Berlin, working in conjunction with its offices in Bonn and London. This revealed that Moskvin had been preparing material to incriminate falsely an unnamed US citizen resident in London. It concluded that the KGB were determined that Moskvin should not be taken alive and questioned by the British.

Bernard Samson was seen firing at Moskvin but his report, given verbally, said that his rounds all went wide. Some people have pointed out that the great preponderance of rounds that Samson has been known to fire, prior to this, hit his targets. Frank Harrington might have thrown some light on the subject, for Frank had been seen on the S-Bahn station brandishing a gun (something that stayed in the minds of those who saw him because Frank had never been seen with a pistol before, or since), but London Central never asked Frank for an account of it.

Bret Rensselaer was also there but Bret was never questioned specifically. He was hit and severely injured, and by the time he'd recovered sufficiently to contribute an account of it, the reports were complete and the incident had passed into Berlin's crowded history. The doctors at the Steglitz Clinic saved Rensselaer's life. He was in the operating theatre for three hours and went from there into an intensive-care ward. Next day his brother flew in on some specially assigned US Air Force jet that came complete with doctors and nurses. He took Bret back to America with him.

23

England. March, 1987.

Bernard Samson was spending that Saturday at home with Gloria in their little house at 13, Balaklava Road, Raynes Park, in London's commuter belt. He was clearing all sorts of unwanted oddments from the garden shed. Most of them were still in the big cardboard boxes bearing the name of the moving company which had brought their furniture here.

Gloria was upstairs in the bedroom. The wardrobe door was open to reveal a long mirror in which she was studying herself. In front of her she was holding a dress she had found in one of the cardboard boxes. It was an expensive dress with a Paris label, a dramatic low-cut cocktail dress of grey and black, the barber-pole stripes sweeping diagonally with the bias cut. It belonged to Fiona Samson.

As she held it up she tried to imagine herself wearing it. She tried to imagine what Fiona was really like and what sort of a marriage she had enjoyed with Bernard and the children.

Bernard was wearing his carpet slippers and came noiselessly upstairs. Entering the room without knocking he exclaimed, 'Oh!' Then he recognized the dress she was holding and said, 'Far too small! And grey is not your colour, my love.'

Embarrassed to be caught with it, Gloria put the dress on the rail in the wardrobe and closed the door. 'She has been away four years. She will never come back, Bernard, will she?'

'I don't know.'

'Don't be angry. Every time I try to talk about her you become bad-tempered. It's a way of blackmailing me into keeping quiet about her.'

'Is that the way you see it?'

Still selfconscious, she touched her hair. 'It's the way it is, Bernard. You want to have me here with you; and you also want to hang on to the increasingly unlikely chance that you will ever see her again.'

Bernard went close and put his arm round her. At first her anger seemed assuaged, but as Bernard went to kiss her she showed a sudden anger. 'Don't! You always try to wriggle out of it. You kiss me; you say you love me; and you shut me up.'

693

'You keep asking me these questions and I tell you the truth. The truth is that I don't know the answers.'

'You make me feel so bloody insecure,' said Gloria.

'I'm always here. I don't get drunk or run around with other women.'

It was the sort of indignant answer he always gave: a typically male response. He really couldn't understand that that wasn't enough. She tried male logic: 'How long will you wait before you assume she's gone for ever?'

'I love you. We are happy together. Isn't that enough? Why do women want guarantees of permanence? Tomorrow I could fall under a train or go crazy. *There is no way that you can be happy ever after*. Can't you understand that?'

'Why are you looking at the clock?' she asked, and tried to move apart from him, but he held her.

'I'm sorry. The D-G is going down to Whitelands to see Silas Gaunt this afternoon. I think they are going to talk about Fiona. I'd give anything to know what they say.'

'You think Fiona is still working for London, don't you?'

The question came like an accusation, and it shook him. He made no move whatsoever and yet that stillness of his face revealed the way his mind was spinning. He had never told Gloria of that belief.

'That's why you won't talk of marriage,' she said.

'No.'

'You're lying. I can always tell. You think your wife was sent there to spy.'

'We'll never know the truth,' said Bernard lamely, and hoped that would end the conversation.

'I must be mad not to have seen that right from the beginning. I was just the stand-in. I was just someone to bed, someone to look after your children and keep the house tidy and shop and cook. No wonder you discouraged all my plans to go to college. You bastard! You've made a fool of me.'

'No, I haven't.'

'Now I understand why you keep all her clothes.'

'You know it's not like that, Gloria. Please don't cry.'

'I'm not bloody crying. I hate you, you bastard.'

'Will you listen!' He shook her roughly. 'Fiona is a Soviet agent. She's gone for ever. Now stop this imagining.'

'Do you swear?'

He stepped back from her. There was a fierce look in her eyes and he was dismayed by it. 'Yes, I swear,' he said.

She didn't believe him. She could always tell when he was lying.

At that moment the meeting between the Director-General and Silas Gaunt was in full swing.

'How long has Mrs Samson been in place now?' asked Silas Gaunt. It was a rhetorical question but he wanted the Director-General to share his pleasure.

'She went over there in eighty-three, so it must be about four years,' said Sir Henry Clevemore. The two men had worked wonders and were rightly proud of what they had achieved. The East German economy was cracking at the seams, the government had become senile and could muster neither will nor resource to tackle the problems. Fiona's information said that the Russian troops would be confined to barracks no matter what political changes came. The USSR had problems of its own. Bret Rensselaer's heady prediction about the Wall coming down by 1990 – considered at the time no more than the natural hyperbole that all SIS projections were prone to – now looked like a real possibility.

They had got some fine material from Fiona Samson that had enabled the two of them to master-mind the campaign as well as facilitating contact with the most level-headed opposition groups. To protect her they had given her a few little victories and a few accolades. Now they were enjoying the feeling of great satisfaction.

These two were alike in many ways. Their family background, education, bearing and deportment were comparable, but Silas Gaunt's service abroad had made him cosmopolitan, which could never be said of the aloof and formal Sir Henry Clevemore. Silas Gaunt was earthy, wily, adaptable and unscrupulous, and despite their years together Sir Henry always had reservations about his friend.

'Do you remember when young Volkmann came knocking at your door in the dead of night?' said Silas.

'The bloody fool had forgotten my phone number.'

'You were in despair,' said Silas.

'Certainly not.'

'I'm sorry to contradict you, Henry, but when you arrived here you said that Fiona Samson had made a dire error of judgement.'

'It did seem somewhat ominous.' He gave a dry chuckle. 'It was the only damn thing he had to commit to memory, and he'd forgotten it.'

'Volkmann turned up trumps. I didn't know he had it in him.'

'I'll get him something,' said the D-G. 'When it's over I'll get him some sort of award. I know he'd like a gong; he's that sort of chap.'

'You know his banking business is being wound down?' said Silas, although he'd briefed the D-G on that already.

'He's taking over that flea-bitten hotel run by that dreadful old German woman. What's her name?'

'Lisl Hennig.'

'That's the one, an absolute Medusa.'

'All good things come to an end,' said Silas.

'There were times,' said the Director-General, 'when I thought we would simply have to pull Mrs Samson out and give up.'

'Samson's a bull-headed young fool,' said Silas Gaunt, voicing what was in the minds of both men. They were sitting in the little-used drawing room of Gaunt's house, while in the next room workmen were slowly rebuilding the fireplace of Gaunt's little study. This room had been virtually unchanged for a hundred years. Like all such farmhouse rooms, with thick stone walls and small windows, it was gloomy all the year round. A big sideboard held well-used willow-pattern plates, and a vase filled with freshly cut daffodils.

Upon the lumpy sofa Silas sprawled, lit by the flickering flames of a log fire. Above him some steely-eyed ancestor squinted through the coach varnish of a big painting, and there was a small table upon which, for the time being, Silas Gaunt was eating his meals. Sir Henry Clevemore had made the journey to Whitelands after hearing that Silas was recuperating after falling from a horse. The old fool shouldn't have gone near a horse at his age, thought the D-G, and had resolved to say as much. But in the event he hadn't done so.

'Samson?' said the D-G. 'You mustn't be hard on him. I blame myself really. Bret Rensselaer always said we should have told Samson the truth.'

'I never thought I'd hear you say that, Henry. You were the one who . . .'

'Yes, I know. But Samson could have been told at the end of that first year.'

'There's nothing to be gained from a post-mortem,' said Silas. There was a tartan car-blanket over him, and every now and again he pulled at it and rearranged it round his legs. 'Or is this leading up to the suggestion that we tell him now?'

'No, no, no,' said the D-G. 'But when he started prying into the way the bank drafts came from Central Funding, I thought we'd be forced to tell him.'

Silas grinned. 'Trying to arrest him when he arrived in Berlin was not the best way to go about it, D-G, if you'll permit me to say so.'

That fiasco was not something the D-G was willing to pursue. He got to his feet and went to the mullioned window. From here there was a view of the front drive and the hills beyond. 'Your elms are looking rather sick, Silas.' There were three of them; massive great fellows planted equidistant across the lawn like Greek columns. They were the first thing you saw from the gatehouse, even before the house came into view. 'Very sick.'

Suddenly Silas felt sick too. Every day he looked at the elms and prayed that the deformed, discoloured leaves would become green and healthy again. 'The gardener says it's due to the frost.'

'Frost fiddlesticks! You should get your local forestry fellow to look at them. If it's Dutch elm disease they must be felled immediately.'

'The frost did terrible damage this year,' said Silas, hoping for a reprieve, or at least reassurance. Even unconvincing reassurance, of the sort the resourceful Mrs Porter his housekeeper gave him, was better than this sort of brutal diagnosis. Silas pleaded, 'You can see that, Henry, from the roses and the colour of the lawn.'

'Get the forestry expert in, Silas. Dutch elm disease has already run through most of the elms in this part of the world. Let it go and you'll make yourself damned unpopular with your neighbours.'

'Perhaps you're right, Henry, but I don't believe it's anything serious.'

'There are still a lot of unanswered questions, Silas. If the time has come to pull her out why don't we just do it without ceremony?'

Silas looked at him for a moment before being sure he was talking about Fiona Samson. 'Because we have a mountain of material that we can't use without jeopardizing her. And when finally she comes back she'll bring more material out with her.'

'We've had a good innings, Silas,' said the D-G, returning to the chintz-covered armchair where he'd been sitting, and giving a little grunt as he dropped into it.

'Let's not cut and run, Henry. In my memory, and privileged knowledge, Fiona Samson has proved the best agent in place the Department has ever had. It wouldn't be fair to her to throw away what is still to come.'

'I really don't understand this plan to keep her alive,' said the D-G.

Silas sighed. The D-G could be rather dense at times: he'd still not understood. Silas would have to say it in simple language. 'The plan is to convince the Soviets she is dead.'

'While she is back here being debriefed?'

'Exactly. If they know she's alive and talking to us they will be able to limit the damage we'll do to them.'

697

'Convince them?' asked the D-G.

'It's been done in the past with other agents.'

'But convince them how? I really don't see.'

'To give you an extreme example; she is seen going into a house. There is an earthquake and the whole street disappears. They think she's dead.'

'Is that a joke, Silas? Earthquake?'

'No, Director, it is simply an example. But the substitution of a corpse is a trick as old as history.'

'Our opponents are very sophisticated these days, Silas. They might tumble to it.'

'Yes, they might. But if they did, it would not be the end of the world. It would be a set-back but it wouldn't be the end of the world.'

'Providing she was safe.'

'Yes, that's what I mean,' said Silas.

The D-G was silent for a moment or two. 'The Americans are going to be dejected at the prospect of losing the source.'

'You don't think they guess where it's coming from?'

'I don't think so. Washington gets it from Bret in California, and by that time anything that would identify her is removed.'

'That business with Bret worked out well.'

'He took a dashed long time before he understood that I couldn't have called off that arrest team without revealing the part he played in running Fiona Samson.'

'I didn't mean that, so much as the way he went to convalesce in California.'

'Yes, Bret has organized himself very well over there, and using him as the conduit distances us from the Berlin material.'

'I shouldn't think Fiona Samson submits anything that would identify her,' said Silas. He never handled the material and there were times when he resented that.

'I'm sure she doesn't,' said the D-G, to indicate that he didn't directly handle the material either. 'She is an extremely clever woman. Will you use Bernard Samson to pull her out?'

'I think he should be involved,' said Silas. 'By now I think he guesses what is going on.'

'Yes,' said the D-G. 'That's why you want to bring her home, isn't it?'

'Not entirely,' said Silas. 'But it is a part of it.'

'The Soviets would leave someone like that in place for ever and ever,' said the D-G.

'We are not the Soviets,' said Silas. 'Are you feeling all right, Henry?'

'Just a palpitation. I shouldn't have smoked that cigar. I promised my doctor I would give them up.'

'Doctors are all the same,' said Silas, who had abstained and sniffed enviously while the D-G went through a big Havana after lunch.

The D-G sat back and breathed slowly and deeply before speaking again. 'This business . . . this business about switching the corpse. I don't see how we are going to handle that, Silas.'

'I know of an American . . . A very competent fellow.'

'American? Is that wise?'

'He's the perfect choice. Free-lance; expert and independent. He's even done a couple of jobs for the opposition . . .'

'Now wait a moment, Silas. I don't want some KGB thug in on this.'

'Hear me out, Henry. We need someone who knows his way around over there; someone who knows the Russian mind. And this chap is on the CIA's "most wanted" list, so he'll not be telling the story to the chaps in Grosvenor Square.'

Sir Henry sniffed to indicate doubt. 'When you put it like that . . .'

'Persona grata with the KGB, unconnected with the CIA and arm's length from us. The perfect man for the job. He'll take on the whole show for a flat fee.'

'The whole show? What does that mean?'

'There will be blood spilled, Henry. There's no avoiding that.'

'I don't want any repercussions,' said the D-G anxiously. 'I'm still answering questions about the Moskvin fracas.'

Silas Gaunt painfully lowered his feet to the floor and leaned across to the table to find some bone-handled knives in the cutlery drawer. He put three of them on the table and picked them up one by one. 'Let me improvise a possible outcome. Body number one; slightly burned but easily identified. Body number two; badly burned but identified by plentiful forensic evidence.' He looked at Sir Henry before picking up the third knife. 'Body number three; burned to a cinder but dental evidence proves it to be Fiona Samson.'

'Very convincing,' said the D-G after a moment's reflection.

'It will work,' said Silas, grabbing the knives and tossing them into the drawer with a loud crash.

'But isn't someone going to ask why?'

'You have been following the reports about Erich Stinnes and his drug racket?'

'Drugs. It's true then?'

'Our KGB colleagues have wide-ranging powers. Security,

intelligence, counter-intelligence, border controls, political crimes, fraud, corruption and drugs have become a very big worry for the Soviets.' He didn't want to go into detail about the drugs. It was a vital part of the operation: it ensnared Stinnes as a trafficker and Tessa Kosinski as an addict, but the D-G would get very jumpy if he knew everything about the drugs.

'Stinnes,' said the D-G. 'Has he given us any decent material since going back there?'

'He's playing both ends against the middle. He feels safe from arrest by us, and safe from his KGB masters too. That's what led him into his drug racket I suppose. He must be making a fortune.'

'I think I see what you have in mind: some drug-running gangsters engage in a shoot-out and Fiona Samson disappears.'

'Precisely. That's why we have to time events to coincide with the shipment of drugs. When Stinnes brings the consignment of heroin from the airport we'll bring Mrs Samson to one of his contact points on the Autobahn – still in the DDR of course – and have Samson there waiting for her. Stinnes will believe it's simply a rendezvous to tranship the drugs. We'll supply a vehicle: a diplomatic vehicle would be best for this sort of show.'

'And send Samson to get her?'

'Yes. But not Samson alone. Deserted husband and errant wife reunited after all that time: a recipe for trouble. I'll have someone else, someone calm and dependable, there to make sure it all goes smoothly.'

'And you say we have to bring in this American fellow? Couldn't we do it with our own people?'

Silas looked at him. 'No, Henry, we couldn't.'

'May I ask why, Silas?'

'The American has had dealings with Stinnes already.'

'Drug dealings you mean?'

Silas hesitated and suppressed a sigh. He didn't want to go into details. There would be problems getting everyone there. They would all have to be told a different story and Silas hadn't yet worked it out. Like the rest of them in London Central, Sir Henry had only the barest idea of what went on in the field. Silas had been closer. 'Let me give you an idea of what's entailed, Henry. We will have to have a body there to substitute for Mrs Samson, the body of a youngish woman. I don't propose we take a dead body through the checkpoints, especially not in a diplomatic vehicle, because if something happened the publicity would be horrendous. We'll also need to leave there a skull with the right dentistry. We don't want the Russians to start asking why there is an extra skull so the body will have to be decapitated. Decapitated on the spot.'

'So how *will* you get the body there?' said the D-G still puzzling over it.

'The body will walk there, go there, drive there . . . I'm not sure yet.'

'You mean alive?' Sir Henry was deeply shocked. His body stiffened and he sat bolt upright. 'What woman? How will he do this?'

'Better you don't ask, Henry,' said Silas Gaunt gently. 'But now you see why we can't use our own people.' He waited for a moment to let the D-G regain his composure. 'Bernard Samson will be there of course, but we'll use young Samson simply to bring his wife out. He will see nothing of the other business.'

'Won't he. . . ?'

'The American sub-contractor will stay behind and make sure the evidence is arranged to tell the story we want the Soviets to believe.'

'And you'll deal with this American direct?'

'No, Henry. I think that would reveal the Department's participation too obviously. I'll use a go-between. There is a fellow named Prettyman whom Bret uses for rough jobs. He's done a couple of things for us in the past. Very able, although not quite right for what I have in mind. I shall use him as a contact. No one will be told the full story, of course. Absolutely no one.'

'As long as you think you can manage this end.'

'Without Bret Rensselaer looking over my shoulder, you mean?' Silas pulled a face. 'We've managed this long.'

'I'll be glad when it's all done, Silas.'

'Of course you will, Henry. But we two old crocks have shown the youngsters a thing or two, haven't we?' They exchanged satisfied smiles.

There was a knock at the door and Mrs Porter brought tea for them. Tea was an elaborate affair at Whitelands, thanks to Mrs Porter. She arranged it on Silas' little table and the D-G pulled a chair up to it. There was buttered toast and honeycomb and caraway seed cake that only Mrs Porter could make so perfectly. That seed cake took the D-G back to his schooldays: he loved it. She poured the tea and left them.

For a few minutes they happily drank their tea and ate their toast like two little boys at a picnic.

'What was the truth about Samson's father?' the D-G asked as Silas poured more tea for them both. 'The real story, I mean. About the two Germans he was supposed to have shot?'

'Well, that's going back a bit. I . . .'

701

'There's no harm now, Silas. Brian Samson is dead, God rest his soul, and so is Max Busby.'

Silas Gaunt hesitated. He'd kept silent so long that some of the details were forgotten. At first the D-G thought he was going to refuse to talk about it, but eventually he said, 'You have to remember the atmosphere back in those days when Hitler was newly beaten. Europe was in ruins and everyone was expecting Nazi "werewolves" to suddenly emerge from the woodwork and start fighting all over again.'

'I remember it only too well,' said the D-G. 'I wish I could forget it. Or rather, I wish I were too young to have been there.'

'The Americans had no real intelligence service. Their OSS people were wasting their time looking for dead Nazis; Martin Bormann was at the top of the list.'

'Berchtesgaden. It's coming back to me now,' said the D-G. 'There was some sort of trap?'

'They had captured a Nazi war criminal named Esser – Reichsminister Esser – in a mountain hut near Hitler's Berghof. There had been a lot of Reichsbank gold found in that neighbourhood. Tons and tons of it was stolen by middle-rank US officers and never recovered. After they took Esser away, the Counter Intelligence Corps kept the hut – it was a house, really, a rather grand chalet in fact – kept it under observation. Martin Bormann's house was between Hitler's Berghof and this place they found Esser. The story was that there was penicillin and money and God knows what else hidden there for Martin Bormann to collect and get away to South America. It was all nonsense of course, but at the time it didn't seem so unlikely.'

'What was Brian Samson doing, there in the American Zone?'

'He was responsible for a prisoner from London: a German civilian named Winter,' said Silas. He offered the seed cake.

The D-G took a slice of cake. 'Winter, yes, of course.' He bit into it and savoured it like old wine.

'Paul Winter was a Nazi lawyer who worked for the Gestapo and who seemed to have an unhealthy amount of influence in Washington . . . a Congressman or someone. There was a tug of war between the State Department who wanted him released, the US Army who wanted him jailed, and the International Military Tribunal who wanted him as a defence lawyer. Meanwhile we had the blighter locked up in London.'

'He had an American mother: Veronica Winter. Her other son went to America and came strutting back in the uniform of a US Army colonel. Reckless people, Americans, eh? He wasn't even naturalized.'

'Very pragmatic,' said Silas, unwilling to make such generalizations.

'I seem to remember that the mother came of a good family. I heard that she'd died of pneumonia in one of those dreadful postwar winters. She was a friend of "Boy" Piper. Sir Alan Piper who was the D-G at one time.'

'Yes, "Boy" Piper was the one who sent me there to sort it out for the Department.'

'Go on, Silas. I want to hear the story.'

'There's not much to tell. The wife . . . Winter's wife that is, sent her husband a message . . .'

'Now this is the Nazi fellow?'

'Yes, Paul Winter the Nazi lawyer.'

'In prison?' asked the D-G, who wanted to get it quite clear.

'He wasn't in prison, in a billet. He'd been released in order to defend Esser. The Nazis accused at Nuremberg were permitted to choose anyone they wanted, even POWs from a prison cage, as their lawyers. The message said she was in this damned mountain hut, so off he dashed. He hadn't seen his wife since the war ended. His brother was a US colonel as you said: he got a military car or a jeep or something and they both cleared off without waiting for permission.'

'To Berchtesgaden?'

'And in particularly foul winter weather. I remember that winter very well. When this fellow Paul Winter got to the mountain house, his wife Inge was waiting for him. She'd had a child; she wanted money.'

'Did he have money?'

'There was a metal chest buried up there. Esser had taken it there and hidden it. During their sessions together he told Paul where it was. Then I suppose Esser must have told Inge Winter that her husband knew. They dug it up. It was gold; a mixed collection of stuff Esser had collected from the Berlin Reichsbank vaults, leaving a signed receipt for it.'

'And her child was Esser's,' supplied the D-G.

'How did you know?'

'It's the only part of the story that sticks in my mind.'

'Yes. Paul Winter must have suspected it wasn't his. They'd been married for ages and never been able to have a child. I can imagine how he felt.'

'And the two Winter boys were killed. But how did they get shot?'

'That's the question, isn't it? If you want the truth they were shot by a drunken US sergeant who thought they were werewolves or deserters or gangsters or some other sort of toughs who might hurt him. That region was plagued with deserters from both sides who'd formed gangs. They stole army supplies on a massive scale, ambushed supply convoys, robbed banks and weren't too fussy about who they hurt.'

'The story I heard . . .'

'Yes, there were lots of stories. Some people said that the Winters were shot by mistake: by someone who was trying to kill Samson and the General who was with him. Some said they were shot by the sergeant acting on secret orders from Washington. Some said Max Busby shot them because he was in love with Paul Winter's wife, or, in another version, involved in some black-market racket with her. It's impossible to prove any of those stories wrong, but believe me, I went into it thoroughly. It was as I told you.'

'But the report said Brian Samson had shot them,' said the D-G. 'I remember distinctly. He was bitter about it right up to the day he died.'

'Ah, yes. That was later. But at the time no one had any doubts. It was the drunken sergeant who was arrested and taken back to the cells. Only when the Americans asked for Samson to go and give evidence to their inquiry did things change. We couldn't let Samson face any sort of questioning of course: that's been Departmental policy since the beginning of time. When we refused to let Samson go down there, the Yanks suddenly saw a chance to get it all over quickly and quietly. By the time I arrived there, all the depositions were scrapped and new ones written. Suddenly they could produce eyewitnesses prepared to swear that Samson accidentally shot the two men.'

'That's despicable,' said the D-G. 'That verdict went on Samson's record.'

'You're preaching to the converted, Henry. I protested about it. And when "Boy" Piper wouldn't support me I made a devil of a fuss. Sometimes I think I blotted my copybook then. I was forever marked as a troublemaker.'

'I'm sure that's not true,' protested the D-G without putting much effort into it.

'I don't blame the Americans for trying it on; but I was furious that they could get away with it,' said Silas mildly. 'You couldn't entirely blame the men who perjured themselves. They were American soldiers, draftees who hadn't seen their families for ages. An inquiry might easily have kept them in Europe for another year.'

'Was Busby a party to this?'

'Busby was the Duty Ops Officer at the Nuremberg CIC office that night. He was getting a lot of stick because he was in command of the party. He preferred an accident with some foreign officer as the guilty party.'

'I can see why there was such bad feeling between him and Samson when he came to work in Berlin.'

'That's why Busby went to work for Lange's people: Brian Samson wouldn't have him.'

'And the wife?'

'She took the gold, probably changed her name and disappeared from the story. There was no sign of her by the time Samson got to the house, and I never found her. She left Esser to face the hangman, and took her daughter and went into hiding; perhaps that's what Esser wanted her to do. She was a very resolute and resourceful young woman. She worked in a nightclub in Garmisch, so she would have had no trouble in contacting the people from whom she could buy permission to live in the French Zone, which is what she did. That removed her from the British and the US jurisdiction. Eventually she got a French passport and took her gold and her baby . . .'

'And lived affluently ever after,' supplied the D-G caustically.

'Crime does sometimes pay,' said Silas. 'We may not like to concede it but it's true.' He drank some tea.

'How much gold was there?' asked the D-G, helping himself to a second piece of seed cake.

'I saw the large metal box. It had been buried – the dirt was still on it. It was provost exhibit number one. About this big.' Silas extended his hands to show the size of a small steamer trunk.

'Do you have any idea what that would weigh?' said the D-G.

'What are you getting at, Sir Henry?'

'No one could carry gold of that dimension; it would weigh a ton.'

'If she couldn't carry it, what would she do with it? Why would you dig it out in the first place, unless you were going to take it away?'

The D-G smiled knowingly. 'Speaking personally, I might dig it up because too many people know where it is.'

'Her husband and Esser and so on?'

'And perhaps many other people,' said the D-G.

'And bury it again,' said Silas, following the D-G's thought processes. 'Ummm.'

'Now there would be only three people who know where it is.'

'And two of them are dead a few minutes later.'

'So only Inge Winter knows where it is.'

'Are you suggesting that she got this American sergeant to shoot her husband and her brother-in-law?'

'I've never met any of them,' said the D-G. 'I'm simply responding to the story you've told me.'

Silas Gaunt said nothing. He tried to remember the evidence he'd examined and the soldiers he'd talked to. The sergeant was a flashy youngster with jewellery and a vintage Mercedes that he was taking home to America. Was he really drunk that night, or was that a ruse to make the 'accident' more convincing? And there was, of course, the sergeant's missing woman friend, who was a singer with a dance band. Silas never did find her. Were the woman friend and Inge Winter one and the same person? Well it was too late now. He poured more tea, drank it and put the mystery out of his mind.

Soon, reflected Silas, the D-G would retire, and that would sever his last remaining link with the Department. Silas found the prospect bleak.

The D-G got up, flicked some cake crumbs from his tie and said, 'I want you to promise me you'll have someone to look at those trees, Silas. It's a beetle, you know.'

'I don't think I could bear to lose those elms, Henry. They must be about two hundred years old. My grandfather adored them: he had a photo taken of the house when they were half the size they are now. There were four of them in those days. They say one of them blew down the night Grandfather died.'

'I've never heard such maudlin nonsense. Elms don't blow down, they're too deep-rooted.'

'My mother told me it fell when Grandfather died,' said Silas, as if the honour of his family rested upon the truth of it.

'Don't be such a fool, Silas. Sometimes you have to sacrifice the things you love. It has to be done. You know that.'

'I suppose so.'

'I'm going to send Mrs Samson over to Bret when she comes out. California. What do you think?'

'Yes, capital,' said Silas. 'She'll be well away from any sort of interference. And Bernard Samson too?'

'No. Unless you. . . ?'

'Well, I do, Henry. Leave Samson here and he'll roar around trying to locate her and make himself a nuisance. Bundle him off and let Bret take care of them both.'

'Very well.' The grandfather clock, which Silas had moved to this room because he didn't trust the work-men not to damage it, struck five p.m. 'Is that really the time? I must be going.'

'Now, you're leaving all the arrangements to me, Henry?' Silas wanted to get it clear; he wanted no recriminations. 'There is a great deal to be done. I'll have to have matching dentistry prepared, and that takes ages.'

'I leave it to you, Silas. If you need money, call Bret.'

'I suppose the special funding mechanism will be wound up once she is safe,' said Silas.

'No. It will be a slush fund for future emergencies. It cost us so much to set up that it would be senseless to dismantle it.'

'I thought Samson's probing into the money end might have made it too public.'

'Samson will be in California,' mused the D-G. 'The more I think of that idea the better I like it. Volkmann said that Mrs Samson has aged a lot lately. We'll send her husband there to look after her.'

24

'How stunning to have the Müggelsee all to ourselves,' said Harry Kennedy. He was at the tiller of a privately owned six-metre racing yacht: Fiona was crewing.

On a hot summer day the lake was crowded with sailing boats, but today was chilly and the lake was entirely theirs. It was late afternoon. The sun, sinking behind bits of cumulus – ragged and shrinking in the cooling air – provided fleeting golden haloes and sudden shadows but little warmth.

The wind was growing stronger, pressing upon the sail steadily like a craftsman's hand, so that the hull cut through the water with a loud hiss, and left a wake of curly white trimmings.

Fiona was sitting well forward, huddled in her bright yellow hooded jacket complete with heavy Guernsey sweater and Harry's scarf, but still she shivered. She liked the broad expanse of the lake, for it enabled her to sit still and not have all the work of tacking and jibing and trimming which Harry liked doing so much. Or rather liked to watch her doing. He never seemed to feel the cold when he was sailing. He became another man when dressed in casual clothes. The short red anorak and jeans made him look younger: this was the intrepid man who flew planes over the desert and the tundra, the man who fretted behind a desk.

She had seen a lot of him during that year he'd spent at the Charité. He'd taken her mind off the miseries of separation at a time she'd most needed someone to love and care for her. Now that he was working in London again, he saw her only when he could get a really long weekend, and that meant every six weeks or so. Sometimes he arranged to borrow this sailing boat from a friend he'd made at the hospital, and she brought sandwiches and a vacuum flask of coffee so they could spend all the day on the lake. These trips must have involved him in a lot of trouble and expense, but he never complained of that. She couldn't help wondering if it was all part of his assigned duty of monitoring her, but she didn't think so.

Neither had he ever suggested the impossible: that she should come to London to see him. He knew about her, of course, or at least he knew as much as he needed to know. Once late at night in her apartment after too much wine he'd blurted out, 'I was sent.' But he'd immediately made it into some sort of metaphysical observation about their being meant for each other and she'd let it go at that. There was nothing to be gained from hinting that she knew the real story behind that first meeting. It was better to have this arm's-length love affair: each of them examining the thoughts and emotions of the other, neither of them entirely truthful.

'Happy?' he called suddenly.

She nodded. It wasn't a lie: everything was relative. She was as happy as she could be in the circumstances. Harry sat lounging knee-bent at the stern – head turned, arm outstretched, elbow on knee, fingers extended to the tiller – looking like Adam painted on the Sistine ceiling. 'Very happy,' she said. He beckoned to her and she moved to sit close beside him.

'Why can't it always be just like this?' he asked in that forlorn way that her children had sometimes posed similarly silly questions. She would never understand him, just as she had never been able to understand Bernard. She would never understand men and the way their minds could be both mature and selfishly childlike at the same time.

'Ever been to the Danube Delta? There is a vast nature reserve. Ships – like floating hotels – go right down the Danube to the Black Sea. It would be a wonderful vacation for us. Would you like that?'

'Let me think about it.'

'I have all the details. One of the heart men at the Charité took his wife: they had a great time.'

She wasn't listening to him. She was thinking all the time of the recent brief meeting she'd had with Bernard. They had met in a farmhouse in Czechoslovakia and Bernard had urged her to come back to him. It should have made her happy to see him again, but it had made her feel inadequate and sad. It had reawakened all her fears about the difficulties of being reunited with her family. Bernard had changed, she had changed, and there could be no doubt that the children would have changed immensely. How could she ever be one of them again?

'I'm sorry, Harry,' she said.

'About what?'

'I'm not good company. I know I'm not.'

'You're tired: you work too hard.'

'Yes.' In fact she'd become worried at her lapses of memory.

709

Sometimes she could not remember what she had been doing the previous day. Curiously the distant past was not so elusive: she remembered those glorious days with Bernard when the children were small and they were all so happy together.

'Why won't you marry me?' he said without preamble.

'Harry, please.'

'As a resident of the DDR you could get a divorce with the minimum of formalities.'

'How do you know?'

'I explored it.'

'I wish you hadn't.' If he had talked to a lawyer it might have drawn attention to her in a way that was undesirable.

'Fiona, darling. Your husband is living happily with another woman.'

'How do you know?'

'I saw them together one evening. I almost stumbled into them in the crush at Waterloo Station. They were catching the Epsom train.'

'You recognized them?'

'Of course. You showed me a photo of him once. The woman with him was blonde and very tall.'

'Yes, that's her.' It hurt like a dagger in the heart. She'd known, of course, but it hurt even more when she heard it from Harry.

'You know her?' he said.

'I've met her,' said Fiona. 'She's pretty.'

'I don't want to make you miserable but we should talk about it. It's madness for us to go on like this.'

'Let's see what happens.'

'You've been saying that since the time we first met. Do you know how long ago that is?'

'Yes. No . . . A long time.'

'Living without you is Hell for me: but being separated from me doesn't make you miserable,' he admonished her, hoping for a contradiction, but she only shrugged. 'We haven't got much time, Fiona.'

She kissed his cheek. 'Harry. We are happy enough this way. And we have lots of time.' It was the same conversation they'd had many times before.

'Not if we were to start a family. Not much time.'

'Is that what you want?'

'You know it is. Our children, Fiona. It's everything I want.'

'You'd come and live here?' She was testing him now.

710

'I lived here before.'

'That's not the same thing as living here permanently,' she said.

'Do I hear a discordant note in the Marxist harmony?'

'I'm stating a fact.'

'You don't have to be defensive, honey.'

'You said you were a Marxist,' she reminded him. It was unfair to remind him of something he'd said only once, and that in a heated argument.

'Yes. I said I *was* a Marxist. I *was* a Marxist a long time ago.' The sail began drumming.

'But no longer?'

He pulled the mainsheet to adjust the sail before turning his head to answer. He was a good sailor, quick and expert in handling the boat and everything else he did. 'I asked myself a question,' he said.

'And?'

'That's all. Marxism is not a creed for those who question.'

'No matter what the answer? Is that true?'

'Yes. Whatever the answer: one question gives birth to another. A thousand questions follow. Nothing can sustain a thousand questions.'

'Nothing? Not even love?'

'Don't mock me.' They were near the shore now: all forest, no sign of people anywhere. 'Ready about!' said Harry in the flat voice he used when commanding the boat.

Stepping carefully she went forward, released the front sail and watched him as he swung the tiller. The boom crashed across the boat as they passed through the wind and instinctively he ducked his head to avoid it. She pulled in the jib and set the front sail before going back to sit down.

'Do you ever play let's pretend?' he said as he settled back on the seat. It was another aspect of his childishness. Flying planes was childish too: perhaps he'd joined the Communist Party as some silly adventure.

'No,' she said.

'I do. Sitting here, just the two of us in the boat, cruising across the Müggelsee, I pretend that you are an alluring Mata Hari and that I am the heroic young fellow in your spell who has come to rescue you.'

She said nothing. She didn't like the drift of this conversation but it was better to see what came of it.

'Pursued by black-hearted villains, the other shore is safety: a place where we'll live happily ever after, and raise our family.'

'Sounds like *A Farewell to Arms*,' said Fiona without putting too much enthusiasm into the idea. 'Did you ever read that?'

'The journey across the lake to Switzerland. Hemingway. Yes, I did it for my high school English. Perhaps that was where I got it.'

'The woman dies,' said Fiona. 'They get to Switzerland but the woman dies in hospital.' She turned to look at him and he seemed so utterly miserable that she almost laughed.

'Don't make jokes,' he said. 'Everything is perfect.' She hugged him in reassurance.

Yes, everything had been perfect for Harry. It was easy for him. But Fiona was coming near to the end of her resources. She was desperately depressed, even out here on the lake with a man who loved her. Depression, she'd found, was no respecter of logical truth; it was some dark chemical cloud that descended upon her at random and reduced her to jelly.

It was no good telling herself that it was nonsense. She'd given up her children and her marriage. Was she being paranoid to think that Bernard would have completely poisoned the children's minds against her by now? She had run away, why wouldn't they be hurt by such rejection? How could she hope to become wife and mother again?

The children were the most terrible sacrifice she had made, but there were other wounds too. She had lost friends and family who now despised her as a traitor. And what was it all for? She had no way to judge the results, or the contribution she'd made. She'd begun to suspect that she was the lamb slaughtered at the altar of Bret Rensselaer's ambition. Bret's wounds were corporeal: his reputation intact. Bret Rensselaer was the winner. So were Silas and the D-G. Three old men had sent her here: and those three would be the victors. What did they care about her? She was expendable: as useful and as readily discarded as a Kleenex tissue.

Fiona was the loser: Fiona, her husband and her children. They would never recover from what she had done. Was any political – or as Bret so liked to have it: economic – victory worth it? The answer was no.

Sometimes she felt like salvaging what little she had left. She felt like grabbing a chance of happiness with Harry, of severing her contact with London and just settling down in East Berlin as a Hausfrau. But that would be no more than a temporary salve. The real loss was Bernard and the children: she wanted them to love her and need her.

'A penny for them?' said Harry.

'I was thinking about my hair,' she said. 'About having it cut shorter.' Men were always ready to believe that women were thinking about their hair.

712

He smiled and nodded. She was looking much older lately: they both were. A vacation in the Danube Delta would be good for both of them.

That evening she had a meeting with Werner Volkmann. She waited there alone in her old-fashioned apartment looking out over the Frankfurter Allee, the wide main road that led eventually to Moscow and, perhaps for that reason, was once called Stalin Allee. It was a part of the procedure that agents running back and forth did not come up to the office. They met privately. She looked at her watch: Werner was late.

She tried to read but was too jittery to concentrate. She found herself trying not to look at *Pariser Platz*, which was hanging over her bed. It was in a neat black ebony frame. One evening she had taken it down and opened the frame in order to replace Kirchner's kitsch gaiety with an abstract print more to her taste. Behind the street scene she had been horrified to come across a coloured print of Lochner's *The Last Judgment*. As such medieval paintings go, it was a mild example of the violent horrors waiting for sinners in the next world, but Fiona, alone and tired and troubled, had been thunderstruck by the demented and distorted figures and terrifying demons. It was as if she was meant to find it lurking under the cosiness of the Berlin street scene. With trembling hands she'd replaced *The Last Judgment* back under the Kirchner and fixed it into its frame, but from that time onwards she was never unaware of the presence of that tormented world that lurked under the frolicsome *Pariser Platz*.

Werner apologized for being late. He was rainswept and weary. He said it was the strain of winding down his banking business and trying to run Lisl Hennig's hotel at the same time, but Fiona wondered if it was the stress of being a double agent. Werner was a West German national. If the security services became convinced that he was betraying them he would simply disappear without trace or, worse still, become a patient in the Pankow clinic.

They chatted for ten minutes, the sort of unimportant talk they might have had if Werner was what he purported to be. Only then did Fiona disconnect the voice-actuated microphone which she had discovered on the first day she got here. Senior staff had their conversations recorded only by random checks, but it was better to be safe.

'Did you see the children?' Before answering he went and sat in the only comfortable chair with his overcoat still on. He wasn't feeling cold: Werner often kept his overcoat on. It was as if he wanted to be ready to leave at short notice. He'd even kept hold of his hat, and now he was fidgeting with it, holding it in both hands like the steering wheel of a heavy truck that he was negotiating along a busy road.

'I will see them next week,' said Werner. He saw the disappointment in her face. 'It's not easy to arrange it without Bernard asking awkward questions. But they are fit and well, I can assure you of that. Bernard is a good father.'

'Yes, I know,' said Fiona, and Werner realized that she had taken it as a reproach. He found it difficult to have a conversation with Fiona these days. She could be damned touchy. She was worn out. He'd told the D-G that over and over again. She said, 'It might be easier if I were in Moscow or China, but it is impossible to forget that everything I love is so near at hand.'

'Soon you'll be home. Here everything is changing,' said Werner. 'I even see diehard communists beginning to discover that man does not live by bread alone.'

'Nothing will ever change,' said Fiona. 'You can't build a capitalist paradise upon a Leninist boneyard.'

'Why so glum, Fiona?' She seldom revealed her personal views.

'Even if you waved a magic wand and declared Eastern Europe totally free, it would not stir. Bret's sanguine ideas about the economy don't take into account the human factor or the immense difficulties of change evident to anyone who comes and looks for themselves. He talks about "the market" but all Eastern Bloc economies are going to remain dominated by the public sector for many many years to come. How will they fix market prices? Who is likely to buy decrepit steel works, ancient textile plants or loss-making factories? Bret says the East will revive its private sector. How? Eastern Europeans have spent their whole working lives slacking off in over-manned jobs. No one here takes risks. Even in the KGB/Stasi office I find people are reluctant to take on new responsibility or make a decision. Forty years of socialism has produced a population incapable of decision-making. People here don't want to think for themselves. Capitalism will not appear just because there is no longer any law against it.' She stopped. It was an unusual outburst. 'I'm sorry, Werner. Sometimes I think I've been here too long.'

'London think so too. The D-G is going to pull you out,' said Werner.

She closed her eyes. 'How soon?'

'Very soon. You should start to tidy things up.' He waited for a stronger reaction and then said, 'You'll be with Bernard and the children again.'

She nodded and smiled bleakly.

'Are you frightened?' he asked, without really believing it was true.

'No.'

'There is nothing to be frightened of, Fiona. They love you, they want you back.'

For a moment she gave no sign of having heard him, then she said, 'Suppose I forget?'

'Forget what?'

She became flustered. 'Things about them. I do forget things, Werner. What will they think of me?' She gave him no chance to answer, and moved on to other things. 'How will it be done, Werner?'

'It might be changed, but at present the plan is to leave a car parked in the street outside. The keys will be under the seat. With the keys there will be an identity card. Use it only as far as the Autobahn then throw it into a ditch somewhere where it won't be found. You'll drive down the Autobahn, dump the car at the roadside and get into one with British plates. The driver will have a UK diplomatic passport for you.'

'You make it sound simple, Werner.' London always made things sound simple. They believed it gave agents confidence.

He smiled and twirled the hat on the finger of one hand. 'London want you to list your contacts here, Fiona.' For years she'd thought of Werner as some soft woolly creature, hen-pecked by his awful wife. Since using him as her contact with London Central she'd discovered that the real Werner was as hard as nails and far more ruthless than Bernard.

'I have none,' she said.

'Contacts: good and bad. I'd give the bad ones careful consideration, Fiona. Office staff? Janitor? Has anyone said anything to you, even in jest?' He pinched his nose between finger and thumb, looking up at her mournfully while he did it.

'What sort of anything?'

'Jokes about you working for the British . . . Jokes about you being a spy.'

'Nothing to be taken seriously.'

'This is not something to gamble with, Fiona. You'd better tell me.' He placed his hat on the floor so that he could wrap the skirt of his overcoat over his knees.

'Harry Kennedy . . . He's a doctor who visits Berlin sometimes.'

'I know.'

'You know?'

'London has had him under surveillance since the day you first came here.'

715

'My God, Werner! Why did you never tell me?'

'I had nothing to tell.'

'I was with him today. Do you know that too?'

'Yes. London tells me of his movements. Working in the hospital means he has to make his plans well in advance.'

'I'm sure he's not . . .'

'There to monitor you? But of course he is. He must be KGB and assigned to you. Kennedy arranged that first meeting with you in London; Bret is certain of it.'

'Have you talked to Bret? I thought Bret was in California.'

'California is served by scheduled flights, phones and fax.'

'Who else knows?' she asked anxiously.

He didn't answer that one. 'Kennedy is a party member from way back. Don't say you haven't checked him out, Fiona?'

She looked at Werner. 'Yes, I have.'

'Of course you have. I told Bret that you would be sure to. What woman could resist an opportunity like that?'

'That sounds very patronizing, Werner.'

'Does it? I'm sorry. But why not tell me the truth right from the start?'

'Today he said how wonderful it would be if I were Mata Hari escaping to the West with him. Or some tosh of that kind.'

Werner tugged at his nose, got up and went to the window. It was night and, under floodlamps, workmen were decorating the Frankfurter Allee with the colourful banners and flags of some African state. All visiting dignitaries were paraded along this boulevard to see their colours thus displayed. It was a mandatory part of the Foreign Ministry's schedule.

In the other direction, the whole sky was pink with the neon and glitter of the West. How near it was, as near and as available as the moon. Werner turned back to her. Fiona was still as beautiful as she had ever been, but she had aged prematurely. Her face was pale and strained, as if she was trying to see into a bright light.

Werner said, 'If Kennedy happened to be here at the time you were pulled out, he'd have to be neutralized, Fiona.'

'Why would he be here at the time I am pulled out?'

'Why indeed?' said Werner. He picked up his hat, flicked at the brim of it and put it on his head. Fiona climbed up on the chair to connect the microphone again.

25

Berlin. June 1987.

It was his wavy hair that made 'Deuce' Thurkettle look younger than his true age. He was sixty-one years old but regular exercise, and careful attention to what he ate, kept him in good physical condition. He put on his bifocals to read the menu but he could manage most things without them, including shooting people, which was what he did for a living. 'Steak and salad,' he said. 'Rare.'

'The Tafelspitz is on today,' said Werner.

'No thanks; too fattening,' said Thurkettle. He knew what it was, a local version of a New England dinner: boiled beef, boiled potatoes and boiled root vegetables. He never wanted to see that concoction again. It was what he'd eaten in prison. Just the sight or smell of a plate of boiled beef and cabbage was enough to remind him of those years he'd spent cooped up on death row, waiting for the executioner, in a high-security prison along with a lot of other men found guilty of multiple murders.

'Perhaps I shouldn't eat Tafelspitz either,' said Werner regretfully. 'Rare steak and salad: twice,' he told the waiter.

It was Sunday morning. They were in West Berlin: Leuschner's, a popular barn-like café, with gilt-framed mirrors on the whole of one wall and a long counter behind which one of the Leuschner brothers served. Coming from the jukebox there was a Beatles tune played by the Band of the Irish Guards. The jukebox used to have hard rock records but one of the Leuschners had decided to refill it with music of his own taste. Werner looked round at the familiar faces. On such Sunday mornings, this otherwise unfashionable place attracted a noisy crowd of off-duty gamblers, musicians, touts, cabbies, pimps and hookers who gathered at the bar. It was not a group much depleted by church-going.

Thurkettle nodded his head to the music. With his bow tie, neatly trimmed beard and suit of distinctly American style, he looked like a tourist. But Thurkettle was here to commit a murder on the orders of London Central. He wondered how much Werner had been told.

Werner's task was to show him some identity photos and offer him any help and assistance he might require. After the job was done Werner was to meet him on the Autobahn, in the small hours of the morning, and pay him his fee in cash. 'You have transport arranged?' asked Werner.

'A motor bike: it's quick and nicely inconspicuous for this sort of caper.'

Werner looked out of the window. People in the street were bent under shiny umbrellas. 'You'll get wet,' said Werner. 'The forecast says storms.'

'Don't worry about me,' said Thurkettle. 'This hit on the Autobahn is just a routine job for me. Rain is the least of my problems.'

It had been a sudden last-minute decision and a rush to get it all arranged. A message from Erich Stinnes had come announcing that a consignment of heroin had arrived at East Berlin's airport. He would bring it through tonight. Once he knew this, Thurkettle sent a signal to London that Fiona Samson could be brought out of East Berlin tonight. Werner had sent affirmation that Fiona was ready.

'These are the people you will see at the rendezvous.' Werner produced photos from his pocket and passed them across the table. What exactly was going to happen, who was to be murdered and why, Werner had not been told. His presence at the rendezvous was not required. It was just as well, for tonight he was committed to a big celebration at Tante Lisl's: a fancy-dress party with all the trimmings. Just about everyone he knew in West Berlin would be there. But now the evening would be spoiled for him: he'd spend all the night worrying about Fiona Samson's escape.

Thurkettle pretended to study the passport-style pictures, but he had seen all these people before at some time or other. Thurkettle prepared carefully for each job, that's why he was highly paid, and that's why he was so successful. After a minute or two he passed the pictures back.

Werner tapped the photo of Stinnes. 'This is your drug peddling contact. Right?'

Thurkettle grunted assent.

'Stinnes will arrive with this woman.' Werner indicated Fiona Samson's photo. 'She will depart with this man.' He indicated the photo of Bernard Samson. 'Probably this man will also be there.' He showed him a photo of Harry Kennedy.

Thurkettle looked at Werner, at the photos, and then at Werner again. 'I'll take care of them.'

Werner said, 'Don't take care of the wrong people.'

'I won't,' said Thurkettle with a cold smile.

'Bernard Samson and Fiona Samson. Make sure they are safe.'

Thurkettle nodded. Now he felt sure that Werner Volkmann was not a party to the real secret: the way that Tessa was to die and change identity with her sister.

'The Brandenburg exit,' added Werner, who was anxious that there should be no misunderstanding.

'No sweat. I know the place. The half-completed highway widening work. I went there yesterday and took a look-see. I'll have a shovel, overalls and a can of gas.'

'Gas? Petrol?' Werner put a map on the table.

'To torch the car. The guy in London, who gave me my orders, wants the car burned.'

'Afterwards you'll meet me here.' He showed Thurkettle on the Autobahn map. 'The cash will be in a leather case. If you don't want to carry a case, you'd better have something to put it in. When you are paid, come back up the Autobahn and through the Border Control Point at Drewitz into West Berlin. You'll go through without any trouble. In Berlin phone the number I gave you and say the job is finished. From then on you are on your own. You have the airline ticket? Don't go back into East Berlin.'

'I won't go back to the East.'

'Have you arranged about a gun? I was told to make sure you had a gun if you needed it.'

'The last time I found myself without a gun was in Memphis, Tennessee. I strangled two guys with my bare hands.' He put a cardboard box on the table. 'Here's one of them,' he said, loosening the lid and holding it open an inch or two.

Werner looked into Thurkettle's cold eyes trying to decide whether it was a joke but, unable to tell, he looked down into the box. '*Gott im Himmel!*' said Werner as he caught sight of the contents. It was a human skull.

'So don't baby me,' said Thurkettle, closing the box and putting it beside him on the chair. 'Just have the dough ready.'

'I will have the money ready.'

'If you want to call it off, this is your final chance,' said Thurkettle. 'But once the job is done I'm like the Pied Piper of Hamelin; if I don't get paid I come back and do the job all over again. Get me?'

'I get you.'

'Used fifty-dollar bills,' said Thurkettle grimly.

Werner sighed and printed circles upon the table with his wet beer-glass. 'I told you: I will have it ready, exactly as I said.'

'You do your thing the way you were told: I do my thing the way I was told: we get along just fine. But if you foul up, old buddy . . .' He left

719

the rest of it unsaid. He'd not yet encountered anyone so dumb as to default in payment to a hired killer. 'Just one more time: I meet you on the Autubahn, direction west. I take the exit marked Ziesar and Görzke. You'll be waiting on the exit ramp. Going off the Autobahn is illegal for Westerners, just wait at the bottom of the ramp.'

They'd been all through it before. 'I'll be there,' said Werner. He wondered if the skull was real or one of those plastic ones they make for medical students. It certainly looked real: very real. He was still wondering about that when the steaks arrived. They were big entrecotes, seared and perfect, cooked and delivered to the table by Willi Leuschner himself. He put down a big pot of home-made horseradish sauce, knowing that Werner liked it. Willi had been at school with Werner and the two men spent a moment exchanging the usual sort of pleasant remarks. The Leuschners were both coming to Werner's fancy-dress party that night. It seemed as if half of Berlin were planning to be there.

'More beer?' asked Willi finally.

'No,' said Werner, 'we both have to keep clear heads.' Willi scribbled the account on a beer-mat and dropped it back on the table.

Deuce Thurkettle left Werner to pay the bill. His BMW bike was outside. It was a big machine with two panniers in which he stowed all his gear. The engine roared and he gave a flip to the accelerator before settling into the saddle. With a quick wave of the hand as he passed the restaurant window he sped away.

He had a lot to do before getting to the rendezvous on the Autobahn, but seeing Werner was necessary. Thurkettle made a point of threatening his clients in that way. It was a part of the fastidious attention to detail that made him so effective.

Another reason for his success was knowing when to keep his mouth shut. Whoever had briefed Werner Volkmann had obviously told him some fairy story. The briefing that Thurkettle had been given by Prettyman in a fancy suite in the London Hilton had been rather more complete and certainly more specific. Prettyman had told him that under no circumstance must anyone be left alive except Bernard and Fiona Samson. No one left alive. Prettyman had been very insistent upon that.

The Brandenburg exit – the place arranged for Fiona Samson to change from one car to the other – was on East Germany's section of Hitler's Autobahn, built to connect Berlin to Holland and all points westwards. As well as being a major East German highway, this was one of the

720

authorized routes along which Westerners were permitted to drive to West Berlin.

On this flat region immediately to the west of Berlin the rivers have spread to become lakes. It is a region of farmland and forest, and once outside the towns the traveller finds little cobble-streeted villages where little has changed since the Kaiser's photo hung in the schoolrooms.

Even one of East Germany's two-stroke motor cars can get there from Berlin in well under an hour; for Thurkettle's powerful motor cycle it was nothing. He arrived before dark. The workers from the construction site had gone: their earth-moving machines were neatly lined up, like tanks for an inspecting general.

Thurkettle broke the lock off the door of the portable hut used by the construction gangs. He used a flashlight to check his guns and ammunition and the stainless steel butcher's hacksaw he'd brought with him. Then he put on his coveralls and plastic medical gloves and looked at the skull and its neat dentistry. That done, he sat down, watched the pouring rain and waited patiently for it to get dark.

These things never go exactly according to plan. That was the most important of the lessons he'd learned over the years. Prettyman had told him that Erich Stinnes would be collecting Fiona Samson and bringing her to the rendezvous. Someone like her would remain there.

Thurkettle had been told that someone of exactly the same build as Fiona Samson must be killed and left at the rendezvous. It was Thurkettle who thought of the idea of using Fiona Samson's sister, and he was pleased with that. She was a drug addict, and such people were easy to control. His task was to put Fiona Samson into the car with her husband and let them depart alive. He then had to kill Stinnes and the sister, bury Stinnes in the excavated ditch the roadworkers had so conveniently provided close by, and burn the car with the sister's body inside it.

The Soviet investigators would never find Stinnes' body because by the time they realized that Stinnes had not gone over the frontier with Samson, there would be a hundred tons of solid concrete and a section of Autobahn over the burial place. The burned body would be identified as Fiona Samson because the two women were very much alike except for the dentistry, and the skull he'd shown Werner had been prepared for exactly that deception. The trickiest task was decapitating the sister, but her head would have to go in the ditch with the Stinnes corpse. Otherwise the forensic team examining the car would find a burned body with two heads, and that would alert even the doziest laboratory assistant.

It all went amiss; right from the very start. Tessa – unreliable in the way that addicts usually are – did not arrive on time. Despite everything Thurkettle had arranged, she went off to Werner's fancy-dress party. Tessa should have arrived first. Thurkettle became so anxious that he went off on his motor cycle, but came back when he recognized the car with Fiona and Stinnes in it. When finally Tessa did arrive, it was in the back of the Ford van with Bernard Samson. Stinnes had arrived in a Wartburg bringing Fiona Samson and Harry Kennedy too. And who could have guessed that Bernard Samson would arrive with some lunatic from London Central who perhaps thought it would be amusing to come directly from Werner's party wearing his fancy dress? A gorilla costume! Their Ford van was there within five minutes of the Wartburg, and parked in what Thurkettle approved as a good getaway position. The Wartburg was parked nose-out, with its sidelights on. Thurkettle expected Stinnes to bring the heroin consignment out of the car but no one emerged.

Everyone seemed to be waiting for something to happen. Thurkettle remained in the darkness and watched. He was standing behind one of the bulldozers when it all started: a slim man, dressed as a gorilla, leapt from the Ford van, and started jumping around, shouting and waving a gun.

A gorilla. It looked so damned convincing for a moment that Thurkettle thought it was a real gorilla. It took a lot to surprise Thurkettle but that took him off guard. It must have taken Stinnes, or whoever was in the driver's seat of the Wartburg, off guard too, for someone switched on the car's full beams to see the gorilla more clearly.

The gorilla raised his pistol and was about to fire at the Wartburg. Thurkettle suddenly saw his reputation threatened and his fee in jeopardy. The Samson woman had to get away safely. Prettyman in London had been most specific about that. If Fiona did not arrive safely in the West, no fee would be paid beyond the small initial 'contract' payment.

So Thurkettle fired at this crazy gorilla. His silenced gun made no more noise than a carefully opened bottle of wine. But by this time Thurkettle was rattled and his shot missed.

Then the gorilla fired. He must have heard Thurkettle's shot, for he was virtually in line with the barrel, where the silencer has least effect. The glass of the Wartburg's windscreen smashed and Thurkettle thought Fiona Samson had been hurt, but then he saw her get out of the car. She shouted something, and then her doped-out sister came floating into view. Tessa came dancing, arms outstretched to display a long yellow diaphanous dress that was some sort of fancy costume.

There must be no mistakes this time. Thurkettle picked up the shotgun and aimed low. Tessa seemed to see him. She grinned as he pulled the trigger twice, hitting her with both shots. As she went down, the gorilla fired again and this time his round put out one of the Wartburg's headlights. Thurkettle didn't like the way it was developing. Given the darkness one or two of these people could get away. But he wasn't by any means certain how many people were there.

There were more shots, fired in rapid succession, a sign of nerves. Stinnes probably, he could be trigger-happy. One of them had to find a mark. The gorilla screamed, ran, stumbled and crashed into the mud. Thurkettle stayed in the darkness. Somewhere in this muddy arena Bernard Samson lurked, and Samson was a pro. Then Stinnes stepped out to make sure the gorilla was dead. What a reckless thing to do. Thurkettle remained very still in the darkness and kept silent.

'It's safe,' called Stinnes. He beckoned to a second man: a tall fellow in a smart trenchcoat: Kennedy.

'How many did they send?' Kennedy asked. He looked round nervously and the light from the single passing headlight caught his face. From his position Thurkettle could see both men clearly and identified them beyond chance of mistake: yes, Erich Stinnes and Harry Kennedy.

Then Fiona Samson walked forward. Some instinct, or understandable trepidation, made her walk so as to avoid the pool of light. London must have briefed her to go for the van, for she was heading towards it, past the men, when two shots were fired. They came from somewhere so close to Thurkettle that the sound made him jump half out of his skin. Fiona Samson disappeared. Damn!

Bang. Some damned great handgun. Kennedy jumped back, arms flailing like a rag doll as he was knocked over, and lay in the mud as still as a bundle of old clothes. He was unmistakably dead. Sometimes it goes like that, a lucky accident and one shot is enough.

Bang. Again the cannon went off. Stinnes lurched round, firing his gun with one hand and clutching his neck with the other, the blood spraying through his fingers. It went everywhere and spattered Fiona. That shot was enough to tell Thurkettle that these were not lucky accidents. There was someone, a too damned close to him someone, who'd silently clambered up on to a piece of heavy machinery to get a better vantage point; some cold-blooded someone who didn't say hands up; someone who hadn't perfected his shooting on the range: Samson.

Thurkettle's mouth went dry. He always made it a rule not to tangle with professional hit men or pros like Samson. It was bad enough facing these KGB goons but Samson was a number one no-no.

The remaining headlight of the Wartburg was switched off. It was dark now except when the lights of passing traffic swept across the mud and debris and the bodies. Thurkettle froze and hoped he hadn't been spotted. Neither Bernard Samson nor his wife had been told of Thurkettle's role in this drama. Only Tessa and Stinnes had expected him to be here, and they were both dead.

Thurkettle crouched lower behind the tracks of the bulldozer and looked at the eastern horizon. Soon it would be dawn. He didn't want to be here when it got light: any passing driver on the Autobahn might spot him. Cops might arrive. 'Are we going to wait here all night, Samson?' he called finally. 'You can take the woman and take the Ford and go. Take your gorilla too. I don't want any of you.' When there was still no response he called, 'Do you hear me? I'm working your side of the street. Get going. I've got work to do.'

It was a breach of contract but only a minor breach: the two Samsons were on the side of the man who employed him. They'd just have to keep their mouths shut. Anyway by the time they were debriefed Thurkettle would have his money and be over the hills and far away.

Fiona Samson might still have been sitting there had she not used every last atom of will-power to get to her feet. Something inside her had snapped. Was this the breakdown of will that she had been dreading for so long? Inside her head there was a noise that she couldn't recognize. It blotted out her thoughts and distorted her vision. She didn't know who she was and couldn't remember where she was supposed to be.

With the sluggish posture of a sleep-walker Fiona Samson emerged from the dark. Spattered with blood, and stumbling in the soft ground, she inched towards the Ford van. She was totally disabled by seeing Kennedy, dear sweet Harry whom she loved, so brutally shot dead, and not by an avenging husband but by a professional and indifferent one. Tessa too. The sister she cherished more than she could say was dead in a pool of blood.

This was that *Last Judgment* she'd discovered with such a shock. Here were the monsters come to torment her for all eternity. Wracked with sin, she had stepped beyond the cosy world of the Pariser Platz into the bloody nightmare on the wall, and there would be no escape. Her mind numbed, and suffering an anguish from which she would never completely recover, she moved through her frenzied world like an automaton.

724

Bernard Samson watched Fiona get into the van. Then, suspicious to the last, he ran to get behind cover. When no shots were fired at him he climbed into the Ford van beside his wife. The engine started and, slowly and carefully, bumping over the pot-holes, the van moved off. Only when the site was clear did Thurkettle decide it was safe enough to emerge from his hiding place.

Left alone, Deuce Thurkettle took off his trenchcoat so that only his coveralls would get soiled. He got his hacksaw and hastily but carefully started his grisly work. When the head was severed he dragged Tessa's body into the car and arranged it with the skull he'd brought with him. The other bodies – the man in the gorilla suit, Harry Kennedy and Stinnes – ended up in the deep part of the excavations.

Thurkettle heaved a sigh of relief as he threw his blood-saturated coveralls into the muddy ditch with them. He tossed the guns after them and, using the shovel, covered everything there with mud and debris.

Setting fire to the car was easier. He watched the Wartburg burn and made sure that everything inside it was going to be thoroughly consumed in the flames. Only then did he mount his motor cycle and ride away to collect his money.

Werner Volkmann was sitting in a Skoda car at the Ziesar exit ramp, as arranged with Thurkettle. Werner had spent the evening at a fancy-dress party of which he was the nominal host. He had drunk only mineral water but now he was tired. Werner had always wanted to be a secret agent. He'd started doing little jobs for the British when he was still a teenager and the whole business of espionage still intrigued him. This was the finale. He knew that. The D-G had shaken hands with him and muttered something about an award: not money, some sort of medal or certificate. On his last visit to California Bret Rensselaer had said what Werner recognized as a final goodbye. By tomorrow morning Werner would be back in his West Berlin hotel and a private citizen again: his career in espionage over. He'd never tell anyone. Secrets shared were not his idea of what secrets should be.

He looked at the pistol that London Central had supplied to him that morning. He'd hoped they would give him something that would satisfy his romantic yearnings: a lovely Colt Model 1911, a stylish Walther P.38 or a classic Luger. Instead London had sent him another of these cheap little 'chamberless expendables'. It looked like a gadget used to ignite the flame on a gas stove. Its surface was hatched to provide a grip but also to eliminate any surface upon which a fingerprint could remain. It used triangular-sectioned cartridges – 'trounds' – in a 'strip clip', and almost everything was made by a plastics corporation in America. It was new, unidentifiable and in perfect working order, but it did not give Werner the satisfaction that he would have got from an old-fashioned weapon. Oh well, one had to move with the times. He put the gun in his inside pocket where it would be easy to reach.

Dawn was breaking as Werner spotted Thurkettle arriving on his motor cycle. He waved airily to Werner and gave a little flip to the accelerator. Deuce enjoyed riding the big bike but now the time had come for him to dispose of it. He'd parked a Volkswagen camper nearby. As soon as he'd collected his payment from this lugubrious schmo, he'd walk to where he'd left the camper. In it there were clean clothes, soap, towels and food. Buried nearby he'd left a Swiss passport wrapped in plastic. The passport had a visa for a three-week camping tour of East Germany. He'd shave off his beard, change his appearance and drift around seeing the sights like a tourist until the heat died down. Then he'd drive north and take the ferry boat to Sweden.

Thurkettle got off his bike and walked over to the car. The rain had soaked him to the skin and the exertions had left his muscles stiff. He remembered that the VW camper had a shower in it, and wondered how long it would take for the water to get hot.

Werner lowered the car window. 'Was there any difficulty?' he asked.

'Nothing I couldn't handle. But Fiona Samson is dead,' said Thurkettle. It was what he'd been told to say. 'One of the Russkie goons wasted her. Bernard Samson got away: so did some other woman. I don't know who she was: she was in a long yellow dress. She went with Bernard Samson.'

Werner knew who the other woman was: it was Tessa. He'd seen her leave the party with Bernard. 'Fiona Samson is dead? Are you sure?'

'It's not something I'd make a mistake about,' said Thurkettle. He smiled: he liked secrets. The switch of identities he'd arranged for the two women was a secret Prettyman had told him to keep entirely to himself. 'All the others are dead.'

'Kennedy too?'

'Yeah, Kennedy too. And a guy dressed as a gorilla. There was a shoot-out. I was lucky to get away in one piece.' He always embellished events when he came to collect his fee. Clients always wanted to feel they were getting value for their money. 'Those Russkie sons of bitches came there all set to blow me away. If I hadn't been there, Bernard Samson would never have made it.'

726

'My God! Poor Fiona,' said Werner. He'd come to adore her over the months they'd worked together. She should never have taken on a task like that, the strain was too much for her. He'd seen her fading under the stress of it. At one meeting recently she had had a momentary black-out. She'd said it was too many late nights and made him promise to keep it a secret. Poor Fiona. He got out of the car and went round to the trunk. It was raining. He looked round him in the brightening dawn. There wasn't much time.

'Yeah, well, that's the way it goes,' said Thurkettle philosophically. He smiled at Werner. He seemed like a genial fellow and Werner smiled too.

'I didn't realize it was still raining,' said Werner.

'Is that right?' said Thurkettle, who was soaked to the skin.

'Do you want to sit in the car and count it?' Werner asked. 'I don't want to stand here getting wet.' He was going through his keys to find the one for the trunk.

'We'll just take a peek at it so I can see it's real.'

'It's real,' said Werner. 'Used notes. Exactly as you specified. I got it from the Commerzbank on Friday.'

He reached into the trunk of the car to get a leather document case. Carefully he put the case into Thurkettle's hands, saying, 'Don't rest it on the car. The paintwork is brand new.'

Thurkettle smiled pitifully. He was used to the sort of nervousness that Volkmann displayed. Clients were always timorous when dealing with a hit man. He held the case with both hands while Werner bent forward and fiddled with the lock. 'It's a combination lock,' explained Werner. He could smell the blood and filth on Thurkettle's clothes: it was the stink of the slaughter-house. 'You can make the combination into anything you choose. I made it 123. You can't forget 123 can you?'

'No,' said Thurkettle. Werner snapped the lock open, and pulled up the lid. There it was: fifty-dollar bills: line upon line of them. 'You can't forget 1, 2, 3.'

It was while Thurkettle was standing there, holding the new leather document case with both hands, that Werner, gripping the curious-looking gun so it was hidden under the case, pulled the trigger. A strip clip of eight rounds fired as fast as a machine gun. They all went into Thurkettle's belly.

Eight rounds. It was only a little 'expendable', but at point-blank range a weapon doesn't have to be a masterpiece of the gunsmith's art for its effect to prove fatal.

The impact of these little medium-velocity rounds did not knock

727

Thurkettle down, he just staggered backwards a couple of paces still holding the case in both hands and staring at Werner in uncomprehending disbelief. Thurkettle's jerky movements caused the money to spill over, and a gust of rainy wind started to carry it away. Thurkettle watched his money blowing away. He grabbed at some notes but winced in pain. This couldn't be happening to him. He was shot. Thurkettle was a professional killer and this jerk was a nothing . . .

As he staggered back, more and more money fluttered away and he tasted the blood gushing up into his mouth and knew he was done for. By now he was clutching the document case against his chest as if it might prove protection against more shots or comfort him in his final moments, and he embraced it tight like a lover, and the bloodsoaked money fell around his feet.

It was just before he fell down that Deuce Thurkettle understood exactly how he'd been tricked. His eyes opened wide in fury. Deuce Thurkettle was the only one who knew for certain that Fiona Samson was still alive. Even this clown who had shot him thought that Samson had escaped with Tessa.

Well, he'd tell the world. He opened his mouth to tell the truth but only blood came out. Lots of it. Then he toppled to the ground.

Werner threw away his little 'expendable'. That was the convenient thing about them. He watched Thurkettle die, for he knew that London would want a positive answer. Werner didn't feel compassion for him. He was a psychopath and society is better off when such people are dead. Any last feeling he might have shown for Thurkettle had been removed when he heard that Fiona was dead. He'd told Thurkettle that getting Bernard and Fiona to safety was of paramount importance and he'd failed to do it.

Werner prodded the body with the toe of his shoe, and kicked it to tip it into the ditch. He'd chosen this spot because of that deep ditch. He moved the motor cycle too. It would be found eventually – someone would spot the dollar bills beflagging the fields – but it was better to get the bike out of sight. He pushed the leather case into the grass, and the rest of the money fluttered aside. He didn't pick any of it up. The notes were probably marked, or counterfeit. London Central had provided the money and the British were very careful about money, it was one of the things he'd discovered soon after starting to work for them.

Bret Rensselaer was at La Buona Nova, the hillside estate in Ventura County, California. He was having an early breakfast by the pool when the coded message came telling him that Fiona and Bernard Samson were on the way to join him in California.

It was a truly beautiful morning. Bret drank his orange juice and poured himself the first cup of coffee of the day. He so enjoyed sitting outdoors inhaling the clear cool air that came off the ocean. Around the pool there were whitewashed walls where the jasmine, roses and bougainvillaea seemed to bloom almost all the year round. There were trees bearing oranges, trees bearing lemons and trees bearing the maja fruit that his hostess called 'Brets'. It looked like a lemon but tasted like an orange, and calling it a Bret was perhaps her way of saying that Bret was sweet and sour. Or British yet American too. Bret didn't know what was implied but he went along with her joke: they had known each other a long long time.

People who had known Bret for a long time would say that he'd aged since being badly wounded at the Berlin shoot-out, but to the casual observer he was as trim and fit and agile as a senior citizen had any right to be. He was swimming and skiing and doing a routine of exercises. He wanted to look good when the visitors arrived.

He could not suppress a smile of satisfaction: they were coming. His plan to get an agent in the Kremlin, as Nikki had sardonically put it, had worked exactly as he'd predicted it would when he first took it to the D-G just after she ran out on him. Now there was only the long and interesting work of debriefing.

Bernard Samson would be here too. He had tried to get the old man to send Bernard elsewhere but it was good security to have him here where he could be supervised. Tessa's disappearance had to be accounted for; the idea that she had run away with Bernard was in every way believable.

This morning Bret would go right through all his notes again so as to be prepared for Fiona's arrival. This would be the last job he'd ever do for London Central and he was determined that it should end perfectly. Werner Volkmann's last report said that Fiona was on the verge of a nervous breakdown, but Bret didn't give it much credence. He'd heard that too often about other working agents: it was usually the preamble to a demand for more money. Fiona would be all right. Good food, sleep and the California air would soon bring her back to being her old self again.

Bernard Samson would go nowhere, of course. His career was at an end. It was strange to think how near Bernard had come to a senior position on the SIS staff. That evening long ago when Bret had gone to see the D-G, he had been all set to promote Bernard to German Stations

729

Controller. From there he would have gone to the top floor and perhaps ended up as Director-General. Heaven knows, he wouldn't be facing any fierce opposition from the line-up of deadbeats that now occupied the top floor. Would Sir Henry and Silas and Frank Harrington, and the rest of that cabal which really ran things, have gone along with Bernard Samson in a top job? They were always saying what a splendid fellow Bernard was, and many of them thought that the Department owed him something for the shabby way his father had been treated. But D-G? Any chance of Bernard as D-G had been eliminated that night when Sir Henry had revealed that Fiona was his choice to go over there.

Bret put down his coffee cup as a sudden thought came to him. The D-G must have known that choosing Fiona meant eliminating Bernard. There were others he could have chosen instead of Fiona: good people, he'd admitted that many times. So, had the D-G's choice of Fiona been influenced by the fact that it would prevent Bernard getting the top job?

Bret drank his coffee and thought about it. There was always another layer of onion no matter how deep you went. Well, if it was true, the old man would never admit it, and he was the only one who knew the answer. Bret knew that he could never really become English. They were very strange people: tribal in their complex allegiances. He finished his coffee and dismissed such thoughts from his mind. There was a lot of work to do.